JOHN
le CARRÉ

THE RUSSIA HOUSE
THE SECRET PILGRIM
A MURDER OF QUALITY

JOHN le CARRÉ

THE RUSSIA HOUSE
THE SECRET PILGRIM
A MURDER OF QUALITY

CHANCELLOR PRESS

The Russia House
first published in Great Britain in 1989 by Hodder & Stoughton Ltd
The Secret Pilgrim
first published in Great Britain in 1991 by Hodder & Stoughton Ltd
A Murder of Quality
first published in Great Britain in 1962 by Victor Gollancz Ltd

This collected volume first published in Great Britain in 1993 by
Chancellor Press an imprint of
Reed Consumer Books Ltd
Michelin House, 81 Fulham Road, London SW3 6RB
and Auckland, Melbourne, Singapore and Toronto

by arrangement with Hodder & Stoughton Ltd

ISBN 1 85152 441 X

A CIP catalogue record for this book is available at the British Library

Printed in Great Britain by the Bath Press

Contents

'Indeed, I think that people want peace
so much that one of these days
governments had better get out of their
way and let them have it.'

DWIGHT D. EISENHOWER

'One must think like a hero to
behave like a merely decent human being.'

MAY SARTON

Foreword

Acknowledgements in novels can be as tedious as credits at the cinema, yet I am constantly touched by the willingness of busy people to give their time and wisdom to such a frivolous undertaking as mine, and I cannot miss this opportunity to thank them.

I recall with particular gratitude the help of Strobe Talbott, the illustrious Washington journalist, Sovietologist and writer on nuclear defence. If there are errors in this book they are surely not his, and there would have been many more without him. Professor Lawrence Freedman, the author of several standard works on the modern conflict, also allowed me to sit at his feet, but must not be blamed for my simplicities.

Frank Geritty, for many years an agent of the Federal Bureau of Investigation, introduced me to the mysteries of the lie-detector, now sadly called the polygraph, and if my characters are not as complimentary about its powers as he is, the reader should blame them, not him.

I must also offer a disclaimer on behalf of John Roberts and his staff at the Great Britain-USSR Association, of which he is Director. It was he who accompanied me on my first visit to the USSR, opening all sorts of doors for me that might otherwise have stayed shut. But he knew nothing of my dark intent, neither did he probe. Of his staff, I may mention particularly Anne Vaughan.

My Soviet hosts at the Writers' Union showed a similar discretion, and a largeness of spirit that took me by surprise. Nobody who visits the Soviet Union in these extraordinary years, and is privileged to conduct the conversations that were granted me, can come away without an enduring love for its people and a sense of awe at the scale of the problems that face them. I hope that my Soviet friends will find reflected in this fable a little of the warmth that I felt in their company, and of the hopes we shared for a saner and more companionable future.

Jazz is a great unifier and I did not want for friends when it came to Barley's saxophone. Wally Fawkes, the celebrated cartoonist and jazz player, lent me his musician's ear, and John Calley his perfect pitch both in words and music. If such men would only run the world I should have no more conflicts to write about.

John le Carré

The Russia House

1

I n a broad Moscow street not two hundred yards from the Leningrad station, on the upper floor of an ornate and hideous hotel built by Stalin in the style known to Muscovites as Empire During the Plague, the British Council's first ever audio fair for the teaching of the English language and the spread of British culture was grinding to its excruciating end. The time was half past five, the summer weather erratic. After fierce rain showers all day long, a false sunlight was blazing in the puddles and raising vapour from the pavements. Of the passers-by, the younger ones wore jeans and sneakers, but their elders were still huddled in their warms.

The room the Council had rented was not expensive but neither was it appropriate to the occasion. I have seen it – Not long ago, in Moscow on quite another mission, I tiptoed up the great empty staircase and, with a diplomatic passport in my pocket, stood in the eternal dusk that shrouds old ballrooms when they are asleep – With its plump brown pillars and gilded mirrors, it was better suited to the last hours of a sinking liner than the launch of a great initiative. On the ceiling, snarling Russians in proletarian caps shook their fists at Lenin. Their vigour contrasted unhelpfully with the chipped green racks of sound cassettes along the walls, featuring *Winnie-the-Pooh* and *Advanced Computer English in Three Hours*. The sackcloth sound-booths, locally procured and lacking many of their promised features, had the sadness of deck chairs on a rainy beach. The exhibitors' stands, crammed under the shadow of an overhanging gallery, seemed as blasphemous as betting shops in a tabernacle.

Nevertheless a fair of sorts had taken place. People had come, as Moscow people do, provided they have the documents and status to satisfy the hard-eyed boys in leather jackets at the door. Out of politeness. Out of curiosity. To talk to Westerners. Because it is there. And now on the fifth and final evening the great farewell cocktail party of exhibitors and invited guests was getting into its stride. A handful of the small *nomenclatura* of the Soviet cultural bureaucracy was gathering under the chandelier, the ladies in their beehive hairstyles and flowered frocks designed for slenderer frames, the gentlemen slimmed by the shiny

French-tailored suits that signified access to the special clothing stores. Only their British hosts, in despondent shades of grey, observed the monotone of socialist austerity. The hubbub rose, a brigade of pinafored governesses distributed the curling salami sandwiches and warm white wine. A senior British diplomat who was not quite the Ambassador shook the better hands and said he was delighted.

Only Niki Landau among them had withheld himself from the celebrations. He was stooped over the table in his empty stand, totting up his last orders and checking his dockets against expenses, for it was a maxim of Landau's never to go out and play until he had wrapped up his day's business.

And in the corner of his eye – an anxious blue blur was all that she amounted to – this Soviet woman he was deliberately ignoring. *Trouble*, he was thinking as he laboured. *Avoid*.

The air of festivity had not communicated itself to Landau, festive by temperament though he was. For one thing, he had a lifelong aversion to British officialdom, ever since his father had been forcibly returned to Poland. The British themselves, he told me later, he would hear no wrong of them. He was one of them by adoption and he had the poker-backed reverence of the convert. But the Foreign Office flunkeys were another matter. And the loftier they were, and the more they twitched and smirked and raised their stupid eyebrows at him, the more he hated them and thought about his dad. For another thing, if he had been left to himself, he would never have come to the audio fair in the first place. He'd have been tucked up in Brighton with a nice new little friend he had, called Lydia, in a nice little private hotel he knew for taking little friends.

'Better to keep our powder dry till the Moscow book fair in September,' Landau had advised his clients at their headquarters on the Western bypass. 'The Russkies love a book, you see, Bernard, but the audio market scares them and they aren't geared for it. Go in with the book fair, we'll clean up. Go in with the audio fair, we're dead.'

But Landau's clients were young and rich and did not believe in death. 'Niki boy,' said Bernard, walking round behind him and putting a hand on his shoulder, which Landau didn't like, 'in the world today, we've got to show the flag. We're patriots, see, Niki? Like you. That's why we're an offshore company. With the *glasnost* today, the Soviet Union, it's the Mount Everest of the recording business. And you're going to put us on the top, Niki. Because if you're not, we'll find somebody who will. Somebody younger, Niki, right? Somebody with the drive and the class.'

The drive Landau had still. But the class, as he himself was the first to tell you, the class, forget it. He was a card, that's what he liked to be. A pushy, short-arsed Polish card and proud of it. He was Old Nik the cheeky chappie of the Eastward-facing reps, capable, he liked to boast, of selling filthy pictures to a Georgian convent or hair tonic to a Rumanian billiard ball. He was Landau the undersized bedroom athlete, who wore raised heels to give his Slav body the English scale he admired, and ritzy suits that whistled 'here I am'. When Old Nik set up his stand, his travelling colleagues assured our unattributable enquirers, you could hear the tinkle of the handbell on his Polish vendor's barrow.

And little Landau shared the joke with them, he played their game. 'Boys, I'm the Pole you wouldn't touch with a barge,' he would declare proudly as he ordered up another round. Which was his way of getting them to laugh with him. Instead of at him. And then most likely, to demonstrate his point, he would whip a comb from his top pocket and drop into a crouch. And with the aid of a picture on the wall, or any other polished surface, he'd sweep back his too-black hair in preparation for fresh conquest, using both his little hands to coax it into manliness. 'Who's that comely one I'm looking at over there in the corner, then?' he'd ask, in his godless blend of ghetto Polish and East End cockney. 'Hullo there, sweetheart! Why are we suffering all alone tonight?' And once out of five times he'd score, which in Landau's book was an acceptable rate of return, always provided you kept asking.

But this evening Landau wasn't thinking of scoring or even asking. He was thinking that yet again he had worked his heart out all week for a pittance – or as he put it more graphically to me, a tart's kiss. And that every fair these days, whether it was a book fair or an audio fair or any other kind of fair, took a little more out of him than he liked to admit to himself, just as every woman did. And gave him a fraction too little in return. And that tomorrow's plane back to London couldn't come too soon. And that if this Russian bird in blue didn't stop insinuating herself into his attention when he was trying to close his books and put on his party smile and join the jubilant throng, he would very likely say something to her in her own language that both of them would live to regret.

That she was Russian went without saying. Only a Russian woman would have a plastic perhaps-bag dangling from her arm in readiness for the chance purchase that is the triumph of everyday life, even if most perhaps-bags were of string. Only a Russian would be so nosy as to stand close enough to check a man's arithmetic. And only a Russian would preface her interruption with one of those fastidious grunts, which in a man always reminded Landau of his father doing up his shoe laces, and in a woman, Harry, bed.

'Excuse me, sir. Are you the gentleman from Abercrombie & Blair?' she asked.

'Not here, dear,' said Landau without lifting his head. She had spoken English, so he had spoken English in return, which was the way he played it always.

'Mr. Barley?'

'Not Barley, dear. Landau.'

'But this is Mr. Barley's stand.'

'This is not Barley's stand. This is my stand. Abercrombie & Blair are next door.'

Still without looking up, Landau jabbed his pencil-end to the left, towards the empty stand on the other side of the partition, where a green and gold board proclaimed the ancient publishing house of Abercrombie & Blair of Norfolk Street, Strand.

'But that stand is empty. No one is there,' the woman objected. 'It was empty yesterday also.'

'Correct. Right on,' Landau retorted in a tone that was final enough for anybody. Then he ostentatiously lowered himself further into his account book, waiting for the blue blur to remove itself. Which was rude of him, he knew, and her continuing presence made him feel ruder.

'But where is Scott Blair? Where is the man they call Barley? I must speak to him. It is very urgent.'

Landau was by now hating the woman with unreasoning ferocity.

'*Mr.* Scott Blair,' he began as he snapped up his head and stared at her full on, 'more commonly known to his intimates as Barley, is *awol*, madam. That means absent without leave. His company booked a stand – yes. And Mr. Scott Blair is chairman, president, governor-general and for all I know lifetime dictator of that company. However, he did not occupy his stand – ' but here, having caught her eye, he began to lose his footing. 'Listen, dear, I happen to be trying to make a living here, right? I am not making it for Mr. Barley Scott Blair, love him as I may.'

Then he stopped, as a chivalrous concern replaced his momentary anger. The woman was trembling. Not only with the hands that held her brown perhaps-bag, but at the neck, for her prim blue dress was finished with a collar of old lace and Landau could see how it shook against her skin and how her skin was actually whiter than the lace. Yet her mouth and jaw were set with determination and her expression commanded him.

'Please, sir, you must be very kind and help me,' she said as if there were no choice.

Now Landau prided himself on knowing women. It was another of his irksome boasts but it was not without foundation. 'Women, they're my hobby, my life's study and my consuming passion, Harry,' he confided to me, and the conviction in his voice was as solemn as a Mason's pledge. He could no longer tell you how many he had had, but he was pleased to say that the figure ran into the hundreds and there was not one of them who had cause to regret the experience. 'I play straight, I choose wisely, Harry,' he assured me, tapping one side of his nose with his forefinger. 'No cut wrists, no broken marriages, no harsh words afterwards.' How true this was, nobody would ever know, myself included, but there can be no doubt that the instincts that had guided him through his philanderings came rushing to his assistance as he formed his judgments about the woman.

She was earnest. She was intelligent. She was determined. She was scared, even though her dark eyes were lit with humour. And she had that rare quality which Landau in his flowery way liked to call the Class That Only Nature Can Bestow. In other words, she had quality as well as strength. And since in moments of crisis our thoughts do not run consecutively but rather sweep over us in waves of intuition and experience, he sensed all these things at once and was on terms with them by the time she spoke to him again.

'A Soviet friend of mine has written a creative and important work of literature,' she said after taking a deep breath. 'It is a novel. A great novel. Its message is important for all mankind.'

She had dried up.

'A novel,' Landau prompted. And then, for no reason he could afterwards think of, 'What's its title, dear?'

The strength in her, he decided, came neither from bravado nor insanity but from conviction.

'What's its message then, if it hasn't got a title?'

'It concerns actions before words. It rejects the gradualism of the *perestroika*. It demands action and rejects all cosmetic change.'

'Nice,' said Landau, impressed.

She spoke like my mother used to, Harry: chin up and straight into your face.

'In spite of *glasnost* and the supposed liberalism of the new guidelines, my friend's novel cannot yet be published in the Soviet Union,' she continued. 'Mr. Scott Blair has undertaken to publish it with discretion.'

'Lady,' said Landau kindly, his face now close to hers. 'If your friend's novel is published by the great house of Abercrombie & Blair, believe me, you can be assured of total secrecy.'

He said this partly as a joke he couldn't resist and partly because his instincts told him to take the stiffness out of their conversation and make it less conspicuous to anybody watching. And whether she understood the joke or not, the woman smiled also, a swift warm smile of self-encouragement that was like a victory over her fears.

'Then, Mr. Landau, if you love peace, please take this manuscript with you back to England and give it immediately to Mr. Scott Blair. Only to Mr. Scott Blair. It is a gift of trust.'

What happened next happened quickly, a street-corner transaction, willing seller to willing buyer. The first thing Landau did was look behind her, past her shoulder. He did that for his own preservation as well as hers. It was his experience that when the Russkies wanted to get up to a piece of mischief, they always had other people close by. But his end of the assembly room was empty, the area beneath the gallery where the stands were was dark and the party at the centre of the room was by now in full cry. The three boys in leather jackets at the front door were talking stodgily among themselves.

His survey completed, he read the girl's plastic name badge on her lapel, which was something he would normally have done earlier but her black-brown eyes had distracted him. Yekaterina Orlova, he read. And underneath, the word 'October', given in both English and Russian, this being the name of one of Moscow's smaller State publishing houses specialising in translations of Soviet books for export, mainly to other Socialist countries, which I am afraid condemned it to a certain dowdiness.

Next he told her what to do, or perhaps he was already telling her by the time he read her badge. Landau was a street kid, up to all the tricks. The woman might be as brave as six lions and by the look of her probably was. But she was no conspirator. Therefore he took her unhesitatingly into his protection. And in doing so he spoke to her as he would to any woman who needed his basic counsel, such as where to find his hotel bedroom or what to tell her hubby when she got home.

'Got it with you then, have you, dear?' he asked, peering down at the perhaps-bag and smiling like a friend.

'Yes.'

'In there, is it?'

'Yes.'

'Then give me the whole bag normally,' Landau said, talking her through her act. 'That's the way. Now give me a friendly Russian kiss. The formal sort. Nice. You've brought me an official farewell gift on the last evening of the fair, you see. Something that will cement Anglo-Soviet relations and make me overweight on the flight home unless I dump it in the dustbin at the airport. Very normal transaction. 1 must have received half a dozen such gifts today already.'

Part of this was spoken while he crouched with his back to her. For, reaching into the bag, he had already slipped out the brown-paper parcel that was inside it and was dropping it deftly into his briefcase, which was of the home-filing variety, very compendious, with compartments that opened in a fan.

'Married, are we, Katya?'

No answer. Maybe she hadn't heard. Or she was too busy watching him.

'Is it your husband who's written the novel, then?' said Landau, undeterred by her silence.

'It is dangerous for you,' she whispered. 'You must believe in what you are doing. Then everything is clear.'

As if he had not heard this warning at all, Landau selected, from a pile of samples that he had kept to give away tonight, a four-pack of the Royal Shakespeare Company's specially commissioned reading of A *Midsummer Night's Dream*, which he placed ostentatiously on the table and signed for her on the plastic casing with a felt-tip pen: 'From Niki to Katya, Peace', and the date. Then he put the four-pack ceremoniously into the perhaps-bag for her, and gathered the handles of the bag together and pressed them into her hand, because she was becoming lifeless and he was worried she might break down or cease to function. Only then did he give her the reassurance that she seemed to be asking for, while he continued to hold her hand, which was cold, he told me, but nice.

'All of us have got to do something risky now and then, haven't we, dear?' Landau said lightly. 'Going to adorn the party, are we?'

'No.'

'Like a nice dinner out somewhere?'

'It is not convenient.'

'You want me to take you to the door?'

'It doesn't matter.'

'I think we've got to smile, dear,' he said, still in English as he walked her across the room, chatting to her like the good salesman he had once again become.

Reaching the great landing, he shook her hand. 'See you at the book fair, then? September. And thanks for warning me, okay? I'll bear it in mind. Still, the main thing is, we've got a deal. Which is always nice. Right?'

She took his hand and seemed to draw courage from it, for she smiled again and her smile was dazed but grateful, and almost irresistibly warm.

'My friend has made a great gesture,' she explained as she pushed back an unruly lock of hair. 'Please be sure that Mr. Barley is aware of this.'

'I'll tell him. Don't you worry,' said Landau jauntily.

He would have liked another smile just for himself, but she had lost interest in him. She was delving in her bag for her card, which he knew she had forgotten till this moment. 'ORLOVA, Yekaterina Borisovna,' it read, in Cyrillic one side and Roman the other, again with the name October in both renderings. She gave it to him, then walked stiffly down the pompous staircase, head up and one hand on the broad marble balustrade, the other hand trailing the perhaps-bag. The boys in leather jackets watched her all the way down to the hall. And Landau, while he popped the card into his top pocket with the half-dozen others he'd collected in the last two hours, saw them watch her and gave the boys a wink. And the boys after due reflection winked back at him, because this was the new season of openness when a pair of good Russian hips could be acknowledged for what they were, even to a foreigner.

For the fifty minutes of revelry that remained, Niki Landau threw his heart into the party. Sang and danced for a grim-faced Scottish librarian in pearls. Recited a witty political anecdote about Mrs. Thatcher for a pair of pale listeners from the State Copyright Agency, VAAP, till they suddenly emitted wild laughter. Buttered up three ladies from Progress Publishers and, in a series of nimble journeys to his briefcase, presented each with a memento of his stay, for Landau was a natural giver and remembered names and promises, just as he remembered so many other things, with the directness of an unencumbered mind. But all the while he kept the briefcase unobtrusively in view, and even before the guests had left, he was holding it in his spare hand while he made his farewells. And when he boarded the private bus that was waiting to take the reps back to their hotel, he sat with it on his knees while he joined in a tuneful unison of rugby songs, led as usual by Spikey Morgan.

'Ladies present now, boys,' Landau warned and, standing up, commanded silence at the passages that he considered too broad. But even when he was playing the great conductor he contrived to keep a firm grip on the briefcase.

At the hotel entrance the usual gaggle of pimps, drug-pushers and currency dealers hung around and, together with their KGB minders, watched the group enter. But Landau saw nothing in their behaviour to concern him, whether over-watchful or over-casual. The crippled old warrior who guarded the passageway to the lifts demanded as usual to see his hotel pass, but when Landau, who had already presented him with a hundred Marlboros, asked him accusingly in Russian why he wasn't out flirting with his girlfriend tonight, he gave a rasping laugh and punched him on the shoulder in goodfellowship.

'If they're trying to frame me, I thought, they'd better be quick about it or the trail will be cold, Harry,' he told me, taking the part of the opposition rather than his own. 'When you frame, Harry, you've got to move in fast while the evidence is still planted on the victim,' he explained, as if he had been framing people all his life.

'Bar of the National, nine o'clock then,' Spikey Morgan said to him wearily when they had fought their way out at the fourth floor.

'Could be, could be not, Spikey,' Landau replied. 'I'm not quite myself, to be honest.'

'Thank God for that,' said Spikey through a yawn, and plodded off into his own dark corridor watched by the evil-eyed floor concierge in her horsebox.

Reaching his bedroom door Landau braced himself before putting the key into the lock. They'd do it now, he thought. Here and now would be the best time to snatch me and the manuscript.

But when he stepped inside, the room was empty and undisturbed and he felt foolish for having suspected it of being any different. Still alive, he thought, and set the briefcase on the bed.

Then he pulled the handkerchief-sized curtains as close as they would go, which was halfway, and hung the useless 'Do Not Disturb' notice on the door, which he then locked. He emptied the pockets of his suit, including the pocket where he stored incoming business cards, pulled off his jacket and tie, his metal armbands, finally his shirt. From the fridge he poured himself half an inch of lemon vodka and took a sip. Landau was not a drinker really, he explained to me, but when in Moscow he did like a nice lemon vodka to end his day. Taking his glass to the bathroom, he stood before the mirror and for a good ten minutes anxiously examined the roots of his hair for signs of white, touching out offending spots with the aid of a new formula that was working wonders. Having completed this labour to his satisfaction, he bound his skull with an elaborate rubber turban like a bathing cap and showered, while he sang 'I am the very model of a modern major-general' rather well. Then he towelled himself, vigorously for the sake of his muscle-tone, slipped into a bold flowered bathrobe and marched back to the bedroom still singing.

And he did these things partly because he always did them and needed the steadying familiarity of his own routines, but partly also because he was proud of having thrown caution to the winds for once and not found twenty-five sound reasons for doing nothing, which these days he might have done.

She was a lady, she was afraid, she needed help, Harry. When did Niki Landau ever refuse a lady? And if he was wrong about her, well then she'd made a crying fool of him and he might as well pack up his toothbrush and report himself at the front door of the Lubyanka for five years' study of their excellent graffiti without the option. Because he'd rather be made a fool of twenty times over than turn away that woman without a reason. And so saying, if only in his mind, for he was always alert to the possibility of microphones, Landau drew her parcel from the briefcase and with a certain shyness set to work untying the string but not cutting it, just the way he had been taught by his sainted mother, whose photograph at this moment nestled faithfully in his wallet. They've got the same glow, he thought in pleasant recognition as he worried patiently at the knot. It's the Slav skin. It's the Slav eyes, the smile. Two nice Slav girls together. The only difference was that Katya hadn't finished up in Treblinka.

The knot finally yielded. Landau coiled up the string and laid it on the bed. I have to know, you see, dear, he explained to the woman Yekaterina Borisovna in his mind. I don't want to pry, I'm not the nosy one, but if I've got to con my way through Moscow customs, I'd better know what I'm conning them out of because it helps.

Delicately so as not to tear it, using both hands, Landau parted the brown paper. He did not see himself as any sort of a hero, or not yet. What was a danger to a Moscow beauty might not be a danger to him. He had grown up hard, it was true. The East End of London had been no rest cure for a ten-year-old Polish immigrant, and Landau had taken his share of split lips, broken noses, smashed knuckles and hunger. But if you had asked him now or at any time in the last thirty years what his definition of a hero was, he would have replied without a second's thought that a hero was the first man out of the back door when they started yelling for volunteers.

One thing he did know as he stared at the contents of that brown-paper parcel: he had the buzz on him. Why he had it was something he could sort out later when there weren't better things to do. But if dodgy work needed to be done tonight, Niki Landau was your man. Because when Niki has the buzz, Harry, no one buzzes better, as the girls all know.

The first thing he saw was the envelope. He registered the three note-books underneath it and saw that the envelope and notebooks were joined with a thick elastic band, the kind he always saved but never found a use for. But it was the envelope that held him because it had her writing on it – a strict copybook kind of writing that confirmed his pure image of her. One square brown envelope, glued rather messily and addressed 'Personal for Mr. Bartholomew Scott Blair, urgent'.

Slipping it free of the elastic band, Landau held it to the light but it was opaque and revealed no shadow. He explored it with his finger and thumb. One sheet of thin paper inside, two at most. *Mr. Scott Blair has undertaken to publish it with discretion*, he remembered. *Mr. Landau, if you love peace . . . give it immediately to Mr. Scott Blair. Only to Mr. Scott Blair . . . it is a gift of trust.*

She trusts me too, he thought. He turned the envelope over. The back was blank.

And there being only so much that one may learn from a sealed brown envelope, and since Landau drew the line at reading Barley's or anybody else's personal mail, he opened his briefcase again and, peering into the stationery compartment, extracted from it a plain manila envelope of his own, with the words 'From the desk of Mr. Nicholas P. Landau' inscribed tastefully on the flap. Then he popped the brown envelope inside the manila one and sealed it. Then he scribbled the name 'Barley' on it and filed it in the compartment marked 'Social', which contained such oddities as visiting cards that had been pressed on him by strangers and notes of odd commissions he had undertaken to perform for people – such as the publishing lady who needed refills for her Parker pen or the Ministry of Culture official who wanted a Snoopy T-shirt for his nephew or the lady from October who simply happened to be passing while he was wrapping up his stand.

And Landau did this because with the tradecraft that was instinctive in him, if totally untaught, he knew that his first job was to keep the envelope as far away as possible from the notebooks. If the notebooks were trouble, then he wanted nothing that would link them with the letter. And vice versa. And in this he was entirely right. Our most versatile and erudite trainers, dyed in all the oceans of our Service folklore, would not have told it to him one whit differently.

Only then did he take up the three notebooks and slip off the elastic band while he kept one ear cocked for footfalls in the corridor. Three grubby Russian notebooks, he reflected, selecting the top one and turning it slowly over. Bound in crudely illustrated board, the spine in fraying cloth. Two hundred and twenty-four pages of poor-quality, feint-ruled quarto, if Landau remembered correctly from the days when he peddled stationery, Soviet price around twenty kopeks retail from any good stationer, always provided that the delivery had arrived and that you were standing in the right queue on the right day.

Finally he opened the notebook and stared at the first page.

She's daft, he thought, fighting off his disgust.

She's in the hands of a nutter. Poor kid.

Meaningless scribblings, done by a lunatic with a mapping pen, in Indian ink at breakneck speed and furious angles. In the margins, sideways, longways. Diagonally across itself like a doctor's writing on the blink. Peppered with stupid exclamation marks and underlinings. Some of it Cyrillic, some English. 'The Creator creates creators,' he read in English. 'To be. Not to be. To counter-be.' Followed by a burst of stupid French about the warfare of folly and the folly of warfare, followed by a barbed-wire entanglement. Thank you very much, he thought, and flipped to another page, then another, both so dense with crazy writing you could hardly see the paper. 'Having spent seventy years destroying the popular will, we cannot expect it suddenly to rise up and save us,' he read. A quote? A night thought? There was no way to tell. References to writers, Russian, Latin and European. Talk of Nietzsche, Kalka and people he'd never heard of, let alone read. More talk of war, this time in English: 'The old declare it, the young fight it, but today the babies and old people fight it too.' He turned another page and came on nothing but a round brown stain. He lifted the notebook to his nose and sniffed. Booze, he thought with contempt. Stinks like a brewery. No wonder he's a mate of Barley Blair's. A double page devoted to a series of hysterical proclamations.

– OUR GREATEST PROGRESS IS IN THE FIELD OF BACK-WARDNESS!

– SOVIET PARALYSIS IS THE MOST PROGRESSIVE IN THE WORLD!

– OUR BACKWARDNESS IS OUR GREATEST MILITARY SECRET!

– IF WE DON'T KNOW OUR OWN INTENTIONS AND OUR OWN CAPACITIES, HOW CAN WE KNOW YOURS?

– THE TRUE ENEMY IS OUR OWN INCOMPETENCE!

And on the next page, a poem, painstakingly copied from Lord knew where:

> He wires in and wires out.
> And leaves the people still in doubt
> Whether the snake that made the track,
> Was going south or coming back.

Scrambling to his feet, Landau strode angrily to the window which gave on to a glum courtyard full of uncollected rubbish.

'A blooming word-artist, Harry. That's what I thought he was. Some long-haired, drug-ridden, self-indulgent genius, and she's gone and thrown herself away on him same as they all do.'

She was lucky there was no Moscow telephone directory or he'd have rung her up and told her what she'd got.

To stoke his anger, he took up the second book, licked his fingertip and whisked contemptuously through it page by page, which was how he came upon the drawings. Then everything went blank for him for a moment, like a flash of empty screen in the middle of a film, while he cursed himself for being an impetuous little Slav instead of a cool calm Englishman. Then he sat down on the bed again, but gently, as if there were someone resting in it, someone he had hurt with his premature condemnations.

For if Landau despised what too often passed for literature, his pleasure in technical matters was unconfined. Even when he didn't follow what he was looking at, he could relish a good page of mathematics all day long. And he knew at one glance, as he had known of the woman Katya, that what he was looking at here was quality. Not your ruled drawing, it was true. Light sketches but all the better for it. Drawn freehand without instruments by somebody who could think with a pencil. Tangents, parabolas, cones. And in between the drawings, businesslike descriptions that architects and engineers use, words like 'aimpoint' and 'captive carry' and 'bias' and gravity and trajectory – 'some in your English, Harry, and some in your Russian.'

Though Harry is not my real name.

Yet when he began to compare the lettering of these beautifully-written words in the second book with the rambling jungle in the first, he discovered to his astonishment certain unmistakable similarities. So that he had the sensation of looking at a kind of schizophrenic's diary with Dr. Jekyll writing one volume and Mr. Hyde the other.

He looked in the third notebook, which was as orderly and purposeful as the second but arranged like a kind of mathematical log with dates and numbers and formulae and the word 'error' repeating itself frequently, often underlined or lifted with an exclamation mark. Then suddenly Landau stared, and continued staring, and could not remove his eyes from what he was reading. The cosy obscurity of the writer's technical jargon had ended with a bang. So had his philosophical ramblings and classy annotated drawings. The words came off the page with a blazoned clarity.

'The American strategists can sleep in peace. Their nightmares cannot be realised. The Soviet knight is dying inside his armour. He is a secondary power like you British. He can start a war but cannot continue one and cannot win one. Believe me.'

Landau looked no further. A sense of respect, mingled with a strong instinct for self-preservation, advised him that he had disturbed the tomb enough. Taking up the elastic band he put the three notebooks together

and snapped it back over them. That's it, he thought. From here on I mind
my business and do my duty. Which is to take the manuscript to my
adopted England and give it immediately to Mr. Bartholomew *alias* Barley
Scott Blair.

Barley Blair, he thought in amazement as he opened his wardrobe and
hauled out the large aluminium hand-case where he kept his samples.
Well, well. We often wondered whether we were nurturing a spy in our
midst and now we know.

Landau's calm was absolute, he assured me. The Englishman had once
more taken command of the Pole. 'If Barley could do it, I could, Harry,
that's what I said to myself.' And it was what he said to me too, when for
a short spell he appointed me his confessor. People do that to me sometimes. They sense the unrealised part of me and talk to it as if it were the
reality.

Lifting the case on to the bed he snapped the locks and drew out two
audio-visual kits that the Soviet officials had ordered him to remove from
his display – one pictorial history of the twentieth century with spoken
commentary which they had arbitrarily ruled to be anti-Soviet, one handbook of the human body with action photographs and a keep-fit exercise
cassette, which, after gazing longingly at the pliant young goddess in the
leotard, the officials had decided was pornographic.

The history kit was a glossy affair, built as a coffee-table book and
containing a quantity of interior pockets for cassettes, parallel texts,
progressive vocabulary cards and students' notes. Having emptied the
pockets of their contents, Landau offered the notebooks to each in turn
but found none large enough. He decided to convert two pockets into one.
He fetched a pair of nail scissors from his sponge bag and set to work with
steady hands, easing the steel staples out of the centre divide.

Barley Blair, he thought again as he inserted the point of the nail scissors.
I should have guessed, if only because you were the one it couldn't possibly
be. Mr. Bartholomew Scott Blair, surviving scion of Abercrombie & Blair
– spy. The first staple had come loose. He gingerly extracted it. Barley
Blair, who couldn't sell hay to a rich horse to save his dying mother on her
birthday, we used to say: spy. He began prising the second staple. Whose
principal claim to fame was that two years ago at the Belgrade book fair
he had drunk Spikey Morgan under the table on straight vodkas, then
played tenor sax with the band so beautifully that even the police were
clapping. Spy. Gentleman spy. Well, here's a letter from your lady, as they
say in the nursery rhyme.

Landau picked up the notebooks and offered them to the space he had
prepared but it was still not big enough. He would have to make one
pocket out of three.

Playing the drunk, thought Landau, his mind still on Barley. Playing the
fool and fooling us. Burning up the last of your family money, running
the old firm deeper into the ground. Oh yes. Except that somehow or

another you always managed to find one of those smart City banking houses to bail you out in the nick of time, didn't you? And what about your chess-playing then? *That* should have been a clue, if Landau had only had eyes for it! How does a man who's drunk himself silly beat all comers at chess then, Harry – straight games – if he isn't a trained spy?

The three pockets had become one pocket, the notebooks fitted more or less inside, the printed indication above them still read 'Student Notes'.

'Notes,' Landau explained in his mind to the inquisitive young customs officer at Sheremetyevo airport. 'Notes, you see, son, like it says. Student's notes. That's why there's a pocket here for notes. And these notes that you are holding in your hand are the work of an actual student following the course. That's why they're here, son, do you see? They are *demonstration notes*. And the drawings here, they're to do with the – '

With socio-economic patterns, son. With demographic population shifts. With vital statistics that you Russkies can never get enough of, can you? Here, seen one of these? It's called a body book.

Which might or might not save Landau's hide, depending on how smart the boy was, and how much they knew, and how they felt about their wives that day.

But for the long night ahead of him, and for the dawn raid when they kicked the door down and burst in on him with drawn pistols and shouted, 'All right, Landau, give us the notebooks!' – for that happy moment, the kit wouldn't do at all. 'Notebooks, Officer? Notebooks? Oh, you mean that bunch of junk some loony Russian beauty pressed on me at the fair tonight. I think you'll probably find them in the rubbish basket, Officer, if the maid hasn't emptied it for once in her life.'

For this contingency also, Landau now meticulously set the scene. Removing the notebooks from the pocket of the history kit, he placed them artistically in the wastepaper basket exactly as if he had flung them there in the rage he had felt when he had taken his first look. To keep them company, he tossed in his surplus trade literature and brochures, as well as a couple of useless farewell gifts he had received: the thin volume of yet another Russian poet, a tin-backed blotter. As a final touch, he added a pair of undarned socks that only your rich Westerner throws away.

Once again I must marvel, as later we all did, at Landau's untutored ingenuity.

Landau did not go out and play that night. He endured the familiar imprisonment of his Moscow hotel room. From his window he watched the long dusk turn to darkness and the dim lights of the city reluctantly brighten. He made himself tea in his little travelling kettle and ate a couple of fruit bars from his iron rations. He dwelt gratefully upon the most rewarding of his conquests. He smiled ruefully at others. He braced himself for pain and solitude and summoned up his hard childhood to help him. He went through the contents of his wallet and his briefcase and his pockets and took out everything that was particularly private to him which he would not wish to answer for across a bare table – a hot letter a little friend sent him years ago that could still revive his appetites, membership of a certain video-by-mail club that he belonged to. His first instinct was to 'burn them like in the movies' but he was restrained by the sight of the smoke detectors in the ceiling, though he'd have laid any money they didn't work.

So he found a paper bag and, having torn up everything very small, he put the pieces in the bag, dropped the bag out of the window and saw it join the rubbish in the courtyard. Then he stretched himself out on the bed and watched the dark go by. Sometimes he felt brave, sometimes he was so scared that he had to drive his fingernails into his palms to hold himself together. Once he turned on the television set, hoping for nubile girl gymnasts, which he liked. But instead he got the Emperor himself telling his bemused children for the umpteenth time that the old order had no clothes. And when Spikey Morgan, half drunk at best, telephoned from the bar of the National, Landau kept him on the line for company till old Spikey fell asleep.

Only once and at his lowest point did it cross Landau's mind to present himself at the British Embassy and seek the assistance of the diplomatic bag. His momentary weakness angered him. 'Those flunkeys?' he asked himself in scorn. 'The ones who sent my dad back to Poland? I wouldn't trust them with a picture postcard of the Eiffel Tower, Harry.'

Besides, that wasn't what she had asked him to do.

In the morning he dressed himself for his own execution, in his best suit, with the photograph of his mother inside his shirt.

And that is how I see Niki Landau still, whenever I dip into his file, or receive him for what we call a six-monthly top-up, which is when he likes to relive his hour of glory before signing yet another declaration of the Official Secrets Act. I see him stepping jauntily into the Moscow street with the metal suitcase in his hand, not knowing from Adam what's in it, but determined to risk his brave little neck for it anyway.

How he sees me, if he ever thinks of me, I dare not wonder. Hannah, whom I loved but failed, would have no doubt at all. 'As another of those Englishmen with hope in their faces and none in their hearts,' she would say, flushing with anger. For I am afraid she says whatever comes to her these days. Much of her old forbearance is gone.

2

T he whole of Whitehall was agreed that no story should ever begin that way again. Indoctrinated ministers were furious about it. They set up a frightfully secret committee of enquiry to find out what went wrong, hear witnesses, name names, spare no blushes, point fingers, close gaps, prevent a recurrence, appoint me chairman and draft a report. What conclusions our committee reached, if any, remains the loftiest secret of them all, particularly from those of us who sat on it. For the function of such committees, as we all well knew, is to talk earnestly until the dust has settled, and then ourselves return to dust. Which, like a disgruntled Cheshire cat, our committee duly did, leaving nothing behind us but our frightfully secret frown, a meaningless interim working paper, and a bunch of secret annexes in the Treasury archives.

It began, in the less sparing language of Ned and his colleagues at the Russia House, with an imperial cock-up, between the hours of five and eight-thirty on a warm Sunday evening, when one Nicholas P. Landau, travelling salesman and taxpayer in good standing, if of Polish origin, with nothing recorded against, presented himself at the doors of no fewer than four separate Whitehall ministries to plead an urgent interview with an officer of the British Intelligence Branch, as he was pleased to call it, only to be ridiculed, fobbed off and in one instance physically manhandled. Though whether the two temporary doormen at the Defence Ministry went so far as to grab Landau by the collar and the seat of his pants, as he maintained they did, and frogmarch him to the door, or whether they merely assisted him back into the street, to use *their* words, is a point on which we were unable to achieve a consensus.

But why, our committee asked sternly, did the two doormen feel obliged to provide this assistance in the first place?

Mr. Landau refused to let us look inside his briefcase, sir. Yes, he offered to let us take charge of the briefcase while he waited, provided he kept charge of the key, sir. But that wasn't regulations. And yes, he shook it in our faces, patted it for us, tossed it about in his hands, apparently in order to demonstrate that there was nothing in it that any of us needed to be afraid of. But that wasn't regulations either. And when we tried with a minimum of force to relieve him of the said briefcase, this *gentleman* – as Landau in their testimony had belatedly become – resisted our efforts, sir, and shouted loudly in a foreign accent, causing a disturbance.

But what did he shout? we asked, distressed by the notion of anybody shouting in Whitehall on a Sunday.

Well, sir, so far as we were able to make him out, him in his emotional state, he shouted that this briefcase of his contained highly secret papers, sir. Which had been entrusted to him by a Russian, sir, in Moscow.

And him a rampageous little Pole, sir, they might have added. On a hot cricketing Sunday in London, sir, and us watching the replay of the Pakistanis against Botham in the back room.

Even at the Foreign Office, that freezing hearth of official British hospitality, where the despairing Landau presented himself as a last resort and with the greatest of reluctance, it was only by dint of high entreaty and some honest-to-God Slav tears that he fought his way to the rarefied ear of the Honourable Palmer Wellow, author of a discerning monograph on Liszt.

And if Landau had not used a new tactic, probably the Slav tears would not have helped. Because this time he placed the briefcase open on the counter so that the doorman, who was young but sceptical, could crane his pomaded head to the recently installed armoured glass and scowl down into it with his indolent eyes, and see for himself that it was only a bunch of dirty old notebooks in there and a brown envelope, not bombs.

'Come-back-Monday-ten-to-five,' the doorman said through the wonderfully-new electric speaker, as if announcing a Welsh railway station, and slumped back into the darkness of his box.

The gate stood ajar. Landau looked at the young man, and looked past him at the great portico built a hundred years earlier to daunt the unruly princes of the Raj. And the next thing anyone knew, he had picked up his briefcase and, defeating all the seemingly impenetrable defences set up to prevent exactly such an onslaught, was pelting hell-for-leather with it – 'like a bloomin' Springbok, sir' – across the hallowed courtyard up the steps into the enormous hall. And he was in luck. Palmer Wellow, whatever else he was, belonged to the appeasement side of the Foreign Office. And it was Palmer's day on.

'Hullo, *hullo*,' Palmer murmured as he descended the great steps and beheld the disordered figure of Landau panting between two stout guards. 'Well you *are* in a muck. My name's Wellow. I'm a resident clerk here.' He held his left fist to his shoulder as if he hated dogs. But his right hand was extended in greeting.

'I don't want a clerk,' said Landau. 'I want a high officer or nothing.'

'Well, a clerk is *fairly* high,' Palmer modestly assured him. 'I expect you're put off by the language.'

It was only right to record – and our committee did – that nobody could fault Palmer Wellow's performance thus far. He was droll but he was effective. He put no polished foot wrong. He led Landau to an interviewing room and sat him down, all attention. He ordered a cup of tea for him with sugar for his shock, and offered him a digestive biscuit. With a costly fountain pen given him by a friend, he wrote down Landau's name and address and those of the companies that hired his services. He wrote down the number of Landau's British passport and his date and place of birth, 1930 in Warsaw. He insisted with disarming truthfulness that he had no knowledge of intelligence matters, but undertook to pass on Landau's material to the 'competent people', who would no doubt give it whatever attention it deserved. And because Landau once again insisted on it, he improvised a receipt for him on a sheet of Foreign Office blue draft, signed it and had the janitor add a date-and-time stamp. He told him that if there was anything further the authorities wished to discuss they would very probably get in touch with him, perhaps by means of the telephone.

Only then did Landau hesitatingly pass his scruffy package across the table and watch with lingering regret as Palmer's languid hand enfolded it.

'But why don't you simply give it to Mr. Scott Blair?' Palmer asked after he had studied the name on the envelope.

'I tried, for Christ's sake!' Landau burst out in fresh exasperation. 'I told you. I rang him everywhere. I've rung him till I'm blue in the face, I tell you. He's not at his home, he's not at work, he's not at his club, he's not at anywhere,' Landau protested, his English grammar slipping in despair. 'From the airport I tried. All right, it's a Saturday.'

'But it's Sunday,' Palmer objected with a forgiving smile.

'So it was a Saturday yesterday, wasn't it! I try his firm. I get an electronic howl. I look in the phone book. There's one in Hammersmith. Not his initials but Scott Blair. I get an angry lady, tells me to go to hell. There's a rep I know, Archie Parr, does the West Country for him. I ask Archie: "Archie, for Christ's sake, how do I get hold of Barley in a hurry?" "He's skedaddled, Niki. Done one of his bunks. Hasn't been seen in the shop for weeks." Enquiries, I try. London, the Home Counties. Not listed, not a Bartholomew. Well he wouldn't be, would he, not if he's a – '

'Not if he's a what?' said Palmer, intrigued.

'Look, he's vanished, right? He's vanished before. There could be reasons why he vanishes. Reasons that you don't know of because you're not meant to. Lives are at stake, could be. Not only his either. It's top urgent, she told me. And top secret. Now get on with it. Please.'

The same evening, there being not much doing on the world front apart from a dreary crisis in the Gulf and a squalid television scandal about soldiers and money in Washington, Palmer took himself off to a rather good party in Montpelier Square that was being thrown by a group of his year from Cambridge – bachelors like himself, but fun. An account of this occasion, too, reached our committee's ears.

'Have any of you heard of a Somebody Scott Blair, by the by?' Wellow asked them at a late hour when his memory of Landau happened to have been revived by some bars of Chopin he was playing on the piano. 'Wasn't there a Scott Blair who was up with us or something?' he asked again when he failed to get through the noise.

'Couple of years ahead of us. Trinity,' came a fogged reply from across the room. 'Read History. Jazz fiend. Wanted to blow his saxophone for a living. Old man wouldn't wear it. Barley Blair. Pissed as a rat from daybreak.'

Palmer Wellow played a thunderous chord that stunned the garrulous company to silence. 'I said, is he a poisonous spy?' he enunciated.

'The father? He's dead.'

'The son, ass. Barley.'

Like someone stepping from behind a curtain, his informant emerged from the crowd of young and less young men and stood before him, glass in hand. And Palmer to his pleasure recognised him as a dear chum from Trinity a hundred years ago.

'I really don't know whether Barley's a poisonous spy or not, I'm afraid,' said Palmer's chum, with an asperity habitual to him, as the background babel rose to its former roar. 'He's certainly a failure, if that's a qualification.'

His curiosity whetted still further, Palmer returned to his spacious rooms at the Foreign Office and to Landau's envelope and notebooks, which he had entrusted to the janitor for safekeeping. And it is at this point that his actions, in the words of our interim working paper, took an unhelpful course. Or in the harsher words of Ned and his colleagues in the Russia House, this was where, in any civilised country, P. Wellow would have been strung by his thumbs from a high point in the city and left there in peace to reflect upon his attainments.

For what Palmer did was have a nice time with the notebooks. For two nights and one and a half days. Because he found them so amusing. He did not open the buff envelope – which was by now marked in Landau's handwriting 'Extremely Private for the attention of Mr. B. Scott Blair or a top member of the Intelligence' – because like Landau he was of a school that felt it unbecoming to read other people's mail. In any case it was glued at both ends, and Palmer was not a man to grapple with physical obstacles. But the notebook – with its crazed aphorisms and quotations, its exhaustive loathing of politicians and soldiery, its scatter-shot references to Pushkin the pure Renaissance man and to Kleist the pure suicide – held him fascinated.

He felt little sense of urgency, none of responsibility. He was a diplomat, not a Friend, as the spies were called. And Friends in Palmer's zoology were people without the intellectual horsepower to be what Palmer was. Indeed it was his outspoken resentment that the orthodox Foreign Office to which he belonged resembled more and more a cover organisation for the Friends' disgraceful activities. For Palmer too was a man of impressive erudition, if of a random kind. He had read Arabic and taken a First in Modern History. He had added Russian and Sanskrit in his spare time. He had everything but mathematics and common sense, which explains why he passed over the dreary pages of algebraic formulae, equations and diagrams that made up the other two notebooks, and in contrast to the writer's philosophical ramblings had a boringly disciplined appearance. And which also explains – though the committee had difficulty accepting such an explanation – why Palmer chose to ignore the Standing Order to

Resident Clerks relating to Defectors and Offers of Intelligence whether solicited or otherwise, and to do his own thing.

'He makes the most frantic connections right across the board, Tig,' he told a rather senior colleague in Research Department on the Tuesday, having decided that it was finally time to share his acquisition. 'You simply must read him.'

'But how do we know it's a he, Palms?'

Palmer just felt it, Tig. The vibes.

Palmer's senior colleague glanced at the first notebook, then at the second, then sat down and stared at the third. Then he looked at the drawings in the second book. Then his professional self took over in the emergency.

'I think I'd get this lot across to them fairly sharpish if I were you, Palms,' he said. But on second thoughts he got it across to them himself very sharpish indeed, having first telephoned Ned on the green line and told him to stand by.

Upon which, two days late, hell broke loose. At four o'clock on the Wednesday morning the lights on the top floor of Ned's stubby brick out-station in Victoria known as the Russia House were still burning brightly as the first bemused meeting of what later became the Bluebird team drew to a close. Five hours after that, having sat out two more meetings in the Service's headquarters in a grand new high-rise block on the Embankment, Ned was back at his desk, the files gathering around him as giddily as if the girls in Registry had decided to erect a street barricade.

'God may move in a mysterious way,' Ned was heard to remark to his red-headed assistant Brock in a lull between deliveries, 'but it's nothing to the way He picks his joes.'

A joe in the parlance is a live source, and a live source in sane English is a spy. Was Ned referring to Landau when he spoke of joes? To Katya? To the unchristened writer of the notebooks? Or was his mind already fixed upon the vaporous outlines of that great British gentleman spy, Mr. Bartholomew Scott Blair? Brock did not know or care. He came from Glasgow but of Lithuanian parents and abstract concepts made him angry.

As to myself, I had to wait another week before Ned decided with a proper reluctance that it was time to haul in old Palfrey. I've been old Palfrey since I can remember. To this day I have never understood what happened to my Christian names. 'Where's old Palfrey?' they say. 'Where's our tame legal eagle? Get the old lawbender in! Better chuck this one at Palfrey!'

I am quickly dealt with. You need not stumble on me long. Horatio Benedict dePalfrey are my names but you may forget the first two immediately, and somehow nobody has ever remembered the 'de' at all. In the Service I am Harry so, quite often, being an obedient soul, I am Harry to myself. Alone in my poky little bachelor flat of an evening, I am quite inclined to call myself Harry while I cook my chop. Legal adviser to the illegals, that's me, and sometime junior partner to the extinct house of Mackie, Mackie & dePalfrey, Solicitors and Commissioners for Oaths, of Chancery Lane. But that was twenty years ago. For twenty years I have been your most humble secret servant, ready at any time to rob the scales of the same blind goddess whom my young heart was brought up to revere.

A palfrey, I am told, was neither a warhorse nor a hunter, but a saddle horse deemed suitable for ladies. Well, there's only one little lady who ever rode this Palfrey any distance, but she rode him nearly to his grave and her name was Hannah. And it was because of Hannah that I scurried for shelter inside the secret citadel where passion has no place, where the walls are so thick I cannot hear her beating fists or tearful voice imploring me to let her in and brave the scandal that so terrified a young solicitor at the threshold of a respectable career.

Hope in my face and nothing in my heart, she said. A wiser woman might have kept such observations to herself, it has always seemed to me. Sometimes the truth is by way of being a self-indulgence. 'Then why do you pursue a hopeless case?' I would protest to her. 'If the patient is dead, why keep trying to revive him?'

Because she was a woman, seemed to be the answer. Because she believed in the redemption of male souls. Because I had not paid enough for being inadequate.

But I have paid now, believe me.

It is because of Hannah that I walk the secret corridors to this day, calling my cowardice duty and my weakness sacrifice.

It is because of Hannah that I sit here late at night, in my grey box of an office with LEGAL on the door, files and tapes and films stacked around me like the case of Jarndyce v. Jarndyce without the pink string, while I draft our official whitewash of the operation we called the Bluebird and of its protagonist, Bartholomew, alias Barley, Scott Blair.

It is because of Hannah also that even while he scribbles at his exculpation this old Palfrey now and then puts down his pen and lifts his head and dreams.

Niki Landau's recall to the British colours, if he had ever seriously abandoned them, took place exactly forty-eight hours after the notebooks hit Ned's desk. Ever since his miserable passage through Whitehall, Landau had been sick with anger and mortification. He hadn't gone to work, he hadn't bothered with his little flat in Golders Green which he normally buffed and pampered as if it were the lantern of his life. Not even Lydia could rouse him from his melancholy. I myself had hastily arranged the Home Office warrant to tap his phone. When she telephoned, we listened to him putting her off. And when she made a tragic appearance at his front door, our watchers reported that he let her stay for a cup of tea and then dismissed her.

'I don't know what I've done wrong but whatever it is, I'm sorry,' they heard her remark sadly as she left.

She was hardly in the street before Ned rang. Afterwards Landau shrewdly wondered to me whether that was a coincidence.

'Niki Landau?' Ned enquired in a voice you didn't feel like fooling with.

'I could be,' said Landau, sitting up straight.

'My name's Ned. I think we have a mutual friend. No need to mention names. You kindly dropped a letter in for him the other day. Rather against the odds, I'm afraid. A package too.'

Landau thrilled to the voice immediately. Capable and commanding. The voice of a good officer, not a cynic, Harry.

'Well, yes, I did,' he said, but Ned was already talking again.

'I don't think we need to go into a lot of details over the telephone, but I do think you and I need to have a long chat and I think we need to shake your hand. Rather soon. When can we do that?'

'Whenever you say,' said Landau. And had to stop himself from saying 'sir'.

'I always think now's a good time. How do you feel about that?'

'I feel a whole lot better, Ned,' said Landau with a grin in his voice.

'I'm going to send a car for you. Won't be at all long, so perhaps you'd just stay where you are and wait for your front doorbell to ring. It's a green Rover, B registration. The driver's name is Sam. If you're worried, ask him to show you his card. If you're still worried, phone the number on it. Think you'll manage?'

'Our friend's all right, is he?' said Landau, unable to resist asking, but Ned had rung off.

The doorbell pealed a couple of minutes afterwards. They had the car waiting round the corner, thought Landau as he floated downstairs in a dream. This is it. I'm in the hands of the professionals. The house was in smart Belgravia, one of a terrace recently restored. Its newly painted white front glistened wholesomely at him in the evening sun. A palace of excellence, a shrine to the secret powers that rule our lives. A polished-brass sign on the pillared doorway said FOREIGN LIAISON STAFF. The door was already opening as Landau climbed the steps. And as the uniformed janitor closed it behind him Landau saw a slender, straight-built man in his early forties advance towards him through the sunbeams, first the trim silhouette, then the no-nonsense handsome healthy features, then the handshake: discreet but loyal as a naval salute.

'Well done, Niki. Come on in.'

Good voices do not always belong to good faces, but Ned's did. As Landau followed him into the oval study, he felt he could say anything in the world to him, and Ned would still be on his side. Landau in fact saw a whole lot of things in Ned that he liked at once, which was Ned's Pied Piper gift: the careful charm, the restrained good looks, the power of quiet leadership and the 'Come on in.' Landau also sniffed the polyglot in him, for he was one himself. He had only to drop a Russian name or phrase for Ned to reach out for it and smile, and match it with a phrase of his own. He was one of us, Harry. If you had a secret, this was the man to tell it to, not that flunkey in the Foreign Office.

But then Landau had not realised, until he began talking, how desperately he had been needing to confide. He opened his mouth, he was away. All he could do from then on was listen to himself in amazement, because he wasn't just talking about Katya and the notebooks, and why he had accepted them, and how he had hidden them, but about his whole life till now, his confusions about being a Slav, his love of Russia despite everything, and his feeling of being suspended between two cultures. Yet Ned did not lead him or check him in any way. He was a born listener. He hardly stirred except to write himself neat notes on bits of card, and if he interrupted, it was only to clear up a rare point of detail – the moment at Sheremetyevo, for example, when Landau was waved through to the departure lounge without a glance.

'Now did all your group receive that treatment or only you?'

'The lot of us. One nod, we were through.'

'You didn't feel singled out in any way?'

'What for?'

'You didn't have the impression you might be getting a different kind of treatment from other people? A better one, for instance?'

'We went through like a bunch of sheep. A flock,' Landau corrected himself. 'We handed in our visas, that was it.'

'Were other groups going through at the same rate, did you notice?'

'The Russkies didn't seem to be bothering at all. Maybe it was the summer Saturday. Maybe it was the *glasnost*. They pulled a few out to inspect and let the others through. I felt a fool, to be truthful. I didn't need to have taken the precautions that I did.'

'You were no sort of fool. You did marvellously,' said Ned, without a hint of patronising while he wrote again. 'And on the plane, who did you sit next to, remember?'

'Spikey Morgan.'

'Who else?'

'No one. I had the window.'

'Which seat was that?'

Landau knew the seat number off pat. It was the one he pre-booked whenever he could.

'Did you talk much on the flight?'

'Quite a lot, as a matter of fact.'

'What about?'

'Women, mainly. Spikey's moved in with a pair of freewheelers in Notting Hill.'

Ned gave a pleasant laugh. 'And did you tell Spikey about the note-books? In your relief, Niki? It would have been perfectly natural in the circumstances. To confide.'

'I wouldn't dream of it, Ned. Not to a soul. I never did, I never will. I'm only telling you because he's vanished and you're official.'

'How about Lydia?'

The offence to Landau's dignity momentarily outweighed his admiration of Ned, and even his surprise at Ned's familiarity with his affairs.

'My ladies, Ned, they know a little about me. They may even think they know more than they do,' he replied. 'But they do not share my secrets because they are not invited to.'

Ned continued writing. And somehow the trim movement of the pen, coupled with the suggestion that he could have been indiscreet, provoked Landau into chancing his hand, because he had noticed already that every time he started to talk about Barley, a kind of freeze settled over Ned's quietly reassuring features.

'And Barley's really all right, is he? He hasn't had an accident or anything?'

Ned seemed not to hear. He took a fresh card and resumed his writing.

'I suppose Barley would have used the Embassy, wouldn't he?' said Landau. 'Him being a professional. Barley. It's the chess that gives him away, if you want to know. He shouldn't play it, in my opinion. Not in public.'

Then and only then did Ned's head rise slowly from the page. And Landau saw a stony expression in his face that was more frightening than his words. 'We never mention names like that, Niki,' said Ned very quietly. 'Not even among ourselves. You couldn't know, so you've done nothing wrong. Just please don't do it again.'

Then seeing perhaps the effect that he had had on Landau, he got up and strolled to a satinwood sidetable and poured two glasses of sherry from a decanter and handed one to Landau. 'And yes, he's all right,' he said.

So they drank a silent toast to Barley, whose name Landau had by then sworn to himself ten times already would never again cross his lips.

'We don't want you to go to Gdansk next week,' said Ned. 'We've arranged a medical certificate and compensation for you. You're ill. Suspected ulcer. And stay away from work in the meantime, do you mind?'

'I'll do whatever you say,' said Landau.

But before he left he signed a declaration of the Official Secrets Act while Ned benignly looked on. It's a weaselly document in legal terms, calculated to impress the signatory and no one else. But then the Act itself is scarcely a credit to its drafters either.

After that, Ned switched off the microphones and the hidden video cameras that the twelfth floor had insisted on because it was becoming that kind of operation.

And this far, Ned did everything alone, which was his good right as head of the Russia House. Fieldmen are nothing if not loners. He didn't even call in old Palfrey to read the riot act. Not yet.

If Landau had felt neglected until that afternoon, for the rest of the week he was swamped with attention. Early the next morning, Ned telephoned asking him with his customary courtesy to present himself to an address in Pimlico. It turned out to be a 1930s block of flats, with curved steel-framed windows painted green and an entrance that should have led to a cinema. In the presence of two men whom he did not introduce, Ned took Landau crisply through his story a second time, then threw him to the wolves.

The first to speak was a distraught, floating man with baby-pink cheeks and baby-clear eyes and a flaxen jacket to match his straggling flaxen hair. His voice floated too. 'You said a blue dress, I think? My name's Walter,' he added, as if himself startled by the news.

'I did, sir.'

'You're sure?' he piped, rolling his head and peering crookedly at him from under his silken brow.

'Totally, sir. A blue dress with a brown perhaps-bag. Most perhaps-bags are made of string. Hers was brown plastic. "Now Niki," I said to myself "today is not the day, but if you were ever thinking of having a tumble with this lady at a future date, which you might, you could always bring her a nice blue handbag from London to match her blue dress, couldn't you?" That's how I remember, you see. I have the connection in my head, sir.'

And it is always an oddity of the tapes when I replay them that Landau called Walter 'sir', while he never called Ned anything but Ned. But this was no great sign of respect in Landau so much as of a certain squeamishness that Walter inspired. After all, Landau was a ladies' man and Walter was quite the opposite.

'And the hair *black*, you say?' Walter sang, as if black hair strained credulity.

'Black, sir. Black and silky. Verging towards the raven. Definitely.'

'Not dyed, you don't think?'

'I know the difference, sir,' said Landau, touching his own head, for he wanted to give them everything by now, even the secret of his eternal youth.

'You said earlier she was Leningrad. Why did you say that?'

'The bearing, sir. I saw quality, I saw a Russian woman of Rome. That's how I think of her. Petersburg.'

'But you didn't see Armenian? Or Georgian? Or Jewish, for example?'

Landau dwelt on the last suggestion but rejected it. 'I'm Jewish myself you see. I won't say it takes one to know one but I'll say I didn't go ting-a-ling inside.'

A silence that could have been embarrassment seemed to encourage him to continue. 'I think being Jewish is overdone, to be frank. If that's what you want to be, good luck I say. But if you don't need it, nobody should make you have it. Myself, I'm a Brit first, a Pole second and everything else comes afterwards. Never mind there's a lot would have it the other way round. That's their problem.'

'Oh well said!' Walter cried energetically, flapping his fingers and giggling. 'Oh that *does* put it in a nutshell. And you say her English was really rather good?'

'More than good, sir. Classic. A lesson to us all.'

'Like a schoolteacher, you said.'

'That was my impression,' said Landau. 'A teacher, a professor. I felt the learning. The intellect. The will.'

'Could she not be an interpreter, you see?'

'Good interpreters efface themselves, in my opinion, sir. This lady projected herself.'

'Oh well I say, that's rather a good answer,' said Walter, shooting his pink cuffs. 'And she was wearing a wedding ring. Well done.'

'She certainly was, sir. A betrothal ring and a marriage ring. That's the first thing I look at after the usual, and in Russia it's not England, you have to look the wrong way round because the girls wear their wedding rings on the right hand. Single Russian women are a pest and divorce is off the peg. Give me a nice solid hubby and a couple of little ones for them to go home to any day. Then I might oblige.'

'Let's ask you about that. You think she had children as well, do you, or not?'

'I am convinced of it, sir.'

'Oh come, you can't be,' Walter said peevishly, with a sudden downturn of the mouth. 'You're not psychic, are you?'

'The hips, sir. The hips, the dignity even when she was scared. She was not a Juno, she was not a sylph. She was a mother.'

'Height?' Walter shrieked in a descant as his hairless eyebrows bucked upwards in alarm. 'Can you do her height for us? Think of yourself. Measure her against you. Are you looking up or down?'

'Above the normal. I told you.'

'Taller than you, then?'

'Yes.'

'Five six? Five seven?'

'More like the second,' said Landau sullenly.

'And her age again? You fumbled it before.'

'If she's over thirty-five, she doesn't know it. A lovely skin, a fine form, a fine woman in her prime, especially the spirit, sir,' Landau replied with a defeated grin, for while he might find Walter unsavoury, in some way he still had the Pole's weakness for eccentrics.

'It's a Sunday. Imagine she's English. Would you expect her to be going to church?'

'She'd definitely have given the problem a good going over,' said Landau to his great surprise before he had time to think of an answer. 'She might have said there was *no* God. She might have said there *was* a God. But she wouldn't have let it drift away from her like most of us. She'd have gone for it and come to a decision and done something about it if she thought she should.'

Suddenly all Walter's quaint ways had resolved themselves into a long rubbery smile. 'Oh you *are* good,' he declared enviously. 'Now do you know any science?' he continued as his voice again soared into the clouds.

'A bit. Kitchen science, really. What I pick up.'

'Physics?'

'O-level, not more, sir. I used to sell the course books. I'm not sure I'd scrape through the exam, mind, even now. But they did enable me to improve myself, put it that way.'

'What does telemetry mean?'

'Never heard of it.'

'Not in English, not in Russian?'

'Not in any language, sir, I'm afraid. Telemetry has passed me by.'

'How about CEP?'

'The what, sir?'

'Circular-error-probable. My goodness, he wrote enough about it, didn't he, in those funny notebooks that you brought us? Don't tell me CEP hasn't stuck in your mind.'

'I didn't notice it. I skipped. That's all I did.'

'Until you came to his point about the Soviet knight dying inside his armour. Where you stopped skipping. Why?'

'I didn't come to it. I *happened* to come to it.'

'All right you happened to come to it. And you formed a view. Is that right? Of what the writer was telling us. What view?'

'Incompetence, I suppose. They're no good at it. The Russkies. They're duff.'

'Duff at what?'

'The rockets. They make errors.'

'What sort of errors?'

'All sorts. *Magnetic* errors. *Bias* errors, whatever those are. I don't know. That's your job, isn't it?'

But Landau's defensive surliness only emphasised his virtue as a witness. For where he wished to shine and could not, his failure reassured them, as Walter's airy gesture of relief now testified.

'Well I think he's done terribly well,' he declared as if Landau were nowhere within earshot, flinging up his hands again, this time in a theatrical gesture of conclusion. 'He tells us what he remembers. He doesn't make things up to spin a better tale. You won't do that, will you, Niki?' he added anxiously, uncrossing his legs as if his crotch were nipping him.

'No, sir, you may rest assured.'

'And you haven't? I mean, because sooner or later we'd find out. Then everything you've given us would lose its lustre.'

'No, sir. It's the way I told it. No more, no less.'

'I'm sure it is,' said Walter to his colleagues in a tone of simple trust as he again sat back. 'The hardest thing in our trade or anybody else's is to say "I believe." Niki's a natural source and rare as hen's teeth. If there were more of *him*, nobody would need *us*.'

'This is Johnny,' Ned explained, playing the aide-de-camp.

Johnny had wavy greying hair and a broad jaw and a file full of official-looking telegrams. With his gold watch-chain and tailored charcoal suit, he might have been a foreign barmaid's vision of an Englishman but he certainly wasn't Landau's.

'Niki, first we have to thank you, pal,' Johnny said, in lazy East Coast American. We the larger beneficiaries, his munificent tone suggested. We the majority shareholders. I'm afraid Johnny is like that. A good officer, but unable to keep his American supremacy inside its box. I sometimes think that is the difference between American spies and our own. Americans, with their frank enjoyment of power and money, flaunt their luck. They lack the instinct to dissemble that comes so naturally to us British.

Anyway, Landau's hackles went up in a flash.

'Mind if I ask you a couple of questions?' Johnny said.

'If it's all right by Ned,' said Landau.

'Of course it is,' said Ned.

'So we're at the audio fair that night. Okay, pal?'

'Well, evening really, Johnny.'

'You escort the woman Yekaterina Orlova across the room to the top of the staircase. Where the guards are. You say goodbye to her.'

'She's holding my arm.'

'She's holding your arm, great. In front of the guards. You watch her down the stairs. Do you also watch her into the street, pal?'

I had not heard Johnny use 'pal' before, so I took it that he was trying to needle Landau somehow, a thing that Agency people learn from their in-house psychologists.

'Correct,' Landau snapped.

'Right into the street? Pause and think,' he suggested, with the attorney's false expansiveness.

'Into the street and out of my life.'

Johnny waited till he was sure everyone was aware that he was waiting, and Landau more aware than anybody. 'Niki, pal, we've had people stand at the top of that staircase in the last twenty-four hours. No one sees the street from the top of that staircase.'

Landau's face darkened. Not in embarrassment. In anger. 'I saw her walk down the stairs. I saw her cross the lobby to where the street is. She did not return. So unless somebody has moved the street in the last twenty-four hours, which I grant you under Stalin was always possible – '

'Let's go on, shall we?' said Ned.

'See anyone walk out after her?' Johnny asked, riding Landau a little harder.

'Down the stairs or into the street?'

'Both, pal. Both.'

'No, I didn't. I didn't see her go into the street, did I, because you just told me I didn't. So why don't you answer the questions and I'll ask them?'

While Johnny sat idly back, Ned intervened. 'Niki, some things have to be very carefully examined. There's a lot at stake and Johnny has his orders.'

'I'm at stake too,' said Landau. 'My word's on the line and I don't like having it made a fool of by an American who's not even British.'

Johnny had returned to the file. 'Niki, will you please describe the security arrangements for the fair, as you yourself observed them?'

Landau took a tense breath. 'Well then,' he said, and started again. 'We had these two young uniformed policemen hanging about the hotel lobby. Those are the boys who keep the lists of all the Russians who come and go, which is normal. Then upstairs inside the hall we had the nasties. Those are the plainclothes boys. The dawdlers, they call them, the *toptuny*,' he added for Johnny's enlightenment. 'After a couple of days you know the *toptuny* by heart. They don't buy, they don't steal the exhibits or ask for freebies and there's always one of them with the butter-blond hair, don't ask me why. We had three boys and they didn't change all week. They were the ones who watched her go down the stairs.'

'That everyone, pal?'

'As far as I know it is everyone but I'm waiting to be told I'm wrong.'

'Were you not also aware of two ladies of indeterminate age, grey-haired persons who were also present every day of the fair, came early, left late, who also didn't buy, didn't enter negotiations with any of the standholders or exhibitors, or appear to have any legitimate purpose for attending the fair?'

'You're talking about Gert and Daisy, I suppose.'

'Excuse me?'

'There was two old biddies from the Council of Libraries. They came for the beer. Their main pleasure was whipping brochures off the stands and cadging free handouts. We christened them Gert and Daisy after a certain British radio show popular in the war years and after.'

'It did not occur to you that these ladies might also be performing a surveillance function?'

Ned's powerful hand was already out to restrain Landau but he was too late.

'Johnny,' said Landau, boiling over. 'This is Moscow, right? Moscow, Russia, *pal*. If I stopped to consider who had a surveillance function and who didn't, I wouldn't get out of bed in the morning and I wouldn't get into it at night. The birds in the trees are wired for all I know.'

Yet again Johnny was at his telegrams. 'You say that Yekaterina Borisovna Orlova referred to the adjoining stand of Abercrombie & Blair as having been empty on the previous day, correct?'

'I do say so, yes.'

'But you didn't see her the day before? Is that also correct?'

'It is.'

'You also say that you have an eye for a pretty lady.'

'I do, thank you, and may it long remain vigilant.'

'Don't you think you should have noticed her then?'

'I do sometimes miss one,' Landau confessed, colouring again. 'If my back is turned, if I am bent over a desk or relieving myself in the toilet, it is possible my attention may flag for a moment.'

But Johnny's nervelessness was acquiring its own authority. 'You have relatives in Poland, do you not, Mr. Landau?' The 'pal' had evidently done its work, for listening to the tape I noticed he had dropped it.

'I do.'

'Do you not have an elder sister highly placed in the Polish administration?'

'My sister works in the Polish Health Ministry as a hospital inspector. She is not highly placed and she is past retiring age.'

'Have you at any time directly or indirectly been the witting target of pressure or blackmail by Communist bloc agencies or third parties acting in their behalf?'

Landau turned to Ned. 'A what target? My English isn't very good, I'm afraid.'

'Conscious,' said Ned with a warning smile. 'Aware. Knowing.'

'No, I haven't,' said Landau.

'In your travels to Eastern bloc countries, have you been intimate with women of those countries?'

'I've been to bed with some. I haven't been intimate.'

Like a naughty schoolboy Walter let out a squeak of choked laughter, lifting his shoulders to his neck and cupping his hand over his dreadful teeth. But Johnny soldiered doggedly on: 'Mr. Landau, have you ever prior to this time had contacts with any intelligence agency of any hostile or friendly country anywhere?'

'Negative.'

'Have you ever sold information to any person of whatever status or profession – newspaper, enquiry agency, police, military – for any purpose, however innocuous?'

'Negative.'

'And you are not and never have been a member of a Communist party or any peace organisation or group sympathetic to its aims?'

'I'm a British subject,' Landau retorted, thrusting out his little Polish jaw.

'And you have no idea, however vague, however mistily formed, of the overall message contained in the material you handled?'

'I didn't handle it. I passed it on.'

'But you read it along the way.'

'What I could, I read. Some. Then I gave up. As I told you.'

'Why?'

'From a sense of decency, if you want to know. Something which I begin to suspect you are not troubled by.'

But Johnny, far from blushing, was digging patiently in his file. He drew out an envelope and from the envelope a pack of postcard-size photographs which he dealt on to the table like playing-cards. Some were fuzzy, all were grainy. A few had foreground obstructions. They showed women coming down the steps of a bleak office building, some in groups, some singly. Some carried perhaps-bags, some had their heads down and carried nothing. And Landau remembered hearing that it was Moscow practice for ladies slipping out for lunchtime shopping to stuff whatever they needed into their pockets and leave their handbags lying on their desks in order to show the world they had only gone down the corridor.

'This one,' said Landau suddenly, pointing with his forefinger.

Johnny played another of his courtroom tricks. He was really too intelligent for all this nonsense but that didn't stop him. He looked disappointed and mighty unbelieving. He looked as if he had caught Landau in a lie. The video film shows him overacting quite outrageously. 'How can you be so damn sure, for God's sake? You never even *saw* her in an overcoat.'

Landau is undismayed. 'That's the lady. Katya,' he says firmly. 'I'd recognise her anywhere. Katya. She's done her hair up, but it's her. Katya. That's her bag too, plastic.' He continues staring at the photograph. 'And her wedding ring.' For a moment he seems to forget he is not alone. 'I'd do the same for her tomorrow,' he says. '*And* the day after.'

Which marked the satisfactory end to Johnny's hostile examination of the witness.

As the days progressed and one enigmatic interview followed another, never the same place twice, never the same people except for Ned, Landau had increasingly the feeling that things were advancing to a climax. In a sound laboratory behind Portland Place, they played him women's voices, Russians speaking Russian and Russians speaking English. But he didn't recognise Katya's. Another day, to his alarm, was devoted to money. Not theirs but Landau's. His bank statements – where the hell did they get them from? His tax returns, salary slips, savings, mortgage, endowment policy, worse than the Inland Revenue.

'Trust us, Niki,' said Ned – but with such an honest, reassuring smile that Landau had the feeling that Ned had been out there fighting for him somehow, and that things were on the verge of coming right.

They're going to offer me a job, he thought on the Monday. They're going to turn me into a spy like Barley.

They're trying to put it right about my father twenty years after his death, he thought on the Tuesday.

Then on the Wednesday morning, Sam the driver pressed his doorbell for the last time and everything came clear.

'Where is it today then, Sam?' Landau asked him cheerfully. 'The Bloody Tower?'

'Sing Sing,' said Sam, and they had a good laugh.

But Sam delivered him not to the Tower and not to Sing Sing either, but to the side entrance of one of the very Whitehall ministries that Landau only eleven days earlier had attempted unsuccessfully to storm. The grey-eyed Brock guided him up a back staircase and disappeared. Landau entered a great room that looked on to the Thames. A row of men sat at a table facing him. To the left sat Walter with his tie set straight and his hair slicked down. To the right sat Ned. Both looked solemn. And between them, with his cuffed hands resting flat on the table and lines of refusal round his neat jaw, sat a younger, sharp-suited man whom Landau rightly assumed to be senior in rank to both of them, and who, as Landau later put it, looked as though he had stepped out of a different movie. He was sleek and tight-lipped and groomed for television. He was rich in more than money. He was forty and rising, but the worst thing about him was his innocence. He looked too young to be charged with adult crimes.

'My name's Clive,' he said in an underpowered voice. 'Come in, Landau. We've got a problem about what to do with you.'

And beyond Clive – beyond all of them, in fact – Niki Landau as an afterthought saw me. Old Palfrey. And Ned saw him see me and Ned smiled and made a pleasant show of introducing us.

'Ah now, Niki, this is Harry,' he said untruthfully.

Nobody else had earned a trade description till then but Ned provided one for me: 'Harry's our in-house umpire, Niki. He makes sure everyone gets a fair deal.'

'Nice,' said Landau.

Which is where, in the history of the affair, I made my own modest entrance, as legal errand boy, as fixer and bit player, and pleaser, and finally as chronicler; now Rosencrantz, now Guildenstern, and just occasionally Palfrey.

And to take even more care of Landau there was Reg, who was big and ginger and reassuring. Reg led Landau to a dunce's chair at the centre of the room, then sat beside him on another. And Landau took to Reg at once, which was usual, for Reg was by trade a welfarer and his clients included defectors, grounded fieldmen and blown agents, and other men and women whose bonds to England might have worn a little thin if old Reg Wattle and his cosy wife Berenice had not been there to hold their hands.

'You've done a good job but we can't tell you why it's good, because that would be insecure,' Clive continued in his arid voice when Landau was comfortably settled. 'Even the little you know is too much. And we can't let you wander round Eastern Europe with our secrets in your head. It's too dangerous. For you and the people involved. So while you've performed a valuable service for us, you've also become a serious worry. If this were wartime, we could lock you up or shoot you or something. But it isn't, not officially.'

Somewhere on his prudent little journey to power, Clive had taught himself to smile. It was an unfair weapon to use on friendly people, rather like silence on the telephone. But Clive knew nothing of unfairness because he knew nothing of its opposite. As to passion, it was what you used when you needed to persuade people.

'After all, you could point the finger at some very important people, couldn't you?' he continued so quietly that everyone kept still to hear him. 'I know you wouldn't do that deliberately but when one's handcuffed to a radiator one doesn't have much choice. Not in the end.'

And when Clive thought he had scared Landau just enough he glanced to me, and nodded to me, and watched me while I opened up the pompous leather folder I had brought with me and handed Landau the long document I had prepared, of which the purport was that Landau renounce in perpetuity all travel behind the Iron Curtain, that he never leave the country without first advising Reg so many days in advance, the details to be arranged between the two of them, and that Reg should look after Landau's passport in order to prevent mishaps. And that he accept irrevocably into his life the role of Reg or whomever the authorities should appoint in Reg's place as confidant, philosopher and discreet arbiter of his affairs of every kind – including the ticklish problem of how to handle the taxation on the cashier's cheque attached, drawn on the Fulham branch of a very boring British bank, in the sum of a hundred thousand pounds.

And that, in order that he be regularly scared by Authority, he should present himself every six months to the Service's Legal Adviser, Harry, for a top-up on the subject of Secrecy – to old Palfrey, Hannah's sometime lover, a man so bowed by life that he can be safely charged with keeping others upright. And that further to the above and pursuant to it and consequent upon it, the whole matter relating to a certain Russian woman and to her friend's literary manuscript, and to the contents of said manuscript – however much or little he may have understood their import – and to the part played by a certain British publisher, be as of this moment solemnly declared void, dead, inoperative and expunged, henceforth and for all time. Amen.

There was one copy and it would live in my safe till it was shredded or fell apart of old age. Landau read it twice while Reg read it over his shoulder. Then Landau disappeared into his own thoughts for a while without much regard for who was watching him or who was willing him to sign and cease to be a problem. Because Landau knew that in this instance he was the buyer, not the seller.

He saw himself standing at the window of his Moscow hotel room. He remembered how he had wished he could hang up his traveller's boots and settle to a less arduous life. And the amusing notion came to him that his Maker must have taken him at his word and fixed things accordingly, which to everyone's unease caused him to break out in a little burst of laughter.

'Well I hope old Johnny the Yank is footing the bill for this, Harry,' he said.

But the joke did not receive the applause it deserved, since it happened to be true. So Landau took Reg's pen and signed, and handed me the document and watched me add my own signature as a witness, Horatio B. dePalfrey, which after twenty years has such a practised illegibility that if I had signed it Heinz's Tomato Soup neither Landau nor anybody else could have told the difference, and put it back inside its leather coffin and patted down the lid. There was handshaking, mutual assurances were exchanged, and Clive murmured, 'We're grateful to you, Niki,' just like in the movie that Landau periodically convinced himself he was part of.

Then everybody shook Landau's hand yet again and, having watched him ride nobly into the sunset or more accurately walk jauntily off down the corridor chatting away at Reg Wattle, who was twice his size, they waited fretfully for the 'take' on the intercepts for which I had already obtained the warrants under the infallible plea of intense American interest.

They tapped his office and home telephones, read his mail and fitted an electronic limpet to the rear axle of his beloved drop-head Triumph.

They followed him in his leisure hours and recruited a typist in his office to keep an eye on him as a 'suspect foreigner' while he served out the last weeks of his notice.

They put potential lady-friends alongside him in the bars where he liked to do his hunting. Yet despite these cumbersome and needless precautions, dictated by that same intense American interest, they drew a blank. No hint of bragging or indiscretion reached their ears. Landau never complained, never boasted, never attempted to go public. He became, in fact, one of the few finished and perfectly happy short stories of the trade.

He was the perfect prologue. He never came back.

He never attempted to get in touch with Barley Scott Blair, the great British spy. He lived in awe of him for ever. Even for the grand opening of the video shop, when he would have loved more than anything in the world to bask in the presence of this real-life secret British hero, he never tried to stretch the rules. Perhaps it was satisfaction enough for him to know that one night in Moscow, when the old country had called on him, he too had behaved like the English gentleman he sometimes longed to be. Or perhaps the Pole in him was content to have cocked a snook at the Russian bear next door. Or perhaps it was the memory of Katya that kept him faithful, Katya the strong, the virtuous, Katya the brave and beautiful, who even in her own fear had taken care to warn him of the dangers to himself. 'You must believe in what you are doing.'

And Landau had believed. And Landau was proud as Punch that he had, as any of us should be.

Even his video shop flourished. It was a sensation. A little rich for some people's blood now and then, including that of the Golders Green police, with whom I had to have a friendly word. But for others pure balm.

Above all, we were able to love him, because he saw us as we wished to be seen, as the omniscient, capable and heroic custodians of our great nation's inner health. It was a view of us that Barley never quite seemed able to share – any more, I have to say, than Hannah could, though she only ever knew it from outside, as the place to which she could not follow me, as the shrine of ultimate compromise and therefore, in her unrelenting view, despair.

'They are definitely not the cure, Palfrey,' she had told me only a few weeks before, when for some reason I was trying to extol the Service. 'And they sound to *me* more likely to be the disease.'

3

T here is no such thing, we older hands like to say, as an intelligence operation that does not occasionally run to farce. The bigger the operation, the bigger the belly laughs, and it is a matter of Service history that the week-long manhunt for Bartholomew alias Barley Scott Blair generated enough frenzy and frustration to power a dozen secret networks. Orthodox young novices like Brock from the Russia House learned to hate Barley's life before they even found the man who led it.

After five days of chasing after him, they thought they knew everything about Barley except where he was. They knew his free-thinking parentage and his expensive education, both wasted, and the unedifying details of his marriages, all broken. They knew the café in Camden Town where he played his chess with any layabout spirit who happened to drift in. A regular gentleman, even if he was the guilty party, they told Wicklow, who was posing as a divorce agent. Under the usual tacky but effective pretexts, they had doorstepped a sister in Hove who despaired of him, tradesmen in Hampstead who were writing to him, a married daughter in Grantham who adored him and a grey-wolf son in the City who was so withdrawn he might have taken a vow of silence.

They had talked to members of a scratch jazz band for whom he had occasionally played saxophone, to the almoner at the hospital where he was enrolled as a visitor and to the vicar at the Kentish Town church where to everyone's amazement he sang tenor. 'Such a lovely voice when he shows up.' said the vicar indulgently. But when they tried, with old Palfrey's help again, to tap his phone to get more of this lovely voice, there was nothing to tap because he hadn't paid his bill.

They even found a trace on him in our own records. Or rather the Americans found it for them, which did not add to their enchantment. For it turned out that in the early 'sixties, when any Englishman who had the misfortune to possess a double-barrelled name was in danger of being recruited to the Secret Service, Barley's had been passed to New York for vetting under some partially observed bilateral security treaty. Furious, Brock checked again with Central Registry who, after first denying all knowledge of Barley, dug up his card from a cut in the white index that was still waiting to be transferred to the computer. And from the white card, behold a white file containing the original vetting form and corre-spondence. Brock rushed into Ned's room as if he had found the clue to everything. Age, 22! Hobbies, theatre and music! Sports, nil! Reasons for considering him, a cousin named Lionel in the Life Guards!

The payoff alone was lacking. The recruiting officer had lunched Barley at the Athenaeum and stamped his file 'No Further Action', taking the trouble to add the word 'ever' in his own hand.

Nevertheless this quaint episode of more than twenty years ago had a certain oblique effect on their attitude towards him, just as they had puzzled uneasily for a while over the bizarre left-wing attachments of old Salisbury Blair, his father. It undermined Barley's independence in their eyes. Not in Ned's, for Ned was made of stronger stuff. But in the others, Brock and the younger ones. It led them to feel they owned him somehow, if only as the unsuccessful aspirant to their mystique.

A further frustration was provided by Barley's disgraceful car, which the police found parked illegally in Lexham Gardens with the offside wing bashed in and the licence out of date and a half bottle of Scotch stuck in the glove compartment with a sheaf of love letters in Barley's hand. Neighbours had been complaining about it for weeks.

'Tow it, boot it, charge it or just crush it?' the obliging superintendent of traffic asked Ned over the phone.

'Forget it,' Ned replied wearily. Nevertheless he and Brock hastened round there in the vain hope of a clue. The love letters turned out to have been written to a lady of the Gardens but she had given them back to him. She was the last person in the world, she assured them with a tragic air, to know where Barley was now.

It wasn't till the following Thursday, when Ned was patiently checking Barley's monthly bank statements, that he discovered among the overdrawn columns a quarterly standing order in favour of a property company in Lisbon, a hundred and something pounds to Real Somebody Limitada. He stared at it unbelievingly. He kept staring. Then he said a foul word where normally he never swore. Then he phoned Travel in a hurry and had them check old flightlists from Gatwick and Heathrow. When Travel phoned back, Ned swore again. They were home. Days of phone calls, interviews and banging on doors, the rules bent in all directions, watch lists, cables to friendly liaison services in half the capitals of the world, their vaunted Records Section humiliated in front of the Americans. Yet nobody they had spoken to and no researches had revealed the one crucial, indispensable, idiotic fact they needed to know: that ten years ago on a whim Barley Blair, having inherited a stray couple of thousand from a remote aunt, bought himself a scruffy pied-à-terre in Lisbon, where he was accustomed to take periodic rests from the burden of his many-sided soul. It could have been Cornwall, it could have been Provence or Timbuktu. But Lisbon by an accident had got him, down on the waterfront, next to a bit of rough parkland, and too near the fish market for a lot of people's sensitivities.

An embattled calm settled over the Russia House with this discovery and Brock's bony face took on a sallow fury.

'Who's our Brother Lisbon these days?' Ned asked him, light as a summer breeze once more.

Then he telephoned old Palfrey alias Harry and put him on permanent standby which, as Hannah would have said, described my situation nicely.

Barley was sitting at the bar when Merridew walked in on him. He was perched on a stool and shooting his mouth off about human nature to a drink-sodden expatriate major of artillery named Graves: Major Arthur Winslow Graves, later whitelisted as a Barley contact, his only claim on history and he never knew it. Barley's long pliant back was arched away from the open door and the door led off the courtyard, so Merridew, who was a fat boy of thirty, was able to collect some much-needed breath before he made his pitch. He had been chasing Barley half the day, missing him everywhere and getting more furious with each rebuff:

At Barley's flat, not five minutes' walk from here, where an Englishwoman with a common accent had told him through the letterbox to get stuffed.

At the British Library, where the lady librarian had reported that Barley

had spent an afternoon browsing, by which she appeared to imply –
though promptly denied it when directly asked – that he was in an
alcoholic stupor.

And at a revolting Tudor tavern in Estoril, where Barley and friends had
enjoyed a liquid supper under plastic muskets and noisily departed not
half an hour before.

The hotel – it prefers to call itself a humble *pensão* – was an old convent,
a place the English loved. To reach it Merridew had to scale a cobbled
stairway overhung with vines and, having scaled it and taken a first
cautious look, he had to hurry down it again in order to tell Brock to run,
'and I mean really run,' and telephone Ned from the café on the corner.
Then scale it yet again, which was why he was feeling so puffed and even
more than usually put-upon. Smells of cool sandstone and fresh-ground
coffee mingled with the night plants. Merridew was impervious to them.
He lacked breath. The sob of distant trams and the honking of boats
provided the only background sounds to Barley's monologue. Merridew
had no awareness of them.

'Blind children cannot *chew*, Gravey, my dear old charmer,' Barley was
explaining patiently while he rested the point of his spidery forefinger on
the major's navel and his elbow on the bar beside an unfinished game of
chess. 'Fact of science, Gravey. Blind children have to be taught to bite.
Come here. Close your eyes.'

Tenderly taking hold of the major's head in both his hands, Barley
guided it towards him, parted the unresisting jaws, and popped in a couple
of cashews. 'There's a lad. On the command champ, champ. Mind your
tongue. Champ. Repeat.'

Taking this as his cue Merridew hoisted his hail-fellow smile and ventured a step into the bar, where he was surprised by two life-sized carvings
of mulatto ladies in court dress standing either side of him at the doorway.
Colour of hair chestnut, colour of eyes green, he rehearsed, checking off
Barley's points as if he were a horse. Height six foot nothing, clean-shaven,
well-spoken, slender build, idiosyncratic dress. Idiosyncratic, my foot,
thought tubby Merridew, still winded, while he examined Barley's linen
bush-jacket, grey flannels and sandals. What do the fools in London
expect him to wear on a hot night in Lisbon? Mink?

'Ah, excuse me,' Merridew said pleasingly. 'I'm actually *looking* for
someone. I wonder if you can help me.'

'Which proves, my dear old mother's arse,' Barley resumed, when he
had carefully restored the major to an upright position, 'quoting the
celebrated song, that notwithstanding the fact that the big juju man made
us of meat, eating people is wrong.'

'I say, do pardon me, but I rather think you're Mr. Bartholomew Scott
Blair,' said Merridew. 'Yes? Correct?'

Keeping a grasp upon the major's lapel in order to avert a military
disaster, Barley cautiously turned himself half-circle on his stool and

looked Merridew over, beginning with his shoes and ending with his smile.

'My name's Merridew from the Embassy, you see. Only I'm the Commercial Second Secretary here. I'm frightfully sorry. We've received a rather pressing telegram for you over our link. We think you should pop round and read it straight away. Would you mind?'

Then unwisely Merridew permitted himself a mannerism peculiar to plump officials. He flung an arm out, cupped his hand and passed it officiously over the top of his head as if to confirm that his hair and his cover were still in their proper places. And this large gesture, performed by a fat man in a low room, seemed to raise fears in Barley that might otherwise have slumbered, for he became disconcertingly sober.

'Are you telling me somebody's dead, old boy?' he asked with a smile so tense it looked ready for the worst of jokes.

'Oh my dear sir. Don't be so Gothic, please. It's a commercial thing, not consular. Why else would it come over our link?' He tried a placatory giggle.

But Barley had not yielded. Not by an inch. He was still looking into the pit, wherever Merridew might choose to look himself. 'So what the hell are we telling ourselves, actually?' he asked.

'Nothing,' Merridew retorted, scared. 'A pressing telegram. Don't take it so personally. Diplomatic wireless.'

'Who's doing the pressing?'

'No one. I can't give you a précis in front of everyone. It's confidential. Our eyes only.'

They forgot his spectacles, thought Merridew, while he returned Barley's stare. Round. Black-framed. Too small for his eyes. Slips them to the tip of his nose when he scowls at you. Gets you in his sights.

'Never knew an honest debt that couldn't wait till Monday,' Barley declared, returning to the major. 'Loosen your girdle, Mr. Merridew. Take a drink with the unwashed.'

Merridew might not have been the slenderest of men or the tallest. But he had grip, he had cunning and like many fat men he had unexpected resources of indignation which he was able to turn on like a flood when they were needed.

'Look here, Scott Blair, your affairs are not my concern, I am glad to say. I am not a bailiff, I am not a common messenger. I am a diplomat and I have a certain standing. I've spent half the day traipsing round after you, I have a car and a clerk waiting outside and I have certain rights over my own life. I'm sorry.'

Their duet might have continued indefinitely had not the major staged an unexpected revival. Jerking back his shoulders, he thrust his fists to the seams of his trousers and tucked his chin into a rictal grimace of respect. 'Royal summons, Barley,' he barked. 'Embassy's the local Buck House. Invitation's a command. Mustn't insult Her Majesty.'

'He's not Her Majesty,' Barley objected patiently. 'He isn't wearing a crown.'

Merridew wondered whether he should summon Brock. He tried smiling winningly but Barley's attention had wandered to the alcove, where a vase of dried flowers hid an empty grate. He tried calling, 'Okay? All set?' much as he might have called to a wife when she was keeping him waiting for a dinner party. But Barley's haggard gaze remained on the dead flowers. He seemed to see his whole life in them, every wrong turning and false step from there to here. Then just as Merridew was giving up hope, Barley began loading his junk into his bush-jacket pockets, ritualistically, as if setting off on a safari: his bent wallet, full of uncashed cheques and cancelled credit cards; his passport, mildewed with sweat and too much travel; the notebook and pencil he kept handy for penning gems of alcoholic wisdom to himself for contemplation when he was sober. And when he had done all this he dumped a large banknote on the bar like somebody who wouldn't be needing money for a long while.

'See the major into his cab, Manuel. That means help him down the steps and into the back seat and pay the driver in advance. When you've done that, you can keep the change. So long, Gravey. Thanks for the laughs.'

Dew was falling. A young moon lay on its back among the moist stars. They descended the stairway, Merridew first, urging Barley to be sure and mind his step. The harbour was filled with roving lights. A black saloon with CD plates waited at the curbside. Brock lurked restively beside it in the darkness. A second unmarked car lay further back.

'Ah now, this is Eddie,' said Merridew, making the introductions. 'Eddie, I'm afraid we took our time. I trust you have made your phone call?'

'All done,' said Brock.

'And everybody at home is happy, I trust, Eddie? The little ones all tucked up and so forth? You won't get flak from the missus?'

'It's all right,' Brock growled in a tone that said shut up.

Barley sat in the front seat, his head pitched back on the rest, eyes closed. Merridew drove. Brock sat very still in the back. The second car pulled out slowly, in the way good watchers do.

'This the way you usually go to the Embassy?' Barley asked in his seeming doze.

'Ah now, the duty dog took the telegram to his house, you see,' Merridew explained lavishly, as if responding to a particularly well-taken point. 'I'm afraid that, come weekends; we have to batten down the Embassy against the Irish. Yes.' He switched on the radio. A deep-throated woman began sobbing a succulent lament. 'Fado,' he declared. 'I adore Fado. I think it's why I'm here. I'm sure it is. I'm sure I put Fado on my post request.' He began conducting with his spare hand. 'Fado,' he explained.

'Are you the people who've been snooping round my daughter, asking her a lot of stupid questions?' Barley asked.

'Oh we're just commercial, I'm afraid,' Merridew said, and kept conducting for all that he was worth. But inside himself he was by now gravely disturbed by Barley's want of innocence. Sooner them than me, he thought, feeling Barley's untamed gaze upon his right cheek. If this is what Head Office has to reckon with these days, God preserve me from a home posting.

They had rented the town house of a former member of the Service, a British banker with a second house in Cintra. Old Palfrey had clinched the deal for them. They wanted no official premises, nothing that could afterwards be held against them. Yet the sense of age and place had its own particular eloquence. A wrought-iron coaching lamp lit the vaulted entrance. The granite flagstones had been hacked to stop the horses slipping. Merridew rang the bell. Brock had closed in tight in case of accidents.

'Hullo. Come on in,' said Ned pleasantly, opening the huge scrolled door.

'Well I'll be off won't I,' said Merridew. 'Marvellous, terrific.' Still burbling covering fire, he scampered back to his car before anyone could contradict him. And as he did so the second car cruised by like one good friend who has seen another to his doorstep on a dangerous night.

For a long moment, while Brock stood off observing them, Ned and Barley appraised one another as only Englishmen can who are of the same height and class and shape of head. And though Ned in appearance was the very archetype of quiet British self-command and balance, and in most ways therefore the exact reverse of Barley – and though Barley was loose-limbed and angular with a face that even in repose seemed determined to explore beyond the obvious – there was still enough of the other in each of them to permit a recognition. Through a closed door came the murmur of male voices, but Ned made as though he hadn't heard it. He led Barley down the passage to a library and said, 'In here,' while Brock stayed in the hall.

'How drunk are you?' Ned asked, lowering his voice and handing Barley a glass of iced water.

'Not,' said Barley. 'Who's hijacking me? What goes on?'

'My name's Ned. I'm about to move the goalposts. There's no telegram, no crisis in your affairs beyond the usual. No one's being hijacked. I'm from British Intelligence. So are the people waiting for you next door. You once applied to join us. Now's your chance to help.'

A silence settled between them while Ned waited for Barley to respond. Ned was Barley's age exactly. For twenty-five years, in one guise or another, he had been revealing himself as a British secret agent to people he needed to obtain. But this was the first time that his client had failed to speak, blink, smile, step back or show the smallest sign of surprise.

'I don't know anything,' said Barley.

'Maybe we want you to find something out.'

'Find it out for yourselves.'

'We can't. Not without you. That's why we're here.'

Drifting over to the bookshelves, Barley tilted his head to one side and peered over the top of his round spectacles at the titles while he went on drinking his water.

'First you're commercial, now you're spies,' he said.

'Why don't you have a word with the Ambassador?'

'He's a fool. I was at Cambridge with him.' He took down a bound book and glanced at the frontispiece. 'Crap,' he pronounced with contempt. 'Must buy them by the yard. Who owns this place?'

'The Ambassador will verify me. If you ask him whether he can manage golf on Thursday, he'll tell you not till five o'clock.'

'I don't play golf,' said Barley, taking down another volume. 'I don't play anything actually. I've retired from all games.'

'Except chess,' Ned suggested, holding out the open telephone directory to him. With a shrug Barley dialled the number. Hearing the Ambassador, he gave a raffish if rather puzzled smile. 'Is that Tubby? Barley Blair here. How about a spot of the golf on Thursday for your liver?'

An acid voice said it was engaged till five o'clock.

'Five won't do at all,' Barley retorted. 'We'll be playing in the dark at that rate – bugger's rung off,' he complained, shaking the dead receiver. Then he saw Ned's hand on the telephone cradle.

'It isn't a joke, I'm afraid,' said Ned. 'It's actually very serious.'

Lost once more in his own contemplations, Barley slowly replaced the receiver. 'The line between actually very serious and actually very funny is actually very thin,' he remarked.

'Well let's cross it, shall we?' said Ned.

The talk behind the door had ceased. Barley turned the handle and walked in. Ned followed. Brock stayed in the hall to guard the door. We had been listening to everything over the relay.

If Barley was curious as to what he would face in there, so were we. It's an odd game, turning a man's life inside out without meeting him. He entered slowly. He took a few paces into the room and stopped, his long arms dangling wide of his sides while Ned, halfway to the table, made the all-male introductions.

'This is Clive, this is Walter, and over here is Bob. This is Harry. Meet Barley, everyone.'

Barley scarcely nodded as the names were spoken. He seemed to prefer the evidence of his eyes to anything he was being told.

The ornate furniture and the coppice of vulgar indoor plants interested him. So did an orange tree. He touched a fruit, caressed a leaf then delicately sniffed his thumb and finger as if assuring himself that they were real. There was a passive anger about him that went ahead of finding out the cause. Anger at being woken, I thought. At being singled out and named – a thing Hannah said I always feared the most.

I also remember thinking he was elegant. Not, God knows, by virtue of his shabby clothes. But in his gestures, in his faded chivalry. In his natural courtesy, even if he resisted it.

'You don't run to surnames, by any chance, do you?' Barley enquired when he had completed his inspection of the room.

'I'm afraid not,' said Clive.

'Because a Mr. Rigby called on my daughter Anthea last week. Said he was a tax inspector. Some bilge about wanting to adjust an unfair assessment. Was he one of you clowns?'

'By the sound of him I should think he probably was,' said Clive, with the arrogance of someone who can't be bothered to lie.

Barley looked at Clive, who had one of those English faces that seemed to have been embalmed while he was still a boy king, at his hard clever eyes with nothing behind them, at the ash beneath his skin. He turned to Walter, so round, wispy and amused, a teased-out Falstaff of the richer common rooms. And from Walter his gaze moved on to Bob, taking in the patrician scale of him, his greater age, his avuncular ease, the browns he wore instead of greys and blues. Bob was lounging with his legs stretched out, one arm flung proprietorially over a chair. Gold-framed half-glasses peeked from his handkerchief pocket. The soles of his cracked mahogany shoes were like flat-irons.

'Barley, I am the odd man out in this family,' Bob announced comfortably in a rich Bostonian drawl. 'I guess I am also the oldest and I don't want to be sitting here under a false flag. I am fifty-eight years old, God help me, I work for the Central Intelligence Agency, which as you probably know is based in Langley in the state of Virginia. I do have a surname but I will not insult you by offering you one because it surely would not be much like the real thing.' He raised a liver-spotted hand in leisurely salute. 'Proud to meet you, Barley. Let's have fun. Let's do some good.'

Barley turned back to Ned. 'Now that *is* jolly,' he said, though with no detectable animus. 'So where are we all off to? Nicaragua? Chile? Salvador? Iran? If you want a Third World leader assassinated, I'm your man.'

'Don't rant,' Clive drawled, though ranting was about the last thing Barley had been guilty of. 'We're as bad as Bob's lot and we do the same things. We also have an Official Secrets Act, which they don't, and we expect you to sign it.'

At which Clive nodded in my direction, causing Barley to take proper if belated notice of my existence. I always try to sit a little apart on these occasions and I was doing so that night. Some residual fantasy, I suppose, about being an Officer of the Court. Barley looked at me and I was momentarily disconcerted by the animal straightness of his stare. It somehow did not fit our untidy portrait of him. And Barley, after running his eye over me and seeing I know not what, undertook a more detailed examination of the room.

It was plush and perhaps he thought Clive owned it. It would certainly have been Clive's taste, for Clive was only middle class in the sense that he was unaware there was a better taste. It had carved thrones and chintz sofas and electric candles on the walls. The team's table, which could have sat an entire Armistice ceremony, stood in a raised alcove lined with sprawling rubber-plants in Ali Baba jars.

'Why didn't you go to Moscow?' Clive asked without waiting any longer for Barley to settle. 'You were expected. You rented a stand, booked your flight and your hotel. But you didn't show up and you haven't paid. You came to Lisbon with a woman instead. Why?'

'Would you rather I came here with a man?' Barley asked. 'What's it got to do with you and the CIA whether I came here with a woman or a Muscovy duck?'

He pulled back a chair and sat down, more in protest than obedience.

Clive nodded to me and I did my routine number. I rose, I walked round the preposterous table and set the Official Secrets Act form in front of him. I drew an important pen from my waistcoat pocket and offered it to him with funereal gravity. But his eyes were fixed on a spot outside the room, which was a thing that tonight and in the months that followed I noticed in him often, his way of looking beyond the present company into some troubled private territory of his own; of bursting into noisy talk as a means of exorcising ghosts that no one else had seen; of snapping his fingers without cause, as if to say, 'That's settled then,' where, so far as anybody else knew, nothing had been proposed in the first place.

'Are you going to sign that thing?' said Clive.

'What do you do if I don't?' Barley asked.

'Nothing. Because I'm telling you now, formally and in front of witnesses, that this meeting and everything that passes between us is secret. Harry's a lawyer.'

'I'm afraid that's true,' I said.

Barley pushed the unsigned form away from him across the table. 'And I'm telling you that if I feel the urge I'll paint it on the rooftops,' he said with equal calm.

I resumed my place, taking my important pen with me.

'You seem to have made a pretty good mess of London, too, before you left,' Clive remarked as he returned the form to his folder. 'Debts everywhere. No one knowing where you are. Trails of weeping mistresses. Are you trying to destroy yourself or what?'

'I inherited a romantic list,' Barley said.

'What on earth does that mean?' said Clive, unabashed by his own ignorance. 'Are we using a smart word for dirty books?'

'My grandfather made a corner in novels for the housemaid. In those days people had housemaids. My father called them "Novels for the Masses" and continued the tradition.'

Bob alone felt moved to offer solace. 'God damn it, Barley,' he cried, 'what's so wrong with romantic literature? Better than some of the horse manure they put out. My wife reads the stuff in bucketfuls. Never did *her* any harm.'

'If you don't like the books you publish, why don't you change them?' Clive asked, who never read anything except Service files and the right-wing press.

'I have a Board,' Barley replied wearily, as if to a tiresome child. 'I have Trustees. I have family shareholders. I have aunts. They like the old safe lines. How-to's. Romances. Tie-ins. Birds of the British Empire.' A glance at Bob. 'Inside the CIA.'

'Why didn't you go to the Moscow audio fair?' Clive repeated.

'The aunts cancelled the match.'

'Will you explain that?'

'I thought I'd take the firm into audio cassettes. The family found out and thought I wouldn't. End of story.'

'So you ran away,' said Clive. 'Is that what you normally do when somebody thwarts you? Perhaps you'd better tell us what this letter's about,' he suggested and, without looking at Barley, slid it along the table to Ned.

Not the original. That was in Langley, being tested for everything from fingerprints to Legionnaires' disease by the unchallengeable forces of technology. A facsimile, prepared to Ned's meticulous instruction, down to the sealed brown envelope marked 'Personal for Mr. Bartholomew Scott Blair, urgent', in Katya's hand, then slit with a paperknife to show it had been opened along the way. Clive handed it to Ned. Ned handed it to Barley. Walter scrabbled at his scalp with his paw and Bob looked on magnanimously like the nice guy who had donated the money. Barley shot a look in my direction, as if he had appointed himself my client. What do I do with this? he was asking with his glance. Do I read it or do I chuck it back at them? I remained, I hope, impassive. I didn't have clients any more. I had the Service.

'Read it slowly,' Ned warned.

'Take all the time in the world, Barley,' said Bob.

How often had we all of us not read the same letter during the last week? I wondered, watching Barley examine the envelope front and back, hold it away from him, hold it close, his round spectacles raised like goggles to his forehead. How many opinions had they not listened to and discarded? It was written in a train, six experts in Langley had pronounced. In bed, said three more in London. In the back of a car. In haste, in jest, in love, in terror. By a woman, by a man, they had said. The writer is left-handed, right-handed. Is someone whose script of origin is Cyrillic, is Roman, is both, is neither.

As a final twist of the comedy, they had even consulted old Palfrey. 'Under our own copyright law the recipient owns the physical letter but the writer owns the copyright,' I had told them. 'I don't imagine anyone will take you through the Soviet courts.' I couldn't tell whether they were worried or relieved by my opinion.

'Do you recognise the handwriting or not?' Clive asked Barley.

Poking his long fingers into the envelope, Barley finally fished out the letter – but disdainfully, as if still half expecting it to be a bill. Then paused. And removed his quaint round spectacles and laid them on the table. Then turned his chair and himself away from everyone. And as he began to read, his face buckled into a frown. He finished the first page then glanced at the end of the letter for the signature. He turned to the second page and read the rest of the letter clean through. Then he read the whole of it over again in one run from 'My beloved Barley' to 'Your loving K.' After which he clutched the letter jealously into his lap with both hands and craned his trunk over it so that by design or accident his face was hidden from everyone and his forelock hung down like a hook and his private prayers stayed private to himself.

'She's potty,' he pronounced into the blackness below him. 'Certifiably, totally barmy. She wasn't even there.'

Nobody asked, who's *she?* or where's *there?* Even Clive knew the value of a good silence.

'K short for Katya, short for Yekaterina, I take it,' piped Walter after a further wait. "The patronymic is Borisovna.' He was wearing a crooked bow tie, yellow, with a brown-and-orange motif.

'Don't know a K, don't know a Katya, don't know a Yekaterina,' Barley said. 'Borisovna ditto. Never screwed one, never flirted with one, never proposed to one, never even married one. Never *met* one, far as I remember. Yes, I did.'

They waited, I waited; and we would have waited all night and there would not have been the creak of a chair or the clearing of a throat while Barley ransacked his memory for a Katya.

'Old cow in Aurora,' Barley resumed. 'Tried to flog me some art prints of Russian painters. I didn't bite. Aunts would have blown their corks.'

'Aurora?' Clive asked, not knowing whether it was a city or a State agency.

'Publishers.'

'Do you remember her other name?'

Barley shook his head, his face still out of sight. 'Beard,' he said. 'Katya of the beard. Ninety in the shade.'

Bob's rich voice had a stereophonic quality, and a knack of changing things simply by its reach. 'Want to read it aloud, Barley?' he called with the homeliness of an old scouting buddy. 'Maybe reading it aloud will freshen up your memory. Want to try, Barley?'

Barley, Barley, everyone his friend except Clive, who never once, to my memory, called him anything but Blair.

'Yes, do that, will you. Read it aloud,' said Clive, making an order of it, and Barley to my surprise seemed to think it a good idea. Sitting himself up with one jointless movement of his back, he arranged his torso in such a way that both the letter and his face were in the light. Frowning as before, he started reading aloud in a tone of studied mystification.

'*My beloved Barley.*' He tilted the letter and began again. '*My beloved Barley, Do you remember a promise you made to me one night in Peredelkino as we lay on the verandah of our friends' dacha and recited to each other the poetry of a great Russian mystic who loved England? You swore to me that you would always prefer humanity to nations and that when the day came you would act like a decent human being.*'

He had stopped again.

'Is none of that true?' said Clive.

'I told you. I never *met* the hag!'

There was a force in Barley's denial that was not there before. He was shoving back something that was threatening him.

'*So now I am asking you to redeem your promise, though not in the way we might have imagined that night when we agreed to become lovers.* Total balls,' he muttered. 'Silly cow's got it all mixed up. *I ask you to show this book to English people who think as we do. Publish it for me, using the arguments you expressed with so much fire. Show it to your scientists and artists and intelligentsia and tell them it is the first stone of a great avalanche and they must throw the next stone for themselves. Tell them that with the new openness we can move together to destroy the destruction and castrate the monster we have created. Ask them which is more dangerous to mankind: to conform like a slave or resist like a man? Act like a decent human being, Barley. I love Herzen's England and you. Your loving K.* Who the hell is she? She's off her tree. They both are.'

Leaving the letter on the table, Barley wandered off into the dark end of the room, softly cursing, hammering his right fist downward onto the air. 'Hell's the woman up to?' he protested. 'She's taken two completely different stories and twisted them together. Anyway, where's the book?' He had remembered us and was facing us again.

'The book is safe,' said Clive, with a sideways glance at me. 'Where is it, please? It's mine.'

'We rather thought it was her friend's,' said Clive.

'I've been charged with it. You saw what he wrote. I'm his publisher. It's mine. You've no right to it.'

He had landed with both feet in the very ground we wished him not to enter. But Clive was quick to distract him.

'*He?*' Clive repeated. 'You mean Katya's a man? Why do you say *he?*

You really are confusing us, you know. You're a confusing person, I suppose.'

I had been expecting the outburst sooner. I had sensed already that Barley's submissiveness was a truce and not a victory, and that each time Clive reined him in he brought him nearer to revolt. So that when Barley sauntered up to the table, leaned across it and slackly raised his hands, palms forward, from his sides, in what might well have been a docile gesture of helplessness, I did not necessarily expect him to offer Clive a sweetly reasoned answer to his question. But not even I had reckoned with the scale of the detonation.

'You have no damned right!' Barley bellowed straight into Clive's face, smashing his palms on to the table so hard that my papers bounced up and down in front of me. Brock came rushing from the hall. Ned had to order him back. 'That's *my* manuscript. Sent to me by *my* author. For *my* consideration in *my* good time. You have no right to steal it, read it or keep it. So give me the book and go home to your squalid island.' He flung out an arm at Bob. 'And take your Boston Brahmin with you.'

'*Our* island,' Clive reminded him. 'The book, as you call it, is not a book at all and neither you nor we have any right to it,' he continued frigidly and untruthfully. 'I'm not interested in your precious publishing ethics. Nobody here is. All we know is, the manuscript in question contains military secrets about the Soviet Union that, assuming they are true, are vital to the defence of the West. To which hemisphere you also belong – I take it, thankfully. What would you do in our place? Ignore it? Throw it into the sea? Or try to find out how it came to be addressed to a derelict British publisher?'

'He wants it published! By me! Not hidden in your vaults!'

'Quite,' said Clive with another glance at me.

'The manuscript has been officially impounded and classified as top secret,' I said. 'It's subject to the same restrictions as this meeting. But even more so.' My old law tutor would have turned in his grave – not, I am afraid, for the first time. But it's always wonderful what a lawyer can achieve when nobody knows the law.

One minute and fourteen seconds was how long the silence lasted on the tape. Ned timed it with his stopwatch when he got back to the Russia House. He had been waiting for it, even relishing it, but he still began to fear that he had hit one of those maddening faults that always seem to happen with recorders at the crucial moment. But when he listened harder he caught the grumble of a distant car and a scrap of girl's laughter carrying to the window, because Barley by then had thrown the curtains open and was staring down into the square. For one minute and fourteen seconds, then, we watched Barley's strangely articulate back silhouetted against the Lisbon night. Then comes a most frightful crash like the shattering of several window panes at once, followed by an oil gush, and you would suppose that Barley had staged his long-delayed breakout, taking the ornamental Portuguese wall plates and curly flower vases with him. But the truth is, the whole rumpus is only the sound of Barley discovering the drinks table and dumping three cubes of ice into a crystal tumbler and pouring a decent measure of Scotch over them, all within a couple of inches' range of a microphone that Brock with his characteristic over-production had concealed in one of the richly carved compartments.

4

H e made base camp at his own end of the room on a stiff school chair as far away from us as he could get. He perched on it sideways to us, stooped over his whisky glass, which he held in both hands, peering into it like a great thinker or at least a lonely one. He spoke not to us but to himself emphatically and scathingly, not stirring except to take a sip from his glass or duck his head in affirmation of some private and usually abstracted point of narrative. He spoke in the mixture of pedantry and disbelief that people use to reconstruct a disastrous episode, such as a death or a traffic accident. So I was *here* and you were *there* and the other chap came from over *there*.

'It was last Moscow book fair. The Sunday. Not the Sunday before, the Sunday after,' he said.

'September,' Ned suggested, at which Barley rolled his head around and muttered 'Thanks,' as if genuinely grateful to be prodded. Then he wrinkled his nose and fussed his spectacles and began again.

'We were knackered,' he said. 'Most of the exhibitors had got out on the Friday. It was only a bunch of us who hung around. Those who had contracts to tidy up, or no particular reason to get back in a hurry.'

He was a compelling man and he had centre stage. It was difficult not to attach to him a little, stuck out there on his own. It was difficult not to think, 'There, but for the grace of God, go I.' And the more so since none of us knew where he was going.

'We got drunk on Saturday night and on the Sunday we all drove out to Peredelkino in Jumbo's car.' Once again he seemed to have to remind himself that he had an audience. 'Peredelkino is the Soviet writers' village,' he said as if none of us had heard of it. 'They get dachas there for as long as they behave themselves. Writers' Union runs it on a members-only basis – who gets a dacha, who writes best in prison, who doesn't write at all.'

'Who's Jumbo?' said Ned – a rare interjection.

'Jumbo Oliphant. Peter Oliphant. Chairman of Lupus Books. Closet Scottish Fascist. Black belt Freemason. Thinks he's got a special wavelength to the Sovs. Gold card.' Remembering Bob, he tilted his head at him. 'Not American Express, I'm afraid. A Moscow book fair gold card, dished out by the Russian organisers, saying what a big boy he is. Free car, free translator, free hotel, free caviar. Jumbo was born with a gold card in his mouth.'

Bob grinned too broadly in order to show the joke was taken in good part. Yet he was a large-hearted man and Barley had spotted this. Barley, it occurred to me, was one of those people from whom good natures cannot hide, just as he could not disguise his own accessibility.

'So off we all went,' Barley resumed, returning to his reverie. 'Oliphant from Lupus, Emery from the Bodley Head. And some girl from Penguin, can't remember her name. Yes, I can. Magda. How the hell could I forget a Magda? And Blair from A & B.'

Riding like nabobs in Jumbo's stupid limo, said Barley, tossing out short sentences like old clothes from his memory box. Ordinary car not good enough for our Jumbo, had to be a damn great Chaika with curtains in the bedroom, no brakes and a gorilla with bad breath for a driver. The plan was to take a look at Pasternak's dacha which rumour had it was about to be declared a museum, though another rumour insisted that the bastards were about to pull it down. Maybe his grave as well. Jumbo Oliphant didn't know who Pasternak was at first but Magda murmured 'Zhivago' and Jumbo had seen the film, said Barley. There was no earthly hurry, all they wanted was a bit of a walk and a peck of country air. But Jumbo's driver used the special lane reserved for official roadhogs in Chaikas, so they did the journey in about ten seconds flat instead of an hour, parked in a puddle and schlepped up to the cemetery still trembling with gratitude from the drive.

'Cemetery on a hillside among a lot of trees. Driver stays in the car. Raining. Not much, but he's worried about his awful suit.' He paused in contemplation of the driver. 'Mad ape,' he muttered.

But I had the feeling Barley was railing at himself and not the driver. I seemed to hear a whole self-accusing chorus in Barley, and I wondered whether the others were hearing it as well. He had people inside himself who really drove him mad.

Point was, Barley explained, that as luck would have it they had hit a day when the liberated masses were out in force. In the past, he said, whenever he'd been there, the place had been deserted. Just the fenced-in tombs and the creepy trees. But on that September Sunday with the unfamiliar smells of freedom in the air, there were about two hundred fans crammed round the grave and more by the time they left, all shapes and sizes. Grave was knee-deep in flowers, Barley said. Offerings pouring in all the time. People passing bouquets over the heads to get them on the heap.

Then the readings began. Little chap read poetry. Big girl read prose. Then a filthy little aeroplane flew so low overhead you couldn't hear a thing. Then it flew back the other way. Then back the same way.

'Wang, wang!' Barley yelled, his long wrist whipping back and forth through the air. 'Wee-ah, wee-ah,' he whined through his nose in disgust.

But the plane couldn't damp the enthusiasm of the crowd any more than the rain could. Someone began singing, the punters took up the refrain and it became a knees-up. Finally the plane pushed off, presumably because it was low on fuel. But that wasn't what you felt, said Barley. Not a bit. You felt the singing had shot the little swine out of the sky.

The singing grew stronger and deeper and more mystical. Barley knew three words of Russian, and the others none. Didn't stop them joining in. Didn't stop the girl Magda from crying her eyes out. Or Jumbo Oliphant from swearing to God, through lumps in his throat, as they walked away down the hill that he was going to publish every word Pasternak had written, not just the film but the other stuff, so help me, and subsidise it out of his very own personal pocket as soon as he got back to his damask castle in the docklands.

'Jumbo has these hot flushes of enthusiasm,' Barley explained with a disarming grin, returning to his audience, but principally to Ned. 'Sometimes they don't die down for minutes on end.' Then he paused and frowned again and pulled off his strange round spectacles that seemed to be more an infliction than a help, and peered at everybody in turn as if to remind himself of his situation.

They were still walking down the hill, he said, and still having a good cry when this same little Russian chap came darting up to them holding his cigarette to one side of his face like a candle, asking in English whether they were Americans.

Once again Clive was ahead of all of us. His head slowly lifted. There was a knife-edge to his managerial drawl. 'Same? What same little Russian chap? We haven't had one.'

Unpleasantly reminded of Clive's presence, Barley screwed up his face in a renewal of distaste. 'He was the reader, for goodness' sake,' he said. 'Chap who'd read Pasternak's poetry at the graveside. He asked if we were American. I said no, thank God, British.'

And I noticed, as I supposed we all did, that it was Barley himself not Oliphant or Emery or the girl Magda, who had become the appointed spokesman of their group.

Barley had fallen into direct dialogue. He had the mynah bird's ear. He had a Russian accent for the little chap and a Scottish woof-woof voice for Oliphant. The mimicry slipped out of him as if he were unaware of it.

'You are writers?' the little chap asked, in Barley's voice for him.

'No, alas. Just publishers,' said Barley, in his own.

'English publishers?'

'Here for the Moscow book fair. I run a corner shop called Abercrombie & Blair and this is the Chairman Himself of Lupus Books. Very rich bloke. Be a knight one day. Gold card and bar. Right, Jumbo?'

Oliphant protested that Barley was saying far too much. But the little chap wanted more.

'May I ask then what were you doing at Pasternak's grave?' said the little chap.

'Chance visit,' Oliphant said, barging in again. 'Total chance. We saw a crowd, we came up to see what was going on. Pure chance. Let's go.'

But Barley had no intention of going. He was annoyed by Oliphant's manners, he said, and he wasn't going to stand by while a fat Scottish millionaire gave the brush-off to an undernourished Russian stranger.

'We're doing what everyone else here's doing,' Barley replied. 'We're paying our respects to a great writer. We liked your reading too. Very moving. Great stuff. Ace.'

'You respect Boris Pasternak?' the little chap asked.

Oliphant again, the great civil rights activist, rendered by a gruff voice and a twisted jaw. 'We have no position on the matter of Boris Pasternak or any other Soviet writer,' he said. 'We're here as guests. Solely as guests. We have no opinions on internal Soviet affairs.'

'We think he's marvellous,' Barley said. 'World class. A star.'

'But why?' asked the little chap, provoking the conflict.

Barley needed no urging. Never mind he wasn't totally convinced that Pasternak was the genius he was cracked up to be, he said. Never mind that, as a matter of fact, he thought Pasternak quite seriously overpraised. That was publisher's opinion, whereas this was war.

'We respect his talent and his art,' Barley replied. 'We respect his humanity. We respect his family and his culture. And tenthly or whatever it is, we respect his capacity to reach the hearts of the Russian people despite the fact that he had the daylights hounded out of him by a bunch of bureau-rats who are very probably the same little beasts who sent us that aeroplane.'

'Can you quote him?' the little chap asked.

Barley had that kind of memory, he explained to us awkwardly. 'I gave him the first lines of "Nobel Prize". I thought it was appropriate after that foul aeroplane.'

'Give it to us now, please, will you?' said Clive as if everything had to be checked.

Barley mumbled, and it crossed my mind that he might actually be a very shy man.

'Like a beast in the pen I'm cut off
From my friends, freedom, the sun

But the hunters are gaining ground
I've nowhere else to run.'

The little chap was frowning at the lighted end of his cigarette while he listened to this, said Barley, and for a moment he really did wonder whether they had walked into a provocation, as Oliphant feared.

'If you respect Pasternak so much, why don't you come and meet some friends of mine?' the little chap suggested. 'We are writers here. We have a dacha. We would be honoured to talk to distinguished British publishers.'

Oliphant had only to hear the first half of this speech to develop a severe case of the bends, said Barley. Jumbo knew all about accepting invitations from strange Russians. He was an expert on it. He knew how they ensnared you, drugged you, compromised you with disgraceful photographs and obliged you to resign your directorships and give up your chances of a knighthood. He was also in the middle of an ambitious joint publishing deal through VAAP and the last thing he needed was to be found in the company of undesirables. Oliphant boomed all this to Barley in a theatrical whisper that assumed the little stranger was deaf.

'Anyway,' Oliphant ended triumphantly, 'it's raining. What are we going to do about the car?'

Oliphant looked at his watch. The girl Magda looked at the ground. The bloke Emery looked at the girl Magda and thought there could be worse things to do on a Sunday afternoon in Moscow. But Barley, as he told it, took another look at the stranger and decided to like what he saw. He had no designs on the girl or on a knighthood. He had already decided he would rather be photographed in the raw with any number of Russian tarts than fully dressed on the arm of Jumbo Oliphant. So he waved them all off in Jumbo's car, and threw in his lot with the stranger.

'Nezhdanov,' Barley declared abruptly to the silent room, interrupting his own flow. 'I've remembered the chap's name. Nezhdanov. Playwright. Ran one of these studio theatres, couldn't put on his own plays.'

Walter spoke, his soaring voice shattering the momentary lull. 'My dear boy, Vitaly Nezhdanov is a latter-day *hero*. He has *three* one-acters opening in Moscow just five weeks from now, and everyone has the most exotic hopes for them. Not that he's a blind bit of good, but we're not allowed to say that because he's a dissident. Or was.'

For the first time since I had set eyes on him, Barley's face took on a sublimely happy aspect, and at once I had the feeling that this was the real man, whom the clouds till now had hidden. 'Oh, now that's really great,' he said with the simple pleasure of someone able to enjoy another man's success. 'Fantastic. That's just what Vitaly needed. Thanks for telling me,' he said, looking a fraction of his age.

Then once again his face darkened over and he began drinking his whisky in little nips. 'Well, there we all were,' he murmured vaguely. 'More the merrier. Meet my cousin. Have a sausage roll.' But his eyes, I noticed, like his words, had acquired a remote quality, as if he were already looking forward to an ordeal.

I glanced along the table. Bob smiling. Bob would smile on his deathbed, but with an old scout's sincerity. Clive in profile, his face keen as an axe and about as profound. Walter never at rest. Walter with his clever head thrown back, twisting a hank of hair around his spongy forefinger while he smirked at the ornate ceiling, writhed and sweated. And Ned, the leader – capable, resourceful Ned – Ned the linguist and the warrior, the doer and the planner – sitting as he had sat from the beginning, to attention, waiting for the order to advance. Some people, I reflected, watching him, are cursed with too much loyalty, for a day could come when there was nothing left for them to serve.

Big, rambling house, Barley was reciting in the telegraphese he had resorted to. Edwardian clapboard, fretted verandahs, overgrown garden, birch forest. Rotting benches, charcoal fire, smell of a cricket ground on a rainy day, ivy. About thirty people, mostly men, sitting and standing around in the garden, cooking, drinking, ignoring the bad weather just like the English. Lousy old cars parked along the roadside, just like English cars used to be before Thatcher's pigs in clover took over the ship. Good faces, fluent voices, arty *nomenclatura*. Enter Nezhdanov leading Barley. No heads turn.

'Hostess was a poet,' Barley said. 'Tamara something. Dikey lady, white hair, jolly. Husband editor of one of the science magazines. Nezhdanov was his brother-in-law. Everyone was someone's brother-in-law. The lit. scene has clout over there. If you've got a voice and they let you use it, you've got a public.'

In his arbitrary memory, Barley now split the occasion into three parts. Lunch, which began around two-thirty when the rain stopped. Night, which followed immediately upon lunch. And what he called 'the last bit', which was when whatever happened had happened, and which so far as any of us could ever fathom occurred in the blurred hours between about two and four when Barley, to use his own words, was drifting painlessly between nirvana and a near terminal hangover.

Until lunch came along, Barley had pottered from group to group, he said – first with Nezhdanov then alone, having a shmooze with whoever felt like talking to him.

'Shmooze?' Clive repeated suspiciously, as if he had learned of a new vice.

Bob hastened to interpret. 'A chat, Clive,' he explained in his friendly way. 'A chat and a drink. Nothing sinister.'

But when lunch was called, said Barley, they sat themselves at a trestle table with Barley up one end and Nezhdanov the other and bottles of Georgian white between them, and everyone talking their best English about whether truth was truth if it was not convenient to the great proletarian so-called Revolution, and whether we should revert to the spiritual values of our ancestors and whether the *perestroika* was having any positive effect on the lives of the common people, and how if you really wanted to know what was wrong with the Soviet Union the best way to find out was to try sending a refrigerator from Novosibirsk to Leningrad.

To my secret irritation, Clive again cut in. Like a man bored by irrelevances he wanted names. Barley slapped his forehead with his palm, his hostility to Clive forgotten. Names, Clive, God. One chap a professor at Moscow State but I never caught his name, you see. Another chap in chemical procurement, that was Nezhdanov's half-brother, they called him the Apothecary. Somebody in the Soviet Academy of Sciences, Gregor, but I didn't get round to finding out what his name was, let alone his angle.

'Any women at the table?' Ned asked.

'Two, but no Katya,' said Barley, and Ned like myself was visibly impressed by the pace of his perception.

'But there was *someone* else, wasn't there?' Ned suggested.

Barley leaned himself slowly backwards to drink. Then forward again as he planted the glass between his knees and stooped over it, nose down, inhaling its wisdom.

'Sure, sure, sure, there was someone else,' he agreed. 'There always is, isn't there?' he added enigmatically. 'Not Katya. Someone else.'

His voice had changed. From what to what I couldn't fathom. A shorter ring. A hint of regret or remorse. I waited as we all did. I think we all sensed even then that something extraordinary was appearing on the horizon.

'Thin bearded chap,' Barley went on, staring into the gloom as if he were making him out at last. 'Tall. Dark suit, black tie. Hollow face. Must be why he grew a beard. Sleeves too short. Black hair. Drunk.'

'Did he have a name?' asked Ned.

Barley was still staring at the half-dark, describing what none of us could see.

'Goethe,' he said at last. 'Like the poet. They called him Goethe. Meet our distinguished writer, Goethe. Could have been fifty, could have been eighteen. Thin as a boy. These dabs of colour on his cheeks, very high up. Beard.'

Which, as Ned remarked later, when he was playing over the tape to the team, was operationally speaking the moment when the Bluebird spread his wings. It is not marked by any awesome silence or the intake of breath around the table. Instead Barley chose this moment to be assailed by a sneezing fit, his first of many in our experience of him. It began as a series of single rounds, then accelerated to a grand salvo. Then it slowly petered out again while he beat his face with his handkerchief and cursed between convulsions.

'Bloody kennel cough,' he explained apologetically.

*

'I was brilliant,' Barley resumed. 'Couldn't put a hoof wrong.'

He had refilled his glass, this time with water. He was sipping from it in slow rhythmic movements like one of those plastic drinking birds that used to bob up and down between the miniatures on every gloomy English bar in the days before television sets replaced them.

'Mr. Wonderful, that was me. Star of stage and screen. Western, courteous and specious. That's why I go there, isn't it? Sovs are the only people daft enough to listen to my bullshit.' His forelock dipped towards his glass again. 'It's the way it happens there. You go for a walk in the countryside and end up arguing with a bunch of drunk poets about freedom versus responsibility. You take a leak in some filthy public loo, somebody leans over from the next stall and asks you whether there's life after death. Because you're a Westerner. So you know. And you tell them. And they remember. Nothing goes away.'

He seemed to be in danger of ceasing to talk at all.

'Why don't you just tell us what happened and leave the reproaches to us?' Clive suggested, somehow implying that the reproaches were above Barley's station.

'I shone. That's what happened. A glib mind had a field day. Forget it.'

But forgetting was the last thing anybody intended, as Bob's cheerful smile showed. 'Barley, I think you are being too hard on yourself. Nobody should blame themselves for being entertaining, for Pete's sake. All you did was sing for your supper, by the sounds of it.'

'What did you talk about?' said Clive, undeflected by Bob's goodheartedness.

Barley shrugged. 'How to rebuild the Russian Empire between lunch and teatime. Peace, progress and *glasnost* by the bottleful. Instant disarmament without the option.'

'Are these subjects you frequently enlarge upon?'

'When I'm in Russia, yes they are,' Barley retorted, provoked again by Clive's tone, but never for long.

'May we know what you said?'

But Barley was not telling his story to Clive. He was telling it to himself and to the room and whoever was in it, to his fellow passengers, point for point, an inventory of his folly. 'Disarmament was not a military matter and not a political one, I said. It was a matter of human will. We had to decide whether we wanted peace or war and prepare for it. Because what we prepared for was going to be what we got.' He broke off. 'It was top-of-my-head stuff,' he explained, again selecting Ned. 'Warmed-up arguments I'd read around the place.'

As if he felt more explanation was required, he started again. 'It so happened I was an expert that week. I'd thought the firm might commission a quick book. Some tout at the book fair wanted me to take UK rights in a book on *glasnost* and the crisis of peace. Essays by past and present hawks, reappraisals of strategy. Could real peace break out after all? They'd signed up some of the old American warhorses from the 'sixties and shown how a lot of them had turned full circle since they left office.'

He was apologising and I wondered why. What was he preparing us for? Why did he feel he should lessen the shock in advance? Bob, who was no kind of fool, for all his candour, must have been asking himself the same question.

'Sounds a fine enough idea to me, Barley. *I* can see money in that. Might even take a piece of it myself,' he added with a locker-room chuckle.

'So you had the patter,' Clive said in his barbed undertone. 'And you regurgitated it. Is that what you're telling us? I'm sure it isn't easy to reconstruct one's alcoholic flights of fancy but we'd be grateful if you'd do your best.'

What had Clive studied, I wondered, if he ever had? Where? Who bore him, sired him? Where did the Service find these dead suburban souls with all their values, or lack of them, perfectly in place?

Yet Barley remained compliant in the face of this renewed onslaught. 'I said I believed in Gorbachev,' he said equably, giving himself a sip of water. 'They mightn't, I did. I said the West's job was to find the other half of him, and the East's was to recognise the importance of the half they had. I said that if the Americans had ever bothered as much about disarmament as they had about putting some fool on the moon or pink stripes into toothpaste, we'd have had disarmament long ago. I said the West's great sin was to believe we could bankrupt the Soviet system by raising the bidding on the arms race, because that way we were gambling with the fate of mankind. I said that by shaking our sabres the West had given the Soviet leaders the excuse to keep their gates locked and run a garrison state.'

Walter let out a whinnying laugh and cupped his gappy teeth with his hairless hand. 'Oh my Lord! So *we're* to blame for Russia's ills. Oh, I think that's *marvellously* rich! You don't think that by any chance they did it to themselves, for instance? Locked themselves up inside their own paranoia? No, he doesn't. I can see.'

Undeterred, Barley resumed his confession. 'Somebody asked me, didn't I think nuclear weapons had kept the peace for forty years? I said that was Jesuitical bollocks. Might as well say gunpowder had kept the peace between Waterloo and Sarajevo. Anyway, I said, what's peace? The bomb didn't stop Korea and it didn't stop Vietnam. It didn't stop anyone from pinching Czecho or blockading Berlin or building the Berlin Wall or going into Afghanistan. If that's peace, let's try it without the bomb. I said what was needed was not experiments in space but experiments in human nature. The superpowers should police the world together. I was flying.'

'And did you *believe* any of this nonsense?' Clive asked.

Barley didn't seem to know. He seemed suddenly to regard himself as facile by definition, and became shamefaced. 'Then we talked about jazz,' he said. 'Bix Beiderbecke, Louis Armstrong, Lester Young. I played some.'

'You mean somebody had a *saxophone?*' Bob cried in spontaneous amusement. 'What else did they have? Bass drums? A ten-piece? Barley, I'm not believing this!'

I thought at first that Barley was walking out. He unwound himself and clambered to his feet. He peered round for the door, then headed apologetically towards it, so that Ned rose in alarm, afraid that Brock would get to him first. But Barley had halted halfway across the room where a low carved table stood. Stooping before it, he began lightly slapping his fingertips on the edge while he sang 'pah-pah-paah, pah-pah-pah-pah,' through his nose, to the simulated accompaniment of cymbals, wire brushes and drums.

Bob was already applauding, Walter too. So was I, and Ned was laughing. Clive alone found nothing to entertain him. Barley took a sobering pull from his glass and sat down again.

'Then they asked me what could be done,' he said as if he'd never left his chair.

'Who did?' said Clive, with that maddening note of disbelief he had.

'One of the people at the table. What does it matter?'

'Let's assume everything matters,' said Clive.

Barley was doing his Russian voice again, clogged and pressing. ' "All right, Barley. Given is all as you say. Who will conduct these experiments in human nature?" You will, I said. They were very surprised. Why us? I said because, when it came to radical change, the Sovs had it easier than the West. They had a small leadership and an intelligentsia with great traditional influence. In a Western democracy it was much harder to make yourself heard above the crowd. They were pleased by the paradox. So was I.'

Not even this frontal assault upon the great democratic values could ruffle Bob's genial forbearance. 'Well, Barley, that's a broad-brush judgment but I guess there's some truth in it at that.'

'But did you suggest what should be *done?*' Clive insisted.

'I said there was only Utopia left. I said that what had looked like a pipe dream twenty years ago was today our only hope, whether we're talking disarmament or ecology or plain human survival. Gorbachev understood that, the West didn't want to. I said that Western intellectuals must find their voice. I said the West should be setting the example, not following it. It was everyone's duty to start the avalanche.'

'So unilateral disarmament,' said Clive, clamping his hands together in a knot. 'Aldermaston, here we come. Well, well. Yes.' Except that he didn't say 'yes' so much as 'ears' which was how he said yes when he meant no.

But Bob was impressed. 'And all this eloquence just from reading around the subject a little?' he said. 'Barley, I think that's extraordinary. Why, if I could absorb that way, I'd be a proud man.'

Perhaps *too* extraordinary, he was also suggesting, but the implications evidently passed Barley by.

'And while you were saving us from our worst instincts, what was the man called Goethe doing?' asked Clive.

'Nothing. The others joined in. Goethe didn't.'

'But he listened? Wide-eyed, I should imagine.'

'We were redesigning the world by then. Yalta all over again. Everyone was talking at once. Except Goethe. He didn't eat, he didn't talk. I kept tossing ideas at him, simply because he wasn't joining in. All he did was grow paler and drink more. I gave him up.'

And Goethe never spoke, Barley continued in the same tone of mystified self-recrimination. All through the afternoon not a dickybird, Barley said. Goethe would listen, he'd glare into some invisible crystal ball. He'd laugh, though not by any means when there was anything much to laugh about. Or he'd get up and cut a straightish line to the drinks table to fetch himself another vodka when everyone else was drinking wine, and come back with a tumbler of the stuff, which he knocked off in a couple of swigs whenever anyone proposed a fitting toast. But Goethe, he proposed no toasts at all, said Barley. He was one of those people who exert a moral influence by their silence, he said, so that you end up wondering whether they're dying of a secret illness or riding on some great accomplishment.

When Nezhdanov led the group indoors to listen to Count Basie on the stereo, Goethe tagged obediently along. It wasn't till late into the night, when Barley had given up all thought of him, that he finally heard Goethe speak.

Once again Ned permitted himself a rare question. 'How did the others behave towards him?'

'They respected him. He was their mascot. "Let's see what Goethe thinks." He'd raise his glass and drink to them and we'd all laugh except Goethe.'

'The women too?'

'Everyone. They deferred to him. Practically made way for him. The great Goethe, here he comes.'

'And no one told you where he lived or worked?'

'They said he was on holiday from somewhere where drinking wasn't approved of. So it was a drinking holiday. They kept drinking to his drinking holiday. He was someone's brother. Tamara's, I don't know. Maybe cousin. I didn't catch it.'

'Do you think they were protecting him?' said Clive.

Barley's pauses are like nobody else's, I thought. He has his own tenuous hold on present things. His mind leaves the room and you wait on tenterhooks to see whether it will come back.

'Yes,' said Barley suddenly, sounding surprised by his own answer. 'Yes, yes, they were protecting him. That's right. They were his supporters' club, of course they were.'

'Protecting him from what?'

Another pause.

'Maybe from having to explain himself. I didn't think that at the time. But I think it now. Yes I do.'

'And why should he not explain himself? Can you suggest a reason without inventing one?' asked Clive, determined apparently to hold Barley to the angry edge.

But Barley didn't rise. 'I don't invent,' he said, and I think we all knew that was true. He was gone again. 'He was high-powered. You felt it in him,' he said, returning.

'What does that mean?'

'The eloquent silence. All you hear at a hundred miles an hour is the ticking of the brain.'

'But no one told you, "He's a genius," or whatever?'

'No one told me. No one needed to.'

Barley glanced at Ned to find him nodding his understanding. A field-man to his fingertips, if necessarily a grounded one, Ned had a way of popping up ahead of you when you thought he was still trying to catch you up.

Bob had another question. 'Anyone take you by the elbow and explain to you just *why* Goethe had a drinking problem, Barley?'

Barley let out an unfettered laugh. His momentary freedoms were a little frightening. 'You don't have to have a *reason* to drink in Russia, for Christ's sake! Name me a single Russian worth his salt who could face the problems of his country sober!'

He dropped into silence again, grimacing into the shadows. He wrinkled up his eyes and muttered an imprecation of some kind, I assumed against himself. Then snapped out of it. 'Woke with a jolt round midnight,' he laughed. ' "Christ. Where am I?" Lying in a deck chair on a verandah with a bloody blanket over me! Thought I was in the States at first. One of those New England screened porches with panels of mosquito gauze and the garden beyond. Couldn't think how I'd got to America so fast after a pleasant lunch in Peredelkino. Then I remembered they'd stopped talking to me and I'd got bored. Nothing personal. They were drunk and they were tired of being drunk in a foreign language. So I'd settled on the verandah with a bottle of Scotch. Somebody had thrown a blanket over me to keep the dew off. The moon must have woken me, I thought. Big full moon. Bloodshot. Then I heard this chap talking to me. Very sombre. Immaculate English. Christ, I thought, new guests at this hour. "Some things are necessary evils, Mr. Barley. Some things are more evil than necessary," he says. He's quoting me from lunch. Part of my world-shaking lecture on peace. I don't know who I was quoting. Then I take a closer look around and I make out this nine-foot-tall bearded vulture hovering over me, clutching a bottle of vodka, hair flapping round his face in the breeze. Next thing I know he's crouching beside me with his knees up round his ears, filling up his glass. "Hullo, Goethe," I say. "Why aren't you dead yet? Nice to see you about." '

Whatever had set Barley free had put him back in prison again, for his face had once more clouded over.

'Then he gives me back another of my lunchtime pearls. "All victims are equal. None are more equal than others."

'I laugh. But not too much. I'm embarrassed, I suppose. Queasy. Feel I've been spied on. Chap sits there all through lunch, drunk, doesn't eat, doesn't say a word. All of a sudden ten hours later he's quoting me like a tape recorder. It's not comfortable.

' "Who are you, Goethe?" I say. "What do you do for a living when you're not drinking and listening?"

' "I'm a moral outcast," he says. "I trade in defiled theories."

' "Always nice to meet a writer," I say. "What sort of stuff are you turning out these days?"

' "Everything," he says. "History, comedy, lies, romances. Then off he goes into some drivel he wrote about a lump of butter melting in the sun because it lacked a consistent point of view. Only thing was, he didn't talk like a writer. Too diffident. He was laughing at himself and for all I knew he was laughing at me too. Not that he hadn't every right to, but that didn't make it any funnier.'

Once more we waited, watching Barley's silhouette. Was the tension in us or in him? He took a sip from his glass. He rolled his head around and muttered something like 'not well' or possibly 'to hell' which neither his audience nor the microphones ever completely caught. We heard his chair crackle like wet firewood. On the tape it sounds like an armed attack.

'So then he says to me, "Come on, Mr. Barley. You're a publisher. Aren't you going to ask me where I get my ideas from?" And I thought, That's not what publishers ask actually, old boy, but what the hell? "Okay, Goethe," I say. "Where do you get your ideas from?"

' "Mr. Barley. My ideas are obtained from – one" – he starts counting.'

Barley too had spread his long fingers and was counting on them, using only the lightest Russian intonations. And once again I was struck by the delicacy of his musical memory, which he seemed to achieve less by repeating words than by retrieving them from some cursed echoing chamber where nothing ever faded from his hearing.

' "My ideas are obtained from – one, the paper tablecloths of Berlin cafés in the 1930s." Then he takes a heave of vodka and a great noisy snort of night air both at once. He creaks. Know what I mean? Those chaps with bubbling chests? "Two," he says, "from the publications of my more gifted competitors. Three, from the obscene fantasies of generals and politicians of all nations. Four, from the liberated intellects of press-ganged Nazi scientists. Five, from the great Soviet people, whose every democratic wish is filtered upwards by means of consultation at all levels, then dumped in the Neva. And six, very occasionally from the mind of a

distinguished Western intellectual who happens to drop into my life."
That's me, apparently, because he glues his eyes on me to see how I take
it. Staring and staring like a precocious child. Transmitting these life-
important signals. Then suddenly he changes and becomes suspicious.
Russians do that. "That was quite a performance you gave at lunch," he
says. "How did you persuade Nezhdanov to invite you?" It's a sneer.
Saying I don't believe you.

' "I didn't persuade him," I say. "It was his idea. What are you trying to
hang on me?"

' "There is no ownership of ideas," he says. "You put it into his head.
You are a clever fellow. Cunning work, I would say. Congratulations."

'Then instead of sneering at me he's clutching on to my shoulders as if
he's drowning. I don't know whether he's ill or he's lost his balance. I've
got a nasty feeling he may want to be sick. I try to help him but I don't
know how. He's hot as hell and sweating. His sweat's dripping on to me.
Hair's all wet. These wild childish eyes. I'll loosen his collar, I think. Then
I get his voice, shoved right down my ear, lips and hot breath all at once. I
can't hear him at first, he's too near. I back away but he comes with
me.

' "I believe every word you said," he whispers. "You spoke into my
heart. Promise me you are not a British spy and I'll make you a promise in
return."

'His words exactly,' Barley said, as if he were ashamed of them. 'He
remembered every word I'd said. And I remember every word of his.'

It was not the first time that Barley had spoken of memory as if it were
an affliction, and perhaps that is why I found myself as so often, thinking
of Hannah.

'Poor Palfrey,' she had taunted me in one of her cruel moods, studying
her naked body in the mirror as she sipped her vodka and tonic and
prepared to go back to her husband. 'With a memory like yours, how will
you ever forget a girl like me?'

Did Barley have that effect on everyone? I wondered – touch their
central nerve unconsciously, send them rushing to their closest thoughts?
Perhaps that was what he had done to Goethe too.

The passage that followed was never paraphrased, never condensed, never
'reconstrued'. For the initiated, either the unedited tape was played or else
the transcript was offered in its entirety. For the uninitiated it never
existed. It was the crux of everything that followed and it was called with
deliberate obfuscation 'the Lisbon Approach'. When the alchemists and
theologians and endusers on both sides of the Atlantic had their turn, this
was the passage they picked out and ran through their magic boxes to
justify the preselected arguments that characterised their artful camps.

' "Not a spy actually, Goethe, old boy. Not now, never have been, never will. May be your line of country, not mine. How about chess? Fond of chess? Let's talk about chess."

'Doesn't seem to hear. "And you are not an American? You are nobody's spy, not even ours?"

' "Goethe, listen," I say. "I'm getting a bit jumpy, to be honest. I'm nobody's spy. I'm me. Let's either talk about chess or you try a different address, okay?" I thought that would shut him up, but it didn't. Knew all about chess, he said. In chess, one chap has a strategy, and if the other chap doesn't spot it or if he relaxes his watch, you win. In chess, the theory is the reality. But in life, in certain types of life, you can have a situation where a player has such grotesque fantasies about another one that he ends up by inventing the enemy he needs. Do I agree? Goethe, I agree totally. Then suddenly it's not chess any more and he's explaining himself the way Russians do when they're drunk. Why he's on the earth, for my ears only. Says he was born with two souls, just like Faust, which is why they call him Goethe. Says his mother was a painter but she painted what she saw, so naturally she wasn't allowed to exhibit or buy materials. Because anything we see is a State secret. Also if it's an illusion it's a State secret. Even if it doesn't work and never will, it's a State secret. And if it's a lie from top to bottom, then it's the hottest State secret of the lot. Says his father did twelve years in the camps and died of a surfeit of intellectual ability. Says the problem with his father was, he was a martyr. Victims are bad enough, saints are worse, he says, but martyrs are the living end. Do I agree?

'I agree. Don't know why I agree but I'm a polite soul and when a chap who is clutching my head tells me his father's done twelve years then died, I'm not about to quarrel with him even when I'm tight.

'I ask him his real name. Says he hasn't got one. His father took it with him. Says that in any decent society they shoot the ignorant, but in Russia it's the other way round, so they shot his father because, unlike his mother, he refused to die of a broken heart. Says he wants to make me this promise. Says he loves the English. The English are the moral leaders of Europe, the secret steadiers, the unifiers of the great European ideal. Says the English understand the relationship between words and action whereas in Russia nobody believes in action any more, so words have become a substitute, all the way up to the top, a substitute for the truth that nobody wants to hear because they can't change it, or they'll lose their jobs if they change it, or maybe they simply don't know *how* to change it. Says the Russians' misfortune is that they long to be European but their destiny is to become American, and that the Americans have poisoned the world with materialistic logic. If my neighbour has a car, I must have two cars. If my neighbour has a gun, I must have two guns. If my neighbour has a bomb, I must have a bigger bomb and more of them, never mind they can't reach their targets. So all I have to do is imagine my neighbour's gun and double it and I have the justification for whatever I want to manufacture. Do I agree?'

It is a miracle that nobody interrupted here, not even Walter. But he didn't, he held his tongue, as they all did. You don't even hear a chair creak before Barley goes on.

'So I agree. Yes, Goethe, I agree with you to the hilt. Anything's better than being asked whether I'm a British spy. Starts talking about the great nineteenth-century poet and mystic Piturin.'

'Pecherin,' says a high sharp voice. Walter has finally brimmed over.

'That's right. Pecherin,' Barley agrees. 'Vladimir Pecherin. Pecherin wanted to sacrifice himself for mankind, die on the cross with his mother at his feet. Have I heard of him? I haven't. Pecherin went to Ireland, became a monk, he says. But Goethe can't do that because he can't get a visa and anyway he doesn't like God. Pecherin liked God and didn't like science unless it took account of the human soul. I ask him how old he is. Goethe, not Pecherin. He looks about seven by now, going on a hundred. He says he's nearer to death than life. He says he's fifty but he's just been born.'

Walter chimes in, but softly, like someone in church, not his usual squeak at all. 'Why did you ask him his *age?* Of all the questions you could have asked? What on earth does it matter at that moment how many teeth he's got?'

'He's unsettling. Not a wrinkle on him till he scowled.'

'And he said science. Not physics. Science?'

'Science. Then he starts reciting Pecherin. Translating as he goes. The Russian first, then the English. *How sweet it is to hate one's native land and avidly await its ruin . . . and in its ruin to discern the dawn of universal renaissance.* I may not have got it quite right but that's the gist. Pecherin understood that it was possible to love your country at the same time as hating its system, he says. Pecherin was nuts about England, just as Goethe is. England as the home of justice, truth and liberty. Pecherin showed there was nothing disloyal in betrayal provided you betrayed what you hated and fought for what you loved. Now supposing Pecherin had possessed great secrets about the Russian soul. What would he have done? Obvious. He'd have given them to the English.

'I'm wanting him out of my hair by now. I'm getting panicky. He's coming close again. Face against face. Wheezing and grinding like a steam engine. Heart breaking out of his chest. These big brown saucer eyes. "What have you been drinking?" I said. "Cortisone?"

' "You know what else you said at lunch?" he says.

' "Nothing," I say. "I wasn't there. It was two other blokes and they hit me first." He's not hearing me again.

' "You said, 'Today one must think like a hero to behave like a merely decent human being.' "

' "That's not original," I say. "None of it is. It's stuff I picked up. It's not me. Now just forget everything I said and go back to your own people."

Doesn't listen. Grabs my arm. Hands like a girl's but they grip like iron. "Promise me that if ever I find the courage to think like a hero, you will act like a merely decent human being."

' "Look," I say. "Leave this out and let's get something to eat. They've got some soup in there. I can smell it. You like soup? Soup?"

'He's not crying as far as I can tell but his face is absolutely soaked. Like a pain sweat all over this white skin. Hanging on to my wrist as if I were his priest. "Promise me," he says.

' "But what am I supposed to be promising, for God's sake?"

' "Promise you'll behave like a gentleman."

' "I'm not a gentleman. I'm a publisher."

'Then he laughs. First time. Huge laughter with a sort of weird click in it. "You cannot imagine how much confidence I derive from your rejection," he says.

'That's where I stand up. Nice and easy, not to alarm him. While he goes on clutching me.

' "I commit the sin of science every day," he says. "I turn ploughshares into swords. I mislead our masters. I mislead yours. I perpetuate the lie. I murder the humanity in myself every day. Listen to me."

' "Got to go now, Goethe, old lad. All those nice lady concierges at my hotel sitting up and worrying about me. Let me loose, will you, you're breaking my arm."

'Hugs me. Pulls me right on to him. Makes me feel like a fat boy, he's so thin. Wet beard, wet hair, this burning heat.

' "Promise," he says.

'Squeezed it out of me. Fervour. Never saw anything like it. "Promise! Promise!"

' "All right," I say. "If you ever manage to be a hero, I'll be a decent human being. It's a deal. Okay? Now let me go, there's a good chap."

' "Promise," he says.

' "I promise," I say and shove him off me.'

Walter is shouting. None of our preliminary warnings, no furious glares from Ned or Clive or myself could switch him off any longer. 'But did you *believe* him, Barley? Was he conning you? You're a sharp cookie underneath the flannel. What did you *feel*?'

Silence. And more silence. Then finally, 'He was drunk. Maybe twice in my life I've been as drunk as he was. Call it three times. He'd been on the white stuff all day long and he was still drinking it like water. But he'd hit one of those clear spells. I believed him. He's not the kind of chap you don't believe.'

Walter again, furious.

'But *what* did you believe? What did you think he was talking to you about? What did you think he *did*? All this chatter about things not reaching their targets, lying to his masters and yours, chess that isn't chess but something else? You can *add*, can't you? Why didn't you come to us?

I know why! You put your head in the sand. "Don't know because don't *want* to know." That's you.'

And the next sound on the tape after that is Barley cursing himself again as he stomps round the room. 'Damn, damn, damn,' he whispers. On and on. Until, cutting through him, we hear Clive's voice. If it ever falls to Clive to order the destruction of the universe, I imagine him using this same deserted tone.

'I'm sorry but I'm afraid we're going to need your rather serious help,' he says.

Ironically I believe Clive *was* sorry. He was a technology man, not at ease with live sources, a suburban espiocrat of the modern school. He believed that facts were the only kind of information and he despised whoever was not ruled by them. If he liked anything at all in life apart from his own advancement and his silver Mercedes car, which he refused to take out of the garage if it had so much as a scratch on it, then it was hardware and powerful Americans in that order. For Clive to sparkle, the Bluebird should have been a broken code, a satellite or an Inter Agency committee. Then Barley need never have been born.

Whereas Ned was all the other way, and more at risk on account of it. He was by temperament and training an agent-runner and captain of men. Live sources were his element and, so far as he knew the word, his passion. He despised the in-fighting of intelligence politics and left all that happily to Clive, just as he left the analysis to Walter. In that sense he was the determined primitive, as people who deal in human nature have to be, while Clive, to whom human nature was one vast unsavoury quagmire, enjoyed the reputation of a modernist.

5

We had moved to the library where Ned and Barley had begun. Brock had set up a screen and projector. He had put chairs in a horseshoe with a special person in his mind for each chair, for Brock, like other violent minds, had an exaggerated appetite for menial labour. He had been listening to the interview over the relay and despite his sinister inklings about Barley a glow of excitement smouldered in his pale Baltic eyes. Barley, deep in thought, lounged in the front row between Bob and Clive, a privileged if distracted guest at a private screening. I watched his head in silhouette as Brock switched on the projector, first turned downward in contemplation, then sharply upward as the first frame struck the screen. Ned sat beside me. Not a word, but I could feel the disciplined intensity of his excitement. Twenty male faces flicked across our vision, most of them Soviet scientists who on a first hasty search around the Registries of London and Langley were deemed to' have had possible access to the Bluebird information. Some were featured more than once: first with beards then with their beards touched out. Others were shown when they were twenty years younger because that was all the archives had of them.

'Not among those present,' Barley pronounced when the parade was over, suddenly shoving his hand to his head as if he had been stung.

Bob just couldn't believe this. His incredulities were as charming as his credulities. 'Not even a perhaps or a maybe, Barley? You sound pretty sure of yourself for a man who was drinking well when he made the original sighting. Jesus, *I've* been to parties where I couldn't remember my own name.'

'Not a tickle, old boy,' said Barley, and returned to his thoughts.

Now it was Katya's turn, though Barley couldn't know it. Bob advanced on her cautiously, a Langley professional showing us his footwork.

'Barley, these are some of the boys and girls around the Moscow publishing scene,' he said over-casually as Brock ran up the first stills. 'People you might have bumped into during your Russian travels, people at receptions, book fairs, people on the circuit. If you see anybody you know, holler.'

'Bless us, that's Leonora!' Barley cut in with pleasure while Bob was still talking. On the screen a splendid burly woman with a backside like a football field was marching across a stretch of open tarmac. 'Leni's top gun with SK,' Barley added.

'SK?' Clive echoed as if he had unearthed a secret society.

'Soyuzkniga. SK order and distribute foreign books throughout the Soviet Union. Whether the books get there is another matter. Leni's a riot.'

'Know her other name?'

'Zinovieva.'

Confirmed, said Bob's smile to the knowing.

They showed him others and he picked the ones they knew he knew, but when they showed him the photograph of Katya that they had shown to Landau – Katya in her overcoat with her hair up, coming down the steps with her perhaps-bag – Barley muttered, 'Pass,' as he had to all the others he didn't know.

But Bob was delightfully upset. Bob said, 'Hold her there, please,' so unhappily that a babe in arms would have guessed that this picture had unrecognised significance.

So Brock held, as we all did: held our breath.

'Barley, the little lady here with the dark hair and big eyes in this picture is with the October Publishing Company, Moscow. Speaks a fine English, classical like yours and Goethe's. We understand she's a *redaktor*, commissioning and approving English language translations of Soviet works. No bells?'

'No such luck,' said Barley.

At which Clive handed him to me. With a tip of his head. Take him, Palfrey. Your witness. Scare him.

I do a special voice for my indoctrination sessions. It's supposed to instil the terror of the marriage vow and I hate it because it is the voice that Hannah hates. If my profession had a false white coat, this would be the moment where I administered the wicked injection. But that night as soon as I was alone with him, I chose a more protective tone and became a different and perhaps rejuvenated Palfrey, the one that Hannah used to swear could overcome. I addressed Barley not as I would some raw probationer but as a friend I was seeking to forewarn.

Here's the deal, I said, using the most non-legal jargon I could think of. Here's the noose we're putting round your neck. Take care. Consider.

Other people, I make them sit. I let Barley roam because I had seen that he was more at ease when he was able to pace and fidget and chuck his arms back in a luxurious stretch. Empathy is a curse even when it is short-lived, and not all the bad law in England can protect me from it.

And while I temporarily warmed to him I noticed a number of things about him I had not registered in the larger company. How his body leaned away from me, as if he were guarding himself against his deep-rooted disposition to give himself to the first person who asked for him. How his arms, despite their striving for self-discipline, remained unruly, particularly at the elbows, which like renegades seemed to be wanting to break free of whatever uniform they were pressed into.

And I noticed my own frustration that I could still not observe him closely enough, but cast round for other glimpses of him in the gilded mirrors as he passed them. Even to this day, I think of him as being a long way off.

And I noticed the pensiveness in him as he dipped in and out of my homily, taking a point or two then swinging away from me in order to digest it, so that suddenly I was facing a breadth of powerful back that was not to be reconciled with the unreconciled front.

And how, as he returned to me, his eyes lacked the subservience that in other recipients of my wise words so often sickened me. He was not daunted. He was not even touched. His eyes disturbed me nonetheless, as they had the first time they appraised me. They were too truthful, too clear, too undefended. None of his milling gestures could protect them. I felt that I or anyone else could have waded into them and claimed possession of him, and the feeling scared me as if it were a threat. It made me fear for my own security.

I thought about his file. So many headlong crashes, acts of seeming self-destruction, so little prudence. His frightful school record. His efforts to earn himself a few laurels by boxing, for which he ended up in the school sanatorium with a broken jaw. His expulsion for being drunk while reading the Epistle at Sung Eucharist. 'I was drunk from the night before, sir. It was not intentional.' Flogged and expelled.

How convenient, I thought, for him and me, if I could have pointed to some great crime that haunted him, some act of cowardice or omission. But Ned had shown me his entire life, secret annexes and all, medical history, money, women, wives, children. And it was small stuff all the way. No big bang, no big crime. No big anything – which may have been the explanation of him. Was it for want of a greater sea that he had repeatedly wrecked himself against life's little rocks, challenging his Maker to come up with something bigger or stop bothering him? Would he be so headlong when faced with greater odds?

Then abruptly, before I am aware of it, our rôles are reversed. He is standing over me, peering down. The team is still waiting in the library and I hear sounds of their restlessness. The declaration form lies before me on the table. But it is me that he is reading, not the form.

'So have you any questions?' I ask up at him, conscious of his height. 'Anything you want to know before you sign?' I am using my special voice after all, for self-protection.

He is at first puzzled, then amused. 'Why? Have you got more answers you want to tell me?'

'It's an unfair business,' I warn him sternly. 'You've had a big secret thrust on you. You didn't ask for it but you can't unknow it. You know enough to hang a man and probably a woman. That places you in a certain category. It brings obligations you can't escape.'

And, God help me, I think of Hannah again. He has woken the pain of her in me as if she were a brand-new wound.

He shrugs, brushing off the burden. 'I don't know what I know,' he says.

There is a thump on the door.

'The point is, they may want to tell you more,' I say, softening again, trying to make him aware of my concern for him. 'What you know already may be only the beginning of what they want you to find out.'

He is signing. Without reading. He is a nightmare client. He could be signing his life away and he wouldn't know it and wouldn't care. They are knocking but I have still to add my name as witness.

'Thanks,' he says.

'What for?'

I put away my pen. Got him, I think, in ice-cold triumph, just as Clive and the rest of them march in. A tricky customer but I signed him up.

But the other half of me is ashamed and mysteriously alarmed. I feel I have lit a fire inside our own camp, and there is no knowing how it will spread or who will put it out.

The only merit of the next act was that it was brief. I was sorry for Bob. He was never a sly man and he was certainly not a bigot. He was transparent, but that is not yet a crime, even in the secret world. He was more in Ned's stamp than Clive's, and nearer to the Service's way of doing things than to Langley's. There was a time when Langley had a lot of Bob's sort, and was the better for it.

'Barley, do you have any concept at all of the nature of the material that the source you call Goethe has so far provided? Of its overall message, shall we say?' Bob enquired awkwardly, putting up his broad smile.

Johnny had pitched the same sort of question at Landau, I remembered. And burned his fingers.

'How can I?' Barley replied. 'I haven't set eyes on the stuff. You won't let me.'

'Are you quite certain Goethe himself gave you no advance indication? No whispered word, author to publisher, of what he *might* – one day, if you both kept your promises – supply? Beyond what you have already accounted for in Peredelkino – the broad talk of weaponry and unreal enemies?'

'I've told you everything I remember,' said Barley, shaking his head in confusion.

Also like Johnny before him, Bob began squinting at the brief he held below the table. But in Bob's case with genuine discomfort. 'Barley, in the six visits you have made to the Soviet Union over the last seven years have you formed any connection, however briefly, with peaceniks, dissidents or other unofficial groups of that nature?'

'Is that a crime?'

Clive cut in. 'Answer the question, will you?'

Amazingly, Barley obliged. Sometimes Clive was simply too small to reach him. 'You meet all sorts, Bob. Jazz people, book people, intellectuals, journalists, artists – it's an impossible question. Sorry.'

'Then can I turn it around a little and ask whether you are acquainted with any peace people back in England at all?'

'I've no idea.'

'Barley, would you be aware that two members of a certain blues group you played with between 1977 and 1980 were involved with the Campaign for Nuclear Disarmament, as well as other peace outfits?'

Barley seemed puzzled but a little enchanted. 'Really? Do they have names?'

'Would it amaze you if I said Maxi Burns and Bert Wunderley?'

To the amusement of everyone but Clive, Barley broke out in jolly laughter. 'Oh my Lord! Forget the peace label, Bob. Maxi was a red-toothed Com. He'd have blown up the Houses of Parliament if he'd had a bomb. And Bert would have held his hand while he did it.'

'I take it they were homosexual?' said Bob, with an old dog's smile.

'Gay as trivets,' Barley agreed contentedly.

At which, with evident relief Bob folded up his piece of paper and gave Clive a glance to say he'd finished, and Ned proposed to Barley that they take some air. Walter moved invitingly to the door and opened it. Ned must have wanted him as a foil, for Walter would never have dared otherwise. Barley hesitated a moment, then picked up a bottle of Scotch and a glass and dropped them one into each side pocket of his bush-jacket, in what I suspect was a gesture designed to shock us. Thus equipped he ambled after them leaving the three of us alone without a word between us.

'Were those Russell Sheriton's questions you were shooting at him?' I asked Bob amiably enough.

'Russell's too bright for all that damn stuff these days, Harry,' Bob replied with evident distaste. 'Russell's come a long way.'

Langley's power struggles were a mystery even to those who were involved in them, and certainly – however much we pretended otherwise – to our barons of the twelfth floor. But in the seethings and jockeyings, Sheriton's name had featured frequently as the man likely to come out at the top of the heap.

'So who authorised them?' I asked, still upon the questions. 'Who drafted them, Bob?'

'Maybe Russell.'

'You just said Russell was too bright!'

'Maybe he has to keep his boyars quiet,' Bob said uncomfortably, lighting up his pipe and swinging out the match.

We settled down to wait on Ned.

The shade tree is in a public garden near the waterfront. I have stood under it and sat under it and watched the dawn rise over the harbour while the dew made teardrops on my grey raincoat. I have listened, without understanding, to an old mystic with a saintly face who likes to receive his disciples there, in that self-same spot by daylight. They are of all ages, and call him the Professor. The bench is built round its trunk and divided by iron arm-rests into seats. Barley sat at the centre with Ned and Walter either side of him. They had talked first in a sleepy sailors' tavern, then on a hilltop, Barley said, but Ned for some reason refuses to remember the hilltop. Now they had come back into the valley for their final place. Brock sat wakefully in the hired car keeping a view of them across the grass. From the warehouses on the other side of the road came a whine of cranes, a pumping of lorries and the yells of fishermen. It was five in the morning but the harbour is awake from three. The first clouds of dawn were shaping and breaking like the First Day.

'Choose somebody else,' Barley said. He had said it before in several different ways. 'I'm not your man.'

'We didn't choose you,' Ned said. 'Goethe did. If we knew a way of getting back to him without you, we'd jump at it. He's taken a fix on you. Probably been waiting ten years for someone like you to turn up.'

'He chose me because I wasn't a spy,' said Barley. 'Because I sang my bloody aria.'

'And you won't be a spy now,' said Ned. 'You'll be a publisher. His. All you'll be doing is collaborating with your author and with us at the same time. What's wrong with that?'

'You've got the draw, you've got the wits,' said Walter. 'No wonder you drink. You've been under-used for twenty years. Now's your chance to shine. You're lucky.'

'I shone at Peredelkino. Every time I shine, the lights go out.'

'You might even be solvent,' said Ned. 'Three weeks of preparation back in London while you're waiting for your visa, a jolly week in Moscow and you'll be off the hook for ever.'

With the prudence that was innate in him, Ned had avoided the word 'training'.

Back comes Walter, a touch of the whip, a piece of flattery, both over the top, but Ned let him run. 'Oh never mind the money, Barley's *far* too grand! It's one shot for your country and a lot of people never get the chance. They dream of it, they write in for it but it never comes their way. And afterwards, when you've done your bit, you can sit back and enjoy the benefits of being British, knowing you've earned them even if you sneer at them, which is your good right, something that has to be fought for like everything else.'

And Ned had judged rightly. Barley laughed and told Walter 'Come off it,' or something of the kind.

'One shot for your author too, if you think about it,' Ned cut in, with his plain man's talk. 'You'll be saving his neck for him. If he's going to hand over State secrets, the least you can do for him is put him on to the competent people. You're a Harrow man, aren't you?' he added as if he had just remembered this. 'Didn't I read somewhere you'd been educated at Harrow?'

'I just went to school there,' Barley said and Walter let out one of his hoots of laughter, in which Barley out of politeness joined.

'Why did you apply to us all those years ago? Do you remember what prompted you?' Ned asked. 'Some sense of duty, was it?'

'I wanted to stay out of my father's firm. My tutor said teach at a prep school. My cousin Lionel said join the spies. You turned me down.'

'Yes, well I'm afraid we can't do you the favour a second time,' said Ned.

Like old companions the three men silently surveyed the waterfront. A chain of naval ships straddled the harbour mouth, their rigging drawn in necklaces of lights.

'Do you know, I've always dreamed there'd be one?' Walter sang suddenly, talking out to sea. 'I'm a God man at heart, I'm sure I am. Or else a failed Marxist. I always believed that sooner or later their history had to throw one up. How much science have you got? None. You wouldn't. You're that generation – the last of the arts virgins. If I asked you what a rate of burn was, you'd probably think I was talking about baking a cake.'

'Probably,' Barley agreed, laughing again despite himself.

'CEP? Not a concept?'

'Don't like initials, I'm afraid.'

'Circular-error-probable then. How's that?'

'Illiterate,' Barley snapped, in one of his unpredictable fits of tetchiness.

'Recalibrate? Whom or what do I recalibrate, and what with?'

Barley didn't bother to reply.

'Very well, then. What's the Big Motherfucker, familiarly known in circles as the BMF? That won't offend your ear for English, will it? Nice Anglo-Saxon words?'

Barley shrugged.

'The BMF was the Soviet SS9 super rocket,' Walter said. 'It was wheeled out at a May Day parade in the dark years of the Cold War. Its dimensions were breathtaking and it was later credited with a notorious *footprint*. Also not a name to you? Footprint? Never mind, it will be. The footprint in this case was three huge holes in the Russian wastes, that looked like the pattern of the Minuteman silo group with its command centre. The argument was whether they were made by independently targetable warheads, and could the Sovs therefore hit three American silos at once? Those who didn't want to believe they could called the footprints a fluke. Those who did upped the ante and said the warheads were for destroying cities not silos. The believers won the day and got themselves a green light for the ABM programme. Never mind their theory was discredited three years later. They squeezed through. I'm losing you, I see.'

'You never had me,' Barley said.

'But he's a fast learner, of course he is,' Walter assured Ned contentedly across Barley's body. 'Publishers can get their minds halfway round anything.'

'What's wrong with *finding out?*' Ned complained in the tone of a good man confused by smart talk. 'That's what I never understand. We're not asking you to build the beastly rockets or push the button. We're asking you to help us improve our knowledge of the enemy. If you don't like the nuclear business, so much the better. And if the enemy turns out to be a friend where's the harm?'

'I thought the Cold War was supposed to be over,' Barley said.

At which Ned, in what appeared to be genuine alarm, exclaimed, 'Oh my dear Lord,' under his breath.

But Walter showed no such restraint. Walter pretended to be indignant, and perhaps he was. He could be anything at any moment and often several things at once. 'Cheap political theatricals and feigned friendships!' he snorted. 'Here we are, locked into the biggest ideological face-off in history and you tell me it's all over because a handful of statesmen find it convenient to hold hands in public and scrap a few obsolete toys. The evil empire's on its knees, oh yes! Their economy's a disaster, their ideology's up the spout and their back-yard's blowing up in their faces. Just don't tell me that's a reason for unbuckling our guns, because I won't believe a word of you. It's a reason for spying the living daylights out of them twenty-five hours a day and kicking them in the balls every time they try to get off the floor. God *knows* who they won't think they are ten years from now!'

'I suppose you do realise that if you walk out on Goethe you'll be leaving him to the Americans?' said Ned on a practical point of information. 'Bob won't let him go, why should he? Don't be fooled by those old Yalie manners of his. How will you live with yourself *then*?'

'I don't want to live with myself' said Barley. 'I can't think of anybody worse to live with.'

A slate-coloured cloud slid across the red sunpath before shattering into fragments.

'It comes down to this,' said Ned. 'It's crude and un-English but I'll say it anyway. Do you want to be a passive or an active player in the defence of your country?'

Barley was still hunting for an answer when Walter supplied it for him, and with an air of finality that brooked no contradiction. 'You're from a free society. You've no choice,' he said.

The din of the harbour rose with the advancing daylight. Barley slowly stood up and rubbed his back. He seemed to have a permanent patch of pain there, just above the waistband. Perhaps it accounted for his slope.

'Any decent Church would have burned you bastards at the stake long ago,' he remarked wearily. He turned to Ned, peering down at him through his too-small spectacles. 'I'm the wrong man,' he warned him. 'And you're a fool for using me.'

'We're all the wrong men,' said Ned. 'We're dealing with wrong things.'

Barley walked across the grass, beating his pockets for his keys. He entered a side street and vanished from their view as Brock went softly after him. The house was a wedge, narrow on the street, broad at the back. Barley unlocked the front door and closed it behind him. He pressed the time switch and began climbing the stairs, keeping an even pace because he had a long way to go.

She was a good woman and nothing was her fault. They were all good women. They were women with a mission to him, just as Hannah once had a mission to me – to save him, to straighten him out, to get his oh-so-many talents working in one direction, to help him make the fresh start that would get him clear of all the fresh starts he had made before. And Barley had encouraged her as he had encouraged all of them. He had stood beside them at the patient's bedside as if he were not himself the patient but a member of the healing team. 'So what shall we do about this poor old chap that will get him up and functioning again?'

The only difference was, he had never believed in the remedy, any more than I had.

She lay face down, exhausted and possibly asleep. She had cleaned the flat. As prisoners clean cells and the bereaved tend tombs, she had scoured the surface of a world she couldn't alter. Other people might tell Barley he was too hard on himself. Women said it to him often. How he mustn't hold himself responsible for both halves of every relationship that collapsed on him. Barley knew better. He knew the distance between himself and everything. In those days he was still the unequalled expert on his own incurability.

He touched her shoulder but she didn't stir, so he knew she was awake.

'I had to go to the Embassy,' he said. 'People in London baying for my blood. I've got to go back and face the music or they'll take away my passport.'

He fished a suitcase from under the bed and began filling it with the shirts she'd ironed for him.

'You said this time you weren't going back,' she told him. 'You'd served your English stretch, you said. You'd done your time.'

'They've put me on the early flight. There's nothing I can do. There's a car coming for me in a few minutes.' He went to the bathroom for his toothbrush and shaving gear. 'They're throwing the whole book at me,' he called. 'There's nothing I can do.'

'And I go back to my husband,' she said.

'Stay here. Use the flat. Whatever. It'll only take a few weeks. Then it's done.'

'If you just hadn't said all that stuff we'd have been fine. I'd have been happy just having an affair. You should see your letters. Hear yourself.'

Barley didn't look at her. He was stooped over his suitcase.

'Just don't do it to anyone else,' she said.

That was as far as her calm could stretch. She began sobbing and was sobbing when he left, and she was still sobbing next morning when I pitched her some line and pushed a declaration form under her nose as I asked her how much he'd told her. Nothing. She blabbed out the whole story yet defended him to the death. Hannah would have done the same. Does it still, a surfeit of loyalty to this day, even though her illusions are destroyed.

*

Three weeks were all that Ned and his Russia House people had to knock Barley into shape. Three weekends and fifteen days that didn't start till five when Barley slipped away from his office.

But Ned drove the job through as only Ned was able. Ned would have kept the trainers up all night and himself all night and day. And Barley, with the changefulness that was innate in him, swung and turned with every breeze, until he settled down and found a steady face and, as the day of his departure approached, a serious one as well. Often he seemed to embrace the entire ethic of our trade without demur. After all, he declared to Walter, was not seeming the only kind of being? Oh my *God*, yes! Walter cried, delighted – and not only in our trade! And was not the whole of man's identity a cover? Barley insisted; and was not the only world worth living in the secret one? Walter assured him that it was, and advised him to take up permanent residence there before prices rose.

Barley had loved Walter from the start, loved the fragility in him and, as I see it now, the transience. He seemed to know from the outset that he was holding the hand of a man who was on his way to the breaker's yard. At other times Barley's own face became as empty as the open grave. He would not have been Barley if he hadn't been a pendulum.

Most of all he took to the family atmosphere which Ned, with his instinct for the unanchored joe, assiduously tended – the chatty suppers, the sharing and being the star of the family, the games of chess with old Palfrey, whom Ned cunningly harnessed to Barley's wagon to redress the disturbingly ephemeral influence of Walter.

'Drop in whenever you're in the mood,' Ned told me, with a friendly pat.

So I became Barley's old Harry.

Old Harry, give us a game of chess, damn you! Old Harry, why aren't you staying for supper? Old Harry, where's your bloody glass, man?

Ned invited Bob sparingly and Clive not at all. It was Ned's show, Ned's joe. And he had a shrewd eye for Barley's flashpoints.

For the safe house Ned had chosen a pretty Edwardian cottage in Knightsbridge, an area of London where Barley had no connection. Clive winced at the cost but the Americans were paying so his fastidiousness was misplaced. The house lay in a cul-de-sac not five minutes' walk from Harrods and I rented it in the name of the Ethical Research & Action Group, a charitable body I had registered years before and locked away for a rainy day. A cosy Service housekeeper named Miss Coad was placed in charge, and I duly swore her on to the Bluebird indoctrination list. The top-floor nursery was converted into a modest lecture room and, like the rest of the rooms, which were snug and well furnished, it was microphoned.

'This is your home from home for the duration,' Ned told Barley, as we showed him round. 'Here's your bedroom when you need one, here's your key. Use the phone as much as you like but I'm afraid we'll be listening, so if it's private you'd do better from the box across the road.'

For good measure, I had extended the Home Office warrant to cover the phone box too. Intense American interest.

Since Barley and I were not long sleepers, we played our chess when the others had turned in. He was an impulsive opponent and often a brilliant one, but there is a calculating streak in me that he never possessed and I was more attuned to his weaknesses than he to mine. After all, I had read his file. But I still remember games where he saw a whole campaign at a glance and with three or four moves and a bellow of amusement forced me to resign.

'Got you, Harry! Say you're sorry! Hang your head!'

But when we set them up again, I could feel the patience drain out of him. He would start to prowl and flick his hands around and let his mind take one of its journeys.

'Married, Harry?'

'Not so you'd notice,' I replied.

'Hell does that mean?'

'I have a wife in the country. I live in the town.'

'Had her long?'

'Couple of lifetimes,' I said carelessly, already wishing I had given him a different answer.

'Love her?'

'My dear chap!' But he was staring at me, wanting to know. 'From a distance, I suppose. Yes,' I added grudgingly.

'She love you back?'

'I assume so. It's some time since I asked her.'

'Kiddywinks?'

'A boy. In his thirties.'

'Ever see him?'

'A card at Christmas. Funerals and weddings. We're good enough friends in our way.'

'What's he do?'

'He flirted with the law. Now he makes money.'

'Is he happy?'

I was angry, which these days is unusual in me. Definitions of happiness and love were none of his damned business. He was a joe. It was my right to come close to him, not the other way round. But it was more unusual still that I should let my anger show. Yet I must have done, for I caught him gazing at me with concern, wondering no doubt whether he had accidentally touched upon some family tragedy. Then he coloured and swung away, looking for a distraction that would get us off the hook.

'He's not fighting it, sir, I'll put it that way,' a Mr. Candyman, specialist in the latest thing in body microphones, told Ned. 'I won't say he's a natural but he does listen and my goodness he does remember.'

'He's a gentleman, Mr. Ned, which is what I like,' said a lady watcher entrusted with teaching Barley the rudiments of streetcraft. 'He's got the brains and he's got a sense of humour, which I often say is halfway to an eye.'

Later she confessed that she had declined his advances in accordance with Service rules, but that he had successfully introduced her to the work of Scott Fitzgerald.

'Whole thing's a load of hocus-pocus,' Barley pronounced raucously at the end of a wearying session on the techniques of secret writing. But he clearly enjoyed it, all the same.

And as the day of reckoning drew nearer his submissiveness became total. Even when I wheeled in the Service accountant, a dreary stick called Christopher, who had devoted five days to an awed inspection of the Abercrombie & Blair books, Barley showed none of the rebelliousness I had expected.

'But every last swine in publishing is broke, Chris old boy!' he protested, pacing the pretty drawing-room to the rhythms of his own humming, holding his whisky glass wide while he dipped at the knees for the long steps. 'The big fellows like Jumbo eat the leaves and we gnaw the bark.' A German voice: 'You hef your methods, ve hef ours.'

But neither Ned nor I gave a cuss about every last swine. Neither did Chris. We cared about the operation and were haunted by the nightmare that Barley might go bankrupt on us in the middle of it.

'But I don't *want* a bloody editor!' Barley cried, waving his long-suffering spectacles at us. 'I can't *pay* a bloody editor. My sainted aunts in Ely will pop their *garters* if I hire a bloody editor!'

But I had already squared the sainted aunts. Over luncheon at Rules I had wooed and won the Lady Pandora Weir-Scott, better known to Barley as the Sacred Cow on account of her High Anglican beliefs. Posing as a Foreign Office Pontiff, I had explained to her in the greatest confidence that the house of Abercrombie & Blair was about to be the recipient of an under-the-counter Rockefeller grant to promote Anglo-Soviet cultural relations. But not a word, or the money would be whisked away and given to another deserving house.

'Well *I'm* a bloody sight more deserving than *anybody*,' Lady Pandora averred, spreading her elbows wide to get the last scrap out of her lobster. '*You* try running Ammerford on thirty thousand a year.'

Mischievously, I asked her whether I could safely approach her nephew.

'Not on your nelly. Leave him to me. He doesn't know money from muck and he can't lie for toffee.'

The need to provide Barley with a minder seemed suddenly more pressing. 'You advertised for him,' Ned explained, brandishing a small-ad from a recent edition of the cultural press in Barley's face. *Old Established British Publisher seeks qualified Russian reader for promotion to editor, 25–45, fiction and technical, curriculum vitae.*

And on the next afternoon Leonard Carl Wicklow presented himself for interview at the much-mortgaged premises of Abercrombie & Blair of Norfolk Street, Strand.

'I have an angel for you, Mr. Barley,' boomed Mrs. Dunbar's gin-soaked voice over the ancient intercom. 'Shall I ask him to fly in?'

An angel in bicycle clips, a webbing kitbag slung across his chest. A high angelic brow, not a worry on it, blond angelic curls. Angelic blue eyes that knew no evil. An angelic nose, so mysteriously knocked off course that your first instinct on meeting him was to reach out and switch it straight again. Interview him as you would anybody, Ned had told Barley. Leonard Carl Wicklow, born Brighton 1964, honours graduate, School of Slavonic & East European Studies, University of London.

'Oh yes, you. Marvellous. Sit down,' Barley grumbled. 'Hell brings you to publishing? Lousy trade.' He had lunched with one of his more strident lady novelists, and was still digesting the experience.

'Well, it's been kind of an on-going thing of mine for years, actually, sir,' said Wicklow, with a smile of angelic enthusiasm.

'Well, if you do come to us you certainly won't *on-go*,' Barley warned, bridling at this unprovoked assault on the English language. 'You may *continue*. You may *endure*. You may even *prevail*. But you jolly well won't *on-go* while *I'm* in the driving seat.'

'Don't know whether the bugger barks or purrs,' he growled to Ned, the same evening back in Knightsbridge, as the three of us loped up the narrow stairs for our evening tryst with Walter.

'He does both rather well, actually,' said Ned.

And Walter's seminars held Barley in their thrall, a sell-out every time. Barley loved anyone whose hold on life was tenuous, and Walter looked as if he were in danger of falling off the edge of the world each time he left his chair. They would talk tradecraft, they would talk nuclear theology, they would talk the horror story of Soviet science that the Bluebird, whoever he might be, was inescapably heir to. Walter was too good a tutor to reveal what his subject was, and Barley was too interested to enquire.

'*Control?*' Walter the ultimate hawk shouted at him indignantly. 'Can you honestly not distinguish between *control* and *disarmament*, you ninny? Defuse world crisis, did I hear? What *Guardian* bilge is that? Our leaders *adore* crisis. Our leaders *feast* on crisis. Our leaders spend their lives quartering the globe in search of crisis to revive their flagging libidos!'

And Barley, far from taking offence, would crane forward in his chair, groan and clap and bay for more. He would challenge Walter, leap to his feet and pound the room shouting '*But* – hang on, damn you – *but!*' He had the memory, he had the aptitude, as Walter had predicted. And his scientific virginity yielded at the first assault, when Walter delivered his introductory lecture on the balance of terror, which he had contrived to turn into an inventory of all the follies of mankind.

'There's no way out,' he announced with satisfaction, 'and no amount of wishful dreaming will produce one. The demon won't go back in its bottle, the face-off is forever, the embrace gets tighter and the toys cleverer with every generation, and there's no such thing for either side as enough security. Not for the main players, not for the nasty little newcomers who each year run themselves up a suitcase bomb and join the club. We get tired of believing that, because we're human. We may even con ourselves into believing the threat has gone away. It never will. Never, never, never.'

'So who'll save us, Walt?' Barley asked. 'You and Nedsky?'

'Vanity, if anything will, which I doubt,' Walter retorted. 'No leader wants to go down in history as the ass who destroyed his country in an afternoon. And funk, I suppose. Most of our gallant politicians do have a narcissistic objection to suicide, thank God.'

'Otherwise no hope?'

'Not for man alone,' said Walter contentedly, who more than once had seriously considered taking Holy Orders rather than the Service's.

'So what's Goethe trying to achieve?' Barley asked another time, with a hint of exasperation.

'Oh, save the world, I'm sure. We'd all like to do *that*.'

'*How* save it? What's his message?'

'That's for you to find out, isn't it?'

'What's he told us so far? Why can't I know?'

'My dear boy, don't be so childish,' Walter exclaimed petulantly, but Ned stepped quickly in.

'You know all you need to know,' he said with a calming authority. 'You're the messenger. It's what you're equipped to be, it's what he wants you to be. He's told us that a lot of things on the Soviet side don't work. He's painted a picture of failure at every level – inaccuracy, incompetence, mismanagement and, on top of that, falsified test results sent to Moscow. Perhaps it's true, perhaps he's made it up. Perhaps somebody made it up for him. It's a beguiling enough story as it stands.'

'Do *we* think it's true?' Barley persisted stubbornly.

'You can't know.'

'Why not?'

'Because under interrogation everybody talks. There are no heroes any more. You talk, I talk, Walter talks, Goethe talks, she talks. So if we tell you what we know about them, we risk compromising our capacity to spy on them. Do we know a particular secret about them? If the answer is no, then they know we lack the software, or the device, or the formula, or the super-secret ground station to find it out. But if the answer is yes, they'll take evasive action to make sure we can't go on watching and hearing them by that method.'

Barley and I played chess.

'Do you reckon marriage only works from a distance then?' he asked me, resuming our earlier conversation as if we had never abandoned it.

'I'm quite sure love does,' I replied with an exaggerated shudder, and quickly moved the subject to less intimate paths.

For his last evening, Miss Coad prepared a salmon trout and polished the silver plate. Bob was commanded, and produced a rare malt whisky and two bottles of Sancerre. But our festivities caught Barley in the same introspective mood, until Walter's spirited Final Sermon rescued him from the doldrums.

'The issue is *why*,' Walter trilled suddenly, his cranky voice flying all over the room, while he helped himself to my glass of Sancerre. 'That's what we're after. Not the substance, but the motive. *Why?* If we trust the motive, we trust the man. Then we trust his material. In the beginning was not the word, not the deed, not the silly serpent. In the beginning was *why?* Why did she pluck the apple? Was she bored? Was she inquisitive? Was she paid? Did Adam put her up to it? If not, who did? The Devil is every girl's cover story. Ignore him. Was she fronting for somebody? It's not enough to say, "Because the apple is there." That may do for Everest. It may even do for Paradise. But it won't do for Goethe and it won't do for us and it *certainly* won't do for our gallant American allies, will it, Bobby?'

And when we all burst out laughing he squeezed his eyes shut and raised his voice still higher.

'Or take the ravishing Katya! Why does Goethe pick on *her?* Why does he put *her* life at risk? And why does she let him? We don't know. But we must. We must know everything we can about her because in our profession the couriers are the message. If Goethe is genuine, the girl's head is on the block. That's a given. If he's not, what does that make her? Did she invent the stuff herself? Is she really in touch with him? Is she in touch with someone different and if so who?' He thrust a strengthless forefinger at Barley's face. 'Then there's *you*, sir. Does Goethe think you're a spy or doesn't he? Did other people *tell* him you were a spy? Be a hamster. Store every nugget you can get. God bless you and all who sail in you.'

I discreetly filled another glass and we drank. And I remember how in the deep quiet we distinctly heard the chimes of Big Ben floating up the river from Westminster.

It was not till early next morning when Barley's departure was only hours off that we granted him a limited sight of the documents he had so stridently demanded in Lisbon – Goethe's notebooks, re-created in facsimile by Langley under draconian conditions of secrecy, down to the thick Russian board backs and line-block drawings of jolly Soviet schoolkids on the covers.

Silently accepting them in both hands, Barley became pure publisher while the rest of us watched the transformation. He opened the first notebook, peered at the gutter, felt the weight and flipped to the back, seeming to work out how long it would take him to read it. He reached for the second, sliced it open at a random page, and seeing tightly-written lines pulled a face that as good as complained that the script was single-spaced and handwritten.

Then he ranged across all three notebooks at once, puzzling his way from illustration to text and text to literary effusion, while he kept his head stiffly backwards and to one side, as if determined to reserve his judgment.

But I noticed how, when he raised his eyes, they had lost their sense of place, and appeared to be fixed on some far mountain of his own.

A routine search of Barley's Hampstead flat conducted by Ned and Brock after his departure revealed no hard clues to his state of mind. An old notebook in which he was accustomed to make his jottings was found in the litter of his desk. The last entries looked recent, the most apt was probably a couplet he had culled from the later work of Stevie Smith.

> 'I am not so afraid of the dark night
> As the friends I do not know.'

Ned conscientiously entered it on the file but refused to make anything of it. Name him a joe who didn't get butterflies in his stomach on the eve of his first run.

And on the back of an old bill tossed into the wastepaper basket Brock came on a quotation which he eventually traced to Roethke, and which for his own dark reasons he only mentioned weeks later.

> 'I learn by going where I have to go.'

6

Katya woke sharply and, as she afterwards persuaded herself, with an immediate awareness that today was the day. She was an emancipated Soviet woman but superstition died hard in her.

'It was meant,' she told herself later.

Through the threadbare curtains a white sun was appearing over the cement parade grounds of her north Moscow suburb. All round her the brick apartment blocks, decked with washing, rose like tattered pink giants into an empty sky.

It's Monday, she thought. I'm in my own bed. I'm free of the street after all. She was thinking of her dream.

Having woken she lay still a moment, patrolling her secret world and trying to shake her mind free of its bad thoughts. And when this didn't work she sprang from her bed and impulsively, as she did most things, ducked with practised deftness between the hanging clothes and crumbling bathroom fittings and showered herself.

She was a beautiful woman as Landau had observed. Her tall body was full but not plump, with a fine neat waist and strong legs. Her black hair was luxuriant and, when she was in a mood to neglect it, rampant. Her face was puckish but intelligent and seemed to animate everything around her. Whether clothed or naked she could make no gesture that did not have its grace.

When she had showered, she turned the taps as hard as they would go, then finished them off with a wallop of the wooden mallet that said, 'Take that!' Humming to herself she picked up the little mirror and strode back to her bedroom to dress. The street again: where was it? In Leningrad or Moscow? The shower had not washed her dream away.

Her bedroom was very small, the smallest of the three rooms that made up her tiny apartment, an alcove with a cupboard and a bed. But Katya was accustomed to these confinements and her swift movements as she brushed out her hair, twisted it and pinned it for the office, had a sensual if haphazard elegance. Indeed the apartment might have been a lot smaller had not Katya been entitled to an extra twenty metres for her work. Uncle Matvey was worth another nine; the twins and her own resourcefulness accounted for the rest. She had no quarrel with the apartment.

Maybe the street was in Kiev, she thought, recalling a recent visit there. No. The Kiev streets are wide but mine was narrow.

While she dressed, the block began to wake up and Katya gratefully counted off the rituals of the normal world. First through the adjoining wall came the Goglidzes' alarm clock sounding six-thirty, followed by their crazy borzoi howling to be let out. The poor Goglidzes, I must take them a gift, she thought. Last month Natasha had lost her mother and on Friday Otar's father had been rushed to hospital with a brain tumour. I'll give them some honey, she thought – and in the same instant found herself smiling a wry greeting to a former lover, a refusenik painter who against all the odds of Nature had contrived to keep a swarm of illegal bees on a rooftop behind the Arbat. He had treated her disgracefully, her friends assured her. But Katya always defended him in her mind. He was an artist, after all, perhaps a genius. He was a beautiful lover and between his rages he had made her laugh. Above all, she had loved him for achieving the impossible.

After the Goglidzes came the grizzling of the Volkhovs' baby daughter cutting her first teeth and a moment later through the floorboards the beat of their new Japanese stereo thumping out the latest American rock. How on earth could they afford such things, Katya wondered in another leap of empathy – Elizabeth always pregnant and Sasha on a hundred and sixty a month? After the Volkhovs came the unsmiling Karpovs, nothing but Radio Moscow for them. A week ago, the Karpovs' balcony had fallen down, killing a policeman and a dog. The wits in the block had wanted to get up a collection for the dog.

She became Katya the provider. On Mondays there was a chance of fresh chickens and vegetables brought privately from the country over the weekend. Her friend Tanya had a cousin who functioned informally as a dealer for smallholders. Phone Tanya.

Thinking this, she also thought about the concert tickets. She had taken her decision. As soon as she got to the office she would collect the two tickets for the Philharmonic which the editor Barzin had promised her as amends for his drunken advances at the May Day party. She had never even noticed his advances, but Barzin was always torturing himself about something, and who was she to stand in the way of his guilt – particularly if it took the form of concert tickets?

At lunchtime after shopping she would trade the tickets with the porter Morozov who had pledged her twenty-four bars of imported soap wrapped in decorative paper. With the fancy soap she would buy the bolt of green check cloth of pure wool that the manager of the clothing shop was keeping locked in his storeroom for her. Katya resolutely refused to wonder why. This afternoon after the Hungarian reception she would hand the cloth to Olga Stanislavsky who, in return for favours to be negotiated, would make two cowboy shirts on the East German sewing machine she had recently traded for her ancient family Singer, one for each twin in time for their birthday. And there might even be enough cloth left over to squeeze them both a private check-up from the dentist.

So goodbye concert. It was done.

The telephone was in the living room where her Uncle Matvey slept, a precious red one from Poland. Volodya had smuggled it from his factory and had the goodness not to take it with him when he made his final exit. Tiptoeing past the sleeping Matvey – and vouchsafing him a tender glance along the way, for Matvey had been her father's favourite brother – she carried the phone across the corridor on its long flex, set it on her bed and began dialling before she had decided whom to talk to first.

For twenty minutes she rang round her friends, trading gossip mostly about where things might be had, but some of it more intimate. Twice when she put the phone down, somebody rang her. The newest Czech film director was at Zoya's last night. Alexandra said he was devastating and today she would take her life in her hands and ring him up, but what could she use for a pretext? Katya racked her brains and came up with a suggestion. Three avant-garde sculptors, till now banned, were to hold their own exhibition at the Railway Workers' Union. Why not invite him to accompany her to the exhibition? Alexandra was delighted. Katya always had the best ideas.

Black-market beef could be bought every Thursday evening from the back of a refrigeration van on the road to Sheremetyevo, said Lyuba; ask for a Tartar named Jan, but don't let him near you! Cuban pineapples were on sale from a shop behind Kropotkin Street, said Olga; mention Dimitri and pay double what they ask.

Ringing off, Katya discovered she was being persecuted by the American book on disarmament that Nasayan had lent her, blue with Roman lettering. Nasayan was October's new non-fiction editor. Nobody liked him, nobody understood how he had got the job. But it was noted that he kept the key to the one copying machine, which placed him squarely in the murkier ranks of officialdom. Her bookshelves were in the corridor, crammed from floor to ceiling and overflowing. She hunted hard. The book was a Trojan horse. She wanted it out of her house, and Nasayan with it.

'Is somebody going to translate it then?' she had asked him sternly as he padded round her office, squinting at her letters, poking through her heap of unread manuscripts. 'Is this why you wish me to read it?'

'I thought it was something that might interest you,' he had replied. 'You're a mother. A liberal, whatever that means. You got on your high horse over Chernobyl and the rivers and the Armenians. If you don't want to borrow it, don't.'

Discovering his wretched book jammed between Hugh Walpole and Thomas Hardy, she wrapped it in newspaper, stuffed it in her perhaps-bag, then hung the bag on the front doorknob because, just as she remembered everything these days, so she forgot everything.

The doorknob that we bought together from the flea market! she thought with a surge of compassion. Volodya, my poor dear intolerable husband, reduced to nursing your historical nostalgia in a communal flat with five ill-smelling grass widowers like yourself!

Her telephoning over, she hastily watered her plants, then went to wake the twins. They were sleeping diagonally in their single bed. Standing over them, Katya gazed at them in awe, for a moment not brave enough to touch them. Then she smiled so that they would be sure to see her smile as they woke.

For an hour after that, she gave herself to them totally, which was how she planned each day. She cooked their *kasha*, peeled their oranges and sang daft songs with them, ending with the 'Enthusiasts' March', their absolute favourite, which they growled in unison, chins on chests, like heroes of the Revolution – not knowing, though Katya knew and was repeatedly amused by it, that they were also singing the melody of a Nazi marching song. While they drank their tea she made their packed lunch, white bread for Sergey, black bread for Anna, a meat-cake inside for each of them. And after that she fastened Sergey's button-on collar and straightened Anna's red neckerchief and kissed them both before she brushed their hair because their school principal was a Pan-Slavist who preached that tidiness was an act of homage to the State.

And when she had done all this, she dropped into a crouch and gathered the twins into her arms, as she had each Monday for the last four weeks.

'So what do you do if Mummy doesn't come back one evening, if she's had to dash off to a conference or visit somebody who is ill?' she asked brightly.

'Telephone Daddy and tell him to come and stay with us,' said Sergey, tugging himself free.

'And I look after Uncle Matvey,' said Anna.

'And if Daddy is away too, what do you do then?'

They began giggling, Sergey because the notion unsettled him and Anna because she was thrilled by the prospect of disaster.

'Go to Auntie Olga's!' Anna cried. 'Wind up Auntie Olga's clockwork canary! Make it sing!'

'And what is Auntie Olga's telephone number? Can you sing that too?'

They sang it, hooting with laughter, all three of them. The twins were still laughing as they clattered ahead of her down the stinking stairwell that served the adolescents as a love-nest and the alcoholics as a bar, and seemingly everybody except themselves as a lavatory. Stepping into the sunlight, they marched hand in hand with her across the park to school, Katya in the middle.

'And what is the objective purpose of your life today, Comrade?' Katya demanded of Sergey with mock ferocity as she straightened his collar once more.

'To serve the people and the Party with all my strength.'

'*And?*'

'Not to let Vitaly Rogov pinch my lunch!'

More laughter as the twins ran away from her up the stone steps, Katya waving till they had disappeared.

In the metro she saw everything too brightly and from a distance. She noticed how glum the passengers were, as if she were not one of them herself and how they all seemed to be reading Moscow newspapers, a sight that would have been unthinkable a year ago when newspapers were good for nothing but toilet paper and closing off draughts. On other days Katya might have read one too; or if not, a book or manuscript for work. But today, despite her efforts to rid herself of her stupid dream, she was living too many lives at once. She was cooking fish soup for her father to make up for some act of wilfulness. She was enduring a piano lesson at the elderly Tatyana Sergeyevna's and being rebuked for levity. She was running in the street, unable to wake. Or the street was running after her. Which was probably why she almost forgot to change trains.

Reaching her office, which was a half-heartedly modern affair of flaking

wood and weeping concrete – more suited to a public swimming pool, she
always thought, than to a State publishing house – she was surprised by
the sight of workmen hammering and sawing in the entrance hall, and for
a second she gave way to the disgusting notion that they were building a
scaffold for her public execution.

'It's our *appropriation,*' wheezed old Morozov, who always had to steal
a word with her. 'The money was allocated to us six years ago. Now some
bureaucrat has consented to sign the order.'

The lift was being repaired as usual. Lifts and churches, she thought, in
Russia always under repair. She took the stairs, climbing swiftly without
knowing what the hurry was, yelling cheerful good mornings at whoever
needed one. Thinking afterwards about her haste, she wondered whether
the ringing of her telephone had drawn her forward subconsciously,
because as she entered her room there it was on her desk howling to be
put out of its pain.

She grabbed the receiver and said 'Da,' out of breath, but evidently she
spoke too soon, for the first thing she heard was a man's voice asking in
English for Madame Orlova.

'This is Madame Orlova,' she said, also in English.

'Madame Yekaterina Orlova?'

'Who is this, please?' she asked, smiling. 'It is Lord Peter Wimsey
perhaps? Who is this?'

One of my silly friends playing a joke. Lyuba's husband again, hoping
for a date. Then her mouth dried.

'Ah well, you don't know me, I'm afraid. My name's Scott Blair. Barley
Scott Blair from Abercrombie & Blair in London, publishers, over here on
a business trip. I think we have a mutual friend in Niki Landau. Niki was
very insistent I should give you a call. How do you do?'

'How do you do,' Katya heard herself say, and felt a hot cloud come over
her and a pain start at the centre of her stomach just below the rib cage.
At the same moment Nasayan strolled in, hands in pockets and unshaven,
which was his way of showing intellectual depth. Seeing her talking, he
hunched his shoulders and struck his ugly face at her in a resentful pout,
willing her to get off the line.

'*Bonjour* to you, Katya Borisovna,' he said sarcastically.

But the voice in the telephone was already talking again, pressing itself
upon her. It was a strong voice so she assumed someone tall. It was
confident so she assumed someone arrogant, the kind of Englishman who
wears expensive suits, has no culture and walks with his hands behind his
back.

'Look, I'll tell you why I'm calling,' he was saying. 'Apparently Niki
promised to look out some old editions of Jane Austen for you with the
original drawings, is that right?' He gave her no time to say whether it was
right or wrong. 'Only I've brought a couple over with me – rather nice

ones, actually – and I wondered whether we could possibly arrange a handover at some mutually convenient point?'

Tired of glowering, Nasayan was picking through the papers in her in-tray after his usual habit.

'You are very kind,' she said into the mouthpiece, using her dullest voice. She had closed her face, making it lifeless and official. That was for Nasayan. She had closed her mind. That was for herself.

'Niki's also sent you about a ton of Jackson's tea,' the voice continued.

'A *ton?*' said Katya. 'What are you talking about?'

'I didn't even know Jackson's were still in business, to be honest. They used to have a marvellous shop in Piccadilly a few doors down from Hatchard's. Anyway, I've got three different kinds of their tea sitting here in front of me – '

He had disappeared.

They have arrested him, she thought. He never rang. It's my dream again. God in Heaven, what do I do next?

' – Assam, Darjeeling and Orange Pekoe. What on earth's a pekoe? Sounds more like an exotic bird to me.'

'I don't know. I suspect it will be a plant.'

'I suspect you'll be right at that. Anyway the question is, how can I give them to you? Can I bring them to you somewhere? Or can you drop in at the hotel and could we have a quick drink and a formal presentation?'

She was learning to appreciate his long-windedness. He was giving her time to steady herself. She pushed her fingers through her hair, discovering to her surprise that it was tidy.

'You have not told me which hotel you are staying at,' she objected severely.

Nasayan's head jerked round to her in disapproval.

'Well, neither I did now. How ridiculous of me. I'm at the Odessa, know the Odessa? Just up the road from the old bath house? I've become quite fond of it. Always ask for it, don't always get it. My day times are rather taken up with meetings – always the way when one's over on a flying visit – but evenings are relatively free at the moment, if that's any good to you. I mean how about tonight – no time like the present – would tonight be any good for you?'

Nasayan was lighting one of his filthy cigarettes, though the whole office knew she hated smoking. Having lit it, he hoisted it in the air and sucked from it with his woman's lips. She grimaced at him but he ignored her.

'That is actually quite convenient,' Katya said in her most military manner. 'Tonight I have to attend an official reception in your district. It is for an important delegation from Hungary,' she added, not sure whom she was meaning to impress. 'We have been looking forward to it for many weeks.'

'Great. Marvellous. Suggest a time. Six? Eight? What suits you best?'

'The reception is at six o'clock. I shall come at perhaps eight-fifteen.'

'Perhaps-eight-fifteen it is. You got the name, did you? Scott Blair. Scott like the Antarctic, Blair like a trumpet. I'm tall and seedy, about two hundred years old, with spectacles I can't see through. But Niki tells me you're the Soviet answer to the Venus de Milo so I expect I'll recognise you anyway.'

'That is most ridiculous!' she exclaimed, laughing despite herself.

'I'll be hanging around the lobby looking out for you, but why don't I give you my room telephone number just in case. Got a pencil?'

As she rang off the contrary passions that had been gathering in her burst their banks and she turned on Nasayan with flashing eyes.

'Grigory Tigranovich. Whatever your position here, you have no right to haunt my room like this, inspect my correspondence and listen to my telephone conversations. Here is your book. If you have something to say to me, say it later.'

Then she scooped up a sheaf of translator's manuscript on the achievements of Cuban agricultural cooperatives and with cold hands began leafing through the pages, pretending to count them. A full hour passed before she telephoned Nasayan.

'You must forgive my anger,' she said. 'A close friend of mine died at the weekend. I was not myself.'

By lunchtime she had changed her plans. Morozov could wait for his tickets, the shopkeeper for his bars of fancy soap, Olga Stanislavsky for her cloth. She walked, she took a bus, not a cab. She walked again, crossing one courtyard after another until she found the down-at-heel blockhouse she was looking for and the alley that ran beside it. 'This is how you get hold of me when you need me,' he had said. 'The janitor is a friend of mine. He will not even know who made the sign.'

You have to believe in what you are doing, she reminded herself.

I do. I absolutely do.

She had the picture postcard in her hand, a Rembrandt from the Hermitage in Leningrad. 'Love to you all,' her message read, signed 'Alina', and a heart.

She had found the street. She was standing in it. It was the street of her bad dream. She pressed the bell, three rings, then shoved the card under the door.

A perfect Moscow morning, alight and beckoning, the air alpine, a day to forgive all sins. The telephone call behind him, Barley stepped out of his hotel and, standing on the warm pavement, loosened his wrists and shoulders and rolled his head round his collar while he turned his mind outward and let the city drown his fears with its conflicting smells and voices. The stink of Russian petrol, tobacco, cheap scent and river water – hullo! Two more days here I shan't know I'm smelling you. The sporadic cavalry charges of the commuter cars – hullo! The belching brown lorries thundering through the pot-holes in pursuit. The eerie emptiness between. The limousines with their blackened windows, the unmarked buildings splitting before their time – are you a block of offices, a barracks or a school? The dough-faced boys smoking in the doorways, waiting. The chauffeurs, reading newspapers in their parked cars, waiting. The unspeaking group of solemn men in hats, staring at a closed door, waiting.

Why did it always draw me? he wondered, contemplating his life in the past tense, which had recently become his habit. Why did I keep coming back here? He was feeling high and bright, he couldn't help it. He was not used to fear.

Because of their making do, he decided. Because they can rough it better than we can. Because of their love of anarchy and their terror of chaos, and the tension in between.

Because God always found excuses not to come here.

Because of their universal ignorance, and the brilliance that bursts through it. Because of their sense of humour, as good as ours and better.

Because they are the last great frontier in an over-discovered world. Because they try so hard to be like us and start from so far back.

Because of the huge heart beating inside the huge shambles. Because the shambles is my own.

I shall come at perhaps-eight-fifteen, she had said. What had he heard in her voice? Guardedness? Guarding whom? Herself? Him? Me? In our profession, the couriers are the message.

Look outwards, Barley told himself. Outwards is the only place to be.

From the metro a group of teenage girls in cotton frocks and boys in denim jackets trotted purposefully to work or instruction, their glum expressions switching to laughter at a word. Spotting the foreigner they studied him with cool glances – his rounded, pop-eye spectacles, his shabby handmade shoes, his old imperialist suit. In Moscow, if nowhere else, Barley Blair observed the bourgeois proprieties of dress.

Joining the stream he let it carry him, not caring which way he went. By contrast with his determinedly contented mood the early food queues had a restless and unsettled look. The grim-suited labour heroes and war veterans, their breastplates of medals jingling in the sunlight as they waded . through the crowds, had an air of being late for wherever they were marching. Even their sloth seemed to have an air of protest. In the new climate, doing nothing was itself an act of opposition. Because by doing nothing we change nothing. And by changing nothing we hang on to what we understand, even if it is the bars of our own gaol.

I shall come at perhaps-eight-fifteen.

Reaching the wide river Barley again dawdled. On the far bank the fairytale domes of the Kremlin lifted into a cloudless heaven. A Jerusalem with its tongue pulled out, he thought. So many towers, scarcely a bell. So many churches, barely a spoken prayer.

Hearing a voice close beside him he swung round too sharply and discovered an old couple in their best clothes asking him the way to somewhere. But Barley of the perfect memory had few words of Russian. It was a music he had listened to often, without summoning the nerve to penetrate its mysteries.

He laughed and made an apologetic face. 'Don't speak it, old boy. I'm an imperialist hyena. English!'

The old man grasped his wrist in friendship.

In every foreign city he had ever been, strangers asked him the way to places he didn't know in languages he didn't understand. Only in Moscow did they bless him for his ignorance.

He retraced his steps, pausing at unswept windows, pretending to examine what they offered. Painted wooden dolls. Who for? Dusty tins of fruit, or were they fish? Battered packets hanging from red string, contents a mystery, perhaps pekoes. Jars of pickled medical samples, lit by ten-watt bulbs. He was approaching his hotel again. A drunk-eyed peasant woman pushed a bunch of dying tulips at him, wrapped in newspaper.

'Awfully kind of you,' he cried and, rummaging through his pockets, found among the junk a rouble note.

A green Lada was parked outside the hotel entrance, the radiator smashed. A hand-inked card in the windscreen said VAAP. The driver was leaning over the bonnet detaching the wiper blades as a precaution against theft.

'Scott Blair?' Barley asked him. 'You looking for me?' The driver paid him not the slightest attention but continued with his work. 'Blair?' said Barley. 'Scott?'

'Those for me, dear?' Wicklow enquired, coming up behind him. 'You're fine,' he added quietly. 'Clean as a whistle.'

Wicklow will watch your back for you, Ned had said. Wicklow, if anybody, will know whether you're being followed. Wicklow and who else? Barley wondered. Last night, as soon as they had checked in to the hotel, Wicklow had vanished until after midnight, and as Barley had put himself to bed he had seen him from his window, standing in the street talking to two young men in jeans.

They got into the car. Barley tossed the tulips on to the back ledge. Wicklow sat in the front seat chatting cheerily to the driver in his perfect Russian. The driver let out a great bellow of laughter. Wicklow laughed too.

'Want to share it?' Barley asked.

Wicklow was already doing so. 'I asked him whether he'd like to drive the Queen when she came here on her State visit. There's a saying here. If you steal, steal a million. If you screw, screw a queen.'

Barley lowered his window and tapped out a tune on the sill. Life was a romp till perhaps-eight-fifteen.

*

'Barley! Welcome to Barbary, my dear chap. For God's sake, man, don't shake hands with me across the threshold, we have enough troubles as it is! You look positively healthy,' Alik Zapadny complained in alarm when they had time to examine each other. 'Why have you no hangover, may I ask? Are you in love, Barley? Are you divorced again? What have you been up to that you require to confess to me?'

Zapadny's drawn face examined him with desperate intelligence, the shadows of confinement stamped for ever in his hollowed cheeks. When Barley had first known him, Zapadny had been a dubious translator in disgrace working under other names. Now he was a dubious hero of the Reconstruction, dressed in a larger man's white collar and black suit.

'I've heard the Voice, Alik,' Barley explained, with a rush of the old fondness as he slipped him a bunch of back-numbers of *The Times* wrapped in brown paper. 'In bed with a good book every night at ten. Meet Len Wicklow, our Russian specialist. Knows more about you than you do, don't we, Leonard Carl?'

'Well, thank God somebody does!' Zapadny protested, careful not to acknowledge the gift. 'We are becoming so unsure of ourselves these days, now that our great Russian mystery is being held up to public view. How much do you know about your new boss, by the way, Mr. Wicklow? Have you heard, for instance, how he undertook the re-education of the Soviet Union singlehanded? Oh yes. He had a charming vision of a hundred million under-educated Soviet workers longing to improve themselves in their leisure. He was going to sell them a great range of titles about how to teach themselves Greek and trigonometry and basic housekeeping. We had to explain to him that the Soviet man-in-the-street regards himself as finite and in his leisure hours he is drunk. Do you know what we bought from him instead to keep him happy? A golf book! You would not imagine how many of our worthy citizens are fascinated by your capitalist golf.' And in haste, still a dangerous joke – 'Not that we have any capitalists *here*. Oh my God, no.'

They sat ten strong at a yellow table under an icon of Lenin made in wood veneers. Zapadny was the speaker, the others were listeners and smokers. Not one of them, so far as Barley knew, was competent to sign a contract or approve a deal.

'Now Barley, what is this total nonsense you are putting about that you have come here in order to buy Soviet books, please?' Zapadny demanded by way of opening courtesies, lifting his hooped eyebrows and placing the tips of his fingers together like Sherlock Holmes. 'You British *never* buy our books. You make us buy yours instead. Besides, you are broke, or so our friends from London tell us. A. & B. are living off God's good air and Scotch whisky, they say. Personally I consider that an excellent diet. But why have you come? I think you only wanted an excuse to visit us again.'

Time was passing. The yellow table floated in the sunbeams. A pall of cigarette smoke floated over it. Black-and-white images of Katya in photographic form came and went in Barley's mind. The Devil is every girl's cover story. They drank tea out of pretty Leningrad cups. Zapadny was delivering his standard caveat against trying to make deals directly with Soviet publishers, selecting Wicklow as his audience: the day-and-night war between VAAP and the rest of the world was evidently raging well. Two pale men wandered in to listen and wandered out again. Wicklow was earning favour by handing round blue Gauloises.

'We've had an injection of capital, Alik,' Barley heard himself explaining from a long way off. 'Times have changed. Russia's top of the cops these days. I've only got to tell the money boys I'm building up a Russian list and they come rushing after me as fast as their short fat legs will carry them.'

'But, Barley, these *boys*, as you call them, can grow into *men* very quickly,' Zapadny, the great sophisticate, warned to a fresh burst of docile laughter. 'Particularly when they are wishing to be repaid, I would say.'

'It's the way I described it in my telex, Alik. Maybe you haven't had time to read it,' said Barley, showing a little muscle. 'If things work out as we plan, A. & B. will be launching a brand-new imprint devoted entirely to things Russian within the year. Fiction, non-fiction, poetry, juveniles, the sciences. We've got a new line in popular medicine, all paperback. The subjects travel, so do the reputations of the authors. We'd like real Soviet doctors and scientists to contribute. We don't want sheep farming in Outer Mongolia or fish farming in the Arctic Circle but if you have sensible subjects you want to suggest we're here to listen and buy. We'll announce our list at the next Moscow book fair and if things go well we'll bring out our first six titles next spring.'

'And have you, forgive me, a sales force these days, Barley, or are you relying on divine intervention as before?' Zapadny enquired with his showy delicacy.

Resisting the temptation to tell Zapadny to watch his manners, Barley struggled on. 'We're negotiating a distribution deal with several major publishers and we'll make an announcement soon. Except for fiction. For the fiction we'll use our own expanded team,' he said, unable to remember for the life of him why they had settled on this bizarre arrangement or indeed whether they had.

'Fiction is still the A. & B. flagship, sir,' Wicklow explained devoutly, helping Barley out.

'Fiction should *always* be one's flagship,' Zapadny corrected him. 'I would say that the novel is the greatest of all marathons. That is only my personal opinion, naturally. It is the highest form of art. Higher than poetry, higher than the short story. But please don't quote me.'

'Well, it is for us literary superpowers, sir, put it that way,' said Wicklow smarmily.

Very gratified, Zapadny turned to Barley. 'On fiction, we should like in this special case to provide our own translator and take a further five per cent royalty on the translation,' he said.

'No problem,' Barley said genially in his sleep. 'These days, that's the kind of money A. & B. puts under the plate.'

But to Barley's amazement Wicklow briskly intervened. 'Excuse me, sir, that means a double royalty. I don't think we can swallow that and live. You must have misheard what Mr. Zapadny was saying.'

'He's right,' said Barley, sitting up sharply. 'How the hell can we afford another five per cent?'

Feeling like a conjuror who is proceeding to his next bogus act, Barley fished a folder from his briefcase and scattered half a dozen copies of a glossy prospectus at the sunbeams. 'Our American connection is described on page two,' he announced. 'Potomac Boston is our partner in the project, A. & B. to buy full English language rights in any Soviet work, and sell off North America to Potomac. They have a sister company in Toronto, so we'll throw in Canada. Right, Wickers?'

'Yes, sir.'

How the hell did Wicklow learn all this junk so quickly? Barley thought.

Zapadny was still studying the prospectus, turning one stiff, immaculate page after another. 'Did *you* print this shit, Barley?' he enquired politely.

'Potomac did,' said Barley.

'But the Potomac river is so far from the city of Boston,' Zapadny objected, airing his knowledge of American geography for the few who shared it. 'Unless they have recently moved it, it is in Washington. What mutual attraction can they have, I ask myself the city of Boston and this river? Are we speaking of an *old* company, Barley, or a *new* one?'

'New in the field. Old in business. They're merchants, ex Washington now in Boston. Venture capital. Diversified portfolio. Film production, carparks, slot machines, call-girls and cocaine. All the usual. Publishing's just one of their sidelines.'

But in his mind's ear as the laughter rose it was Ned who was doing the talking. 'Congratulations, Barley. Bob here has come up with a wealthy Boston chum who's willing to take you on as a partner. All you have to do is spend his money.'

And Bob, with his flat-iron feet and tweedy jacket, smiling the buyer's smile.

Eleven-thirty. Eight hours and forty-five minutes until perhaps-eight-fifteen.

'The driver wants to know what to expect when he meets the Queen,' Wicklow was yelling enthusiastically over the back of his seat. 'It's really getting to him. Does she take bribes? Does she have people executed for small offences? How does it feel to live in a country ruled by two fierce women?'

'Tell him it's exhausting but we're equal to it,' Barley said with a huge yawn.

And having refreshed himself with a nip from his flask he leaned back in the cushions and woke to find himself following Wicklow down a prison corridor. Except that instead of the cries of the incarcerated, it was the whistle of a tea kettle that he heard and the clicking of an abacus echoing through the gloom. A moment later, Wicklow and Barley are standing in the offices of a British railway company, vintage 1935. Flyblown light bulbs and defunct electric fans dangle from the cast-iron rafters. Amazons in headscarves preside over antiquated Cyrillic typewriters large as ovens. Ledgers cram the dusty shelves. Stacks of shoeboxes stuffed with buff folders rise from the floorboards to the sills.

'Barley! Jesus! Welcome to Prometheus Unbound! They tell me you got some money finally. Who gave it you?' yells a middle-aged figure in Fidel Castro battle gear leaping at them through the clutter. 'We deal direct, okay? To hell with those arseholes in VAAP?'

'Yuri, marvellous to see you! Meet Len Wicklow, our Russian-speaking editor.'

'You a spy?'

'Only in my spare time, sir.'

'Jesus! Nice chap! Reminds me of my kid brother.'

They are in Madison Avenue. Venetian blinds, wall charts and armchairs. Yuri is fat, exuberant and Jewish. Barley has brought him a bottle of Black Label and tights for his beautiful new wife. Tossing away the whisky cap, Yuri insists on pouring tots into the teacups. They enter the Russian ether. Talk of Bulgakov, Platonov, Akhmatova. Will Solzhenitsyn be permitted? Will Brodsky? Talk of a ragtag list of contemporary British writers who have arbitrarily found official favour and therefore fame in Russia. Barley has not heard of some, loathes others. Gusts of laughter, toasts, news of English friends, death to the arseholes in VAAP. Russia is changing by the hour, has Barley heard? Did he see that piece in *Moscow News* last Thursday about the neo-Fascist crazies in Pamyat, with their way-out nationalism and their anti-Semitism and their anti-everyone except themselves? And how about that piece in *Ogonyok* about Sigmund Freud? And *Novy Mir's* stand on Nabokov? Editors, designers, translators proliferate in the usual amazing numbers, but no Katyas. Everyone is drunk, even those who have declined the alcohol. A great writer named Misha is presented and seated where his audience can watch him.

'Misha hasn't been to prison yet,' Yuri explains apologetically, to huge laughter. 'But maybe if he's lucky, they'll send him before it's too late, so that he can get published in the West!'

They talk the latest Soviet masterpieces of fiction. Yuri has chosen a mere eight from his own list – every one of them a sure bestseller, Barley.

Publish them and you will be able to open a Swiss bank account for me. A hunt for plastic carrier bags before Wicklow takes charge of the carbon copies of eight unpublishable manuscripts, for this is a world in which the photocopier and electric typewriter are still the forbidden instruments of sedition.

They talk theatre and Afghanistan. 'Soon we shall all meet in London!' Yuri cries, like a mad gambler staking all. 'I send you my son, okay? Will you send me yours? Listen, we exchange hostages and that way nobody bombs each other!'

Everyone falls silent when Barley speaks, and stays silent for Misha the great writer. Wicklow translates while Yuri and three others object to Wicklow's translation. Misha objects to the objections. The downturn has begun.

Somebody demands to know why Britain is still run by the Fascist Conservative Party. Why doesn't the proletariat kick the bastards out? Barley offers something unoriginal about democracy being the worst of systems except for the others. No one laughs. Perhaps they have heard it, perhaps they don't like it. In the wake of the whisky it is time to get out while the smiles are still fading. How can the English preach human rights, somebody sullenly demands, when they are enslaving the Irish and the Scots? Why do you support the disgusting government in South Africa? yells a ninety-year-old blonde in a ball-dress. I don't, says Barley. I truly don't.

'Listen,' says Yuri, at the door. 'Stay away from that bastard Zapadny, okay? I don't say he's KGB. All I say is, he needed some damn good friends to get him back into circulation. You're a nice fellow. Know what I mean?'

They have already embraced many times.

'Yuri,' says Barley. 'My old mother brought me up to believe that all of you were KGB.'

'Me too?'

'You specially. She said you were the worst.'

'I love you. Hear me? Send me your son. What's his name?'

One-thirty and they are an hour late for their next step along the hard road to perhaps-eight-fifteen.

Dark timber, splendid food, respectful menials, the atmosphere of a baronial hunting lodge. They are sitting at the long table below the balcony in the Writers' Union, Alik Zapadny once again presiding. Several promising young writers of sixty stroll over, listen and stroll away again, taking their great thoughts with them. Zapadny points out those recently released from prison and those who he hopes will soon replace them. Literary bureaucrats pull up chairs and practise their English. Wicklow interprets, Barley sparkles, all on fruit juice and the residue of Black Label. The world is going to be a better place, Barley assures Zapadny, as if he were an expert on the world.

Rashly he quotes Zinoviev. 'When will it all end? When people stop queuing for the Tomb?' – a reference to Lenin's mausoleum.

The applause this time is not so deafening.

At two o'clock in conformity with the new drinking laws and in the nick of time, the waiter brings a carafe of wine and Zapadny in Barley's honour extracts a bottle of pepper vodka from his worm-eaten briefcase.

'Did Yuri tell you I was KGB?' he asks mournfully.

'Of course he didn't,' says Barley stoutly.

'Please do not regard yourself as singled out. He tells it to all Westerners. As a matter of fact, I sometimes worry a little bit about Yuri. He's a nice fellow but everyone knows he is a lousy publisher, so how does a Jew like him get his position? His little boy was christened at Zagorsk last week. How do you explain this?'

'It's not my problem, Alik. Live and let live. Finito.' And aside: 'Wickers, get me out of here, I'm getting sober.'

By six, after two more enormously eloquent meetings, and having miraculously succeeded in declining half a dozen invitations for the evening, Barley is back in his hotel room, fighting with the shower to sober up while Wicklow shouts cheerful publishing talk at him through the door for the benefit of the microphones. For Wicklow has Ned's orders to stay with Barley till the last moment in case he gets stage fright or fluffs his lines.

7

T he Odessa Hotel in that third year of the Great Soviet Reconstruction was not the jewel of Moscow's rugged tourist trade but it was not the worst piece either. It was dilapidated, it was down-at-heel, it was selective in its favours. Tied to the rouble rather than to the dollar, it lacked such refinements as foreign currency bars and groups of travel-weary Minnesotans appealing tearfully for their missing luggage. It was so ill-lit that the brass lamps and blackamoors and galleried dining room recalled the bad old past at the point of its collapse rather than the Socialist phoenix rising from the ashes. And when you stepped from the juddering lift and braved the frown of your floor concierge, crouching in her box surrounded by blackened room-keys and mossy telephones, you were quite likely to have the sensation of being returned to the vilest institutions of your youth.

But then the Reconstruction was not yet a visual medium. It was strictly in the audio stage.

Nevertheless, for those who looked for it, the Odessa in those days had soul, and with luck has it still. The good ladies of reception keep a kindly heart behind their iron stares; the porters have been known to wink you to the lift without demanding to see your hotel pass for the fifth time in one day. The restaurant manager, given the right encouragement, will usher you graciously to your alcove and likes a good face in return. And in the evenings between six and nine the lobby becomes an impromptu pageant of the hundred nations of the Empire. Smartly dressed administrators from Tashkent, flaxen schoolteachers from Estonia, fiery-eyed Party functionaries from Turkmenia and Georgia, factory managers from Kiev, naval engineers from Archangel – not to mention Cubans, Afghans, Poles, Rumanians and a platoon of dowdily arrogant East Germans – pour out of their airport charabancs and descend from the sunlight of the street into the quelling darkness of the lobby in order to pay their homage to Rome and shift their luggage in metric stages towards the tribune.

And Barley, himself a reluctant emissary though from a different empire, that evening took his place among them.

First he sat, only to have an old lady thump him on the shoulder and demand his seat. Then he hovered in an alcove near the lift until he risked being walled in by a rampart of cardboard suitcases and brown parcels. Finally he removed himself to the protection of a central pillar and there he remained, apologising to everyone, watching the glass door turn off and on, and shuffling out of everybody's light, then into it again, while he brandished Jane Austen's *Emma* at his chest and in his other hand a lurid carrier bag from Heathrow airport.

It was a good thing that Katya arrived to save him.

There was no secret to their meeting, nothing secretive in their behaviour. Each caught the other's eye at the same instant, while Katya was still being buffeted through the door. Barley threw up an arm, waving Jane Austen.

'Hullo, it's me. Blair. Jolly good!' he yelled.

Katya vanished and reappeared victorious. Did she hear him? She smiled anyway and lifted her eyes to Heaven in mute show, making excuses for her lateness. She shoved back a lock of black hair and Barley saw Landau's wedding and betrothal rings.

'You should have seen me trying to get away,' she was signalling across the heads. Or: 'Couldn't get a cab for love nor money.'

'Doesn't matter a bit,' Barley was signalling back.

Then she cut him dead while she scowled and rummaged in her handbag for her identity card to show to the plainclothes boy, whose agreeable job that night was to challenge all attractive ladies entering the hotel. It was a red card that she produced so Barley divined the Writers' Union.

Then Barley himself was distracted while he tried in his passable if clotted French to explain to a tall Palestinian that no, he was afraid he was *not* a member of the Peace Group, old boy, and alas *not* the manager of the hotel either, and he doubted very much whether there was one.

Wicklow, who had observed these events from halfway up the staircase, reported later that he had never seen an overt encounter better done.

As actors Barley and Katya were dressed for different plays: Katya for high drama in her blue dress and old lace collar that had so taken Landau's fancy; and Barley for low English comedy in a pinstripe suit of his father's that was too short for him in the sleeve, and a pair of very scuffed buckskin boots by Ducker's of Oxford that only a collector of bygones could have regarded as still splendid.

When they met they surprised each other. After all they were still strangers, closer to the forces that had brought them here than to one another. Discarding the impulse to give her a formal peck on the cheek, Barley found himself instead puzzling over her eyes, which were not only very dark and full of light at the same time but heavily fringed, so that he couldn't help wondering whether she was endowed with a double set of eyelashes.

And since Barley on his side wore that indefinably foolish expression which overcomes certain Englishmen in the presence of beautiful women, it was Katya's suspicion that her first instinct on the telephone had been right and he was haughty.

Meanwhile they were standing close enough to feel the warmth of each other's bodies and for Barley to smell her make-up. The Babel of foreign languages continued round them.

'You are Mr. Barley, I think,' she told him breathlessly and laid a hand along his forearm, for she had a way of touching people as if seeking to assure herself that they were real.

'Yes indeed, the same, hullo, well done, and you're Katya Orlova, Niki's friend. Wonderful you could make it. Masterpiece of timing. How are you?'

Photographs don't lie but they don't tell the truth either, Barley was thinking, watching her breast rise and fall with her breathing. They don't catch the glow of a girl who looks as though she's just witnessed a miracle and you're the person she's chosen to tell first.

The restless crowd in the lobby brought him to his senses. No two people, however purposefully united, could have survived for long exchanging pleasantries in the centre of that turmoil.

'Tell you what,' he said, as if he had had a bright idea on the spur of the moment. 'Why don't I buy you a bun? Niki was determined I should make a fuss of you. You met each other at that fair, he tells me. What a character. Heart of gold,' he continued cheerfully as he led her towards the staircase and a sign that read 'Buffet'. 'Salt of the earth. A pain in the neck as well, of course, but who isn't?'

'Oh Mr. Landau is a *very* kind man,' she said, speaking much as

Barley was for the benefit of an unidentified audience, but sounding very persuasive nevertheless.

'And reliable,' Barley called approvingly as they gained the first-floor landing. Now Barley too was for some reason out of breath. 'Ask Niki to do a thing, he does it. In his own way, it's true. But he does it and keeps his thoughts to himself. I always think that's the sign of a good friend, don't you?'

'I would say that without discretion there can be no friendship,' she replied as if quoting from a marriage book. 'True friendship must be based on mutual trust.'

And Barley while responding warmly to such profundity could not fail to recognise the similarity of her cadences to those of Goethe.

In a curtained area stood a thirty-foot food counter with a single tray of sugar biscuits on it. Behind it three bulky ladies in white uniforms and helmets of transparent plastic had mounted guard over a regimental samovar while they argued among themselves.

'Sound judge of a book too, in his own way, old Niki,' Barley observed, stretching out the topic as they took up their places before the rope barrier. '*Bête intellectuelle*, as the French say. Tea, please, ladies. Marvellous.'

The ladies went on haranguing each other. Katya stared at them with no expression on her face. Suddenly to Barley's astonishment she drew out her red pass and snarled – there was no other word for it – with the result that one of them detached herself from her companions long enough to yank two cups from a rack and slap them viciously on two saucers as if she were breech-loading an old rifle. Still furious, she filled a huge kettle. And having with further signs of rage unearthed a modern box of matches, she turned up a gas ring and dumped the kettle on it before returning to her comrades.

'Care for a biscuit?' Barley asked. '*Foie gras?*'

'Thank you. I ate cake already at the reception.'

'Oh my God. Good cake?'

'It was not very interesting.'

'But nice Hungarians?'

'The speeches were not significant. I would say they were banal. I blame our Soviet side for this. We are not sufficiently relaxed with foreigners even when they are from Socialist countries.'

Both for a moment had run out of lines. Barley was remembering a girl he had known at university, a general's daughter with skin like rose petals who lived only for the rights of animals until she hurriedly married a groom from the local hunt. Katya was staring gloomily into the further end of the room where a dozen stand-up tables were placed in strict lines. At one of them stood Leonard Wicklow sharing a joke with a young man his own age. At another an elderly *Rittmeister* in riding boots was drinking lemonade with a girl in jeans and throwing out his arms as if to describe his lost estates.

'Can't think why I didn't offer you dinner,' Barley said, meeting her eyes again with the feeling of falling straight into them. 'One doesn't want to be too forward, I suppose. Not unless one can get away with it.'

'It would not have been convenient,' she replied, frowning.

The kettle began chugging but the war-hardened women of the buffet kept their backs to it.

'Always so difficult, performing on the telephone, don't you think?' Barley said, for small talk. 'Addressing oneself to a sort of plastic flower, I mean, instead of a human face. Hate the beastly thing personally, don't you?'

'Hate what, please?'

'The telephone. Talking at a distance.' The kettle began spitting on the gas. 'You get the silliest ideas about people when you can't see them.'

Jump, he told himself. *Now.*

'I was saying the very same thing to a publishing friend of mine only the other day,' he went on, at the same jolly, conversational level. 'We were discussing a new novel someone sent me. I'd shown it to him, strictly confidentially, and hc was absolutely knocked out by it. Said it was the best thing he'd seen for years. Dynamite, in fact.' Her eyes fixed on his own and they were scaringly direct. 'But so *odd* not to have any sort of picture of the writer,' he continued airily. 'I don't even know the chap's name. Let alone where he gets all his information from, learnt his craft and so forth. Know what I mean? Like hearing a bit of music and not being sure whether it's Brahms or Cole Porter.'

She was frowning. She had drawn in her lips and seemed to be moistening them inside her mouth. 'I do not regard such personal questions as appropriate to an artist. Some writers can work only in obscurity. Talent is talent. It does not require explanations.'

'Well I wasn't talking so much about explanations, you see, as about authenticity,' Barley explained. A path of down followed the line of her cheekbone but unlike the hair on her head it was gold. 'I mean, *you* know publishing. If a fellow's written a novel about the hill tribes of Northern Burma, for instance, one's entitled to ask whether he's ever been south of Minsk. Specially if it's a really important novel, which this one is. A potential world-beater, according to my chum. In a case like that, I reckon you're entitled to insist that the writer should stand up and declare his qualifications.'

Bolder than the others, the senior lady was pouring boiling water into the samovar. A second was unlocking the regimental cash box. A third was scooping rations of tea into a handscale. Searching in his pockets Barley came up with a three-rouble note. At the sight of it the woman at the cash box broke into a despairing tirade.

'I expect she wants change,' Barley said stupidly. 'Don't we all?'

Then he saw that Katya had put thirty kopeks on the counter and that she had two very small dimples when she smiled. He took the books and bag. She followed him with the teacups on a tray. But as they reached their table she addressed him with an expression of challenge.

'If an author is obliged to prove that he is saying the truth, so also is his publisher,' she said.

'Oh, I'm for honesty on all sides. The more people put their cards on the table, the better off we'll *all* be.'

'I am informed that the author was inspired by a Russian poet.'

'Pecherin,' Barley replied. 'Looked him up. Born 1807 in Dymerka, province of Kiev.'

Her lips were near the brim of her cup, her eyes down. And though he had plenty of other things on his mind, Barley noticed that her right ear, protruding from her hair, had become transparent in the evening light from the window.

'The author was also inspired by certain opinions of an Englishman concerning world peace,' she said with the utmost severity.

'Do you think he would like to meet that Englishman again?'

'This can be established. It is not known.'

'Well the Englishman would like to meet *him*,' said Barley. 'They've got an awful lot to say to each other. Where do you live?'

'With my children.'

'Where are your children?'

A pause while Barley again had the uncomfortable sensation of having offended against some unfamiliar ethic.

'We live close to the Aeroport metro station. There is no airport there any more. There are apartments. How long are you staying in Moscow, please, Mr. Barley?'

'A week. Any address for your apartment?'

'It is not convenient. You are staying all the time here at the Hotel Odessa?'

'Unless they chuck me out. What does your husband do?'

'It is not important.'

'Is he in publishing?'

'No.'

'Is he a writer?'

'No.'

'So what is he? A composer? A frontier guard? A cook? How does he maintain you in the style to which you are accustomed?'

He had made her laugh again, which seemed to please her as much as it did him. 'He was manager of a timber concern,' she said.

'What's he manager of now?'

'His factory prefabricates houses for rural areas. We are divorced, like everyone else in Moscow.'

'What are the kids? Boys? Girls? How old?'

And that put an end to laughter. For a moment he thought she would walk out on him. Her head lifted, her face closed and an angry fire filled her eyes. 'I have a boy and a girl. They are twins, eight years old. It is not relevant.'

'You speak beautiful English. Better than I do. It's like well water.'

'Thank you, I have a natural comprehension of foreign languages.'

'It's better than that. It's unearthly. It's as if English had stopped at Jane Austen. Where did you learn it?' .

'In Leningrad. I was at school there. English is also my passion.'

'Where were you at university?'

'Also in Leningrad.'

'When did you come to Moscow?'

'When I married.'

'How did you meet him?'

'My husband and I knew each other from childhood. While we were at school, we attended summer camps together.'

'Did you catch fish?'

'Also rabbits,' she said as her smile came back again to light the whole room. 'Volodya is a Siberian boy. He knows how to sleep in the snow, skin a rabbit and catch fish through the ice. At the time I married him I was in retreat from intellectual values. I thought the most important thing a man could know was how to skin a rabbit.'

'I was *really* wondering how you met the author,' Barley explained.

He watched her wrestle with her indecision, noticing how readily her eyes reflected her changing emotions, now coming to him, now retreating. Until he lost her altogether as she stooped below the level of the table, pushed away her flying hair and picked up her handbag. 'Please thank Mr. Landau for the books and the tea,' she said. 'I shall thank him myself next time he comes to Moscow.'

'Don't go. Please. I need your advice.' He lowered his voice and it was suddenly very serious. 'I need your instructions about what to do with that crazy manuscript. I can't fly solo. Who wrote it? Who's Goethe?'

'Unfortunately I have to return to my children.'

'Isn't somebody looking after them?'

'Naturally.'

'Ring up. Say you're running late. Say you've met a fascinating man who wants to talk literature to you all night. We've hardly met. I need time. I've got masses of questions for you.'

Gathering up the volumes of Jane Austen she started towards the door. And like a persistent salesman Barley stumbled at her side.

'Please,' he said. 'Look. I'm a lousy English publisher with about ten thousand enormously serious things to discuss with a beautiful Russian woman. I don't bite, I don't lie. Have dinner with me.'

'It is not convenient.'

'Is another night convenient? What do I do? Burn joss? Put a candle in my window? You're what I came here for. Help me to help you.'

His appeal had confused her.

'Can I have your home number?' he insisted.

'It is not convenient,' she muttered.

They were descending the wide staircase. Glancing at the sea of heads Barley saw Wicklow and his friend among them. He grasped Katya's arm, not fiercely but nevertheless causing her to stand still.

'When?' he said.

He was still holding her arm at the bicep, just above the inside of the elbow where it was firmest and most full.

'Perhaps I shall call you late tonight,' she replied, relenting.

'Not perhaps.'

'I shall call you.'

Remaining on the stair he watched her approach the edge of the crowd then seem to take a breath before spreading her arms and barging her way to the door. He was sweating. A damp shawl hung over his back and shoulders. He wanted a drink. Above all he wanted to get rid of the microphone harness. He wanted to smash it into very small pieces and trample on them and send them registered and personal to Ned.

Wicklow, with his crooked nose, was skipping up the stairs to him, grinning like a thief and talking some bilge about a Soviet biography of Bernard Shaw.

She walked quickly, looking for a taxi but needing movement. Clouds had gathered and there were no stars, just the wide streets and the glow of arc-lights from Petrovka. She needed distance from him and from herself. A panic born not of fear but of a violent aversion was threatening to seize hold of her. He should not have mentioned the twins. He had no right to knock down the paper walls between one life and another. He should not pester her with bureaucratic questions. She had trusted him: why did he not trust her?

She turned a corner and kept walking. He is a typical imperialist, false, importunate and untrusting. A taxi passed, not heeding her. A second slowed down long enough to hear her call her destination then sped away in search of a more lucrative assignment – to ferry whores, to carry furniture, to deliver black-market vegetables, meat and vodka, to work the tourist traps. The rain was beginning, big drops, well aimed.

His humour, so ill-placed. His inquisitions, so impertinent. I shall never go near him again. She should take the metro but dreaded the confinement. Attractive, naturally, as many Englishmen are. That graceful clumsiness. He was witty and without doubt sensitive. She had not expected him to come so close. Or perhaps it was she who went too close to him.

She kept walking, steadying herself looking for a taxi. The rain fell harder. She pulled a folding umbrella from her bag and opened it. East German, a present from a short-lived lover she had not been proud of. Reaching a crossroads she was about to step into the street when a boy in a blue Lada pulled up beside her. She had not hailed him.

'How's business, sister?'

Was he a taxi, was he a freebooter? She jumped in and gave her destination. The boy started to argue. The rain was thundering on the car roof.

'It's urgent,' she said, and handed him two three-rouble notes. 'It's urgent,' she repeated and glanced at her watch, at the same time wondering whether glancing at watches was something people did when they were in a hurry to get to hospital.

The boy seemed to have taken her cause to heart. He was driving and talking at breakneck speed while the rain poured through his open window. His sick mother in Novgorod had fainted while picking apples from a ladder and woken up with both legs in plaster, he said. The windscreen was a torrent of gushing water. He had not stopped to attach the wipers.

'How is she now?' Katya asked, tying a scarf round her hair. A woman in a hurry to get to hospital does not exchange small talk about the plight of others, she thought.

The boy hauled the car to a halt. She saw the gates. The sky was calm again, the night warm and sweet-smelling. She wondered whether it had rained at all.

'Here,' said the boy, holding out her three-rouble notes. 'Next time, okay? What's your name? You like fresh fruit, coffee, vodka?'

'Keep it,' she snapped, and pushed the money back at him.

The gates stood open, leading to what could have been an office block with a few lights dimly burning. A flight of stone steps, half-buried in mud and rubbish, rose to an overhead walkway. The walkway led across a sliproad. Looking down, Katya saw parked ambulances, their blue lights lazily rotating, drivers and attendants smoking in a group. At their feet lay a woman on a stretcher, her smashed face wrenched to one side as if to escape a second blow.

He took care of me, she thought as her mind returned to Barley for a moment.

She hurried towards the grey block that rose ahead of her. A clinic designed by Dante and built by Franz Kafka, she remembered. The staff go there to steal medicines and sell them on the black market; the doctors are all moonlighting to feed their families, she remembered. A place for the lowlife and riffraff of our empire, for the luckless proletariat with neither the influence nor connections of the few. The voice in her head had a rhythm that marched with her as she strode confidently through the double doors. A woman snapped at her, and Katya, rather than show her card, handed her a rouble. The lobby echoed like a swimming pool. Behind a marble counter, more women ignored everyone except one another. An old man in blue uniform sat dozing in a chair, his open eyes staring at a defunct television set. She strode past him and entered a corridor lined with patients' beds. Last time there had been no beds in the corridor.

Perhaps they cleared them out to make room for someone important. An exhausted trainee was giving blood to an old woman, assisted by a nurse in open overalls and jeans. Nobody groaned, nobody complained. Nobody asked why they must die in a corridor. An illuminated sign gave the first letters of the word 'Emergency'. She followed it. Look as though you own the place, he had advised her the first time. And it had worked. It still did.

The waiting room was a discarded lecture hall lit like a night ward. On the platform, a matron with a saintly face sat at the head of a line of applicants as long as a retreating army. In the auditorium, the wretched of the earth growled and whispered in the twilight, nursed their children. Men with half-dressed injuries lay on benches. Drunks lolled and swore. The air stank of antiseptic, wine and old blood.

Ten minutes to wait. Yet again she found her mind slipping back to Barley. His straight familiar eyes, his air of hopeless valour. Why would I not give him my home telephone number? His hand on her arm as if it had been there for ever. 'You're what I came here for.' Selecting a broken bench near the rear door marked 'Lavatories', she sat and peered ahead of her. You can die there and nobody will ask your name, he had said. There is the door, there is the alcove for the cloakroom, she rehearsed. Then there are the lavatories. The telephone is in the cloakroom but it is never used because nobody knows it is there. Nobody can get through to the hospital on the open line, but this line was put in for a bigwig doctor who wanted to keep in touch with his private patients and his mistress, until he got himself transferred. Some idiot installed it out of sight behind a pillar. It's been there ever since.

How do you know about such places? she had asked him. This entrance, this wing, this telephone, sit down and wait. How do you know?

I walk, he had replied, and she had had a vision of him striding the Moscow streets without sleep, food or herself walking. I am the wandering Gentile, he had told her. I walk to keep company with my mind, I drink to hide from it. When I walk, you are beside me; I can see your face at my shoulder.

He will walk until he falls, she thought. And I shall follow him.

On the bench beside her a peasant woman in a saffron headscarf had begun to pray in Ukrainian. She was holding a small icon in both hands and bowing her head over it, deeper each time, till she was prodding her hairless forehead with the tin frame. Her eyes grew bright and as they closed Katya saw tears come out from between the lids. In the blink of a star I shall look like you, she thought.

She remembered how he had told her about visiting a mortuary in Siberia, a factory for the dead, situated in one of the phantom cities where he worked. How the corpses came out of a chute and were passed round a carousel, male and female mixed, to be hosed and labelled and stripped of their gold by the old women of the night. Death is a secret like any other, he had told her; a secret is something that is revealed to one person at a time.

Why do you always try to educate me to the meaning of death? she had demanded of him, sickened. Because you have taught me how to live, he had replied.

The telephone is the safest in Russia, he had said. Even our lunatics in the security *Organs* would not think of tapping the unused telephone of an emergency hospital.

She remembered their last meeting in Moscow, in the deepest part of winter. He had picked up a slow train at a backwater station, a place with no name in the centre of nowhere. He had bought no ticket and travelled hard class, pushing ten roubles into the conductor's palm like everybody else. Our gallant *competent Organs* are so bourgeois these days they no longer know how to mix with the workers, he had said. She pictured him a waif in his thick underclothes, lying in semi-darkness on the top berth reserved for luggage, listening to the smokers' coughing and the grumble of the drunks, suffocating from the stink of humanity and the leaky water-heater while he stared at the appalling things he knew and never spoke of. What kind of hell must that be, she wondered, to be tormented by your own creations? To know that the absolute best you can do in your career is the absolute worst for mankind?

She saw herself waiting for him to arrive, bivouacked among the thousands of other waiting-wounded at the Kazansky railway station under the foul fluorescent lights. The train is delayed, is cancelled, is derailed, said the rumours. Heavy snowfalls all the way to Moscow. The train is arriving, it never started, I need never have bothered to tell so many lies. The station staff had poured formaldehyde into the lavatories and the whole concourse stank of it. She was wearing Volodya's fur hat because it hid more of her face. Her mohair scarf covered her chin, her sheepskin coat the rest of her. She had never known such desire for anyone. It was a heat and a hunger at once inside the fur.

When he stepped off the train and walked towards her through the slush, her body was stiff and embarrassed like a boy's. As she stood beside him in the crowded metro, she nearly screamed in the silence as he pressed against her. She had borrowed Alexandra's apartment. Alexandra had gone to the Ukraine with her husband. She unlocked the front door and made him go ahead. Sometimes he seemed not to know where he was or, after all her planning, not to care. Sometimes she was scared to touch him, he was too frail. But not today. Today she ran at him, grasped him with all her force, gathering him to her without skill or tenderness, punishing him for her months and nights of fruitless longing.

But he? He embraced her as her father used to, keeping his waist clear of her and his shoulders firm. And as she pulled away from him she knew that the time was past when he could bury his torment in her body.

You are the only religion I have, he whispered, kissing her brow with closed lips. Listen to me, Katya, while I tell you what I have decided to do.

The peasant woman was kneeling on the floor, loving her icon, pressing it to her breast and lips. Katya had to climb over her to reach the gangway. A pale young man in a leather jacket had sat himself at the end of the bench. He had one arm tucked into his shirt, so she supposed it was his wrist that was broken. His head had fallen forward and as she squeezed past him she noticed that his nose was broken, too, though healed.

The alcove was in darkness. A broken light bulb dangled uselessly. A massive wooden counter barred her way to the cloakroom. She tried to lift the flap but it was too heavy so she wriggled under it. She was standing among empty coat-racks and hangers and uncollected hats. The pillar was a metre across. A handwritten sign said NO CHANGE GIVEN and she read it by the light of an opening and closing door. The telephone was in its usual place on the other side, but when she placed herself before it she could hardly see it in the dark.

She stared at it, willing it to ring. Her panic was over. She was strong again. Where are you? she wondered. In one of your postal numbers, one of your blurs on the map? In Kazakhstan? In the Middle Volga? In the Urals? He visited all of them, she knew. In the old days she had been able to tell by his complexion when he had been working outdoors. At other times he looked as though he had been underground for months. Where are you with your dreadful guilt? she wondered. Where are you with your terrifying decision? In a dark place like this? In a small-town telegraph office that is open round the clock? She imagined him arrested, the way she sometimes dreamed of him, trussed and white in a hut, tied to a wooden horse, scarcely bucking any more as they went on beating him. The phone was ringing. She lifted the receiver and heard a flat voice.

'This is Pyotr,' he said, which was their code to protect each other – if I am in their hands, and they force me to call you, I shall tell them a different name so that you can hide.

'And this is Alina,' she replied, amazed that she could speak at all. After that she didn't care. He's alive. He hasn't been arrested. They are not beating him. They have not tied him to a wooden horse. She felt lazy and bored. He was alive, he was speaking to her. Facts, no emotion, his voice at first remote and only half familiar. Backwards and forwards, only facts. Do this. He said this. I said this. Tell him I thank him for coming to Moscow. Tell him he is behaving like a reasonable human being. I am well. How are you?

She rang off too weak to talk any more. She returned to the lecture hall and sat on a bench with the rest of them, reaching for breath, knowing nobody would care.

The boy in the leather jacket was still lounging on the bench. She noticed his bent nose again, perfect yet off-true. She remembered Barley again and was grateful for his existence.

*

He lay on his bed in his shirt-sleeves. His bedroom was an airless box hacked from a grand bedchamber and filled with the water-chorus of every Russian hotel, the snuffle of the taps, the trickle of the cistern from the tiny bathroom, the gulping of the huge black radiator, the groan of the refrigerator as it flung itself upon a fresh cycle of convulsions. He was sipping whisky from a toothmug, pretending to read by the useless bedlight. The telephone lay at his elbow, and beside the telephone lay his notebook for messages and great thoughts. Phones can be alive whether or not they're on their cradles, Ned had warned him. Not this one, it isn't, thought Barley. This one's dead as a dodo till she rings. He was reading wonderful Marquez but the print was like barbed wire to him; he kept stumbling and having to go back.

A car went by in the street, then a pedestrian. Then it was the turn of the rain, cracking like tired shot against the window panes. Without a scream or a laugh or a cry of anger, Moscow had returned herself to the great spaces.

He remembered her eyes. What did they see in me? A relic, he decided. Dressed in my father's suit. A lousy actor concealed by his own performance, and behind the greasepaint nothing. She was looking for the conviction in me and saw instead the moral bankruptcy of my English class and time. She was looking for future hope and finding vestiges of a finished history. She was looking for connection and saw the notice on me saying 'reserved'. So she took one look at me and ran.

Reserved for whom? For what great day or passion have I reserved myself?

He tried to imagine her body. With a face like that, who needs a body anyway?

He drank. She's courage. She's trouble. He drank again. Katya, if that's who you are, I am reserved for you.

If.

He wondered what else there was to know of her. Nothing except the truth. There had been an epoch, long forgotten, when he had mistaken beauty for intelligence, but Katya was so obviously intelligent there could be no problem this time of confusing the two qualities. There had been another epoch, God help him, when he had mistaken beauty for virtue. But in Katya he had sensed such iridescent virtue that if she were to pop her head round the door at this moment and tell him she had just murdered her children, he would instantly find six ways of assuring her she was not to blame.

If.

He took another pull of Scotch and with a jolt remembered Andy.

Andy Macready, trumpeter, lying in hospital with his head cut off. Thyroid, said his missus vaguely. When they'd first discovered it, Andy didn't want the surgery. He'd prefer to take the long swim and not come back, he said, so they got drunk together and planned the trip to Capri, one last great meal, a gallon of red and the long swim to nowhere through the filthy Mediterranean. But when the thyroid really got to him Andy discovered he preferred life to death, so he voted for the surgery instead. And they cut his head off his body, all but the vertebrae, and kept him going on tubes. So Andy was alive still, with nothing to live for and nothing to die of, cursing that he hadn't done the swim in time, and trying to find a meaning for himself that death wouldn't take away.

Phone Andy's missus, he thought. Ask her how her old man is. He peered at his watch, calculating what time it was in the real or unreal world of Mrs. Macready. His hand started for the phone but didn't pick it up in case it rang.

He thought of his daughter Anthea. Good old Ant.

He thought of his son Hal in the City. Sorry I screwed it up for you, Hal, but you've still got a bit of time left to get it right.

He thought of his flat in Lisbon and the girl crying her heart out, and he wondered with a shudder what had become of her. He thought of his other women, but his guilts weren't quite up to their usual, so he wondered about that too. He thought of Katya again and realised he had been thinking of her all the time.

A tap at the door. She has come to me. She is wearing a simple housecoat and is naked underneath. Barley, she whispers, darling. Will you still love me afterwards?

She does nothing of the kind. She has no precedent and no sequel. She is not part of the familiar, well-thumbed series.

It was Wicklow, his guardian angel, checking on his ward.

'Come on in, Wickers. Care for a spot?'

Wicklow raised his eyebrows, asking has she phoned? He was wearing a leather jacket and there were drops of rain on it. Barley shook his head. Wicklow poured himself a glass of mineral water.

'I've been running through some of the books they pushed at us today, sir,' he said, in the fancy tone they both adopted for the microphones. 'I wondered whether you'd like an update on some of the non-fiction titles.'

'Wickers, date me up,' said Barley hospitably, stretching himself on the bed again while Wicklow took the chair.

'Well there is just *one* of their submissions I'd like to share with you, sir. It's that fitness handbook on dieting and exercises. I think we might consider it for one of our co-production splashes. I wondered whether we could sign one of their top illustrators and raise the Russian impact level.'

'Raise it. Sky's the limit.'

'Well I'll have to ask Yuri first.'

'Ask him.'

Hiatus. Let's run that through again, thought Barley.

'Oh, by the way, sir. You were asking why so many Russians use the word "convenient".'

'Well now, so I was,' said Barley, who had been asking nothing of the kind.

'The word they're thinking of is *udobno*. It means convenient but it also means proper, which must be a bit confusing sometimes. I mean it's one thing not to be convenient. It's another not to be proper.'

'It is indeed,' Barley agreed after long thought while he sipped his Scotch.

Then he must have dozed because the next thing he knew he was sitting bolt upright with the receiver to his ear and Wicklow standing over him. This was Russia, so she didn't say her name.

'Come round,' he said.

'I am sorry to call so late. Do I disturb you?'

'Of course you do. All the time. That was a great cup of tea. Wish it could have lasted longer. Where are you?'

'You invited me for dinner tomorrow night, I think.'

He was reaching for his notebook. Wicklow held it ready.

'Lunch, tea, dinner, all three of them,' he said. 'Where do I send the glass coach?' He scribbled down an address. 'What's your home telephone number, by the way, in case I get lost or you do?' She gave him that too, reluctantly, a departure from principle, but she gave it all the same. Wicklow watched him write it all down, then softly left the room as they continued talking.

You never know, Barley thought, steadying his mind with another long pull of Scotch when he had rung off. With beautiful, intelligent, virtuous women, you simply never know where they stand. Is she pining for me, or am I a face in her crowd?

Then suddenly the Moscow fear hit him at gale force. It sprang out at him when he was least expecting it, after he had fought it off all day. The muffled terrors of the city burst thundering upon his ears and after them the piping voice of Walter.

'Is she really in touch with him? Did she invent the stuff herself? Is she in touch with someone different, and if so who?'

8

In the situation room in the basement of the Russia House the atmosphere was of a tense and permanent night air-raid. Ned sat at his command desk before a bank of telephones. Sometimes one winked and he spoke into it in terse monosyllables. Two female assistants softly put round the telegrams and cleared the out-trays. Two illuminated post-office clocks, one London time, one Moscow time, shone like twin moons from the end wall. In Moscow it was midnight. In London nine. Ned scarcely looked up as his head janitor unlocked the door to me.

It was the earliest I had been able to get away. I had spent the morning at the Treasury solicitors' and the afternoon with the lawyers from Cheltenham. Supper was helping to entertain a delegation of espiocrats from Sweden before they were packed off to the obligatory musical.

Walter and Bob were bowed over a Moscow street map. Brock was on the internal telephone to the cypher room. Ned was immersed in what seemed to be a lengthy inventory. He waved me to a chair and shoved a batch of incoming signals at me, scribbled messages from the front.

0954 hrs Barley has successfully telephoned Katya at October. They have made an appointment for 2015 at the Odessa tonight. More.

1320 hrs irregulars have followed Katya to number 14 so-and-so street. She posted a letter at what appears to be an empty house. Photographs to follow soonest by bag. More.

2018 hrs Katya has arrived at the Odessa Hotel. Barley and Katya are talking in the canteen. Wicklow and one irregular observing. More.

2105 hrs Katya departs Odessa. Summary of conversation to follow. Tapes to follow soonest by bag. More.

2200 hrs interim. Katya has promised to telephone Barley tonight. More.

2250 hrs Katya followed to the so-and-so hospital. Wicklow and one irregular covering. More.

2325 hrs Katya receives phone call on disused hospital telephone. Speaks three minutes twenty seconds. More.

And now suddenly, no more.

Spying is normality taken to extremes. Spying is waiting.

'Is Clive Without India receiving tonight?' Ned asked, as if my presence had reminded him of something.

I replied that Clive would be in his suite all evening. He had been locked up in the American Embassy all day, and he had told me he proposed to be on call.

I had a car so we drove to Head Office together.

'Have you seen this bloody document?' Ned asked me, tapping the folder on his lap.

'Which bloody document is that?'

'The Bluebird distribution list. Bluebird readers and their satraps.'

I was cautiously non-committal. Ned's bad temper in mid-operation was legendary. The light on the door of Clive's office was green, meaning come in if you dare. The brass plate said 'Deputy' in lettering to outshine the Royal Mint.

'What the devil's happened to the need-to-know, Clive?' Ned asked him, waving the distribution list as soon as we were in the presence. 'We give Langley one batch of highly sensitive, unsourced material and overnight they've recruited more cooks than broth. I mean what is this? Hollywood? We've got a live joe out there. We've got a defector in place we've never met.'

Clive toured the gold carpet. He had a habit when he was arguing with Ned of turning his whole body at once, like a playing-card. He did so now.

'So you think the Bluebird readership list too long?' he enquired in the tone of one taking evidence.

'Yes, and so should you. And so should Russell Sheriton. Who the devil are the Pentagon Scientific Liaison Board? What's the White House Academic Advisory Team when it's at home?'

'You would prefer me to take a high line and insist Bluebird be confined to their Inter Agency Committee? Principals only, no staff, no aides? Is that what you are telling me?'

'If you think you can get the toothpaste back in the tube, yes.'

Clive affected to consider this on its merits. But I knew, and so did Ned, that Clive considered nothing on its merits. He considered who was in favour of something and who was against it. Then he considered who was the better ally.

'Firstly, not a single one of those elevated gentlemen I have mentioned is capable of making head or tail of the Bluebird material without expert guidance,' Clive resumed in his bloodless voice. 'Either we let them flounder in ignorance or we admit their appendages and accept the price. The same goes for their Defense Intelligence team, their Navy, Army, Air Force and White House evaluators.'

'Is this Russell Sheriton speaking or you?' Ned demanded.

'How can we tell them not to call in their scientific panels when we offer them immensely complex material in the same breath?' Clive persisted, neatly letting Ned's question pass him by. 'If Bluebird's genuine, they're going to need all the help they can get.'

'If,' Ned echoed, flaring. 'If he's genuine. My God, Clive, you're worse than they are. There are two hundred and forty people on that list and every one of them has a wife, a mistress and fifteen best friends.'

'And *secondly*,' Clive went on, when we had forgotten there had been a firstly, 'it's not *our* intelligence to dispose of. It's Langley's.' He had swung on me before Ned could get in his reply. 'Palfrey. Confirm. Under our sharing treaty with the Americans, is it not the case that we give Langley first rights on all strategic material?'

'In strategic matters our dependence on Langley is total,' I conceded. 'They give us what they want us to know. In return we are obliged to give them whatever we find out. It isn't often much but that's the deal.'

Clive listened carefully to this and approved it. His coldness had an unaccustomed ferocity and I wondered why. If he had possessed a conscience, I would have said it was uneasy. What had he been doing at the Embassy all day? What had he given away to whom for what?

'It is a common misapprehension of this Service,' Clive continued, talking straight at Ned now, 'that we and the Americans are in the same boat. We're not. Not when it comes to strategy. We haven't a defence analyst in the country who is capable of holding a candle to his American counterpart on matters of strategy. Where strategy is concerned, we are a tiny, ignorant British coracle and they are the *Queen Elizabeth*. It is not our place to tell them how to run their ship.'

We were still marvelling at the vigour of this declaration when Clive's hot line began ringing and he went for it greedily, for he always loved answering his hot line in front of his subordinates. He was unlucky. It was Brock calling for Ned.

Katya had just phoned Barley at the Odessa and they had agreed a meeting for tomorrow evening, said Brock. Moscow station required Ned's urgent approval of their operational proposals for the encounter. Ned left at once.

'What are you brewing with the Americans?' I asked Clive, but he didn't bother with me.

All next day I spent talking to my Swedes. In the Russia House, life was scarcely more enlivening. Spying is waiting. Around four I slipped back to my room and telephoned Hannah. Sometimes I do that. By four she is back from the Cancer Institute where she works part time, and her husband never comes home before seven. She told me how her day had gone. I scarcely listened. I gave her some story about my son, Alan, who was in deep water with a nurse up in Birmingham, a nice enough girl but really not Alan's class.

'I may ring you later,' she said.

Sometimes she said that, but she never rang.

Barley walked at Katya's side and he could hear her footsteps like a tighter echo of his own. The flaking mansions of Dickensian Moscow were bathed in stale twilight. The first courtyard was gloomy, the second dark. Cats stared at them from the rubbish. Two long-haired boys who might have been students were playing tennis across a row of packing cases. A third leaned against the wall. A door stood ahead of them, daubed with graffiti and a red crescent moon. 'Watch for the red marks,' Wicklow had advised. She was pale and he wondered if he was pale too, because it would be a

living miracle if he wasn't. Some men will never be heroes, some heroes
will never be men, he thought, with urgent acknowledgements to Joseph
Conrad. And Barley Blair, he'll never be either. He grabbed the doorhandle
and yanked it. She kept her distance. She was wearing a headscarf and a
raincoat. The handle turned but the door wouldn't budge. He shoved it
with both hands then shoved harder. The tennis players yelled at him in
Russian. He stopped dead, feeling fire on his back.

'They say you should please kick it,' Katya said, and to his amazement
he saw that she was smiling.

'If you can smile now,' he said, 'how do you look when you're happy?'

But he must have said it to himself because she didn't answer. He kicked
it and it gave, the grit beneath it screaming. The boys laughed and went
back to their game. He stepped into the black and she followed him. He
pressed a switch but no light came. The door slammed shut behind them
and when he groped for the handle he couldn't find it. They stood in deep
darkness, smelling cats and onions and cooking oil and listening to bits of
music and argument from other people's lives. He struck a match. Three
steps appeared, then half a bicycle, then the entrance to a filthy lift. Then
his fingers burned. You go to the fourth floor, Wicklow had said. Watch
for the red marks. How the devil do I watch for red marks in the dark?
God answered him with a pale light from the floor above.

'Where are we, please?' she asked politely.

'It's a friend of mine,' he said. 'A painter.'

He pulled back the lift door, then the grille. He said 'Please' but she was
already past him, standing in the lift and looking upward, willing it to
rise.

'He's away for a few days. It's just somewhere to talk,' he said.

He noticed her eyelashes again, the moisture in her eyes. He wanted to
console her but she wasn't sad enough.

'He's a painter,' he said again, as if that legitimised a friend.

'Official?'

'No. I don't think so. I don't know.'

Why hadn't Wicklow told him which kind of bloody painter the man
was supposed to be?

He was about to press the button when a small girl in tortoiseshell
spectacles hopped in after them hugging a plastic bear. She called a greeting
and Katya's face lit up as she greeted her in return. The lift juddered
upwards, the buttons popping like cap pistols at each floor. At the third
the child politely said goodbye, and Barley and Katya said goodbye in
unison. At the fourth the lift bumped to a halt as if it had hit the ceiling
and perhaps it had. He shoved her ashore and leapt after her. A passage
opened before them, filled with the stench of baby, perhaps a lot of babies.
At the end of it, on what seemed to be a blank wall, a red arrow directed
them left. They came on a narrow wooden staircase leading upwards. On
the bottom step Wicklow crouched like a leprechaun reading a weighty

book by the aid of a mechanic's light. He did not lift his head as they
climbed past him but Barley saw Katya stare at him all the same.

'What's the matter? Seen a ghost?' he asked her.

Could she hear him? Could he hear himself? Had he spoken? They were
in a long attic. Chinks of sky pierced the tiles, bats' mess smeared the
rafters. A path of scaffolders' boards had been laid over the joists. Barley
took her hand. Her palm was broad and strong and dry. Its nakedness
against his own was like the gift of her entire body.

He advanced cautiously, smelling turpentine and linseed and hearing
the tapping of an unexpected wind. He squeezed between a pair of iron
cisterns and saw a life-sized paper sea-gull in full flight strung from a
beam, turning on its thread. He pulled her after him. Beyond it, fixed to
a shower-rail, hung a striped curtain. If there's no sea-gull there's no
meeting, Wicklow had said. No sea-gull means abort. That's my epitaph,
thought Barley. 'There was no sea-gull, so he aborted.' He swept the
curtain aside and entered a painter's studio, once more drawing her after
him. At its centre stood an easel and a model's upholstered box. An aged
chesterfield rested on its stuffing. It's a one-time facility, Wicklow had said.
So am I, Wickers, so am I. A homemade skylight was cut into the slope of
the roof. A red mark was daubed on its frame. Russians don't trust walls,
Wicklow had explained, she'll talk better in the open air.

The skylight opened, to the consternation of a colony of doves and
sparrows. He nodded her through first, noticing the easy flow of her long
body as she stooped. He clambered after her, barking his spine and saying
'Damn' exactly as he knew he would. They were standing between two
gables in a leaded valley only wide enough for their feet. The pulse of
traffic rose from streets they couldn't see. She was facing him and close.
Let's live up here, he thought. Your eyes, me, the sky. He was rubbing his
back, screwing up his eyes against the pain.

'You are hurt?'

'Just a fractured spine.'

'Who is that man on the stairs?' she said.

'He works for me. He's my editor. He's keeping a lookout while we
talk.'

'He was at the hospital last night.'

'What hospital?'

'Last night after seeing you, I was obliged to visit a certain hospital.'

'Are you ill? Why did you go to hospital?' Barley asked, no longer
rubbing his back.

'It is not important. He was there. He appeared to have a broken arm.'

'He can't have been there,' Barley said, not believing himself. 'He was
with me the whole evening after you left. We had a discussion about
Russian books.'

He saw the suspicion slowly leave her eyes. 'I am tired. You must excuse
me.'

'Let me tell you what I've worked out, then you can tell me it's no good. We talk, then I take you out to dinner. If the People's custodians were listening to our call last night they'll expect that anyway. The studio belongs to a painter friend of mine, a jazz nut like me. I never told you his name because I couldn't remember it and perhaps I never knew it. I thought we could bring him a drink and look at his pictures but he didn't appear. We went on to dinner, talked literature and world peace. Despite my reputation I did not make a pass at you. I was too much in awe of your beauty. How's that?'

'It is convenient.'

Dropping into a crouch, he produced a half bottle of Scotch and unscrewed the cap. 'Do you drink this stuff?'

'No.'

'Me neither.' He hoped she would settle beside him but she remained standing. He poured a tot into the cap and set the bottle at his feet.

'What's his name?' he said. 'The author's. Goethe. Who is he?'

'It is not important.'

'What's his unit? Firm? Postbox number? Ministry? Laboratory? Where's he working? We haven't time to fool around.'

'I don't know.'

'Where's he stationed? You won't tell me that either, will you?'

'In many places. It depends where he is working.'

'How did you meet him?'

'I don't know. I don't know what I may tell you.'

'What did he tell you to tell me?'

She faltered, as if he had caught her out. She frowned. 'Whatever is necessary. I should trust you. He was generous. It is his nature.'

'So what's holding you up?' Nothing. 'Why do you think I'm here?' Nothing. 'Do you think I enjoy playing cops-and-robbers in Moscow?'

'I don't know.'

'Why did you send me the book if you don't trust me?'

'It was for him that I sent it. I did not select you. He did,' she replied moodily.

'Where is he now? At the hospital? How do you speak to him?' He looked up at her, waiting for her answer. 'Why don't you just start talking and see how it goes?' he suggested. 'Who he is, who you are. What he does for a living.'

'I don't know.'

'Who was in the woodshed at three a.m. on the night of the crime.' More nothing. 'Tell me why you've dragged me into this. You started this. I didn't. Katya? It's me. I'm Barley Blair. I do jokes, I do bird noises, I drink. I'm a friend.'

He loved her grave silences while she stared at him. He loved her listening with her eyes and the sense of recovered companionship each time she spoke.

'There has been no crime,' she said. 'He is my friend. His name and occupation are unimportant.'

Barley took a sip while he thought about this. 'So is this what you usually do for friends? Smuggle their illicit manuscripts to the West for them?' She thinks with her eyes as well, he thought. 'Did he happen to mention to you what his manuscript was about?'

'Naturally. He would not endanger me without my consent.'

He caught the protectiveness in her voice and resented it. 'What did he tell you was in it?' he asked.

'The manuscript describes my country's involvement in the preparation of anti-humanitarian weapons of mass destruction over many years. It paints a portrait of corruption and incompetence in all fields of the defence-industrial complex. Also of criminal mismanagement and ethical shortcomings.'

'That's quite a mouthful. Do you know any details beyond that?'

'I am not acquainted with military matters.'

'So he's a soldier.'

'No.'

'So what is he?'

Silence.

'But you approve of that? Passing that stuff out to the West?'

'He is not passing it to the West or to any bloc. He respects the British but that is not important. His gesture will ensure true openness among scientists of all nations. It will help to destroy the arms race. She had still to come to him. She was speaking flatly as if she had learned her lines by heart. 'He believes there is no time left. We must destroy the abuse of science and the political systems responsible for it. When he speaks philosophy, he speaks English,' she added.

And you listen, he thought. With your eyes. In English. While you wonder whether you can trust me.

'Is he a scientist?' he asked.

'Yes. He is a scientist.'

'I hate them all. What branch? Is he a physicist?'

'Perhaps. I don't know.'

'His information comes from across the board. Accuracy, aimpoints, command and control, rocket motors. Is he one man? Who gives him the material? How does he know so much?'

'I don't know. He is one man. That is obvious. I do not have so many friends. He is not a group. Perhaps he also supervises the work of others. I don't know.'

'Is he high up? A big boss? Is he working here in Moscow? Is he a headquarters man? What is he?'

She shook her head at each question. 'He does not work in Moscow. Otherwise I have not asked him and he does not tell me.'

'Does he test things?'

'I don't know. He goes to many places. All over the Soviet Union. Sometimes he has been in the sun, sometimes he has been very cold, sometimes both. I don't know.'

'Has he ever mentioned his unit?'

'No.'

'Box numbers? The names of his bosses? The name of a colleague or subordinate?'

'He is not interested to tell me such things.'

And he believed her. While he was with her, he would believe that north was south and babies grew on jacaranda trees.

She was watching him, waiting for his next question.

'Does he understand the consequences of publishing this stuff?' he asked. 'To himself, I mean? Does he know what he's playing with?'

'He says that there are times when our actions must come first and we must consider consequences only when they occur.' She seemed to expect him to say something but he was learning to slow down. 'If we see one goal clearly we may advance one step. If we contemplate all goals at once we shall not advance at all.'

'How about you? Has he thought about the consequences to you at all if any of this comes to light?'

'He is reconciled.'

'Are you?'

'Naturally. It was my decision also. Why else would I support him?'

'And the children?' he asked.

'It is for them and for their generation,' she said with a resolution bordering on anger.

'What about the consequences to Mother Russia?'

'We regard the destruction of Russia as preferable to the destruction of all mankind. The greatest burden is the past. For all nations, not only Russia. We regard ourselves as the executioners of the past. He says that if we cannot execute our past, how shall we construct our future? We shall not build a new world until we have got rid of the mentalities of the old. In order to express truth we must also be prepared to be the apostles of negation. He quotes Turgenev. A nihilist is a person who does not take anything for granted, however much that principle is revered.'

'And you?'

'I am not a nihilist. I am a humanist. If it is given to us to play a part for the future, we must play it.'

He was searching her voice for a hint of doubt. He found none. She was tone perfect.

'How long's he been talking like this? Always? Or is it only recent?'

'He has always been idealistic. That is his nature. He has always been extremely critical in a constructive sense. There was a time when he was able to convince himself that the weapons of annihilation were so terrible they would have the effect of abolishing war. He believed they would produce an alteration in the mind of the military establishments. He was persuaded by the paradox that the greatest weapons contained within them the greatest capacity for peace. He was in this regard an enthusiast of American strategic opinions.'

She was starting towards him. He could feel it in her, the stirring of a need. She was waking and approaching him. Under the Moscow sky, she was shedding her mistrust after too much loneliness and deprival.

'So what changed him?'

'He has experienced for many years the incompetence and arrogance of our military and bureaucratic organisations. He has seen how it drags on the feet of progress. That is his expression. He is inspired by the *perestroika* and by the prospect of world peace. But he is not Utopian, he is not passive. He knows that nothing will come of its own accord. He knows that our people are deluded and lack collective power. The new revolution must be imposed from above. By intellectuals. By artists. By administrators. By scientists. He wishes to make his own irreversible contribution in accordance with the exhortations of our leadership. He quotes a Russian saying: "If the ice is thin, one must walk fast." He says we have lived too long in an era we no longer need. Progress can only be achieved when the era is finished.'

'And you agree?'

'Yes, and so do you!' Heat, now. Fire in her eyes. An English too perfect, learned in the cloister, from permitted classics of the past. 'He says that he heard you criticise your own country in similar terms!'

'Does he have any small thoughts?' Barley asked. 'I mean, does he like the movies? What car does he drive?'

She had turned away from him and he had the side view of her face cut against the empty sky. He took another nip of Scotch.

'You said he might be a physicist,' he reminded her.

'He was trained as a physicist. I believe he has also qualified in aspects of engineering. In the field in which he works, I believe that the distinctions are not always closely observed.'

'Where was he trained?'

'Already at school he was regarded as a prodigy. At fourteen he won a Mathematics Olympiad. His success was printed in the Leningrad newspapers. He went to the Litmo, afterwards to postgraduate studies at the University. He is extremely brilliant.'

'When I was at school those were the people I hated,' said Barley, but to his alarm she scowled.

'But you did not hate Goethe. You inspired him. He often quotes his friend Scott Blair. "If there is to be hope, we must all betray our countries." Did you really say this?'

'What's a Litmo?' said Barley.

'Litmo is the Leningrad Institute for Mechanical and Optical Science. From university he was sent to Novosibirsk to study at the scientific city of Akademgorodok. He made candidate of sciences, doctor of sciences. He made everything.'

He wanted to press her about the everything, but he was scared of rushing her so he let her speak about herself instead. 'So how did you get mixed up with him?'

'When I was a child.'

'How old was the child?'

He felt her reticence collect again and then dissolve as if she had to remind herself she was in safe company – or in company so unsafe that to be further compromised made little difference.

'I was a great intellectual of sixteen,' she said, with a grave smile.

'How old was the prodigy?'

'Thirty.'

'What year are we talking about?'

'1968. He was still an idealist for peace. He said they would never send in the tanks. "The Czechs are our friends," he said. "They are like the Serbs and the Bulgarians. If it were Warsaw, perhaps they would send in the tanks. But against our Czechs, never, never." '

She had turned her whole back to him. She was too many women at once. She had her back to him and was talking to the sky, yet she was drawing him into her life and appointing him her confidant.

It was August in Leningrad, she said, she was sixteen and studying French and German in her last year at school. She was a star pupil and a peace-dreamer and a revolutionary of the most romantic kind. She was on the brink of womanhood and thought herself mature. She was speaking of herself with irony. She had read Erich Fromm and Ortega y Gasset and Kafka and seen *Dr. Strangelove*. She regarded Sakharov as right in his thinking but wrong in his method. She was concerned about the Russian Jews but shared her father's view that they had brought their troubles on themselves. Her father was Professor of Humanities at the University, and her school was for sons and daughters of the Leningrad *nomenclatura*. It was August 1968 but Katya and her friends were still able to live in political hope. Barley tried to remember whether he had ever lived in political hope and decided it was unlikely. She was talking as if nothing would ever stop her talking again. He wished he could hold her hand again as he had held it on the stairs. He wished he could hold any part of her but best of all her face, and kiss her instead of listening to her love story.

'We believed that East and West were drawing closer together,' she said. 'When the American students demonstrated against Vietnam, we were proud of them and regarded them as our comrades. When the students of Paris rioted, we wished we could be beside them at the barricades, wearing their nice French clothes.'

She turned and smiled at him again over her shoulder. A horned moon had appeared above the stars at her left side and Barley had some vague literary memory that it boded bad luck. A flock of gulls had settled on a roof across the street. I'll never leave you, he thought.

'There was a man in our courtyard who had been absent for nine years,' she was saying. 'One morning he was back, pretending he had never been away. My father invited him to dinner and played him music all evening. I had never consciously met anyone who had been freshly persecuted so I naturally hoped that he would talk of the horrors of the camps. But all he wished to do was listen to Shostakovich. I did not understand in those days that some suffering cannot be described. From Czechoslovakia we heard of extraordinary reforms. We believed that these reforms would soon come to the Soviet Union and that we would have hard currency and be free to travel.'

'Where was your mother?'

'Dead.'

'How did she die?'

'Of tuberculosis. She was already ill when I was born. On 20th August there was a closed showing of a Godard film at the Club of Scientists.' Her voice had become strict against herself. 'The invitations were for two persons. My father, after making enquiries about the moral content of the film, was reluctant to take me but I insisted. In the end he decided I should accompany him for the sake of my French studies. Do you know the Club of Scientists in Leningrad?'

'I can't say I do,' he said, leaning back.

'Have you seen *A bout de souffle?*'

'I starred in it,' he said, and she broke out laughing while he sipped his Scotch.

'Then you will remember that it is a very tense film. Yes?'

'Yes.'

'It was the most powerful film I had ever seen. Everyone was greatly impressed by it, but for me it was a thunderbolt. The Club of Scientists is on the embankment of the river Neva. It is full of old glory, with marble staircases and very low sofas which are difficult to sit on in a tight skirt.' She was sideways to him again, her head forward. 'There is a beautiful winter-garden and a room like a mosque with heavy curtains and rich carpets. My father loved me very much but he was concerned for me and he was strict. When the film was over we moved to a dining room with wood panels. It was beautiful. We sat at long tables and that was where I met Yakov. My father introduced us. "Here is a new genius from the world of physics," he said. My father had the fault of sometimes being sarcastic with young men. Also Yakov was beautiful. I had heard something about him but nobody had told me how vulnerable he was, more like an artist than a scientist. I asked him what he was doing and he replied that he had returned to Leningrad to recover his innocence. I laughed and for a girl of sixteen produced an impressive response. I said

I found it strange that a scientist of all people should be seeking innocence. He explained that in Akademgorodok he had shown too much brilliance in certain fields and had made himself too attractive to the military. It appears that in matters of physics the distinction between peaceful and military research is often very small. Now they were offering him everything – privileges, money to make his researches – but he was still refusing them because he wished to preserve his energies for peaceful means. This made them angry because they customarily recruit the cream of our scientists and do not expect refusal. So he had returned to his old university in order to recover his innocence. He proposed initially to study theoretical physics and was looking for influential people to support him, but they were reluctant because of his attitude. He had no permit to reside in Leningrad. He spoke very freely, as our scientists may. Also he was full of enthusiasm for the Gorodok. He spoke of the foreigners who in those days passed through, the brilliant young Americans from Stanford and MIT, also the English. He described the painters who were forbidden in Moscow but permitted to exhibit in the Gorodok. The seminars, the intensity of life, the free exchanges of ideas – and, as I was sure, of love. "In what other country but Russia would Richter and Rostropovich come and play their music specially for the scientists, Okudzhava sing and Voznesensky read his poems! This is the world that we scientists must build for others!" He made jokes and I laughed like a mature woman. He was very witty in those days but also vulnerable, as he is today. There is a part of him that refuses to grow up. It is the artist in him, but it is the perfectionist also. Already in those days he was an outspoken critic of the incompetence of the authorities. He said there were so many eggs and sausages in the Gorodok supermarket that the shoppers poured out by bus from Novosibirsk and emptied the shelves by ten in the morning. Why could not the eggs make the journey instead of the people? This would be much better! Nobody collected the rubbish, he said, and the electricity kept cutting off. Sometimes the rubbish was knee-deep in the streets. And they call it a scientific Paradise! I made another precocious comment. "That's the trouble with Paradise," I said. "There is nobody to collect the rubbish." Everyone was very amused. I was a success. He described the old guard trying to come to grips with the ideas of the new men and going away shaking their heads like peasants who have seen a tractor for the first time. Never mind, he said. Progress will prevail. He said that the armoured train of the Revolution which Stalin had derailed was at last in motion again and the next stop would be Mars. That was when my father interrupted with one of his cynical opinions. He was finding Yakov too vociferous. "But, Yakov Yefremovich," he said, "was not Mars the god of war?" Immediately Yakov became reflective. I had not imagined a man could change so quickly, one minute bold, the next so lonely and distressed. I blamed my father. I was furious with him.

Yakov tried to recover but my father had thrown him into despair. Did Yakov talk to you about his father?'

She was sitting across the valley from him, propped against the opposing slope of the rooftiles, her long legs stretched before her, her dress drawn tightly over her body. The sky was darkening behind her, the moon and stars were growing.

'He told me his father died of an overdose of intelligence,' Barley replied.

'He took part in a camp uprising. He was in despair. Yakov did not know of his father's death for many years. One day an old man came to Yakov's house and said he had shot Yakov's father. He had been a guard at the camp and was ordered to take part in the execution of the rebels. They were shot down in dozens by machine guns near the Vorkuta railway terminal. The guard was weeping. Yakov was only fourteen at the time but he gave the old man his forgiveness and some vodka.'

I can't do this, Barley thought. I'm not equal to these dimensions.

'What year was his father shot?' he asked. Be a hamster. It's about the only thing you're fit for.

'I think it was the spring of 1952. While Yakov remained silent, everybody at the table began to talk vehemently about Czechoslovakia,' she continued in her perfect archaeological English. 'Some said the ruling gang would send in the tanks. My father was sure of it. Some said they would be justified in doing so. My father said they would do it whether they were justified or not. The red Czars would do exactly as they pleased, he said, just as the white Czars had done. The system would win because the system always won and the system was our curse. This was my father's conviction as it later became Yakov's. But Yakov was at that time still determined to believe in the Revolution. He wished his own father's death to have been worthwhile. He listened intently to what my father had to say but then he became aggressive. "They will never send in the tanks!" he said. "The Revolution will survive!" He beat the table with his fist. You have seen his hands? Like a pianist's, so white and thin? He had been drinking. So had my father and my father also became angry. He wished to be left in peace with his pessimism. As a distinguished humanist, he did not like to be contradicted by a young scientist whom he regarded as an upstart. Perhaps also my father was jealous, because while they quarrelled, I fell completely in love with Yakov.'

Barley took another sip of Scotch.

'You don't find that shocking?' she demanded indignantly as her smile leapt back to her face. 'A girl of sixteen, for an experienced man of thirty?'

Barley wasn't feeling very quick-witted, but she seemed to need his reassurance. 'I'm speechless but on the whole I'd say they were both very lucky,' he said.

'When the reception ended I asked my father for three roubles to go to the Café Sever to eat ice-cream with my companions. There were several daughters of academics at the reception, some were my school comrades. We made a group and I invited Yakov to join us. On the way I asked him where he lived and he told me: in the street of Professor Popov. He asked me, "Who was Popov?" I laughed. Everyone knows who Popov is, I said. Popov was the great Russian inventor of radio who transmitted a signal even before Marconi, I told him. Yakov was not so sure. "Perhaps Popov never existed," he replied. "Perhaps the Party invented him in order to satisfy our Russian obsession with being the first to invent everything." From this I knew that he was still struggling with doubts about what they would do concerning Czechoslovakia.'

Feeling anything but wise, Barley gave a wise nod.

'I asked him whether his apartment was a communal or a separate one. He said it was a room which he shared with an old acquaintance from the Litmo who was working in a special night laboratory, so they seldom met. I said, "Then show me where you live. I wish to know that you are comfortable." He was my first lover,' she said simply. 'He was extremely delicate, as I had expected him to be, but also passionate.'

'Bravo,' said Barley so softly that perhaps she didn't hear.

'I stayed with him three hours and took the last metro home. My father was waiting up for me and I talked to him like a stranger visiting his house. I did not sleep. Next day I heard the news in English on the BBC. The tanks had gone into Prague. My father, who had predicted this, was in despair. But I was not concerned for my father. Instead of going to school I went back to look for Yakov. His room-mate told me I would find him at the Saigon, which was the informal name of a cafeteria on the Nevsky Prospekt, a place for poets and drug-pedlars and speculators, not professors' daughters. He was drinking coffee but he was drunk. He had been drinking vodka since he heard the news. "Your father is right," he said. "The system will always win. We talk freedom but we are oppressors." Three months later he had returned to Novosibirsk. He was bitter with himself but he still went. "It is a choice between dying of obscurity or dying of compromise," he said. "Since that is a choice between death and death, we may as well choose the more comfortable alternative." '

'Where did that leave you?' Barley asked.

'I was ashamed of him. I told him that he was my ideal and that he had disappointed me. I had been reading the novels of Stendhal, so I addressed him like a great French heroine. Nevertheless I believed that he had taken an immoral decision. He had talked one thing and done the opposite. In the Soviet Union, I told him, too many people do this. I told him I would never speak to him again until he had corrected his immoral choice. I reminded him of E. M. Forster, whom we both admired. I told him that he must connect. That his thoughts and actions must be one. Naturally I soon relented and for a while we resumed our relationship, but it was no longer romantic and when he took up his new work he corresponded without warmth. I was ashamed for him. Perhaps also for myself.'

'And so you married Volodya,' Barley said.

'That is correct.'

'And you kept Yakov going on the side?' he suggested, as if it were the most normal thing in the world.

She was blushing and scowling at once. 'For a while, it is true, Yakov and I maintained a clandestine relationship. Not often, but sometimes. He said we were a novel that had not been finished. Each of us was looking to the other to complete his destiny. He was correct, but I had not realised the strength of his influence over me or of mine over him. I thought that if we met more we might become free of each other. When I realised this was not the case I ceased to see him. I loved him but I refused to see him. Also I was pregnant from Volodya.'

'When did you get together again?'

'After the last Moscow book fair. You were his catalyst. He had been on vacation and drinking very heavily. He had written many internal papers and registered many official complaints. None of them had made any impression on the system, though I think he had succeeded in annoying the authorities. Now you had spoken into his heart. You had put his thoughts into words at a crucial moment in his life, and you had related words to actions, which Yakov does not find easy. The next day, he telephoned me at my office, using a pretext. He had borrowed the apartment of a friend. My relationship with Volodya was by then disintegrating, although we were still living together because Volodya had to wait for an apartment. While we sat in the room of Yakov's friend, he spoke very much about you. You had made everything come clear for him. That was his phrase to me. "The Englishman has given me the solution. From now on, there is only action, there is only sacrifice," he said. "Words are the curse of our Russian society. They are a substitute for deeds." Yakov knew that I had contact with Western publishers, so he told me to look for your name among our lists of foreign visitors. He set to work at once to prepare a manuscript. I should give it to you. He was drinking a great deal. I was scared for him. "How can you write if you are drunk?" He replied that he drank to survive.'

Barley took another nip of whisky. 'Did you tell Volodya about Yakov?'

'No.'

'Did Volodya find out?'

'No.'

'So who does know?'

It seemed she had been asking herself the same question, for she replied with great promptness.

'Yakov tells his friends nothing. This I know. If I am the one who borrows the apartment, I say only that it is for a private matter. In Russia we have secrecy and we have loneliness, but we have no word for privacy.'

'What about your girlfriends? Not a hint to them?'

'We are not angels. If I ask them for certain favours, they make certain assumptions. Sometimes it is I who provide the favours. That is all.'

'And nobody helped Yakov compile his manuscript?'

'No.'

'None of his drinking friends?'

'No.'

'How can you be certain?'

'Because I am certain that in his thoughts he is completely alone.'

'Are you happy with him?'

'Please?'

'Do you like him – as well as love him? Does he make you laugh?'

'I believe that Yakov is a great and vulnerable man who cannot survive without me. To be a perfectionist is to be a child. It is also to be impractical. I believe that without me he would break.'

'Do you think he's broken now?'

'Yakov would say, which one is sane? The one who plans the extermination of mankind, or the one who takes steps to prevent it?'

'How about the one who does both?'

She didn't reply. He was provoking her and she knew it. He was jealous, wanting to erode the edges of her faith.

'Is he married?' he asked.

An angry look swept across her face. 'I do not believe he is married but it is not important.'

'Has he got kids?'

'These are ridiculous questions.'

'It's a pretty ridiculous situation.'

'He says that human beings are the only creatures to make victims of their children. He is determined to provide no victims.'

Except yours, Barley thought: but he managed not to say it.

'So, you followed his career with interest,' he suggested roughly, returning to the question of Goethe's access.

'From a distance, and without detail.'

'And all that time you didn't know what work he did? Is that what you're saying?'

'What I knew, I deduced only from our discussions of ethical problems. "How much of mankind should we exterminate in order to preserve mankind? How can we talk of a struggle for peace when we plan only terrible wars? How can we speak of selective targets when we have not the accuracy to hit them?" When we discuss these matters, I am naturally aware of his involvement. When he tells me that the greatest danger to mankind is not the reality of Soviet power but the illusion of it, I do not question him. I encourage him. I urge him to be consistent and if necessary brave. But I do not question him.'

'Rogov? He never mentioned a Rogov? Professor Arkady Rogov?'

'I told you. He does not discuss his colleagues.'

'Who said Rogov was a colleague?'

'I assumed this from your questions,' she retorted hotly and yet again he believed her.

'How do you communicate with him?' he asked, recovering his gentler tone.

'It is not important. When a certain friend of his receives a certain message, he informs Yakov and Yakov telephones me.'

'Does the certain friend know who the certain message is from?'

'He has no reason. He knows it is a woman. That is all.'

'Is Yakov afraid?'

'Since he talks so much about courage, I assume he is afraid. He quotes Nietzsche. "The ultimate goodness is not to be afraid." He quotes Pasternak. "The root of beauty – " '

'Are you?'

She stared away from him. In the houses across the street, home lights were appearing in the windows.

'I must think not of my children but of *all* children,' she said, and he noticed two tears lying neglected on her cheeks. He took another pull of whisky and hummed a few bars of Basie. When he looked again, the tears had gone.

'He talks about the great lie,' she said, as if she had just remembered.

'What great lie?'

'Everything is part of the same great lie, down to the smallest spare part of the least significant weapon. Even the results that are sent to Moscow are subject to the great lie.'

'Results? What results? Results of what?'

'I don't know.'

'Of testing?'

She seemed to have forgotten her denial. 'I believe, of testing. I believe he is saying that the results of testing are deliberately distorted in order to satisfy the orders of the generals and the official production requirements of the bureaucrats. Perhaps it is he personally who distorts them. He is very complicated. Sometimes he talks about his many privileges of which he has become ashamed.'

The shopping list, Walter had called it. With a deadened sense of duty, Barley crossed off the last items. 'Has he mentioned particular projects?'

'No.'

'Has he mentioned being involved in command systems? How the field commander is controlled?'

'No.'

'Has he ever told you what steps are taken to prevent mistaken launches?'

'No.'

'Has he ever suggested he might be engaged in data processing?'

She was tired. 'No.'

'Does he get promoted now and then? Medals? Big parties as he moves up the ladder?'

'He does not speak of promotion except that it is all corrupt. I told you already that maybe he has been too loud in his criticisms of the system. I do not know.'

She had withdrawn from him. Her face was out of sight behind the curtain of her hair.

'You will do best to ask him all further questions for yourself,' she said, in the tone of someone packing up to leave. 'He wishes you to meet him in Leningrad on Friday. He is attending an important conference at one of the military scientific institutions.'

First the sky swayed, then Barley became aware of the evening chill. It had closed over him like an icy cloud, though the sky was dark and clear and the new moon, when it finally kept still, shed a warming glow.

'He has proposed three places and three times,' she continued in the same flat tone. 'You will please keep each appointment until he is success-ful. He will keep one of them if he can. He sends you his greetings and his thanks. He loves you.'

She dictated three addresses and watched him while he wrote them in his diary, using his apology for a code. Then she waited while he had a sneezing fit, watching him as he heaved and cursed his Maker.

They dined like exhausted lovers in a cellar with an old grey dog and a gypsy who sang blues to a guitar. Who owned the place, who allowed it to exist or why, were mysteries Barley had never troubled to solve. All he knew was that in some previous incarnation, at some forgotten book fair, he had arrived here drunk with a group of crazy Polish publishers and played 'Bless This House' on someone's saxophone.

They talked stiffly, and as they talked the gap between them widened until it seemed to Barley to engulf the totality of his insignificance. He gazed at her and felt that he had nothing to offer her that she did not have tenfold. In the ordinary way, he would have made a passionate declaration of love to her. A lunge into absolutes would have been essential to his need to break the tension of a new relationship. But in Katya's presence he could find no absolutes to put opposite her own. He saw his life as a series of useless resurrections, one failure supplanted by another. He was appalled to think that he belonged to a society that existed only in materialism and gave so little thought to its great themes. But he could tell her none of this. To tell her anything was to assail the image that she had of him, and he had nothing to offer in its place.

They discussed books and he watched her slipping away from him. Her face became distracted, her voice prosaic. He went after her, he sang and danced, but she had gone. She was making the same flat statements he had been listening to all day long while he had been waiting to meet her. In a minute, he thought, I'll be telling her about Potomac Boston and explaining how the river and the city are not joined. And God help him, he was, doing just that.

It was not till eleven o'clock, when the management put the lights out and he walked her down the lifeless street to the metro station, that it dawned on him against all sane reckoning that he might have made an impression upon her that in some modest way compared with the impression she had made on him. She had taken his arm. Her fingers lay along the inside of his forearm and she had fallen into a wide stride in order to keep pace with him. The white mouth of the elevator shafts stood open to receive her. The chandeliers twinkled above them like inverted Christmas trees as he took her in the formal Russian embrace: left cheek, right cheek, left cheek and goodnight.

'Mr. Blair, sir! Thought I spotted you! Quite a coincidence! Come aboard, we'll run you home!'

Barley climbed in and Wicklow with his acrobat's agility spirited himself into the back seat where he set to work to dislodge the recorder from the small of Barley's back.

They drove him to the Odessa and dropped him. They had work to do. The lobby was like an airport terminal in thick fog. In every sofa and armchair, unofficial guests who had paid the going rate slumbered in the gloom. Barley peered benignly round them, wrinkling his nose. Some wore jumpsuits. Others were more formally dressed.

'Snoot, anybody?' he called, quite loud. No response. 'Anyone care for a glass of *whisky* at all?' he enquired, fishing his bottle, still two-thirds full, from the poacher's pocket of his raincoat. He gave himself a long pull by way of example, then passed the bottle along the line.

And that was how Wicklow found him two hours later – in the lobby, squatted companionably among a group of grateful night souls, enjoying a last one before turning in.

9

'Who on earth are Clive's new Americans?' I murmured to Ned as we assembled like early worshippers round Brock's tape recorder in the situation room.

The London clock said six. Victoria Street had not yet begun its morning growl. The squeaking of the spool sounded like a chorus of starlings as Brock wound the tape in place. It had arrived by courier half an hour ago, having travelled overland by bag to Helsinki, then by special plane to Northolt. If Ned had been willing to listen to the technological tempters, we could have avoided the whole costly process, for the Langley wizards were swearing by a new device that transmitted spoken word securely. But Ned was Ned and he preferred his own tried methods.

He sat at his desk and was putting his signature to a document which he was shielding with his hand. He folded the paper, put it in its envelope and sealed the flap before handing it to tall Emma, one of his assistants. By then I had given up expecting a reply, so that his vehemence startled me.

'They're bloody carpetbaggers,' he snapped.

'From Langley?'

'God knows. Security.'

'Whose?' I insisted.

He shook his head, too furious to answer. Was it the document he had just signed that was annoying him, or the presence of the American interlopers? There were two of them. Johnny from their London station was escorting them. They wore navy blazers and short hair, and they had a Mormon cleanliness that I found slightly revolting. Clive stood between them, but Bob had sat himself demonstratively at the far end of the room with Walter, who looked wretched – I supposed at first because of the hour. Even Johnny seemed discomfited by their presence, and so immediately was I. These dull, unfamiliar faces had no place at the heart of our operation, and at such a crucial moment. They were like a gathering of mourners in advance of an anticipated death. But whose? I looked again at Walter and my anxieties were compounded.

I looked again at the new Americans, so slight, so trim, so characterless. Security, Ned had said. Yet why? And why *now*? Why did they look at everyone except Walter? Why did Walter look at everyone except them? And why did Bob sit apart from them, and Johnny go on staring at his hands? I was grateful to have my thoughts interrupted.

We heard the boom of footsteps on wood stairs. Brock had started the recorder. We heard clunks and Barley's oath as he barked his back on the window frame. Then the shuffling of feet again as they clambered on to the rooftop.

It's a seance, I thought, as their first words reached us. Barley and Katya are addressing us from the great beyond. The immobile strangers with their executioners' faces were forgotten.

Ned was the only one of us with earphones. They made a difference, I later discovered when I tried them. You hear the Moscow doves shuffling on the gable and the rapid breathing inside Katya's voice. You hear the beating of your own joe's heart through the body mikes.

Brock played the whole rooftop scene before Ned ordered a break. Only our new Americans seemed unaffected. Their brown glances brushed each one of us but settled nowhere. Walter was blushing.

Brock played the dinner scene and still no one stirred: not a sigh or a creak or a handclap, not even when he stopped the spool and wound it back.

Ned pulled off his earphones.

'Yakov Yefremovich, last name unknown, physicist, aged thirty in 1968, ergo born 1938,' he announced as he grabbed a pink trace request from the pile before him and scribbled on it. 'Walter, offers?'

Walter had to gather himself. He seemed distraught, and his voice had none of its usual flightiness. 'Yefrem, Soviet scientist, other names unknown, father of Yakov Yefremovich q.v., shot in Vorkuta after an uprising in the spring of '52,' he declared without looking at his pad. 'There can't be *that* many scientific Yefrems who were executed for an overdose of intelligence, even in dear Stalin's day,' he added rather pathetically.

It was absurd, but I fancied I saw tears in his eyes. Perhaps someone really *has* died, I thought, glancing once more at our two Mormons.

'Johnny?' said Ned, writing.

'Ned, we think we'll take Boris, other names unknown, widower, Professor of Humanities, Leningrad University, late 'sixties, one daughter Yekaterina,' said Johnny, still to his hands.

Ned seized another trace form, filled it in and tossed it into his out-tray like money he was pleased to throw away.

'Palfrey. Want to play?'

'Put me down for the Leningrad newspapers, will you please, Ned?' I said as airily as I could, given that Clive's Americans had turned their brown gaze full upon me. 'I'd like runners, starters and winners of the Mathematics Olympiad of 1952,' I said amid laughter. 'And for safety's sake perhaps you'd throw in '51 and '53 as well. And shall we add his academic medals, please, somewhere along the line? "He made candidate of sciences, he made doctor of sciences. He made everything," she said. Can we have that, please? Thank you.'

When all the bids were in, Ned glared around for Emma to take the trace forms down to Registry. But that wasn't good enough for Walter who was suddenly determined to be counted – for, leaping to his feet, he marched fussily to Ned's desk, all five foot nothing of him, his little wrists flying out in front of him.

'I shall do *all* the ferreting myself,' he announced, in far too grand a tone, as he grabbed the pink bundle to his breast. 'This war is *far* too important to be left to our blue-rinse generals of Registry, irresistible though they may be.'

And I remember noticing how our Mormons watched him all the way to the door, then watched each other as we listened to his merry little heels prinking down the corridor. And I do not think I am speaking with hindsight when I tell you that my blood ran chill for Walter, without my having the smallest idea why.

'A breath of country air,' Ned told me on the internal telephone an hour later when I was barely back at my desk at Head Office. 'Tell Clive I need you.'

'Then you'd better go, hadn't you?' said Clive, still closeted with his Mormons.

We had borrowed a fast Ford from the car pool. As Ned drove, he brushed aside my few attempts at conversation and handed me the file to read instead. We entered the Berkshire countryside but he still didn't talk. And when Brock rang on the carphone to give him some elliptical confirmation he required, he merely grunted, 'Then tell him,' and returned to his brooding.

We were forty miles from London, on the foulest planet of man's discovery. We were in the slums of modern science, where the grass is always nicely cut. The ancient gateposts were mastered by eroded sand-stone lions. A polite man in a brown sports jacket opened Ned's door. His colleague poked a detector underneath the chassis. Politely, they patted us both down.

'Taking the briefcase, are we, gentlemen?'

'Yes,' said Ned.

'Care to open it, sir?'

'No.'

'Dip it in the box, can we, gentlemen? We're not talking unexposed film, I presume, sir?'

'Please,' I said. 'Dip it in the box.'

We watched while they lowered the briefcase into what looked like a green coal bin, and took it out again.

'Thank you,' I said, taking it back.

'It's my pleasure, sir. Not at all, I'm sure.'

The blue van said FOLLOW ME. An Alsatian dog frowned at us from its barred rear window. The gates opened electronically and beyond them lay mounds of clipped grass like mass graves grown over. Olive downs stretched towards the sunset. A mushroom-shaped cloud would have looked entirely natural. We entered parkland. A pair of buzzards wheeled in the cloudless sky. High wire fenced off the hay fields. Smokeless brick buildings nestled in artful hollows. A noticeboard urged protective cloth-ing in Zones D to K. A skull and crossbones said 'You Have Been Warned.' The van ahead of us was moving at a funeral's pace. We lumbered round a bend and saw empty tennis courts and aluminium towers. Lanes of col-oured pipe jogged beside us, guiding us to a cluster of green sheds. At their centre, on a hilltop, stood the last vestige of the pre-nuclear age, a Berk-shire cottage of brick and flint with 'Administrator' stencilled on the gate. A burly man came tripping down the crazy-paving path to greet us. He wore a blazer of British racing green and a tie with gold squash rackets on it, and a handkerchief shoved into his cuff.

'You're from the Firm. Well done. I'm O'Mara. Which of you is who? I've told him to kick his heels in the lab till we whistle for him.'

'Good,' said Ned.

O'Mara had grey-blond hair and an offhand regimental voice cracked by alcohol. His neck was puffy and his athlete's fingers were stained mahogany with nicotine. 'O'Mara keeps the long-haired scientists in line,' Ned had told me in one of our rare exchanges during the drive. 'He's half personnel, half security, all shit.'

The drawing-room had the air of being tended by Napoleonic prisoners of war. Even the bricks of the fireplace had been polished and the plaster lines between them picked out in loving white. We sat in rose-patterned armchairs drinking gin and tonic, lots of ice. Horse-brasses twinkled from the glistening black beams.

'Just come back from the States,' O'Mara recalled, as if accounting for our recent separation. He raised his glass and ducked his mouth to it, meeting it halfway. 'You fellows go there a lot?'

'Occasionally,' said Ned.

'Now and then,' I said. 'When duty calls.'

'We send quite a few of our chaps out there on loan, actually. Oklahoma. Nevada. Utah. Most of them like it pretty well. A few get the heebie-jeebies, run for home.' He drank and took a moment to swallow. 'Visited their weapons laboratory at Livermore, out in California. Nice enough place. Decent guest house. Money galore. Asked us to attend a seminar on death. Bloody macabre if you think about it, but the shrinks seemed to believe it would do everybody good and the wines were extraordinary. I suppose if you're planning to consign large chunks of humanity to the flames you might as well know how it works.' He drank again, all the time in the world. The hilltop at that hour was a very quiet place. 'Surprising how many people hadn't given the subject much thought. Specially the young. The older ones were a bit more squeamish. They could remember the age of innocence, if it ever existed. You're a prompt fatality if you die straight off, and a soft one if you do it the slow way. I never realised. Gives a new meaning to the value of being at the centre of things, I suppose. Still, we're into the fourth generation now. Dulls the pangs. You chaps golfers?'

'No,' said Ned.

'I'm afraid not,' I said. 'I used to take lessons but they somehow never made much difference.'

'Marvellous courses but they made us hire bloody Noddy carts. Wouldn't be seen dead in the things over here.' He drank again, the same slow ritual. 'Wintle's an oddball,' he explained when he had swallowed. 'They're all oddballs but Wintle's got odder balls than most. He's done Socialism, he's done Jesus. Now he's into contemplation and Tai Chi.

Married, thank God. Grammar school but talks proper. Three years to go.'

'How much have you told him?' Ned asked.

'They always think they're under suspicion. I've told him he isn't, and I've told him to keep his stupid mouth shut when it's over.'

'And do you think he will?' I asked.

O'Mara shook his head. 'Don't know how to, most of 'em, however hard we boot 'em.'

There was a knock at the door and Wintle came in, an eternal student of fifty-seven. He was tall but crooked, with a curly grey head that shot off at an angle, and an air of brilliance almost extinguished. He wore a sleeveless Fair Isle pullover, Oxford bags and moccasins. He sat with his knees together and held his sherry glass away from him like a chemical retort he wasn't sure of.

Ned had turned professional. His tantrums were set aside. 'We're in the business of tracking Soviet scientists,' he said, managing to make himself sound dull. 'Watching the snakes and ladders of their defence establishment. Nothing very sexy, I'm afraid.'

'So you're Intelligence,' said Wintle. 'I thought as much, though I didn't say anything.'

It occurred to me that he was a very lonely man.

'Mind your own fucking business what they are,' O'Mara advised him perfectly pleasantly. 'They're English and they've got a job to do, same as you.'

Ned fished a couple of typed sheets from a folder and handed them to Wintle, who put down his glass to take them. His hands had a way of finishing knuckles down and fingers curled, like a man begging to be freed.

'We're trying to maximalise some of our neglected old material,' Ned said, falling into a jargon he would otherwise have eschewed. 'This is an account of your debriefing when you returned from a visit to Akademgorodok in August, 1963. Do you remember a Major Vauxhall? It's not exactly a literary masterpiece but you mention the names of two or three Soviet scientists we'd be grateful to catch up with, if they're still around and you remember them.'

As if to protect himself from a gas attack, Wintle pulled on a pair of extraordinarily ugly steel-framed spectacles.

'As I recall that debriefing, *Major* Vauxhall gave me his *word* of honour that everything I said was *entirely* voluntary and confidential,' he declared with a didactic jerkiness. 'I am therefore *very* surprised to see my name *and* my words lying about in open Ministerial archives a full twenty-five *years* after the event.'

'Well it's the nearest you'll ever get to immortality, sport, so I should shut up and enjoy it,' O'Mara advised.

I interposed myself like somebody separating belligerents in a family row. If Wintle could just expand a little on the interviewer's rather bald account, I suggested. Maybe flesh out one or two of the Soviet scientists whose names are listed on the final page, and perhaps throw in some account of the Cambridge team while he was about it? If he wouldn't mind answering just one or two questions which might tilt the scales?

' "Team" is *not* a word I would use in this context, thank you,' Wintle retorted, pouncing on the word like some bony predator. 'Not on the British side anyway. *Team* suggests common purpose. We were a Cambridge *group*, yes. A *team*, no. Some went for the ride, some went for the self-aggrandisement. I refer particularly to Professor Callow who had a *highly* exaggerated opinion of his work on accelerators, since refuted.' His Birmingham accent had escaped from its confinement. 'A very small minority *indeed* had ideological motives. They happened to believe in science without borders. A free exchange of knowledge for the common benefit of mankind.'

'Wankers,' O'Mara explained to us helpfully.

'We'd the French there, Americans galore, the Swedes, Dutch, even one or two Germans, Wintle continued, oblivious to O'Mara's jibe. 'All of them had hope, in my opinion, and the Russians had it in bucketfuls. It was us British who were dragging our feet. We still are.'

O'Mara groaned and took a restorative pull of gin. But Ned's good smile, even if a little battered, encouraged Wintle to run on.

'It was the height of the Khrushchev era, as you will doubtless recall. Kennedy this side, Khrushchev that side. A golden age was beckoning, said some. People in those days talked about Khrushchev very much as they talk of Gorbachev now, I'm sure. Though I do have to say that, in my opinion, our enthusiasm *then* was more genuine and spontaneous than the so-called enthusiasm *now*.'

O'Mara yawned and fixed his pouchy gaze disconcertingly upon myself.

'*We* told them whatever *we* knew. *They* did the same,' Wintle was saying as his voice gathered assurance. '*We* read *our* papers. *They* read *theirs*. Callow didn't cut any ice, I'm bound to say. They rumbled *him* in no time. But we'd Panson on cybernetics and *he* flew the flag all right, and we had me. *My* modest lecture was quite a success, though I do say it myself. I haven't heard applause like it since, to be frank. I wouldn't be surprised if they still talk about it over there. The barricades came down so fast you could *literally* hear them crashing in the lecture hall. "Flow, not demarcation." That was our slogan. "Flow" wasn't the word for it either, not if you saw the vodka that was drunk at the late-night parties. *Or* the girls there. Or heard the chat. The KGB was listening, of course. We knew *all* about that. We'd had the pep talk before we left, though several objected to it. Not me, I'm a patriot. But there wasn't a blind thing that any of them could do, not *their* KGB and not *ours*.' He had evidently hit a favourite theme for he straightened himself to deliver a prepared speech. 'I'd like to add here that *their* KGB is greatly misjudged, in my opinion. I have it on *good* authority that the Soviet KGB has very *frequently* sheltered some of the most tolerant elements of the Soviet intelligentsia.'

'Jesus – well don't tell me ours hasn't,' O'Mara said.

'Furthermore I've no doubt whatever that the Soviet authorities very *rightly* argued that in any trade-off of scientific knowledge with the West, the Soviet Union had more to *gain* than *lose*.' Wintle's slanted head was switching from one to another of us like a railway signal, and his upturned hand was resting on his thigh in anguish. 'They had the culture too. None of your Arts-Sciences divide for *them*, thank you. They had the Renaissance dream of rounded man, still do have. I'm not much of a one for culture myself. I don't have the time. But it was all there for those who had the *interest*. And reasonably charged too, I understand. Some of the events were complimentary.'

Wintle needed to blow his nose. And to blow his nose Wintle needed first to spread his handkerchief on his knee, then poke it into operational mode with his fingertips. Ned seized upon the natural break.

'Well now, I wonder whether we could take a look at one or two of those Soviet scientists whose names you kindly gave to Major Vauxhall,' he suggested, taking the sheaf of papers I was holding out to him.

We had arrived at the moment we had come for. Of the four of us in the room, I suspected only Wintle was unaware of this, for O'Mara's yellowed eyes had lifted to Ned's face and he was studying him with a dyspeptic shrewdness.

Ned led with his discards, as I would have done. He had marked them for himself in green. Two were known to be dead, a third was in disgrace. He was testing Wintle's memory, rehearsing him for the real thing when it came. Sergey? said Wintle. My goodness yes, Sergey! But what was his other name then? Popov? Popovich? That's right, Protopopov! Sergey Protopopov, engineer specialising in fuels!

Ned coaxed him patiently along, three names, a fourth, guiding his memory, exercising it: 'Well now, just think about him a second before you say no again. Really no? Okay. Let's try Savelyev.'

'Come again?'

Wintle's memory, I noticed, had the Englishman's embarrassment with Russian surnames. It preferred first names that it could anglicise.

'Savelyev,' Ned repeated. Again I caught O'Mara's eye upon him. Ned peered at the report in his hand, perhaps a mite too carelessly. 'That's it. Savelyev.' He spelt it. ' "Young, idealistic, talkative, called himself a humanitarian. Working on particles, brought up in Leningrad." Those were your words, according to Major Vauxhall all those lifetimes ago. Anything more I might add? You didn't keep up with him, for instance? Savelyev?'

Wintle was smiling in marvel. 'Was that his name, then? Savelyev? Well I'm blowed. There you are. I'd forgotten. To me he's still Yakov, you see.'

'Fine. Yakov Savelyev. Remember his patronymic?'

Wintle shook his head, still smiling.

'Anything to add to your original description?'

We had to wait. Wintle had a different sense of time from ours. And to judge by his smirk, a different sense of humour.

'Very sensitive fellow, Yakov was. Wouldn't dare ask his questions in the plenum. Had to hang back and pluck your sleeve when it was over. "Excuse me, sir, but what do you think of so-and-so?" Good questions, mind. A very cultural man, too, they say, in his way. I'm told he cut quite a dash at some of the poetry readings. And the art shows.'

Wintle's voice trailed off and I feared he was about to fabricate, which is a thing people do often when they have run out of information but want to keep their ascendancy. But to my relief he was merely retrieving memories from his store – or rather milking them out of the ether with his upright fingers.

'Always going from one group to another, Yakov was,' he said, with the same irritating smile of superiority. 'Standing himself at the edge of a discussion, very earnest. Perching on the edge of a chair. There was some mystery about his father, I never knew what. They say he was a scientist too, but executed. Well a lot were, weren't they, scientists. They killed them off like fruit flies, I've read about it. If they didn't kill them, they kept them in prison. Tupolev, Petliakov, Korolev – some of their greatest stars of aircraft technology designed their best stuff in prison. Ramzin invented a new boiler for heat engines in prison. Their first rocketry research unit was set up in prison. Korolev ran it.'

'Bloody well done, old boy,' said O'Mara, bored again.

'Gave me this piece of rock,' Wintle continued.

And I saw his hand, upward on his knee again, opening and closing round the imaginary gift.

'*Rock?*' said Ned. 'Yakov gave it to you? Do you mean music? No, you mean a geological sample of some kind.'

'When we Westerners left Akadem,' Wintle resumed, as if launching himself and us upon an entirely new story, 'we *stripped* ourselves of our possessions. *Literally.* If you'd seen our group on that last day, you would *not* have believed it. We'd our Russian hosts crying *their eyes* out, hugging and embracing, flowers on the buses, even Callow was having a weep if you can believe it. And us Westerners unloading everything we had: books, papers, pens, watches, razors, toothpaste, even our *toothbrushes.* Gramophone records if we'd brought them. Spare underclothes, ties, shoes, shirts, socks, everything except the minimum we needed for our decency to fly home in. We didn't *agree* to do it. We hadn't even *discussed* it. It happened *spontaneously.* There was some did more, of course. Particularly the Americans, being impulsive. I heard of one fellow offering a marriage of convenience to a girl who was desperate to get out. I didn't do that. I wouldn't. I'm a patriot.'

'But you gave some of your goodies to Yakov,' Ned suggested, while he affected to write painstakingly in a diary.

'I started to, yes. It's a bit like feeding the birds in the park, handing out your treasures is. You pick the one who's not getting his share and you try to fatten him up. Besides, I'd taken to young Yakov, you couldn't help it, him being so soulful.'

The hand had frozen round the empty shape, the fingertips striving to unite. The other hand had risen to his brow and taken hold of a sizable pinch of flesh.

' "Here you are, Yakov," I said. "Don't be slow in coming forward. You're too shy for your own health, you are." I'd an electric shaver in those days. Plus batteries, transformer, all in a nice carrying case. But he didn't seem to be that comfortable with them. He put them aside, sort of thing, and kept shuffling about. Then I realised he was trying to give something to *me*. It was this rock, wrapped in newspaper. They'd no fancy wrapping, naturally. "It's a piece of my country," he says. "To thank you for your lecture," he says. He wanted me to love the good in it always, however bad it might sometimes seem from outside. Spoke a beautiful English, mind, better than half of *us*. I was a bit embarrassed, frankly, if you want to know. I kept that piece of old rock for very many years. Then my wife threw it out during one of her spring-cleans. I thought of writing to him sometimes, I never did. He was arrogant, mind, in his way. Well a lot of them were. I dare say *we* were in *our* way, too. We all thought science could rule the world. Well I suppose it does now, though not in the way it was meant to, I'm sure.'

'Did he write to you?' said Ned.

Wintle wondered about this for a long time. 'You can never tell, can you? You never know what's been stopped in the post. Or who by.'

From the briefcase I passed Ned the bunch of photographs. Ned passed them to Wintle while O'Mara watched. Wintle leafed through them and suddenly let out a cry.

'That's him! Yakov! The man who gave me the rock.' He thrust the picture back at Ned. 'Look for yourself! Look at those eyes! *Then* tell me he's not a dreamer!'

Extracted from the Leningrad evening paper dated 5th January 1954 and reconstituted by Photographic Section, Yakov Yefremovich Savelyev as a teenaged genius.

There were other names, and Ned took Wintle laboriously through each one of them, laying false trails, brushing over his tracks until he was satisfied that in Wintle's mind at least Savelyev meant no more than the rest.

'Clever of you to hide your trump in the middle of your hand,' O'Mara remarked as, glass in hand, he walked us down the drive to the car. 'Last time I heard of Savelyev he was running their testing range in darkest Kazakhstan, dreaming up ways to read their own telemetry without everyone reading it over their shoulder. What's he up to now? Selling the shop?'

It is not often I take pleasure in my work but our meeting and the place had sickened me, and O'Mara had sickened me more than both. It is not often that I seize someone by the arm either, and have to recoil, and loosen my grip.

'I take it you have signed the Official Secrets Act?' I asked him quietly enough.

'Practically wrote the bloody thing,' O'Mara retorted, very surprised.

'Then you will know that all knowledge that comes to you officially and all speculation based upon that knowledge are in the perpetual property of the Crown.' Another legal distortion, but never mind. I released him. 'So if you like your job here, and you are hoping for promotion, and if you are looking forward to your pension, I suggest you never think of this meeting again or of any name associated with it. Thank you so much for the gin. Goodbye.'

On the journey back, with the identification of Bluebird confirmed and phoned ahead of us in wordcode to the Russia House, Ned remained withdrawn. Yet when we reached Victoria Street he was suddenly determined not to let me go. 'You stick around,' he ordered me, and guided me ahead of him down the basement steps.

At first glance the scene in the situation room was one of purest joy. The centrepiece was Walter, poised like an artist before a whiteboard as big as he was, drawing up the details of Savelyev's life in coloured crayons. If he had been wearing a broad-brimmed hat and smock, he could not have looked more rakish. Only at second glance did I recall my eerie apprehensions of that morning.

Around him – which meant behind him, for the whiteboard was propped against the wall beneath the clocks – stood Brock and Bob, and Jack our cypher clerk, and Ned's girl Emma, and a senior girl called Pat who was one of the mainstays of Soviet Registry. They held glasses of champagne and each of them in his different way was smiling, though Bob's smile was more like a grimace of pain suppressed.

'A lonely decider,' Walter declaimed rhapsodically. He froze a moment as he heard us, but did not turn his head. 'A fifty-year-old achiever shaking his mid-life bars, looking at mortality and a wasted life. Well, aren't we all?'

He stood back. Then skipped forward again and chalked in a date. Then took a swig of champagne. And I sensed something ghoulish and scaring about him, like make-up on the dying.

'Living at their secret centre all his adult life,' he continued gaily. 'But keeping his mouth shut. Taking his own decisions, all by himself in the dark, bless him. Getting his own back on history if it kills him, which it probably will.' Another date, and the word OLYMPIAD. 'He's the vintage year. Any younger, he'd be brainwashed. Any older, he'd be looking for an old fart's sinecure.'

He drank, his back still turned to us. I glanced at Bob for enlightenment but he was looking studiously at the floor. I glanced at Ned. His eyes were on Walter but his face was expressionless. I glanced at Walter again and saw that his breath was coming to him in defiant gasps.

'I invented him, I'm sure I did,' Walter declared, seemingly oblivious to the dismay around him. 'I've been predicting him for years.' He wrote the words FATHER EXECUTED. 'Even after they'd drafted him, the poor lamb tried so *hard* to be good. He wasn't sneaky. He wasn't resentful. He had his doubts but, as scientists go, he was a good soldier. Until one day – *bingo!* He wakes up and discovers it's all a load of junk and he's wasted his genius on a bunch of incompetent gangsters and brought the world to the edge of ruin into the bargain.' He was writing in fierce strokes while the sweat ran down his temples: WORKING UNDER ROGOV AT 109 TESTING SITE KAZAKHSTAN. He doesn't know it but he's joined the great Russian male menopausal revolution of the 'eighties. He's had all the lies, he's had Stalin, the Khrushchev chink of light and the long dark of Brezhnev. But he's still got one last shot in him, one last menopausal chance to print himself on the world. And the new buzz-words are ringing in his ears: revolution from above, openness, peace, change, courage, reconstruction. He's even being *encouraged* to revolt.'

He was writing faster than ever, shortwinded or not: TELEMETRY, ACCURACY. 'Where will they land?' he was asking rhetorically between gasps. 'How close will how many get to how many targets when? What's the expansion and temperature of the skin? What's gravity up to? Crucial questions and the Bluebird knows the answers. He knows because he's in charge of making the missiles talk while they go along – without the Americans hearing, which is his skill. Because he's contrived the encryption systems that dodge the American super-listeners in Turkey and mainland China. He sees all the answers in clear, before Brother Rogov fudges them for his lords and masters in Moscow. Which according to the Bluebird is Rogov's speciality. "Professor Vitaly Rogov is an arse-licking toady," he tells us in notebook two. A fair judgment. That's what Vitaly Rogov is. A verifiable, fully-paid-up, spineless, arse-licking toady, meeting his norms and earning his medals and his privileges. Who does that remind us of? No one. Certainly not our own dear Clive. So Bluebird blows his lid. He confesses his agony to Katya and Katya says, "Don't just whimper, do something." And by golly, he does it. He gives us every bloody thing he can lay his hands on. The Crown Jewels doubled and re-doubled. Encryptions decrypted. Telemetry *en clair*. Retrospective code-breaks to help us check it out. The unbuggered head-on truth, before it gets repainted for Moscow consumption. All right, he's potty. Who isn't, who's any good?' He took a last swig from his glass and I saw that the centre of his face was a crimson mass of pain and embarrassment and indignation.

'Life's a botch,' he explained, as he shoved the glass into my hand.

The next I knew, he had slipped past us up the stairs and we heard the steel doors successively open and slam shut behind him till he had reached the street.

'Walter was a liability,' Clive explained to me tersely next morning, when I bearded him. 'To us he was merely eccentric perhaps. But to others – ' It was the nearest I had ever known him come to acknowledging the existence of sex. He quickly censored himself. 'I've given him to Training Section,' he continued with a return to his most frigid manner. 'He raised too many eyebrows on the other side.'

He meant, on the other side of the Atlantic.

So Walter, wonderful Walter, disappeared and I was right, we never saw the Mormons again and Clive never once referred to them. Were they mere messengers from Langley, or had they formed their verdict and exacted their punishment? Were they from Langley at all, or from one of the mushrooming groups of initials that Ned had so objected to when he complained to Clive about the Bluebird distribution list? Or were they Ned's greatest of all pet hates – tame psychiatrists?

Whatever they were, the effect of them was felt all through the Russia House, and Walter's absence yawned at us like a shell-hole made by our best ally's guns. Bob felt it and was ashamed. Even hard-faced Johnny remained ill at ease.

'I'll want you nearer to the operation,' Ned told me.

It seemed a wretched consolation for Walter's disappearance.

'You're on edge again,' said Hannah as we walked.

It was lunchtime. Her office was close to Regent's Park. Sometimes on warm days we would share a sandwich together. Sometimes we even did a bit of zoo. Sometimes she gave the Cancer Institute a rest and we ended up in bed.

I asked after her husband, Derek. He was one of the few subjects we had in common. Had Derek lost his temper again? Had he beaten her up? Sometimes, in the days when we had been full-time lovers, I used to think it was Derek who held us together. But today she didn't want to talk about Derek. She wanted to know why I was on edge.

'They sacked a man I rather liked,' I said. 'Well, not sacked, but threw him on the rubbish heap.'

'What did he do wrong?'

'Nothing at all. They just decided to see him in a different light.'

'Why?'

'Because it suited them. They withdrew their tolerance of him in order to satisfy certain requirements.'

She thought about this. 'You mean that convention got the better of them,' she suggested. Like you, she was saying. Like us.

Why do I keep coming back to her, I wondered. To visit the scene of the crime? To seek, for the thousandth time, her absolution? Or do I visit her as we visit our old schools, trying to understand what happened to our youth?

Hannah is still a beautiful woman, which is a consolation. The greying and the broadening have yet to come. When I catch her face backlit, and glimpse her valiant, vulnerable smile, I see her as I saw her twenty years ago, and tell myself I have not ruined her after all. 'She's all right. Look at her. She's smiling and undamaged. It's Derek, not you, who kicks her around.'

But I am never sure. Never sure at all.

The Union Jack that had so enraged the dictator Stalin when he observed it from the battlements of the Kremlin dangled dispiritedly from its mast in the British Embassy forecourt. The cream-coloured palace behind it resembled an old wedding cake waiting to be cut, the river lay docile as the morning downpour flailed its oily back. At the iron gates two Russian policemen studied Barley's passport while the rain smeared the ink. The younger copied out his name. The elder dubiously compared his harrowed features with his photograph. Barley was wearing a drenched brown mackintosh. His hair was plastered to his scalp. He looked a little shorter than his usual height.

'Well, *honestly*, what a day!' cried the well-bred girl in a pleated tartan skirt, waiting in the lobby. 'Hullo, I'm Felicity. You *are* who I think you are, aren't you? A jolly wet Scott Blair? The Economic Counsellor *is* expecting you.'

'I thought the Economic people were in the other building.'

'Oh, that's Commercial. They're *quite* different.'

Barley followed her swinging tail up the ancestral staircase. As always when he entered a British mission, a sense of dislocation overtook him, but this morning it was absolute. The tuneless whistling came from his local paper boy in Hampstead. The huffing and bumping of the floor polisher was the Co-op milk van. It was eight in the morning, and official Britain was not yet officially awake. The Economic Counsellor was a stubby Scotsman with silver hair. His name was Craig.

'Mr. Blair, sir! How do you do? Sit you down! Do you take the tea or the coffee? They both taste the same, I'm afraid, but we're working on it. Gradually, but we'll get there.'

Seizing Barley's mackintosh, he impaled it on a Ministry of Works coat-tree. Above the desk a framed photograph showed the Queen in riding habit. A notice beside her warned that speech in this room was not secure. Felicity brought tea and Garibaldi biscuits. Craig talked vigorously, as if he couldn't wait to get rid of his news. His red face was shiny from shaving.

'Oh and I hear you've been having the most *fantastic* runaround from those brigands in VAAP! Have they been making any sense at all? Are you getting anywhere, or are they just giving you the usual Moscow flannel? It's all *makework* here, you see. Seldom but seldom is anything actually transacted. The profit motive, somewhat like diligence, is unknown to them. It's all Brownie points and scratching one another's you-know-whats. The impossible combination, I always say, of incurable idleness harnessed to unattainable visions. The Ambassador used my very phrase in a despatch recently. No credit given, none asked. How do they ever come to grips, I ask you, with an economy built upon sloth, tribalism and hidden unemployment? Answer, they don't! When will they ever break free? What will happen if they do? Answer, God alone knows. I'm seeing the book-world here as a microcosm for their entire dilemma, follow me?'

He roared on until he seemed to decide that Barley and the microphones had had their fill. 'Well, I've surely relished our little conversation here this morning. You've given me much food for thought, I don't mind telling you. There's a great danger in our business of getting cut off from the source here. Will you allow me to pass you around a little now? Our Chancery people will never forgive me if I don't.'

With a nod of command, he led the way along a passage to a metal door with an evil eyehole in it. The door opened as they reached it and closed as Barley stepped inside.

Craig is your link, Ned had said. He's hell on earth but he'll take you to your leader.

Barley's first impression was that he was in a darkened ward, his next that the ward was a sauna, for the only light came from a corner of the floor and there was a smell of resin. Then he decided that the sauna was suspended for he detected a rocking underfoot.

Seating himself gingerly on a bridge chair, he discerned two figures behind a table. Above the first hung a curling poster of a Beefeater defending London Bridge. Above the second, Lake Windermere languished under a British Rail sunset.

'Bravo, Barley,' exclaimed a sturdy English voice, not unlike Ned's, from below the Beefeater. 'My name's Paddy, short for Patrick, and this gent is Cy. He's American.'

'Hi, Barley,' said Cy.

'We're just the local messenger boys here,' Paddy explained. 'We're rather limited in what we can do, naturally. Our main job is to supply the camels and hot meals. Ned sends his very special greetings. So does Clive. If they weren't so sullied they'd have come over and done their nail-biting with us. Hazard of the profession. Comes to us all, I'm afraid.'

As he spoke, the poor light released him. He was shaggy but lithe, with the craggy brows and faraway eyes of an explorer. Cy was sleek and urban and younger by a dozen years. Their four hands lay on a street map of

Leningrad. Paddy's shirtcuffs were frayed. Cy's were drip dry.

'I'm to ask you whether you want to go on, by the by,' Paddy said, as if that were a rather good joke. 'If you want to bail out that's your good right and no hard feelings. Want to bail out? What do you say?'

'Zapadny will kill me,' Barley muttered.

'Why's that?'

'I'm his guest. He's footing my bill, fixing my programme.' Lifting his hand to his forehead, he scrubbed at it as a way of reviving communication with his brain. 'What do I tell him? I can't just up-sticks, bye-bye, I'm off to Leningrad. He'd think I was loony.'

'But you *are* saying Leningrad, not London?' Paddy persisted kindly enough.

'I haven't got a visa. I've got Moscow. I haven't got Leningrad.'

'But assuming.'

Another lengthy delay.

'I need to talk to him,' Barley said, as if that were an explanation.

'To Zapadny?'

'Goethe. Got to talk to him.'

Dragging the back of his right wrist across his mouth in one of his habitual gestures, Barley looked at it as if expecting blood. 'I won't lie to him,' he muttered.

'There's no question of your lying to him. Ned wants a partnership, not a deception.'

'That goes for us too,' said Cy.

'I won't be sly with him. I'll talk to him straight or not at all.'

'Ned wouldn't wish it any other way,' said Paddy. 'We want to give him everything he needs.'

'Us too,' said Cy.

'Potomac Boston, Incorporated, Barley, your new American trading partner,' Paddy proposed in a fresh voice, glancing at a paper before him. 'The head of their publishing operation is a Mr. Henziger, is that right?'

'J. P.,' Barley said.

'Ever met him?'

Barley shook his head and winced. 'Name on the contract,' he said.

'That the nearest you've got to him?'

'We've spoken on the phone a couple of times. Ned thought we ought to be heard on the transatlantic line. Cover.'

'But you've no mental portrait of him otherwise?' Paddy persisted, in the way he had of forcing clear replies even if it made a pedant of him. 'He's not a drawn character for you in some way?'

'He's a name with money and offices in Boston and he's a voice on the phone. That's all he's ever been.'

'And in your conversations with local third parties – with Zapadny, say – J. P. Henziger has not featured as some kind of horror figure? You haven't given him a false beard or a wooden leg or a lurid sexlife? Nothing one might have to take into account if one were making him flesh, as it were?'

Barley considered the question but seemed to lose hold of it.

'No?' asked Paddy.

'No,' Barley said, and again unwisely shook his head.

'So a situation that might have arisen is this,' said Paddy. 'Mr. J. P. Henziger of Potomac Boston, young, dynamic, pushy, is presently to be found on holiday in Europe with his wife. It's the season. They are at this moment, let us say, at the Marski Hotel in Helsinki. Know the Marski?'

'I've had a drink there,' Barley said, as if he were ashamed of it.

'And in this impulsive American way they have, the Henzigers have taken it into their heads to make a lightning trip to Leningrad. Over to you, I think, Cy.'

Cy unlocked his smile and obliged. He had a sharp face when it came alive and an intelligent if snappish way of talking.

'The Henzigers take a three-day guided tour, Barley. Visas at the Finnish border, the guide, the bus, the whole nine yards. They're straightforward people, decent. This is Russia and it's their first time. *Glasnost* is news back home in Boston. He has money invested in you. Knowing you are in Moscow spending it, he requires you to drop everything, hurry to Leningrad, carry his bags for him and report progress. That's normal practice, typical of a young tycoon. You see a problem? Some way it doesn't play for you?'

Barley's head was clearing and his vision with it.

'No. It plays. I can make it work if you can.'

'First thing this morning UK time, J. P. calls your London office from the Marski, gets your machine,' Cy continued. 'J. P. does not talk to machines. An hour from now he telexes you care of Zapadny at VAAP, copy to Craig here at the British Embassy, Moscow, requesting you to meet with him this Friday at the Hotel Evropeiskaya, alias the Europe, Leningrad, which is where his tour-group is staying. Zapadny will wriggle, maybe raise a cry of pain. But since you are spending J. P.'s cash, it's our prediction Zapadny will have no choice but to bow to market forces. Figure?'

'Yes,' said Barley.

Paddy took back the story. 'If he's got any sense he'll help you get your visas changed. If he sulks, Wicklow can whisk them across to OVIR and they'll change them while he waits. You wouldn't make too much of it to Zapadny, in our view. You wouldn't grovel or apologise, not to Zapadny. You'd make a virtue of it. Tell him that's how life is lived these days in the fast lane.'

'J. P. Henziger is family,' Cy said. 'He's a fine officer. So's his wife.'

He stopped abruptly.

Like an umpire who has spotted a foul, Barley had flung out an arm and was pointing it at Paddy's chest.

'Hang on, you two! Hold your water. Half a mo! What use will *either* of them be, however *fine* they are, if they're riding round Leningrad locked in a bloody tour-bus all day?'

Paddy took only a moment to recover from this unexpected onslaught. 'You tell him, Cy,' he said.

'Barley, on their arrival at the Hotel Europe Thursday evening Mrs. Henziger will contract a severe dose of Leningrad tummy. J. P. will have no taste for sightseeing while his lovely lady is laid low with the runs. He'll dig in with her at the hotel. No problem.'

Paddy set the lamp and power pack next to the map of Leningrad. Katya's three addresses were ringed in red.

It was late afternoon before Barley telephoned her, about the time when he reckoned she would be locking away her paperclips. He had taken a nap and followed it with a couple of Scotches to bring himself up to par. But when he started talking he discovered that his voice was too high, and he had to bring it down.

'Ah. Hullo! You got home all right,' he said, sounding like someone he'd never met. 'Train didn't turn into a pumpkin or anything?'

'Thank you, it was not a problem.'

'Great. Well, I just rang to find out, really. Yes. Say thank you for a marvellous evening. Mmhmh. And goodbye for the time being.'

'Thank you also. It was productive.'

'Hoped we might have had another chance to meet, you see. Trouble is, I've got to go to Leningrad. Some stupid bit of business has cropped up and made me change my plans.'

A prolonged silence. 'Then you must sit down,' she said.

Barley wondered which of them had gone mad. 'Why?'

'It is our custom, when we are preparing for a long journey, first to sit down. You are sitting now?'

He could hear the happiness in her voice and it made him happy too.

'I'm lying down, actually. Will that do?'

'I have not heard of it. You are supposed to sit on your luggage or a bench, sigh a little and then cross yourself. But I expect that lying down will have the same effect.'

'It does.'

'Will you come back to Moscow from Leningrad?'

'Well not on this trip. I think we'll fly straight back to school.'

'School?'

'England. Stupid expression of mine.'

'What does it denote?'

'Obligations. Immaturity. Ignorance. The usual English vices.'

'You have many obligations?'

'Suitcases of 'em. But I'm learning to sort them out. I actually said no yesterday and astonished everybody.'

'Why do you have to say no? Why not say. yes? Perhaps they would be even more astonished.'

'Yes, well that was the trouble with last night, wasn't it? I never got round to talking about myself. We talked about you, the great poets down the ages, Mr. Gorbachev, publishing. But we left out the main topic. Me. I'll have to make a special trip just to come and bore you.'

'I am sure you will not bore me.'

'Is there anything I can bring you?'

'Please?'

'Next time I come. Any special wishes? An electric toothbrush? Paper curlers? More Jane Austen?'

A long delicious pause.

'I wish you a good journey, Barley,' she said.

The last lunch with Zapadny was a wake without a corpse. They sat fourteen, all men, the only guests in the enormous upstairs restaurant of an unfinished new hotel. Waiters brought food and vanished to the distant outskirts. Zapadny had to send scouts to find them. There was no drink and precious little conversation unless Barley and Zapadny contrived it between them. There was canned music of the 'fifties. There was a lot of hammering.

'But we have arranged a great party for you, Barley,' Zapadny protested. 'Vassily is bringing his drums, Victor will lend you his saxophone, a friend of mine who makes his own moonshine has promised us six bottles, there will be some mad painters and writers. It has all the makings of a most disreputable evening and you have the weekend to recover. Tell your American Potomac bastard to go to hell. We do not like you so serious.'

'Our tycoons are your bureaucrats, Alik. We ignore them at our peril. So do you.'

Zapadny's smile was neither warm nor forgiving. 'We even thought you might have lost your heart a little to one of our celebrated Moscow beauties. Can't the delicious Katya persuade you to stay?'

'Who's Katya?' Barley heard himself reply while he was still wondering why the ceiling hadn't fallen in.

A buzz of eager amusement rose from around the table.

'This is Moscow, Barley,' Zapadny reminded him, very pleased with himself. 'Nothing happens without something happening. The intelligentsia is small, we are all broke and local telephone calls are free. You cannot dine with Katya Orlova in an intimate and rather crazy restaurant without at least fifteen of us being advised of it next morning.'

'It was strictly business,' Barley said.

'Then why didn't you take Mr. Wicklow along with you?'

'He's much too young,' said Barley, and scored another peal of Russian merriment.

*

The night sleeper to Leningrad leaves Moscow at a few minutes before midnight, traditionally so that Russia's numberless bureaucrats may claim a second day's subsistence for the journey. The compartment had four berths, and Wicklow and Barley had the lower pair until a heavyweight blond lady insisted Barley exchange places with her. The fourth berth was occupied by a quiet man of apparent means who spoke elegant English and carried an air of private grief about him. First he wore a lawyer's dark suit, then he wore wildly striped pyjamas that would have graced a clown, but his mood did not brighten with his costume. There was more business when the blond lady refused to take off even her hat until the three men had removed themselves to the corridor. Harmony was restored when she called them back and, clad in a pink tracksuit with pompoms on the shoulders, fed them homemade pastries in gratitude for their gallantry. And when Barley produced whisky she was so impressed she made them eat her sausage too, insisting they drink the health of Mrs. Thatcher more than once.

'Where do you come from?' the sad man asked Barley across the divide as they settled for the night.

'London,' said Barley.

'London in England. Not from the moon, not from the stars, but London in England,' the sad man confirmed and, unlike Barley, soon appeared to fall asleep. But a couple of hours later as they pulled into a station, he resumed their conversation. 'Do you know where we are now?' he asked without bothering to establish whether Barley was awake.

'I don't think I do.'

'If Anna Karenina were travelling with us tonight and had her wits about her, this would be the place where she would abandon the unsatisfactory Vronsky.'

'Marvellous,' said Barley quite mystified. His whisky was gone but the sad man had Georgian brandy.

'It was a swamp before, it is a swamp today,' the sad man said. 'If you are studying the Russian disease, you must live in the Russian swamp.'

He was talking about Leningrad.

10

A low cottonwool sky hung over the imported palaces, making them dreary in their fancy dress. Summer music played in the parks but the summer clung behind the clouds, leaving a chalky Nordic mist to trick and tremble on the Venetian waterways. Barley walked and, as always when he was in Leningrad, he had the sensation of walking through other cities, now Prague, now Vienna, now a bit of Paris or a corner of Regent's Park. No other city that he knew hid its shame behind so many sweet façades or asked such terrible questions with its smile. Who worshipped in these locked, unreal churches? And whose God? How many bodies had choked these graceful canals or floated frozen to the sea? Where else on earth has so much barbarism built itself such pretty monuments? Even the people in the street, so slow spoken, decorous, reserved, seemed joined to one another by their monstrous dissembling. And Barley, as he loitered and gazed like any tourist – and like any spy counted off the minutes – Barley felt himself a part of their duplicity.

He had shaken hands with an American tycoon who was not a tycoon, and commiserated with him about his sick wife who was not sick and probably not his wife.

He had instructed a subordinate who was not his subordinate to give succour in an emergency that did not exist.

He was on his way to keep a rendezvous with an author who was not an author but was seeking martyrdom in a city where martyrdom could be had free across the counter, whether or not you happened to stand in line for it.

He was scared numb and had a hangover for the fourth day running.

He was a citizen of Leningrad at last.

Finding himself in the Nevsky Prospekt he realised he was looking for the cafeteria called informally the Saigon, a place for poets, drug-pedlars and speculators, not professors' daughters. 'Your father is right,' he heard her say. 'The system will always win.'

He had his own street map, courtesy of Paddy – German, with a multi-lingual text. From Cy he had a copy of *Crime and Punishment*, a battered Penguin paperback in a translation to drive him to despair. He had put them both in a plastic carrier bag. Wicklow had insisted. Not just any bag but this bag, advertising some beastly American cigarette and recognisable at five hundred metres. Now his only mission in life was to trail Raskolni-kov on his fateful journey to murder the old lady, which was why he was searching for a courtyard leading off the Griboyedev Canal. Iron gates opened to it, a spreading tree gave it shade. He wandered in it slowly, peering at his Penguin book, then guardedly at the grimy windows as if expecting the old pawnbroker's blood to come seeping down the yellowing paintwork. Only occasionally did he allow his gaze to stray into that unfocused middle distance which is the preserve of the English upper classes, and which comprises such extraneous objects as passers-by, or those not passing by but doing nothing; or the gate that led to Plekhanova Street which only very local people knew of, said Paddy, such as scientists who in their youth had studied at the Litmo around the corner, but who, so far as Barley could see from his casual searching of the approaches, showed no sign of returning.

He was out of breath. A bubble of nausea like an airpocket filled his lower chest. He reached the gate and opened it. He passed through an entrance hall. He climbed the short flight of steps to the street. He glanced both ways and made another show of comparing his findings while Wicklow's hated microphone harness sawed his back. He turned round and sauntered back through the courtyard and under the spreading tree until he was once more alongside the canal. He sat on a bench and unfolded the street map. Ten minutes, Paddy had said, handing him a scratched sportswatch in place of his unreliable heirloom. Five before, five after, then abort.

'You are lost?' asked a pale man who looked too old to be a tout. He was wearing Italian racing-driver glasses and Nike sneakers. His Russian English had an American accent.

'I'm always lost, old boy, thank you,' said Barley politely. 'It's the way I like it.'

'You want to sell me something? Cigarettes? Scotch? Fountain pen? You want to trade drugs or currency or something like this?'

'Thanks, but I'm very nice as I am,' Barley replied, relieved to hear himself speaking normally. 'If you'd just move out of the sun a little, I'll be even nicer.'

'You want to meet an international group of people including girls? I can show you the real Russia nobody ever gets to see.'

'Old boy, to be perfectly honest, I don't believe you'd know the real Russia if it got up and bit you in the balls,' said Barley, returning to his map. The man drifted away.

On Fridays even the great scientists will be doing what everyone else is doing, Paddy had said. They'll be closing down the week and getting drunk. They'll have had their three-day knees-up, they'll have shown each other their achievements and traded their researches. Their Leningrad hosts will be feeding them a lavish lunch but leaving them time to get at the shops before they return to their postbox numbers. That will be your friend's first chance to slip away from the group if he's going to.

My friend. *My* Raskolnikov friend. Not *his* friend. Mine. In case I come unstuck.

One rendezvous down and two to go.

Barley stood up, rubbed his back and with time to waste continued his literary tour of Leningrad. Recrossing the Nevsky Prospekt, he gazed at the weathered faces of the shoppers and in a rush of empathy prayed to be assumed into their ranks: 'I'm one of you! I share your confusions! Accept me! Hide me! Ignore me!' He steadied himself. Look round. Look foolish. Gawp.

Behind him stood the Kazan Cathedral. Ahead of him rose the House of Books, where as a good publisher Barley now lingered, squinting into the windows and upward at the stubby tower with its vile globe. But he did not stay for long in case he was recognised by somebody from one of the editorial offices upstairs. He entered Zhelyabova Street and approached one of the great department stores of Leningrad, with its wartime English fashions in the window and fur hats out of season. He placed himself conspicuously at the main entrance, hooking the carrier bag over his middle finger and unfolding his map for refuge.

Not here, he thought. For Christ's sake, not here. Give us a decent privacy, Goethe, please. Not here.

'If he selects the shop, he's reckoning on a very public meeting,' Paddy had said. 'He's got to fling up his arms and shout, "Scott Blair, can it be you?" '

For the next ten minutes Barley thought of nothing. He stared at the map, lifted his head and stared at buildings. He stared at girls, and in Leningrad that summer's day the girls were staring back. But their alertness did not reassure him and he ducked back into his map. Sweat was running like marbles over his rib cage. He had a fantasy that the microphones would short-circuit. Twice he cleared his throat because he feared he wouldn't be able to speak. But when he tried to moisten his lips he discovered that his tongue had withered.

The ten minutes were up but he waited another two because he owed them: to himself, to Katya, to Goethe. He folded the map, not making the right folds, but then he had never managed that anyway. He stuffed the map into the gaudy plastic bag. He rejoined the crowds and discovered that after all he could walk like everybody else, no sudden lurches, no bone-cracking falls headlong to the pavement.

He strolled back down the Nevsky towards the Anichkov Bridge, looking for the No. 7 trolleybus to Smolny for his third and final appearance before the assembled spies of Leningrad.

Two boys in jeans stood ahead of him in the queue. Three babushkas stood behind him. The trolleybus arrived and the boys leapt in. Barley followed them aboard. The two boys chatted noisily. An old man stood up in order to let one of the babushkas sit. We're a good crowd in here, Barley thought in another lurch of dependence upon those he was deceiving; let's stay together all day and enjoy each other. A small boy was frowning into his face, asking him something. On an inspiration, Barley pulled back his sleeve and showed him Paddy's steel wristwatch.

The boy studied it and gave a hiss of rage. The trolleybus clanged to a halt.

He's funked it, thought Barley in relief as he entered the park. The sun broke clear of the clouds. He's chickened and who can blame him?

But by then he had spotted him. Goethe, precisely as advertised. Goethe, the great lover and thinker, seated on the third bench to your left as you enter the gravel path, a nihilist who takes no principle for granted.

Goethe. Reading his newspaper. Sober and half his original size, dressed in a black suit certainly, but looking like his smaller, older brother. Barley's heart sank, then leapt, at the sight of such sheer ordinariness. The shadow of the great poet was extinct. Lines of age marked the once-smooth face. The mercurial had no place in this clerkish, bearded Russian taking his midday air on a park bench.

But Goethe nonetheless, and seated amid a cluster of warring Russian shrines: not a pistol shot from the fiery statues of Marx, Engels and Lenin, who forced their bronze scowls on him from strangely separated plinths; not a musket shot from the sacred Room Sixty-Seven, where Lenin had set up his revolutionary headquarters in a boarding school for the better class of Petersburg girl; not a funeral march from Rastrelli's blue baroque cathedral built to ease the declining years of an empress; not a blindfold walk from the Leningrad Party Headquarters with its oversize policemen glowering at the liberated masses.

Smola means tar, Barley recalled stupidly in this continuing moment of monstrous normality. In Smolny, Peter the Great stored his tar for the first Russian Navy.

Those nearest to Goethe were as normal as the man himself. The day might have started dull but the new sunlight had worked miracles and the good citizens were stripping off as if a common urge had seized them. Boys bare to the waist, girls like thrownaway flowers, hulking women in satin brassieres lay sprawled at Goethe's feet, playing radios, munching sandwiches and discussing whatever it was that made them grimace, ponder and laugh in swift succession.

A chip path ran close to the bench. Barley launched himself upon it studying the *Informationen* at the back of the folded map. In the field, Ned had said, in a session devoted to the macabre etiquette of tradecraft, the source is the star and the star decides whether to make the meeting or abort.

Fifty yards separated Barley from his star but the path joined them like a ruled line. Was he walking too fast or too slowly? One moment he was pressing up against the couple in front of him, the next he was being shoved aside from behind. If he ignores you, wait five minutes then try a second pass, Paddy had said. Squinting over his map, Barley saw Goethe's face lift as if he had scented his approach. He saw the whiteness of his

cheeks and the unlit hollows of his eyes; then the whiteness of the
newspaper as he folded it together like a camper's blanket. He saw that
there was something angular and not quite reconciled about his movements, so that he resembled in Barley's racing mind a figure of over-orderly
clockwork in a Swiss town: now I will lift my white face, now I strike
twelve with my white flag, now I stand up and march away. The newspaper
folded, Goethe put it in his pocket and gave a pedagogic glance at his
wristwatch. Then with the same mechanical air of being someone else's
invention, he took his place in the army of pedestrians and loped among
them towards the river.

Now Barley's pace was set, for it was Goethe's. His quarry was following the path towards a row of parked cars. Eyes and brain clear, Barley
walked after him and, reaching the cars, saw him standing against the
fast-flowing Neva, his jacket puffed out by the river breeze. A pleasure
steamer passed but the passengers gave no sign of pleasure. A coaling boat
hobbled by, dappled in red lead, and the filthy smoke from its funnel was
beautiful in the dancing river light. Goethe leaned over the balustrade and
peered down at the current as if calculating its speed. Barley headed
towards him, slurring his feet while he orientated himself from his map
with increasing diligence. Even when he heard himself addressed, in the
immaculate English that had woken him on the verandah in Peredelkino,
he did not immediately respond.

'Sir? Excuse me, sir. I think we are acquainted.'

But Barley at first refused to hear. The voice was too nervous, too
tentative. He went on frowning at his *Informationen*. Must be another
tout, he was saying to himself. Another of those drug-pedlars or pimps.

'Sir?' Goethe repeated, as if he himself were now unsure.

Only now, won over by the stranger's insistence, did Barley reluctantly
raise his head.

'I think you are Mr. Scott Blair, sir, the distinguished publisher from
England.'

At which Barley finally persuaded himself to recognise the man addressing him, first with doubt then unfeigned but muted pleasure as he thrust
out his hand.

'Well, I'm damned,' he said quietly. 'Good God. The great Goethe, as I
live and breathe. We met at that disgraceful literary party. We were the
only two people sober. How are you?'

'Oh, I am *very* well,' Goethe said as his strained voice gathered courage.
But his hand when Barley shook it was slippery with sweat. 'I do not know
how I could be better at this moment. Welcome to Leningrad, Mr. Barley.
What a pity I have an appointment this afternoon. You can walk a little?
We can exchange ideas?' His voice barely fell. 'It is safest to keep moving,'
he explained.

He had grasped Barley's arm and was propelling him swiftly along the
embankment. His urgency had driven every tactical thought from Barley's

mind. Barley glanced at the bobbing figure beside him, at the pallor of his racked cheeks, the tracks of pain or fear or worry that ran down them. He saw the hunted eyes flicking nervously at every passing face. And his only instinct was to protect him: for Goethe's own sake and for Katya's.

'If we could walk for half an hour, we would see the battleship *Aurora*, which fired the blank shot to launch the Revolution. But the next revolution shall begin with a few gentle phrases of Bach. It is time. Do you agree?'

'And no conductor,' said Barley, with a grin.

'Or maybe some of that jazz you play so beautifully. Yes, yes! I have it! You shall announce our revolution by playing Lester Young on the saxophone. You have read the new Rybakov novel? Twenty years suppressed and therefore a great Russian masterpiece? It is a rape of time, I think.'

'It hasn't appeared in English yet.'

'You have read mine?' The thin hand had tightened on his arm. The pressed-in voice had fallen to a murmur.

'What I could understand of it, yes.'

'What do you think?'

'It's brave.'

'No more than that?'

'It's sensational. What I could understand of it. Great.'

'We recognised each other that night. It was magic. You know our Russian saying "One fisherman always sees another from afar"? We are fishermen. We shall feed the thousands with our truth.'

'Maybe we will at that,' said Barley doubtfully, and felt the gaunt head swing round to him. 'I have to discuss it with you a bit, Goethe. We've got one or two problems.'

'That's why you have come. I too. Thank you for coming to Leningrad. When will you publish? It must be soon. The writers here, they wait three, five years for publication even if they are not Rybakov. I can't do that. Russia has no time. Neither have I.'

A line of tugs drew by, a two-man scull flicked cheekily in their wake. Two lovers were embracing at the parapet. And in the shadow of the cathedral a young woman stood rocking a pram while she read from the book she was holding in her spare hand.

'When I didn't show up at the Moscow audio fair, Katya gave your manuscript to a colleague of mine,' Barley said cautiously.

'I know. She had to take a chance.'

'What you don't know is that the colleague couldn't find me when he got back to England. So he gave it to the authorities. People of discretion. Experts.'

Goethe turned sharply to Barley in alarm and the shadow of dismay spread swiftly over his fraught features. 'I do not *like* experts,' he said. 'They are our gaolers. I despise experts more than anyone on earth.'

'You're one yourself, aren't you?'

'Therefore I know! Experts are addicts. They solve nothing! They are servants of whatever system hires them. They perpetuate it. When we are tortured, we shall be tortured by experts. When we are hanged, experts will hang us. Did you not read what I wrote? When the world is destroyed, it will be destroyed not by its madmen but by the sanity of its experts and the superior ignorance of its bureaucrats. You have betrayed me.'

'Nobody's betrayed you,' Barley said angrily. 'The manuscript went astray, that's all. Our bureaucrats are not your bureaucrats. They've read it, they admire it, but they need to know more about you. They can't believe the message unless they can believe the source.'

'But do they want to publish it?'

'First of all they need to reassure themselves you're not a trick, and their best way to do that is to talk to you.'

Goethe was striding too fast, taking Barley with him. He was staring out ahead of him. Sweat was running down his temples.

'I'm an arts man, Goethe,' Barley said breathlessly to his averted face. 'All I know about physics is *Beowulf*, girls and warm beer. I'm out of my depth. So's Katya. If you want to go this road, go it with the experts and leave us out. That's what I came to tell you.'

They crossed a path and struck out across another segment of lawn. A group of schoolchildren broke ranks to let them through.

'You came to tell me that you refuse to publish me?'

'How *can* I publish you?' Barley retorted, in turn fired by Goethe's desperation. 'Even if we could knock the material into shape, what about Katya? She's your courier, remember? She's passed Soviet defence secrets to a foreign power. That's not exactly a laugh a minute over here. If they ever find out about the two of you, she'll be dead the day the first copy hits the stands. What sort of part is that for a publisher to play? Do you think I'm going to sit in London and press the button on the two of you here?'

Goethe was panting, but his eyes had ceased to scan the crowds and were turned to Barley.

'Listen to me,' Barley pleaded. 'Just hold on a minute. I understand. I really think I understand. You had a talent and it was put to unfair uses. You know all the ways the system stinks and you want to wash your soul. But you're not Christ and you're not Pecherin. You're out of court. If you want to kill yourself, that's your business. But you'll kill her too. And if you don't care who you kill, why should you care who you save?'

They were heading for a picnic place with chairs and tables cut from logs. They sat side by side and Barley spread his map. They bent over it, pretending to examine it together. Goethe was still measuring Barley's words, matching them against his purposes.

'There is only *now*,' he explained finally, his voice not above a murmur. 'There is no other dimension but *now*. In the past we have done everything badly for the sake of the future. Now we must do everything right for the sake of the present. To lose time is to lose everything. Our Russian history does not give us second chances. When we leap across an abyss, she does not give us the opportunity for a second step. And when we fail she gives us what we deserve: another Stalin, another Brezhnev, another purge, another ice age of terrified monotony. If the present momentum continues, I shall have been in the vanguard. If it stops or goes back, I shall be another statistic of our post-Revolutionary history.

'So will Katya,' Barley said.

Goethe's finger, unable to stay still, was travelling across the map. He glanced round him, then continued. 'We are in Leningrad, Barley, the cradle of our great Revolution. Nobody triumphs here without sacrifice. You said we needed an experiment in human nature. Why are you so shocked when I put your words into practice?'

'You got me wrong that day. I'm not the man you took me for. I'm the original useless mouth. You just met me when the wind was in the right direction.'

With a frightening control Goethe opened his hands and spread them palms downward on the map. 'You do not need to remind me that man is not equal to his rhetoric,' he said. 'Our new people talk about openness, disarmament, peace. So let them have their openness. And their disarmament. And their peace. Let us call their bluff and give them what they ask. And make sure that this time they cannot put the clock back.' He was standing, no longer able to bear the confinement of the table.

Barley stood beside him. 'Goethe, for God's sake. Take it easy.'

'To the devil with easy! It is easy that kills!' He began striding again. 'We do not break the curse of secrecy by passing our secrets from hand to hand like thieves! I have lived a great lie! And you tell me to keep it secret! How did the lie survive? By secrecy. How did our great vision crumble to this dreadful mess? By secrecy. How do you keep your own people ignorant of the insanity of your war plans? By secrecy. By keeping out the light. Show my work to your spies if that's what you must do. But publish me as well. That is what you promised and I shall believe your promise. I have dropped a notebook containing further chapters into your carrier bag. No doubt it answers many of the questions the idiots wish to put to me.'

The breeze of the river washed over Barley's heated face as they strode along. Glancing at Goethe's glistening features, he fancied he glimpsed traces of the hurt innocence that seemed to be the source of his outrage.

'I shall wish a book jacket that is only letters,' he announced. 'No drawing, please, no sensational design. You heard me?'

'We haven't even got a title,' Barley objected.

'You will please use my own name as the author. No evasions, no pseudonyms. To use a pseudonym is to invent another secret.'

'I don't even *know* your name.'

'They will know it. After what Katya told you, and with the new chapters, they will have no problem. Keep correct accounts. Every six months, please send the money to a deserving cause. Nobody shall say I did this for my own profit.'

Through the approaching trees the strains of martial music vied with the clatter of invisible trams.

'Goethe,' said Barley.

'What is the matter? Are you afraid?'

'Come to England. They'll smuggle you out. They're smart. Then you can tell the world everything you want. We'll rent the Albert Hall for you. Put you on television, radio – you name it. And when it's over, they'll give you a passport and money and you can live happily ever after in Australia.'

They had stopped again. Had Goethe heard? Had he understood? Still nothing stirred behind his unblinking stare. His eyes were fixed on Barley as if he were a distant spot upon a vast horizon.

'I am not a defector, Barley. I am a Russian, and my future is here, even if it is a short one. Will you publish me or not? I need to know.'

Buying time, Barley delved into his jacket pocket and pulled out Cy's worn paperback. 'I'm to give you this,' he said. 'A memento of our meeting. Their questions are bound into the text, together with an address in Finland you can write to and a phone number in Moscow with instructions on what to say when you call. If you'll do business with them direct, they've got all sorts of clever toys they can give you to make communication easier.' He placed it in Goethe's open hand and it remained there.

'Will you publish me? Yes or no.'

'How do they get hold of you? They have to know.'

'Tell them I can be reached through my publisher.'

'Take Katya out of the equation. Stay with the spies and keep away from her.'

Goethe's gaze had descended to Barley's suit and remained there, as if the sight of it troubled him. His sad smile was like a last holiday.

'You are wearing grey today, Barley. My father was sent to prison by grey men. He was shot by an old man who wore a grey uniform. It is the grey men who have ruined my beautiful profession. Take care or they will ruin yours too. Will you publish me or must I start again in my search for a decent human being?'

For a while Barley could not answer. His mechanisms of evasion had run out.

'If I can get control of the material, and find a way through it to a book, I'll publish you,' he replied.

'I asked you, yes or no.'

Promise him anything he asks within reason, Paddy had said. But what was reason? 'All right,' he replied. 'Yes.'

Goethe handed Barley back the paperback book and Barley in a daze returned it to his pocket. They embraced and Barley smelt sweat and stale tobacco smoke and felt again the desperate strength of their farewell in Peredelkino. As abruptly as Goethe had seized him, so he now released him and with another nervous glance round him set off quickly towards the trolleybus stop. And as Barley watched him he noticed how the old couple from the outdoor café was watching his departure too, standing in the shadow of the dark blue trees.

Barley sneezed, then started sneezing seriously. Then really sneezed. He walked back into the park, his face buried in his handkerchief while he shook his shoulders and sneezed and shook again.

'Why, *Scott!*' J. P. Henziger exclaimed, with the overbright enthusiasm of a busy man kept waiting, as he snatched back the door of the largest bedroom in the Hotel Europe. 'Scott, this is a day when we discover who our friends are. Come in, please. What kept you? Say hullo to Maisie.'

He was mid-forties, muscular and prehensile, but he had the kind of ugly friendly face that Barley would normally have warmed to instantly. He wore an elephant hair round one wrist and a gold-link bracelet round the other. Half-moons of sweat blackened his denim armpits. Wicklow appeared behind him and quickly closed the door.

Twin beds, draped in olive counterpanes, commanded the centre of the room. In one of them languished Mrs. Henziger, a thirty-five-year-old kitten without her make-up, her combed-out tresses spread tragically over her freckled shoulders. A man in a black suit hovered uneasily at her side. He wore liver-coloured spectacles. A medical practitioner's case lay open on the bed. Henziger continued vamping for the microphones.

'Scott, I want you to meet Dr. Pete Bernstorf from the US Consulate General here in Leningrad, a fine physician. We are indebted to him. Maisie is improving fast. We are indebted to Mr. Wicklow also. Leonard fixed the hotel, the tour people, the pharmacy. How was your day?'

'One bloody long laugh,' Barley blurted, and for a moment the script threatened to go badly wrong.

Barley tossed the carrier bag on to the bed and with it the rejected paperback book from his jacket pocket. With shaking hands he pulled off his jacket, tore the microphone harness out of his shirt and flung it after the bag and the book. He reached behind him into his waistband and, brushing aside Wicklow's offer of assistance, extracted the grey recording box from the small of his back and threw that on the bed as well, so that Maisie let out a stifled 'shit' and moved her legs quickly to one side. Marching to the washbasin, he emptied his whisky flask into a toothmug, hugging his other arm across his chest as if he had been shot. Then he drank and went on drinking, oblivious to the perfect drill unfolding round him.

Henziger, light as a cat for all his bulk, grabbed the carrier bag, picked out the notebook and shoved it at Bernstorf who spirited it into his medical case among the phials and instruments, where it mysteriously disappeared.

Henziger passed him the paperback, which also vanished. Wicklow swept up the recorder and harness. They too went into the case, which Bernstorf snapped shut while he issued departing instructions to the patient: no solids for forty-eight hours, Mrs. Henziger, tea, a piece of brown bread if you must, make sure you complete the course of antibiotics whether or not you feel better. He had not finished before Henziger chimed in.

'And Doctor, if ever you are in Boston, and you need anything, because I mean *anything*, here's my card and here's my promise and here's . . .'

Toothmug in hand, Barley remained facing the washbasin, glowering in the mirror as the Good Samaritan's case made its journey to the door.

Of all his nights in Russia and, come to think of it, of all his nights anywhere in the world, this was Barley's worst.

Henziger had heard that a cooperative restaurant had just opened in Leningrad, cooperative being the new codeword for private. Wicklow had tracked it down and reported it full, but rejection for Henziger was challenge. By dint of heavy telephoning and heavier tipping, an extra table was laid for them, three foot from the worst and noisiest gypsy opera Barley ever hoped to hear.

And there they now sat, celebrating Mrs. Henziger's miraculous recovery. The mewing of the singers was amplified by electronic bullhorns. There was no remission between numbers.

And all round them sat the Russia that the slumbering puritan in Barley had long hated but never seen: the not-so-secret czars of capitalism, the industrial parvenus and conspicuous consumers, the Party fat-cats and racketeers, their jewelled women reeking of Western perfumes and Russian deodorant, the waiters doting on the richest tables. The singers' frightful voices rose, the music rose to drown them, the voices rose again and Henziger's voice rose above them all.

'Scott, I want you to know something,' he bellowed to Barley, leaning excitedly across the table. 'This little country is on the move. I smell hope here, I smell change, I smell commerce. And we in Potomac are buying ourselves a piece of it. I'm proud.' But his voice had been taken away from him by the band. 'Proud,' his lips repeated soundlessly to a million gypsy decibels.

And the trouble was, Henziger was a nice fellow and Maisie was a sport, which made it worse. As the agony dragged on, Barley entered the blessed state of deafness. Inside the cacophony he discovered his own safe room. From its arrow-slit windows his secret self stared into the white Leningrad night. Where have you gone, Goethe? he asked. Who stands in for her when she isn't there? Who darns your black socks and cooks your washed-out soup for you while you drag her by the hair along your noble altruistic path to self-destruction?

Somehow without his being aware of it they must have returned to the hotel, for he woke to discover himself propped on Wicklow's arm among the Finnish alcoholics stumbling shamefacedly round the lobby.

'Great party,' he told anyone who would hear him. 'Splendid band. Thank you for coming to Leningrad.'

But as Wicklow patiently hauled him up to bed the undrunk part of Barley glanced over his shoulder, down the wide staircase. And in the darkness near the entrance, he saw Katya, seated with her legs crossed, her perhaps-bag on her lap. She was wearing a pinched black jacket. A white silk scarf was knotted under her chin, and her face was pressed towards him with that tense smile she had, sad and hopeful, open to love.

But as his gaze cleared he saw her say something saucy out of the corner of her mouth to the porter, and he realised she was just another Leningrad tart looking for a trick.

And next day, to the fanfare of the most discreet of British trumpets, our hero came home.

Ned wanted no display, no Americans and certainly no Clive, but he was determined on a gesture, so we drove to Gatwick and, having posted Brock at the Arrivals barrier with a card saying 'Potomac', we installed ourselves in a hospitality lounge that the Service shared uneasily with the Foreign Office amid endless argument about who had drunk the gin.

We waited, the plane was delayed. Clive phoned from Grosvenor Square to ask 'Has he arrived, Palfrey?' as if he half expected him to stay in Russia.

Another half-hour passed before Clive phoned again and this time Ned himself took the call. He had scarcely slammed the phone down before the door opened and Wicklow slipped in grinning like a choirboy but contriving at the same time to shoot his eyes in warning.

Seconds after him, enter Barley looking like his own surveillance photographs, except that he was white-faced. 'Buggers cheered!' he blurted before Brock had got the door shut. 'That prissy captain with his Surrey vowels! I'll kill the swine.'

While Barley stormed on, Wicklow discreetly explained the cause of his distress. Their charter flight out of Leningrad had been occupied by a delegation of young British traders whom Barley had arbitrarily branded yuppies of the vilest sort, which by the sound of them they were. Several were drunk by the time they boarded, the rest were quick to catch up. They had not been more than a few minutes in the air when the captain, who in Barley's view was the provocateur of the incident, announced that the plane had left Soviet airspace. A roar went up while the air hostesses scampered up and down the aisle doling out champagne. Then they all broke into 'Rule, Britannia!'

'Give me Aeroflot every time,' Barley raged at the assembled faces. 'I'm going to write to the airline. I'm going to – '

'You're going to do nothing of the kind,' Ned kindly interrupted him. 'You're going to let us make an enormous fuss of you. You can have your tantrum later.'

As he said this, he went on shaking Barley's hand until Barley eventually smiled.

'Where's Walt?' he asked, peering round.

'I'm afraid he's off on a job,' said Ned but Barley had already lost interest. His hand trembled violently as he drank and he wept a bit, which Ned assured me was par for the course for joes coming back from the field.

11

T he pattern of the next three days, like the wreck of a smashed aeroplane, was afterwards minutely examined for technical faults, though few were found.

After his outburst at the airport Barley entered the bright stage, smiling a lot to himself on the car journey, greeting familiar landmarks with his habitual shy affection. He also had a sneezing fit.

As soon as we reached the Knightsbridge house, where Ned was determined Barley should spend the night before returning to his flat, he dumped his luggage in the hall, flung his arms round Miss Coad and, declaring his undying love for her, presented her with a splendid lynx-fur hat which neither Wicklow nor anyone else could afterwards remember him buying.

At this point I removed myself. Clive had commanded me to the twelfth floor for what he termed 'a crucial discussion', though it turned out that what he really wanted was to tap me. Was Scott Blair nervous? Was he above himself? How was he, Palfrey? Johnny was there, listening but scarcely speaking. Bob, he said, had been recalled to Langley for consultations. I told them what I had seen, no less, certainly no more. Both were puzzled by Barley's tears.

'You mean he said he was going back?' said Clive.

The same night Ned dined with Barley alone. This was not yet the debriefing. It was the coming down. The tapes reveal Barley in staccato mood and his voice a key higher than usual. By the time I joined them for coffee he was talking about Goethe but with artificial objectivity.

Goethe had aged, had lost his bounce.

Goethe was really shot up.

Goethe seemed to have stopped drinking. He was getting his highs elsewhere. 'You should have seen his hands, Harry, shaking over that map.'

You should have seen yours, I thought, when you were drinking champagne at the airport.

He referred to Katya only once that evening, also in a deliberately unemotional way. I think he was determined we should know that he had no feelings that were not ours to control. That was not deviousness on Barley's part. With the exception of what we had taught him, he was incapable of it. It was his fear of where his feelings might end up if they were no longer anchored to us.

Katya was more scared for her kids than she was for herself, he said, again with studied detachment. He supposed most mothers were. On the other hand her children were the cyphers for the world she wished to save. So in a sense what she was doing was a kind of absolute version of mother love, don't you agree, Nedsky?

Ned agreed. Nothing harder than to experiment with one's own children, Barley, he said.

But a marvellous girl, Barley insisted, now in patronising mode. A bit too hell-bent for Barley's personal taste these days, but if you liked your women to have the moral fibre of Joan of Arc, then Katya was for you. And she was beautiful. No question. A bit too haywire to be classical, if we knew what he meant, but undeniably striking.

We couldn't tell him we had been admiring photographs of her for the last week, so we took his word for it.

At eleven, complaining of the time difference, Barley flopped. We stood in the hall watching him haul himself upstairs to bed.

'Anyway it was good stuff, was it?' he asked as he clung to the banister and grinned down at us through his little round spectacles. 'The new notebook he gave us. You've looked at it?'

'The boffins are burning the midnight oil over it at this moment,' Ned replied. He could hardly say they were fighting over it like cats and dogs.

'Experts are addicts,' Barley said, with another grin.

But he remained on the half-landing swaying, while he seemed to search for an appropriate exit line.

'Somebody ought to do a bit of work on those body microphones, Nedsky. Bloody saddle-sores all over my back. The next bloke you send had better have a thicker hide. Where's Uncle Bob, by the by?'

'He sends love,' said Ned. 'Business is brisk at the moment. He hopes to catch up with you soon.'

'Is he out hunting with Walt?'

'If I knew I wouldn't tell you,' said Ned, and we all laughed.

That night, I remember, I received a particularly irrelevant phone call

from Margaret, my wife, about a parking ticket she had picked up in
Basingstoke – in her view, unfairly.

'It was *my* space, I had put my indicator out when this bloody little man
in a brand-new Jaguar, a white one, with slicked black hair – '

Unwisely I laughed, and suggested to her that Jaguars with slicked black
hair had no special dispensation at parking meters. Humour was never
Margaret's strong point.

The next morning, the Sunday, Clive again required my attendance, first
to pump me about the previous night, then to hear me 'talk turkey' with
Johnny on such esoteric matters as whether Barley could legally be styled
an employee of our Service and, if so, whether by taking our shilling he
had renounced certain rights – his right to legal representation in the event
of a dispute with us, for instance. I was Delphic, which annoyed them, but
basically I said the answer was 'yes'. Yes, he had renounced those rights.
Or more exactly, yes, we could gull him into thinking he had, whether he
had in law or not.

Johnny, if I have not mentioned it already, had graduated from Harvard
Law School, so for once it was not necessary for Langley to send us a
chorus of legal advisers.

In the afternoon, Barley being restless and the day sunny, we drove to
Maidenhead and walked the towpath beside the Thames. By the time we
returned, I suppose you could say Barley had been debriefed: for what with
no questions coming down to us from our analysts, and his operational
encounters already covered by technical means, there was really very little
left to debrief him about.

Was Barley affected by our worries? We were as jolly as we could
be, but I couldn't help wondering whether the atmosphere of menacing
stagnation was getting through to him. Or perhaps his feelings were such
a maelstrom of confusion and anticlimax that he merely lumped us in with
them.

On the Sunday night we ate supper together in Knightsbridge and Barley
was so mild-mannered and reposed that Ned decided – as I would have
done – that it was safe to send him back to Hampstead.

His flat was in a Victorian block off East Heath Road and the static
surveillance post was situated directly below it, manned by a bright
young Service couple. The rightful tenants had been temporarily resettled
elsewhere. Around eleven, the couple reported that Barley was in his flat
alone but prowling. They could hear but not see him. Ned had drawn the
line at video. He was doing a lot of talking to himself, they said, and when
he opened his mail, curses and groans came over the monitors.

Ned was unbothered. He had read Barley's mail already and knew it
contained no horrors beyond the usual.

Around one a.m., Barley rang his daughter Anthea in Grantham.

'What's an ig?'

'An Eskimo house without a loo. How was Moscow?'

'What do you get if you cross the Atlantic with the *Titanic?*'

'About halfway. How was Moscow?'

'What do you get if you cross a sheep with a kangaroo?'

'I asked you how Moscow was.'

'A woolly jumper. How's your boring husband?'

'Asleep, trying to be. What became of the cream bun you took to Lisbon?'

'Rained off.'

'I thought she was permanent.'

'She is. I'm not.'

Barley next telephoned two women, the first a former wife over whom he had retained visiting rights, the second not previously listed. Neither could oblige him at such short notice, not least because they were in bed with their men.

At one-forty the couple reported that Barley's bedroom lights were out. Ned gratefully went to sleep, but I was already in my little flat and sleep was the last thing in my mind. Memories of Hannah were teeming through my head, mixed with images of Barley in the Knightsbridge house. I remembered his falsely casual way of talking about Katya and her children and I kept comparing it with my own repeated denials of my love for Hannah, back in the days when it endangered me. *Hannah looks a bit down in the mouth*, some innocent would remark every five minutes of my day. *Is that husband of hers leading her a dance or what?* And I'd smile. *I gather he likes to knock her around a bit*, I'd say, with exactly that same superior tone of detachment that I had heard in Barley, while the cancerous secret fires inside me ate away my heart.

Next morning Barley went to his office to resume work, but it was agreed that he would drop by the Knightsbridge house on his way home from work in case there were points to clear up. This was not quite the loose arrangement that it sounds, for Ned by now was locked in a serious shoot-out with the twelfth floor, and it was likely that by evening he would either have to give ground or face a full-scale battle with the mandarins.

But by then Barley had disappeared.

According to Brock's watchers Barley left his office in Norfolk Street a little earlier than expected, at four-forty-three, carrying his saxophone in its case. Wicklow, who was in Abercrombie & Blair's back office typing up an account of the Moscow trip, was unaware of his departure. But a pair of Brock's boys in jeans followed Barley west down the Strand and, when he changed his mind, crossed with him into Soho where he went to earth in an afternoon watering-hole frequented by publishers and agents. He spent twenty minutes there, emerged still carrying his saxophone and looking perfectly steady. He hailed a cab, and one of the boys was close enough to hear him give the address of the safe house. The same boy bleeped Brock, who called Ned in Knightsbridge to say 'Stand by, your guest is on his way.' I was elsewhere, fighting other wars.

Thus far nobody was to blame, except that neither of the boys thought to take the cab's number, an oversight that later cost them dear. It was rush hour. A trip between the Strand and Knightsbridge could take an age. It was not till seven-thirty that Ned gave up waiting and, worried but not yet alarmed, returned to the Russia House.

At nine when nobody had any sensible suggestions Ned reluctantly declared an in-house alert, which by definition excluded the Americans. As usual, Ned was operational cool. Perhaps subconsciously he had steeled himself for such a crisis, for Brock later commented that he slipped into a prepared routine. He did not inform Clive, but as he explained to me later, telling Clive in the present poisoned atmosphere was as good as sending a singing telegram to Langley.

Ned drove himself first to Bloomsbury where the Service listeners owned a run of cellars under Russell Square. He used a car from the pool and must have driven like the wind. The head duty listener was Mary, a compulsive eater of forty, rose-faced and spinsterish. Her only known loves were unattainable voices. Ned handed her a list of Barley's contacts, compiled by the departed Walter from intercepts and watch reports. Could Mary cover them immediately? Like now?

Mary damn well could not. 'Stretching regulations is one thing, Ned. A dozen illegal taps is completely another, can't you even *see*?'

Ned might have argued that the extra numbers were covered by the existing Home Office warrant but he didn't bother. He phoned me in Pimlico just as I was uncorking the bottle of burgundy with which I proposed to console myself after a dirty day. It's a rather awful little flat and I had the window open to get out the smell of frying. I remember closing the window while we talked.

Phone warrants are in theory signed by the Home Secretary or in his absence by his Minister. But there is a trick to this, for he has provided the Legal Adviser with a delegated authority to be used only in emergency and accounted for in writing within twenty-four hours. I scribbled out my authority, signed it, turned off the gas – I was still boiling the Brussels sprouts – clambered into a cab and twenty minutes later handed the authority to Mary. Within the hour the telephones of Barley's twelve contacts were covered.

What was I thinking as I did all this? Did I think Barley had done away with himself? No, I did not. His concerns were for the living. The last thing he wished to do was leave them to their fate.

But I considered the possibility that he had broken ranks, and I suppose my worst fantasy was of Barley loudly clapping as the Aeroflot pilot announced that his plane had re-entered Soviet airspace.

In the meantime, on Ned's orders, Brock had persuaded the police to put out an emergency call for any metropolitan cab-driver who had picked up a tall man with a saxophone on the corner of Old Compton Street at five-thirty, destination Knightsbridge but probably changed en route. Yes, a tenor saxophone – a baritone sax was twice the size. By ten they had their man. The cab had started out for Knightsbridge but at Trafalgar Square Barley had indeed changed his mind and asked to be driven to Harley Street. The fare came to three pounds. Barley gave the driver a fiver and told him to keep the change.

By a small miracle of quick thinking, assisted by the late Walter's records, Ned made the connection – Andrew George Macready, alias Andy, former jazz trumpeter and listed Barley contact, had been admitted to the Sisters of Mercy Hospice, Harley Street, three weeks ago, see scrawled letter intercept in pencil, Mrs. Macready to Hampstead, serial 47A, and Walter's lapidary comment on the minute sheet: *Macready is Barley's guru on mortality.*

I still remember how I clung to the grab handle of Ned's car with both hands. We arrived at the hospice to be told Macready was under sedation. Barley had sat with him for an hour and they had managed to exchange a few words. The night matron, who had just come on duty, had taken Barley a cup of tea, no milk or sugar. Barley had topped it up with whisky from a flask. He had offered the matron a dram but she declined. He asked her whether he might 'play old Andy a couple of his favourite numbers'. He played softly for ten minutes exactly, which was what she had allowed him. Several of the nuns had gathered in the corridor to listen, and one of them recognised the tune as Basie's 'Blue and Sentimental'. He left his phone number and a cheque for a hundred pounds 'for the croupier' on a brass collection plate at the door. The matron had told him he could come back whenever he wanted.

'You're not police, are you?' she asked me unhappily as we made for the door.

'Good Lord, no. Whyever should we be?'

She shook her head and would not answer, but I thought I knew what she had seen in him. A man in flight, hiding from his own actions.

Using the car telephone as we sped back to the Russia House Ned ordered Brock to list all clubs, concert halls and pubs in the London area where jazz was being played tonight. He should distribute as many watchers as he could muster over these events.

For good measure I added the lawyer's ten cents worth. In no circumstances was Brock or any watcher physically to restrain Barley or close with him. Whatever other rights Barley might have waived, he had not waived his right to defend himself and he was a powerful man.

We were settling for a long wait when Mary the head listener rang, this time all sweetness and oil. 'Ned, I think you ought to get round here a tiny bit fastish. Some of your eggs have hatched.'

We tear back to Russell Square, Ned leaning the car against the curves at sixty miles an hour.

In her cellar lair Mary received us with the doting smile she reserved for moments of disaster. A favourite girl called Pepsi stood beside her, dressed in green overalls. A tape recorder turned on the desk.

'Who the hell's *that* at this hour?' a stentorian voice demanded and I recognised immediately Barley's formidable Aunt Pandora, the Sacred Cow whom I had entertained to lunch. Hiatus while coins were fed into the machine. Followed by Barley's courteous voice.

'I'm rather afraid I've had it, Pan. I'm kissing the firm goodbye.'

'Don't talk cock,' Aunt Pandora retorted. 'Some fool girl's been getting at you again.'

'I'm serious, Pan. This time it's for real. I had to tell you.'

'You're *always* serious. That's why you're such a fraud pretending to be frivolous.'

'I'm going to talk to Guy in the morning.' Guy Solomons, family solicitor, listed Barley contact. 'Wicklow, the new man, can take it over. He's a tough little runt and he's a fast learner.'

'Did you trace the phone box?' Ned asked Mary as Barley rang off.

'No time,' said Mary proudly.

From the tape we heard the renewed ring of a phone. Barley again. 'Reggie? I'm having a blow tonight. Come and play.'

Mary handed us a piece of card on which she had written, *Canon Reginald Cowan, drummer and clerk in holy orders.*

'Can't,' said Reggie. 'Bloody Confirmation class.'

'Ditch them,' said Barley.

'Can't. Buggers are here with me now.'

'We need you, Reggie. Old Andy's dying.'

'So are we all. All the bloody time.'

As the tape was ending, Brock came through on a live call from the Russia House asking for Ned urgently. His watchers had reported that Barley had looked in on his Soho drinking club an hour ago, drunk five whiskies then moved on to the Noah's Arch at King's Cross.

'Noah's *Arch?* You mean Ark.'

'Arch. It's an arch under the railway line. Noah's an eight-foot West Indian. Barley's joined the band.'

'Alone?'

'So far.'

'What sort of place?'

'Diner and boozer. Sixty tables, stage, brick walls, whores, the usual.' Brock thought all pretty girls were whores.

'How full?' said Ned.

'Two-thirds and rising.'

'What's he playing?'

' "Lover Man", Duke Ellington.'

'How many exits?'

'One.'

'Put together one team of three men and park them at a table near the door. If he leaves, straddle him but don't touch him. Call Resources and tell them I want Ben Lugg to get his cab over to the Noah's Arch immediately and wait with his flag down. He'll know what to do.' Lugg was the Service's tame cabby. 'Are there any public phones in the club?'

'Two.'

'Have them occupied till I get there. Has he seen you?'

'No.'

'Don't let him. What's across the road?'

'A launderette.'

'Is it open?'

'No.'

'Wait for me in front of it.' He swung round on Mary, who was still smiling. 'There are two phones at the Noah's Arch, King's Cross,' he said, speaking very slowly. 'Have them faulted *now*. If the management's got its own line, have that faulted too. *Now*. I don't care how short-staffed the engineers are, fault them *now*. If there are phone boxes in the street outside, fault the lot. *Now*.'

We abandoned the Service car and hailed a cab. Brock was waiting as ordered in the doorway of the launderette. Ben Lugg was parked at the curbside. Tickets were five ninety-five at the door. Ned led me past the watchers' table without a glance and shoved his way to the front.

Nobody was dancing. The band's front line was taking a break. Barley was standing centre stage in front of a gold chair, playing with the gentle backing of the double bass and drums. A brick arch made a sound chamber over him. He was still wearing his publishing suit and seemed to have forgotten to remove his jacket. Rotating coloured lights wandered over him, occasionally closing on his face which was running sweat. His expression was nerveless and remote. He was holding the long notes and I knew they were a requiem for Andy and for whoever else was occupying his beleaguered mind. A couple of girls had sat themselves in the band seats and were staring at him with unblinking eyes. A line of beers was also awaiting his attention. Beside him stood the immense Noah with his arms folded across his chest, listening with his head down. The piece ended. Deliberately and tenderly, as if he were dressing a friend's wound, Barley cleaned out his sax and laid it to rest in its case. Noah did not allow applause but there was a scuffling noise while everyone snapped their fingers and there were calls of 'encore' but Barley didn't bother with them. He drained a couple of the beers, gave a wave round and picked his way delicately through the crowd to the door. We went after him and as we stepped into the street Ben Lugg drew alongside with his flag up.

'Mo's,' Barley ordered as he flopped into the back seat. He had another flask of Scotch from somewhere and was unscrewing the cap. 'Hullo, Harry. How's love at a distance?'

'Great, thanks. I recommend it.'

'Where on earth's Mo's?' Ned asked as he settled beside him and I parked myself on the jump seat.

'Tufnell Park. Underneath the Falmouth Arms.'

'Good sound?' Ned asked.

'The best.'

But it was not Barley's false cheerfulness that alarmed me. It was the remoteness of him, the deadness of his eyes, the way he kept himself confined inside the fastness of his English courtesy.

Mo was a blonde in her fifties and she spent a long time kissing Barley before she would let us sit at her table. Barley played blues and Mo wanted him to stay, I think for the night, but Barley could stay nowhere long, so we went to a music pizza house in Islington where he played another solo and Ben Lugg came in with us to have a cup of tea and a listen. Ben was a boxer in his day and still talked about the fight game. From Islington we crossed the river to the Elephant to hear a black group playing soul in a bus garage. It was four-fifteen but Barley was showing no sign of sleep; he preferred to sit with the group drinking spiked cocoa out of pint-sized china mugs. When we at last gentled him towards Ben's cab, the two girls from Noah's reappeared from nowhere and sat themselves either side of him in the back seat.

'Now then, you girls,' said Ben while Ned and I waited on the pavement. 'Hop it.'

'Stay where you are, I should,' Barley advised them.

'It's not your cab, dears. It's this bloke's' – indicating Ned – 'now piss off, like good girls.'

Barley swung his fist at Ben's head, which was adorned with a black Homburg hat. Ben blocked the blow like a man waving away a cobweb, and in the same movement drew Barley carefully out of the cab and handed him over to Ned, who took him equally carefully in an arm-lock.

Still in his Homburg, Ben disappeared into the back of the cab and came out with a girl in each hand.

'Why don't we all get a bit of fresh air?' Ned suggested while Ben gave the girls a tenner each to get lost.

'Good idea,' said Barley.

So we crossed the river in slow procession, with Brock's watchers bringing up the rear and Ben Lugg's cab crawling along behind us. A dirty brown dawn was rising over dockland.

'Sorry about that,' said Barley after a while. 'No harm done, is there, Nedsky?'

'None that I know of,' said Ned.

'Be alert,' Barley advised. 'Your Country Needs Lerts. Right, Nedsky? Just felt like making a spot of music,' he explained to me. 'You a musical man, Harry? Chum of mine used to play to his girl over the phone. Only piano, mind, not sax, but he said it did the trick. You could try it out on your missus.'

'We're leaving for America tomorrow,' said Ned.

Barley took the news conversationally. 'Nice for you. Nice time of year. Country looking at its best, I'd say.'

'It's nice for you too, actually,' said Ned. 'We thought we'd take you along.'

'Casual, is it?' Barley asked. 'Or better pack a dinner jacket to be on the safe side?'

12

We flew to the island in a small plane, arriving at dusk. The small plane belonged to a grand American corporation. Nobody said who owned the island. It was narrow and wooded, its middle sagged into the sea and its ends were propped up by conical peaks, so that my impression from the air was of a Bedouin tent collapsing into the Atlantic. I put it at two miles long. We saw the New England mansion and its grounds at one end, and the tiny white dock at the other, though I learned later that the mansion was called a summer house because nobody went there in winter. It had been built at the turn of the century by a rich Bostonian, in the days when such people called themselves rusticators. We felt the wings rock and smelt salt sea through the rattling cabin windows. We saw sunspots flicking over the waves like searchlights at a tattoo, and cormorants warring in the wind. We saw a light-beacon on the mainland to the west. We had been following the coast of Maine for fifty-eight minutes by my watch. The trees came up either side of us, the sky vanished, and suddenly we were bouncing and swinging along a grass avenue with Randy and his boys waiting with a jeep at the end of it. Randy was wholesome as only privileged Americans can be. He wore a windcheater and a tie. I felt I knew his mother.

'I'm your host here, gentlemen, for as long as you elect to stay, and welcome to our island.' He shook Barley's hand first. They must have shown him photographs. 'Mr. Brown, sir, this is a real honour. Ned? Harry?'

'Jolly nice of you,' said Barley.

The pine trees, as we wound down the hillside, stood black against the
sea. The boys followed in a second car.

'You gentlemen fly British? Mrs. Thatcher really got a hold of that line!'
said Randy.

'Time she went down with the ship,' Barley said.

Randy laughed as if laughing were something he'd learned on the
course. Brown was Barley's workname for the trip. Even his passport,
which Ned carried, said that he was Brown.

We bumped across a causeway to the gatehouse. The gates opened and
closed behind us. We were on our own headland. At the top of it stood the
mansion lit by arc-lights hidden in the bushes. Lawns and wind-burned
shrubs fell away from it to either side. The posts of a broken jetty stepped
precariously out to sea. Randy parked the jeep and, taking Barley's luggage, led us along an illuminated path between hydrangeas to a boat-
house. On our crossing to Boston, Barley had dozed and drunk and
groaned at the film. On our small plane he had frowned at the New
England landscape as if its beauty troubled him. But once we landed he
seemed to re-enter his own world.

'Mr. Brown, sir, my orders are to accommodate you in the bridal suite,'
said Randy.

'Can't think of anywhere nicer, old boy,' said Barley politely.

'You really *say* that, Mr. Brown: *old boy?*'

Randy ushered us through a stone-flagged hall to a captain's cabin. The
style was designer homestead. A reproduction brass bed stood in a corner,
a reproduction scrubwood writing desk at the window. Doubtful ship's
fittings hung on the walls. In the alcove where the all-American kitchen
was, Barley identified the refrigerator, pulled it open and peered hopefully
inside.

'Mr. Brown likes a bottle of Scotch in his room of an evening, Randy. If
you've such a thing in your locker he'd be grateful.'

The summer house was a museum of golden childhoods. In the porch,
honey-coloured croquet mallets lay propped against a dusty goat-cart
laden with lobster buoys gathered from the beach. There were smells of
beeswax and leather. In the hall, portraits of young men and women in
broad hats hung beside primitive paintings of whalers. We followed Randy
up a wide polished staircase, Barley trailing behind us. On each landing,
arched windows bordered with stained glass made jewelled gateways to
the sea. We entered a corridor of blue bedrooms. The largest was reserved
for Clive. From our balconies we could look down the gardens to the
boat-house and across the sea to the mainland. The dusk was turning to
dark.

In a white-raftered dining room, a Langley vestal managed not to look
at us while she served Maine lobster and white wine.

While we ate, Randy explained the rules of the house. 'No fraternising
with the staff, please, gentlemen, just a good morning and hullo. Anything

needs saying to them, best let me say it for you. The guards are for your convenience and safety, gentlemen, but we would like you to remain within the confines of the property. Please. Thank you.'

Dinner and speeches over, Randy took Ned to the communications room and I walked Barley back to the boat-house. A fierce wind was ripping over the gardens. As we passed in and out of the light-cones Barley seemed to be smiling into it recklessly. Boys with handsets watched us pass.

'How about chess?' I asked him as we reached his door.

I wished I could see his face more clearly but I had lost it, just as I had lost his mood. I felt a pat on the arm as he wished me goodnight. His door opened and closed again, but not before I had glimpsed the spectral figure of a sentry standing not two yards from us in the darkness.

'A wise lawyer, a fine officer,' Russell Sheriton advised me next morning in a reverential murmur, knowing I was neither, as his strong, soft palms enveloped my hand. 'One of the true greats. Harry, how are you doing?'

Little had changed in him since his tour of duty in London: the rings beneath the eyes a little doggier, a little sadder, the blue suit a size or two larger, the same white-shirted paunch. The same mortician's aftershave, six years on, anointed the Agency's newest head of Soviet operations.

A group of his young men stood respectfully apart from him, clutching their travel bags and looking like stranded passengers at an airport. Clive and Bob were mounted either side of him like cohorts. Bob looked older by ten years. A chastened smile had replaced his old-world self-assurance. He greeted us too effusively, as if he had been warned to stay away from us.

The Island Conference, as it euphemistically became known, was about to begin.

There is an underlying pleasantness to the events of the next days, an air of good men going about their business, which I am in danger of forgetting as I recall the rest.

It is the hardest point for me to make, yet I owe it to Barley to try, for he never took against our hosts – he never blamed them for anything that happened to him, then or later. He could grumble about Americans in general, but no sooner had he met them individually than he spoke of them as decent fellows all. There was not a man among them he wouldn't have been happy to swap a drink with any evening at the local, if we'd had one. And of course Barley always saw the force of any argument that was directed against him, just as he was always vastly impressed by other people's industry.

And my goodness, were they industrious! If numbers, money and sheer endeavour alone could have produced intelligence, the Agency would have had it by the cartload – except that, alas, the human head is not a cart, and there is such a thing as unintelligence as well.

And how deeply they yearned to be loved! – and Barley warmed immediately to their need. Even as they tore into him, they needed to be loved. And by Barley, too! Just as to this day they need to be loved for all their staged putsches, destabilisations and wild adventures against The Enemy Out There.

Yet it was this very mystery of good hearts turned inside out that gave our week its underlying terror.

Years ago I talked to a man who had been flogged, an English mercenary who was doing us a few favours in Africa and needed paying off. What he remembered most was not the lash but the orange juice they gave him afterwards. He remembers being helped back to his hut, he remembers being laid face down on the straw. But what he really remembers is the glass of fresh orange juice that a warder set at his head, then crouched beside him, waiting patiently, till he was strong enough to drink some. Yet it was this same warder who had flogged him.

We too had our glasses of orange juice. And we had our decent warders, even if they were disguised behind headsets and a surface animosity that quickly melted before Barley's warmth. Within a day of our arrival, the same guards with whom we were forbidden to fraternise were tiptoeing at any odd moment in and out of Barley's boat-house, stealing a Coke or a Scotch from him before slipping back to their posts. They sensed he was that kind of man. And as Americans they were fascinated by his celebrity.

There was one old hand called Edgar, an ex-Marine, who gave him quite a run for his money at chess. Barley, I learned later, got his name and address out of him, against every known canon of the trade, so that they could play a contest by post 'when all this is over'.

Not only warders either. In Sheriton's chorus of young men, as in Sheriton himself there was a moderation that was like an even beat of sanity against the hysterical highs and lows of those whom Sheriton himself dubbed collectively the egomaniacs.

But that, I suppose, is the tragedy of great nations. So much talent bursting to be used, so much goodness longing to come out. Yet all so miserably spoken for, that sometimes we could scarcely believe it was America speaking to us at all.

But it was. The lash was real.

The interrogations took place in the billiards room. The wooden floor had been painted dark red for dancing and the billiards table replaced by a ring of chairs. But an ivory scorer and a row of initialled cue-cases still lined the wall, and the long downlight made a pool at the centre where Barley was obliged to sit. Ned fetched him from the boat-house.

'Mr. Brown, sir, I am proud to shake your hand and I have just decided that my name for the duration of our relationship is Haggarty,' Sheriton declared. 'I took one look at you, I felt Irish. Don't ask me why.' He was leading Barley at a good pace across the room. 'Most of all, I wish to congratulate you. You have all the virtues: memory, observation, British grit, saxophone.'

This in one hypnotic flow while Barley grinned sheepishly and allowed himself to be settled in the place of honour.

But Ned already sat stiffly, arms folded across his chest, and Clive, though he was of the circle, had managed to paint himself out of the picture. He sat among Sheriton's young men and had pushed his chair back till they hid him.

Sheriton remained standing before Barley and was talking down at him, even when his words said he was addressing someone else. 'Clive, would you permit me to bombard Mr. Brown with some impertinent questions? Ned, will you tell Mr. Brown, please, that he is in the United States of America and that if he doesn't care to answer anything he needn't, because his silence will be taken as clear evidence of his guilt?'

'Mr. Brown can look after himself,' Barley said – but still grinning, still not quite believing in the tension.

'He can? That's great, Mr. Brown! Because for the next couple of days that's exactly what we hope you'll do!'

Sheriton went to the sideboard and poured himself some coffee and came back with it. His voice struck the calmer note of common sense. 'Mr. Brown, we are buying a Picasso, okay? Everybody round this room is buying the same Picasso. Blue, saignant, well-done, what the fuck? There are about three people in the world who understand it. But when you get to the bottom line there's one question counts. Did Picasso paint it, or did J. P. Shmuck Jr. of South Bend, Indiana, or Omsk, Russia, paste it together in his potato barn? Because remember this.' He was prodding his own soft chest and holding his coffee cup in his spare hand. 'No resale. This is not London. This is Washington. And for Washington, intelligence has to be useful, and that means it has to be used, not contemplated in Socratic detachment.' He lowered his voice in reverent commiseration. 'And you're the guy who's selling it to us, Mr. Brown. Like it or not, you personally are the nearest we shall get to the source until the day we persuade the man you call Goethe to change his ways and work to us direct. If we ever do. Doubtful. Very, very doubtful.'

Sheriton took a turn and moved to the edge of the ring. 'You are the linchpin, Mr. Brown. You are *the man*. You are *it*. But how much of *it* are you? A little of it? Some of it? Or all of it? Do you write the script, act, produce and direct? Or are you the bit part you say you are, the innocent bystander we all have yet to meet?'

Sheriton sighed, as if it were a little hard on a man of his tender sensitivities. 'Mr. Brown, do you have a regular girl these days, or are you screwing the backlist?'

Ned was halfway to his feet but Barley had already answered. Yet his voice was not abrasive, even now, it was not hostile. It was as if he were unwilling to disturb the good atmosphere all of us were enjoying.

'Well now, how about you, sunshine? Does Mrs. Haggarty oblige or are we reduced to the habits of our youth?'

Sheriton was not even interested.

'Mr. Brown, we are buying *your* Picasso, not mine. Washington doesn't like its assets cruising the singles bars. We have to play this very frank, very honest. No English reticence, no old-school persiflage. We've fallen for that horse manure before and we will never, *never* fall for it again.'

This, I thought, for Bob, whose head was once again turned downward to his hands.

'Mr. Brown is not cruising the singles bars,' Ned cut in hotly. 'And it's not his material. It's Goethe's. I don't see that his private life has the least to do with it.'

Keep your thoughts to yourself Clive had told me. His eyes repeated the message to Ned now.

'Oh Ned, come on now, come *on!*' Sheriton protested. 'The way Washington is these days, you have to be married and born again before you can get on a fucking bus. What takes you to Russia every five minutes, Mr. Brown? Are you buying property there?'

Barley was grinning, but no longer so pleasantly. Sheriton was getting to him, which was exactly what Sheriton intended.

'As a matter of fact, old boy, it's a role I rather inherited. My old father always preferred the Soviet Union to the United States, and went to a lot of trouble publishing their books. He was a Fabian. A kind of New Dealer. If he'd been one of your people he'd have been blacklisted.'

'He'd have been framed, fried and immortalised. I read his record. It's awful. Tell us more about him, Mr. Brown. What did he bequeath to you that you inherited?'

'What the devil's that to anyone?' said Ned.

He was right. The matter of Barley's eccentric father had been aired and dismissed as irrelevant by the twelfth floor long ago. But not apparently by the Agency. Or not any more.

'And in the 'thirties, as you no doubt also know, then,' Barley continued in his calmer tone, 'he started up a Russian Book Club. It didn't last long but he had a go. And in the war when he could get the paper he'd publish pro-Soviet propaganda, most of it glorifying Stalin.'

'And after the war what did he do then? Go help them build the Berlin Wall on weekends?'

'He had hopes, then he packed them in,' Barley replied after reflection. The contemplative part of him had regained the upper hand. 'He could have forgiven the Russians most things, but not the Terror, not the camps and not the deportations. It broke his heart.'

'Would his heart have been broken if the Sovs had used less muscular methods?'

'I don't expect so. I think he'd have died a happy man.'

Sheriton wiped his palms on his handkerchief and like an overweight Oliver Twist carried his coffee cup in both hands back to the refreshments table, where he unscrewed the thermos jug and peered mournfully inside before pouring himself a fresh cup.

'Acorns,' he complained. 'They gather acorns and press them and make coffee out of them. That's what they do out here.' There was an empty chair beside Bob. Sheriton lowered himself into it and sighed. 'Mr. Brown, will you let me spell it out for you a little? There is no longer the space in life to take each humble member of the human family on his merits, okay? So everybody who is anybody has a record. Here's yours. Your father was a Communist sympathiser, latterly disenchanted. In the eight years since he died you have made no fewer than six visits to the Soviet Union. You have sold the Sovs precisely four very lousy books from your own list and published precisely three of theirs. Two awful modern novels which didn't do a damn thing, a piece of crap about acupuncture which did eighteen copies in the trade edition. You're on the verge of bankruptcy, yet we calculate your outlay for these trips at twelve thousand pounds and your revenue at nineteen hundred. You're divorced, freestyle and British public school. You drink like you're watering the desert single-handed and you pick jazz friends with records that make Benedict Arnold look like Shirley Temple. Seen from Washington, you're rampant. Seen from here, you're very nice, but how will I explain this to the next Congressional sub-committee of Bible-belt knuckle-draggers who take it into their heads to pillory Goethe's material because it endangers Fortress America?'

'Why does it do that?' said Barley.

I think we were all surprised by his calm. Sheriton certainly was. He was looking at Barley over his shoulder until then, affecting a slightly pitiful stance as he explained his dilemma. Now he straightened up, and faced Barley full on with an alert and quizzical directness.

'Pardon me, Mr. Brown?'

'Why does Goethe's material scare them? If the Russians can't shoot straight, Fortress America should be jumping for joy.'

'Oh we are, Mr. Brown, we are. We're ecstatic. Never mind that the entire American military might is invested in the belief that the Soviet hardware is accurate as hell. Never mind that a perception of Soviet accuracy is *all* in this game. That with accuracy, you can sneak up on your enemy while he's out playing golf, take out his ICBM's unawares and leave him unable to respond in kind. Whereas without accuracy, you'd damn well better not try it, because that's when your enemy turns right around and takes out your twenty favourite towns. Never mind that zillions of taxpayers' dollars and whole junk-yards of political rhetoric have been lavished on the fond nightmare of a Soviet first strike and the American window of vulnerability. Never mind that even today the idea of Soviet supremacy is the main argument in favour of Star Wars, and the principal strategic fun-game at Washington cocktail parties.' To my astonishment, Sheriton abruptly changed voices and broke into the accents of a Deep South hillbilly. 'Time we blew those mothers apart before they do the same to us, Mr. Brown. This li'l ole planet just ain't big enough for two superpowers, Mr. Brown. Which one do *you* favour, Mr. Brown, when poo-ush comes to sheu-uve?'

Then he waited, while his pouchy face resumed its contemplation of life's many injustices.

'And I *believe* in Goethe,' he went on in a startled-voice. 'I am on record as buying Goethe outright from the day he stepped out of the closet. Retail. Goethe for my money is a source whose time has come. And do you know what that tells me? It tells me that I also have to believe in Mr. Brown here and that Mr. Brown needs to be very candid with me or I'm dead.' He cupped a paw reverently over his left breast. 'I believe in Mr. Brown, I believe in Goethe, I believe in the material. And I'm scared shitless.'

Some people change their minds, I was thinking. Some people have a change of heart. But it takes Russell Sheriton to announce that he has seen the light on the road to Damascus. Ned was staring at him in disbelief. Clive had chosen to admire the cue-cases. But Sheriton remained pouting at his coffee, reflecting on his bad luck. Of his young men, one had his chin in his hand while he studied the toe-cap of his Harvard shoe. Another was peering at the sea through the window as if the truth might rather lie out there.

But nobody was looking at Barley, nobody seemed to have the nerve. He was sitting still and looking young. We had told him a little, but nothing like this. Least of all had we told him that the Bluebird material had set the industrial-military factions at one another's throats and raised roars of outrage from some of Washington's most sleazy lobbies.

Old Palfrey spoke for the first time. As I did so, I had a sense of performing in the theatre of the absurd. It was as if the real world were slipping out from under our feet.

'What Haggarty is asking you is this,' I said. 'Will you voluntarily submit to questioning by the Americans so that they can take a view of the source once and for all? You can say no. It's your choice. Is that right, Clive?'

Clive didn't like me for that but he gave his reluctant assent before once more ducking below the horizon.

The faces round the ring had turned to Barley like flowers in the sun.

'What do you say?' I asked him.

For a while he said nothing. He stretched, he drew the back of his wrist across his mouth, he looked vaguely embarrassed. He shrugged. He looked towards Ned but could not find his eye, so he looked back at me, rather foolishly. What was he thinking, if anything? That to say 'no' would be to cut him off from Goethe for good? From Katya? Had he even got that far in his mind? To this day I have no idea. He grinned, apparently in embarrassment.

'What do *you* think Harry? In for a penny? What does my mouthpiece say?'

'It's more a question of what the client says,' I answered glossily, smiling back at him.

'We'll never know if we don't give it a try, will we?'

'I suppose we never will,' I said.

Which seems to be the nearest he ever came to saying, 'I'll do it.'

'Yale has these secret societies, you see, Harry,' Bob was explaining to me. 'Why, the place is shot through with them. If you've heard of Scull and Bones, Scroll and Key, you've still only heard the tip of the iceberg. And these societies, they emphasise the team. Harvard now – why, Harvard goes all the other way and puts its money on individual brilliance. So the Agency, when it's fishing for recruits in those waters, has a way of picking its team players from Yale and its high flyers from Harvard. I won't go so far as to say that every Harvard man is a prima donna or every Yale man gives blind obedience to the cause. But that's the broad tradition. Are you a Yale man, Mr. Quinn?'

'West Point,' said Quinn.

It was evening and the first delegation had just flown in. We sat in the same room with the same red floor under the same billiards light, waiting for Barley. Quinn sat at the head and Todd and Larry sat to either side of him. Todd and Larry were Quinn's people. They were clean-limbed and pretty and, for a man of my age, ludicrously youthful.

'Quinn's from way up there,' Sheriton had told us. 'Quinn talks to Defense, he talks to the corporations, he talks to God.'

'But who hires him?' Ned had asked.

Sheriton seemed genuinely puzzled by the question. He smiled as if pardoning a solecism in a foreigner.

'Well now, Ned, I guess we all do,' he said.

Quinn was six foot one, wide-shouldered and big-eared. He wore his suit like body armour. There were no medals on it, no badges of rank. His rank was in his stubborn jaw and shaded empty eyes, and in the smile of enraged inferiority that overcame him in the presence of civilians.

Ned entered first, then came Barley. Nobody stood up. From his deliberately humble place in the centre of the American row, Sheriton meekly made the introductions.

Quinn likes them plain, he had warned us. Tell your man not to be too damn clever. Sheriton was following his own advice.

It was right that Larry should open the questioning because Larry was the outgoing one. Todd was virginal and withdrawn, but Larry wore an overlarge wedding ring and had the colourful tie and did the laughing for them both.

'Mr. Brown, sir, we have to think this thing through from the point of view of your detractors,' he explained with elaborate insincerity. 'In our business, there's unverified intelligence and there's verified intelligence. We'd like to verify your intelligence. That's our job and that's what we're paid for. Please don't take any hint of suspicion personally, Mr. Brown. Analysis is a science apart. We have to respect its laws.'

'We have to imagine it's an organised put-together,' Todd blurted belligerently from Larry's side. '*Smoke.*'

Amusement, until Larry laughingly explained to Barley that he was not being offered a cigarette: 'smoke' was the trade word for deception.

'Mr. Brown, sir, whose idea was it, please, to go out to Peredelkino that day, fall two years ago?' asked Larry.

'Mine, probably.'

'Are you sure of that, sir?'

'We were drunk when we made the plan, but I'm pretty sure it was me who proposed it.'

'You drink quite a lot, don't you, Mr. Brown?' said Larry.

Quinn's enormous hands had settled round a pencil as if they proposed to strangle it.

'Fair amount.'

'Does drinking make you forget things, sir?'

'Sometimes.'

'And sometimes not. After all, we have long verbatims between you and Goethe when you were both totally inebriated. Had you ever been to Peredelkino before that day, sir?'

'Yes.'

'Often?'

'Two or three times. Maybe four.'

'Did you visit with friends out there?'

'I visited friends, yes,' said Barley, instinctively bridling at the American usage.

'Soviet friends?'

'Of course.'

Larry paused long enough to make Soviet friends sound like a confession.

'Care to identify these friends, please, sir, names?'

Barley identified the friends. A writer. A woman poet. A literary bureaucrat. Larry wrote them down, moving his pencil slowly for effect. Smiling as he wrote, while Quinn's shadowed eyes continued glowering at Barley on fixed lines down the table.

'On the day of your trip then, Mr. Brown,' Larry resumed, 'On this Day One, as we may call it, did it not occur to you to press a few doorbells of

' "He's a nice chap." That means you like him?'

'He's an irritating little sod but I liked him, yes. Still do.'

'You never did deals with him? Any deal?'

'He worked for other houses. I was my own boss. What deals could we do?'

'Ever *buy* anything from him?'

'Why should I?'

'I would like to know, please, what you and Niki Landau transacted together on the occasions when you were alone, often in Communist capital cities.'

'He boasted about his conquests. He liked good music. Classical stuff.'

'He ever discuss his *sister* with you? His *sister* still in Poland?'

'No.'

'He ever express his resentment to you regarding the alleged ill-treatment of his father by the British authorities?'

'No.'

'When was your last intimate conversation with Niki Landau, please?'

Barley finally allowed himself to betray a certain irritation. 'You make us sound like a pair of queens,' he complained.

Quinn's face did not flicker. Perhaps he had made that deduction already.

'The question was *when*, Mr. Brown,' said Todd, in a tone suggesting that his patience was being stretched.

'Frankfurt, I suppose. Last year. Couple of belts in the Hessischer Hof.'

'That the Frankfurt book fair?'

'One doesn't go to Frankfurt for fun, old boy.'

'No dialogue with Landau since?'

'Don't recall one.'

'Nothing at the London book fair this spring?'

Barley appeared to rack his brains. 'Oh my hat. Stella. You're right.'

'I beg your pardon?'

'Niki had spotted a girl who used to work for me. Stella. Decided he fancied her. He fancied everybody really. By way of being a stoat. Wanted me to introduce them.'

'And you did?'

'Tried to.'

'You pimped for him. That the term?'

'That's right, old boy.'

'What transpired, please?'

'I asked her for a drink at the Roebuck round the corner, six o'clock. Niki turned up, she didn't.'

'So you were left alone with Landau? One on one?'

'That's right. One to one.'

'What did you talk about?'

'Stella, I suppose. The weather. Might have been anything.'

'Mr. Brown, do you have anything very much to do with past or former Soviet citizens in the United Kingdom?'

'Cultural Attaché, now and then. When he can be bothered to answer, which isn't often. If a Sov writer comes over and the Embassy gives a binge for him, I'll probably go along.'

'We understand you like to play chess at a certain café in the area of Camden Town, London.'

'So?'

'Is this not a café frequented by Russian exiles, Mr. Brown?'

Barley raised his voice but otherwise held steady. 'So I know Leo. Leo likes to lead from weakness. I know Josef. Josef charges at anything that moves. I don't go to bed with them and I don't trade secrets with them.'

'You do have a very selective memory, though, don't you, Mr. Brown? Considering the extraordinarily detailed accounts you give of other episodes and persons?'

Still Barley did not flare, which made his reply all the more devastating. For a moment, indeed, it seemed he would not even answer; the tolerance that was now so deeply seated in him seemed to tell him not to bother.

'I remember what's important to me, old boy. If I haven't got a dirty enough mind to match yours, that's your bloody business.'

Todd coloured. And went on colouring. Larry's smile widened till it nearly split his face. Quinn had put on a sentry's scowl. Clive had not heard a thing.

But Ned was pink with pleasure and even Russell Sheriton, sunk in a crocodile's sleep, seemed to be remembering, among so many disappointments, something vaguely beautiful.

The same evening as I was taking a walk along the beach, I came on Barley and two of his guards, out of sight of the mansion, skimming flat stones to see who could get the most bounces.

'Got you! Got you!' he was shouting, leaning back and flinging his arms at the clouds.

'The mullahs are smelling heresy,' Sheriton declared over dinner, regaling us with the latest state of play. Barley had pleaded a headache and asked for an omelette in the boat-house. 'Most of these guys came to town on a Margin of Safety ticket. That means raise military spending and develop any new system however crazy that will bring peace and prosperity to the arms industry for the next fifty years. If they're not sleeping with the manufacturers, they're sure as hell eating with them. The Bluebird is telling them a very bad story.'

'And if it's the truth?' I asked.

Sheriton sadly helped himself to another piece of pecan pie. 'The truth? The Sovs can't play? They're cost-cutting at every corner and the buffoons in Moscow don't know one half of the bad news because the buffoons in the field cheat on them so they can earn their gold watches and free caviar? You think *that's* the truth?' He took a huge mouthful but it didn't alter the shape of his face. 'You think that certain unpleasant *comparisons* aren't made?' He poured himself some coffee. 'You know what's the worst thing for our democratically-elected neanderthals? The total worst? It's the implications against *us*. Moribund on the Sov side means moribund *our* side. The mullahs hate that. So do the manufacturers.' He shook his head in disapproval. 'To hear the Sovs can't do solid fuel from shit, their rocket motors suck instead of blow? Their early-warning errors worse than ours? Their heavies can't even get out of the kennel? That our intelligence estimates are ludicrously exaggerated? The mullahs get terrible vibes from these things.' He reflected on the inconstancy of mullahs. 'How do you peddle the arms race when the only asshole you have to race against is yourself? Bluebird is life-threatening intelligence. A lot of highly-paid favourite sons are in serious danger of having their rice-bowls broken, all on account of Bluebird. You want truth, that's it.'

'So why stick your neck out?' I objected. 'If it's not a popular ticket, why run on it?'

And suddenly I didn't know where to put myself.

It isn't often that old Palfrey stops a conversation, causes every head to swing round at him in amazement. And I certainly hadn't meant to this time. Yet Ned and Bob and Clive were staring at me as if I had taken leave of my senses, and Sheriton's young men – we had two of them, if I remember rightly – independently put down their forks and began independently wiping their fingers on their napkins.

Only Sheriton didn't seem to have heard. He had decided that a little cheese wouldn't hurt him after all. He had pulled the trolley to him, and was morosely examining the display. But none of us imagined that cheese was uppermost in his mind, and it was clear to me that he was buying time while he wondered whether to reply and how.

'Harry,' he began carefully, addressing not me but a piece of Danish blue. 'Harry, I swear to God. You have before you a man committed to peace and brotherly love. By this I mean that my primary ambition is to knock so much shit out of the Pentagon firebreathers that they will never again tell the President of the United States that twenty rabbits make a tiger, or that every fucking sardine fisherman three miles out of port is a Soviet nuclear submarine in drag. I also wish to hear no more bullshit about digging little holes in the ground and surviving nuclear war. I am a glasnostic, Harry. I have made certain discoveries about myself. I was born a glasnostic, my parents are old glasnostics from way back. For me, glasnosticism is a way of life. I want my children to live. Quote me and enjoy me.'

'I didn't know you had any children,' said Ned.

'Figurative,' said Sheriton.

But Sheriton, if you pulled away the wrapping, was telling us a truthful version of his new self. Ned sensed it, I sensed it. And if Clive didn't, that was only because he had deliberately abbreviated his perceptions. It was a truth that lay not so much in his words, which as often as not were designed to obscure his feelings rather than express them, but in a new and irrepressible humility that had entered his manner since his cut-throat days in London. At the age of fifty, after quarter of a century as a Cold War brawler, Russell Sheriton, to use Walter's expression, was shaking his mid-life bars. It had never occurred to me that I could like him, but that evening I began to.

'Brady's bright,' Sheriton warned us with a yawn as we turned in. 'Brady can hear the grass growing.'

And Brady, parse him how you would, was bright as boot-buttons.

You spotted it in his clever face and in the nerveless immobility of his courteous body. His ancient sports coat was older than he was, and as he came into the room you knew he took pleasure in being unspectacular. His young assistant wore a sports coat too and, like his master, had a classy dowdiness.

'Looks like you've done a fine thing, Barley,' Brady said cheerfully in his Southern lilt, setting his briefcase on the table. 'Anybody say thank you along the way? I'm Brady and I'm too damned old to fool around with funny names. This is Skelton. *Thank you.*'

The billiards room again but without Quinn's table and upright chairs. Instead, we lounged gratefully in deep cushions. A storm was brewing. Randy's vestals had closed the shutters and put on lights. As the wind rose, the mansion began clinking like restless bottles on a shelf. Brady unpopped his briefcase, a gem from the days when they knew how to make them. Like the university professor he occasionally was, he wore a polka-dot blue tie.

'Barley, did I read somewhere, or am I dreaming, you once played sax in the great Ray Noble's band?'

'Beardless boy in those days, Brady.'

'Wasn't Ray just the sweetest man you ever knew? Didn't he make the best sound ever?' Brady asked as only Southerners can.

'Ray was a prince.' Barley hummed a few bars from 'Cherokee'.

'Too bad about his politics,' Brady said, smiling. 'We all tried to talk him out of that nonsense, but Ray would go his way. Ever play chess with him?'

'Yes I did, as a matter of fact.'

'Who won?'

'Me, I think. Not sure. Yes, me.'

Brady smiled. 'So did I.'

Skelton smiled too.

They talked London and which part of Hampstead Barley lived in:

'Barley, I just love that area. Hampstead is my idea of civilisation.' They talked the bands Barley had played. 'My God, don't tell me *he's* still around! At his age I wouldn't even buy unripe bananas!' They talked British politics and Brady just *had* to know what it was that Barley thought so wrong with Mrs. T.

Barley appeared to have to think about that, and at first came up with no suggestions. Perhaps he had caught Ned's warning eye.

'Hell, Barley, it's not *her* fault she hasn't any worthwhile opponents, is it?'

'Woman's a bloody Red,' Barley growled, to the secret alarm of the British side.

Brady didn't laugh, just raised his eyebrows and waited, as we all did.

'Elective dictatorship,' Barley continued, quietly gathering steam. 'A thousand legs good, two legs lousy. God bless the corporation and bugger the individual.'

He seemed to be about to enlarge on this thesis, then changed his mind, and to our relief, let it rest.

Nevertheless it was a light enough beginning, and after ten minutes of it Barley must have been feeling pretty much at ease. Until in his languid way Brady came to 'this present thing you've gotten yourself into, Barley,' and proposed that Barley should go over the turf again in his own words, 'but homing in on that historic eye-to-eye you two fellows had in Leningrad.'

Barley did as Brady wanted, and though I like to think I listened quite as sharply as Brady, I heard nothing in Barley's narrative that seemed to me contradictory or particularly revealing beyond what was already on the record.

And at first blush Brady didn't seem to hear anything surprising either, for when Barley had finished, Brady gave him a reassuring smile and said, 'Well now, thank you, Barley,' in a voice of apparent approval. His slender fingers poked among his papers. 'Worst thing about spying, I always say, is the hanging around. Must be like being a fighter pilot,' he said, selecting a page and peering at it. 'One minute sitting home eating your chicken dinner, next minute frightening the hell out of yourself at eight hundred miles an hour. Then it's back home in time to wash the dishes.' He had apparently found what he was looking for. 'Is that how it felt to you, Barley, stuck out there in Muscovy without a prayer?'

'A bit.'

'Hanging around waiting for Katya? Hanging around waiting for Goethe? You seemed to do quite some hanging around after you and Goethe had finished your little pow-wow, didn't you?'

Perching his spectacles on the tip of his nose, Brady was studying the paper before passing it to Skelton. I knew the pause was contrived but it scared me all the same, and I think it scared Ned for he glanced at Sheriton, then anxiously back to Barley. 'According to our field reports, you and

Goethe broke up around fourteen thirty-three Leningrad time. Seen the picture? Show it to him, Skelton.'

All of us had seen it. All but Barley. It portrayed the two men in the gardens of the Smolny after they had said goodbye. Goethe had turned away. Barley's hands were still held out to him from their farewell embrace. The electronic timeprint in the top left corner said fourteen thirty-three and twenty seconds.

'Remember your last words to him?' Brady asked, with an air of sweet reminiscence.

'I said I'd publish him.'

'Remember *his* last words to *you?*'

'He wanted to know whether he should look for another decent human being.'

'One hell of a goodbye,' Brady remarked comfortably, while Barley continued to look at the photograph, and Brady and Skelton looked at Barley. 'What did you do then, Barley?'

'Went back to the Europe. Handed over his stuff.'

'What route did you take? Remember?'

'Same way I got there. Trolleybus into town, then walked a bit.'

'Have to wait long for the trolleybus?' Brady asked, while his Southern accent became, to my ear at least, more of a mocking-bird than a regional digression.

'Not that I remember.'

'How long?'

'Five minutes. Maybe longer.'

I could not remember one occasion until now when Barley had pleaded an imperfect memory.

'Many people in line?'

'Not many. A few. I didn't count.'

'The trolleybus runs every ten minutes. The ride into town takes another ten. The walk to the Europe, at your pace, ten. Our people have timed it all ways up. Ten's the outside. But according to Mr. and Mrs. Henziger, you didn't show up in their hotel room till fifteen fifty-five. That leaves us with quite a tidy hole, Barley. Like a hole in time. Mind telling me how we're going to fill it? I don't expect you went on a drinking spree, did you? You were carrying some pretty valuable merchandise. I'd have thought you wanted to unload it pretty quick.'

Barley was becoming wary and Brady must have seen that he was, for his hospitable Southern smile was offering a new kind of encouragement, the kind that said 'come clean'.

As to Ned, he was sitting stock still with both feet flat on the ground, and his straight gaze was fixed on Barley's troubled face.

Only Clive and Sheriton seemed to have pledged themselves to display no emotions at all.

'What were you doing, Barley?' Brady said.

'I mooched,' said Barley, not lying at all well.

'Carrying Goethe's notebook? The notebook he had *entrusted* to you with his life? Mooched? You picked a damned odd afternoon to mooch for fifty minutes, Barley. Where d'you go?'

'I wandered back along the river. Where we'd been. Paddy had told me to take my time. Not to rush back to the hotel but to go at a leisurely speed.'

'That's true,' Ned murmured. 'Those were my instructions via Moscow station.'

'For fifty minutes?' Brady persisted, ignoring Ned's intervention.

'I don't know how long it was. I wasn't looking at my watch. If you take time, you take time.'

'And it didn't cross your mind that with a tape and a power-pack in your pants, and a notebook full of potentially priceless intelligence material in your carrier bag, the shortest distance between two points might *just* be a straight line?'

Barley was getting dangerously angry but the danger was to himself as Ned's expression, and I fear my own, could have warned him.

'Look, you're not listening, are you?' he said rudely. 'I told you. Paddy told me to take time. They trained me that way in London, on our stupid little runs. Take time. Never hurry if you're carrying something. Better to make the conscious effort to go slowly.'

Yet again, brave Ned did his best. 'That's what he was taught,' he said.

But he was watching Barley as he spoke.

Brady was also watching Barley. 'So you mooched *away* from the trolleybus stop, *towards* the Communist Party Headquarters in the Smolny Institute – not to mention the Komsomol and a couple of other Party shrines – *carrying* Goethe's notebook – in your bag? Why did you do that, Barley? Fellows in the field do some damned strange things, you don't have to tell me that, but this strikes me as plain suicidal.'

'I was obeying orders, blast you, Brady! I was taking my time! How often do I have to tell you?'

But even as he flared it occurred to me that Barley was caught not so much in a lie as in a dilemma. There was too much honesty in his appeal, too much loneliness in his assailed eyes. And Brady to his credit seemed to understand this too, for he showed no sign of triumph at Barley's distress, preferring to befriend him rather than to goad.

'You see, Barley, a lot of people around here would attach a heap of suspicion to a gap like that,' Brady said. 'They would have a picture of you sitting in somebody's office or car while that somebody photographed Goethe's notebook or gave you orders. Did you do any of that? I guess now's the time to say so if you did. There's never going to be a good time, but this is about as good as we're likely to get.'

'No.'

'No, you won't tell?'

'That's not what happened.'

'Well, something happened. Do you remember what was in your mind while you mooched?'

'Goethe. Publishing him. Bringing down the temple if he had to.'

'What temple's that, exactly? Can we get away from the metaphysical a little?'

'Katya. The children. Taking them with him if he gets caught. I don't know who has the right to do that. I can't work it out.'

'So you mooched and tried to work it out.'

Maybe Barley did mooch, maybe he didn't. He had clammed up.

'Wouldn't it have been more normal to hand over the notebook first and try to work out the ethics afterwards? I'm surprised you were able to think clearly with that damn thing burning a hole in your carrier bag. I'm not suggesting we're any of us very logical in these situations, but even by the laws of *un*logic, I would feel you had put yourself in a damned uncomfortable situation. I think you did something. I think you think so too.'

'I bought a hat.'

'What kind of hat?'

'A fur hat. A woman's hat.'

'Who for?'

'Miss Coad.'

'That a girlfriend?'

'She's the housekeeper at the safe house in Knightsbridge,' Ned cut in before Barley could reply.

'Where'd you buy it?'

'On the way between the tram stop and the hotel. I don't know where. A shop.'

'That all?'

'Just a hat. One hat.'

'How long did that take you?'

'I had to queue.'

'How long did it take?'

'I don't know.'

'What else did you do?'

'Nothing. I bought a hat.'

'You're lying, Barley. Not gravely, but you are undoubtedly lying. What else did you do?'

'I phoned her.'

'Miss Coad?'

'Katya.'

'Where from?'

'A post office.'

'Which one?'

Ned had put a hand across his forehead as if to shield his eyes from the sun. But the storm had taken hold, and outside the window both sea and sky were black.

'Don't know. Big place. Phone cabins under a sort of iron balcony.'

'You called her at her office or at her home?'

'Office. It was office hours. Her office.'

'Why don't we hear you do that on the body tapes?'

'I switched them off.'

'What was the purpose of the call?'

'I wanted to make sure she was all right.'

'How did you go about that?'

'I said hullo. She said hullo. I said I was in Leningrad, I'd met my contact, business was going along fine. Anyone listening would think I was talking about Henziger. Katya would know I was talking about Goethe.'

'Makes pretty good sense to me,' said Brady with a forgiving smile.

'I said, so goodbye again till the Moscow book fair and take care. She said she would. Take care, I mean. Goodbye.'

'Anything else?'

'I told her to destroy the Jane Austens I'd given her. I said they were the wrong edition. I'd bring her some new ones.'

'Why'd you do that?'

'The Jane Austens had questions for Goethe printed into the text. They were duplicates of the questions in the paperback he wouldn't take from me. In case she got to him and I didn't. They were a danger to her. Since he wasn't going to answer them anyway, I didn't want them lying around her house.'

Nothing stirred in the room. Just the sea wind making the shutters crack, and puffing in the eaves.

'How long did your call with Katya take, Barley?'

'I don't know.'

'How much money did it cost you?'

'I don't know. I paid at the desk. Two roubles something. I talked a lot about the book fair. So did she. I wanted to listen to her.'

This time it was Brady's turn to keep quiet.

'I had a feeling that as long as I was talking, life was normal. She was all right.'

Brady took a while, then against all our expectation closed the show: 'So, small talk,' he suggested as he began to pack his wares into his grandfather's attaché case.

'That's it,' Barley agreed. 'Small talk. Chitchat.'

'As between acquaintances,' Brady suggested, popping the case shut. 'Thank you, Barley. I admire you.'

We sat in the huge drawing-room, Brady at our centre, Barley gone.

'Drop him down a hole, Clive,' Brady advised, in a voice still steeped in courtesy. 'He's flakey, he's a liability and he thinks too damn much.

Bluebird is making waves you would not believe. The fiefdoms are up in arms, the Air generals are in spasm, Defense say he's a charter to give away the store, the Pentagon's accusing the Agency of promoting bogus goods. Your only hope is throw this man out and put in a professional, one of ours.'

'Bluebird won't deal with a professional,' said Ned, and I heard the fury simmering in his voice and knew it was about to boil over.

Skelton too had a suggestion. It was the first time I had heard him speak, and I had to crane my head to catch his cultured college voice.

'Fuck Bluebird,' he said. 'Bluebird's got no business calling the shots. He's a traitor and a guilt-driven crazy and who knows what else he is besides? Hold his feet to the fire. Tell him if he stops producing we'll sell him to his own people and the girl with him.'

'If Goethe's a good boy, he gets the jackpot, I'll see to it,' Brady promised. 'A million's no problem. Ten million's better. If you frighten him enough and pay him enough, maybe the neanderthals will believe he's on the level. Russell, give my love. Clive, it's been a pleasure. Harry. Ned.'

With Skelton at his side he started to move towards the door.

But Ned wasn't saying goodbye. He didn't raise his voice or bang the table but neither did he hold back the dark glow in his eyes or the edge of outrage in his words.

'Brady!'

'Something on your mind, Ned?'

'Bluebird won't be bullied. Not by them, not by you. Blackmail may look nice in the planning room but it won't play on the ground. Listen to the tapes if you don't believe me. Bluebird's in search of martyrdom. You don't threaten martyrs.'

'So what do I do with them, Ned?'

'Did Barley lie to you?'

'Not unduly.'

'He's straight. It's a straight case. Do you remember straight? While you're thinking round corners, Bluebird's going straight for goal. And he's chosen Barley as his running mate. Barley's the only chance we have.'

'He's in love with the girl,' said Brady. 'He's complicated. He's a liability.'

'He's in love with hundreds of girls. He proposes to every girl he meets. That's who he is. It's not Barley who thinks too much. It's you people.'

Brady was interested. Not in his own conviction, if he had any, but in Ned's.

'I've done all kinds,' Ned went on. 'So have you. Some cases are never straight, even when they're over. This one was straight from the first day, and if anyone is shoving it off course, we are.'

I had never heard him speak with so much fervour. Neither had Sheriton, for he was transfixed, and perhaps it was for this reason that Clive felt obliged to interpose himself with a fanfare of civil servant's exit music.

'Yes, well I think we have ample food for thought here, Brady. Russell, we must talk this through. Perhaps there's a middle way. I rather think there may be. Why don't we take soundings? Kick it around a little. Run over it one more time?'

But nobody had left. Brady, for all Clive's ushering platitudes, had remained exactly where he was, and I observed a raw kindliness in his features that was like the real man beneath the mask.

'Nobody hired us for our brotherly love, Ned. That's just not what they put us spooks on earth for. We knew that when we signed up.' He smiled. 'Guess if plain decency was the name of the game, you'd be running the show in place of Deputy Clive here.'

Clive was not pleased by this suggestion, but it did not prevent him from escorting Brady to his jeep.

For a moment I thought I was alone with Ned and Sheriton, until I saw Randy our host framed in the doorway, wearing an expression of star-struck disbelief. 'Was that *the* Brady?' he asked breathlessly. 'The Brady who did like *everything?*'

'It was Greta Garbo,' Sheriton said. 'Go away, Randy. Please.'

I should play you more of that steadying music while Sheriton's young men take Barley back again, and walk with him on the beach and joke with him and produce the street map of Leningrad for him, and painstak-ingly log the very shop where Miss Coad's lynx hat was bought, and how he paid for it and where the receipt might have got to if there ever was one, and whether Barley had declared the hat to customs at Gatwick, and the very post office where he must have made his telephone call.

I should describe to you the spare hours Ned and I spent sitting around Barley's boat-house in the evenings, hunting for ways to shake him from his introspections and finding none.

For Barley's journey away from us – I felt it even then – had not flagged from the moment when he first agreed to be interrogated. He had become a solitary pilgrim, but where to? Where from? Who for?

Then comes the morning following – a real sparkler, as they call it there; I think it must have been the Thursday – when the little plane from Logan airport brought us Merv and Stanley in time for their favourite breakfast of pancakes and bacon and pure maple syrup.

Randy's kitchen was well acquainted with their tastes.

They were bearish, kindly men of the soil, with pumice-stone faces and big hands, and they arrived looking like a vaudeville duo, wearing dark trilby hats and humping a salesman's suitcase which they kept close to them while they ate and later set down gingerly on the red-painted floor of the billiards room.

Their profession had made their faces dull, but they were the type our own Service likes best – straightforward, loyal, uncomplicated foot-soldiers with a job to do and kids to feed, who loved their country without making a to-do of it.

Merv's hair was cropped to a moleskin fuzz. Stanley had bandy legs and wore some sort of loyal badge in his lapel.

'You can be Jesus Christ, Mr. Brown. You can be a fifteen-hundred-a-month typist,' Sheriton had said as we stood around in Barley's boat-house in a state of shifty supplication. 'It's voodoo, it's alchemy, it's the ouija board, it's reading fucking tea-leaves. And if you don't go through with it, you're dead.'

Clive spoke next. Clive could find reasons for anything. 'If he's nothing to hide, why should he be bothered?' he said. 'It's their version of the Official Secrets Act.'

'What does Ned say?' Barley asked.

Not Nedsky any more. Ned.

There was a defeat in Ned's reply that I shall never forget, and in his eyes as well. Brady's interrogation of Barley had shaken his faith in himself and even in his joe.

'It's your choice,' he said lamely. And as if to himself, 'A pretty disgusting one too, if you ask me.'

Barley turned to me, exactly as he had done before, when I had first asked him whether he would submit to the American questioning.

'Harry? What do I do?'

Why did he insist on my opinion? It was unfair. I expect I looked as uncomfortable as Ned. I certainly felt so, though I managed a light-hearted shrug. 'Either humour them and go along with it or tell them to go to hell. It's up to you,' I replied, much as I had on the first occasion.

Thus the eternal lawyer.

Barley's stillness again. His indecision slowly giving way to resignation. His separation from us as he stares through the window at the sea. 'Well, let's hope they don't catch me telling the truth,' he says.

He stands up and flips his wrists around, loosening his shoulders, while the rest of us like so many butlers confirm among ourselves by furtive looks and nods that our master has said yes.

At their work Merv and Stanley had the respectful nimbleness of executioners. Either they had brought the chair with them or the island kept one for them as a permanency, an upright wooden throne with a scalloped arm-rest on the left side. Merv set it handy for the electric socket while Stanley spoke to Barley like a grandfather.

'Mr Brown, sir, this is not a situation where you should expect hostility. It is our wish you should not be troubled by a relationship with your examiners. The examiner is not adversarial, he is an impartial functionary, it's the machine that does the work. Kindly remove your jacket, no need to roll back your sleeves, sir, or unbutton your shirt, thank you. Very easy now, please, nice and relaxed.'

Meanwhile with the greatest delicacy Merv slipped a doctor's blood-pressure cuff over Barley's left bicep until it was flush with the artery inside his elbow. Then he inflated the cuff until the dial said fifty milligrams while Stanley, with the devotion of a boxing second, fitted a one-inch diameter rubberised tube round Barley's chest, careful to avoid the nipples so that it didn't chafe. Then Stanley fitted a second tube across Barley's abdomen while Merv slipped a double finger stall over the two central fingers of Barley's left hand, with an electrode inside it to pick up the sweat glands and the galvanised skin response and the changes of skin temperature over which the subject, provided he has a conscience, has no control – or so preach the converted, for I had had it all explained to me by Stanley beforehand, much as a concerned relative will inform himself in advance about the details of a loved one's surgical operation. Some polygraphers, Harry, they liked an extra band around the head like an encephalograph. Not Stanley. Some polygraphers, they liked to shout and rage at the subject. Not Stanley. Stanley reckoned that a lot of people got disturbed by an accusatory question, whether or not they were guilty.

'Mr. Brown, sir, we ask you to make no movement, fast or slow,' Merv was saying. 'If you do make such a movement we are liable to get a violent disturbance in the pattern which will necessitate further testing and a repetition of the questions. Thank you. First we like to establish a norm. By norm we mean a level of voice, a level of physical response, imagine a seismograph, you are the earth, you provide the disturbance. Thank you, sir. Answer to be "yes" or "no" only, please, always answer truthfully. We break off after every eight questions, that will be to loosen the pressure cuff in order to prevent discomfort. While the cuff is loosened we shall engage in normal conversation, but no humour, please, no undue excitation of any kind. Is your name Brown?'

'No.'

'Do you have a different name from the one you are using?'

'Yes.'

'Are you British born, Mr. Brown?'

'Yes.'

'Did you fly here, Mr. Brown?'

'Yes.'

'Did you come here by boat, Mr. Brown?'

'No.'

'Have you truthfully answered my questions so far, Mr. Brown?'

'Yes.'

'Do you intend to answer my questions truthfully throughout the remainder of this test, Mr. Brown?'

'Yes.'

'Thank you,' said Merv, with a gentle smile while Stanley released the air from the cuff. 'Those are what we call the non-relevant questions. Married?'

'Not at the moment.'

'Kids?'

'Two, actually.'

'Boys or girls?'

'One of each.'

'Wise man. Alrighty?' He began pumping up the cuff again. 'Now we go relevant. Easy now. That's nice. That's very nice.'

In the open suitcase the four spectral wire claws described their four mauve skylines across the graph paper, while the four black needles nodded inside their dials. Merv had taken up a sheaf of questions and settled himself at a small table at Barley's side. Not even Russell Sheriton had been allowed to know the questions the faceless desk inquisitors in Langley had selected. No casual tampering by Barley's terrestrial co-habitants was to be allowed to breathe upon the mystic powers of the box.

Merv spoke tonelessly. Merv, I was sure, prided himself upon the impartiality of his voice. He was the March of Time. He was Houston Control.

'I am knowingly engaged in a conspiracy to supply untrue information to the intelligence services of Britain and the United States of America. Yes, I am so engaged. No, I am not so engaged.'

'No.'

'My motive is to promote peace between nations. Yes or no?'

'No.'

'I am operating in collusion with Soviet Intelligence.'

'No.'

'I am proud of my mission on behalf of world Communism.'

'No.'

'I am operating in collusion with Niki Landau.'

'No.'

'Niki Landau is my lover.'

'No.'

'Was my lover.'

'No.'

'I am homosexual.'

'No.'

A break while Stanley once more eased the pressure. 'How's it feeling, Mr. Brown? Not too much pain?'

'Never enough, old boy. I thrive on it.'

But we didn't look at him in these breaks, I noticed. We looked at the floor or at our hands, or at the beckoning wind-bent trees outside the window. It was Stanley's turn. A cosier tone, but the same mechanical flatness.

'I am operating in collusion with the woman Katya Orlova and her lover.'

'No.'

'The man I call Goethe is known to me as a plant of Soviet Intelligence.'

'No.'

'The material he has passed to me has been prepared by Soviet Intelligence.'

'No.'

'I am the victim of sexual entrapment.'

'No.'

'I am being blackmailed.'

'No.'

'I am being coerced.'

'Yes.'

'By the Soviets?'

'No.'

'I am being threatened with financial ruin if I do not collaborate with the Soviets.'

'No.'

Another break. Round Three. Merv's turn.

'I lied when I said I had telephoned Katya Orlova from Leningrad.'

'No.'

'From Leningrad I called my Soviet Control and told him of my discussion with Goethe.'

'No.'

'I am the lover of Katya Orlova.'

'No.'

'I have been the lover of Katya Orlova at some time.'

'No.'

'I am being blackmailed regarding my relationship with Katya Orlova.'

'No.'

'I have told the truth so far throughout this interview.'

'Yes.'

'I am an enemy of the United States of America.'

'No.'

'My aim is to undermine the military preparedness of the United States of America.'

'Do you mind running that one by me again, old boy?'

'Hold it,' said Merv, and at the suitcase Stanley held it, while Merv made a pencilled annotation on the graph paper. 'Don't break the rhythm, please, Mr. Brown. We have people do that on purpose when they want to shake off a bad question.'

Round Four and Stanley's turn again. The questions droned on and it was clear they would not stop until they had reached the nadir of their vulgarity. Barley's 'no's' had acquired a deadened rhythm and a mocking passivity. He remained sitting exactly as they had placed him. I had never seen him so still for so long.

They broke again but Barley no longer relaxed between rounds. His stillness was becoming unbearable. His chin was lifted, his eyes were closed and he appeared to be smiling, God alone knew what about. Sometimes his 'no' fell before the end of a sentence. Sometimes he waited so long that the two men paused and looked up, the one from his dials and the other from his papers, and they seemed to me to have the torturer's anxiety that they might have taxed their man too hard. Till the 'no' finally fell again, neither louder nor quieter, a letter delayed in the mail.

Where does he get his stoicism from? No, no, to everything. Why does he sit there like a man preparing himself for the indignities of age, meekly mouthing 'no'? What does this meekness mean, *no, yes, no, no*, till lunchtime, when they take him off the machine?

But in another part of my head, I think I knew the answer, even if I could not yet put it into words: his reality had moved elsewhere.

Spying is waiting.

We waited three days, and you may still count the hours in my grey hairs. We had split on lines of seniority: Sheriton to go with Bob and Clive to Langley; Ned to stay on the island with his joe, Palfrey to remain with them on standby, though what I was standing by for was a mystery to me. I hated the island by then and I suspected that Ned and Barley did too, though I could get no nearer to Ned than I could to Barley. He had become remote and for the time being humourless. Something had happened to his pride.

So we waited. And played distracted chess, seldom finishing a game. And listened to Randy talk about his yacht. And listened for the telephone. And to the screaming of the birds and the pulse of the sea.

It was a mad time, and the vagaries of the isolated place with its fuming skies and storms and patches of idyllic beauty made it madder. A 'dungeon fog', as Randy called it, enveloped us and with it a mindless fear that we would never leave the island. The fog cleared but we were still there. The shared intimacy should have drawn us closer, but both men had withdrawn to their kingdoms, Ned to his room and Barley to the outdoor. With the rain whipping over the island like grapeshot I would peer through the streaming window and glimpse Barley pounding over the cliff in his oilskins, picking up his knees as if wrestling with uncomfortable shoes – or once, playing solitary cricket on the beach with Edgar the guard, a piece of driftwood and a tennis ball. In sunny spells he sported an old blue sailing cap which he had unearthed from a sea-chest in his room. He wore it with a grim face, eyes upon unconquered colonies. One day Edgar appeared with an old yellow dog he had unearthed from somewhere and they made it run back and forth between them. On another day there was a regatta off the mainland and a shoal of white yachts clustered in a ring like tiny teeth. Barley stood watching them interminably, seemingly delighted by the carnival, while Edgar stood off watching Barley.

He's thinking of his Hannah, I thought. He's waiting for life to provide him with the moment of choice. It did not occur to me till much later that some people do not take their decisions in quite that way.

My last image of the island has the convenient distortions of a dream. I had spoken to Clive only twice on the telephone, which for him was virtually a blackout. Once he wished to know 'how your friends are bearing up' and I gathered from Ned that he had already asked him the same question. And once he needed to hear about the arrangements I had made for Barley's compensation, including the subsidies to his company, and whether the monies would come from our own funds or in the form of a supplementary estimate. I had a few notes with me and was able to enlighten him.

It is midday and *The New York Times* and *Washington Post* have just arrived on the table in the sunroom. I am stooped over them when I hear Randy yelling at the guards to get Ned to the telephone. As I turn, I see Ned himself entering from the garden side and striding across the hall to the communications room. I glance beyond him, up to the first-floor landing, and I see Barley, a motionless silhouette. There are some old bookcases up there, and that morning he has persuaded Randy to unlock them so that he can browse. It is the landing with the semi-circular window, the one that looks over the hydrangeas to the sea.

He is standing with his back turned and a book hanging from one long hand, and he is staring at the Atlantic. His feet are apart, his spare hand is raised, as it often is, to somewhere near his head, as if to fend off a blow. He must have heard everything that is going on – Randy's yell, then Ned's hasty footsteps across the hall, followed by the slam of the communications room door. The landing floor is tiled and footsteps come chiming up that stairwell like squeaky church bells. I can hear them now as Ned emerges from the communications room, goes a few steps and halts.

'Harry! Where's Barley?'

'Up here,' says Barley quietly over the banister.

'They've given you the thumbs-up!' Ned shouts, jubilant as a schoolboy. 'They apologise. I spoke to Bob, I spoke to Clive, I spoke to Haggarty. Goethe's is the most important stuff they've handled for years. Official. They'll go for him a hundred per cent. There'll be no turning back any more. You've beaten their whole apparatus.'

Ned was used to Barley's distracted ways by then, so he should not have been surprised when Barley gave no sign of having heard him. His gaze was still fixed on the Atlantic. Did he think he saw a small boat founder? Everybody does. Watch the Maine seas for long enough and you see them everywhere, a sail, a hull, now the speck of a survivor's head or hand, ducking under the sea's swell never to resurface. You must go on watching for a long time to know you are looking at ospreys and cormorants going about their hunting.

But Ned in his excitement manages to be wounded. It is one of those rare moments in him when the professional drops his guard and reveals the unfinished man inside.

'You're going back to Moscow, Barley! That's what you wanted, isn't it? To see it through?'

And Barley at last, concerned that he has hurt Ned's feelings. Barley half-turning so that Ned can see his smile. 'Yes, old boy. Of course it is. Just what I wanted.'

Meanwhile it is my turn in the communications room. Randy is beckoning me in.

'Is that you, Palfrey?'

It is I.

'*Langley* are taking over the case,' says Clive, as if this were the other part of the great news. 'They're giving it a full-facility grading, Palfrey. That's the highest they go,' he adds quellingly.

'Oh well. Congratulations,' I say and, taking the telephone from my ear, stare at it in disbelief while Clive's drawl continues to ooze out of it like a tap nothing can turn off. 'I want you to draw up a document of understanding immediately, Palfrey, and prepare a full-length agreement to cover the usual contingencies. We've got them eating out of our hand, so I expect you to be firm. Firm but fair. We're dealing with very realistic people, Palfrey. Hard-nosed.'

More. Still more. And more yet. Langley to take over Barley's pension and resettlement as earnest of their total operational control. Langley to share equally in the running of the source, but to have a casting vote in the event of disagreement.

'They're preparing a full-scale shopping list, Palfrey, a grand slam. They're taking it to State, Defense, the Pentagon and the scientific bodies. All the biggest questions of the day will be canvassed and set down for the Bluebird to respond to. They know the risks but that isn't deterring them. Nothing ventured, nothing gained, they reason. That takes courage.'

It is his Despatch Box voice. Clive has India at last. 'In the great offence-defence stand-off, Palfrey, nothing exists in a vacuum, he explains loftily, quoting, I had no doubt, what somebody had said to him an hour before. 'It's a matter of the finest tuning. Every question is as important as every answer. They know that. They see it clearly. They can pay the source no higher compliment than to prepare a no-holds-barred questionnaire for him. It's a thing they haven't done for many, many years. It breaks precedent. Recent precedent anyway.'

'Does Ned know?' I ask, when I can get a word in.

'He can't. None of us can. We're talking the highest strategic classifications.'

'I meant, does he know you've made them a present of his joe?'

'I want you to come down to Langley immediately and thrash out terms with your opposite numbers here. Randy will arrange transport. Palfrey?'

'Does he know?' I repeat.

Clive makes one of his telephone silences, in which you are supposed to work out all the ways in which you are at fault.

'Ned will be brought up to date when he gets back to London, thank you. That will be quite soon enough. Until then I shall expect you to say nothing. The role of the Russia House will be respected. Sheriton values the link. It will even be enlarged in certain ways, perhaps permanently. Ned should be grateful.'

The news was nowhere more joyfully received than in the British trade press. *Marriage with a Future*, trumpeted *Booknews* a few weeks later in, its trailer for the Moscow book fair. *The long-rumoured engagement between Abercrombie & Blair of Norfolk Street, Strand, and Potomac Traders, Inc. of Boston, Mass., is ON! Seventeen-stone entrepreneur Jack Henziger has finally weighed in beside Barley Scott Blair of A. & B. with a new joint company titled Potomac & Blair, which plans an aggressive campaign in the fast-opening East Bloc markets. 'This is a shop window on tomorrow,' declares confident Henziger.*

Moscow Book Fair, here they come!

The newsflash was accompanied by a warming photograph of Barley and Jack Henziger shaking hands across a bowl of flowers. The photograph was taken by the Service photographer in the safe house in Knightsbridge. Flowers by Miss Coad.

I met Hannah the day following my return from the island and I assumed we would make love. She looked tall and golden, which is the way she always looks when I have not seen her for a while. A Thursday, so she was taking her fourteen-year-old son Giles to some spurious consultant behind Harley Street. I have never cared for Giles, probably because I know that he was conceived on the rebound, too soon after I had sent her back to Derek. We sat in our usual evil café drinking rancid tea, while she waited for him to come out, and smoked, a thing I hate. But I wanted her, and she knew it.

'Whereabouts in America?' she said, as if it mattered.

'I don't know. Some island full of ospreys and bad weather.'

'I bet they weren't real ospreys.'

'They were, actually. They're common there.'

And I saw by the strain in her eyes that she wanted me too.

'Anyway, I've got to take Giles home,' she said, when we had sufficiently read each other's thoughts.

'Put him in a cab,' I suggested.

But by then we were opposed to each other once more, and the moment was dead.

13

K atya collected Barley at ten o'clock on the Sunday morning from
the forecourt of the immense Mezhdunarodnaya, which was where
Henziger had insisted they stay. Westerners know it familiarly as 'the
Mezh'. Both Wicklow and Henziger, seated in the hotel's preposterous
Great Hall, contrived to witness their happy reunion and departure.

The day was fine and autumn-scented and Barley had started waiting
for her early, hovering in the forecourt amid the blind limousines that
fetched and disgorged their Third World chieftains in a steady flow. Then
at last her red Lada popped up among them like a burst of fun at a
funeral, with Anna's white hand streaming out of the rear window like a
handkerchief and Sergey, upright as a commissar beside her, clutching his
fishing net.

It was important to Barley to notice the children first. He had thought
about it and told himself it was what he would do, because nothing was
insignificant any more, nothing could be left to chance. Only when he had
waved enthusiastically at both of them therefore and pulled a face at Anna
through the back window, did he allow himself to peer into the front,
where Uncle Matvey sat squarely in the passenger seat, his polished brown
face glowing like a chestnut and his sailor's eyes twinkling under the brim
of his plaid cap. Sunshine or storm, Matvey had put on his best things to
honour the great Englishman: his twill jacket, his best boots and bow tie.
The crossed enamelled flags of the Revolution were pinned to his lapel.
Matvey lowered his window and Barley reached through it, grasping his
hand and yelling 'Hullo, *hullo*' at him several times. Only then did he
venture to look at Katya. And there was a kind of hiatus as if he had
forgotten his lines or his cover story, or simply how beautiful she was,
before he hoisted his smile.

But Katya showed no such reticence.

She leapt out of the car. She was wearing badly-cut slacks and looked
marvellous in them. She rushed round to him beaming with happiness and
trust. She yelled, 'Barley!' And by the time she reached him she had flung
her arms so wide that her body was cheerfully and unthinkingly open to
him for his embrace – which as a good Russian girl she then decorously
curtailed, standing back from him but still holding on to him, examining
his face, his hair, his ancient outdoor gear, while she chatted away in a
flood of spontaneous goodfellowship.

'It is so *good*, Barley. Really so good to see you!' she was exclaiming.
'Welcome to the book fair, welcome to Moscow again. Matvey could not
believe it, your phone call from London! "The English were always our
friends," he said. "They taught Peter how to sail, and if he had not known

how to sail, we would not today have a navy." He is speaking of Peter the Great, you see. Matvey lives only for Leningrad. Do you not admire Volodya's fine car? I am so grateful he has something he can love at last.'

She released him and, like the happy idiot he by now was looking, Barley let out a cry of 'God, nearly forgot!' He meant the carrier bags. He had propped them against the wall of the hotel beside the entrance and by the time he reappeared with them, Matvey was trying to climb out of the car to make room for him in the front, but Barley would have none of it.

'No, no, no, *no!* I'll be absolutely fine with the twins! Bless you all the same, Matvey.' Then he threaded and backed his long body into the rear seat as if he were parking an articulated lorry, while he handed round his parcels and the twins giggled at him in awe: this giant Westerner with so many joints and bits left over, who has brought us English chocolates, and Swiss crayons, and drawing books, one each, and the works of Beatrix Potter in English to share, and a beautiful new pipe for Uncle Matvey, which Katya is saying will make him happier than is possible to imagine, with a pouch of English tobacco to smoke in it.

And for Katya everything she could want for the rest of her life – lipsticks and a pullover and scents and a French silk scarf too beautiful to wear.

All this by the time Katya drove out of the Mezh forecourt and bumped on to a pockmarked highway, chatting about the book fair that was opening tomorrow, and steering inaccurately between the flooded craters.

They were heading roughly east. The friendly gold September sun hung ahead of them, making even the Moscow suburbs beautiful. They entered the sad flatland of Moscow's outskirts, with its proprietorless fields, desolate churches and fenced-in transformers. Clusters of old dachas were scattered like ancient beachhuts along the roadside, and their sculptured gables and boxed gardens reminded Barley as always of the English country railway stations of his youth. From his seat in the front, Matvey was poisoning them all with his new pipe and proclaiming his ecstasy through the clouds of smoke. But Katya was too busy pointing out the sights to pay him much attention.

'Over *that* hill lies the so-and-so metal foundry, Barley. The shabby cement building to your left is a collective farm.'

'Great!' said Barley. 'Fascinating! What a day, though, wow!'

Anna had emptied her crayons on to her lap and discovered that if she licked the points they left wet trails of paint. Sergey was urging her to put them back in their tin and Barley was trying to keep the peace by drawing animals in her sketch book for her to colour, but Moscow road surfaces are not kind to artists.

'Not *green*, you chump,' he told her. 'Who ever saw a green cow? Katya, for heaven's sake, your daughter thinks cows are green.'

'Oh Anna is *completely* impractical!' Katya cried laughing, and spoke quickly to Anna over her shoulder, who giggled up at Barley.

And all this had to be heard over Matvey's continued monologue and Anna's immense hilarity and Sergey's troubled interjections, not to mention the anguished thunder of the little engine, until nobody could hear anything except themselves. Suddenly they swung off the road, across a grass field and up a hill without even a track to guide them, to huge laughter from the children and from Katya too, while Matvey clutched his hat with one hand, and his pipe with the other.

'You see?' Katya was demanding of Barley above the din, as if she had proved a long-contested point between lovers. 'In Russia we may go *exactly* where our fancy takes us, provided we do not trespass into the estates of our millionaires or government officials.'

They crested the hill amid more riotous laughter and plunged into a grass dip, then rose again like a brave little boat on a wave to join a farm track that ran beside a stream. The stream entered a birch grove, the track raced beside it. Katya somehow hauled the car to a halt, heaving on the handbrake as if she were slowing down a sledge. They were alone in Paradise with the stream to dam, and a bank to picnic on, and space to play *lapta* with Sergey's stick and ball from the boot of the car, which required everybody to stand in a ring, and one to bowl and one to bat.

Anna, it quickly became apparent, was frivolous about *lapta*. Her ambition was to get through it with as much laughter as possible, then settle down to lunch and flirt with Barley. But Sergey the soldier was a believer and Matvey the sailor was a zealot. While Katya spread out the picnic, she explained the mystical importance of *lapta* to the development of Western culture.

'Matvey assures me it is the origin of American baseball and your English cricket. He believes it was introduced to you by Russian immigrants. I am sure he also believes that it was invented by Peter the Great.'

'If it's true, it's the death of the Empire,' said Barley gravely.

Lying in the grass, Matvey is still talking volubly while he puffs at his new pipe. His generous blue eyes, receding into their glorious Leningrad past, are filled with a heroic light. But Katya hears him as if he were a radio that can't be switched off. She picks on the odd point and is deaf to all the rest. Marching across the grass, she climbs into the car and closes the door behind her, to reappear in shorts, carrying the picnic in an oilcloth bag, with sandwiches wrapped in newspaper. She has prepared cold *kotleti* and cold chicken and meat pies. She has salted cucumber and hard-boiled eggs. She has brought bottles of Zhiguli beer, Barley has brought Scotch, with which Matvey fervently toasts some absent monarch, perhaps Peter himself.

Sergey stands on the bank, raking the water with his net. His dream, Katya explains, is to catch a fish and cook it for everyone who depends on him. Anna is drawing. Ostentatiously, leaning away from her work so that others may admire it. She wishes to give Barley a portrait of herself to hang in his room in London.

'She is asking, are you married?' Katya says, yielding to her daughter's importuning.

'No, not at present, but I'm always available.'

Anna asks another question but Katya blushes and rebukes her. His loyalist duties completed, Matvey is lying on his back with his cap over his eyes, rattling on about heaven knows what, except that, whatever it is, it is all delightful to him.

'Soon he will describe the siege of Leningrad,' Katya calls with a fond smile.

A pause while she glances at Barley. She means, 'Now we can talk.'

The grey lorry was leaving, and high time too. Barley had been resenting it over her shoulder for quite a while, hoping it was friendly but wishing it would leave them alone. The side windows of its cab were dark with dust. Gratefully he saw it lumber to the road then lumber out of sight and mind.

'Oh, he is *very* well,' Katya was saying. 'He wrote me a long letter and everything is excellent with him. He was ill but he is completely recovered, I am sure. He has many matters to discuss with you and he will make a special visit to Moscow during the fair in order to meet you and hear the progress concerning his book. He would like to see some prepared manuscript soon, perhaps only a page. My opinion is that this would be dangerous but he is so impatient. He wants proposals about the title, translations, even illustrations. I think he is becoming a typical dictatorial writer. He will confirm everything very soon and he will also find an apartment where you can meet. He wishes to make all the arrangements himself, can you imagine? I think you have been a very good influence for him.'

She was searching in her handbag. A red car had parked on the other side of the birch grove but she seemed oblivious to everything but her own good spirits. 'Personally I believe his work will soon be regarded as redundant. With the disarmament talks advancing so rapidly and the new atmosphere of international cooperation, all these terrible things will shortly belong to the past. Naturally the Americans are suspicious of us. Naturally we are suspicious of them. But when we have joined our forces, we can disarm completely and between us prevent all further trouble in the world.' It was her didactic voice, brooking no argument.

'How do we prevent all further trouble in the world if we haven't got any arms to prevent it with?' Barley objected, and won a sharp look for his temerity.

'Barley, you are being Western and negative, I think,' she retorted as she drew the envelope from her handbag. 'It was you, not I, who told Yakov that we required an experiment in human nature.'

No stamp, Barley noticed. No postmark. Just 'Katya' in Cyrillic, in what looked like Goethe's handwriting, but who could tell? He felt a sudden sense of warning in his head and shoulders, like a poison, or an allergy coming on.

'What's he been recovering from?' he asked.

'Was he nervous when you met him in Leningrad?'

'We both were. It was the weather,' Barley replied, still waiting for an answer. He was feeling slightly drunk as well. Must be something he had eaten.

'It was because he was ill. Quite soon after your meeting he had a bad collapse and it was so sudden and severe that even his colleagues did not know where he had disappeared to. They had the worst suspicions. A trusted friend told me they feared he might be dead.'

'I didn't know he had any trusted friends except you.'

'He has appointed me his representative to you. He naturally has other friends for other things.' She drew out the letter but did not give it to him.

'That's not quite what you told me before,' he said feebly, while he continued to battle with his multiplying symptoms of mistrust.

She was unmoved by his objection. 'Why should one tell everything at a first encounter? One has to protect oneself. It is normal.'

'I suppose it is,' he agreed.

Anna had finished her self-portrait and needed immediate recognition. It showed her picking flowers on a rooftop.

'Superb!' Barley cried. 'Tell her I'll hang it above my fireplace, know just the spot. There's a picture of Anthea skiing on one side, and Hal sailing on the other. Anna goes in the middle.'

'She asks how old is Hal?' Katya said.

He really had to think. He had first to remember Hal's birth year, then the year it was now, then laboriously subtract the one from the other while he fought off the singing in his ears.

'Ah well now, Hal's twenty-four. But I'm afraid he's made a rather foolish marriage.'

Anna was disappointed. She stared reproachfully at them as Katya resumed their conversation.

'As soon as I heard he had disappeared I tried to contact him by all the usual means but I was not successful. I was extremely distressed.' She passed him the letter at last, her eyes alight with pleasure and relief. As he took it from her, his hand closed distractedly over hers and she let it. 'Then eight days ago, a week ago yesterday which was Saturday, just two days after you telephoned from London, Igor telephoned me at my house. "I have some medicine for you. Let us have a coffee and I will give it to you." Medicine is our code for a letter. He meant a letter from Yakov. I was amazed and very happy. It is even years since Yakov has sent me a letter. And such a letter!'

'Who's Igor?' Barley said, speaking rather loudly in order to defeat the uproar inside his head.

There were five pages of it, written on good unobtainable white writing paper, in an orderly, regular script. Barley had not imagined Goethe capable of such a conventional-looking document. She took back her hand, but gently.

'Igor is a friend of Yakov from Leningrad. They studied together.'

'Great. What does he do now?'

She was annoyed by his question and impatient to have his good reaction to the letter, even if he could only judge it by appearance. 'He is a scientist of some kind with one of the ministries. What does it matter how Igor is employed? Do you wish me to translate it to you or not?'

'What's his other name?'

She told him, and in the midst of his confusion he was exalted by her abrasiveness. We should have had years, he thought, not hours. We should have pulled each other's hair when we were kids. We should have done everything we never did, before it was too late. He held the letter for her and she knelt herself carelessly behind him on the grass, steadying herself with one hand on his shoulder, while with the other she pointed past him at the lines as she translated. He could feel her breasts brushing against his back. He could feel his world steady itself inside him, as the monstrosity of his first suspicions made way for a more analytical frame of mind.

'Here is the address, just a box number, that is normal,' she said, her fingertip on the top right corner. 'He is in a special hospital, perhaps in a special town. He wrote the letter in bed – you see how well he writes when he is sober? – he gave it to a friend who was on his way to Moscow. The friend gave it to Igor. It is normal. "My darling Katya" – that is not exactly how he begins, it is a different endearment, never mind. "I have been struck down with some variety of hepatitis but illness is very instructive and I am alive." That is so typical of him, to draw at once the moral lesson.' She was pointing again. 'This word makes the hepatitis worse. It is "irritated".'

'Aggravated,' Barley said quite calmly.

The hand on his shoulder gave him a reproving squeeze. 'What does it matter what is the right word? You want me to fetch a dictionary? "I have had a high temperature and much fantasy – " '

'Hallucination,' Barley said.

'The word is *gallutsinatsiya* – ' she began furiously.

'Okay, let's stick with that.'

' "– but now I am recovered and in two days I shall go to a convalescent unit for a week by the sea." He does not say which sea, why should he? "I shall be able to do everything except drink vodka, but that is a bureaucratic limitation which as a good scientist I shall quickly ignore." Is that not typical also? That after hepatitis he thinks immediately of vodka?'

'Absolutely,' Barley agreed, smiling in order to please her – and perhaps to reassure himself.

The lines were dead straight as if written on a ruled page. There was not a single crossing out.

' "If only all Russians could have hospitals like this, what a healthy nation we would soon become." He is always the idealist, even when he is ill. "The nurses are so beautiful and the doctors are young and handsome, it is more a house of love here than a house of sickness." He says this to make me jealous. But do you know something? It is most unusual that he comments on anybody happy. Yakov is a tragedian. He is even a sceptic. I think they have cured his bad moods as well. "Yesterday I took exercise for the first time but I soon felt exhausted like a child. Afterwards I lay on the balcony and got quite a suntan before sleeping like an angel with nothing on my conscience except how badly I have treated you, always exploiting you." Now he writes love talk, I shall not translate it.'

'Does he always do that?'

She laughed. 'I told you. It is not even normal that he writes to me, and it is many months, I would say years, since he spoke of our love, which is now entirely spiritual. I think the illness has made him a little sentimental, so we shall forgive him.' She turned the page in his hand, and again their hands met, but Barley's was as cold as winter and he was secretly surprised that she did not comment on it. 'Now we come to Mr. Barley. You. He is extremely cautious. He does not mention you by name. At least the illness has not affected his discretion. "Please tell our good friend that I shall try my best to see him during his visit, provided that my recovery continues. He should bring his materials and I shall try to do the same. I have to deliver a lecture in Saratov that week" – Igor says that is the military academy, Yakov always gives a lecture there in September, so many things one learns when somebody is ill – "and I shall come to Moscow as soon as possible from there. If you speak to him before I do, please tell him the following. Tell him to bring all further questions because after this I do not wish to answer any more questions for the grey men. Tell him his list should be final and exhaustive." '

Barley listened in silence to Goethe's further instructions which were as emphatic as they had been in Leningrad. And as he listened, the black clouds of his disbelief swept together to make a secret dread inside him, and his nausea returned.

A sample page of translation, but in print, please, print is so much more revealing, she was saying on Goethe's behalf.

I wish for an introduction by Professor Killian of Stockholm, please approach him as soon as possible, she was reading.

Have you had further reactions from your intelligentsia? Kindly advise me.

Publishing dates. Goethe had heard that autumn was the best market, but must one really wait a whole year? she asked, for her lover.

The title again. How about *The Biggest Lie in the World?* The blurb, please let me see a draft. And please send an early copy to Dr. Dagmar Somebody at Stanford and Professor Herman Somebody-else at MIT . . .

Barley painstakingly wrote all this down in his notebook on a page he headed BOOK FAIR.

'What's in the rest of the letter?' he asked.

She was returning it to its envelope. 'I told you. It is love talk. He is at peace with himself and he wishes to resume a full relationship.'

'With you.'

A pause while her eyes considered him. 'Barley, I think you are being a little childish.'

'Lovers then?' Barley insisted. 'Live happily ever after. Is that it?'

'In the past he was scared of the responsibility. Now he is not. That is what he writes and naturally it is out of the question. What has been has been. It cannot be restored.'

'Then why does he write it?' said Barley stubbornly.

'I don't know.'

'Do you believe him?'

She was about to be seriously angry with him when she caught something in his expression that was not envy and not hostility but an intense, almost frightening concern for her safety.

'Why should he spin you the talk just because he's ill? He doesn't usually fool around with people's emotions, does he? He prides himself on speaking the truth.'

And still his penetrating gaze would not relinquish her or the letter.

'He is lonely,' she replied protectively. 'He is missing me so he exaggerates. It is normal. Barley, I think you are being a little bit – '

Either she could not find the word, or on second thoughts she decided against using it, so Barley supplied it for her. 'Jealous,' he said.

And he managed what he knew she was waiting for. He smiled. He composed a good, sincere smile of disinterested friendship and squeezed her hand and clambered to his feet. 'He sounds fantastic,' he said. 'I'm very happy for him. For his recovery.'

And he meant it. Every word. He could hear the true note of conviction in his voice as his eye moved quickly to the parked red car on the other side of the birch grove.

Then to the common delight Barley hurls himself upon the business of becoming a weekend father, a role for which his torn life has amply prepared him. Sergey wants him to try his hand at fishing. Anna wants to know why he hasn't brought his swim suit. Matvey has gone to sleep, smiling from the whisky and his memories. Katya stands in the water in her shorts. She looks more beautiful to him than ever before, and more remote. Even collecting rocks to build a dam, she is the most beautiful woman he has ever seen.

Yet nobody ever worked harder on a dam than Barley that afternoon, nobody had a clearer vision of how the waters should be held at bay. He rolls up his stupid grey flannel trousers and soaks himself to the crotch. He heaves sticks and stones till he is half-dead, while Anna sits astride his shoulders directing operations. He pleases Sergey with his businesslike approach, and Katya with his romantic flourish. A white car has replaced the red one. A couple sit in it with the doors open, eating whatever they are eating, and at Barley's suggestion the children stand on the hilltop and wave to them, but the couple in the white car don't wave back.

Evening falls and a tang of autumn fires drifts through the dying birch leaves. Moscow is made of wood again, and burning. As they load the car, a pair of wild geese fly over them and they are the last two geese in the world.

On the journey back to the hotel, Anna sleeps on Barley's lap while Matvey chatters and Sergey frowns at the pages of *Squirrel Nutkin* as if they are the Party Manifesto.

'When do you speak to him again?' Barley asks.

'It is arranged,' she says enigmatically.

'Did Igor arrange it?'

'Igor arranges nothing. Igor is the messenger.'

'The new messenger,' he corrects her.

'Igor is an old acquaintance and a new messenger. Why not?'

She glances at him and reads his intention. 'You cannot come to the hospital, Barley. It is not safe for you.'

'It's not exactly a holiday for you either,' he replies.

She knows, he thought. She knows but does not know she knows. She has the symptoms, a part of her has made the diagnosis. But the rest of her refuses to admit there's anything amiss.

The Anglo-American situation room was no longer a shabby basement in Victoria but the radiant penthouse of a smart new baby skyscraper off Grosvenor Square. It styled itself the Inter-Allied Conciliation Group and was guarded by shifts of conciliatory American Marines in military plainclothes. An air of thrilled purpose pervaded it as the expanded team of trim young men and women flitted between clean desks, answered winking telephones, spoke to Langley on secure lines, passed papers, typed at silent keyboards or lounged in attitudes of eager relaxation before the rows of television monitors that had replaced the twin clocks of the old Russia House.

It was a deck on two levels, and Ned and Sheriton were seated side by side on the closed bridge, while below them on the other side of the sound-proofed glass their unequal crews went about their duties. Brock and Emma had one wall, Bob, Johnny and their cohorts the other wall and centre aisle. But all were travelling in the same direction. All wore the same obediently purposeful expressions, faced the same banks of screens that rolled and flickered like stock exchange quotations as the automatic decodes came in.

'Truck's safely back in dock,' said Sheriton as the screens abruptly cleared and flashed the codeword BLACKJACK.

The truck itself was a miracle of penetration.

Our own truck! In Moscow! Us! In English it would have been a lorry but here it was a truck in deference to the American proprietorship. An enormous separate operation lay behind its acquisition and deployment. It was a Kamaz, dirty grey and very big, one of a fleet of trucks belonging to SOVTRANSAVTO, hence the acronym daubed in Roman letters across its filthy flank. It had been recruited, together with its driver, by the Agency's enormous Munich station during one of the truck's many forays to West Germany to collect luxury commodities for Moscow's privileged few with access to a special distribution store. Everything from Western shoes to Western tampons to spare parts for Western cars had been shuttled back and forth inside the truck's bowels. As to the driver, he was one of the Long Distance Gunners, as these luckless creatures are known in the Soviet Union – State employees, miserably underpaid, with neither medical nor accident insurance to protect them against misfortune in the West, who even in deepest winter huddle stoically in the lee of their great charges, munching sausage before sharing another night's sleep in their comfortless cabins – but making for themselves, in Russia nevertheless, vast fortunes out of their opportunities in the West.

And now, for yet more immense rewards, this particular Long Distance Gunner had agreed to 'lend' his truck to a 'Western dealer' here in the very heart of Moscow. And this same dealer, who was one of Cy's own army of *toptuny*, lent it to Cy, who in turn stuffed inside it all kinds of ingeniously portable surveillance and audio equipment, which was then swept away again before the truck was returned through intermediaries to its legal driver.

Nothing of the sort had ever happened before. Our own mobile safe room, in Moscow!

Ned alone found the whole idea unsettling. The Long Distance Gunners worked in pairs, as Ned knew better than anyone. By KGB edict, these pairs were deliberately incompatible, and in many cases each man had a responsibility to report upon the other. But when Ned asked if he could read the operational file, it was denied him under the very laws of security he himself held dear.

But the most impressive piece of Langley's new armoury had still to be unveiled, and once again Ned had not been able to hold out against it. From now onwards, sound tapes in Moscow would be encrypted into random codes and transmitted in digital pulses in one-thousandth of the time that the tapes would take to run if you were listening to them in your drawing room. Yet when the pulses were restored to sound by the receiving

station, the Langley wizards insisted, you could never tell the tapes had
had such a rough time.

The word WAIT was forming in pretty pyramids. Spying is waiting.

The word SOUND replaced it. Spying is listening.

Ned and Sheriton put on their headsets as Clive and I slipped into the
spare seats behind them and put on ours.

Katya sat pensively on her bed staring at the telephone, not wanting it to
ring again.

Why do you give your name when none of us give names? she asked
him in her mind.

Why do you give mine?

*Is that Katya? How are you? This is Igor speaking. Just to tell you I
have heard nothing more from him, okay?*

Then why do you ring me to tell me nothing?

The usual time, okay? The usual place. No problem. Just like before.

Why do you repeat what needs no repetition, after I have already told
you I will be at the hospital at the agreed time?

*By then he'll know what his position is, he'll know which plane he can
catch, everything. Then you don't have to worry, okay? How about your
publisher? Did he show up all right?*

'Igor, I do not know which publisher you are referring to.'

And she rang off before he could say more.

I am being ungrateful, she told herself. When people are ill it is normal
that old friends should rally. And if they promote themselves overnight
from casual acquaintance to old friend, and take centre stage when for
years they have hardly spoken to you, it is still a sign of loyalty and there
is nothing sinister about it, even if only six months ago Yakov declared
Igor to be unredeemable – 'Igor has continued along the path I left behind,'
he had remarked after a chance meeting in the street. 'Igor asks too many
questions.'

Yet here was Igor acting as Yakov's closest friend and putting himself
out for him in risky and invaluable ways. '*If you have a letter for Yakov,
you have only to give it to me. I have established an excellent line of
communication to the sanatorium. I know somebody who makes the
journey almost every week,*' he had told her at their last meeting.

'The sanatorium?' she had cried excitedly. 'Then where is he? Where is
it located?'

But it was as if Igor had not yet thought of the answer to this question,
for he had scowled and looked uncomfortable and pleaded State secrecy.
Us, State secrecy, when we are flaunting the State's secrets!

I am being unfair to him, she thought. I am starting to see deception
everywhere. In Igor, even in Barley.

Barley. She frowned. He had no business to criticise Yakov's declaration
of affection. Who does he think he is, this Westerner with his attaching

manners and cynical suspicions? Coming so close so quickly, playing God to Matvey and my children?

I shall never trust a man who was brought up without dogma, she told herself severely.

I can love a believer, I can love a heretic, but I cannot love an Englishman.

She switched on her little radio and ran through the shortwave bands, having first put in the earpiece so as not to disturb the twins. But as she listened to the different voices clamouring for her soul – Deutsche Welle, Voice of America, Radio Liberty, Voice of Israel, Voice of God knew whom, each one so cosy, so superior, so compelling – an angry confusion came over her. I'm a Russian! she wanted to shout back at them. Even in tragedy, I dream of a better world than yours!

But *what* tragedy?

The phone was ringing. She grabbed the receiver. But it was only Nasayan, an altered man these days, checking on tomorrow's plans.

'Listen, I am confirming privately that you really wish to be at the October stand tomorrow. Only we must begin early, you see. If you have to get your kids to school or something of that sort, I can easily instruct Yelizavyeta Alexeyevna to come instead of you. It is no hardship. You have only to tell me.'

'You are very kind, Grigory Tigranovich, and I appreciate your call. But having spent most of last week helping to put up the exhibits, I should naturally like to be present at the official opening. Matvey can manage very well to see the children off to school.'

Thoughtfully, she put the receiver back on its cradle. Nasayan, my God – why do we address each other like characters on the stage? Who do we think is listening to us who requires such rounded sentences? If I can talk to an English stranger as if he is my lover, why can't I talk normally to an Armenian who is my colleague?

He rang, and she knew at once that she had been waiting all this while for his call, because she was already smiling. Unlike Igor, he did not say his name or hers.

'Elope with me,' he said.

'Tonight?'

'Horses are saddled, food for three days.'

'But are you also sober enough to elope?'

'Amazingly, I am.' A pause. 'It's not for want of trying but nothing happened. Must be old age.'

He sounded sober too. Sober and close.

'But what about the book fair? Are you going to desert it as you deserted the audio fair?'

'To hell with the book fair. We've got to do it before or never. Afterwards we'll be too tired. How are you?'

'Oh, I am furious with you. You have completely bewitched my family, and now they ask only when you will come back with more tobacco and crayons.'

Another pause. He was not usually so thoughtful when he was joking.

'That's what I do. I bewitch people, then the moment they're under my spell I cease to feel anything for them.'

'But that's terrible!' she cried, deeply shocked. 'Barley, what are you telling me?'

'Just repeating the wisdom of an early wife, that's all. She said I had impulses but no feelings and I shouldn't wear a duffle coat in London. Anyone tells you something like that, you believe it for the rest of your life. I've never worn a duffle coat since.'

'Barley, that woman – Barley, that was a totally cruel and irresponsible thing for her to say. I am sorry but she is completely wrong. She was provoked, I am sure. But she is wrong.'

'She is, is she? So what do I feel? Enlighten me.'

She broke out laughing, realising she had walked straight into his trap.

'Barley, you are a very, very bad man. I shall have nothing to do with you.'

'Because I don't feel anything?'

'For one thing, you feel protection for people. We all noticed that today, and we were grateful.'

'More.'

'For another, you feel a sense of honour, I would say. You are decadent, naturally, because you are a Westerner. That is normal. But you are redeemed because you feel honour.'

'Are there any pies left over?'

'You mean you feel hunger too?'

'I want to come and eat them.'

'Now?'

'Now.'

'That is completely impossible! We are all in bed already and it's nearly midnight.'

'Tomorrow.'

'Barley, this is too ridiculous. We are about to begin the book fair, both of us have a dozen invitations.'

'What time?'

A beautiful silence was settling between them.

'You may come at perhaps-half-past-seven.'

'I may be early.'

For a long while after that neither of them spoke. But the silence joined them more closely than words could have done. They became two heads on a single pillow, ear to ear. And when he rang off it was not his jokes and self-ironies that stayed with her but the tone of contented sincerity – she would almost say solemnity – that he had seemed unable to keep out of his voice.

*

He was singing.

Inside his head, and outside it too. In his heart and all over his body at last, Barley Blair was singing.

He was in his big grey bedroom at the gloomy Mezh on the eve of the Moscow book fair, and he was singing 'Bless This House' in the recognisable manner of Mahalia Jackson while he pirouetted round the room with a glass of mineral water in his hand, glimpsing his reflection in the immense television screen that was the room's one glory.

Sober.

Hot sober.

Barley Blair.

Alone.

He had drunk nothing. In the safe truck for his debriefing, though he had sweated like a racehorse, nothing. Not even a glass of water while he had regaled Paddy and Cy with a sweetened, unworried version of his day.

At the French publishers' party at the Rossiya with Wicklow, where he had positively shone with confidence, nothing.

At the Swedes' party at the National with Henziger, where he had shone yet more brightly, he had grabbed a glass of Georgian *shampanskoye* in self-protection because Zapadny was so pointedly amazed he was not drinking. But he had contrived to leave it undrunk behind a flower vase. So still nothing.

And at the Doubleday party at the Ukraina with Henziger again, shining like the North Star by now, he had clutched a mineral water with a bit of lemon floating in it to look like gin and tonic.

So nothing. Not out of highmindedness. Not a reformed spirit, God forbid. He had not signed the Pledge or turned over a new leaf. It was merely that he wished nothing to mar the clear-headed, reasoned ecstasy that was collecting in him, this unfamiliar sense of being at dreadful risk and equal to it, of knowing that whatever was happening he had prepared himself for it, and that if nothing was happening he was ready for that too, because his preparedness was an all-round defence with a sacred absolute at its centre.

I have joined the tiny ranks of people who know what they will do first if the ship catches fire in the middle of the night, he thought; and what they will do last, or not do at all. He knew in ordered detail what he considered worth saving and what was unimportant to him. And what was to be shoved aside, stepped over and left for dead.

A great house-cleaning had taken place inside his mind, comprising quite humble details as well as grand themes. Because, as Barley had recently observed, it was in humble detail that grand themes wrought their havoc.

The clarity of his view amazed him. He peered round him, took a turn or two, sang a few bars. He came back to where he was, and knew that nothing had been left out.

Not the momentary inflection of uncertainty in her voice. Or the shadow of doubt flitting across the dark pools of her eyes.

Or Goethe's straight lines of handwriting instead of wild scrawls.

Or Goethe's cumbersome, untypical jokes about bureaucrats and vodka.

Or Goethe's guilty dirge about the way he had treated her, when for twenty years he had treated her however he had damn well felt like, including using her as a throwaway delivery-girl.

Or Goethe's callow promise to make it all up to her in the future, so long as she'll stay in the game for the time being, when it is an article of Goethe's faith that the future no longer interests him, that his whole obsession is with now. 'There is only *now!*'

Yet from these spindrift theories that were most likely nothing more than theories, Barley's mind flew effortlessly to the grandest prize of his clarified perception: that in the context of Goethe's notion of what he was achieving, Goethe was *right*, and that for most of his life Goethe had stood on one side of a corrupt and anachronistic equation while Barley in his ignorance had stood on the other.

And that if Barley were ever called upon to choose, he would rather go Goethe's path than Ned's or anybody else's, because his presence would be urgently required in the extreme middle ground of which he had elected himself a citizen.

And that everything that had happened to Barley since Peredelkino had delivered the proof of this. The old isms were dead, the contest between Communism and capitalism had ended in a wet whimper. Its rhetoric had fled underground into the secret chambers of the grey men who were still dancing away long after the music had ended.

As to his loyalty to his country, Barley saw it only as a question of which England he chose to serve. His last ties to the imperial fantasy were dead. The chauvinist drumbeat revolted him. He would rather be trampled by it than march with it. He knew a better England by far, and it was inside himself.

He lay on his bed, waiting for the fear to seize him, but it wouldn't. Instead, he found himself playing a kind of mental chess, because chess was about possibilities, and it seemed best to contemplate them in tranquillity rather than try and sort through them when the roof was falling in.

Because if Armageddon didn't strike, there was nothing lost. But if Armageddon did, there was much to save.

So Barley began to think. And Barley began to make his preparations with a cool head, exactly as Ned would have advised if Ned were still holding the reins.

He thought till early morning and dozed a bit and when he woke he went on thinking, and by the time he strode cheerfully into breakfast already looking round for the fun of the fair, there was an entire section of his head that was given over full time to thinking what the fools who do it describe as the unthinkable.

14

'Oh come, Ned,' said Clive airily, still elated by the wizardry of the transmission. 'The Bluebird's been ill before. Several times.'

'I know,' said Ned distractedly. 'I know.' And then, 'Maybe I don't mind him being ill. Maybe I mind him writing.'

Sheriton was listening chin in hand, as he had been listening to the tape. An affinity had grown up between Ned and Sheriton, as in an operation it must. They were handling the transfer of power as if it had happened long ago.

'But my dear man, that's what we all do when we're ill,' Clive exclaimed in a misjudged demonstration of human understanding. 'We *write* to the whole world!'

It had never occurred to me that Clive was capable of illness, or that he had friends to write to.

'I mind him handing chatty letters to mysterious intermediaries. And I mind him talking about trying to bring more materials for Barley,' Ned said. 'We know he never normally writes to her. We know he's security conscious to a fault. Suddenly he falls ill and writes her a gushing five-page love letter via Igor. Igor who? Igor when? How?'

'He should have photographed the letter,' said Clive, becoming disapproving of Barley. 'Or taken it off her. One or the other.'

Ned was too wrapped up in his thoughts to give this suggestion the contempt it deserved.

'How could he? She knows him as a publisher. That's all she knows him as.'

'Unless the Bluebird told her otherwise,' said Clive.

'He wouldn't,' Ned retorted, and returned to his thoughts. 'There was a car,' he said. 'A red car then a white car. You saw the watch report. The red car went in first, then the white car took over.'

'That is pure speculation. On a warm Sunday the whole of Moscow takes to the countryside,' said Clive knowledgeably.

He waited for a reaction but in vain, so he returned to the subject of the letter. '*Katya* didn't have any problems with it,' he objected. '*Katya* 's not crying foul. She's jumping for joy. If she didn't smell a rat, and Scott Blair didn't, why should *we* – sitting here in London, doing their worrying for them?'

'He asked for the shopping list,' said Ned, as if still hearing distant music. 'A final and exhaustive list of questions. Why did he do that?'

Sheriton had finally stirred himself. He was flagging Ned down with his big paw. 'Ned, Ned, Ned, Ned. Okay? It's Day One again, so we're jumpy. Let's get some sleep.'

He stood up. So did Clive and so did I. But Ned stayed doggedly rooted where he was, his hands clasped before him on his desk.

Sheriton spoke down at him. With affection, but with force as well. 'Ned, just hear me, Ned, okay? Ned?'

'I'm not deaf.'

'No, but you're tired. Ned, if we bad-mouth this operation one more time, it will never come back. We are going with *your* man, the one *you* brought to *us* in order to persuade *us*. We moved hell on earth to get this far. We have the source. We have the appropriation. We have the influential audience. We are within pissing distance of filling gaps in our knowledge that no smart machines, no electronic heavy breathers, no Pentagon Jesuits can get within light years of. If we keep our nerve, and Barley does, and Bluebird does, we will have landed a bonanza beyond the dreams of the most accomplished fantasists. If we stay in there.'

But Sheriton was speaking with too much conviction, and his face, for all its pudgy inscrutability, was betraying an almost desperate need.

'Ned?'

'Hearing you, Russell. Loud and clear.'

'Ned, this is no longer a cottage industry, for Christ's sake. We played big, now we have to think big. You don't get bigger than this. Presidential findings are not an invitation to doubt our own good judgment. They are in the way of being orders. Ned, I really think you should get some sleep.'

'I don't think I'm tired,' said Ned.

'I think you are. I think everyone will say you are. I think they may even say Ned was very bullish for the Bluebird until the big bad American wolf came and took his joe away. Then all of a sudden the Bluebird was a very iffy source. I think people are going to say you are tired as hell.'

I glanced at Clive.

Clive too was looking down at Ned, but with eyes so cold they chilled my blood. Time to move you on, they were saying. Time to measure you for the drop.

Both Henziger and Wicklow kept a close eye on Barley that day and reported on him frequently, Henziger to Cy by whatever means they used, Wicklow by way of an irregular to Paddy. Both attested to his high spirits and relaxed manner, and in differing language to his sovereignty. Both

described how at breakfast he had enchanted a couple of Finnish publishers who were showing interest in the Trans-Siberian Railway project.

'They were eating out of his hand,' said Wicklow, providing an unconsciously comic picture of breakfast, but at the Mezh anything is possible.

Both recorded with amusement Barley's determination to act as their
tour-guide when they reached the permanent exhibition site, and how he
obliged their taxi to drop them at the end of the grand avenue so that, as
first-time pilgrims from the world of capitalism, they could make their
first approach on foot.

So the two professional spies strolled contentedly through the wet
autumn sunshine with their jackets over their shoulders and their joe
between them while Barley favoured them with his own eccentric guided
tour, extolling the 'late Essoldo period' architecture and the 'Revolutionary Rococo' gardens. He doted on the immense ornamental pool and its
golden fish spewing jets of water at the rumps of fifteen naked golden
nymphs, one for each of the Socialist republics. He insisted that they
dawdle at the white-pillared love bowers and temples of delight – whose
portals, he pointed out, were dedicated not to Venus or Bacchus but to the
fallen goddesses of the Soviet economy – coal, steel and even atomic
energy, Jack!

'He was witty but he wasn't high,' reported Henziger, who had already
taken fondly to Barley in Leningrad. 'He was damn funny.'

And from the temples Barley marched them up the triumphal avenue
itself, the Emperor's Ride, perhaps a mile of it and heaven knows how
broad, celebrating the People's Achievements in the Service of Mankind.
And surely no vision of popular power was ever portrayed in such despotic
images! he proclaimed. Surely no revolution had so perfectly enshrined
everything it had set out to raze to the ground! But by then Barley had to
bellow his irreverences over the din of the loudspeakers, which all day
long pour floods of self-congratulatory messages on to the heads of the
benighted crowds below.

Finally they arrived, as they had to, at the two pavilions housing the
fair.

'On my right, the publishers of Peace, Progress and Goodwill,' Barley
announced, playing the referee at a prize fight. 'On my left, the distributors
of Fascist imperialist lies, the pornographers, the poisoners of truth.
Seconds out. Time.'

They showed their passes and walked in.

The exhibition stand of the newly inaugurated and geographically confusing house of Potomac & Blair was a small but satisfactory sensation of the
fair. Langley's lovingly created P. & B. symbol shone resplendent between
the dowdier displays of Astral Press and Purbeck Media. The stand's
interior design, characterised by its Langley architects as tough but tasty,
was a model of instant impact. The exhibits – many of them, as is

customary, dummies of books still to enter the production line – were prepared with all the attention to detail that intelligence services tradition-ally bestow on fakes. The only good coffee at the fair was to be found bubbling on an ingenious machine in the rear cubby-hole. There was Langley's own Mary Lou to serve it. For the favoured, there was even a forbidden shot of Scotch to help them through the day – forbidden, indeed, by special edict of the organisers, for even literary reconstruction must be the work of sober men.

And Mary Lou, with her homespun schoolgirl smile and billowing tweed skirt, made a natural product of the nicer side of Madison Avenue. Nobody need ever have guessed she had a little of Langley's thread woven into her as well.

Neither was Wicklow, with his polished patter, anything other than the quick-eyed, upwardly-mobile young publisher they make these days.

As to honest Jack Henziger, he was the archetype of the settled bucca-neer of the modern American book trade. He made no secret of his antecedents. Pipelines in the Middle East, humanity in Afghanistan, red beans to opium-growing hill-tribes in Thailand – Henziger had sold them all, whatever he had sold for Langley on the side. But publishing was where his heart was, and he was here to prove it.

And Barley seemed to revel in the artifice. He threw himself upon it as if it were his long-lost reality, shaking hands, receiving the congratulations of his competitors and colleagues, until around eleven he professed himself restless and proposed to Wicklow that they tour the lines and take comfort to the troops.

So off they set, Barley bearing in his arms a bunch of white envelopes of which he occasionally pressed one into a chosen hand as he yelled and greeted his way along the packed alleys of visitors and exhibitors.

'Well blow me over, if it isn't Barley Bloody Blair,' a familiar voice declared from the centre of a multi-lingual display of illustrated Bibles. 'Remember me, do you? Third from the left in the mink jock-strap, back in your humble days?'

'Spikey. They let you in again,' said Barley with pleasure, and handed him his envelope.

'It's when they won't let me *out* I'm worried. This your dad, then?'

Barley presented the distinguished editor Wicklow, and Spikey Morgan bestowed a priestly blessing on him with his nicotine-stained fingers.

They pressed on, only to stumble into Dan Zeppelin a few yards later. Dan did not talk. Dan conspired in a gravedigger's murmur, leaning across his counter at you over folded arms.

'So I mean tell me something, Barley. Okay? Are we pioneers or are we the fucking Mitford sisters? So a few unbooks are books this year. So a few unwriters have been sprung from jail. Big deal. I walk into my own stand this morning, there's some asshole pulling the books out of my shelves. "May I ask you a personal question?" I says. "What the fuck are

you doing with my books?" "Orders," he says. Six books, he confiscated.
Mary G. Ambleside on fucking *Black Consciousness in Song and Word*.
Orders! I mean who are we, Barley? Who are they? What do they think
they're restructuring when there was never a structure in the first place?
How do you restructure a corpse?'

At Lupus Books they were directed to the coffee room, where our
Chairman Himself the newly-knighted Sir Peter Oliphant, had upstaged
even the Russians by reserving a table. A handwritten notice in both
languages confirmed his triumph. The flags of Britain and the Soviet Union
warned off doubters. Flanked by interpreters and high officials, Sir Peter
was dilating on the many advantages to the Soviet Union of subsidising
his generous purchases from them.

'It's the Earl!' cried Barley, handing him an envelope. 'Where's the
coronet?'

With scarcely a flicker of his dusty eyelids, the great man continued his
dissertation.

At the Israeli stand an armed peace reigned. The dark queue was orderly
but mute. Boys in jeans and sneakers lounged against the walls. Lev
Abramovitz was white-haired and overpoweringly tall. He had served in
the Irish Guards.

'Lev. How's Zion?'

'Maybe we're winning, maybe the happy ending's at the beginning,' Lev
said, pocketing Barley's envelope.

And from Israel, with Barley leading at a canter, they pounded across
the concourse to the Pavilion of Peace, Progress and Goodwill, where
there could no longer be any doubt of the massive historical upheaval
taking place, or of who was doing the heaving.

Every banner and spare bit of wall screamed the new Gospel. In every
stand of every republic, the thoughts and writings of the no-longer-new
prophet, with his birthmark turned away and his jaw raised, were blazoned alongside those of his colourless master, Lenin. At the VAAP stand,
where Barley and Wicklow shook a few hands and Barley shed a batch of
envelopes, the Leader's speeches, wrapped in shiny covers and rendered
into English, French, Spanish and German, made a totally resistible
appeal.

'How much more of this shit do we have to take, Barley?' a blond-faced
Moscow publisher demanded *sotto voce* as they went by. 'When will they
start repressing us again to make us comfortable? If our past's a lie, who's
to say our future isn't a lie as well?'

They continued along the stands, Barley leading, Barley greeting, Wicklow following.

'Joseph! Great to see you! Envelope for you. Don't eat it all at once.'

'Barley! My friend! Didn't they give you my message? Maybe I didn't
leave one.'

'Yuri. Great to see you! Envelope for you.'

'Come and drink tonight, Barley! Sasha is coming, so is Rosa. Rudi's giving a concert tomorrow so he wants to stay sober. You heard about the writers they let out? Listen, it's Potemkin village stuff. They let them out, they give them a few meals, show them off and throw them back inside till next year. Come over here, I got to sell you a couple of books to annoy Zapadny.'

At first Wicklow didn't even realise they had arrived at their destination. He saw a Roman standard hung with faded flags and some gold lettering stitched on red bunting. He heard Barley's yell of 'Katya, where are you?' But nothing said who owned the stand and probably that was a part of the display that hadn't arrived. He saw the usual unreadable books on agricultural development in the Ukraine and the traditional dances of Georgia expiring on their shelves under the strain of previous exhibitions. He saw the usual half-dozen broad-hipped women standing around as if they were waiting for a train, and a small unshaven fellow clutching his cigarette in front of him like a conjuror's wand, scowling at Barley's nametag.

Nasayan, Wicklow read in return. *Grigory Tigranovich. Senior Editor, October Publishing*.

'You are looking for Miss Katya Orlova, I think,' Nasayan told Barley in English, holding his cigarette still higher as if to get a clearer look at his visitor.

'I'll say I am!' Barley replied with enthusiasm, and a couple of the women smiled.

A grin of frightful courtesy had spread over Nasayan's face. With a flourish of his cigarette he stepped aside and Wicklow recognised Katya's back as she talked with two very small Asians whom he took to be Burmese. Then an instinct made her turn and she caught sight of Barley first, then Wicklow, then Barley again, while a splendid smile lit her face.

'Katya. Fantastic,' said Barley shyly. 'How are the kids? Did they survive?'

'Oh thank you, they are *very* well!'

Watched by Nasayan and his ladies, as well as by Wicklow, Barley handed her an invitation to the great glasnost launch party of Potomac & Blair.

'Oh by the way, I may skip some of the gay whirl tonight,' Barley remarked as they made their way back to the Western pavilion. 'You and Jack and Mary Lou will have to manage on your own. I'm dining with a beautiful lady.'

'Anyone we know?' Wicklow asked. They both laughed. It was a sunny day.

She's fine, Barley was thinking contentedly. If something is happening, it hasn't happened to her yet.

How much did we know or guess, any of us, of Barley's feelings towards

Katya? In a case so scrupulously monitored and controlled, the question of love received diffident handling.

Wicklow, diligently promiscuous in his own life, was puritanical about Barley's. Perhaps as a young man he still could not take seriously the notion of an older passion. For Wicklow, Barley was merely infatuated, which he usually was anyway. People of Barley's age were not in love.

Henziger, who was Barley's rough contemporary, regarded sex as an unsung perquisite of the secret life, and took it for granted that a square-shooter like Barley would put his body where his duty lay. Like Wicklow, but for different reasons, he found nothing exceptional in Barley's tender feelings towards Katya and operationally much to recommend them.

And in London? There was no sharply defined view. On the island Brady had said a mouthful, but Brady's assault had been repelled and his advice with it.

And Ned? Ned had a wife as soldierly as himself and as unawakened. Name me a joe in a bad country, Ned liked to say with a rueful smile, who doesn't fall for a pretty face if she's on his side against the world.

And Bob, Sheriton and Johnny seem all to have assumed in different ways that Barley's private life and his appetites generally were of such a seedy complexity that they were best left out of the equation.

And Palfrey, what was old Palfrey thinking – hurrying up to Grosvenor Square in any spare hour and, if he couldn't make it, phoning Ned to ask, 'How's the boy?'

Palfrey was thinking about Hannah. The Hannah he had loved and loves still, as only cowards may. The Hannah whose smile was once as warm and deep as Katya's. 'You're a good man, Palfrey,' she will say with terrible control on the days when she is trying to understand me. 'You'll find a way. Maybe not now, but one day.' And oh, Palfrey found a way all right! He pleaded the code – that convenient code that rules that a young solicitor caught in adultery is *ipso facto* excluded from doing anything about it. He pleaded children, hers and his – so many people involved, dear. He pleaded marriage, curse him – how will they cope without us, dear, Derek can't even boil an egg? He pleaded the partnership and, when it was dissolved, he buried his stupid head in the sands of the secret desert where no Hannah would ever be able to see him again. And he had the nerve to plead duty – the Service would never forgive me a mucky divorce, dear – not its legal adviser, it couldn't.

I was thinking about the island too. About the evening Barley and I had stood on the shingle beach watching the fog-bank roll at us across the grey Atlantic.

'They'd never get her out, would they?' Barley said. 'Not if things went wrong.'

I didn't answer and I don't think he expected me to, but he was right. She was a thoroughbred Soviet national and she had committed a thoroughbred Soviet crime. She was nowhere near the swappable class.

'Anyway, she'd never leave her children,' he said, confirming his own doubts.

We watched the sea for a while, his eyes on Katya and mine on Hannah, who would never leave her children either, but wanted to bring them with her, and make an honest man out of a career-obsessed Chancery Lane hack who was sleeping with his senior partner's wife.

'Raymond Chandler!' Uncle Matvey yelled from his chair, over the clamour of neighbours' television sets.

'Terrific,' Barley said.

'Agatha Christie!'

'Ah well, now, *Agatha*.'

'Dashiel Hammett! Dorothy Sayers. Josephine Tey.'

Barley sat on the sofa where Katya had settled him. The living room was tiny. The span of his arms could have bridged the width of it. A glass-fronted corner cupboard contained the family treasures. Katya had already given him the tour of them. The pottery mugs, made by a friend for her wedding, their medallions portraying the bride and groom. The Leningrad coffee set, no longer complete, that had belonged to the lady in the wood frame on the top shelf. The old sepia photograph of a Tolstoyan couple, the man bearded and resolute in his stiff white collar, the girl in her bonnet and fur muff.

'Matvey is passionate for English detective fiction,' Katya called from the kitchen, where she had last things to do.

'Me too,' said Barley untruthfully.

'He is telling you it was not permitted under the Czars. They would never have tolerated such an intrusion into their police system. Do you have vodka? No more for Matvey, please. You must take some food. We are not alcoholics like you Westerners. We do not drink without food.'

Under the pretext of examining her books, Barley stepped into the tiny passage from where he could see her. Jack London, Hemingway and Joyce, Dreiser and John Fowles. Heine, Remarque and Rilke. The twins were in the bathroom chattering. He gazed at her through the open kitchen door. Her gestures had an air of timeless and deliberate delay. She's become a Russian again, he thought. When something works, she's grateful. When it doesn't work, it's life. From the living room Matvey was still talking gaily.

'What's he saying now?' Barley asked.

'He is talking about the siege.'

'I love you.'

'The Leningraders refused to accept that they were beaten.' She was preparing cakes of liver on rice. Her hands kept still a moment, then went on with their work. 'Shostakovich still composed even if the ink froze in his inkwell. The novelists went on writing, you could hear a chapter of a new novel any week if you knew the right cellars to go to.'

'I love you,' he repeated. 'All my failures were preparations for meeting you. Fact.'

She breathed out sharply and they both fell silent, for a moment deaf to Matvey's jolly monologue from the sitting room, and to the sounds of splashing from the bathroom.

'What else does he say?' Barley asked.

'Barley – ' she protested.

'Please. Tell me what he's saying.'

'The Germans were four kilometres from the city on the south side. They covered the outskirts with machine-gun fire and shelled the centre with artillery.' She handed him mats and knives and forks and followed him to the living room. 'Two hundred and fifty grams of bread for a labourer, others a hundred and twenty-five. Are you really so fascinated by Matvey, or are you pretending to be polite, as usual?'

'It's a mature, unselfish, absolute, thrilling love. I've never known any-thing approaching it. I thought you ought to be the first to know.'

Matvey was beaming at Barley in unalloyed adoration. His new English pipe gleamed from his top pocket. Katya held Barley's stare, started to laugh, shook her head, not in negation but in daze. The twins rushed in wearing their dressing-gowns and swung on Barley's hands. Katya settled them to the table and put Matvey at the head. Barley sat beside her while she poured the cabbage soup. With a prodigious show of power Sergey drew the cork from a wine bottle, but Katya would take no more than a half-glass and Matvey was permitted only vodka. Anna broke ranks to fetch a drawing she had made after a visit to the Timiryasev Academy: horses, a real wheatfield, plants that could survive the snow. Matvey was telling the story of the old man in the machine shop across the road, and once more Barley insisted on hearing every word.

'There was an old man Matvey knew, a friend of my father's,' Katya said. 'He had a machine shop. When he was too weak from starving, he strapped himself to the machinery so that he would not collapse. That was how Matvey and my father found him when he died. Strapped to the machinery. Frozen. Matvey also wishes you to know that he personally wore a luminous badge on his coat' – Matvey was proudly indicating the very spot on his pullover – 'so that he didn't knock into his friends in the dark when they took their buckets to fetch water from the Neva. So. That is enough of Leningrad,' she said firmly. 'You have been very gen-erous, Barley, as usual. I hope you are sincere.'

'I have never been so sincere in my life.'

Barley was in the middle of toasting Matvey's health when the telephone started ringing beside the sofa. Katya sprang up but Sergey was ahead of her. He put the receiver to his ear and listened, then replaced it on the cradle with a shake of his head.

'So many misconnections,' Katya said, and handed round plates for the liver cakes.

*

There was only her room. There was only her bed.

The children had gone to their bed and Barley could hear them snuffling in their sleep. Matvey lay on his army bedroll in the living room, already dreaming of Leningrad. Katya sat upright and Barley sat beside her, holding her hand while he watched her face against the uncurtained window.

'I love Matvey too,' he said.

She nodded and gave a short laugh. He put his knuckles against her cheek and discovered that she was weeping.

'Just not in the same way I love you,' he explained. 'I love children, uncles, dogs, cats and musicians. The entire Ark is my personal responsibility. But I love you so profoundly that I am ashamed to be articulate. I would be very grateful if we could find a way to silence me. I look at you, and I am absolutely sick of the sound of my own voice. Do you want that in writing?'

Then with both hands he turned her face to him and kissed her. Then he guided her towards the top of the bed and laid her head on the pillow and kissed her again, first her lips and then her closed wet eyelashes while her arms gathered round his back and drew him down on her. Then she pushed him away from her and sprang up and went to look at the twins before returning. Then she slid the bolt inside her bedroom door.

'If the children come, you must dress and we must be very serious,' she warned, kissing him.

'Can I tell them I love you?'

'If you do I shall not interpret.'

'Can I tell you?'

'If you are very quiet.'

'Will you interpret?'

She was no longer weeping. She was no longer smiling. Black, logical eyes, searching like his own. An embrace without reservation, no hidden codicils, no small print to the agreement.

I had never known Ned in such a mood. He had become the Jonah of his own operation and his rugged stoicism only made his forebodings harder to take. In the situation room he sat at his desk as if he were presiding at a court martial, while Sheriton lolled beside him like an intelligent Teddy bear. And when as a reckless throw I walked him down the road to the Connaught where I occasionally took Hannah and, to ease the waiting, fed him a magical dinner in the Grill, I still could not penetrate the mask of his forbearance.

For the truth was, his pessimism was seriously affecting my own spirits. I was on a see-saw. Clive and Sheriton were up one end, Ned was the dead weight at the other. And since I am no great decision-taker, it was all the more disturbing to watch a man normally so incisive resign himself to ostracism.

'You're seeing ghosts, Ned,' I told him with little of Sheriton's conviction. 'You've gone far beyond whatever anybody else is thinking. All right, it's not your case any more. That doesn't mean it's a shipwreck. And your credibility is, well, ebbing.'

'A final and exhaustive list,' Ned said again, as if the phrase had been dinned into him by a hypnotist. 'Why final? Why exhaustive? Answer me that. When Barley saw him in Leningrad, he wouldn't even accept our preliminary questionnaire. He threw it back in Barley's face. Now he's asking for the whole shopping list in one go. *Asking* for it. The *final* list. The Grand Slam. We're to get it all together for the weekend. After that the Bluebird will answer no more questions from the grey men. "This is your last chance," he's saying. *Why?*'

'Look at it the other way round a minute,' I urged him in a desperate murmur, when the wine waiter had brought us a second decanter of priceless claret. 'All right. The Bluebird has been turned by the Sovs. He's bad. The Sovs are running him. So why do they close it down? Why not sit back and play us along? *You* wouldn't close it down if you were in their shoes. You wouldn't hand us an ultimatum, create deadlines. Would you?'

His reply put paid to the best and most expensive meal I had ever given a fellow officer in my life.

'I might have to,' he said. 'If I were Russian.'

'Why?'

His words were the more chilling for being spoken with a leaden dispassion.

'Because he might not be presentable any more. He might not be able to speak. Or pick up his knife and fork. Or pour salt on his grouse. He might have made a couple of voluntary statements about his charming mistress in Moscow who had no idea, but really no idea, what she was doing. He might have – '

We walked back to Grosvenor Square. Barley had left Katya's apartment at midnight Moscow time and returned to the Mezh, where Henziger had sat up for him in the lobby, ostensibly reading a manuscript.

Barley was in high spirits but had nothing new to report. Just a family evening, he had told Henziger, but good fun all the same. And the hospital visit still on, he added.

The whole of the next day nothing. A space. Spying is waiting. Spying is worrying yourself sick while you watch Ned sink into a decline. Spying is taking Hannah to your flat in Pimlico between the hours of four and six when she is supposed to be having a German lesson, God knows why. Spying is imitating love, and making sure she's home in time to give dear Derek his dinner.

15

They went in Volodya's car. She had borrowed it for the evening. He was to wait for her outside the Aeroport metro station at nine, and at nine exactly the Lada pulled up precariously beside him.

'You should not have insisted,' she said.

The tower blocks glowed above them but in the streets there was already the menacing atmosphere of curfew. Scents of autumn filled the damp night air. A half-moon, draped in shrouds of mist, hung ahead of them. Occasionally their hands brushed. Occasionally their hands grasped each other in a strong embrace. Barley was watching the wing mirror. It was smashed and some of the bits were missing but he could see enough in it to watch the cars that followed without overtaking. Katya turned left but still nothing passed them.

She wasn't speaking so he wasn't either. He wondered how they learned it, where is safe to speak, where isn't. At school? From older girls as they grew up? Or was it your earnest little lecture from the family doctor somewhere round the second year of puberty? 'It's time you learned that cars and walls have ears just like people . . .'

They were bumping over a pitted sliproad into a half-finished carpark.

'Imagine you are a doctor,' she warned him as they faced each other across the roof of the car. 'You must look very strict.'

'I'm a doctor,' Barley said. Neither of them was joking.

They picked their way between a maze of moonlit puddles to a pathway covered in asbestos awning, leading to double doors and an empty reception desk. He caught the first alarming smells of hospital: disinfectant, floor polish, surgical spirit. At a crisp pace she marched him across a circular hallway of mottled concrete, down a linoleum corridor and past a marble counter staffed by sullen women. A clock said ten-twenty-five. Making a consciously officious gesture, Barley compared it with his watch. The clock was ten minutes slow. The next corridor was lined with figures slumped on kitchen chairs.

The waiting-room was a gloomy catacomb supported by immense pillars with a raised platform at one end. At the other, swing doors gave on to the lavatories. Somebody had rigged a temporary light to show the way. By its pale light, Barley could make out empty coat racks behind a wooden counter, parked stretcher trolleys and, fixed to the nearest pillar, an ancient telephone. A bench stood against the wall. Katya sat on it, so Barley sat beside her.

'He tries always to be punctual. Sometimes he is delayed by the connection,' she said.

'Can I speak to him?'

'He would be angry.'

'Why?'

'If they hear English on a long-distance line they will immediately pay attention. It is normal.'

From the swing doors a man in a head-bandage looking like a blinded soldier from the front wandered into the women's lavatory as two women emerged. They grabbed hold of him and redirected him. Katya unclipped her handbag and took out a notebook and a pen.

He will try at ten-forty, she had said. At ten-forty he will attempt the first connection. He will not speak for long, she had said. To speak too long even between safe telephones is unwise.

She stood up and walked to the telephone, ducking like a regular under the cloakroom counter.

Will he tell her he loves her? Barley wondered – 'I love you enough to risk your life for me'? Will he give her the love talk he gave her in his letter? Or will he tell her that she is an acceptable price for the cleansing of his uneasy soul?

She was standing sideways to him, gazing keenly through the swing doors. Had she seen something bad? Had she heard something? Or was her mind already far away with Yakov?

It's how she stands when she's waiting for him, he thought like someone who is prepared to wait all day.

The telephone rang hoarsely, as if it had dust in its larynx. A sixth sense had already guided her towards it, so it had no chance to give a second squawk before she had it in her hand. Barley was only a few feet from her but he was hard put to it to hear her voice above the background clatter of the hospital. She had turned away from him, presumably for privacy, and she had boxed her hand over her free ear so that she could hear her lover in the earpiece. Barley could just hear her say 'yes' and 'yes' again, submissively.

Leave her alone! he thought angrily. I've told you before and I'm going to tell you again at the weekend. Leave her alone, keep her out of this. Deal with the grey men or me!

The notebook lay open on a rickety shelf attached to the pillar, the pen on top of it, but she hadn't touched either one of them. *Yes. Yes. Yes.* I did that on the island. *Yes. Yes. Yes.* He saw her shoulders rise into her neck and stay there and her back stretch as if she had taken a deep breath or enjoyed some pleasurable moment within herself. Her elbow rose from her side to cram the earpiece more firmly into her head. *Yes. Yes.* What about *no* for once? *No, I won't lie down for you!*

Her spare hand had found the pillar and he could see the fingers part and brace themselves as the tips pressed into the dark plaster. He saw the back of her hand whiten as it stiffened, but it didn't move, and suddenly her hand alarmed him. It had found a climbing hold and was clinging to it

for grim life. She was on the cliff face and the fingerhold was all she had
between her lover and the abyss.

She turned, the receiver still pressed to her ear, and he saw her face.
Who was she? What had she become? For the first time since he had met
her she was without expression, and the telephone jammed against her
temple was the gun that somebody was holding there.

She had the hostage stare.

Then her body began sliding down the pillar as if she couldn't be
bothered any more to hold it upright. At first it was only her knees that
gave way, then she crumpled at the waist as well, but Barley was there to
hold her. He flung one arm round her waist and with the other he snatched
the phone from her. He held it to his ear and shouted, 'Goethe!' but all he
got was a dialling tone so he rang off.

It was an odd thing, but Barley had forgotten until now that he was
strong. They started to move but as they did so she was seized with a
violent revulsion against him and lashed out silently with her clenched fist,
cracking him so hard over the cheekbone that for a moment he saw
nothing but a dazzling light. He grappled her hands to her sides and held
them there while he pulled her under the counter and frogmarched her
through the hospital and across the carpark. 'She's a disturbed patient,' he
was explaining in his mind. 'A disturbed patient in a doctor's care.'

Still holding her, he tipped her handbag on to the roof of the car,
found the key, unlocked the passenger door and bundled her inside.
Then he ran round to the driver's side in case she had ideas of taking
over after all.

'I shall go home,' she said.

'I don't know the way.'

'Take me home,' she repeated.

'I don't know the way, Katya! You'll have to tell me right and left, do
you hear?' He grabbed her shoulders. 'Sit up. Look out of the window.
Where's reverse on this bloody thing?'

He fiddled with the gears. She grabbed the lever and slammed it in
reverse, making the gearbox scream.

'Lights,' he said.

He had already found them, but he made her turn them on for him,
willing her by his anger to respond. As he bumped across the carpark he
had to swerve to avoid an ambulance entering at speed. Mud and water
blacked out the windscreen, but there were no wipers because it wasn't
raining. Stopping the car again, he sprang out and smeared the windscreen
halfway clean with his handkerchief, then back into the car.

'Go left,' she ordered. 'Be quick, please.'

'We came the other way before.'

'It's one way. Be quick.'

Her voice was dead and he couldn't rouse it. He offered her his flask.
She pushed it aside. He drove slowly, ignoring her instruction to be quick.

Headlights in the driving mirror, not gaining or losing. It's Wicklow, he thought. It's Paddy, Cy, Henziger, Zapadny, the whole Guards Armoured of them. Her face lit and went out again under the sodium streetlamps but it was lifeless. She was staring into her own head at whatever frightful things she saw in her imagination. Her clenched fist was in her mouth. Its knuckles were wedged between her teeth.

'Do I turn here?' he asked her roughly. And again he shouted at her, 'Tell me where to turn, will you?'

She spoke first in Russian, then in English. 'Now. Right. Go faster.'

Nothing was familiar to him. Every empty street was like the next one and the last one.

'Turn now.'

'Left or right?'

'*Left!*'

She screamed the word at the top of her voice, then screamed it again. After the scream came her tears and they went on coming between choking hopeless sobs. Then gradually the sobs began to falter and by the time he drew up at her apartment block they had ceased. He pulled the handbrake but it was broken. The car was still rolling as she shoved her door open. He reached for her but she was too quick. Somehow she had scrambled on to the pavement and was running across the forecourt with her hand-bag open, foraging for her keys. A boy in a leather jacket was lounging in the doorway and he appeared to want to block her. But by then Barley was level with her so the boy leapt aside for them to pass. She wouldn't wait for the lift or perhaps she'd forgotten that there was one. She ran up the stairs and Barley ran after her, past a couple embracing. On the first landing an old man sat drunk in the corner. They climbed and kept climbing. Now it was an old woman who was drunk. Now it was a boy. They climbed so many flights that Barley began to fear she had forgotten which floor she was supposed to live on. Then suddenly she was turning the locks and they were inside her apartment again, and Katya was in the twins' room, kneeling on their bed with her head struck forward and panting like a desperate swimmer, one arm flung across the body of each sleeping child.

Once more there was only her bedroom. He led her to it because even in that tiny space she no longer knew the way. She sat on the bed unsurely, seeming not to know how high it was. He sat beside her, staring into her dull face, watching her eyes close, half open and close again, not venturing to touch her because she was rigid and appalled and apart from him. She was clasping her wrist as if it were broken. She gave a deep sigh. He said her name but she didn't seem to hear him. He peered round the room, searching. A minuscule worktop was fixed along one wall, a make-up table and writing desk combined. Tossed among old letters lay a ring-backed writing block similar to the sort that Goethe used. A framed

Renoir reproduction hung above the bed. He unhooked it and set it on his lap. The trained spy ripped a page out of the notebook, laid it on the picture glass, took a pen from his pocket and wrote:

Tell me.

He put the paper before her and she read it with indifference without relinquishing her wrist. She gave a faint shrug. Her shoulder was leaning against his, but she was unaware of it. Her blouse was open and her rich black hair was tousled from the running. He wrote again *Tell me*, then he grabbed her by the shoulders while his eyes implored her with a desperate love. Then he stabbed his forefinger at the sheet of paper. He picked up the picture and rammed it into her lap for her to press on. She stared at the paper and at *Tell me*, then she gave a long heartbreaking choke and put her head down until he lost sight of her behind the chaotic curtain of her hair.

They have taken Yakov, she wrote.

He took back the pen.

Who told you?

Yakov, she replied.

What did he say?

He will come to Moscow on Friday. He will meet you at Igor's apartment at eleven o'clock on Friday night. He will bring you more material and answer your questions. Please have a precise list ready. It will be the last time. You should bring him news of publication, dates, details. You should bring good whisky. He loves me.

He grabbed back the pen.

Was it Yakov talking?

She nodded.

Why do you say they've taken him?

He used the wrong name.

What name?

Daniil. It was our rule. Pyotr if he is safe, Daniil if he is taken.

The pen had been passing urgently between them. Now Barley held on to it as he wrote question after question. *He made a mistake?* he wrote.

She shook her head.

He has been ill. He has forgotten your code, he wrote.

She shook her head again.

Has he never got it wrong before? he wrote.

At this she shook her head, took back the pen and wrote in an angry hand, *He called me Mariya. He said, Is that Mariya? Mariya is how I should call myself if there was danger. If I am safe, Alina.*

Write his words.

This is Daniil. Is that Mariya speaking? My lecture was the greatest success of my career. That was a lie.

Why?

He says always, in Russia the only success is not to win. It is a joke we have. He spoke deliberately against our joke. He was telling me we are dead.

Barley went to the window and looked steeply down at the concourse and the street. The whole dark world inside him had fallen into silence. Nothing moved, nothing breathed. But he was prepared. He had been prepared all his life, and never known it. She is Goethe's woman, therefore she is as dead as he is. Not yet, because this far Goethe has protected her with the last bit of courage left in him. But dead as dead can be, any time they care to reach out their long arm and pick her off the tree.

For perhaps an hour he remained there at the window before returning to the bed. She was lying on her side with her eyes open and her knees drawn up. He put his arm round her and drew her into him and he felt her cold body break inside his grasp as she began sobbing with convulsive, soundless heaves, as if she was afraid even to weep within the hearing of the microphones.

He began writing to her again, in bold clear capitals: PAY ATTENTION TO ME.

The screens were rolling every few minutes. Barley has left the Mezh. More. They have arrived at the metro station. More. Have exited (*sic*) the hospital, Katya on Barley's arm. More. Men lie but the computer is infallible. More.

'Why on earth's he driving?' Ned asked sharply as he read this.

Sheriton was too absorbed to reply but Bob was standing behind him and Bob picked up the question.

'Men like to drive women, Ned. The chauvinist age is still upon us.'

'Thank you,' said Ned politely.

Clive was smiling in approval.

Intermission. The screens slip out of sequence as Anastasia takes back the story. Anastasia is an angry old Latvian of sixty who has been on the Russia House books for twenty years. Anastasia alone has been allowed to cover the vestibule.

The legend speaks:

She made two passes, first to the lavatory, then back to the waiting room.

On her first pass, Barley and Katya were sitting on a bench waiting.

On her second, Barley and Katya were standing beside the telephone and appeared to be embracing. Barley had a hand to her face, Katya also had a hand up, the other hung at her side.

Had Bluebird's call come through by then?

Anastasia didn't know. Though she had stood in her lavatory cubicle listening as hard as she could, she hadn't heard the phone ring. So either the call had failed to come through or it was over by the time she made her second pass.

'Why on earth should he be embracing her?' said Ned.

'Maybe she had a fly in her eye,' Sheriton said sourly, still watching the screen.

'He drove,' Ned insisted. 'He's not allowed to drive over there, but he drove. He let her drive all the way out to the country and back. She drove him to the hospital. Then all of a sudden he takes over the wheel. Why?'

Sheriton put down his pencil and ran his forefinger round the inside of his collar. 'So what's the betting, Ned? Did Bluebird make his call or didn't he? Come on.'

Ned still had the decency to give the question honest thought. 'Presumably he made it. Otherwise they would have gone on waiting.'

'Maybe she heard something she didn't like. Some bad news or something,' Sheriton suggested.

The screens had gone out, leaving the room sallow.

Sheriton had a separate office done in rosewood and instant art. We decamped to it, poured ourselves coffee, stood about.

'Hell's he doing in her flat for so long?' Ned asked me aside. 'All he has to do is get the time and place of the meeting out of her. He could have done that two hours ago.'

'Maybe they're having a tender moment,' I said.

'I'd feel better if I thought they were.'

'Maybe he's buying another hat,' said Johnny unpleasantly, overhearing us.

'Geronimo,' said Sheriton as the bell rang, and we trooped back to the situation room.

An illuminated street map of the city showed us Katya's apartment marked by a red pinlight. The pick-up point lay three hundred metres east of it, at the south-east corner of two main streets marked green. Barley must now be heading along the south pavement, keeping close to the curb. As he reached the pick-up point, he should affect to slow down as if hunting for a car. The safe car would pull alongside him. Barley had been instructed to give the driver the name of his hotel in a loud voice and negotiate a price with his hands.

At the second roundabout the car would take a side turning and enter a building site where the safe truck was parked without lights, its driver appearing to doze in his cab. If the truck's wing aerial was extended, the car would make a right-hand circle and return to the truck.

If not, abort.

Paddy's report hit the screens at one a. m. London time. The tapes were available for us less than an hour later, blasted from the roof of the US Embassy. The report has since been torn to pieces in every conceivable way. For me it remains a model of factual field reporting.

Naturally the writer needs to be known, for every writer under the sun has limitations. Paddy was not a mindreader but he was a lot of other things, a former Gurkha turned special forces man turned intelligence officer, a linguist, a planner and improviser in Ned's favourite mould.

For his Moscow persona, he had put on such a skin of English silliness that the uninitiated made a joke of him when they described him to each other: his long shorts in the summer when he took himself on treks through the Moscow woods; his langlaufing in the winter, when he loaded up his Volvo with ancient skis and bamboo poles and iron rations and finally his own egregious self, clad in a fur cap that looked as though it had been kept over from the Arctic convoys. But it takes a clever man to act the fool and get away with it for long, and Paddy was a clever man, however convenient it later became to take his eccentricities at face value.

Also in controlling his motley of pseudo language students, travel clerks, little traders and third-flag nationals, Paddy was first rate. Ned himself could not have bettered him. He tended them like a canny parish priest, and every one of them in his lonely way rose to him. It was not his fault if the qualities that made men come to him also made him vulnerable to deception.

So to Paddy's report. He was struck first by the precision with which Barley gave his account, and the tape bears him out. Barley's voice is more self-assured than in any previous recording.

Paddy was impressed by Barley's resolve and by his devotion to his mission. He compared the Barley he saw before him in the truck with the Barley he had briefed for his Leningrad run and warmed to the improvement. He was right. Barley was an enlarged and altered man.

Barley's account to Paddy tallied also with every checkable fact at Paddy's disposal, from the pick-up at the metro and the drive to the hospital, to the wait on the bench and the stifled bell. Katya had been standing over the phone when it rang, Barley said. Barley himself had scarcely heard it. Then no wonder Anastasia hadn't heard it either, Paddy reasoned. Katya must have been quick as light to grab that receiver.

The conversation between Katya and the Bluebird had been short, two minutes at most, said Barley. Another neat fit. Goethe was known to be scared of long telephone conversations.

With so much collateral available to him therefore, and with Barley navigating his way through it, how on earth can anybody afterwards maintain that Paddy should have driven Barley straight to the Embassy and shipped him back to London bound and gagged? But of course Clive maintained just that, and he was not the only one.

Thus to the three mysteries that by now were sticking in Ned's throat – the embrace, the drive from the hospital with Barley at the wheel, the two hours they spent together in the flat. For Barley's answers, we must see him as Paddy saw him, bowed over the low light on the table in the truck, his face glistening from the heat. There is the whirr from the bafflers in the background. Both men are wearing earphones, a closed-circuit microphone lies between them. Barley whispers his story, half to the microphone, half to his station chief. Not all Paddy's nights of adventure on the North-West Frontier could have yielded a more dramatic atmosphere.

Cy sits in the shadows in a third pair of earphones. It is Cy's truck but he has orders to let Paddy host the feast.

'Then she goes and gets the wobblies,' says Barley, with enough of the man-to-man in his voice to make Paddy smile. 'She'd been winding herself up all week for his call and suddenly it was over and she went pop. Probably didn't help her, me being there. Without me around, I reckon she'd have held it back till she got home.'

'Probably would at that,' Paddy agrees understandingly.

'It was too much for her. Hearing his voice, hearing he'll be in town in a couple of days, her worries about her kids – and about him, and about herself as well – it was just too much for her.'

Paddy understood perfectly. He had known emotional women in his day, and was experienced in the sorts of thing they cried over.

From there everything else flowed naturally. The deception became a symphony. Barley had done what he could to comfort her, he said, but she was in bad shape so he put his arm round her and lugged her to the car and drove her home.

In the car she did some more crying but she was on the mend by the time they got to her flat. Barley made her a cup of tea and patted her hand, until he was confident she was able to cope.

'Well done,' said Paddy. And if, as he says this, he sounds like a nineteenth-century Indian Army officer congratulating his men after a futile cavalry charge, that is only because he is impressed and his mouth is too near the microphone.

There is lastly Barley's question, which is where Cy came in. With hindsight, no doubt, it sounds like a straight declaration of larcenous intent. But Cy didn't hear it that way and neither did Paddy. Neither, in fact, did anyone in London except Ned, whose impotence was by now unnerving. Ned was becoming the pariah of the situation room.

'Oh yes – that's it – what about the shopping list?' says Barley as he prepares to leave. The question emerges as one of several small administrative worries, not a solo. 'When do you get to press the shopping list into my hot little hand?' he asks repetitiously.

'Why?' says Cy from the shadows.

'Well *I* don't know. Shouldn't I bone up on it a bit or something?'

'There's nothing to bone up,' says Cy. 'It's written questions, yes-or-no answers, and it is positively important that you do not know any part of it, thank you.'

'So when do I get it?'

'The shopping list we do as late as possible,' says Cy.

Of Cy's own opinion of Barley's state of mind, one nugget is recorded. 'With the Brits,' he is reported to have said, 'you never know what the hell they're thinking anyway.'

That night at least, Cy had a certain justice on his side.

'There was no bad news,' Ned insisted while Brock played the truck tapes for the third or thirtieth time.

We were back in our own Russia House. We had taken refuge there. It was like the early days all over again. It was dawn, but we were too wakeful to remember sleep.

'There was no *bad* news,' Ned repeated. 'It was all *good* news. "I'm well. I'm safe. I gave a great lecture. I'm catching the plane. See you on Friday. I love you." So she weeps.'

'Oh, I don't know,' I said, talking against my own mood. 'Haven't *you* ever cried when *you* were happy?'

'She weeps so much he has to cart her down the hospital corridor. She weeps so much she can't drive. When they get to her apartment she runs ahead of him to the door as if Barley doesn't exist, because she's so *happy* that the Bluebird's flying in on time. And he comforts her. For all the good news she's had.' Barley's recorded voice had come on again. 'And he's calm. Totally calm. Not a worry in the world. "We're bang on target, Paddy. Everything's fine. That's why she's weeping." Of course it is.'

He sat back and closed his eyes while Barley's trustworthy voice continued to talk to him from the recorder.

'He doesn't belong to us any more,' said Ned. 'He's gone away.'

As also, in a different sense, had Ned. He had launched a great operation. Now all he could do by his own reckoning was watch it hurtle out of control. In my whole life I never saw a man so isolated, with the possible exception of myself.

Spying is waiting.
Spying is worrying.
Spying is being yourself but more so.
The nostrums of the extinct Walter and the living Ned rang in Barley's ears. The apprentice had become heir to the spells of his masters but his magic was more potent than theirs had ever been.

He was on a plateau none of them had ascended. He had the goal, he had the means to reach it and he had what Clive would have called the motivation, which in better mouths was purpose. Everything they had taught him was paying off as he rode calmly into battle to deceive them. But he was not their trickster.

Their flags were nothing to him. They could wave in any wind. But he was not their traitor. He was not his own cause. He knew the battle he had to win and whom he had to win it for. He knew the sacrifice he was prepared to make. He was not their traitor. He was complete.

He did not need their scared labels and their weakling systems. He was one man alone but he was greater than the sum of those who had presumed to take control of him. He knew them as the worst of all bad weapons, because their existence justified their targets.

In a gentle way that was not even all that gentle, he had discovered anger. He could smell its first kindling and hear the crackle of its brushwood.

There was only now. Goethe was right. There was no tomorrow because tomorrow was the excuse. There was now or there was nowhere and Goethe, even nowhere, was still right. We must cut down the grey men inside ourselves, we must burn our grey suits and set our good hearts free, which is the dream of every decent soul, and even – believe it or not – of certain grey men too. But how, with what?

Goethe was right, and it was not his fault or Barley's that each by accident had set the other in motion. With the radiance of spirit that was rising in him, Barley's sense of kinship with his unlikely friend was overwhelming. He brimmed with allegiance to Goethe's frantic dream of unleashing the forces of sanity and opening the doors on dirty rooms.

But Barley did not dwell long on Goethe's agony. Goethe was in hell and very likely Barley would soon be following him. I'll mourn him when I have the time, he thought. Until then his business was with the living whom Goethe had put so shamefully at risk, and in a brave last gesture had attempted to preserve.

For his immediate business Barley must use the grey men's wiles. He must be himself but more so than he has ever been before. He must wait. He must worry. He must be a man reversed, inwardly reconciled, outwardly unfulfilled. He must live secretly on tiptoe, arch as a cat inside his head while he acts the Barley Blair they wish to see, their creature all the way.

Meanwhile the chess-player in him reckons his moves. The slumbering negotiator is becoming unobservably awake. The publisher is achieving what he has never achieved before, he is becoming the cool-headed broker between the necessity and the far vision.

Katya knows, he reasons. *She knows Goethe is caught.*

But they do not know she knows, because she kept her wits about her on the telephone.

And they do not know I know that Katya knows.

In the whole world I am the only person apart from Katya and Goethe who knows that Katya knows.

Katya is still free.

Why?

They have not stolen her children, ransacked her flat, thrown Matvey in the madhouse or displayed any of the delicacy traditionally reserved for Russian ladies playing courier to Soviet defence physicists who have decided to entrust their nation's secrets to a derelict Western publisher.

Why?

I too this far am free. They have not chained my neck to a brick wall.

Why?

Because they do not know we know they know.
So they want more.
They want us, but more than us.
They can wait for us, because they want more.
But what is the more?
What is the clue to their patience?

Everybody talks, Ned had said, stating a fact of life. *With today's methods everybody talks*. He was telling Barley not to try and hold out if he was caught. But Barley was not thinking about himself any more. He was thinking about Katya.

Each night, each day that followed, Barley moved the pieces round in his mind, honing his plan while he waited, as we all did, for Friday's promised meeting with the Bluebird.

At breakfast, Barley punctually on parade, a model publisher and spy. And each day, all day long, the life and soul of the fair.

Goethe. Nothing I can do for you. No power on earth will prise you from their grip.

Katya, still savable. Her children, still savable. Even though everybody talks and Goethe in the end will be no exception.

Myself, unsavable as ever.

Goethe gave me the courage, he thought, as his secret purpose grew in him, *and Katya the love.*

No. Katya gave me both. And gives them to me still.

And the Friday as quiet as the days before, the screens near-blank, as Barley steers himself methodically towards the evening's grand Potomac & Blair Launch Party in the Spirit of Goodwill and Glasnost, as our flowery invitations have it, printed in triptych with deckle edges on the Service's own printing press not two weeks ago.

And intermittently, with a seeming casualness, Barley assures himself of Katya's continuing welfare. He rings her whenever he can. He chats to her and makes her use the word 'convenient' as a safety signal. In return he includes the word 'frankly' in his own careless chatter. Nothing heavy; nothing on the matter of love or death or great German poets. Just:

How are you doing?
Is the fair wearing you out, frankly?
How are the twins?
Is Matvey still enjoying his pipe?

Meaning, I love you, and I love you, and I love you, and I love you frankly.

For further assurance regarding her safety Barley despatches Wicklow to take a passing look at her in the Socialist pavilion. 'She's fine,' Wicklow reports with a smile, humouring Barley's nervousness. 'She's steady as she goes.'

'Thanks,' says Barley. 'Jolly nice of you, old boy.'

The second time, again at Barley's bidding, Henziger himself goes.

Perhaps Barley is saving himself for the evening. Or perhaps he does not trust his own emotions. But she is still there, still alive, still breathing, and she has changed into her party frock.

Yet all the while, even driving back early to town in order to be ahead of his guests, Barley continues to muster his private army of alterable and unalterable facts with a clarity that the most trained and compromised lawyer would be proud of.

16

'**G**yorgy! Marvellous! Fantastic! Where's Varenka?'

'Barley, my friend, for Christ's sake save us! We don't like the twentieth century any better than you English. Let's run away from it together! We leave tonight, okay? You buy the tickets?'

'Yuri. My God, is this your new wife? Leave him. He's a monster.'

'Barley! Listen! Everything is fine! We have no more problems! In the old days we had to assume that everything was a mess! Now we can look in our newspapers and confirm it!'

'Misha! How's the work going? Super!'

'It's war, for Christ's sake, Barley, open war. First we got to hang the old guard, then we got to fight another Stalingrad!'

'Leo! Great to see you! How's Sonya?'

'Barley, pay attention to me! Communism is not a threat! It's a parasite industry that lives off the mistakes of all you stupid assholes in the West!'

The reception was in the mirrored upstairs room of an elderly mid-town hotel. Plainclothes guards stood outside on the pavement. More hovered in the hall and on the staircase and at the entrance to the room.

Potomac & Blair had invited a hundred people. Eight had accepted, nobody had refused, and so far a hundred and fifty had arrived. But until Katya was among them Barley preferred the spaces near the door.

A flock of Western girls swept in, escorted by the usual dubious official interpreters, all men. A portly philosopher who played the clarinet arrived with his newest boyfriend.

'Aleksandr! Fantastic! Marvellous!'

A lonely Siberian called Andrey, already drunk, needed to speak to Barley on a matter of vital urgency. 'One-party Socialism is a disaster,

Barley. It has broken our hearts. Keep your British variety. You will publish my new novel?'

'Well I don't know about that, Andrey,' Barley replied cautiously, glancing towards the door. 'Our Russian editor admires it but he doesn't see an English market. We're thinking about it.'

'You know why I came tonight?' Andrey asked.

'Tell me.'

Another jolly group arrived, but still with no Katya among them.

'In order to wear my fine clothes for you. We Russians know each other's tricks too well. We need your Western mirror. You come here, you depart again with our best images reflected in you and we feel noble. If you have published my first novel, it is only logical that you publish my second.'

'Not if the first one didn't make any money, it isn't, Andrey,' said Barley with rare firmness, and to his relief saw Wicklow slipping towards them across the room.

'You have heard that Anatoly died in prison of a hunger strike in December? After two years of this Great New Russia we are enjoying?' Andrey continued, taking another enormous pull of whisky, supplied courtesy of the American Embassy in support of a more sober Russia.

'Of course we heard about him,' Wicklow cut in soothingly. 'It was disgusting.'

'So why don't you publish my novel?'

Leaving Wicklow to cope, Barley spread his arms and hastened beaming to the door. The superb Natalie of the All-Union State Library of Foreign Literature had arrived, a wise beauty of sixty. They fell into an adoring embrace.

'So whom shall we discuss tonight, Barley? James Joyce or Adrian Mole? Why are you looking so intelligent, suddenly? It is because you have become a capitalist.'

A stampede flung half the company to the further end of the room and caused the guards to peer through the doorway in alarm. The roar of conversation dipped and recovered. The buffet had been unveiled.

But still no Katya.

'Today under the *perestroika* it is all much easier,' Natalie was saying through her irresistible smile. 'Foreign travel is no problem. For example to Bulgaria. All we have to do is describe to our bureaucrats what kind of person we think we are. Naturally the Bulgarians need to know this before we arrive. They must be warned what to expect. Are we an intelligent person, medium intelligent or normal intelligent? The Bulgarians need to prepare themselves, perhaps even train themselves a little. Are we calm or excitable, plain-minded or full of imagination? When we have answered these simple questions and a thousand more of the same sort, we may proceed to the more important issues, such as the address and full names of our maternal grandmother, the date of her death and the number of her death certificate and, if they are feeling like it, perhaps also the name of the doctor who signed it. So you may see that our bureaucrats are doing everything possible to introduce the new, relaxed regulations quickly, and send us all abroad on holiday with our children. Barley, whom are you staring round for? Have I lost my looks or are you bored with me already?'

'So what did you tell them?' Barley asked with a laugh, and willed himself to keep his eyes on her.

'Oh, I said I was very intelligent, I was a calm, amusing person and the Bulgarians would be delighted with my company. The bureaucrats are testing our determination, that is all. They hope that if we have to satisfy so many different departments we shall lose courage and decide to stay at home. But it is getting better. Everything is getting a little better. Maybe you don't believe it, but the *perestroika* is not being run for foreigners. It is run for us.'

'How is your dog, Barley?' a man's gloomy voice murmured at Barley's side. It was Arkady, unofficial sculptor, with his beautiful unofficial girl-friend.

'I haven't got a dog, Arkady. Why do you ask?'

'Because from this moment it has become safer to discuss one's dog than one's fellow human beings, I would say.'

Barley turned his head to follow Arkady's gaze and saw Alik Zapadny standing on the far side of the room in earnest conversation with Katya.

'We Muscovites are talking too dangerously these days,' Arkady continued, his eyes still fixed upon Zapadny. 'We are becoming careless in our excitement. The informers will have a good harvest this autumn, even if nobody else does. Ask him. He is at the peak of his profession, I would say.'

'Alik, you old devil, what are you pestering this poor girl about?' Barley demanded as he embraced Katya first and then Zapadny. 'I could see her blushing from across the room. You want to watch him, Katya. His English is almost as good as yours, and he talks it a lot faster. How are you?'

'Oh thank you,' she said softly. 'I am *very* well.'

She was wearing the dress she had worn at their meeting at the Odessa. She was withdrawn but in command of herself. Her face had the battered eagerness of bereavement. Dan Zeppelin and Mary Lou stood with them.

'We were having rather an interesting discussion on human rights, as a matter of fact, Barley,' Zapadny explained, waving his glass in a circular gesture round the company as if he were taking a collection. 'Weren't we, Mr. Zeppelin? We are always so grateful when Westerners preach to us about how to behave towards our criminals, you see! But then what is the difference, I am asking myself between a country that locks a few extra people in prison, and a country that leaves its gangsters at large? I think I have just found a negotiating point here for our Soviet leaders, actually. Tomorrow morning we shall announce to the so-called Helsinki Watch Committee that we can have nothing further to do with them until they have put the American Mafia behind bars. How would that be, Mr. Zeppelin? We let ours out, you put yours inside. It's a fair deal, I would say.'

'You want the polite answer or the real one?' Dan snapped over Mary Lou's shoulder.

Another polyglot group of guests swept past, followed after a theatrical pause by none other than the great Sir Peter Oliphant himself, surrounded by a retinue of Russian and English bag-carriers. The noise grew, the room filled. Three sickly-looking British correspondents inspected the depleted buffet and departed. Somebody opened the piano and began playing a Ukrainian song. A woman sang well and others joined her.

'No, Barley, I do not know what terrifies you,' Katya was replying, to Barley's surprise, so he must have asked her. 'I am sure you are very brave, like all English.'

In the heat of the room and the swirl of the occasion, his own excitement had turned suddenly against him. He felt drunk but not from alcohol for he had been nursing one tired Scotch all evening.

'Maybe there's nothing there,' he ventured, addressing not just Katya but a ring of unfamiliar faces. 'Out in the woodwork. Talent.' Everyone was waiting, Barley too. He was trying to look at all of them while his eyes saw only Katya. What had he been saying? What had they been hearing? Their faces were still turned to him but there was no light in them, not even Katya's; there was only concern. He stumbled on. 'We had this vision, all of us, for years, of great Russian artists waiting to be discovered.' He faltered. 'Well, didn't we? Epic novels, plays? Great painters, banned, working in secrecy? Attics full of wonderful illegal stuff? Musicians the same? We talked about it. Dreamed about it. The secret continuation of the nineteenth century. "And when the thaw comes, they'll all come out of the ice and dazzle us," we told each other. So where the hell are they, all these geniuses? What if they froze to death in the ice? Maybe the repression worked. That's all I'm saying.'

A spellbound silence followed before Katya came to his aid. 'The Russian talent exists and has always existed, Barley, even in the worst times. It cannot be destroyed,' she declared with a hint of her old strictness. 'Perhaps it will first have to adjust itself to the new circumstances, but soon it will express itself brilliantly. I am sure that is what you wish to say.'

Henziger is making his speech. It is a masterpiece of unconscious hypocrisy. 'May the pioneering venture of Potomac & Blair provide a modest addition to the great new era of East-West understanding!' he declares, puffed up by his conviction. His voice lifts and with it his glass. He is the honest trader, he is every decent American with his heart in the right place.

And no doubt that he is precisely what he thinks he is, for the ham actor in him lies just below the surface. 'Let's make each other rich!' he cries, raising his glass still higher. 'Let's make each other free! Let's trade together, and let's talk together and let's drink together, and let's make the world a better place. Ladies and gentlemen – to you and to Potomac & Blair and to our mutual profit – and to the *perestroika* – good health! Amen!'

They are yelling for Barley. Spikey Morgan starts it, Yuri and Alik Zapadny take it up, all the old hands who know the game yell, 'Barley, Barley!' Soon the whole room is yelling for Barley, some of them without even knowing why, and for a moment none of them see him anyway. Then suddenly he is standing on the buffet table holding a borrowed saxophone and playing 'My Funny Valentine', which he has played at every Moscow book fair since the first, while Jack Henziger accompanies him on the piano in the unmistakable style of Fats Waller.

The guards at the door creep into the room to listen, the guards from the stairs come to the doorway and the guards from the hall come to the stairs as the first notes of Barley's swansong gather clarity and then a splendid power.

'We're going to the new Indian, for Christ's sake,' Henziger protests as they stand on the pavement under the stodgy gaze of the *toptuny*. 'Bring Katya with you! We've booked a table!'

'Sorry, Jack. We're bespoke. Longstanding date.'

Henziger is only putting on a show. 'She needs welfaring,' Barley has confided to him. 'I'm going to take her off and give her a quiet supper somewhere.'

But Barley did not take Katya to dinner for their farewell evening, as the irregulars confirmed before they were stood down. And it was Katya, not Barley this time, who did the taking. She took him to the place known to every urban Russian boy and girl from adolescence, and it is to be found at the top of every purpose-built apartment block in every major city. There is not a Russian of Katya's generation who does not count such places among her memories of early love. And such a place was to be found at the top of Katya's staircase also, at the point where the last flight ends and the attics begin, though it was more sought after in winter than in summer because it included the suppurating hot-water tank and steaming black-bandaged pipes.

But first it was necessary for her to inspect Matvey and the twins and establish that they were still safe, while Barley stood on the landing and waited for her. Then she led him by the hand up several flights until the last, which was of wood. She had a key and it fitted the rusted steel door that ordered all trespassers to keep their distance. And when she had unlocked it and relocked it, she led him across the rafters to the bit of hard floor where she had prepared a makeshift bed, with a muddied view of the stars through the filthy skylight and the chugging of the pipes and the stench of drying clothes for company.

'The letter you gave to Landau went astray,' he said. 'It ended up in the hands of our officials. It was the officials who sent me to you. I'm sorry about that.'

But there was no more time for either of them to be shocked by anything. He had told her little of his plan and he told her no more now. It was understood between them that she knew too much already. And besides, they had more important matters to discuss, for it was on this night also that Katya told Barley the things that afterwards constituted the rest of his knowledge of her. And she confessed her love for him in terms simple enough to sustain him through the separation they both knew lay ahead of them.

Nevertheless Barley did not outstay his welcome. He did not give the men in the field or the men in London cause to be anxious for him. He was back at the Mezh by midnight, in good time for a last one with the boys.

'Oh Jack, Alik Zapadny's summoned me to his traditional farewell snoot for old hands tomorrow afternoon,' he confided to Henziger over a nightcap in the first-floor bar.

'Want me to come along?' asked Henziger. For like the Russians themselves, Henziger harboured no illusions about Zapadny's regrettable connections.

Barley smiled regretfully. 'Your knees aren't brown enough, Jack. It's for us golden oldies from the days when there was no hope.'

'What time?' asked Wicklow, ever practical.

'Four o'clock, I think he said. Seems a damned odd time for a drink. Yes, I'm sure he did. Four.'

Then he wished them all an affectionate goodnight and rode to Heaven in the lift, which in the Mezh is a glass cage that slides up and down the outside of a steel rod, to the private worry of many honest souls below.

It was lunchtime and after all our sleepless nights and wakeful dawns there was something indecent about a sensation that occurred at lunchtime. But a sensation it was. A hand-carried sensation. A sensation inside a yellow envelope inside a locked steel briefcase. Gaunt Johnny from their London station ran into the situation room with it, having brought it under guard from the Embassy across the square. He ran right through the lower level and up the little staircase to the command area before he realised we had moved to Sheriton's rosewood parlour for our sandwiches and coffee.

He handed it to Sheriton and stood over him like a stage messenger while Sheriton read first the covering letter, which he stuffed into his pocket, then the message itself.

Then he stood over Ned while Ned read the message too. It wasn't till

Ned passed it back to me that Johnny seemed to decide he had read it enough times: a signals intercept, transmitted by the Soviet Military out of Leningrad, intercepted in Finland by the Americans and decrypted in Virginia by a bank of computers powerful enough to light London for a year.

Leningrad to Moscow, copy to Saratov.

Professor Yakov Savelyev is authorized to take a recreational weekend in Moscow following his lecture to the military academy in Saratov this Friday. Please arrange transport and facilities.

'Well thank you, Mr. Administration Officer, Leningrad,' Sheriton murmured.

Ned had taken back the signal and was re-reading it. Of all of us, he seemed to be the only one who was not impressed.

'Is this all they broke?' he asked.

'I don't know, Ned,' said Johnny, not bothering to conceal his hostility.

'It says here "one over one". What's that supposed to mean? Find out whether it's the only one in the batch. If it isn't, perhaps you'd be good enough to find out what else they picked up on the same trawl that was worth a damn.' He waited till Johnny had left the room. 'Perfect,' he said acidly. 'Copybook. My God, you'd think we were dealing with the Germans.'

We stood about, nibbling distractedly at our food. Sheriton had shoved his hands into his pockets and turned his back to us while he stared out of the smoked-glass window at the silent traffic. He was wearing a long-haired black cardigan. Through the interior window the rest of us could watch Johnny talking on one of the supposedly safe telephones. He rang off and we watched him come back across the room to us.

'Zero,' he announced.

'What's zero?' Ned said.

' "One over one" means one over one. It's a solo. Nothing either side.'

'A fluke then?' Ned suggested.

'A solo,' Johnny repeated stubbornly.

Ned swung round to Sheriton, who still had his back to us. 'Russell. Read the signs. That intercept is completely on its own. There's nothing anywhere near it and it stinks. They're tossing us a piece of bait.'

Now it was Sheriton's turn to make a second study of the sheet. When he finally spoke, he affected a deep weariness and it was clear he was reaching the limits of his tolerance.

'Ned, I am confidently assured by the cryptographers that the intercept came from low-grade military crap put out on an army squeezebox vintage 1921. Nobody plants deception that way any more. Nobody does those things. It's not the Bluebird that's going off course. It's you.'

'Maybe that's *why* they planted it that way! Isn't that what you and I might do? Come in on the blind side?'

'Well, maybe we would at that,' Sheriton conceded, as if it scarcely mattered to him. 'Once you start thinking that way, it's pretty hard to think any other way.'

Clive at his worst. 'We can hardly ask Sheriton to break off the operation on the grounds that everything is going *well*, Ned,' he said silkily.

'On the grounds of pixie voices,' Sheriton corrected him, his temper gathering as he wandered moodily back into the room. 'On the grounds that anything going our way is a Kremlin plot, and everything we fuck up is evidence of our integrity. Ned, my Agency damn nearly died of that ailment. So did you guys. We're not going that route today. It's my operation and my ass.'

'And my joe,' said Ned. 'We've blown him. And we've blown the Bluebird.'

'Sure, sure,' said Sheriton with icy affability. 'No question.'

He glanced unlovingly at Clive. 'Mr. Deputy?'

Clive had his own ways of sitting on the fence, and they were all of them well tried. 'Russell – if I may say so – Ned. I think you are both being slightly egotistical. We are a service. We live corporate lives. It is our masters, not we ourselves alone, who have given the Bluebird their blessing. There is a corporate will here that is bigger than any of us.'

Wrong again, I thought. It is smaller than all of us. It is an insult to the powers of each of us, except perhaps of Clive who therefore needs it.

Sheriton turned back to Ned, but still did not raise his voice. 'Ned, do you have any idea what will happen in Washington and Langley if I abort *now*? Can you imagine the peals of hyena laughter that will resound across the Atlantic from Defense, the Pentagon and the neanderthals? Can you guess what view might be taken of the Bluebird material until now?' He pointed without apparent rancour at Johnny, who sat skull-eyed, watching each of them in turn. 'Can you see this guy's report? This Judas? We were sowing a little moderation around town, remember? Now you tell me I've got to throw Bluebird to the jackals.'

'I'm telling you not to give him the shopping list.'

Sheriton inclined his ear as if he were a little deaf. '*Barley* the shopping list? Or *Bluebird* the shopping list?'

'Neither of them. Abort.'

Finally Sheriton became very angry indeed. He had been winding himself up for this moment, and now it had arrived. He stood himself before Ned and not two foot from him, and when he flung up his palms in remonstration he wrenched half his fluffy cardigan with him so that he resembled an overweight bat in a fury.

'So okay! Here's our worst-case situation. Cooked Ned-style. Okay? We show Bluebird the shopping list and he turns out to be their asset, not ours. Have I considered that possibility? Ned, night and day I have considered little else. If Bluebird is their guy and not ours, if Barley is, if the girl is, if all or any of the players is less than strictly kosher, the shopping list will shine a very bright light up the anal orifice of the United

States of America.' He began pacing. 'It will show the Sovs what has been given away by their own man. So they'll know what we know. Already bad. It will show the Sovs what we *don't* know, and *how* we don't know it. More bad, but there's worse to come. Cleverly analysed, the shopping list can show them the gaps in our intelligence-gathering machinery and if they're cleverer still, in our own grotesque, fucking ridiculous, incompetent, ludicrously overstocked arsenal. Why? Because in the end we concentrate on what scares us, which is what we can't do and they can. That's the down side. Ned, I have looked at the bank balance. I know the stakes. I know what we can earn ourselves from Bluebird and what he stands to cost us if we screw up. Losing disenchants me. I've seen it done. I am not impressed. If we're wrong, it's shit city. We knew that back on Nowhere Island and we know it a little better now because it's live-ammunition time. But this is *not* the moment to start looking over our shoulders unless we have a cast-iron reason!'

He came back to Ned. '*Bluebird is straight*, Ned! Remember? Your words. I loved you for them! I still do! Bluebird is telling the unpolluted truth as he knows it. And my myopic masters are going to have it shoved up their asses even if it turns their balls to water. Do you read me, Ned? Or have I put you to sleep already?'

But Ned would not rise to Sheriton's black rage. 'Don't give it to him, Russell. We've lost him. If you give him anything at all, give him smoke.'

'*Smoke?* Play Barley *back*, you mean? Admit the Bluebird's bad? Are you joking? Give me *proof* Ned! Don't give me *hunches!* Give me fucking *proof!* Everybody in Washington who hasn't got hair between his toes tells me that Bluebird is the Holy Bible, the Talmud and the Koran! Now *you* tell me, give him smoke! You got us into this, Ned! Don't try and jump off the tiger at the first fucking stop!'

Ned pondered this for a while, and Clive pondered Ned. Finally Ned gave a shrug as if to say perhaps it made no difference anyway. Then he returned to his desk where he sat alone seeming to read papers and I remember wondering suddenly whether he had a Hannah too, whether we all did, some life unled that kept him to the wheel.

Perhaps it was true that VAAP had no small rooms or perhaps Alik Zapadny, after his years in prison, had an understandable aversion to them.

In any case the room he had singled out for their encounter seemed to Barley big enough for a regimental dance, and the only thing small about it was Zapadny himself who crouched at one end of a long table like a mouse on a raft, watching his visitor with darting eyes as he ambled down the parquet floor at him, his long arms dangling at his sides, elbows up a little, and an expression on his face such as neither Zapadny nor perhaps anyone else had ever seen in him before: not apologetic, not vague, not wilfully foolish, but of an almost menacing firmness of intention.

Zapadny had arranged some papers before him, and a heap of books beside the papers and a jug of drinking water and two glasses. And it was evident that he wished to offer Barley an impression of being discovered in the midst of his duties, rather than facing him in cold blood without props or the protection of his numberless assistants.

'Barley, my dear chap, look here it's most kind of you to call by and say your farewells like this, you must be as busy as I am at this moment, my hat,' he began, speaking much too quickly. 'I would say that if our publishing industry continues to expand like this, then I see no way out of it, though it is only my personal and unofficial opinion, we shall have to employ a hundred more staff and most likely apply for larger offices also.' He hummed and fussed his papers and pulled back a chair in what he imagined to be a gesture of old-style European courtesy. But Barley as usual preferred to stand. 'Well it's more than my life is worth to offer you a drink on the premises, when the sun is not even over the yardarm as we say, but I mean do sit down and let us kick a few thoughts around for a few minutes – ' raising his eyebrows and looking at his watch – 'my God, we should have a month of it, not five days! How is the Trans-Siberian Railway progressing? I mean I see no basic difficulties there, provided our own position is respected, and the rules of fair play are observed by all the contracting parties. Are the Finns being too greedy? Perhaps your Mr. Henziger is being greedy? He is certainly a hard-nosed character, I would say.'

He caught Barley's eye again and his discomfort increased. Standing over him, Barley bore no resemblance to a man who wished to discuss the Trans-Siberian Railway.

'I find it actually a little odd that you insisted so dogmatically on speaking to me completely alone, you see,' Zapadny continued rather desperately. 'After all, this one is fairly and squarely in Mrs. Korneyeva's court. It is she and her staff who are directly responsible for the photographer and all the practical arrangements.'

But Barley also had a prepared speech though it was not marred by any of Zapadny's nervousness. 'Alik,' he said, still declining to sit down. 'Does that telephone work?'

'Of course.'

'I need to betray my country and I'm in a hurry. And what I would like you to do is put me in touch with the proper authorities, because there are certain things that have to be hammered out in advance. So don't start telling me you don't know who to get hold of just do it, or you'll lose a lot of Brownie points with the pigs who think they own you.'

It was mid-afternoon but a wintry dusk had settled over London, and Ned's little office in the Russia House was bathed in twilight. He had put his feet on his desk and was sitting back in his chair, eyes closed and a dark whisky at his elbow – not by any means, I quickly realised, his first of the day.

'Is Clive Without India still cloistered with the Whitehall nobles?' he asked me, with a tired levity.

'He's at the American Embassy settling the shopping list.'

'I thought no mere Brit was allowed near the shopping list.'

'They're talking principle. Sheriton has to sign a declaration appointing Barley an honorary American. Clive has to add a citation.'

'Saying what?'

'That he's a man of honour and a fit and proper person.'

'Did you draft it for him?'

'Of course.'

'Silly fellow,' said Ned with an air of dreamy reproof. 'They'll hang you.' He leaned back and closed his eyes.

'Is the shopping list really worth so much?' I asked. I had a sense, for once, of being more practically disposed than Ned was.

'Oh it's worth everything,' Ned replied carelessly. 'If any of it's worth anything, that is.'

'Do you mind telling me why?'

I had not been admitted to the inmost secrets of the Bluebird material, but I knew that if I ever had been I would not have been able to make head or tail of them. But conscientious Ned had taken himself to night-school. He had sat at the feet of our in-house boffins and lunched our grandest defence scientists at the Athenaeum in order to bone up.

'Interface,' he said with contempt. 'Mutually assured bedlam. We track their toys. They track ours. We watch each other's archery contests without either of us knowing which targets the other side is aiming at. If they're aiming for London, will they hit Birmingham? What's error? What's deliberate? Who's approaching zero-CEP?' He caught my bewilderment and was pleased with himself. 'We watch them lob their ICBMs into the Kamchatka peninsula. But can they lob them down a Minuteman silo? We don't know and they don't. Because the big stuff on either side has never been tested under war conditions. The test trajectories are not the trajectories they'll use when the fun starts. The earth, God bless her, is not a perfect globe. How can she be at her age? Her density varies. So does the old girl's gravitational pull when things fly over her, like missiles and warheads. Enter bias. Our targeteers try to compensate for it in their calibrations. Goethe tried. They pour in data from earth-watch satellites, and perhaps they succeed better than Goethe did. Perhaps they don't. We won't know till the blessed balloon goes up, and nor will they, because you can only try the real thing once.' He stretched luxuriously as if the topic pleased him. 'So the camps divide. The hawks cry, "The Sovs are pinpoint! They can knock the smile off the arse of a fly at ten thousand miles!" And all the doves can reply is, "We don't know what the Sovs can do, and the Sovs don't know what the Sovs can do. And nobody who doesn't know whether his gun works or not is going to shoot first. It's the uncertainty that keeps us honest," say the doves. But that is not an argument that satisfies the literal American mind, you see, because the literal American mind does not like to grapple with fuzzy concepts or grand visions. Not at its literal field level. And what Goethe was saying was an even larger heresy. He was saying that the uncertainty was all there was. Which I rather agree with. So the hawks hated him and the doves had a ball and hanged themselves from the chandelier.' He drank again. 'If Goethe had only backed the pinpoint boys instead, everything would have been fine,' he said reprovingly.

'And the shopping list?' I asked him again.

He peered whimsically into his glass. 'The targeting of one side, my dear Palfrey, is based on that side's assumptions about the other side. And vice versa. *Ad infinitum*. Do we harden our silos? If the enemy can't hit them, why should we bother? Do we superharden them – even if we know how – at a cost of billions? We're already doing so, as a matter of fact, though it's not much sung about. Or do we protect them imperfectly with SDI at a cost of more billions? Depends what our prejudices are and who signs our pay cheque. Depends whether we're manufacturers or taxpayers. Do we put our rockets on trains or autobahns or park them in country lanes, which happens to be this month's flavour? Or do we say it's all junk anyway, so to hell with it?'

'So is it ending or beginning?' I asked.

He shrugged. 'When did it ever end? Turn on your television set, what do you see? The leaders of both sides hugging each other. Tears in their eyes. Looking more like each other every day. *Hooray, it's all over!* Bollocks. Listen to the insiders and you realise the picture hasn't altered by a brush-stroke.'

'And if I turn my television off? What will I see then?'

He had ceased to smile. Indeed his good face was more serious than I had ever seen it before, though his anger – if such it was – seemed to be directed at no one but himself.

'You'll see *us*. Hiding behind our grey screens. Telling each other we keep the peace.'

17

The elusive truth that Ned was speaking of came out slowly and in a series of distorted perceptions, which is generally the case in our secret overworld.

At six p. m. Barley was seen to 'exit' the VAAP offices, as our screens now insisted on advising us, and there was a flurry of apprehension that he might be drunk, for Zapadny was a drinking buddy and a farewell vodka with him was likely to be just that. He emerged, Zapadny with him. They embraced fulsomely on the doorstep, Zapadny flushed and a little excitable in his movements and Barley rather rigid, hence the watchers' worry that he was drunk, and their rather odd decision to photograph him – as if by freezing the moment they might somehow sober him up. And since this is the last photograph of him on the file, you may imagine how much attention has been paid to it. Barley has Zapadny in his arms, and there is strength to their embrace, at least on Barley's side. In my imagination, if no one else's, it is as if Barley is holding the poor fellow up in order to give him the courage to keep his half of the bargain; as if he is literally breathing courage into him. And the pink is weird. VAAP is a former school on Bolshaya Bronnaya Street in the centre of Moscow. It was built, I guess, at the turn of the century, with large windows and a plaster facade. And this plaster was painted in that year a light pink, which in the photograph is transformed to a flaming orange, presumably by the last rays of a red sun. The entwined men are thus caught in an unholy scarlet halo like a red flash. One of the watchers even gained the entrance hall on the pretext of visiting the cafeteria, and tried to achieve the reverse shot. But a tall man stood in his way, watching the scene on the pavement. Nobody has identified him. At the news-stand, a second man, also tall, is drinking from a mug, but not with much conviction for his eyes too are turned to the two embracing figures outside.

The watchers took no note of the scores of people who had passed in and out of the VAAP building during the two hours Barley had been in the place, how could they? They had no idea whether the visitors had come to buy copyrights or secrets.

Barley returned to his hotel where he had a drink in the bar with a bunch of publishing cronies, among them Henziger, who was able to confirm, to London's relief, that Barley was not drunk – to the contrary, that he was calm and in thoughtful spirits.

Barley did mention in passing that he was expecting a phone call from one of Zapadny's outriders – 'We're still trying to stitch up the Trans-Siberian thing.' And at about seven p. m. he suddenly confessed himself ravenous, so Henziger and Wicklow took him through to the Japanese restaurant, together with a couple of jolly girls from Simon & Schuster whom Wicklow was counting on for light relief to ease Barley's passage to his evening rendezvous.

Over dinner Barley sparkled so brightly that the girls tried to persuade him to come back to the National with them, where a party was being thrown by a group of American publishers. Barley replied that he had a date but might come on afterwards if it didn't run too long.

Exactly at eight p. m. by Wicklow's watch, Barley was summoned to the telephone and took the call in the restaurant, not five yards from where the party was sitting. Wicklow and Henziger strained, as a matter of routine, to catch his words. Wicklow recalls hearing 'That's all that matters to me.' Henziger thinks he heard 'We've got a deal' but it might have been '*not* a deal' or even 'not yet real'.

Either way, Barley was cross when he resumed his seat and complained to Henziger that the bastards were still holding out for too much money, which Henziger regarded more as a sign of his internal stress than of any great concern for the Trans-Siberian project.

Quarter of an hour later the phone rang again and Barley returned from his conversation smiling. 'We're on,' he told Henziger jubilantly. 'Sealed, signed and delivered. They never go back on a handshake.' At which Henziger and Wicklow broke out clapping and Henziger remarked that 'we could do with a few more of *them* in Moscow.'

It seems not to have occurred to either man that Barley had never before shown so much enthusiasm for a publishing agreement. But then what were they supposed to be looking for, except the night's great coup?

Barley's dinner conversation was later painstakingly reconstructed, without result. He was talkative but not excitable. His subject was jazz, his idol was Slim Gaillard. The great ones were always outlaws, he maintained. Jazz was nothing if not protest. Even its own rules had to be broken by the real improvisers, he said.

And everyone agreed with him, yes, yes, long live dissent, long live the individual over the grey men! Except nobody saw it that way. And again, why should they?

At nine-ten p.m. with less than two hours to kill, Barley announced that he would stretch out in his room for a bit, he had letters to write and business to clear up. Both Wicklow and Henziger offered to give him a hand, for they had orders not to leave him to himself if they could avoid it. But Barley declined their offers and they could not insist.

So Henziger took up his post in the next-door room and Wicklow placed himself in the lobby while Barley stretched out, though in reality he cannot have stretched out even for a second, for what he accomplished verges on the heroic.

Five letters were traced to this short span, not to mention two telephone calls to England, one to each of his children, both monitored within the United Kingdom and bounced through to Grosvenor Square but neither of operational consequence. Barley was merely concerned to catch up with family news and enquire after his grand-daughter, aged four. He insisted she be brought to the telephone, but she was too shy or too tired to talk to him. When his daughter Anthea asked him how his love-life was, he replied 'complete', which was held to be an unusual sort of reply, but then the circumstances were not usual.

Ned alone remarked that Barley had said nothing about returning to England the next day, but Ned was by now a voice in the wilderness and Clive was seriously considering taking him off the case altogether.

Barley also wrote two shorter letters, one to Henziger, one to Wicklow. And since they were not tampered with, so far as the laboratories could afterwards determine, and since – even more remarkable – the hotel delivered them to the correct room numbers promptly at eight o'clock next morning, it was assumed that these letters were in some way part of the package that Barley had negotiated while he was inside the VAAP building.

The letters advised the two men that if they left the country quietly that day, taking Mary Lou with them, no harm would come to them. Barley had a warm word for each.

'Wickers, there's a real publisher in you. Go for it!'

And for Henziger, 'Jack, I hope this won't mean you take premature retirement in Salt Lake City. Tell them you never trusted me anyway. I didn't trust me, so why should you?'

No homilies, no apt quotations from his large, untidy store. Barley, it seemed, was coping very well without the assistance of other people's wisdom.

At ten o'clock, he left the hotel accompanied by Henziger only, and they had themselves dropped on the northern outskirts of the town where Cy and Paddy were once more waiting in the safe truck. This time Paddy was driving. Henziger sat beside him and Barley got in the back with Cy, slipped off his coat and let Cy put on the microphone harness and give him the latest operational intelligence: that Goethe's plane from Saratov had arrived in Moscow on time; and that a figure answering Goethe's description had been observed entering Igor's apartment block forty minutes ago.

Soon afterwards, lights had come up in the windows of the target flat.

Cy then handed Barley two books, one a paperback copy of *From Here to Eternity* which contained the shopping list, the other a fatter volume, leather-bound, which was a concealment device containing a sound-baffler to be activated by pulling open the front cover. Barley had played with one in London and was proficient in its use. His body microphones were tuned to defeat the impulses of the device, but normal wall microphones were not. The disadvantage of the baffler was also known to him. Its presence in the room was detectable. If Igor's flat was microphoned, then the listeners would at once be aware that a baffler was being used. This risk had been passed by both London and Langley as acceptable.

The other risk had not been considered, namely that the device might fall into the hands of the opposition. It was still in the prototype stage and a small fortune and several years of research had been lavished on its development.

At ten-fifty-four p.m. just as Barley was leaving the safe truck, he handed Paddy an envelope and said, 'This is for Ned personally in case anything happens to me.' Paddy slipped the envelope in his inside jacket pocket. He noticed that it was a fat envelope and, so far as he could see in the half-light, it was not addressed.

The most lively account of Barley's walk to the foot of the apartment block was provided not by the military reportese of Paddy, still less by the Haig-speak of Cy, but in the boisterous tones of his good friend Jack Henziger who escorted him to the entrance. Barley did not utter, he said. Neither did Jack. They'd no wish to be identified as foreigners.

'We walked alongside of each other out of step,' Henziger said. 'He has this long step, mine's short. It bothered me we couldn't keep step. The apartment house was one of these brick monsters they have out there with like a mile of concrete round them, and we kept on walking without getting anywhere. It's like one of those dreams, I thought. You keep on running but you don't make any distance. Very hot, the air. Sweaty. I'm sweating, but Barley's cool. He was collected, no question. He looked great. He looked straight into my eyes. He wished me a lot of luck. He was at peace with himself. I felt it.'

Shaking hands, Henziger nevertheless had a momentary impression that Barley was angry about something. Perhaps angry against Henziger, for now in the half-dark he seemed determined to avoid Henziger's eye.

'Then I thought, Maybe he's mad at Bluebird for getting him into this. Then I thought, Maybe he's mad at all of us, but too polite to say it. Like he was being very British somehow, very laid back, very understated, keeping it all inside.'

Ninety seconds later as they were preparing to leave, Cy and Paddy saw a silhouette at Igor's window and took it to be Barley's. The right hand was adjusting the top of the curtain, which was the agreed signal to say 'All's well.' They drove away and left the surveillance of the apartment to the irregulars, who covered each other in shifts all night, but the light in the apartment stayed burning and Barley didn't come out.

One theory out of hundreds is that he never went up to the apartment at all, and that they took him straight through the building and out the other side, and that the figure in the window was one of their own people, for instance one of the tall men in the photograph taken in the VAAP foyer that afternoon. It never seemed to me to matter, but to the experts for some reason it did. When a problem threatens to engulf you, there's nothing like irrelevant detail to keep your head above water.

Speculation about Barley's disappearance began slowly and built throughout the night. Optimists like Bob, and for a while Sheriton, clung on till
dawn and after. Barley and Bluebird had drunk themselves under the table
again, they kept insisting in order to keep each other's spirits up. It was
Peredelkino all over again, a rerun, no question, they told each other.

Then for a short while they worked up a kidnap theory, until soon after
five-thirty in the morning – thanks to the time difference – when Henziger
and Wicklow had their letters and Wicklow without further fuss took a
cab to the British Embassy, where the Soviet guards at the gate did not
obstruct him. The result was a flash signal to Ned, decypher yourself, from
Paddy. Meanwhile, Cy was putting through a similar message to Langley,
Sheriton and anyone else who was still willing to listen to a man whose
Moscow days looked like being over very soon.

Sheriton took the news with his customary phlegm. He read Cy's
telegram, he looked around the room and realised that the whole team
was watching him – the smart girls, the boys in ties, loyal Bob, ambitious
Johnny with his gunman's eyes. And of the Brits, Ned, myself and Brock,
for Clive had prudently discovered urgent business elsewhere. There was
a lot of the actor in Sheriton, just as there was in Henziger, and he used it
now. He stood up, he hauled at his waistband, he massaged his face like a
man reckoning he needed a shave.

'Well, boys. Better put the chairs on the tables till next time.'

Then he walked over to Ned, who was still sitting at his desk studying
Paddy's telegram, and he laid a hand on Ned's shoulder.

'Ned, I owe you dinner some time,' he said.

Then he walked over to the door and unhooked his new Burberry and
buttoned himself into it and departed, followed after a moment by Bob
and Johnny.

Others did not bow out so elegantly, least of all the barons of the twelfth
floor.

Once again, a committee of enquiry was formed.

Names should be named. Nobody should be spared. Heads must roll.

The Deputy to chair it, Palfrey to be secretary.

Another purpose of such committees, I discovered, is to impart a sense
of ceremony to events that have passed off without any. We were extremely
solemn.

The first to be heard, as usual, were the conspiracy theorists, who were
recruited in short order from the Foreign Office, the Defence Ministry and
a rather unlovely body called the Informal Consultants, which consisted
of industrial and academic scientists who fancied themselves as Sunday
spies. These amateur espiocrats commanded huge influence around the
Whitehall bazaars, and were heard at inordinate length by the committee.

A professor from Edinburgh addressed us for five full pipe-loads and nearly gassed us all, but nobody had the nerve to tell him to put the damn thing out.

The first great question was, what would happen next? Would there be expulsions, a scandal? What would become of our Moscow station? Had any of the irregulars been compromised?

The audio truck, though Soviet property, was an American problem, and its abrupt disappearance caused hushed concern among those who had favoured its use.

The question of who is expelled for what is never a plain one, for heads of station in Moscow, Washington and London are these days declared to their host countries. Nobody in Moscow Centre had any illusions about Paddy's activities, or Cy's. Their cover was not designed to protect them from the opposition, but from the gaze of the real world.

In any case, they were not expelled. Nobody was expelled. Nobody was arrested. The irregulars, who were stood down indefinitely, went peaceably about their cover jobs.

The absence of a retaliatory gesture was quickly seen by Western pundits as vastly significant.

A conciliatory move in the season of *glasnost*?

A clear signal to us that the Bluebird was a gambit to obtain the American shopping list?

Or a less clear signal to us that the Bluebird material was accurate, but too embarrassing to acknowledge?

The battle-lines were set. Somewhat along the principle that Ned had already explained to me, doves and hawks on both sides of the Atlantic once more gleefully parted company.

If the Sovs are sending us a signal that the material is accurate, why then clearly the material is inaccurate, said the hawks.

And vice versa, said the doves.

And vice versa again, said the hawks.

Papers written, feuds waged. Promotions, sackings, pensions, medals, lateral postings and downgradings. But no consensus. Just the usual triumph of the fattest, disguised as rational deduction.

In our committee Ned alone refused to join the dance. He seemed cheerfully determined to accept the blame. 'The Bluebird was straight and Barley was straight,' he repeated to the committee over and again, without once losing his good humour. 'There was no deception by anyone, except where we deceived ourselves. It was we who were crooked. Not the Bluebird.'

Soon after he had delivered himself of this judgment, it was agreed he was under mental stress and his attendance was required more sparingly.

Oh, and note was taken. Passively, since active verbs have an unpleasant way of betraying the actor. Very serious note. Taken all over the place.

Note was taken that Ned had failed to advise the twelfth floor of Barley's drunken breakout after his return from Leningrad.

Note was taken that Ned had requisitioned all manner of resources on that same night, for which he had never accounted, among them Ben Lugg and the services of the head listener Mary, who sufficiently overcame her loyalty to a brother officer to give the committee a lurid account of Ned's high-handedness. Demanding illegal taps! Imagine! Faulting telephones! The liberty!

Mary was pensioned off soon after this and now lives in a rage in Malta, where it is feared she is writing her memoirs.

Note was also taken, if regretfully, of the questionable conduct of our Legal Adviser dePalfrey – I even got my *de* back – who had failed to justify his use of the Home Secretary's delegated authority in the full knowledge that this was required of him by the secretly agreed Procedures Governing the Service's Activities as Amended by etcetera, and in accordance with paragraph something of a deniable Home Office protocol.

The heat of battle was however taken into account. The Legal Adviser was not pensioned off, neither did he take himself to Malta. But he was not exonerated either. A partial pardon at best. A Legal Adviser should not have been so close to an operation. An inappropriate use of the Legal Adviser's skills. The word injudicious was passed around.

It was also noted with regret that the same Legal Adviser had drafted a glowing testimonial of Barley for Clive's signature not forty-eight hours before Barley's disappearance, thus enabling Barley to take possession of the shopping list, though presumably not for long.

In my spare hours, I drew up Ned's terms of severance and thought nervously about my own. Life inside the Service might have its limitations but the thought of life outside it terrified me.

The announcement of Bluebird's passing provided a temporary setback to our committee's deliberations, but it soon recovered. The offending item was a six-line affair in *Pravda*, carefully pitched to be neither too much nor too little, reporting the death after illness of the distinguished physicist Professor Yakov Savelyev of Leningrad and listing his several decorations. He had died of natural causes – the bulletin assured us – soon after delivering an important lecture to the military academy at Saratov.

Ned took the day off when this news reached him, and the day became three days, a light flu. But the conspiracy theorists had a ball.

Savelyev was not dead.

He had been dead all along, and the version we had dealt with was an impostor.

He was doing what he had always been doing, running the Scientific Disinformation Section of the KGB.

His material was vindicated, was not vindicated.

It was worthless.

It was pure gold.

It was smoke.

It was a truthful message of peace sent to us at immense risk by the moderates inside Moscow's ruling ranks in order to show us that the Soviet nuclear sword had rusted in its scabbard and the Soviet nuclear shield had more holes in it than a colander.

It was a fiendish plot to persuade the American faint-hearts to take their fingers off the nuclear trigger.

In short, there was enough for everyone to get their teeth into.

And, because in the symbiotic relationship that exists between belligerent states nothing can take place in the one without setting off a mirror reaction in the other, a counter-industry grew up and the history of the American part in the Bluebird affair was hastily rewritten.

Langley knew all along that the Bluebird was bad, said the counter-industry.

Or that Barley was.

Or that both of them were.

Sheriton and Brady were playing double-double games, said the counter-industry. Their one aim was to plant the smoke convincingly and steal another march on the Russians in the endless struggle for the Margin of Safety.

Sheriton was a genius.

Brady was a genius.

They were all, all geniuses!

Sheriton had scored a brilliant coup. Brady had.

The Agency was staffed by nothing but brilliant strategists who were quite unlike their dismal counterparts in the overt world. God preserve the Agency. Where would we be without it?

As if all this were not enough, new tiers of possibility were added to the old. For example, that Sheriton had been the unwitting instrument of the Pentagon and Defense. It was they who had prepared the phoney shopping list and they who had known all along that the Bluebird was a plant.

And each fresh rumour had to be taken seriously in its turn, even if the only real mystery was who had fabricated it or why. The answer, in many cases, appeared to be Russell Sheriton, who was fighting for his hide.

As to the Bluebird, if he had not died of natural causes, he was certainly doing so now.

Ned alone, returned from his self-imposed vigil, was once more so crass as to speak the likely truth. 'The Bluebird was straight and we killed him,' he said roundly, at the first meeting he attended. He was not invited to the next one.

And all this while our search for Barley did not let up, even if there were those of us who were glad not to find him. We edged towards him, round him and, too often, away from him. But we were honourable men. We never let up.

But what had Barley traded – and for what?

What were the Russians prepared to buy from him – from Barley, who till now had only needed an expensive lunch, paid for most likely out of his own pocket, to talk himself into an irreversible loss?

He was blown, after all! To smithereens! Already by the time he went to them! And knew it!

What had he got to offer them that they couldn't help themselves to? We are talking after all of torture, of the foulest methods, and registers of agony from which even the return is unimaginable hell. The Russians might be improving their image, but nobody seriously supposed that they were going to abandon overnight methods that had stood them in good stead for thousands of years.

The first and most obvious answer was the shopping list. Barley could tell the Russians baldly he would not obtain it from his masters until he had the necessary assurances. And that he would sooner boil in oil for the rest of his life than fetch the shopping list for free.

And they believed him. They saw that they would have to go without the shopping list if they didn't play his game. And because the grey men of either side are as scared of self-sacrifice as they are of love, the tender sages of the KGB evidently preferred to deal with the part of him they understood, rather than meddle with the part they didn't.

They knew he had the power to refuse them, to say, 'No, I will not fetch the shopping list. No, I will not walk into Igor's apartment until you have given me your more than solemn word.'

They knew, when they had listened to him, that he had the strength. And, like us, they were a little embarrassed by it.

And Barley – as he had told Henziger and Wicklow at dinner – had never met a Russian yet who could give his solemn word and walk away from it. He was not talking of politics, of course just business.

And in return? What did Barley buy with what he sold?

Katya.

Matvey.

The twins.

Not a bad deal. Real people in exchange for unreal arguments.

For himself? Nothing. Nothing that could conceivably modify the strength of his demand on account of those whom he had taken into his protection.

And little by little it became clear that Barley for once in his life had hammered out a first-rate contract. If the Bluebird was a lost cause, Katya and her children showed every sign of being a saved one. She remained at October, she was sighted at the occasional reception, she answered her telephone at home and at her office. The twins still went to school and sang the same daft songs. Matvey wandered his amiable ways.

Soon, therefore, another great theory added itself to the rest. 'The Sovs are engaging in an internal cover-up,' it ran. 'They do not wish to give currency to Bluebird's revelations of incompetence.'

So the needle swung the other way for a while and Bluebird's material was deemed genuine. But not for long.

'This is what they *want* us to believe,' a man of power cried.

So the needle swung hastily back to where it was before, because nobody wants to be made a fool of.

But Barley's deal held. Katya did not lose her privileges, her red card, her apartment, her job or even, as the months went by, her looks. At first, it was true, the reports spoke of the pallor of widowhood, of an unkempt appearance and long absences from work. And clearly nobody had promised Barley that she would not be invited to make a voluntary statement about her relationship with the late Bluebird.

But gradually, after a becoming period of withdrawal, her ebullience reasserted itself and she was seen about.

And of Barley himself?

The trail went hot, then cold, then very cold indeed.

Formal letters of resignation, postmark Lisbon, were received by his aunts within a few days of the book fair and bore the marks of Barley's earlier style – a general weariness of publishing, the industry has outgrown itself, time to turn his hand to other things while he still has a few good years ahead of him.

As to his immediate plans, he proposed 'to lose himself for a while' and explore unusual places. So it was clear that he was not in Russia any more.

Seemingly clear, that is.

And after all, he said so himself. So did the pretty girl in the Barry Martin Travel Agency, which has its offices in the Mezhdunarodnaya. Mr. Scott Blair had decided he would fly to Lisbon instead of back to London, she said. A courier from VAAP brought his ticket. She rewrote it and booked him on the Aeroflot direct flight, leaving on the Monday at 1120 hours, arriving Lisbon 1530, stopping Prague.

And somebody used that ticket. A tall man, spoke to nobody, a Barley to the life, or nearly. Tall like the man in the VAAP lobby perhaps, but we checked him anyway. We checked him all along the line and the line only stopped when it reached Tina, Barley's Lisbon housekeeper. Yes, yes! Tina had heard from him, she told Merridew – a nice postcard from Moscow saying he'd met a lady-friend and they were going to take a holiday!

Merridew was profoundly relieved to learn that Barley had not, after all, returned to his patch.

*

Then over the next months a picture of Barley's after-life began to form before it disappeared again.

A West German drug-smuggler while in detention heard that a man of Barley's description was under interrogation in a prison near Kiev. A cheerful fellow, said the German. Popular with the inmates. Free. Even the guards gave him the odd grudging smile.

An adventurous French motoring couple returning home had been assisted by a 'tall friendly Englishman' who spoke some French to them when they were involved in a traffic pile-up with a Soviet limousine near Smolensk. Nobody was hurt. Six foot, brown floppy hair, polite, with a big laugh, and tended by these burly Russians.

And one day near Christmas, not long after Ned had formally handed over the Russia House, a signal came in from Havana reporting a Cuban source to the effect that an Englishman was under special detention at a political gaol near Minsk, and that he sang a lot.

Sang? went the outraged signal back. Sang about *what*?

Sang Satchmo, came Havana's reply. Source was a jazz fiend, like the Englishman.

And the text of Barley's letter to Ned?

It remains a small mystery of the affair that it never reached the file, and there is no record of it in the official history of the Bluebird case. I think Ned hung on to it as something he cared about too much to file.

So that should be the end of the story, or rather the story should have no end. Barley in the judgment of the knowing was all set to take his place among the other shadows that haunt the darker byways of Moscow society – the trodden-out defectors and spies, the traded ones and the untrusted ones with their pathetic wives and pallid minders, sharing out their dwindling rations of Western treats and Western memories.

He should have been spotted after a few years, accidentally but on purpose, at a party where a lucky British journalist was mysteriously present. And perhaps, if times remained the same, he would be fitted out with some taunting piece of disinformation, or invited to throw a little pepper into the eyes of his former masters.

And indeed that was the very ritual that seemed to be unfolding when a flash telegram from Paddy's successor reported that a tall sandy Englishman had been sighted – not only sighted, heard – playing tenor saxophone at a newly-opened club in the old town, one year to the day after his disappearance.

Clive was hauled from his bed, signals flew between London and Langley, the Foreign Office was asked to take a view. They did and it was unequivocal for once – *not our problem and not yours*. They seemed to feel the Russians were better equipped to muzzle Barley than we were. After all, the Russians had obliged before.

Next day a second telegram arrived, this time from fat Merridew in Lisbon. Barley's housekeeper Tina, with whom Merridew had reluctantly maintained relations, had been instructed to prepare the flat for the arrival of her master.

But *how* instructed? asked Merridew.

By telephone, she replied, Senhor Barley had telephoned her.

Telephoned you where from, you stupid woman?

Tina hadn't asked and Barley hadn't said. Why should she ask where he was, if he was coming to Lisbon any day?

Merridew was appalled. He was not the only one. We advised the Americans, but Langley had suffered a collective loss of memory. They near as nothing asked us, Barley who? There is a public notion that services such as ours take violent retribution against those who have betrayed their secrets. Well, and sometimes it is true, they do – though seldom against people of Barley's class. But in this case it was immediately clear that nobody, and least of all Langley, had any wish to make a shining beacon out of somebody they would greatly prefer to forget. Better to square him, they agreed – and keep the Americans out of it.

I mounted the staircase apprehensively. I had declined the protective services of Brock, and Merridew's half-hearted offer of support. The stairwell was dark and steep and inhospitable and unpleasantly silent. It was early evening but we knew he was at home. I pressed the bell but did not hear it ring, so I rapped the door with my knuckles. It was a stubby little door, thickly panelled. It reminded me of the boat-house on the island. I heard a step inside and at once stood back, I still don't know quite why, but I suppose it was a kind of fear of animals. Would he be fierce, would he be angry or over-effusive, would he throw me down the stairs or fling his arms round me? I was carrying a briefcase and I remember transferring it to my left hand as if to be ready to protect myself. Though, God knows, I am not a fighting man. I smelt fresh paint. There was no eyehole in the door, and it was flush against its iron lintel. He had no way of knowing who was there before he opened to me. I heard a latch slip. The door swung inward.

'Hullo, Harry,' he said.

So I said, 'Hullo, Barley.' I was wearing a lightweight dark suit, blue in preference to grey. I said, 'Hullo, Barley,' and waited for him to smile.

He was thinner, he was harder and he was straighter, with the result that he had become very tall indeed, taller than me by a head. You're a nerveless traveller, I remember thinking as I waited. It was what Hannah in her early days used to say we should both of us learn to become. The old untidy gestures had left him. The discipline of small spaces had done its work. He was trim. He was wearing jeans and an old cricket shirt with the sleeves rolled to the elbow. He had splashes of white paint on his forearms and a smear of it across his forehead. I saw a step-ladder behind him and a half-whited wall, and at the centre of the room heaps of books and gramophone records partly protected with a dustsheet.

'Come for a game of chess, Harry?' he asked, still not smiling.

'If I could just talk to you,' I said, as I might have said to Hannah, or anybody else to whom I was proposing a half-measure.

'Officially?'

'Well.'

He studied me as if he hadn't heard me, frankly and in his own time, of which he seemed to have a lot – much, I suppose, as one studies cellmates or interrogators in a world where the common courtesies tend to be dispensed with.

But his gaze had nothing downward or shameful in it, nothing of arrogance or shiftiness. It seemed to the contrary even clearer than I remembered it, as if it had settled itself permanently in the far regions to which it used occasionally to drift.

'I've got some cold plonk, if that'll do you,' he said, and stood back to let me pass him while he watched me, before he closed the door and dropped the latch.

But he still didn't smile. His mood was a mystery to me. I felt I could understand nothing of him unless he chose to tell it me. Put another way, I understood everything about him that was within my grasp to understand. The rest, infinity.

There were dustsheets on the chairs as well but he pulled them off and folded them as if they were his bedding. Prison people, I have noticed over the years, take a long time to shake off their pride.

'What do you want?' he asked, pouring us each a glass from a flagon.

'They've asked me to tidy things up,' I said. 'Get some answers out of you. Assurances. Give you some in return.' I had lost my way. 'Whether we can help,' I said. 'Whether you need things. What we can agree on for the future and so on.'

'I've got all the assurances I need, thanks,' he said politely, lighting on the one word that seemed to catch his interest. 'They'll move at their own pace. I've promised to keep my mouth shut.' He smiled at last. 'I've followed your advice, Harry. I've become a long-distance lover, like you.'

'I was in Moscow,' I said, fighting hard to find the flow to our conversation. 'I went to the places. Saw the people. Used my own name.'

'What is it?' he asked with the same courtliness. 'Your name. What is it?'

'Palfrey,' I said, leaving out the *de*.

He smiled as if in sympathy, or recognition.

'The Service sent me over there to look for you. Unofficially but officially, as it were. Ask the Russians about you. Tidy things up. We thought it was time we found out what had happened to you. See if we could help.'

And make sure they were observing the rules, I might have added. That nobody in Moscow was going to rock the boat. No silly leaks or publicity stunts.

'I told you what happened to me,' he said.

'You mean in your letters to Wicklow and Henziger and people?'

'Yes.'

'Well, naturally we knew the letters had been written under duress, if you wrote them at all. Look at poor Goethe's letter.'

'Balls,' he said. 'I wrote them of my own free will.'

I edged a little nearer to my message. And to the briefcase at my side.

'As far as we're concerned, you acted very honourably,' I said, drawing out a file and opening it on my lap. 'Everybody talks under duress and you were no exception. We're grateful for what you did for us and aware of the cost to you. Professionally and personally. We're concerned that you should have your full measure of compensation. On terms, naturally. The sum could be large.'

Where had he learned to watch me like that? To withhold himself so steadily? To impart tension to others, when he seemed impervious to it himself?

I read him the terms, which were somewhat like Landau's in reverse. To stay out of the United Kingdom and only to enter with our prior consent. Full and final settlement of all claims, his silence in perpetuity expressed *ex abundanti cautela* in half a dozen different ways. And a lot of money to sign here, provided – always and only provided – he kept his mouth shut.

He didn't sign, though. He was already bored. He waved my important pen away.

'What did you do with Walt, by the way? I brought a hat for him. Kind of tea-cosy in tiger stripes. Can't find the damn thing.'

'If you send it to me, I'll see he gets it,' I said.

He caught my tone and smiled at me sadly. 'Poor old Walt. They've given him the push, eh?'

'We peak early in our trade,' I said, but I couldn't look him in the eye so I changed the subject. 'I suppose you heard that your aunts have sold out to Lupus Books.'

He laughed – not his old wild laughter, it was true, but a free man's laugh, all the same. 'Jumbo! The old devil! Conned the Sacred Cow! Trust him!'

But he was at ease with the idea. He seemed to take genuine pleasure in the rightness of it. I am scared, as we all are in my trade, of people of good instinct. But I was able to share vicariously in his repose. He seemed to have developed universal tolerance.

She'll come, he told me as he gazed out at the harbour. They promised that one day she would come.

Not at once, and in their time, not in Barley's. But she would come, he had no doubt. Maybe this year, maybe next, he said. But something inside the mountainous bureaucratic Russian belly would heave and give birth to a mouse of compassion. He had no doubt of it. It would be gradual but it would happen. They had promised him.

'They don't break their promises,' he assured me, and in the face of such trust it would have been churlish in me to contradict him. But something else was preventing me from voicing my customary scepticism. It was Hannah again. I felt she was begging me to let him live with his humanity, even if I had destroyed hers. 'You think people never change because you don't,' she had once said to me. 'You only feel safe when you're disenchanted.'

I suggested I take him out for food but he seemed not to hear. He was standing at the long window, staring at the harbour lights while I stared at his back. The same pose that he struck when we had first interviewed him here in Lisbon. The same arm holding out his glass. The same pose as on the island when Ned told him he had won. But straighter. Was he talking to me again? I realised he was. He was watching their ship arrive from Leningrad, he said. He was watching her hurry down the gangway to him with her children at her side. He was sitting with Uncle Matvey under the shade tree in the park below his window, where he had sat with Ned and Walter in the days before his manhood. He was listening to Katya's rendering of Matvey's heroic tales of endurance. He was believing in all the hopes that I had buried with me when I chose the safe bastion of infinite distrust in preference to the dangerous path of love.

I succeeded in persuading him to come to dinner, and as a kindness he let me pay. But I could buy nothing else from him, he signed nothing, he accepted nothing, he wanted nothing, he conceded nothing, he owed nothing and he wished the living lot of us, without anger, to the Devil.

But he had a splendid quiet. He wasn't strident. He was considerate of my feelings, even if he was too courteous to enquire what they were. I had never told him about Hannah, and I knew I never could, because the new Barley would have no patience with my unaltered state.

For the rest, he seemed concerned to make me a gift of his story, so that I would have something to take home to my masters. He brought me back to his flat and insisted I have a nightcap, and that nothing was my fault.

And he talked. For me. For him. Talked and talked. He told me the story as I have tried to tell it to you here, from his side as well as ours. He went on talking till it was light, and when I left at five in the morning, he was wondering whether he might as well finish that bit of wall before turning in. There was a lot to get ready, he explained. Carpets. Curtains. Bookshelves.

'It's going to be all right, Harry,' he assured me as he showed me off the premises. 'Tell them that.'

Spying is waiting.

The author and publisher acknowledge use of the following copyright material:

Lines from 'Nobel Prize' from *Selected Poems* by Boris Pasternak, translated by John Stallworthy and Peter France, copyright © Peter France, 1983, (Allen Lane, 1983); lines from 'Dirge' from Stevie Smith's *Collected Poems*, (Allen Lane, 1975); a line from Theodore Roethke's *Collected Poems*, (Faber, 1985); lines from May Sarton from *Journal of a Solitude*, (Women's Press, 1985).

The Secret Pilgrim

FOR ALEC GUINNESS

with affection and thanks

1

L et me confess to you at once that if I had not, on the spur of the moment, picked up my pen and scribbled a note to George Smiley inviting him to address my passing-out class on the closing evening of their entry course – and had Smiley not, against all my expectations, consented – I would not be making so free to you with my heart.

At the most, I would be offering you the sort of laundered reminiscence with which, if I am honest, I was a bit too inclined to regale my students: feats of secret chivalry, of the dramatic, the resourceful and the brave. And always, of course, the useful. I would be enthralling you with memories of night drops into the Caucasus, hazardous crossings by fast boat, beach landings, winking shore lights, clandestine radio messages that ceased in mid-transmission. Of silent heroes of the Cold War who, having made their contribution, modestly went to earth in the society they had protected. Of defectors-in-place snatched in the nick of time from the jaws of the opposition.

And to a point, yes, that is the life we lived. In our day we did those things, and some even ended well. We had good men in bad countries who risked their lives for us. And usually they were believed, and sometimes their intelligence was wisely used. I hope so, for the greatest spy on earth is worth nothing when it isn't.

And for the lighter note, over a second whisky in the Probationers' Mess, I would have picked out for them the occasion when a three-man reception team from the Circus, operating inside East Germany, and gallantly led by myself, lay freezing on a ridge in the Harz Mountains, praying for the flutter of an unmarked plane with its engines cut, and the blessed black parachute floating in its wake. And what did we find when our prayer was answered and we had slithered down an icefield to claim our treasure? Stones, I would tell my wide-eyed students. Chunks of honest Argyll granite. The despatchers at our Scottish airbase had sent us the training cannister by mistake.

That tale, at least, found a certain echo, even if some of my other offerings tended to lose their audience halfway through.

I suspect that my impulse to write to Smiley had been brewing in me longer than I realised. The idea was conceived during one of my regular visits to Personnel to discuss the progress of my students. Dropping in on the Senior Officers' Bar for a sandwich and a beer, I had bumped into Peter Guillam. Peter had played Watson to George's Sherlock Holmes in the long search for the Circus traitor, who turned out to be our Head of Operations, Bill Haydon. Peter had not heard from George for – oh, a year now, more. George had bought this cottage in North Cornwall somewhere, he said, and was indulging his dislike of the telephone. He had some kind of sinecure at Exeter University, and was allowed to use their library. Sadly I pictured the rest: George the lonely hermit on an empty landscape, taking his solitary walks and thinking his thoughts. George slipping up to Exeter for a little human warmth in his old age while he waited to take his place in the spies' Valhalla.

And Ann, his wife? I asked Peter, lowering my voice as one does when Ann's name comes up – for it was an open secret, and a painful one, that Bill Haydon had counted among Ann's many lovers.

Ann was Ann, said Peter, with a Gallic shrug. She had bits of family with grand houses on the Helford Estuary. Sometimes she stayed with them, sometimes she stayed with George.

I asked for Smiley's address. 'Don't tell him I gave it you,' said Peter as I wrote it down. With George, there had always been that certain kind of guilt about passing on his whereabouts – I still don't quite know why.

Three weeks later Toby Esterhase came down to Sarratt to give us his celebrated talk on the arts of clandestine surveillance on unfriendly soil. And of course he stayed for lunch, which was greatly enhanced for him by the presence of our first three girls. After a battle lasting as long as I had been at Sarratt, Personnel had finally decided that girls were all right after all.

And I heard myself trailing Smiley's name.

There have been times when I would not have entertained Toby in the woodshed, and others when I thanked my Maker I had him on my side. But with the years, I am pleased to notice, one settles to people.

'Oh look here, my God, Ned!' Toby cried in his incurably Hungarian English, smoothing back his carefully pomaded mane of silver hair. 'You mean you haven't heard?'

'Heard what?' I asked patiently.

'My dear fellow, George is chairing the Fishing Rights Committee. Don't they tell you anything down here in the sticks? I think I better take this up with the Chief actually, one to one. A word in his ear at the Club.'

'Perhaps you'd tell me first what the Fishing Rights Committee is,' I suggested.

'Ned, you know what? I think I get nervous. Maybe they took you off the list.'

'Maybe they did at that,' I said.

He told me anyway, as I knew he would, and I duly acted astonished, which gave him an even greater sense of his importance. And there is a part of me that remains astonished to this day. The Fishing Rights Committee, Toby explained for the benefit of the unblessed, was an informal working party made up of officers from Moscow Centre and the Circus. Its job, said Toby – who I really believe had lost any capacity to be surprised – was to identify intelligence targets of interest to both services and thrash out a system of sharing. 'The idea actually, Ned, was to target the world's trouble spots,' he said with an air of maddening superiority – 'I think they fix first the Middle East. Don't quote me, Ned, okay?'

'And you're telling me Smiley *chairs* this committee?' I asked incredulously when I had attempted to digest this.

'Well, maybe not much longer, Ned – Anno Domini and so forth. But the Russians were so frightfully keen to meet him, we brought him in to snip the tape. Give the old fellow a treat, I say. Stroke him a bit. Bunch of fivers in an envelope.'

I didn't know which to marvel at the more: the notion of Toby Esterhase tripping to the altar with Moscow Centre, or of George Smiley presiding over the marriage. A few days later, with Personnel's permission, I wrote to the Cornish address Guillam had given me, adding diffidently that if George loathed public speaking half as much as I did, he should on no account accept. I had been a bit in the dumps till then, but when his prim little card arrived by return declaring him delighted, I felt a probationer myself, and just as nervous.

Two weeks after that, wearing a brand-new country suit for the occasion, I was standing at the barrier at Paddington Station, watching the elderly trains disgorge their middle-aged commuters. I don't think I had ever been quite so aware of Smiley's anonymity. Wherever I looked, I seemed to see versions of him: tubby, bespectacled gentlemen of a certain seniority, and every one of them with George's air of being slightly late for something he would rather not be doing. Then suddenly we had shaken hands and he was sitting beside me in the back of a Head Office Rover, stockier than I remembered him, and white-haired, it was true, but of a vigour and good humour I had not seen in him since his wife had her fatal fling with Haydon.

'Well, well, Ned. How do you like being a schoolmaster?'

'How do you like retirement?' I countered with a laugh. 'I'll be joining you soon!'

Oh, he loved retirement, he assured me. Couldn't get enough of it, he said wryly; I should have no fears of it at all. A little tutoring here, Ned, the odd paper to deliver there; walks, he'd even acquired a dog.

'I hear they hauled you back to sit on some extraordinary committee,' I said. 'Conspiring with the Bear, they say, against the Thief of Baghdad.'

George does not gossip, but I saw his smile broaden. 'Do they now? And your source would be Toby, no doubt,' he said, and beamed contentedly upon the dismal subtopian landscape while he launched into a diversionary story about two old ladies in his village who hated each other. One owned an antique shop, the other was very rich. But as the Rover continued its progress through once-rural Hertfordshire, I found myself thinking less about the ladies of George's village than about George himself. I was thinking that this was a Smiley reborn, who told stories about old ladies, sat on committees with Russian spies and gazed on the overt world with the relish of someone who has just come out of hospital.

That evening, squeezed into an elderly dinner jacket, the same man sat at my side at Sarratt high table, peering benignly round him at the polished plate candlesticks and old group photographs going back to God knows when. And at the fit, expectant faces of his young audience as they waited on the master's word.

'Ladies and gentlemen, Mr. George Smiley,' I announced severely as I rose to introduce him. 'A legend of the Service. Thank you.'

'Oh, I don't think I'm a legend at all,' Smiley protested as he clambered to his feet. 'I think I'm just a rather fat old man wedged between the pudding and the port.'

Then the legend began talking, and I realised that I had never heard Smiley address a social gathering before. I had assumed it was a thing he would be congenitally bad at, like forcing his opinions on people, or referring to a joe by his real name. So the sovereign way in which he addressed us surprised me before I had begun to fathom the content. I heard his first few sentences and I watched my students' faces – not always so obliging – lift and relax and light to him as they gave him first their attention, then their trust and finally their support. And I thought, with an inner smile of belated recognition: yes, yes, of course, this was George's other nature. This was the actor who had always lain hidden in him, the secret Pied Piper. This was the man Ann Smiley had loved and Bill Haydon had deceived and the rest of us had loyally followed, to the mystification of outsiders.

There is a wise tradition at Sarratt that our dinner speeches are not recorded and no notes are taken, and that no official reference may afterwards be made to what was said. The guest of honour enjoyed what Smiley in his Germanic way called 'the fool's freedom,' though I can think of few people less qualified for the privilege. But I am nothing if not a professional, trained to listen and remember, and you must understand also that Smiley had not spoken many words before I realised – as my students were not slow to notice – that he was speaking straight into my heretical heart. I refer to that other, less obedient person who is also inside me and whom, if I am honest, I had refused to acknowledge since I had embarked on this final lap of my career – to the secret questioner who had been my uncomfortable companion even before a reluctant joe of mine called Barley Blair had stepped across the crumbling Iron Curtain and, for reasons of love, and some sort of honour, had calmly kept on walking, to the incredulity of the Fifth Floor.

The better the restaurant, we say of Personnel, the worse the news. 'It's time you handed on your wisdom to the new boys, Ned,' he had told me over a suspiciously good lunch at the Connaught. '*And* to the new *girls*,' he added, with a loathsome smirk. 'They'll be letting them into the Church next, I suppose.' He returned to happier ground. 'You know the tricks. You've kicked around. You've had an impressive last lap running Secretariat. Time to put it all to advantage. We think you should take over the Nursery and pass the torch to tomorrow's spies.'

He had used a rather similar set of sporting metaphors, if I remembered rightly, when in the wake of Barley Blair's defection he had removed me from my post as Head of the Russia House and consigned me to that knacker's yard, the Interrogators' Pool.

He ordered up two more glasses of Armagnac. 'How's your Mabel, by the way?' he continued, as if he had just remembered her. 'Somebody told me she'd got her handicap down to twelve – ten, by God! Well. I trust you'll keep her away from me! So what do you say? Sarratt in the week, home to Tunbridge Wells at weekends, sounds to me like the triumphant crowning of a career. What do you say?'

So what *do* you say? You say what others have said before you. Those who can, do. Those who can't, teach. And what they teach is what they can't do any more, because either the body or the spirit or both have lost their singleness of purpose; because they have seen too much and suppressed too much and compromised too much, and in the end tasted too little. So they take to rekindling their old dreams in new minds, and warming themselves against the fires of the young.

And that brings me back to the opening bars of Smiley's speech that night, for suddenly his words were reaching out and grasping me. I had invited him because he was a legend of the past. Yet to the delight of all of us, he was turning out to be the iconoclastic prophet of the future.

I'll not bother you with the finer points of Smiley's introductory tour of the globe. He gave them the Middle East, which was obviously on his mind, and he explored the limits of colonial power in supposedly post-colonialist times. He gave them the Third World and the Fourth World and posited a Fifth World, and pondered aloud whether human despair and poverty were the serious concern of any wealthy nation. He seemed pretty confident they weren't. He scoffed at the idea that spying was a dying profession now that the Cold War had ended: with each new nation that came out of the ice, he said, with each new alignment, each rediscovery of old identities and passions, with each erosion of the old status quo, the spies would be working round the clock. He spoke, I discovered afterwards, for twice the customary length, but I didn't hear a chair creak or a glass clink – not even when they dragged him to the library and sat him in the throne of honour before the fire for more of the same, more heresy, more subversion. My children, hardened cases all of them, in love with George! I didn't hear a sound beyond the confident flow of Smiley's voice and the eager burst of laughter at some unexpected self-irony or confession of failure. You're only old once, I thought, as I listened with them, sharing their excitement.

He gave them case histories I had never heard, and which I was certain nobody in Head Office had cleared in advance – certainly not our Legal Adviser Palfrey, who in response to the openness of our former enemies had been battening down and double-locking every useless secret he could lay his obedient hands on.

He dwelt on their future role as agent-runners and, applying it to the altered world, vested in it the traditional Service image of mentor, shepherd, parent and befriender, as prop and marriage counsellor, as pardoner, entertainer and protector; as the man or woman who has the gift of treating the outrageous premise as an everyday affair, and so becomes his agent's partner in illusion. None of that had changed, he said. None of it ever would. He paraphrased Burns: 'A spy's a spy for all that.'

But no sooner had he lulled them with this sweet notion than he warned them of the death of their own natures that could result from the manipulation of their fellow men, and the truncation of their natural feeling.

'By being all things to all spies, one does rather run the risk of becoming nothing to oneself,' he confessed sadly. 'Please don't ever imagine you'll be unscathed by the methods you use. The end may justify the means – if it wasn't supposed to, I dare say you wouldn't be here. But there's a price to pay, and the price does tend to be oneself. Easy to sell one's soul at your age. Harder later.'

He mixed the deadly serious with the deadly frivolous and made the difference small. Between whiles he seemed to be asking the questions I had been asking of myself for most of my working life, but had never managed to express, such as: 'Did it do any good?' And 'What did it do to me?' And 'What will become of us now?' Sometimes his questions were answers: George, we used to say, never asked unless he knew.

He made us laugh, he made us feel and, by means of his inordinate deference, he shocked us with his contrasts. Better still, he put our prejudices at risk. He got rid of the acceptance in me and revived the slumbering rebel that my exile to Sarratt had silenced. George Smiley, out of a clear sky, had renewed my search and confused me wonderfully.

Frightened people never learn, I have read. If that is so, they certainly have no right to teach. I'm not a frightened man – or no more frightened than any other man who has looked at death and knows it is for him. All the same, experience and a little pain had made me a mite too wary of the truth, even towards myself. George Smiley put that right. George was more than a mentor to me, more than a friend. Though not always present, he presided over my life. There were times when I thought of him as some kind of father to replace the one I never knew. George's visit to Sarratt gave back the dangerous edge to my memory. And now that I have the leisure to remember, that's what I mean to do for you, so that you can share my voyage and ask yourself the same questions.

2

'There are some people,' Smiley declared comfortably, favouring with his merry smile the pretty girl from Trinity Oxford whom I had thoughtfully placed across the table from him, 'who, when their past is threatened, get frightened of losing everything they thought they had, and perhaps everything they thought they were as well. Now I don't feel that one bit. The purpose of *my* life was to end the time I lived in. So if my past were still around today, you could say I'd failed. But it's not around. We won. Not that the victory matters a damn. And perhaps we didn't win anyway. Perhaps they just lost. Or perhaps, without the bonds of ideological conflict to restrain us any more, our troubles are just beginning. Never mind. What matters is that a long war is over. What matters is the hope.'

Removing his spectacles from his ears, he fumbled distractedly with his shirt front, looking for I could not imagine what, until I realised that it was the fat end of the necktie on which he was accustomed to polish his lenses. But an awkwardly assembled black bow tie provides no such conveniences, so he used the silk handkerchief from his pocket instead.

'If I regret anything at all, it's the way we wasted our time and skills. All the false alleys, and bogus friends, the misapplication of our energies. All the delusions we had about who we were.' He replaced his spectacles and, as I fancied, turned his smile upon myself. And suddenly I felt like one of my own students. It was the sixties again. I was a fledgling spy, and George Smiley – tolerant, patient, clever George – was observing my first attempts at flight.

We were fine fellows in those days, and the days seemed longer. Probably no finer than my students today, but our patriotic vision was less clouded. By the end of my new-entry course I was ready to save the world if I had to spy on it from end to end. We were ten in my intake and after a couple of years of training – at the Sarratt Nursery, in the glens of Argyll and battle camps of Wiltshire – we waited for our first operational postings like thoroughbreds pining for the chase.

We too in our way had come to maturity at a great moment in history, even if it was the reverse of this one. Stagnation and hostility stared at us from every corner of the globe. The Red Peril was everywhere, not least on our own sacred hearth. The Berlin Wall had been up two years and by the looks of it would stay up for another two hundred. The Middle East was a volcano, just as it is now, except that in those days Nasser was our chosen British hate object, not least because he was giving Arabs back their dignity and playing hookey with the Russians into the bargain. In Cyprus, Africa and South East Asia the lesser breeds without the law were rising against their old colonial masters. And if we few brave British occasionally felt our power diminished by this – well, there was always Cousin America to cut us back into the world's game.

As secret heroes in the making, therefore, we had everything we needed: a righteous cause, an evil enemy, an indulgent ally, a seething world, women to cheer us, but only from the touchline, and best of all the Great Tradition to inherit, for the Circus in those days was still basking in its wartime glory. Almost all our leading men had earned their spurs by spying on the Germans. All of them, when questioned at our earnest, off-the-record seminars, agreed that when it came to protecting mankind against its own excesses, World Communism was an even darker menace than the Hun.

'You gentlemen have inherited a dangerous planet,' Jack Arthur Lumley, our fabled Head of Training, liked to tell us. 'And if you want my personal opinion, you're bloody lucky.'

Oh, we wanted his opinion all right! Jack Arthur was a derring-do man. He had spent three years dropping in and out of Nazi-occupied Europe as if he were a regular house-guest. He had blown up bridges single-handed. He had been caught and escaped and caught again, no one knew how many times. He had killed men with his bare fingers, losing a couple in the fray, and when the Cold War came along to replace the hot one, Jack hardly noticed the difference. At the age of fifty-five he could still shoot you a grin on a man-sized target with a 9-millimetre Browning at twenty paces, pick your door lock with a paper clip, booby-trap a lavatory chain in thirty seconds or pin you helpless to the gym-mat in one throw. Jack Arthur had despatched us by parachute from Stirling bombers and landed us in rubber boats on Cornish beaches and drunk us under the table on mess nights. If Jack Arthur said it was a dangerous planet, we believed him to the hilt!

But it made the waiting all the harder. If I hadn't had Ben Arno Cavendish to share it with, it would have been harder still. There are only so many attachments you can serve around Head Office before your enthusiasm turns to gall.

Ben and I had been born under the same star. We were the same age, the same schooling, the same build, and within an inch of the same height. Trust the Circus to throw us together – we told each other excitedly; they probably knew it all along! We both had foreign mothers, though his was dead – the Arno came from his German side – and were both, perhaps by way of compensation, determinedly of the English extrovert classes – athletic, hedonistic, public-school, male, born to administer if not to rule. Though, as I look at the group photographs of our year, I see that Ben made a rather better job of the part than I did, for he possessed an air of maturity that in those days eluded me – he had the widow's peak and the confirmed jaw, a man superior to his youthfulness.

Which, for all I knew, was why Ben got the coveted Berlin job instead of me, running flesh-and-blood agents inside East Germany, while I was once more put on standby.

'We're lending you to the watchers for a couple of weeks, young Ned,' said Personnel, with an avuncular complacency I was beginning to resent. 'Be good experience for you, and they can do with a spare pair of hands. Plenty of cloak-and-dagger stuff. You like that.'

Anything for a change, I thought, putting a brave face on it. For the past month I had bent my ingenuity to sabotaging the World Peace Conference in – let's say – Belgrade, from a dark desk on the Third Floor. Under the instruction of a slow-spoken superior who lunched for hours on end in the Senior Officers' Bar, I had enthusiastically re-routed delegates' trains, blocked their hotel plumbing and made anonymous bomb threats to their conference hall. For the month before that, I had crouched bravely in a stinking cellar next to the Egyptian Embassy at six every morning, waiting for a venal charlady to bring me, in exchange for a five-pound note, the contents of the Ambassadorial wastepaper basket from the previous day. By such modest standards, a couple of weeks riding around with the world's best watchers sounded like a free holiday.

'They're assigning you to Operation Fat Boy,' Personnel said, and gave me the address of a safe house off Green Street in the West End. I heard the sound of ping-pong as I walked in, and a cracked gramophone record playing Gracie Fields. My heart sank, and once again I sent a prayer of envy to Ben Cavendish and his heroic agents in Berlin, the spy's eternal city. Monty Arbuck, our section leader, briefed us the same evening.

Let me apologise for myself in advance. I knew very little of other ranks in those days. I was of the officer caste – literally, for I had served with the Royal Navy – and found it perfectly natural that I had been born into the upper end of the social system. The Circus is nothing if not a little mirror of the England it protects, so it seemed equally right to me that our watchers and allied trades, such as burglars and eavesdroppers, should be drawn from the artisan community. You cannot follow a man for long in a bowler hat. A honed BBC voice is no passport to unobtrusiveness once you are outside London's golden mile, least of all if you are posing as a street hawker or a window cleaner or a post-office engineer. So you should see me, at best, as a callow young midshipman seated among his more experienced and less privileged shipmates. And you should see Monty not as he was, but as I saw him that evening, as a taut-minded gamekeeper with a chip on his shoulder. We were ten, including Monty: three teams of three, therefore, with a woman to each so that we could cover ladies' lavatories. That was the principle. And Monty our controller.

'Good evening, College,' he said, placing himself before a blackboard and talking straight at me. 'Always nice to have a touch of quality to raise the tone, I say.'

Laughter all round, loudest from myself, a good sport to his men.

'Target for tomorrow, College, is His Right Royal Sovereign Highness Fat Boy, otherwise known as – '

Turning to the blackboard, Monty helped himself to a piece of chalk and laboriously scratched up a long Arab name.

'And the nature of our mission, College, is PR,' he resumed. 'I trust you know what PR is, do you? I have no doubt they teach you that at the spies' Eton?'

'Public Relations,' I said, surprised to occasion so much merriment. For alas it turned out that in the watchers' vernacular the initials stood for Protect and Report, and that our task for tomorrow, and for as long as our royal visitor chose to remain our charge, was to ensure that no harm came to him, and to report to Head Office on his activities, whether social or commercial.

'College, you're with Paul and Nancy,' Monty told me, when he had provided us with the rest of our operational intelligence. 'You'll be number three in the section, College, and you'll kindly do *exactly* as you are told, irregardless.'

But here I prefer to give you the background to Fat Boy's case not in Monty's words but in my own, and with the benefit of twenty-five years of hindsight. Even today, I can blush to think who I thought I was, and how I must have appeared to the likes of Monty, Paul and Nancy.

Understand first that licensed arms dealers in Britain regard themselves as some kind of rough-edged élite – did then, do now – and that they enjoy quite disproportionate privileges at the hands of the police, the bureaucracy and the intelligence services. For reasons I have never understood, their grisly trade puts them in a relationship of confidence with these bodies. Perhaps it's the illusion of reality they impart, of guns as the earthy truth of life and death. Perhaps, in the tethered minds of our officials, their wares suggest the same authority that is exerted by those

who use them. I don't know. But I've seen enough of the street side of life
in the years between to know that more men are in love with war than
ever get a chance to fight one, and that more guns are bought to satisfy
this love than for a pardonable purpose.

Understand also that Fat Boy was a most valued customer of this
industry. And that our task of Protecting and Reporting was only one
small part of a far larger undertaking; namely, the care and cultivation of
a so-called friendly Arab state. By which was meant, and is meant to this
day, currying favour, suborning and flattering its princelings with our
English ways, wheedling favourable concessions in order to satisfy our oil
addiction – and, along the way, selling enough British weaponry to keep
the Satanic mills of Birmingham turning day and night. Which may have
accounted for Monty's rooted distaste for our task. I like to think so
anyway. Old watchers are famous for their moralising – and with reason.
First they watch, later they think. Monty had reached the thinking stage.

As to Fat Boy, his credentials for this treatment were impeccable. He
was the wastrel brother of the ruler of an oil-rich sheikdom. He was
capricious, and prone to forget what he had bought before. And he arrived
as billed, in the ruler's Boeing jet, at a military airport near London
specially cleared for him, to have himself a little fun and do a little
shopping – which we understood would include such fripperies as a couple
of armoured Rolls-Royces for himself, half the trinkets at Cartier's for his
women friends around the globe, a hundred or so of our not quite latest
ground-to-air missile launchers, and a squadron or two of our not quite
latest combat fighters for his royal brother. Not forgetting a succulent
British government contract for spares, services and training which would
keep the Royal Air Force and the arms manufacturers in clover for years
to come. – Oh, and oil. We would have oil to burn. Naturally.

His retinue, apart from private secretaries, astrologers, flatterers, nann-
ies, children and two tutors, comprised a personal doctor and three
bodyguards.

Lastly there was Fat Boy's wife, and her codename is irrelevant because
from Day One Monty's watchers dubbed her 'the Panda' on account of
the dark circles round her eyes when she was unveiled, and her wistful and
solitary deportment, which gave the air of an endangered species. Fat Boy
had a string of wives, but the Panda, though the oldest, was the most
favoured, and perhaps the most tolerant of her husband's pleasures around
town, for he liked nightclubs and he liked to gamble – tastes for which my
fellow watchers cordially loathed him before he arrived, since it was
known of him that he seldom went to bed before six in the morning, and
never without losing about twenty times their combined annual salaries.

The party had rooms at a grand West End hotel, on two floors linked by
a specially installed lift. Fat Boy, like many forty-year-old voluptuaries,
was worried about his heart. He was also worried about microphones,
and liked to use the lift as his safe room. So the Circus listeners had

thoughtfully provided a microphone in the lift for him as well, which was
where they reckoned to pick up their tidbits about the latest palace
intrigues, or any unforeseen threat to Fat Boy's military shopping list.

And everything was running smoothly until Day Three, when one small
unknown Arab man in a black overcoat with velvet collars appeared
silently on our horizon. Or more accurately, in the ladies' lingerie department of a great Knightsbridge department store, where the Panda and
her attendants were picking their way through a stack of frilly white
undergarments spread over the glass counter. For the Panda also had her
spies. And word had reached her that, on the day before, the Fat Boy
himself had brooded fondly over the same articles, and even ordered a few
dozen to be sent to an address in Paris where a favoured lady friend
constantly awaited him in subsidised luxury.

Day Three, I repeat, and the morale of our three-strong unit under strain.
Paul was Paul Skordeno, an inward man with a pocked complexion and a
talent for ferocious invective. Nancy told me he was under a cloud, but
wouldn't say what for.

'He *bit* a girl, Ned,' she said, but I think now that she meant more than
merely hit.

Nancy herself was all of five feet tall and in appearance a kind of
licensed bag-lady. For her standard, as she called it, she wore lisle stockings
and sensible rubber-soled walking shoes, which she seldom changed. What
more she needed – scarves, raincoats, woollen hats of different colours –
she took in a plastic carrier.

On surveillance duty our section worked eight-hour shifts always in the
same formation, Nancy and Paul playing forward, young Ned trailing
along behind as sweep. When I asked Skordeno whether we could vary
the formation, he told me to get used to what I'd got. On our first day we
had followed Fat Boy to Sandhurst, where a lunch had been organised in
his honour. The three of us ate egg-and-chips in a café close to the main
gates while Skordeno railed first against the Arabs, then against the
Western exploitation of them, then to my distress against the Fifth Floor,
whom he described as Fascist golfers.

'You a Freemason, College?'

I assured him I was not.

'Well, you'd best hurry up and join then, hadn't you? Haven't you
noticed the saucy way Personnel shakes your hand? You'll never get to
Berlin if you're not a Mason, College.'

Day Two had been spent hanging around Mount Street while Fat Boy
had himself measured for a pair of Purdy shotguns, first precariously
brandishing a try-gun round the premises, then throwing a tantrum when
he discovered he would have to wait two years before they were ready.
Paul ordered me twice into the shop while this scene was unfolding, and

seemed pleased when I told him the staff were becoming suspicious of my frivolous enquiries.

'I'd have thought it was your kind of place,' he said, with his skull-like grin. 'Huntin', shootin' and fishin' – they like that on the Fifth Floor, College.'

The same night had found us sitting three up in a van outside a shuttered whorehouse in South Audley Street, and Head Office in a state of near panic. Fat Boy had only been holed up there two hours when he had telephoned the hotel and ordered his personal doctor to attend immediately. His heart! we thought in alarm. Should we go in? While Head Office dithered, we entertained visions of our quarry dead of a heart attack in the arms of some over-conscientious whore before he had signed the cheque for his obsolete fighter planes. It was not till four o'clock that the listeners laid our fears to rest. Fat Boy had been afflicted by a spell of impotence, they explained, and his doctor had been summoned to inject an aphrodisiac into the royal rump. We returned home at five, Skordeno drunk with anger, but all of us consoled by the knowledge that Fat Boy was due in Luton at midday to attend a grand demonstration of the nearly latest British tank, and we could count on a day's rest. But our relief was premature.

'The Panda wants to buy herself some pretties,' Monty announced to us benignly on our arrival in Green Street. 'Your lot's on. Sorry about that, College.'

Which brings us to the lingerie department of the great Knightsbridge store, and to my moment of glory. Ben, I was thinking; Ben, I would trade one day of yours for five of mine. Then suddenly I wasn't thinking of Ben any more and I had ceased to envy him. I had drawn back into the privacy of a doorway and was speaking into the mouthpiece of the cumbersome radio set, which in those days was the best there was. I had selected the channel which gave me a direct line to base. It was the one Skordeno had told me not to use.

'The Panda's got a monkey on her back,' I informed Monty in my calmest voice, using the approved watchers' jargon to describe a mysterious follower. 'Five five, black curly hair, heavy moustache, aged forty, black overcoat, rubber-soled black shoes, Arab appearance. He was at the airport when Fat Boy's plane came in. I remember him. It's the same man.'

'Stay on him' came Monty's laconic reply. 'Paul and Nancy stick with the Panda, you stick with the monkey. Which floor?'

'One.'

'Stay on him wherever he goes, keep talking to me.'

'He could be carrying,' I said as my eyes again fixed surreptitiously on the subject of my call.

'You mean he's pregnant?'

I didn't think that very funny.

Let me set the scene precisely, for it was more complicated than you may suppose. Our trio was not alone in following the Panda's retinue on its snail-paced shopping expedition. Wealthy Arab princesses do not arrive unannounced at great Knightsbridge stores. In addition to a pair of floor-walkers in black jackets and striped trousers, two very obvious house detectives had placed themselves at either archway with their feet apart and their hands curled at their sides, ready at any moment to grapple with whirling dervishes. As if that were not enough, Scotland Yard had that morning taken upon itself to provide its own brand of protection in the form of an iron-faced man in a belted raincoat who insisted on placing himself beside the Panda and glowering at anyone who came near. And finally, you must see Paul and Nancy in their Sunday best, their backs turned to everyone while they affected to study trays of negligés, and watched our quarry in the mirrors.

And all of this again, you understand, set in the hushed and scented privacy of the harem; in a world of flimsy undergarments, deep-pile carpets and languorous half-naked dummies – not to mention those kindly grey-haired lady attendants in black crêpe who, at a certain age, are deemed to have achieved a sufficiently unthreatening demeanour to pre-side over shrines of female intimacy.

Other men, I noticed, preferred not to enter the lingerie department at all, or hurried through it with averted gaze. My instinct would have been the same, had it not been for my recognition of this melancholy little man with his black moustache and passionate brown eyes, who unswervingly trailed the Panda's retinue at fifteen paces. If Monty had not appointed me sweep, I might not have seen him at all – or not then. But it was quickly clear that both he and I, by virtue of our different trades, were obliged to keep the same distance from our target – I with nonchalance, he with a kind of intense and mystical dependence. For his gaze never wavered from her. Even when he was unsighted by a pillar or a customer, he still contrived to crane his dark head this way or that until he had locked her once more in his zealous and – I was now convinced – fanatical gaze.

I had first sensed this fervour in him when I had spotted him in the arrivals hall at the airport, pressing himself on tiptoe against the long window as he wriggled to get a better view of the royal couple's approach. I had made nothing so special of him then. I was subjecting everyone to the same critical examination. He had seemed to be just another of the gaggle of diplomats, retainers and hangers-on who formed the royal welcome party. Nevertheless his intensity had struck a chord in me: So this is the Middle East, I had mused as I watched him squeeze his hollowed face against the glass. These are the heathen passions my Service must contain if we are to drive our cars and heat our houses and sell our weaponry in peace.

The monkey had taken a couple of steps forward and was peering at a cabinet of ribbons. His gait – exactly like that of his namesake – was wide but stealthy; he seemed to move entirely from the knees, in conspiratorial strides. I selected a display of garters next to him and peered into it while I again furtively examined him for tell-tale bulges round the waist and armpits. His black overcoat was of the classic gunman's shape: voluminous and without a belt, the kind of coat that covers effortlessly a long-barrelled pistol fitted with a suppressor, or a semi-automatic slung beneath the arm.

I studied his hands, my own nervously prickling. His left hung loosely at his side, but his right, which looked the stronger, kept travelling towards his chest and withholding, as if he were preparing himself to pluck up courage for the final act.

A right-handed cross draw, I thought; most likely to the armpit. Our weapons trainers had taught us all the combinations.

And his eyes those dark, slow-burning, soulful zealot's eyes – even in profile they seemed fixed upon the afterlife. Had he sworn vengeance on her? On her household? Had fanatical mullahs promised him a place in Heaven if he did the deed? My knowledge of Islam was scant, and what there was of it was drawn from a couple of background lectures and the novels of P. C. Wren. Yet it was enough to warn me that I was in the presence of a desperate fanatic who counted his own life cheap.

As to myself, alas, I was unarmed. It was a sore point with me. Watchers would never dream of carrying weapons on normal duty, but covert protection work is a different type of watching, and Paul Skordeno had been allocated a sidearm from Monty's safe.

'One's enough, College,' Monty had told me, with his old man's smile. 'We don't want you starting World War Three, now do we?'

All that was left to me, therefore, as I rose and softly followed him again, was to select in advance one of the blows we had been taught to master in our silent-killing classes. Should I count on attacking him from behind – with a rabbit punch? – with a double simultaneous blow over the ears? Either method could kill him instantly, whereas a live man can still be questioned. Then would I do better breaking his right arm first, hoping to take him with his own weapon? Yet if I let him draw, might I myself not go down in a hail of bullets from the several bodyguards around the room?

She had seen him!

The Panda had looked straight into the eyes of the monkey, and the monkey had returned her stare!

Had she recognised him? I was certain she had. But had she recognised his purpose? And was she, perhaps, in some strange turn of Oriental fatalism, preparing herself for death? The lurid possibilities went racing through my mind as I continued to observe their mysterious exchange. Their eyes met, the Panda froze in mid-gesture. Her jewelled, crabby little hands, plundering the clothing on the counter, kept still – and then, as if to his command, slipped passively to her sides. After which she stood motionless, without will, without even the strength to detach herself from his penetrating stare.

At last, with a forlorn and strangely humble air, she turned away from him, murmured something to her lady companions and, holding out her hand to the counter, released whatever frilly thing she was still clutching in it. She was wearing brown that day – if she had been a man, I would be tempted to say a Franciscan habit – with wide sleeves longer than her arms, and a brown headband bound tightly across her brow.

I saw her sigh, then slowly and, I was sure, resignedly, she led her entourage towards the archway. After her went her personal bodyguard; after him the Scotland Yard policeman. Then came the ladies of her train, followed by the floorwalkers. And finally came Paul and Nancy, who, with a show of indecision, had torn themselves away from their study of the negligés and were sauntering like any shoppers in the party's wake. Paul, who had surely overheard my conversations with Monty, vouchsafed me not the smallest glance. Nancy, who prided herself on her amateur dramatics, was pretending to pick a marital dispute with him. I tried to see whether Paul had unbuttoned his jacket, for he too favoured the cross draw. But his broad back was turned away from me.

'All right, College, show me,' said Monty brightly into my left ear, appearing beside me as if by magic. How long had he been there? I had no idea. It was past midday and our time for standing down, but this was no moment to change the guard. The monkey was not five yards from us, stepping lightly but determinedly after the Panda.

'We can take him at the stairs,' I murmured.

'Speak louder,' Monty advised me, in the same unabashed voice. 'Speak normally, no one listens to you. Mutter, mutter out of the corner of your mouth, they think you've come to rob the till.'

Since we were on the first floor, the Panda's party was sure to take the lift, whether they went up or down. Beside the lift stood a pair of swing doors opening on to what in those days was a stone emergency staircase, rather dank and insanitary, with linoleum treads. My plan, which I out-lined to Monty in staccato sentences as we followed the monkey towards the archway, was simplicity itself. As the party approached the lift, Monty and I would close on him from either side, grab an arm each and sweep him into the staircase. We would subdue him with a blow to the groin, remove his weapon, then spirit him to Green Street where we would invite him to make a voluntary statement. In training exercises we had done such things a dozen times – once, to our embarrassment, to an innocent bank clerk who was hurrying home to his wife and family, and whom we had mistaken for a member of the training staff.

But if Monty heard me, to my frustration he gave no sign of having done so. He was watching the floorwalkers clear a path through the crowd to the lift so that the Panda's party could ride in privacy. And he was smiling like any casual commoner who stumbles on a glimpse of royalty.

'She's going down,' he declared with satisfaction. 'Pound to a penny it's the costume jewellery she's after. You'd think the Gulfies wouldn't bother with the artificial stuff, but they can't get enough of it; they think it's got to be a bargain. Come on, son. This is fun. Let's go and take a look.'

I like to think that even in my perplexity I recognised the excellence of Monty's tradecraft. The Panda's exotic entourage, mostly in Arab dress, was arousing lively curiosity among the shoppers. Monty was just another punter, enjoying the spectacle. And yes, he was right again, their destination was the costume jewellery department, as the monkey also had divined, for as we emerged from our lift the monkey scampered ahead of the party to take up a favoured place alongside the glittering displays, his left shoulder nearest to the wall, exactly as required of a right-handed gunman who draws across his chest.

Yet, far from choosing a strategic position from which to return fire, Monty merely wandered after him, and, having placed himself next to him, beckoned me to join them, and in such a way that I had no alternative but to leave Monty, not the monkey, at the centre of our trio.

'This is why I always come to Knightsbridge, son,' Monty was explaining, loudly enough for half the floor to hear. 'You never know who you're going to meet. I brought your mother last time – *you* remember – we'd gone to the Harrods Food Hall. I thought: "*Hullo*, I know you, you're Rex Harrison." I could have held out my hand and touched him but I didn't. It's the crossroads of the world, Knightsbridge is, don't you agree, sir?' – lifting his hat to the monkey, who smiled wanly in return. 'Now I wonder where this lot would be from. Arabs, by the look of them, with the wealth of Solomon at their fingertips. And they don't even pay taxes, I dare say. Not royalty, well they wouldn't have to. There isn't a royal household in the world pays taxes to itself, it wouldn't be logical. See the big policeman there, son? He'll be Special Branch, you can tell by his stupid scowl.'

The Panda's party meanwhile was distributing itself among the illuminated glass counters while the Panda, in barely concealed agitation, was requiring that the trays be taken out for her inspection. And soon, as in the lingerie department, she was picking out one object after another, turning it critically under the inspection light, then setting it down and taking up another. And yet again, as she continued to appraise and relinquish each piece in turn, I saw her worried gaze slip towards us, first to the monkey, then to myself, as if she had seen in me her one hope of protection.

Yet Monty, when I glanced at him for confirmation, was still smiling.

'That's exactly what happened in the lingerie department,' I whispered, forgetting his instruction to speak normally.

But Monty continued his noisy monologue. 'But underneath, son – I always say this – underneath, royals or not, they're the same as what we are, through and through. We're all born naked, we're all on our way to the grave. Your wealth is your health, better to be rich in friends than money, I say. We've all got the same appetites, the same little weaknesses and naughty ways.' And on he ran, as if in deliberate contrast to my extreme alertness.

She had ordered up more trays. The counter was covered with sumptuous paste tiaras, bracelets and rings. Selecting a three-string necklace of imitation rubies, she held it to her throat, then took up a hand mirror to admire herself.

And was it my imagination? It was not! She was using the mirror to observe the monkey and ourselves! First one dark eye, then the other fixed upon us; then the two of them together, warning us, imploring us, before she set the mirror down again and turned her back to us, and swept as if in anger along the edge of the glass counter, where a fresh display awaited her.

At the same moment, the monkey took a step forward and I saw his hand rise to the opening of his overcoat. Throwing caution aside, I too stepped forward, my right arm drawn back, the fingers of my right hand flexed, palm parallel to the ground in the approved Sarratt manner. I had decided on an elbow to the heart, followed by a side-of-hand to the upper lip, to the point where the nose cartilage joins the top half of the jaw. A complicated network of nerves has its meeting point here, and a well-aimed blow can immobilise the victim for some while. The monkey was opening his mouth and breathing in. I anticipated a cry to Allah, or perhaps the screamed slogan of some fundamentalist sect – though I am no longer sure how much we knew or cared in those days about fundamentalist Arabs. I at once determined to scream myself, not only in order to confuse him, but because a deep breath would put more oxygen into my bloodstream and so increase my striking power. I was actually drawing this breath when I felt Monty's hand lock like an iron ring round my wrist and, with unpredicted power, immobilise me as he drew me back to him.

'Now don't do that, son, this gentleman was before you,' he said in a matter-of-fact voice. 'He's got a little confidential business to transact, haven't you, sir?'

He had indeed. And Monty's grasp did not release me until I had observed the nature of it. The monkey was speaking. Not to the Panda, not to her retinue, but to the two floorwalkers in striped trousers who were inclining their heads to listen to him, at first condescendingly, then with startled interest as their gaze switched to the Panda.

'Alas, gentlemen, Her Royal Highness prefers to make her purchases informally, you see,' he was saying. 'Without the inconvenience of a wrapping or an invoice, let us put it that way. It is her time of life. Three and four years ago, she was a most expert bargainer, you know. Oh yes. She would negotiate a most competitive discount for everything she wished to buy. But today, at her time of life, she is taking matters most literally into her own hands, you see. Or should I say into her sleeve, oh dear? I am therefore charged by His Royal Highness to make a most bountiful settlement for all such informal purchases, on the very clear understanding that no breath of publicity reaches the public ear, gentlemen, whether in the written or the spoken word, if you understand me.'

Then from his pocket he drew not, alas, a deadly Walther automatic, not a Heckler & Koch submachine gun, not even one of our beloved standard Browning 9-millimetres, but a tooled Moroccan leather wallet stuffed with his master's banknotes in a variety of denominations.

'I counted, I believe, three fine rings, sir, one in artificial emerald, two in paste diamond, also a fine artificial ruby necklace, gentlemen, three strings. It is the wish of His Royal Highness that our settlement should take generous account of any inconvenience suffered by your most excellent staff, you see. Also commission to your good selves, on the understanding already stated regarding publicity.'

Monty's grip on me had at last relaxed, and as we walked towards the hall I dared to glance at him, and saw to my relief that his expression, though thoughtful, was surprisingly gentle.

'That's the trouble in our job, Ned,' he explained contentedly, using my Christian name for the first time. 'Life's looking one way, we're looking the other. I like an honest-to-God enemy myself sometimes, I don't mind admitting. Take a lot of finding, though, don't they? Too many nice blokes about.'

3

'**N**ow do please remember,' Smiley piously exhorted his young audience, in much the tone he might have selected if he had been asking them to put their offerings in the collection box as they were leaving, 'that the privately educated Englishman – and Englishwoman, if you will allow me – is the greatest dissembler on earth.' He waited for the laughter to subside. 'Was, is now and ever shall be for as long as our disgraceful school system remains intact. Nobody will charm you so glibly, disguise his feelings from you better, cover his tracks more skilfully or find it harder to confess to you that he's been a damned fool. Nobody acts braver when he's frightened stiff, or happier when he's miserable; nobody can flatter you better when he hates you than your extrovert Englishman or woman of the supposedly privileged classes. He can have a Force Twelve nervous breakdown while he stands next to you in the bus queue, and you may be his best friend, but you'll never be the wiser. Which is why some of our best officers turn out to be our worst. And our worst, our best. And why the most difficult agent you will ever have to run is yourself.'

In his own mind, I had no doubt, Smiley was talking about the greatest deceiver of us all, Bill Haydon. But for me, he was talking about Ben – and yes, though it's harder to admit, about the young Ned, and perhaps the old one too.

It was the afternoon of the day I had failed to immolate the Panda's bodyguard. Tired and dispirited, I arrived at my flat in Battersea to find the door on the latch and two men in grey suits sifting through the papers in my desk.

They barely looked at me as I burst in. The nearer of them was Personnel and the second an owlish, ageless, tubby man in circular spectacles who eyed me with a sort of baleful commiseration.

'When did you last hear from your friend Cavendish?' said Personnel, scarcely glancing at me before returning to my papers.

'He *is* your friend, isn't he?' said the owlish man unhappily while I struggled to collect myself. 'Ben? Arno? Which do you call him?'

'Yes. He is. Ben is. What is this?'

'So when did you last hear from him?' Personnel repeated, shoving aside a pile of letters from my girlfriend of the time. 'Does he ring you? How do you keep in touch?'

'I had a postcard from him a week ago. Why?'

'Where is it?'

'I don't know. I destroyed it. If it isn't in the desk. Will you kindly tell me what's going on?'

'Destroyed it?'

'Threw it away.'

'*Destroy* sounds deliberate, doesn't it? What did it look like?' Personnel said, pulling out another drawer. 'Stay where you are.'

'It had a picture of a girl on one side and a couple of lines from Ben on the other. What does it matter what it had on it? Please get out of here.'

'Saying?'

'Nothing. It said, this is my latest acquisition. "Dear Ned, this is my new catch, so glad you're not here. Love, Ben." Now get out!'

'What did he mean by that?' – pulling out another drawer.

'Glad I wouldn't cut him out with the girl; I suppose. It was a joke.'

'Do you usually cut him out with his women?'

'We've no women in common. We never have had.'

'What *do* you have in common?'

'Friendship,' I said angrily. 'What the hell are you looking for actually? I think you'd better leave at once. Both of you.'

'I can't find it,' Personnel complained to his fat companion as he tossed aside another wad of my private letters. 'No postcard of any kind. You're not lying, are you, Ned?'

The owlish man had not taken his eyes off me. He continued to regard me with a wretched empathy, as if to say it comes to all of us and there's nothing we can do. 'How was the postcard *delivered*, Ned?' he asked. His voice, like his demeanour, was tentative and regretful.

'By post, how else?' I replied rudely.

'The open mail, you mean?' the owlish man suggested sadly. 'Not by Service bag, for instance?'

'By Forces mail,' I replied. 'Field Post Office. Posted Berlin with a British stamp on it. Delivered by the local postman.'

'Do you remember the Field Post Office *number*, by any chance, Ned?' the owlish man enquired with enormous diffidence. 'On the postmark, I mean?'

'It was the ordinary Berlin number, I imagine,' I retorted, struggling to keep up my indignation in the face of someone so exquisitely deferential. 'Forty, I think. Why's it so important? I've had enough of this.'

'But you'd say it was definitely posted in Berlin anyway? I mean, that was your impression at the time? So far as you recall it now? The Berlin number – you're sure?'

'It looked exactly like the others he'd sent me. I didn't submit it to a minute examination,' I said, my anger rising again as I saw Personnel yank yet another drawer from my desk and tip out its contents.

'A pin-up sort of girl, Ned?' the owlish man enquired, with a hangdog smile, which was evidently intended to apologise for Personnel as well as for himself.

'A nude, yes. A tart, I assume, looking over her bare backside. That's why I threw it away. Because of my cleaning lady.'

'Oh, so you remember now!' Personnel cried, swinging round to face me. ' "I threw it away." Pity you didn't bloody say so at once!'

'Oh, I don't know, Rex,' said the owlish man placatingly. 'Ned was very confused when he came in. Who wouldn't be?' His worried gaze settled once more upon myself. 'You're doing a stint with the watchers, isn't that right? Monty says you're rather good. Was she in colour, by the way? Your nude?'

'Yes.'

'Did he always send postcards, or sometimes letters?'

'Only postcards.'

'How many?'

'Three or four since he's been there.'

'Always in colour?'

'I don't remember. Probably. Yes.'

'And always of girls?'

'I think so.'

'Oh, but you remember, really. Of course you do. And always naked too, I expect?'

'Yes.'

'Where are the others?'

'I must have thrown them away too.'

'Because of your cleaning lady?'

'Yes.'

'To protect her sensitivities?'

'Yes!'

The owlish man took his time to consider this. 'So the dirty postcards – forgive me, I don't mean that offensively, really not – they were a sort of running joke between you?'

'On his side, yes.'

'But you didn't send him any in return? Please say if you did. Don't be embarrassed. There isn't time.'

'I'm not embarrassed! I didn't send him any. Yes, they were a running joke. And they were getting increasingly *risqué*. If you want to know, I was becoming slightly bored with seeing them laid out on the hall table for my collection. So was Mr. Simpson. He's the landlord. He suggested I write to Ben and tell him to stop sending them. He said it was getting the house a bad name. Now will you please, one of you, tell me what the hell's going on?'

This time Personnel replied. 'Well, that's what we thought you might be able to tell *us*,' he said in a mournful voice. 'Ben Cavendish has disappeared. So have his agents, in a manner of speaking. A couple of them are featured in this morning's *Neues Deutschland*. British spy ring caught red-handed. The London evening papers are running the story in their late editions. He hasn't been seen for three days. This is Mr. Smiley. He wants to talk to you. You're to tell him whatever you know. And that means anything. I'll see you later.'

I must have lost my bearings for a moment, because when I saw Smiley again he was standing at the centre of my carpet, gloomily peering round him at the havoc he and Personnel had wreaked.

'I've a house across the river in Bywater Street,' he confessed, as if it were a great burden to him. 'Perhaps we ought to pop round there, if it's all the same to you. It's not *terribly* tidy, but it is better than this.'

We drove there in Smiley's humble little Austin, so slowly you would have supposed he was conveying an invalid, which was perhaps how he regarded me. It was dusk. The white lanterns of Albert Bridge floated at us like waterborne coachlights. Ben, I thought desperately, what have we done? Ben, what have they done to you?

Bywater Street was jammed, so we parked in a mews. Parking for Smiley was as complicated as docking a liner, but he managed it and we walked back. I remember how impossible it was to keep alongside him, how his thrusting round-arm waddle somehow ignored my existence. I remember how he steeled himself to turn the key of his own front door, and his alertness as he stepped into the hall. As if home were a dangerous place for him, as I know now that it was. There was a couple of days' milk in the hall and a half-eaten plate of chop and peas in the drawing room. The turntable of a gramophone was silently revolving. It didn't take a genius to surmise that he had been called out in a hurry – presumably by Personnel yesterday evening – while he was tucking into his chop and listening to a spot of music.

He wandered off to the kitchen in search of soda for our whiskies. I followed him. There was something about Smiley that made you responsible for his solitude. Open tins of food lay about and the sink was crammed with dirty plates. While he mixed our whiskies, I started clearing up, so he fished a teacloth from the back of the door and set to work drying and putting away.

'You and Ben were considerable partners, weren't you?' he asked.

'We shared a cabin at Sarratt, yes.'

'So that's what – kitchen, couple of bedrooms, bathroom?'

'No kitchen.'

'But you were twinned for your training course as well?'

'For the last year of it. You choose an oppo and learn to work to each other.'

'Choose? Or have chosen for you?'

'Choose first, then they approve or break you up.'

'And after that, you're landed with each other for better for worse?'

'Pretty much, yes.'

'For the whole of the last year? For half the course, in fact? Day and night, as it were? A total marriage?'

I could not understand why he was pressing me about things he must have known.

'And you do everything together?' he continued. 'Forgive me but it's some time since I was trained. Written, practical, physical, you mess together, share a cabin – a whole life, in fact.'

'We do the syndicate work together, and the strongarm stuff. That's automatic. It begins with being roughly the same weight and physical aptitude.' Despite the disturbing tendency of his questions, I was beginning to feel a great need to talk to him. 'Then the rest sort of follows naturally.'

'Ah.'

'Sometimes they split us up – say, for a special exercise or if they think one person is relying too much on his oppo. But as long as it's fifty-fifty they're happy for you to keep together.'

'And you won everything,' Smiley suggested approvingly, helping himself to another wet plate. 'You were the best pair. You and Ben.'

'It was just that Ben was the best student,' I said. 'Whoever had him would have won.'

'Yes, of course. Well, we all know people like that. Did you know each other before you joined the Service?'

'No. But we'd run parallel. We were at the same school, different houses. We were at Oxford, different colleges. We both read languages but we still never met. He did a short service commission in the army, I did the same in the navy. It took the Circus to bring us together.'

Taking up a delicate bone-china cup, he peered doubtfully into it, as if searching for something I had missed. 'Would *you* have sent Ben to Berlin?'

'Yes, of course I would. Why not?'

'Well, why?'

'He's got perfect German from his mother. He's bright. Resourceful. People do what he wants them to do. His father had this terrific war.'

'So did your mother, as I remember.' He was referring to my mother's work with the Dutch Resistance. 'What did *he* do – Ben's father, I mean?' he continued, as if he really didn't know.

'He broke codes,' I said, with Ben's pride. 'He was a wrangler. A mathematician. A genius, apparently. He helped organise the double-cross system against the Germans – recruit their agents and play them back. My mother was very small beer by comparison.'

'And Ben was impressed by that?'

'Who wouldn't be?'

'He talked of it, I mean,' Smiley insisted. 'Often? It was a big matter for him. You had that impression?'

'He just said it was something he had to live up to. He said it was the up-side of having a German mother.'

'Oh dear,' said Smiley unhappily. 'Poor man. And those were his words? You're not embellishing?'

'Of course I'm not! He said that with a background like his, in England you had to run twice as fast as everyone else, just to keep up.'

Smiley seemed genuinely upset. 'Oh dear,' he said again. 'How unkind. And do you think he has the stamina, would you say?'

He had once more stopped me short. At our age, we really didn't think of stamina as being limited.

'What for?' I asked.

'Oh, I don't know. What kind of stamina would one need for running twice as fast as everyone else in Berlin? A double ration of nerves, I suppose – always a strain. A doubly good head for alcohol – *and* where women are concerned – never easy.'

'I'm sure he's got whatever it takes,' I said loyally.

Smiley hung his teacloth on a bent nail which looked like his own addition to the kitchen. 'Did you ever talk politics, the two of you?' he asked as we took our whiskies to the drawing room.

'Never.'

'Then I'm sure he's sound,' he said, with a sad little laugh, and I laughed too.

Houses always seem to me, at first acquaintance, to be either masculine or feminine, and Smiley's was undoubtedly feminine, with pretty curtains and carved mirrors and clever woman's touches. I wondered who he was living with, or wasn't. We sat down.

'And is there any reason why you *mightn't* have sent Ben to Berlin?' he resumed, smiling kindly over the top of his glass.

'Well, only that I wanted to go myself. Everybody wants a Berlin break. It's the front line.'

'He simply disappeared,' Smiley explained, settling back and appearing to close his eyes. 'We're not keeping anything from you. I'll tell you what we know. Last Thursday he crossed into East Berlin to meet his head agent, a gentleman named Hans Seidl – you can see his photograph in *Neues Deutschland*. It was Ben's first solo meeting with him. A big event. Ben's superior in the Berlin Station is Haggarty. Do you know Haggarty?'

'No.'

'Have you heard of him?'

'No.'

'Ben never mentioned him to you?'

'No. I told you. I've never heard his name.'

'Forgive me. Sometimes an answer can vary with a context, if you follow me.'

I didn't.

'Haggarty is second man in the Station under the Station Commander. Did you not know that either?'

'No.'

'Has Ben a regular girlfriend?'

'Not that I know of.'

'Irregular?'

'You only had to go to a dance with him, they were all over him.'

'And after the dance?'

'He didn't brag. He doesn't. If he slept with them, he wouldn't say. He's not that kind of man.'

'They tell me you and Ben took your bits of leave together. Where did you go?'

'Twickenham. Lord's. Bit of fishing. Mainly we stayed with one another's people.'

'Ah.'

I couldn't understand why Smiley's words were scaring me. Perhaps I was so scared for Ben that I was scared by everything. Increasingly I had the feeling Smiley assumed I was guilty of something, even if we had still to find out what. His recitation of events was like a summary of the evidence.

'First comes *Willis*,' he said, as if we were following a difficult trail. 'Willis is the Berlin Head of Station, Willis has overall command. Then comes *Haggarty*, and Haggarty is the senior field officer under Willis and Ben's direct boss. Haggarty is responsible for the day-to-day servicing of the Seidl network. The network is twelve agents strong, or was – that is to say, nine men and three women, now all under arrest. An illegal network of that size, communicating partly by radio and partly by secret writing, requires a base team of at least the same number to maintain it, and I'm not talking about evaluating or distributing the product.'

'I know.'

'I'm sure you do, but let me tell you all the same,' he continued at the same ponderous pace. 'Then you can help me fill in the gaps. Haggarty is a powerful personality. An Ulsterman. Off duty, he drinks, he's noisy and unpleasant. But when he's working he's none of those things. He's a conscientious officer with a prodigious memory. You're sure Ben never mentioned him to you?'

'I told you. No.'

I had not intended this to sound so adamant. There's always a mystery about how often you can deny a thing without beginning to sound like a liar, even to yourself; and of course this was the very mystery Smiley was playing upon in order to bring hidden things to the surface in me.

'Yes, well you *did* tell me no,' he agreed with his habitual courtesy. 'And I did *hear* you say no. I merely wondered whether I had jogged your memory.'

'No.'

'Haggarty and Seidl were *friends*,' he continued, speaking, if it were possible, even more slowly. 'So far as their business allowed, they were *close* friends. Seidl had been a prisoner of war in England, Haggarty in Germany. While Seidl was working as a farm labourer near Cirencester in 1944, under the relaxed conditions for German prisoners of war that prevailed by then, he succeeded in courting an English landgirl. His guards at the camp took to leaving a bicycle for him outside the main gates with an army greatcoat tossed over the handlebar to cover Seidl's prisoner-of-war tunic. As long as he was back in his own bed by reveille, the guards turned a blind eye. Seidl never forgot his gratitude to the English. When the baby came along, Seidl's guards and fellow prisoners came to the christening. Charming, isn't it? The English at their best. But the story doesn't ring a bell?'

'How could it? You're talking about a joe!'

'A blown joe. One of Ben's. Haggarty's experiences of German prison camp were not so uplifting. Never mind. In 1948, while Haggarty was nominally working with the Control Commission, he picked up Seidl in a bar in Hannover, recruited him and ran him back into East Germany, to his home town of Leipzig. He has been running him ever since. The Haggarty-Seidl friendship has been the linchpin of the Berlin Station for the last fifteen years. At the time of his arrest last week, Seidl was fourth man in the East German Foreign Ministry. He had served as their Ambassador in Havana. But you've never heard of him. Nobody ever mentioned him to you. Not Ben. Not anyone.'

'No,' I said, as wearily as I could manage.

'Once a month Haggarty was accustomed to going into East Berlin and debriefing Seidl – in a car, in a safe flat, on a park bench,wherever – the usual thing. After the Wall there was a suspension of service for a while, before the meetings were cautiously resumed. The game was to cross in a Four Power vehicle – say, an army jeep – introduce a substitute, hop out at the right moment and rejoin the vehicle at an agreed point. It sounds perilous and it was, but with practice it worked. If Haggarty was on leave or sick, there was no meeting. A couple of months ago Head Office ruled that Haggarty should introduce Seidl to a successor. Haggarty is past retiring age, Willis has had Berlin so long he's blown sky high, and besides he knows far too many secrets to go wandering round behind the Curtain. Hence Ben's posting to Berlin. Ben was untarnished. Clean. Haggarty in person briefed him – I gather exhaustively. I'm sure he was not merciful. Haggarty is not a merciful man, and a twelve-strong network can be a complicated matter: who works to whom and why; who knows whose identity; the cut-outs, codes, couriers, cover-names, symbols, radios, dead-letter boxes, inks, cars, salaries, children, birthdays, wives, mistresses. A lot to get into one's head all at once.'

'I know.'

'Ben told you, did he?'

I did not rise to him this time. I was determined not to. 'We learned it on the course. *Ad infinitum,*' I said.

'Yes. Well, I suppose you did. The trouble is, the theory's never quite the same as the real thing, is it? Who's his best friend, apart from you?'

'I don't know.' I was startled by his sudden change of tack. 'Jeremy, I suppose.'

'Jeremy who?'

'Galt. He was on the course.'

'And women?'

'I told you. No one special.'

'Haggarty wanted to take Ben into East Berlin with him, make the introduction himself,' Smiley resumed. 'The Fifth Floor wouldn't wear that. They were trying to wean Haggarty away from his agent, and they don't hold with sending two men into badland where one will do. So Haggarty took Ben through the rendezvous procedures on a street map, and Ben went into East Berlin alone. On the Wednesday, he did a dry run and reconnoitred the location. On the Thursday he went in again, this time for real. He went in legally, driven in a Control Commission Humber

car. He crossed at Checkpoint Charlie at three in the afternoon and slipped
out of the car at the agreed spot. His substitute rode in it for three hours,
all as planned. Ben rejoined the car successfully at six-ten, and recrossed
into West Berlin at six-fifty in the evening. His return was logged by the
checkpoint. He had himself dropped at his flat. A faultless run. Willis and
Haggarty were waiting for him at Station Headquarters, but he telephoned
from his flat instead. He said the rendezvous had gone to plan, but he'd
brought nothing back except a high temperature and a ferocious stomach
bug. Could they postpone their debriefing till morning? Lamentably they
could. They haven't seen him or heard from him since. He sounded
cheerful despite his ailment, which they put down to nerves. Has Ben ever
been ill on you?'

   'No.'

   'He said their mutual friend had been in great form, a real character
and so forth. Obviously he could say no more on the open telephone.
His bed wasn't slept in, he took no extra clothes with him. There's no
proof that he was in his flat when he rang, there's no proof he's been
kidnapped, there's no proof he hasn't been. If he was going to defect,
why didn't he stay in East Berlin? They can't have turned him round
and played him back at us or they wouldn't have arrested his network.
And if they wanted to kidnap him, why not do it while he was their
side of the Wall? There's no hard evidence that he left West Berlin by
any of the approved corridors – train, autobahn, air. The controls are
not efficient, and as you say, he was trained. For all we know, he hasn't
left Berlin at all. On the other hand, we thought he might have come to
you. Don't look so appalled. You're his friend, aren't you? His best
friend? Closer to him than anyone? Young Galt doesn't compare. He
told us so himself. 'Ben's great buddy was Ned,' he said. 'If Ben was
going to turn to any of us, it would have to be Ned.' The evidence rather
bears that out, I'm afraid.'

   'What evidence?'

   No pregnant pause, no dramatic change of tone, no warning of any
kind: just dear old George Smiley being his apologetic self. 'There's a letter
in his flat, addressed to you,' he said. 'It's not dated, just thrown in a
drawer. A scrawl rather than a letter. He was probably drunk. It's a love
letter, I'm afraid.' And, having handed me a photocopy to read, he fetched
us both another whisky.

Perhaps I do it to help me look away from the discomfort of the moment.
But always when I set that scene in my memory I find myself switching to
Smiley's point of view. I imagine how it must have felt to be in his
position.

   What he had before him is easy enough to picture. See a striving trainee
trying to look older than his years, a pipesmoker, a sailor, a wise nodder, a

boy who could not wait for middle age, and you have the young Ned of the early sixties.

But what he had behind him was not half so easy, and it was capable of altering his reading of me drastically. The Circus, though I couldn't know it at the time, was in low water, dogged by unaccountable failure. The arrest of Ben's agents, tragic in itself, was only the latest in a chain of catastrophes reaching across the globe. In northern Japan, an entire Circus listening station and its three-man staff had vanished into thin air. In the Caucasus, our escape lines had been rolled up overnight. We had lost networks in Hungary, Czechoslovakia and Bulgaria, all in a space of months. And in Washington our American Cousins were voicing ever-louder dissatisfaction with our reliability, and threatening to cut the special cord for good.

In such a climate, monstrous theories become daily fare. A bunker mentality develops. Nothing is allowed to be accident, nothing random. If the Circus triumphed, it was because we were allowed to do so by our opponents. Guilt by association was rife. In the American perception, the Circus was nurturing not one mole but burrows of them, each cunningly advancing the career of every other. And what joined them was not so much their pernicious faith in Marx – though that was bad enough – it was their dreadful English homosexuality.

I read Ben's letter. Twenty lines long, unsigned, on white unwatermarked Service stationery, one side. Ben's handwriting but awry, no crossings out. So yes, probably he was drunk.

It called me 'Ned my darling.' It laid Ben's hands along my face and drew my lips to his. It kissed my eyelids and my neck and, thank God, on the physical front it stopped there.

It was without adjectives, without art, and the more appalling for its lack of them. It was not a period piece, it was not affected. It was not arch, Greek or nineteen-twenties. It was an unobstructed cry of homosexual longing from a man I had known only as my good companion.

But when I read it, I knew it was the real Ben who had written it. Ben in torment confessing feelings I had never been aware of, but which when I read them I accepted as true. Perhaps that already made me guilty – I mean, to be the object of his desire, even if I had never consciously attracted it, and did not desire him in return. His letter said sorry, then it ended. I didn't think it was unfinished. He had nothing more to say.

'I didn't know,' I said.

I handed Smiley back the letter. He returned it to his pocket. His eyes didn't leave my face.

'Or you didn't know you knew,' he suggested.

'I didn't know,' I repeated hotly. 'What are you trying to make me say?'

You must try to understand Smiley's eminence, the respect his name awoke in someone of my generation. He waited for me. I shall remember

all my life the compelling power of his patience. A sudden shower of rain
fell, with the handclap that London rain showers make in narrow streets.
If Smiley had told me he commanded the elements, I would not have been
surprised.

'In England you can't tell anyway,' I said sulkily, trying to collect myself.
God alone knows what point I was trying to make. 'Jack Arthur's not
married, is he? Nowhere to go in the evenings. Drinks with the lads till the
bar closes. Then drinks a bit more. No one says Jack Arthur's queer. But if
they arrested him tomorrow in bed with two of the cooks, we'd say we'd
known it all along. Or I would. It's imponderable.' I stumbled on, all
wrong, groping for a path and finding none. I knew that to protest at
all was to protest too much, but I went on protesting all the
same.

'Anyway, where was the letter found?' I demanded, trying to recover
the initiative.

'In a drawer of his desk. I thought I told you.'

'An empty drawer?'

'Does it matter?'

'Yes, it does! If it was jammed in among old papers, that's one thing. If
it was put there to be found by you people, that's another. Maybe he was
forced to write it.'

'Oh, I'm sure he was forced,' said Smiley. 'It's just a question of what
by. Did you know he was so lonely? If there was no one in his life but you,
I'd have thought it would have been rather obvious.'

'Then why wasn't it obvious to Personnel?' I said; bridling again. 'My
God, they grilled us for long enough before they appointed us. Sniffed
round our friends and relations and teachers and dons. They know far
more about Ben than I do.'

'Why don't we just assume that Personnel fell down on the job? He's
human, this is England, we're the clan. Let's begin again with the Ben
who's disappeared. The Ben who wrote to you. There was no one close to
him but you. Not anyone that you knew of, anyway. There could have
been lots of people you *didn't* know of, but that's not your fault. As far as
you knew, there was no one. We have that settled. Don't we?'

'Yes!'

'Very well then, let's talk about what you *did* know. How's that?'

Somehow he brought me down to earth and we talked into the small
grey hours. Long after the rain had stopped and the starlings had begun,
we were talking. Or I was – and Smiley was listening as only Smiley can,
eyes half closed, chins sunk into his neck. I thought I was telling him
everything I knew. Perhaps he thought I was too, though I doubt it, for he
understood far better than I the levels of self-deception that are the means
of our survival. The phone rang. He listened, muttered 'Thank you' and
rang off. 'Ben's still missing and there are no new pointers,' he said. 'You're
still the only clue.' He took no notes that I remember and I don't know to

this day whether he had a recorder running. I doubt it. He hated machines, and besides, his memory was more reliable than theirs.

I talked about Ben but I talked as much about myself, which was what Smiley wanted me to do: myself as the explanation for Ben's actions. I described again the parallel nature of our lives. How I had envied him his heroic father – I, who had no father to remember. I made no secret of our shared excitement, Ben's and mine, when we began to discover how much we had in common. No, no, I said again, I knew of no one woman – except his mother, who was dead. And I believed myself, I am sure I did.

In childhood, I told Smiley, I used to wonder whether somewhere in the world there was not another version of myself, some secret twin who had the same toys and clothes and thoughts that I did, even the same parents. Perhaps I'd read a book based on this story. I was an only child. So was Ben. I told Smiley all this because I was determined to talk directly to him from my thoughts and memories as they came to me, even if they incriminated me in his eyes. I only know that, consciously, I held nothing back from him, even if I reckoned it potentially ruinous to myself. Somehow Smiley had convinced me that this was the least I owed to Ben. Unconsciously – well, that's another matter altogether. Who knows what a man hides, even from himself, when he is telling the truth for his survival?

I told him of our first meeting – mine and Ben's – in the Circus training house in Lambeth where the newly selected entrants were convened. Until then, none of us had met any of his fellow novices. We had hardly met the Circus either, for that matter, beyond the recruiting officer, the selectors and the vetting team. Some of us had only the haziest notion of what we'd joined. Finally we were to be enlightened – about each other, and about our calling – and we gathered in the waiting room like so many characters in a Foreign Legion novel, each with his secret expectations and his secret reasons for being there, each with his overnight bag containing the same quantity of shirts and underpants, marked in Indian ink with his personal number, in obedience to the printed instructions on the unheaded notepaper. My number was nine and Ben's was ten. There were two people ahead of me when I walked into the waiting room, Ben and a stocky little Scot called Jimmy. I nodded at Jimmy, but Ben and I recognised each other at once – I don't mean from school or university but as people who bear a physical and temperamental similarity to one another.

'Enter the third murderer,' he said, shaking my hand. It seemed a wonderfully inappropriate moment to be quoting Shakespeare. 'I'm Ben, this is Jimmy. Apparently we've got no surnames any more. Jimmy left his in Aberdeen.'

So I shook Jimmy's hand as well, and waited on the bench beside Ben to see who came through the door next.

'Five to one he's got a moustache, ten to one a beard, thirty to one green socks,' said Ben.

'And evens on a cloak,' I said.

I told Smiley about the training exercises in unfamiliar towns when we had to invent a cover story, meet a contact and withstand arrest and interrogation. I let him sense how such exploits deepened our companionship, just as sharing our first parachute jumps deepened it, or compass-trekking at night across the Scottish Highlands, or looking out dead-letter boxes in godforsaken inner cities, or making a beach landing by submarine.

I described to him how the directing staff would sometimes drop a veiled reference to Ben's father, just to emphasise their pride in having the son to teach. I told him about our leave weekends, how we would go once to my mother's house in Gloucestershire and once to his father's in Shropshire. And how, each parent being widowed, we had amused ourselves with the notion that we might broker a marriage between them. But the chances in reality were small, for my mother was stubbornly Anglo-Dutch, with jolly sisters and nephews and nieces who all looked like Breughel models, whereas Ben's father had become a scholarly recluse whose only known surviving passion was for Bach.

'And Ben reveres him,' said Smiley, prodding again at the same spot.

'Yes. He adored his mother but she's dead. His father has become some sort of icon for him.'

And I remember noticing to my shame that I had deliberately avoided using the word 'love,' because Ben had used it to describe his feelings for me.

I told him about Ben's drinking, though again I think he knew. How Ben normally drank little and often nothing at all, until an evening would come along – say, a Thursday and the weekend already looming – when he would drink insatiably, Scotch, vodka, anything, a shot for Ben, a shot for Arno. Then reel off to bed, speechless but inoffensive. And how on the morning after, he looked as if he had undergone a fortnight's cure at a health farm.

'And there was really nobody but you?' Smiley mused. 'Poor you, what a burden, coping with all that charm alone.'

I reminisced, I wandered, I told him everything as it came to me, but I knew he was still waiting for me to tell him something I was keeping back, if we could find out what it was. Was I conscious of withholding? I can only reply to you as I afterwards replied to myself: I did not know I knew. It took me a full twenty-four hours more of self-interrogation to winkle my secret out of its dark corner. At four a.m., he told me to go home and get some sleep. I was not to stray from my telephone without telling Personnel what I was up to.

'They'll be watching your flat, naturally,' he warned me as we waited for my cab. 'You won't take it personally, will you? If you imagine being on the loose yourself, there are really very few ports you'd feel safe to head for in a storm. Your flat could rank high on Ben's list. Assuming there isn't anybody else except his father. But he wouldn't go to him, would he? He'd be ashamed. He'd want you. So they watch your flat. It's natural.'

'I understand,' I said as a fresh wave of disgust swept over me.

'After all, there's no one of his age whom he seems to like better than you.'

'It's all right. I understand,' I repeated.

'On the other hand of course, he's not a fool, so he'll know how we're reasoning. And he could hardly imagine you would hide him in your priest-hole without telling us. Well, you wouldn't, would you?'

'No. I couldn't.'

'Which if he's halfway rational he would also know, and that would rule you out for him. Still, he might drop by for advice or assistance, I suppose. Or a drink. It's unlikely, but it's not an assumption we can ignore. You must be far, far and away his best friend. Nobody to compare with you. Is there?'

I was wishing very much he would stop talking like this. Until now, he had shown the greatest delicacy in avoiding the topic of Ben's declared love for me. Suddenly he seemed determined to reopen the wound.

'Of course he *may* have written to other people apart from you,' he remarked speculatively. 'Men or women, both. It's not so unlikely. There are times when one's so desperate that one declares one's love to all sorts of people. If one knows one's dying or contemplating some desperate act. The difference in their case would be, he posted the letters. Still, we can't go round Ben's chums asking them whether he's written them a steamy letter recently – it wouldn't be secure. Besides, where would one start? That's the question. You have to put yourself in Ben's position.'

Did he deliberately plant the germ of self-knowledge in me? Later, I was certain he did. I remember his troubled, perspicacious gaze upon me as he saw me to the cab. I remember looking back as we turned the corner, and seeing his stocky figure standing in the centre of the street as he peered after me, ramming his last words into my departing head. 'You have to put yourself in Ben's position.'

I was in vortex. My day had begun in the small hours in South Audley Street and continued with barely pause for sleep through the Panda's monkey and Ben's letter until now. Smiley's coffee and my sense of being the prisoner of outrageous circumstance had done the rest. But the name of Stefanie, I swear it, was still nowhere in my head – not at the front, not at the back. Stefanie still did not exist. I have never, I am sure, forgotten anyone so thoroughly.

Back in my flat, my periodical spurts of revulsion at Ben's passion gave way to concern for his safety. In the living room I stared theatrically at the sofa where he had so often stretched out after a long day's street training in Lambeth: 'Think I'll bunk down here if you don't mind, old boy. Jollier than home tonight. Arno can sleep at home. Ben sleeps here.' In the kitchen I laid the palm of my hand on the old iron oven where I had fried him his midnight eggs: 'Christ Almighty, Ned, is that a stove? Looks more like what we lost the Crimean War with!'

I remembered his voice, long after I had switched out my bedside light, rattling one crazy idea after another at me through the thin partition – the shared words we had, our insider language.

'You know what we ought to do with Brother Nasser?'

'No, Ben.'

'Give him Israel. Know what we ought to do with the Jews?'

'No, Ben.'

'Give them Egypt.'

'Why, Ben?'

'People are only satisfied with what doesn't belong to them. Know the story of the scorpion and the frog crossing the Nile?'

'Yes, I do. Now shut up and go to sleep.'

Then he'd tell me the story, nevertheless, as a Sarratt case history. The scorpion as penetration agent, needing to contact his stay-behind team on the opposite bank. The frog as double agent, pretending to buy the scorpion's cover story, then blowing it to his paymasters.

And in the morning he was gone, leaving behind him a one-line note saying, 'See you at Borstal,' which was his name for Sarratt. 'Love, Ben.'

Had we talked about Stefanie on those occasions? We hadn't. Stefanie was someone we discussed in motion, glancingly, not side by side through a stationary wall. Stefanie was a phantom shared on the run, an enigma too delightful to dissect. So perhaps that's why I didn't think of her. Or not yet. Not knowingly. There was no dramatic moment when a great light went up and I sprang from my bath shouting, '*Stefanie!*' It simply didn't happen that way, for the reason I am trying to explain to you; somewhere in the no-man's-land between confession and self-preservation, Stefanie floated like a mythic creature who only existed when she was owned up to. As best I remember, the notion of her first came back to me as I was tidying up the mess left by Personnel. Stumbling on my last year's diary, I began flipping through it, thinking how much more of life we live than we remember. And in the month of June, I came on a line drawn diagonally through the two middle weeks, and the numeral '8' written neatly beside it – meaning Camp 8, North Argyll, where we did our paramilitary training. And I began to think – perhaps merely to sense – yes, of course, Stefanie.

And from there, still without any sudden Archimedean revelation, I found myself reliving our night drive over the moonlit Highlands: Ben at the wheel of the open Triumph roadster, and myself beside him making chatty conversation in order to keep him awake; because we were both happily exhausted after a week of pretending we were in the Albanian mountains raising a guerrilla army. And the June air rushing over our faces.

The rest of the intake were travelling back to London on the Sarratt bus. But Ben and I had Stefanie's Triumph roadster because Steff was a sport, Steff was selfless, Steff had driven it all the way from Oban to Glasgow just so that Ben could borrow it for the week and bring it back to her when the course restarted. And that was how Stefanie came back to me – exactly as she had come to me in the car – amorphously, a titillating concept, a shared woman – Ben's.

'So who or what *is* Stefanie, or do I get the usual loud silence?' I asked him as I pulled open the glove compartment and looked in vain for traces of her.

For a while I got the loud silence.

'Stefanie is a light to the ungodly and a paragon to the virtuous,' he replied gravely. And then, more deprecatingly: 'Steff's from the Hun side of the family.' He was from it himself, he liked to say in his more acerbic moods. Steff was from the Arno side, he was saying.

'Is she pretty?' I asked.

'Don't be vulgar.'

'Beautiful?'

'Less vulgar, but still not there.'

'What is she, then?'

'She is perfection. She is luminous. She is peerless.'

'So beautiful, then?'

'No, you lout. Exquisite. *Sans pareil*. Intelligent beyond the dreams of Personnel.'

'And otherwise – to you – what is she? Apart from being a Hun and the owner of this car?'

'She is my mother's eighteenth cousin dozens of times removed. After the war she came and lived with us in Shropshire and we grew up together.'

'So she's your age, then?'

'If the eternal is to be measured, yes.'

'Your proxy sister, as it were?'

'She was. For a few years. We ran wild together, picked mushrooms in the dawn, touched wee-wees. Then I went off to boarding school and she returned to Munich to resume being a Hun. End of childhood idyll and back to Daddy and England.'

I had never known him so forthcoming about any woman, nor about himself.

'And now?'

I feared he had switched off again, but finally he answered me. 'Now is less funny. She went to art school, took up with a mad painter and settled in a dower house in the Western Isles of Scotland.'

'Why's it less funny? Doesn't her painter like you?'

'He doesn't like anyone. He shot himself. Reasons unknown. Left a note to the local council apologising for the mess. No note to Steff. They weren't married, which made it more of a muddle.'

'And now?' I asked him again.

'She still lives there.'

'On the island?'

'Yes.'

'In the dower house?'

'Yes.'

'Alone?'

'Most of the time.'

'You mean you go and see her?'

'I *see* her, yes. So I suppose I *go* too. Yes. I go and see her.'

'Is it serious?'

'Everything to do with Steff is massively serious.'

'What does she do when you're not there?'

'Same as she does when I'm there, I should think. Paints. Talks to the dickie birds. Reads. Plays music. Reads. Plays music. Paints. Thinks. Reads. Lends me her car. Do you want to know any more of my business?'

For a while we remained strangers, until Ben once more relented. 'Tell you what, Ned. Marry her.'

'Stefanie?'

'Who else, you idiot? That's a bloody good idea, come to think of it. I propose to bring the two of you together to discuss it. You shall marry Steff, Steff shall marry you, and I shall come and live with you both, and fish the loch.'

My question sprang from a monstrous, culpable innocence: 'Why don't you marry her yourself?' I asked.

Was it only now, standing in my flat and watching the slow dawn print itself on the walls, that I had the answer? Staring at the ruled-out pages of last June and remembering with a jolt his dreadful letter?

Or was it given to me already in the car, by Ben's silence as we sped through the Scottish night? Did I know even then that Ben was telling me he would never marry any woman?

And was this the reason why I had banished Stefanie from my conscious memory, planting her so deep that not even Smiley, for all his clever delving, had been able to exhume her?

Had I looked at Ben as I asked him my fatal question? Had I looked at him as he refused, and went on refusing, to reply? Had I deliberately *not* looked at him at all? I was used to his silences by then, so perhaps, having waited in vain, I punished him by entering my own thoughts.

All I knew for certain was that Ben never answered my question, and that neither of us ever mentioned Stefanie again.

*

Stefanie his dream woman, I thought as I continued to examine the diary. On her island. Who loved him. But should marry me.

Who had the taint of death about her that Ben's heroes always seemed to need.

Eternal Stefanie, a light to the ungodly, luminous, peerless, German Stefanie, his paragon and proxy sister – mother too, perhaps – waving to him from her tower, offering him sanctuary from his father.

You have to put yourself in Ben's position, Smiley had said.

Yet even now, the open diary in my hands, I did not allow myself the elusive moment of revelation. An idea was forming in me. Gradually it became a possibility. And only gradually again, as my state of physical and mental siege bore in on me, did it harden into conviction, and finally purpose.

It was morning at last. I hoovered the flat. I dusted and polished. I considered my anger. Dispassionately, you understand. I reopened the desk, pulled out my desecrated private papers and burned in the grate whatever I felt had been irrevocably sullied by the intrusion of Smiley and Personnel: the letters from Mabel, the exhortations from my former tutor to 'do something a bit more fun' than mere research work at the War Office.

I did these things with the outside of myself while the rest of me grappled with the correct, the moral, the decent course of action.

Ben, my friend.

Ben, with the dogs after him.

Ben in anguish, and God knew what more besides.

Stefanie.

I took a long bath, then lay on my bed watching the mirror on the chest of drawers because the mirror gave me a view of the street. I could see a couple of men whom I took to be Monty's, dressed in overalls and doing something longwinded with a junction box. Smiley had said I shouldn't take them personally. After all, they only wanted to put Ben in irons.

It is ten o'clock of the same long morning as I stand purposefully to one side of my rear window, peering down into the squalid courtyard, with its creosoted shed that used to be the old privy, and its clapboard gate that opens on the dingy street. The street is empty. Monty is not so perfect after all.

The Western Isles, Ben had said. A dower house on the Western Isles.

But which isle? And Stefanie who? The only safe guess was that if she came from the German side of Ben's family and lived in Munich, and that since Ben's German relatives were grand, she was likely to be titled.

I rang Personnel. I might have rung Smiley but I felt safer lying to Personnel. He recognised my voice before I had a chance to state my business.

'Have you heard anything?' he demanded.

'Afraid not. I want to go out for an hour. Can I do that?'

'Where to?'

'I need a few things. Provisions. Something to read. Thought I'd just pop round to the library.'

Personnel was famous for his disapproving silences.

'Be back by eleven. Ring me as soon as you get in.'

Pleased by my cool performance, I went out by the front door, bought a newspaper and bread. Using shop windows, I checked my back. Nobody was following me, I was sure. I went to the public library and from the reference section drew an old copy of *Who's Who* and a tattered *Almanach de Gotha*. I did not pause to ask myself who on earth, in Battersea of all places, could have worn out the *Almanach de Gotha*. I consulted the *Who's Who* first and turned up Ben's father, who had a knighthood and a battery of decorations: '*1936, married the Gräfin Ilse Arno zu Lotbringen, one son Benjamin Arno.*' I switched to the *Almanach* and turned up the Arno Lothringens. They rated three pages, but it took me no time to identify the distant cousin whose first name was Stefanie. I boldly asked the librarian for a telephone directory for the Western Isles of Scotland. She hadn't one, but allowed me to call enquiries on her telephone, which was fortunate for I had no doubt my own was being tapped. By ten-forty-five I was back at the telephone in my flat talking to Personnel in the same relaxed tone as before.

'Where did you go?' he asked.

'To the newsagent. And the baker's.'

'Didn't you do the library?'

'Library? Oh yes. Yes, I did.'

'And what, pray, did you take out?'

'Nothing, actually. For some reason I find it hard to settle to anything at the moment. What do I do next?'

Waiting for him to reply, I wondered whether I had given too many answers but decided I had not.

'You wait. The same as the rest of us.'

'Can I come in to Head Office?'

'Since you're waiting, you might as well wait there as here.'

'I could go back to Monty, if you like.'

It was probably my over-acute imagination at work, but I had a mental image of Smiley standing at his elbow, telling him how to answer me.

'Just wait where you are,' he said curtly.

I waited, Lord knows how. I pretended to read. I dramatised myself and wrote a pompous letter of resignation to Personnel. I tore up the letter and burned the pieces. I watched television, and in the evening I lay on the bed observing the changing of Monty's guard in the mirror and thinking of Stefanie, then Ben, then Stefanie again, who was now firmly lodged in my imagination, always outside my reach, dressed in white, Stefanie the immaculate, Ben's protector. I was young, let me remind you, and in matters of women less experienced than you would have suspected if you had heard me speak of them. The Adam in me was still pretty much a child, not to be confused with the warrior.

I waited till ten, then slipped downstairs with a bottle of wine for Mr. Simpson and his wife, and sat with them while we drank it, watching more television. Then I took Mr. Simpson aside.

'Chris,' I said. 'I know it's daft but there's a jealous lady stalking me and I'd like to leave by the back way. Would you mind letting me out through your kitchen?'

An hour later, I was on the night sleeper to Glasgow. I had obeyed my counter-surveillance procedures to the letter and I was certain I was not being followed. At Glasgow Central Station, all the same, I took the precaution of dawdling over a pot of tea in the buffet while I cocked an eye for potential watchers. As a further precaution, I hired a cab to Helensburgh on the other side of the Clyde, before joining the Campbeltown bus to West Loch Tarbert. The ferry to the Western Isles sailed three days a week in those days, except for the short summer season. But my luck held: a boat was waiting, and she sailed as soon as I had boarded her, so that by early afternoon we had passed Jura, docked at Port Askaig and were heading out to the open sea again under a darkening northern sky. We were down to three passengers by then, an old couple and myself, and when I went up on deck to fend off their questions, the first mate cheerfully asked me more of his own: Was I on holiday now? Was I a doctor then? Was I married at all? Nevertheless, I was in my element. From the moment I take to the sea, everyone is clear to me, everything possible. Yes, I thought excitedly, surveying the great crags as they approached, and smiling at the shrieking of the gulls, yes, this is where Ben would hide! This is where his Wagnerian demons would find their ease!

You must understand and try to pardon my callow susceptibility in those days to all forms of Nordic abstraction. What Ben was driven by, I pursued. The mythic island – it should have been Ossian's! – the swirling clouds and tossing sea, the priestess in her solitary castle – I could not get enough of them. I was in the middle of my Romantic period, and my soul was lost to Stefanie before I met her.

The dower house was on the other side of the island, they told me at the shop, better ask young Fergus to take you in his jeep. Young Fergus turned out to be seventy, if a day. We passed between a pair of crumbling iron gates. I paid off young Fergus and rang the bell. The door opened; a fair woman stared at me.

She was tall and slim. If it was really true that she was my own age – and it was – she had an authority it would take me another lifetime to acquire. She wore, instead of white, a paint-smeared smock of dark blue. She held a palette knife in one hand, and as I spoke she raised it to her forehead and pushed away a stray bit of hair with the back of her wrist. Then lowered it again to her side, and stood listening to me long after I had finished speaking, while she pondered the resonance of my words inside her head and compared them with the man or boy who stood before her. But the strangest part of this moment is also the hardest for me to relate. It is that Stefanie came closer to the figure of my imagination than made sense. Her pallor, her air of uncorrupted truthfulness, of inner strength, coupled with an almost pitiable fragility, corresponded so exactly with my expectation that, had I bumped into her in another place, I would have known that she was Stefanie.

'My name's Ned,' I said, speaking to her eyes. 'I'm a friend of Ben's. Also a colleague. I'm alone. No one knows I'm here.'

I had meant to go on. I had a pompous speech in my head that said something like 'Please tell him that whatever he's done, it makes no difference to me.' But the steadiness of her gaze prevented me.

'Why should it matter who knows that you are here and who does not?' she asked. She spoke without accent, but with a German cadence, making tiny hesitations before the open vowels. 'He is not hiding. Who is looking for him except you? Why should he hide?'

'I understood he might be in some kind of trouble,' I said, following her into the house.

The hall was half studio, half makeshift living room. Dustsheets covered much of the furniture. The remains of a meal lay on the table: two mugs, two plates, both used.

'What kind of trouble?' she demanded.

'It's to do with his work in Berlin. I thought perhaps he would have told you about it.'

'He has told me nothing. He has never talked to me about his work. Perhaps he knows I am not interested.'

'May I ask what he does talk about?'

She considered this. 'No.' And then, as if relenting, 'At present he does not talk to me at all. He seems to have become a Trappist. Why not? Sometimes he watches me paint, sometimes he fishes, sometimes we eat something or drink a little wine. Quite often he sleeps.'

'How long's he been here?'

She shrugged. 'Three days?'

'Did he come straight from Berlin?'

'He came on the boat. Since he does not speak, that's all I know.'

'He disappeared,' I said. 'There's a hue and cry for him. They thought he might come to me. I don't think they know about you.'

She was listening to me again, listening first to my words and then my silence. She seemed to be without embarrassment, like a listening animal. It's the authority of suffering, I thought, remembering her lover's suicide; she cannot be reached by small worries.

'*They*,' she repeated with puzzlement. 'Who are *they*? What is there to *know* about me that is so particular?'

'Ben was doing secret work,' I said.

'*Ben?*'

'Like his father,' I said. 'He was tremendously proud of following in his father's steps.'

She was shocked and agitated. 'Why? Who for? *Secret* work? What a fool!'

'For British Intelligence. He was in Berlin, attached to the Military Adviser's office, but his real work was intelligence.'

'*Ben?*' she said as the disgust and disbelief gathered in her face. 'All those *lies* he must tell? Ben?'

'Yes, I'm afraid so. But it was duty.'

'How *terrible*.'

Her easel stood with its back to me. Placing herself the other side of it, she began mixing her paints.

'If I could just talk to him,' I said, but she pretended to be too much lost to her painting to hear me.

The back of the house gave on to parkland, then a line of pines hunchbacked by the wind. Beyond the pines lay a loch surrounded by small mauve hills. On its far bank I made out a fisherman standing on a collapsed jetty. He was fishing but not casting. I don't know how long I watched him, but long enough to know that it was Ben, and that he had no interest in catching fish. I pushed open the French windows and stepped into the garden. A cold wind was ruffling the surface of the loch as I tiptoed along the jetty. He was wearing a tweed jacket that was too full for him. I guessed it had belonged to her dead lover. And a hat, a green felt hat that, like all hats with Ben, looked as though it had been made for him. He didn't turn, though he must have felt my footsteps. I placed myself beside him.

'The only thing you'll catch like that is pneumonia, you German ass,' I said.

His face was turned against me, so I remained standing beside him, watching the water with him and sensing the nudge of his shoulder as the rocking jetty threw us carelessly together. I watched the water thicken and the sky turn grey behind the mountains. A few times I watched the red float of his line vanish below the oily surface. But if a fish had struck, Ben made no effort to play it or reel it in. I saw the lights go on in the house, and the figure of Stefanie standing at her easel, adding a brush stroke, then backing her wrist against her brow. The air turned cold and the night gathered, but Ben didn't move. We were in competition with each other, as we had been during our strongarm training. I was demanding, Ben was refusing. Only one of us could have his way. If it took me all night and all tomorrow, and if I starved in the process, I wasn't going to yield till he'd acknowledged me.

A half moon came up, and stars. The wind dropped and a silver ground mist formed across the blackened heather. And still we stood there, waiting for one of us to surrender. I was nearly sleeping on my feet when I heard the rattle of his reel and saw the float lift from the water and the bare line after it, flashing in the moonlight. I didn't move and didn't speak. I let him reel in and make his hook fast. I let him turn to me, because he had to if he wanted to walk past me down the jetty.

We stood face to face in the moonlight. Ben looked downwards, apparently studying my feet to see how he could step round them. His gaze travelled up to my face, but nothing changed in his expression. His locked features stayed locked. If they betrayed anything, it was anger.

'Well,' he said. 'Enter the third murderer.'

This time neither of us laughed.

She must have sensed our approach and removed herself. I heard music playing in another part of the house. When we reached the hall, Ben headed for the stairs but I grabbed his arm.

'You've got to tell me,' I said. 'There's never going to be anyone better to tell. I broke ranks to come here. You've got to tell me what happened to the network.'

There was a long drawing room beyond the hall, with shuttered windows and more dustsheets over the sofas. It was cold, but Ben still had his jacket on and I my greatcoat. I opened the shutters and let the moonlight in. I had an instinct that anything brighter would disturb him. The music was not far away from us. I thought it was Grieg. I wasn't sure. Ben spoke without remorse and without catharsis. He had confessed enough to himself, all day and night, I knew. He talked in the dead tone of somebody describing a disaster he knows that nobody can understand who was not part of it, and the music kept playing below his voice. He had no use for himself. The glamorous hero had given up as one of life's contenders. Perhaps he was a little tired of his guilt. He spoke tersely. I think he wanted me to go.

'Haggarty's a shit,' he said. 'World class. He's a thief, he drinks, he rapes a bit. His one justification was the Seidl network. Head Office were trying to wheedle him away from it and give Seidl to new people. I was the first new person. Haggarty decided to punish me for taking away his network.'

He described the studied insults, the successive night duties and weekends, the hostile reports passed back to Haggarty's supporters' club in Head Office.

'At first he wouldn't tell me anything about the network. Then Head Office bawled him out, so he told me everything. Fifteen years of it. Every tiny detail of their lives, even the joes who'd died on the job. He'd send files to me in pyramids, all flagged and cross-referenced. Read this, remember that. Who's she? Who's he? Note this address, this name, these cover-names, those symbols. Escape procedures. Fallbacks. The recognition codes and safety procedures for the radio. Then he'd test me. Take me to the safe room, sit me across the table, grill me. "You're not up to it. We can't send you in till you know your stuff. You'd better stay in over the weekend and mug it up. I'll test you again on Monday." The network was his life. He wanted me to feel inadequate. I did and I was.'

But Head Office did not give in to Haggarty's bullying, neither did Ben. 'I put myself on an exam footing,' he said.

As the day of his first meeting with Seidl approached, Ben assembled for himself a system of mnemonics and acronyms that would enable him to encompass the network's fifteen years of history. Seated night and day in his office at Station Headquarters, he drew up consciousness charts and communications charts and devised systems for memorising the aliases, covernames, home addresses and places of employment of its agents, sub-agents, couriers and collaborators. Then he transferred his data to plain postcards, writing on one side only. On the other, in one line, he wrote the subject: 'dead-letter boxes,' 'salaries,' 'safe houses.' Each night, before going back to his flat or stretching out in the Station sickroom, he would play a game of memory with himself, first putting the cards face downward on his desk, then comparing what he had remembered with the data on the reverse side.

'I didn't sleep a lot but that's not unusual,' he said. 'As the day came up, I didn't sleep at all. I spent the whole night mugging up my stuff, then I lay on the couch staring at the ceiling. When I got up I couldn't remember any of it. Sort of paralysis. I went to my room, sat down at the desk, put my head in my hands and started to ask myself questions. "If covername Margaret-stroke-two thinks he's under surveillance, whom does he contact how, and what does the contact then do?" The answer was a total blank.

'Haggarty wandered in and asked how I was feeling and I said "fine." To do him justice, he wished me luck and I think he meant it. I thought he'd shoot some trick question at me and I was going to tell him to go to hell. But he just said, "*Komm gut Heim*," and patted my shoulder. I put the cards in my pocket. Don't ask me why. I was scared of failure. That's why we do everything, isn't it? I was scared of failure and I hated Haggarty and Haggarty had put me to the torture. I've got about two hundred other reasons why I took the cards, but none of them help a great deal. Perhaps it was my way of committing suicide. I quite like that idea. I took them and I went across. We used a limousine, specially converted. I sat in the back with my double hidden under the seat. The Vopos weren't allowed to search us, of course. All the same, switching with a double as you turn a sharp corner is a bloody hairy game. You've got to sort of roll out of the car. Seidl had provided a bike for me. He believes in bicycles. His guards used to lend him one when he was a prisoner of war in England.'

Smiley had told me the story already, but I let Ben tell it to me again.

'I had the cards in my jacket pocket,' he went on. 'My inside jacket pocket. It was one of those blazing-hot Berlin days. I think I unbuttoned my jacket while I bicycled. I don't know. When I try to remember, I sometimes unbuttoned it and I sometimes didn't. That's what happens to your memory when you work it to death. It does all the versions for you. I got to the rendezvous early, checked the cars, the usual bullshit, went in. It had all come back to me by then. Taking the cards with me had done the trick. I didn't need them. Seidl was fine. I was fine. We did our business, I briefed him, gave him some money – all just like Sarratt. I rode back to the pickup point, ditched the bike, dived into the car and as we crossed into West Berlin I realised I hadn't got the cards. I was missing the weight of them, or the pressure or something. I was in a panic but I always am. Deep down, I'm in a panic all the time. That's who I am. This was just a bigger panic. I made them drop me at my flat, rang Seidl's emergency number. No one answered. I tried the fallback. No answer. I tried his stand-in, a woman called Lotte. No answer. I took a cab to Tempelhof, made a discreet exit, came here.'

Suddenly there was only Stefanie's music to listen to. Ben had finished his story. I didn't realise at first that this was all there was. I waited, staring at him, expecting him to go on. I had been wanting a kidnapping at least – savage East German secret police rising from the back of his car, sandbagging him, forcing a chloroformed mask on him while they rifled his pockets. It was only gradually that the appalling banality of what he had told me got through to me: that you could lose a network as easily as you could lose a bunch of keys or a cheque book or a pocket handkerchief. I was craving for a greater dignity, but he had none to offer me.

'So where did you last have them?' I said stupidly. I could have been talking to a child about his lost schoolbooks, but he didn't mind, he had no pride any more.

'The cards?' he said. 'Maybe on the bicycle. Maybe rolling out of the car. Maybe getting back into it. The bike has a security chain to lock round the wheel. I had to stoop down to put it on and take it off. Maybe then. It's like losing anything. Till you find it, you never know. Afterwards, it's obvious. But there hasn't been an afterwards.'

'Do you think you were followed?'

'I don't know. I just don't know.'

I wanted to ask him when he had written his love letter to me, but I couldn't bring myself to. Besides, I thought I knew. It was in one of his drinking sessions when Haggarty was riding him hardest and he was in despair. What I really wanted him to tell me was that he had never written it. I wanted to put the clock back and make things the way they had been until a week ago. But the simple questions had died with the simple answers. Our childhoods were over for good.

They must have surrounded the house, and certainly they never rang the bell. Monty was probably standing outside the window when I opened the shutters to let the moonlight in, because when he needed to, he just stepped into the room, looking embarrassed but resolute.

'You did ever so nicely, Ned,' he said consolingly. 'It was the public library gave you away. Your nice librarian lady took a real shine to you. I think she'd have come with us if we'd let her.'

Skordeno followed him, and then Smiley appeared in the other doorway, wearing the apologetic air that frequently accompanied his most ruthless acts. And I recognised with no particular surprise that I had done everything he had wanted me to do. I had put myself in Ben's position and led them to my friend. Ben didn't seem particularly surprised either. Perhaps he was relieved. Monty and Skordeno moved into place either side of him, but Ben remained sitting among the dustsheets, his tweed jacket pulled round him like a rug. Skordeno tapped him on the shoulder; then Monty and Skordeno stooped and, like a pair of furniture removers used to one another's timing, lifted him gently to his feet. When I protested to Ben that I had not knowingly betrayed him, he shook his head to say it didn't matter. Smiley stepped aside to let them by. His myopic gaze was fixed on me enquiringly.

'We've arranged a special sailing,' he said.

'I'm not coming,' I replied.

I looked away from him and when I looked again he was gone. I heard the jeep disappearing down the track. I followed the music across the empty hall into a study crammed with books and magazincs and what appeared to be the manuscript of a novel spread over the floor. She was sitting sideways in a deep chair. She had changed into a housecoat and her pale golden hair hung loose over her shoulders. She was barefoot, and did not lift her head as I entered. She spoke to me as if she had known me all her life, and I suppose in a way she had, in the sense that I was Ben's familiar. She switched off the music.

'Were you his lover?' she asked.

'No. He wanted me to be. I realise that now.'

She smiled. 'And I wanted him to be *my* lover, but that wasn't possible either, was it?' she said.

'It seems not.'

'Have you had women, Ned?'

'No.'

'Had Ben?'

'I don't know. I think he tried. I suppose it didn't work.'

She was breathing deeply and tears were trickling down her cheeks and neck. She climbed to her feet, eyes pressed shut, and, like a blind woman, stretched out her arms for me to embrace her. Her body squeezed against me as she buried her head in my shoulder and shook and wept. I put my arms round her but she pushed me away and led me to the sofa.

'Who made him become one of you?' she said.

'No one. It was his own choice. He wanted to imitate his father.'

'Is that a choice?'

'Of a sort.'

'And you too, you are a volunteer?'

'Yes.'

'Whom are *you* imitating?'

'No one.'

'Ben had no capacity for such a life. They had no business to be charmed by him. He was too persuasive.'

'I know.'

'And you? Do you need them to make a man of you?'

'It's something that has to be done.'

'To make a man of you?'

'The work. It's like emptying the dustbins or cleaning up in hospitals. Somebody has to do it. We can't pretend it isn't there.'

'Oh, I think we can.' She took my hand and wound her fingers stiffly into mine. 'We pretend a lot of things aren't there. Or we pretend that other things are more important. That's how we survive. We shall not defeat liars by lying to them. Will you stay here tonight?'

'I have to go back. I'm not Ben. I'm me. I'm his friend.'

'Let me tell you something. May I? It is very dangerous to play with reality. Will you remember that?'

I have no picture of our leavetaking, so I expect it was too painful and my memory has rejected it. All I know now is, I had to catch the ferry. There was no jeep waiting so I walked. I remember the salt of her tears and the smell of her hair as I hurried through the night wind, and the black clouds writhing round the moon and the thump of the sea as I skirted the rocky bay. I remember the headland and the stubby little lighted steamer starting to cast off. And I know that for the entire journey I stood on the foredeck and that for the last part of it Smiley stood beside me. He must have heard Ben's story by then, and come up on deck to offer me his silent consolation.

I never saw Ben again – they kept me from him as we disembarked – but when I heard he had been discharged from the Service I wrote to Stefanie and asked her to tell me where he was. My letter was returned marked 'Gone Away.'

I would like to be able to tell you that Ben did not cause the destruction of the network, because Bill Haydon had betrayed it long before. Or better, that the network had been set up for us by the East Germans or the Russians in the first place, as a means of keeping us occupied and feeding us disinformation. But I am afraid the truth is otherwise, for in those days Haydon's access was limited by compartmentation, and his work did not take him to Berlin. Smiley even asked Bill, after his capture, whether he had had a hand in it, and Bill had laughed.

'I'd been wanting to get my hooks on that network for years,' he'd replied. 'When I heard what had happened, I'd a bloody good mind to send young Cavendish a bunch of flowers, but I suppose it wouldn't have been secure.'

The best I could tell Ben, if I saw him today, is that if he hadn't blown the network when he did, Haydon would have blown it for him a couple of years later. The best I could tell Stefanie is that she was right in her way, but then so was I, and that her words never left my memory, even after I had ceased to regard her as the fountain of all wisdom. If I never understood who she was – if she belonged, as it were, more to Ben's mystery than my own – she was nevertheless the first of the siren voices that sounded in my ear, warning me that my mission was an ambiguous one. Sometimes I wonder what I was for her, but I'm afraid I know only too well: a callow boy, another Ben, unversed in life, banishing weakness with a show of strength, and taking refuge in a cloistered world.

I went back to Berlin not long ago. It was a few weeks after the Wall had been declared obsolete. An old bit of business took me, and Personnel was pleased to pay my fare. I never was formally stationed there, as it worked out, but I had been a frequent visitor, and for us old cold warriors a visit to Berlin is like returning to the source. And on a damp afternoon I found myself standing at the grimy little bit of fencing known grandly as the Wall of the Unknown Ones, which was the memorial to those killed while trying to escape during the sixties, some of whom did not have the foresight to give their names in advance. I stood among a humble group of East Germans, mostly women, and I noticed that they were examining the inscriptions on the crosses: unknown man, shot on such-and-such a date, in 1965. They were looking for clues, fitting the dates to the little that they knew.

And the sickening notion struck me that they could even have been looking for one of Ben's agents who had made a dash for freedom at the eleventh hour and failed. And the notion was all the more bewildering when I reflected that it was no longer we Western Allies, but East Germany itself, which was struggling to snuff out its existence.

The memorial is gone now. Perhaps it will find a corner in a museum somewhere, but I doubt it. When the Wall came down – hacked to pieces, sold – the memorial came down with it, which strikes me as an appropriate comment on the fickleness of human constancy.

4

S omebody asked Smiley about interrogation, yet again. It was a question that cropped up often 'as the night progressed – mainly because his audience wanted to squeeze more case histories out of him. Children are merciless.

'Oh, there's *some* art to faulting the liar, of course there is,' Smiley conceded doubtfully, and took a sip from his glass. 'But the real art lies in recognising the truth, which is a great deal harder. Under interrogation, nobody behaves normally. People who are stupid act intelligent. Intelligent people act stupid. The guilty look innocent as the day, and the innocent look dreadfully guilty. And just occasionally people act as they are and tell the truth as they know it, and of course they're the poor souls who get caught out every time. There's nobody less convincing to our wretched trade than the blameless man with nothing to hide.'

'Except possibly the blameless woman,' I suggested under my breath.

George had reminded me of Bella and the ambiguous sea captain Brandt.

He was a big, rough flaxen fellow, at first guess Slav or Scandinavian, with the roll of a landed seaman and the far eyes of an adventurer. I first met him in Zurich where he was in hot water with the police. The city superintendent called me in the middle of the night and said, 'Herr Konsul, we have somebody who says he has information for the British. We have orders to put him over the border in the morning.'

I didn't ask which border. The Swiss have four, but when they are throwing somebody out they're not particular. I drove to the district prison and met him in a barred interviewing room: a caged giant in a roll-neck pullover who called himself Sea Captain Brandt, which seemed to be his personal version of *Kapitän zur See*.

'You're a long way from the sea,' I said as I shook his great, padded hand.

As far as the Swiss were concerned, he had everything wrong with him. He had swindled a hotel, which in Switzerland is such a heinous crime it gets its own paragraph in the criminal code. He had caused a disturbance, he was penniless and his West German passport did not bear examination – though the Swiss refused to say this out loud, since a fake passport could prejudice their chances of getting rid of him to another country. He had been picked up drunk and vagrant and he blamed it on a girl. He had broken someone's jaw. He insisted on speaking to me alone.

'You British?' he asked in English, presumably in order to disguise our conversation from the Swiss, though they spoke better English than he did.

'Yes.'

'Prove, please.'

I showed him my official identity card, describing me as Vice-Consul for Economic Affairs.

'You work for British Intelligence?' he asked.

'I work for the British government.'

'Okay, okay,' he said, and in sudden weariness sank his head into his hand so that his long blond hair flopped forward, and he had to toss it back again with a sweep of his arm. His face was chipped and pitted like a boxer's.

'You ever been in prison?' he asked, staring at the scrubbed white table.

'No, thank God.'

'Jesus,' he said, and in bad English told me his story.

He was a Latvian, born in Riga of Latvian and Polish parents. He spoke Latvian, Russian, Polish and German. He was born to the sea, which I sensed immediately, for I was born to it myself. His father and grandfather had been sailors, he had served six years in the Soviet navy, sailing the Arctic Out of Archangel, and the Sea of Japan out of Vladivostok. A year back he had returned to Riga, bought a small boat and taken up smuggling along the Baltic coast, running cheap Russian vodka into Finland with the help of Scandinavian fishermen. He was caught and put in prison near Leningrad, escaped and stowed away to Poland, where he lived illegally with a Polish girl student in Cracow. I tell you this exactly as he told it to me, as if stowing away to Poland from Russia were as self-evident as catching a number 11 bus or popping down the road for a drink. Yet even with my limited familiarity with the obstacles he had overcome, I knew it was an extraordinary feat – and no less so when he performed it a second time. For when the girl left him to marry a Swiss salesman, he headed back to the coast and got himself a ride to Malmö, then down to Hamburg where he had a distant cousin, but the cousin was distant indeed, and told him to go to hell. So he stole the cousin's passport and headed south to Switzerland, determined to get back his Polish girl. When her new husband wouldn't let her go, Brandt broke the poor man's jaw for him, so here he was, a prisoner of the Swiss police.

All this still in English, so I asked him where he'd learned it. From the BBC, when he was out smuggling, he said. From his Polish girl – she was a language student. I had given him a packet of cigarettes and he was devouring them one after another, making a gaschamber of our little room.

'So what's this information you've got for us?' I asked him.

As a Latvian, he said in preamble, he felt no allegiance to Moscow. He had grown up under the lousy Russian tyranny in Latvia, he had served under lousy Russian officers in the navy, he had been sent to prison by lousy Russians and hounded by lousy Russians, and he had no compunction about betraying them. He hated Russians. I asked him the names of the ships he had served on and he told me. I asked him what armament they carried and he described some of the most sophisticated stuff they possessed at that time. I gave him a pencil and paper and he made surprisingly impressive drawings. I asked him what he knew about signals. He knew a lot. He was a qualified signalman and had used their latest toys, even if his memory was a year old. I asked him, 'Why the British?' and he replied that he had known 'a couple of you guys in Leningrad' – British sailors on a goodwill visit. I wrote down their names and the name of their ship, returned to my office and sent a flash telegram to London because we only had a few hours' grace before they put him over the border. Next evening Sea Captain Brandt was undergoing rigorous questioning at a safe house in Surrey. He was on the brink of a dangerous career. He knew every nook and bay along the south Baltic coast; he had good friends who were honest Latvian fishermen, others who were black marketeers, thieves and disaffected drop-outs. He was offering exactly what London was looking for after our recent losses – the chance to build a new supply line in and out of northern Russia, across Poland into Germany.

I have to set the recent history for you here – of the Circus, and of my own efforts to succeed in it.

After Ben, it had been touch and go for me whether they promoted me or threw me out. I think today that I owed more to Smiley's backstairs intervention than I gave him credit for at the time. Left to himself, I don't think Personnel would have kept me five minutes. I had broken bounds while under house arrest, I had withheld my knowledge of Ben's attachment to Stefanie, and if I was not a willing recipient of Ben's amorous declarations, I was guilty by association, so to hell with me.

'We rather thought you might like to consider the British Council,' Personnel had suggested nastily, at a meeting adorned not even by a cup of tea.

But Smiley interceded for me. Smiley, it appeared, had seen beyond my youthful impulsiveness, and Smiley commanded what amounted to his own modest private army of secret sources scattered around Europe. A further reason for my reprieve was provided – though not even Smiley could have known it at the time – by the traitor Bill Haydon, whose London Station was rapidly acquiring a monopoly of Circus operations worldwide. And if Smiley's questing eye had not yet focussed on Bill, he was already convinced that the Fifth Floor was nursing a Moscow Centre mole to its bosom, and determined to assemble a team of officers whose age and access placed them beyond suspicion. By a mercy, I was one.

For a few months I was kept in limbo, devilling in large back rooms, evaluating and distributing low-grade reports to Whitehall clients.

Friendless and bored, I was seriously beginning to wonder whether Personnel had decided to post me to death, when to my joy I was summoned to his office and in Smiley's presence offered the post of second man in Zurich, under a capable old trooper named Eddows, whose stated principle was to leave me to sink or swim.

Within a month I was installed in a small flat in the Altstadt, working round the clock eight days a week. I had a Soviet naval attaché in Geneva who loved Lenin but loved a French air hostess more, and a Czech arms dealer in Lausanne who was having a crisis of conscience about supplying the world's terrorists with weapons and explosives. I had a millionaire Albanian with a chalet in St. Moritz who was risking his neck by returning to his homeland and recruiting members of his former household, and a nervous East German physicist on attachment to the Max Planck Institute in Essen who had secretly converted to Rome. I had a beautiful little microphone operation running against the Polish Embassy in Bern and a telephone tap on a pair of Hungarian spies in Basel. And I was by now beginning to fancy myself seriously in love with Mabel, who had recently been transferred to Vetting Section, and was the toast of the Junior Officers' Bar.

And Smiley's faith in me was not misplaced, for by my own exertions in the field, and his insistence upon rigid need-to-know at home, we succeeded in netting valuable intelligence and even getting it into the right hands – and you would be surprised how rarely that combination is achieved.

So that when after two years of this the Hamburg slot came up – a one-man post, and working directly to London Station, now willy-nilly the operational hub of the Service – I had Smiley's generous blessing to apply for it, whatever his private reservations about Haydon's widening embrace. I angled, I was not brash, I reminded Personnel of my naval background. I let him infer, if I did not say it in as many words, that I was straining at the bonds of Smiley's old-world caution. And it worked. He gave me Hamburg Station on the Haydon ticket, and the same night, after a romantic dinner at Bianchi's, Mabel and I slept together, the first time for each of us.

My sense of the rightness of things was further increased when, on looking over my new stocklist, I saw to my amusement that one Wolf Dittrich, alias Sea Captain Brandt, was a leading player in my new cast of characters. We are talking of the late sixties now. Bill Haydon had three more years to run.

Hamburg had always been a good place to be English, now it was an even better place to spy. After the lakeside gentility of Zurich, Hamburg crackled with energy and sparkled with sea air. The old Hanseatic ties to Poland, northern Russia and the Baltic states were still very much alive. We had commerce, we had banking – well, so had Zurich. But we had shipping too, and immigrants and adventurers. We had brashness and vulgarity galore. We were the German capital of whoredom and the press. And on our doorstep we had the secretive lowlands of Schleswig-Holstein, with their horizontal rainstorms, red farms, green fields and cloudstacked skies. Every man has his price. To this day, my soul can be bought for a jar of Lübeck beer, a pickled herring and a glass of schnapps after a trudge along the dykes.

Everything else about the job was equally pleasing. I was Ned the Assistant Shipping Consul; my humble office was a pretty brick cottage with a brass plate, handy enough for the Consulate General, yet prudently apart from it. Two clerks on secondment from the Admiralty performed my cover work for me, and kept their mouths shut. I had a radio and a Circus cypher clerk. And if Mabel and I were not yet engaged to be married, our relationship had reached a stage when she was ready to clear her decks for me whenever I popped back to London for a consultation with Bill or one of his lieutenants.

To meet my joes, I had a safe flat in Wellingsbüttel overlooking the cemetery, on the upper floor of a flower shop managed by a retired German couple who had belonged to us in the war. Their busiest days were Sundays, and on Monday mornings a queue of kids from the housing estate sold them back the flowers they had sold the day before. I never saw a safer spot. Hearses, covered vans and funeral cortèges rolled past us all day long. But at night the place was literally as quiet as the grave. Even the exotic figure of my sea captain became unremarkable when he donned his black hat and dark suit and swung into the brick archway of our shop and, with his commercial traveller's briefcase bouncing at his side, stomped up the stairs to our innocent front door marked 'Büro.'

I shall go on calling him Brandt. Some people, however much they change their names, have only one.

But the jewel in my crown was the *Margerite* – or, as we called her in English, the *Daisy*. She was a fifty-foot clinker-built, double-ended fishing boat converted to a cabin cruiser, with a wheelhouse, a main saloon and four berths in the foc's'le. She had a mizzen mast and sail to steady her from rolling. She had a dark-green hull with light-green gunnels and a white cabin roof. She was built for stealth, not speed. In poor light and choppy water, she was invisible to the naked eye. She had sparse top-hamper, and lay close to the water, which gave her a harmless image on the radar screens, particularly in heavy weather. The Baltic is a vengeful sea, shallow and tideless. Even in a mild wind, the waves come steep and nasty. At ten knots and full throttle, the *Daisy* pitched and rolled like a pig. The only speedy thing about her was the fourteen-foot Zodiac dinghy hoisted as the ship's lifeboat and lashed to the cabin roof, with a Johnson 50–horsepower to whisk our agents in and out.

For her berth she had the old fishing village of Blankenese on the river

Elbe, just a few short miles out of Hamburg. And there she lay contentedly among her equals, as humble an example of her kind as you could wish. From Blankenese, when she was needed, she could slip upriver to the Kiel Canal, and crawl its sixty miles at five knots before hitting open sea.

She had a Decca navigator that took readings from slave stations on the shore, but so did everyone. She had nothing inside or out that was not consistent with her modesty. Each of her three-man crew could turn his hand to everything. There were no specialists, though each had his particular love. When we needed expert despatchers or fitters, the Royal Navy was on hand to help us.

So you can see that, what with a new dynamic team to back me up at London Station, and a full hand of sources to test my versatility, and the *Daisy* and her crew to manage, I had everything that a Head of Station with salt water in his blood could decently inherit.

And of course I had Brandt.

Brandt's two years before the Circus mast had altered him in ways I at first found hard to define. It was not so much an aging or a hardening I observed in him, as that wearying alertness, that overwakefulness, which the secret world with time imprints upon even the most relaxed of its inhabitants. We met at the safe flat. He entered. He stopped dead and stared at me. His jaw fell open and he let out a great shout of recognition. He seized my arms in a sultan's greeting and nearly broke them. He laughed till the tears came, he held me away to look at, then hauled me back to hug against his black overcoat. But his spontaneity was strained by watchfulness. I knew the signs. I had seen them in other joes.

'God damn, why they don't tell me nothing, Herr Konsul?' he cried as he embraced me yet again. 'What damn game they playing? Listen, we do some good things over there, hear me? We got good people, we beat those damn Russians to death, okay?'

'I know,' I said, laughing back at him. 'I heard.'

And when night fell he insisted on seating me among the coils of rope in the back of his van and driving me at breakneck speed to the remote farmhouse that London had acquired for him. He was determined to introduce me to his crew and I looked forward to it. And I looked forward even more to getting a sight of his girlfriend Bella, because London Station was feeling a little queasy about her recent arrival in his life. She was twenty-two years old and had been with him three months. Brandt was looking hard at fifty. It was midsummer, I remember, and the inside of the van smelt of freesias, for he had bought her a bunch at the market.

'She's a number one girl,' he told me proudly as we entered the house. 'Cooks good, makes good love, learns English, everything. Hey, Bella, I brought you new boyfriend!'

Painters and sailors make the same kind of houses, and Brandt's was no exception. It was scant but homely, with brick floors and low, white-raftered ceilings. Even in the darkness it seemed to usher in the outside light. From the front door we stepped straight down into the drawing room. A wood fire smouldered in the hearth and a ship's lamp shone on the naked flank of a girl as she lay reading on a heap of cushions. Hearing us enter, she sprang excitedly to her feet. Twenty-two and going on eighteen, I thought as she grabbed my hand and gaily pumped it up and down. She was wearing a man's shirt and very short shorts. A gold amulet glinted at her throat, declaring Brandt's possession of her: this is my woman, wearing my badge of ownership. Her face was peasant and Slav and naturally happy, with clear, wide eyes, high cheeks and a tipped-up smile even when her lips were in repose. Her bare legs were long and tanned to the same gold colour as her hair. She had a small waist, high breasts and full hips. It was a very beautiful, very young body, and whatever Brandt was thinking, it belonged to no one of his age, or even mine.

She set his freesias in a vase and fetched black bread and pickles and a bottle of schnapps. She was carelessly provocative in her movements. Either she knew exactly, or not at all, the power of each slight gesture she made. She sat beside him at the table, smiled at me and threw her arm around him, letting her shirt gape. She took possession of his hand and showed me by comparison the slenderness of her own, while Brandt talked recklessly about the network, mentioning joes and places by name, and Bella measured me with her frank eyes.

'Listen,' Brandt said, 'we got to get Aleks another radio, hear me, Ned? They take it apart, they put new spares, batteries, that radio's lousy. That's a bad-luck radio.'

When the phone rang, he answered it imperiously: 'Listen, I'm busy, okay? . . . Leave the package with Stefan, I said. Listen, have you heard from Leonids?'

The room gradually filled up. First to enter was a darting, bandy-legged man with a drooping moustache. He kissed Bella rapturously but chastely on the lips, punched Brandt's forearm and helped himself to a plateful of food.

'That's Kazimirs,' Brandt explained, with a jab of his thumb. 'He's a bastard and I love him. Okay?'

'Very okay,' I said heartily.

Kazimirs had escaped three years ago across the Finnish border, I remembered. He had killed two Soviet frontier guards along his way, and he was crazy about engines – never happier than when he was up to his elbows in oil. He was also the respected ship's cook.

After Kazimirs came the Durba brothers, Antons and Alfreds, stocky and pert like Welshmen, and blue-eyed like Brandt. The Durbas had sworn to their mother that they would never go to sea together, so they took it in turns, for the *Daisy* handled best with three, and we liked to leave space for cargo and unexpected passengers. Soon everyone was talking at once, shooting questions at me, not waiting for the answers, laughing, proposing toasts, smoking, reminiscing, conspiring. Their last run had been bad, really bad, said Kazimirs. That was three weeks ago. *Daisy* had hit a freak storm off the Gulf of Danzig and lost her mizzen. At Ujava on the Latvian coast, they had missed the light signal in the fog, said Antons Durba. They had fired a rocket and God help them, there was this whole damned reception party of crazy Latvians standing on the beach like a delegation of city fathers! Wild laughter, toasts, then a deep Nordic silence while everyone but myself was struck by the same solemn memory.

'To Valdemars,' said Kazimirs, and we drank a toast to Valdemars, a member of their group who had died five years ago. Then Bella took Brandt's glass and drank too, a separate ceremony while she watched me over the brim. 'Valdemars,' she repeated softly, and her solemnity was as beguiling as her smile. Had she known Valdemars? Had he been one of her lovers? Or was she simply drinking to a brave fellow countryman who had died for the Cause?

But I have to tell you a little more about Valdemars – not whether he had slept with Bella or even how he had died, for no one knew for sure. All that was known was that he had been put ashore and never heard of again. One story said he had managed to swallow his pill, another that he had given orders to his bodyguard to shoot him if he walked into a trap. But the bodyguard had disappeared too. And Valdemars was not the only one who had disappeared during what was now remembered by the group as 'the autumn of betrayal.' In the next few months, as the anniversaries of their deaths came round, we drank to four other Latvian heroes who had perished unaccountably in the same ill-starred period – delivered, it was now believed, not to partisans in the forest, nor loyal reception parties on the beach, but straight into the hands of Moscow Centre's chief of Latvian operations. And if new networks had been cautiously rebuilt meanwhile, five years later the stigma of these betrayals still clung to the survivors, as Haydon had been at pains to warn me.

'They're a careless bunch of sods,' he had said with his usual irreverence, 'and when they're not being careless, they're duplicitous. Don't be fooled by all that Nordic phlegm and backslapping.'

I was remembering his words as I continued my mental reconnaissance of Bella. Sometimes she listened resting her head on her clenched fist, sometimes she laid her head on Brandt's forearm, dreaming his thoughts for him while he plotted and drank. But her big, light eyes never ceased visiting me, working me out, this Englishman sent to rule our lives. And occasionally, like a warm cat, she shook herself free of Brandt and took time to groom herself, recrossing her legs and primly correcting the fit of her shorts, or twisting a hank of hair into a plait, or drawing her gold amulet from between her breasts and examining it front and back. I waited for a spark of complicity between herself and other members of the crew, but it was clear to me that Brandt's girl was holy ground. Even the ebullient

Kazimirs deadened his face to talk to her. She fetched another bottle, and when she returned she sat down beside me and took hold of my hand and opened my palm on the table, examining it while she spoke in Latvian to Brandt, who broke into a gust of laughter which the rest of them took up.

'You know what she say?'

'I'm afraid I don't.'

'She says English make damn good husband. If I die, she going to have you instead!'

She clambered back to him and, laughing, wriggled into his embrace. She didn't look at me after that. It was as if she didn't need to. So I avoided her eyes in return, and thought dutifully about her history as told to London Station by Sea Captain Brandt.

She was the daughter of a farmer from a village near Jelgava, who had been shot dead when security police raided a secret meeting of Latvian patriots, Brandt had said. The farmer was a founder member of the group. The police wanted to shoot the girl as well, but she escaped into the forest and joined up with a band of partisans and outlaws who passed her round among them for a summer, which did not seem to have upset her. By stages she had made her way to the coast and, by a route that was still mysterious to us, got word to Brandt, who, without troubling to mention her to London in advance, picked her off a beach while he was landing a new radio operator to replace another who had had a nervous breakdown. Radio operators are the opera stars of every network. If they don't have breakdowns, they have shingles.

'Great guys,' said Brandt enthusiastically as he drove me back to town. 'You like them?'

'They're terrific,' I said, and meant it, for there is no better company anywhere than men who love the sea.

'Bella want to work with us. She want to kill the guys who shoot her father. I say no. She's too young. I love her.'

A fierce white moon shone on the flat meadows, and by its light I saw his craggy face in profile, as if set against the storm to come.

'And you knew him,' I suggested, affecting to recapitulate something I vaguely remembered. 'Her father. Feliks. He was a friend of yours.'

'Sure I knew Feliks! I love him! He was a great guy! The bastards shot him dead.'

'Did he die immediately?'

'They shoot him to pieces. Kalashnikovs. They shoot everybody. Seven guys. All shot.'

'Did anyone see it happen?'

'One guy. He see it, run away.'

'What became of the bodies?'

'Secret police take them. They're scared, those police guys. Don't want no trouble from the people. Shoot the partisans, throw them in a truck, drive away to hell.'

'How well did you know him – her father?'

Brandt made his sweeping gesture with his forearm. 'Feliks? He was my friend. Fought at Leningrad. Prisoner of war in Germany. Stalin didn't like those guys. When they came home from Germany, he sent them to Siberia, shot them, gave them a bad time. What the hell?'

But London Station had picked up a different story, even if at this stage it was only a whisper. The father had been the informant, said the whisper. Recruited in Siberian captivity and sent back to Latvia to penetrate the groups. He had called the meeting, tipped off his masters, then climbed out of the back window while the partisans were being slaughtered. As a reward, he was now managing a collective farm near Kiev, living under a different name. Somebody had recognised him and told somebody else who had told somebody else. The source was delicate, checking would be a lengthy process.

So I was warned. Watch out for Bella.

I was more than warned. I was disturbed. In the next weeks I saw Bella several times, and each time I was obliged to record my impressions on the encounter sheet which London Station now insisted must be completed each time she was sighted. I made a rendezvous with Brandt at the safe flat, and to my alarm he brought her with him. She had spent the day in town, he said. They were on their way back to the farmhouse, why not?

'Relax. She don't speak no English,' he reminded me with a laugh, noticing my discomfort.

So I kept our business short, while she lounged on the sofa and smiled and listened to us with her eyes, but mostly she listened to me.

'My girl's studying,' Brandt told me proudly, patting her on the backside as we prepared to separate. 'One day she be a big professor. *Nicht wahr, Bella? Du wirst ein ganz grosser Professor, du!*'

A week later, when I took a discreet look at the *Daisy* at her berth in Blankenese, Bella was there again, wearing her shorts and scampering over the deck in her bare feet as if we were planning a Mediterranean cruise.

'For heaven's sake. We can't have girls aboard. London will go mad,' I told Brandt that night. 'So will the crew. You know how superstitious they are about having women on the ship. You're the same yourself.'

He brushed me aside. My predecessor had raised no objection, he said. Why should I?

'Bella makes the boys happy,' he insisted. 'She's from home, Ned, she's a kid. She's a family for them, come on!'

When I checked the file, I discovered he was half right. My predecessor, a seconded naval officer, had reported that Bella was 'conscious to' the *Daisy*, even adding that she seemed to 'exert a benign influence as ship's mascot.' And when I read between the lines of his report of the *Daisy*'s most recent operational mission, I realised that Bella had been there on the dockside to wave them off – and no doubt to wave them safely back as well.

Now of course operational security is always relative. I had never imagined that everything in the Brandt organisation was going to be played by Sarratt rules. I was aware that in the cloistered atmosphere of Head Office it was too easy to mistake our tortuous structures of codenames, symbols and cut-outs for life on the ground. Cambridge Circus was one thing. A bunch of volatile Baltic patriots risking their necks was another.

Nevertheless the presence of an uncleared, unrecruited camp-follower at the heart of our operation, privy to our plans and conversations, went beyond anything I had imagined – and all this in the wake of the betrayals five years earlier. And the more I worried over it, the more proprietorial, it seemed to me, did Brandt's devotion to the girl become. His endearments grew increasingly lavish in my presence, his caresses more demonstrative. 'A typical older man's infatuation for a young girl,' I told London, as if I had seen dozens of such cases.

Meanwhile a new mission was being planned for the *Daisy*, the purpose to be revealed to us later. Twice, three times a week, I found myself of necessity driving out to the farmhouse, arriving after dark, then sitting for hours at the table while we studied charts and weather maps and the latest shore observation bulletins. Sometimes the full crew came, sometimes it was just the three of us. To Brandt it made no difference. He clasped Bella to him as if the two of them were in the throes of constant ecstasy, fondling her hair and neck, and once forgetting himself so far as to slip his hand inside her shirt and cup her naked breast while he gave her a prolonged kiss. Yet as I discreetly looked away from these disturbing scenes, what remained longest in my sight was Bella's gaze on me, as if she were telling me she wished that it was I, not Brandt, who was caressing her.

'Explicit embraces appear to be the norm,' I wrote drily on the encounter sheet, Hamburg to London Station, late that night in my office. And in my nightly log: 'Route, weather and sea conditions acceptable. We await firm orders from Head Office. Morale of crew high.'

But my own morale was fighting for survival as one calamity followed upon another.

There was first the unfortunate business of my predecessor, full name Lieutenant Commander Perry de Mornay Lipton, D.S.O., R.N., retd., sometime hero of Jack Arthur Lumley's wartime irregulars. For ten years until my arrival, Lipton had cultivated the rôle of Hamburg character, by day acting the English bloody fool, sporting a monocle and hanging around the expatriate clubs ostensibly to pick up free advice on his investments. But come nightfall, he put on his secret hat and went to work briefing and debriefing his formidable army of secret agents. Or so the legend, as I had heard it from Head Office.

The only thing that had puzzled me was that there had been no formal handover between us, but Personnel had told me tersely Lipton was on a mission elsewhere. I was now admitted to the truth. Lipton had departed, not on some life-and-death adventure in darkest Russia, but to southern Spain, where he had set up house with a former Corporal of Horse named Kenneth, and two hundred thousand pounds of Circus funds, mainly in gold bars and Swiss francs, which he had paid out over several years to brave agents who did not exist.

The mistrust shed by this sad discovery now spilled into every operation Lipton had touched, including inevitably Brandt's. Was Brandt too a Lipton fiction, living high on our secret funds in exchange for ingeniously fabricated intelligence? Were his networks, were his vaunted collaborators and friends, many of whom were drawing liberal salaries?

And Bella – was Bella part of the deception? Had Bella softened his head and weakened his will? Was Brandt too feathering his nest before retiring with his loved one to the south of Spain?

A procession of Circus experts passed through the doors of my little shipping office. First came an improbable man called Captain Plum. Crouched in the privacy of my safe room, Plum and I pored over the *Daisy's* old fuel dockets and mileage records and compared them with the perilous routes that Brandt and the crew claimed to have steered on their missions along the Baltic coast. The ship's logs were sketchy at best, as most logs are, but we read them all, alongside Plum's records of signals intercepts, radar stations, navigational buoys and sightings of Soviet patrol boats.

A week later Plum was back, this time accompanied by a foulmouthed Mancunian called Rose, a former Malayan policeman who had made himself a name as a Circus sniffer dog. Rose questioned me as roughly as if I were myself a part of the deception. But when I was about to lose my temper he disarmed me by declaring that, on the evidence available, the Brandt organisation was innocent of misdoing.

Yet in the minds of such people as this, suspicions of one kind only fired suspicions of another, and the question mark hanging over Bella's father, Feliks, had not gone away. If the father was bad, then the daughter must know it, went the reasoning. And if she knew and had not said it, then she was bad as well. Moscow Centre, like the Circus, was well known for recruiting entire families. A father-and-daughter team was eminently plausible. Soon, without any solid evidence I was aware of, London Station began to peddle the notion that Feliks had been responsible for the betrayals five years ago.

Inevitably, this placed Bella in an even more sinister light. There was talk of ordering her to London and grilling her, but here my authority as

Brandt's case officer held sway. Impossible, I advised London Station. Brandt would never stand for it. Very well, came the answer – typical of Haydon's cavalier approach – bring them both over and Brandt can sit in while we interrogate the girl. This time I was sufficiently moved to fly back to London myself, where I insisted on stating my case personally to Bill. I entered his room to find him stretched out on a chaise longue, for he affected the eccentricity of never sitting at his desk. A joss stick was burning from an old ginger jar.

'Maybe Brother Brandt isn't as prickly as you think, Master Ned,' he said accusingly, peering at me over his half-framed spectacles. 'Maybe *you're* the prickly one?'

'He's besotted with her,' I said.

'Are you?'

'If we start accusing his girl in front of him, he'll go crazy. He lives for her. He'd tell us to go to hell and dismantle the network, and I doubt whether anyone else could run it.'

Haydon pondered this: 'The Garibaldi of the Baltic. Well, well. Still, Garibaldi wasn't much bloody good, was he?' He waited for me to answer but I preferred to take his question as rhetorical. 'Those jokers she shacked up in the forest with,' he drawled finally. 'Does she talk about them?'

'She doesn't talk about any of it. Brandt does, she doesn't.'

'So what does she talk about?'

'Nothing much. If she says anything of significance, it's usually in Latvian and Brandt translates or not as he thinks fit. Otherwise she just smiles and looks.'

'At you?'

'At him.'

'And she's quite a looker, I gather.'

'She's attractive, I suppose. Yes.'

Once more he took his time to consider this. 'Sounds to me like the ideal woman,' he pronounced. 'Smiles and looks, keeps quiet, fucks – what more can you ask?' He again examined me quizzically over his spectacles. 'Do you mean she doesn't even speak *German*? She must do, coming from up there. Don't be daft.'

'She speaks German reluctantly when she's got no choice. Speaking Latvian's a patriotic act. German isn't.'

'Good tits?'

'Not bad.'

'Couldn't you get alongside her a bit more? Without rocking the lovers' boat, obviously. Just the answers to a few basic questions would be a help. Nothing dramatic. Just whether she's the real thing, or whether Brother Brandt smuggled her into the nest in a warming pan – or whether Moscow Centre did, of course. See what you can get out of her. He's not her natural father, you realise that, I suppose. He can't be.'

'Who isn't?' For a confused moment I had thought he was still talking about Brandt.

'Her daddy. Feliks. The one who got shot or didn't. The farmer. According to the record, she was born January '45, wasn't she?'

'Yes.'

'Ergo, conceived around April '44. At which time – if Brother Brandt's to be believed – her supposed daddy was languishing in a prisoner-of-war camp in Germany. Mind you, we shouldn't be too straitlaced about it. No great feat of skill, I suppose, to get yourself knocked up while your old man's in the pen. Still every little helps when we're trying to decide whether to abort a network which may have run its course.'

I was grateful for Mabel's company that night, even if we had not yet found our form as the great lovers we were so anxious to become. But of course I didn't tell her anything of my business, least of all about Bella. As a Vetting girl, Mabel was on the routine side of the Circus. It would have been quite improper for me to share my problems with her. If we had already been married – well, that might have been a different thing. Meanwhile, Bella must remain my secret.

And she did. Back in my solitary bed in Hamburg I thought of Bella and little else. The double mystery of her – as a woman and as a potential traitor – elevated her to an object of almost unlimited danger to me. I saw her no longer as a fringe figure of our organisation but its destiny. Her virtue was ours. If Bella was pure, so was the network. But if she was the plaything of another service – a deceiver planted on us to tempt and weaken and ultimately betray us – then the integrity of those round her was soiled with her own, and the network would indeed, as Haydon put it, have run its course.

I closed my eyes and saw her gaze upon me, sunny and beckoning. I felt again the softness of her kisses each time we greeted one another – always, as it seemed to me, held for a fraction longer than formality required. I pictured her liquid body in its different poses, and turned it over and over in my imagination in the same way that I contemplated the possibilities of her treason. I remembered Haydon's suggestion that I should try to 'get alongside her,' and discovered I was incapable of separating my sense of duty from my desires.

I retold myself the story of her escape, questioning it at every stage. Had she got away before the shooting or during it? And how? Had some lover among the security troops tipped her off? Had there been a shooting at all? And why did she not grieve more for her dead father, instead of making love to Brandt? Even her happiness seemed to speak against her. I imagined her in the forest, with the cut-throats and outlaws. Did each man take her at his will, or did she live now with this one, now with that? I dreamed of her, naked in the forest, and myself naked with her. I awoke ashamed of myself and put through an early-morning call to Mabel.

Did I understand myself? I doubt it. I knew little about women, beautiful women least of all. I am sure it never occurred to me that finding fault with Bella might be my way of weakening her sexual hold on me. Determined on the straight path, I wrote to Mabel daily. Meanwhile I fixed on the *Daisy*'s forthcoming mission as the perfect opportunity to undertake a hostile questioning of Bella. The weather was turning foul, which was what suited the *Daisy* best. It was autumn and the nights were lengthening. The *Daisy* liked the dark too.

'Crew stand by to sail Monday,' said London Station's first signal. The second, which did not arrive till Friday evening, gave their destination as the Narva Bay in northern Estonia, not a hundred miles west of Leningrad. Never before had the *Daisy* ventured so far along the Russian seaboard; only rarely had she been used in support of non-Latvian patriots.

'I would give my eyes,' I told Brandt.

'You're too damn dangerous, Ned,' he replied, clapping me on the shoulder. 'Be seasick four days, lie in your bunk, get in the way, what the hell?'

We both knew it was impossible. The most Head Office had ever granted me was a night spin round the island of Bornholm, and even that had been like drawing teeth.

On the Saturday night we gathered in the farmhouse. Kazimirs and Antons Durba arrived together in the van. It was Antons's turn to go to sea. With such a small operational crew, everyone had to know everything, everyone had to be interchangeable. There was no more drink. From now on, they were a dry ship. Kazimirs had brought lobsters. He cooked them elaborately, with a sauce that he was famous for, while Bella played cabin girl to him, fetching and carrying and being decorative. When we had eaten, Bella cleared the table and I spread the charts under the hanging overhead lamp.

Brandt had said six days. It was an optimistic guess. From the Kieler Förde the *Daisy* would make for open sea, passing Bornholm on the Swedish side. On reaching the Swedish island of Gotland she would put in at Sundre on the southern tip, refuel and top up her provisions. While refuelling, she would be approached by two men, one of whom would ask if they had any herring. They were to reply: 'Only in tins. There have been no herring in these waters for years.' All such exchanges sound fatuous in cold blood, and this one reduced Antons and Kazimirs to fits of nervous laughter. Returning from the kitchen, Bella joined in.

One of the men would then ask to come aboard, I continued. He was an expert – I did not say in sabotage, because the crew had mixed feelings on the matter. His name for the trip would be Volodia. He would be carrying a leather suitcase and, in his coat pocket, a brown button and a white button as proof of his good faith. If he did not know his name, or carried no suitcase, or did not produce the buttons, they were to put him back on shore alive, but return to Kiel at once. There was an agreed radio signal for this eventuality. Otherwise they should make no signals whatever. A moment's silence gripped us, and I heard the sound of Bella's bare feet on the brick floor as she fetched more firewood.

From Gotland they should head northeast through international waters, I said, and steer a central course up the Gulf of Finland, until they were lying off the island of Hogland, where they should idle till dusk, then head due south for Narva Bay, reckoning to make landfall by midnight.

I had brought large-scale charts of the Bay and photographs of the sandy coastline. I spread them on the table and the men gathered to my side to look at them. As they did so, something made me glance up and I caught sight of Bella, curled up in her own corner of the room, her excited eyes full upon me in the firelight.

I showed them the point on the beach that the Zodiac should make for, and the point on the headland where they should watch for signals. The landing party would be wearing ultra-violet glasses, I said; the Estonian reception party would be using an ultra-violet lamp. Nothing would be visible to the naked eye. After the passenger and his suitcase had been landed, the dinghy should wait no more than two minutes for any possible replacement before heading back for the *Daisy* at full speed. The dinghy should be crewed by one man only, so that if necessary he could take a second passenger on the return run. I recited the recognition signals to be exchanged with the reception party, and this time nobody laughed. I gave the shelving and gradients of the landing beach. There would be no moon. Bad weather was expected, and surely hoped for. Bella brought us tea, brushing carelessly against us as she set out the mugs. It was as if she were harnessing her sexuality to our cause. Reaching Brandt, who was still stooped over the beach chart, she gravely caressed his broad back with both her hands as if filling him with her youthful strength.

I returned to my flat at five in the morning with no thought of sleep. In the afternoon I rode with Brandt and Bella to Blankenese in the van. Antons and Kazimirs had been with the boat all day. They were dressed for the voyage, in bobble hats and oilskin trousers. Orange life jackets were airing on the deck. Shaking hands with each man in turn, I passed round the sea-proofed capsules that contained their lethal pills of pure cyanide. A grey drizzle was falling; the little quay was deserted. Brandt walked to the gangway, but when Bella made to follow him, he stopped her.

'No more,' he told her. 'You stay with Ned.'

She was wearing his old duffle coat, and a woollen hat with earflaps, which I suspected she had been wearing when he rescued her. He kissed her and she hugged him till he pushed her off and went aboard, leaving her at my side. Antons stepped into the engine house and we heard the engine cough and come to life. Brandt and Kazimirs cast off. Nobody looked at us any more. The *Daisy* cleared the quay and headed sedately for the centre of the river. The three men's backs remained turned against us. We heard the hoot of her ship's horn, and watched her until she had slipped behind the curtain of grey mist.

Like abandoned children, Bella and I walked hand in hand up the ramp to Brandt's parked van. Neither of us spoke. Neither of us had anything to say. I glanced back for a last sight of the *Daisy*, but the mist had swallowed her. I looked at Bella and saw that her eyes were unusually bright, and that she was breathing fast.

'He'll be all right,' I assured her, releasing her hand while I unlocked the door. 'They're very experienced. He's a great man.' Even in German, it sounded rather silly.

She got into the van beside me and took back my hand. Her fingers were like separate lives inside my palm. Get alongside her, Haydon had kept insisting. In my most recent signal, I had assured him I would try.

At first we drove in companionable silence, joined and separated by our shared experience. I was driving cautiously because I was taut, but my hand still held hers to give her comfort, and when I was obliged to take a firmer grasp of the steering wheel, I saw that her hand stayed beside me, fingers upward, waiting for me to come back. Suddenly I was terribly concerned about where to take her. Absurdly so. I thought of an elegant basement restaurant with tiled alcoves where I took my banking joes. The elderly waiters would provide her with the kind of reassurance she needed. Then I remembered she was wearing Brandt's duffle coat, jeans and rubber boots. I was no better dressed myself. So where? I wondered anxiously. It was getting late. Through the mist, lights were coming on in the cottages.

'Are you hungry?' I asked.

She put her hand back on her lap.

'Should I find us somewhere to eat?' I asked.

She shrugged.

'Shall I take you to the farmhouse?' I suggested.

'What for?'

'Well I mean, how are you going to spend the next few days? What did you do the last time he was away?'

'I rested from him,' she said, with a laugh I had not expected.

'Then tell me how you would like to wait for him,' I suggested magnanimously, with a hint of rank. 'Do you prefer to be alone? Meet up with other exiles and have gossips? What's best?'

'It's not important,' she said, and moved away from me.

'Tell me all the same. Help me.'

'I shall go to cinemas. Look at shops. Read magazines. I shall listen to music. Try to study. Get bored.'

I decided on the safe flat. There would be food in the fridge, I told myself. Give her a meal, a drink, get her talking. Then either drive her to the farmhouse or send her by cab.

We entered the city. I parked two streets away from the safe flat and took her arm as we walked along the tree-lined pavement. I would have done the same for any woman in a dark street, but there was something disturbing about feeling her bare arm inside Brandt's sleeve. The city was unfamiliar to me. In the lighted windows of the houses, people talked and laughed as if we didn't exist. She clasped my arm and drew my hand against her breast – to be precise, the underside of it, I could feel its shape precisely through the layers of clothing. I was remembering the Circus bar-room jokes about certain officers who picked up their best intelligence in bed. I was remembering Haydon asking me whether she had good tits. I felt ashamed, and took back my hand.

There was a man-door to one side of the cemetery gates. As I unlocked it and ushered her ahead of me, she turned and kissed me on the eyes, one after the other, while she held my face in both her hands. I gripped her waist and she seemed weightless. She was very happy. I could see her smile by the yellow cemetery lights.

'Everyone is dead,' she whispered excitedly. 'But we are alive.'

I went ahead of her up the stairs. Halfway, I looked back to make sure she was following me. I was scared that she might have changed her mind. I was scared altogether – not because I was without experience – thanks to Mabel I was not – but because I knew already that I was encountering a different category of woman from any I had known before. She was standing right behind me, holding her shoes in her hands, still smiling.

I opened the door for her. She stepped through and kissed me again, laughing in merriment, just as if I had lifted her up and carried her across the threshold on our wedding day. I remembered stupidly that Russians never shake hands in doorways, and perhaps Latvians didn't either, and perhaps her kisses were some kind of ceremony of exorcism. I would have asked her, except that, near enough, I had lost my voice. I closed the door, then crossed the room to turn up the fire, an electric convector affair which, as long as the room was cold, blew out warm air with enormous vigour, but afterwards only fitfully, like an old dog dreaming.

I went to the kitchen to fetch some wine. When I returned she had disappeared and the light was on under the bathroom door. I set the table carefully with knives and forks and spoons and cheese and cold meat and glasses and paper napkins and anything else that I could possibly think of, because I was taking refuge in the distancing formalities of hospitality.

The bathroom door opened and she emerged wearing Brandt's coat wrapped round her as a dressing-gown and, to judge by her bare legs, little else. Her hair was brushed. In our safe flats, we always keep a brush and comb for hospitality.

And I remember thinking that if she was as bad as Haydon seemed to think she was, it was a pretty terrible thing for her to be wearing Brandt's coat in order to deceive the man she was already betraying; and a pretty terrible thing for me to be the man she had selected, while my agents were heading for high danger with lethal pills in their coat pockets. But I had no sense of guilt. I mention this in order to try to explain that my mind was zigzagging in any number of directions in its effort to still my desire for her.

I kissed her and took off her coat, and I never saw before or since anyone so beautiful. And the truth is that, at that moment and at that age, I had not yet acquired the power to distinguish between truth and beauty. They were one and the same to me, and I could only feel awe for her. If I had ever suspected her of anything, the sight of her naked body convinced me of her innocence.

After that, the images of my memory must tell you their own tale. Even today I see us as two other people, never as ourselves.

Bella naked by the half light of the fire, lying on her side as I had first seen her by the fire in the farmhouse. I had fetched the duvet from the bedroom.

'You're so beautiful,' she whispered.

It had not occurred to me that I could fill her with a comparable wonder.

Bella at the window, the light from the cemetery making a perfect statue of her body, gilding her fleece and drawing light patterns on her breasts.

Bella kissing Ned's face, hundreds of small kisses as she brings him back to life. Bella laughing at the limitless beauty of herself, and of the two of us together. Bella taking laughter into love, a thing that had never happened to me before, until every part of each of us was a matter for celebration, to be kissed and suckled and admired in its own way.

Bella turning away from Ned to offer herself, thrusting back to accept him as she continues whispering to him. Her whispering stops. She begins her ascent, arching backward until she is upright. And suddenly she is crying out, crying to me and the dead, and she is the most living thing on earth.

Ned and Bella calm at last, standing at the window and gazing down into the graveyard.

There is Mabel, I say, but it seems too early to get married.

'It is always too early,' she replies as we start to make love again.

Bella in the bath and myself crammed happily against the taps the other end while she lazily fondles me under the water and talks about her childhood.

Bella on the duvet, drawing my head between her legs.

Bella above me, riding me.

Bella kneeling over me, her secret garden open to my face as she transports me to places I have never imagined, not even lying in my wretched single bed, dreaming over and over of this moment and trying with far too little knowledge to ward off the unknown.

And between whiles you may see Ned dozing on Bella's breast, our untouched food still on the table that I had set so formally in self-protection. With a mind made lucid by our lovemaking, I ask whatever else I can think of that will satisfy Bill Haydon's curiosity, and my own.

I drove her home and reached my flat around seven in the morning. In no mood to sleep for the second night running, I sat down and wrote my encounter report instead, my pen flying because I was still in paradise. There was no message from the *Daisy* but I expected none. Come evening, I received an interim report on her progress. She had passed Kiel and was heading for the Kieler Förde. She would be hitting open sea in a couple of hours. I had a tame German journalist to see that night and a consular meeting in the morning, but I passed the news in veiled terms to Bella on the telephone and promised to come to her soon, for she was determined I should visit her at the farmhouse. When Brandt returned, she said, she wanted to be able to look at all the places in the house where we had made love, and think of me. I suppose it testifies to the power of love's illusion that I found nothing underhand in this, or paradoxical. We had created a world together and she wished to have it round her when I was taken away from her. That was all. She was Brandt's girl. She expected nothing of me but my love.

When I arrived, we made straight for the long drawing room, where this time it was she who had laid the table. We sat at it quite naked, which was what she wanted. She wanted to see me among the familiar furniture. Afterwards we made love in their bed. I suppose I should have been ashamed, but I felt only the excitement of being appointed to the most secret places of their lives. 'These are his hairbrushes,' she said. 'These are his clothes, you are on his side of the bed.' One day I will understand what this means, I thought. And then, more grimly: or is this the pleasure that she takes in betrayal?

Next evening I had arranged to visit an old Pole in Lubeck who had established a clandestine correspondence with a distant nephew in Warsaw. The boy was being trained for cypher work in the Polish diplomatic service, and wanted to spy for us in exchange for resettlement in Australia. London Station was considering a direct approach to him. I returned to Hamburg and slept like the dead. Next morning, while I was still writing my report, a signal from London announced that the *Daisy* had successfully refuelled in Sundre and was on course for the Finnish Gulf with passenger Volodia aboard. I phoned Bella and told her all was still well, and she said, 'Please come to me.'

I spent the morning in the Reeperbahn police station extricating a pair of drunk British merchant sailors who had broken up a brothel, and the afternoon at a ghastly consular wives' tea party to rally support for the Week of the Political Prisoner. I wished the merchant sailors had broken up that brothel too. I arrived at the farmhouse at eight in the evening and we went straight to bed. At two in the morning the phone rang and Bella answered it. It was my cypher clerk calling me from the shipping office: a decypher yourself, flash priority; I was required at once.

I drove like the wind and made the office in forty minutes. As I sat down to the codebooks, I realised that Bella's smells were on my face and hands.

The signal had been transmitted over Haydon's symbol, personal to Head of Station, Hamburg. The *Daisy*'s landing party had come under heavy fire from prepared positions, it said. The dinghy was unaccounted for, and so was everyone aboard it, which meant Antons Durba and his passenger, and very likely whoever was waiting on the beach. There was no word of the Estonian patriots. The *Daisy* had sighted ultra-violet-light signals from the shore, but only one completed series of the agreed pattern, and the assumption was that the Estonian team had been taken captive as soon as they had lured the landing party to its fate. It was a familiar story, even if it was five years old. The fallback radio in Tallinn was not replying.

I was to pass this information to nobody and return to London on the first flight of the morning. A seat had been reserved for me. Toby Esterhase would meet me at Heathrow. I drafted an acknowledgement and handed it to my clerk, who accepted it without comment. He knows, I thought. How could he not? He had telephoned me at the farmhouse and spoken to Bella. The rest he could see in my face and, for all I knew, he could smell it too.

This time there was no joss burning in Haydon's room and he was sitting at his desk. Roy Bland, his Head of Eastern Europe, sat one side of him, Toby Esterhase the other. Toby's jobs were never easily defined, for he liked to keep them vague in the hope that they would multiply. But in practice he was Haydon's poodle, a role which later cost him dear. And I was surprised to see George Smiley sitting unhappily apart from them on the edge of Haydon's chaise longue, even if the symbolism of his posture did not dawn on me till three years later.

'It's an inside job,' Haydon said without preliminaries. 'The mission was blown sky high in advance. If Durba hasn't gone down with the ship, he's already swinging by his thumbs, telling his all. Volodia doesn't know a lot, but that may be his tough luck, because his interrogators aren't going to believe him and he's got a hamper full of explosives to explain. Maybe he took the pill, but I doubt it – he's a ninny.'

'Where's Brandt?' I said.

'Sitting under a bright light in the Sarratt interrogation wing and roaring like a bull. Somewhere somebody blundered. We're asking Brandt whether it might possibly be him. If not, who? It's a carbon-copy fuck-up from the last time round. Each member of the crew is being grilled separately.'

'Where's the *Daisy*?'

'In Helsinki. We've put a navy crew aboard and they're under orders to get her out tonight. The Finns don't fancy being seen providing safe harbour for people teasing the Bear. If the press don't get to hear about it, it'll be a bloody miracle.'

'I see,' I said stupidly.

'Good. I don't. What do we do? You tell me. You've got thirty Baltic agents waiting on your every word. What do you say? Abort? Apologise? Act natural and look busy? All suggestions gratefully acknowledged.'

'The Durbas weren't conscious to the Estonian network,' I objected. 'Antons can't blow what he doesn't know.'

'So who blew Antons, pray? Who blew the landing party, the coordinates, the beach, the time? Who set us up? We asked Brandt the same question, funnily enough. We thought he might suggest Bella, the Baltic strumpet. He suggested it was one of us lot instead, the cheeky bastard.'

He was furious and his fury was directed at me. I would never have imagined that lethargy could convert to such violent anger. Yet he still spoke quietly, in the nasal, upper-class drawl he had. He still managed to remain offhand. Even in passion he conveyed a deadly casualness, which made him all the more formidable.

'So what do *you* say?' he demanded of me.

'What about?'

'About *her*, sweetheart. Pouting Miss Latvia.' He was holding up the encounter report that I had written after our first night together. 'Christ Almighty, I asked for an assessment, not a bloody aria.'

'I think she's innocent,' I said. 'I think she's a simple peasant kid. That's my assessment. I expect it's Brandt's too. She answered my questions, she gave a plausible account of herself.'

Haydon had found his charm again. He could do that at the drop of a hat. He drew you and he repelled you. I remember that exactly. He danced all ways for you, playing your emotions against each other, because he had none of his own.

'Most spies *do* give a plausible account of themselves,' he retorted as he turned the pages of my report. 'The better ones do, anyway. Don't they, Tobe?' – favouring Esterhase.

'Absolutely, Bill. All the way, I would say,' said Esterhase the pleaser.

The others had a copy too. Silence settled while they studied it, pausing at the passages Haydon had sidelined. Roy Bland lifted his head and peered at me. Bland had lectured to us at Sarratt. He was a North Countryman and former don who had spent years behind the Curtain under academic cover. His accent was broad and very flat.

'Bella admits her father's not her father, right, Ned? Her mother was raped by the Germans and got pregnant from it, so she's half German by origin. Right, Ned?'

'Yes. Right, Roy. That's what she told me.'

'So when her father, as she calls him, when Feliks comes back from prisoner-of-war camp, and hears what's happened, he adopts the child.

Her. Bella. Nice of him. She volunteered that to you. She made no secret of it. Right, Ned?'

'Yes. Right, Roy.'

'Then why the fuck doesn't she tell Brandt the same tale as she tells you?'

I had asked her this myself, and so was able to answer him at once. 'When he brought her to the West, she was afraid he wouldn't take her in if he knew she wasn't his best friend's natural daughter. They weren't lovers then. He was offering protection and a life. She was scared. She took it. She'd been living in the forest. It was her first time in the West. Her own father was dead, so she needed another father figure.'

'Brandt, you mean?' said Bland slyly.

'Yes, of course.'

'Well, don't you think it's pretty bloody odd then, Ned, that Brandt didn't know the truth about her *anyway?*' he demanded triumphantly. 'If Brandt was her father's close buddy like he says he was, wouldn't he be bound to know all that? Come on, Ned!'

Smiley cut in, I thought in order to help me: 'Brandt very probably *does* know, Roy. Would *you* tell your best friend's daughter that she was the illegitimate child of a German soldier if you thought she wasn't aware of it? I'm sure *I* wouldn't. *I'd* go to quite some lengths to protect her. Specially if the father was dead and I was in love with the daughter.'

'Bugger love,' said Haydon, turning another page of my report. 'Brandt's a randy old goat. Who's this Tadeo she keeps talking about? Tadeo saw the bodies being loaded into the truck. Tadeo says he saw my father's body go in last. They'd shot most of the men in the face, but my father was shot in the chest and stomach, a machine gun had nearly cut him in two.' I mean, Christ, for a wilting violet she's bloody explicit when it helps her story, I will say.'

'Tadeo was her first lover,' I said.

'Jealous, are we?' Haydon asked me, drawing laughter from the satraps either side of him.

But not from Smiley. And not from me.

'Tadeo was a boy at her school,' I said. 'He'd been ordered to keep guard outside the house while the meeting took place, but he was making love with Bella in a field nearby. That's how she managed to escape. Tadeo told her to run for it, and who to ask for when she reached the partisans. Then he hid in a nearby house and watched what happened before joining her. It's in my report.'

Toby Esterhase added his own kind of sneer, in his own kind of Austro-Hungarian English. 'And Tadeo is most conveniently dead, of course, Ned. Being a witness in Bella's story is actually quite a risk business, I would say.'

'He was shot by a frontier guard,' I said. 'He wasn't even trying to cross.

He was making a reconnaissance. She has the feeling everyone she touches dies,' I added, thinking involuntarily of Ben.

'She could be right, at that,' said Haydon.

Perversely, it seemed to me, Roy Bland now joined in my defence – for increasingly I had the feeling I was in the dock. 'Mind you, Tadeo could be kosher *and* wrong about Feliks's death. Maybe the police faked his death. After all, he did go into the truck last. He'd have been covered with blood anyway in that slaughterhouse. They wouldn't have needed to splash the tomato ketchup on him, would they? It would have been done for them already.'

Smiley took up Bland's cudgels. I was beginning to regret I had lobbied so hard to be posted out of his care.

'Is the father *really* so important to us, Bill?' he objected. 'Feliks can be the Judas of all time, and still have a perfectly honest daughter, can't he?'

'I believe that too,' I said. 'She admires her father. She has no problem talking about him. She honours him. She's still in mourning for him.'

I was remembering how she had looked down into the graveyard. I was remembering her determination to celebrate the gift of life. I refused to believe she had been pretending.

'All right,' said Haydon impatiently, shoving a full-plate photograph at me across the desk. 'We'll stretch a point and trust you. What the hell are we supposed to make of this lot?'

It was a much enlarged photograph and out of register. I guessed it was a photograph of a photograph. It was stamped in red along the top left corner with the one word 'Witchcraft,' which I had heard on the grapevine was London Station's most secret source.

Toby Esterhase's warning to me confirmed this: 'You never saw this photograph actually, Ned,' he told me over Haydon's shoulder, with the kind of smarminess people reserve for the young. 'Also you never saw the word "Witchcraft." When you leave this room, your mind will be a blank, totally.'

It was a group photograph of young men and women arranged against a background of what could have been a barracks, or the campus of a university. They were about sixty strong, and in civilian uniform, the men in suits and ties, the women in high white blouses and long skirts. A group of older men and an evil-looking woman stood to one side of them. The mood, like the clothes and the building and the background, was sullen.

'Second row of the chorus, third from the right,' said Haydon, handing me a magnifying glass. 'Good tits, same as the young man said.'

It was Bella, there was no doubt of it. Bella three or four years younger it was true, and Bella with her hair swept back in what I guessed to be a bun. But Bella's broad, fair eyes and Bella's irrepressible smile, and the high, firm cheeks I adored.

'Did Bella ever whisper in your tiny shell-like that she'd been at language school in Kiev?' Haydon asked me.

'No.'

'Did she give any account of her education at all, apart from how she'd had it off with Tadeo in the hay?'

'No.'

'Of course Kiev *is* more of a holiday school than a school. Not a place many chaps talk about afterwards much. Unless they're confessing. Theoretically it's a school for tomorrow's interpreters but I'm afraid that in practice it's more a spawning ground for Moscow Centre hopefuls. Centre owns it, Centre staffs it, Centre skims the cream. The slops go to their Foreign Office, same as here.'

'Has Brandt seen this?' I asked.

His levity fell from him. 'You're joking, aren't you? Brandt's a hostile witness, so are they all.'

'Can I see Brandt?'

'I wouldn't recommend it.'

'Does that mean no?'

'Yes. It means no.'

'Was Witchcraft also the source of the report against Bella's father?'

'Mind your own bloody business,' he said, but I had caught Toby's startled eye and sensed that I was right.

'Does Moscow Centre always take class photographs of its white hopes?' I asked, emboldened as Smiley's head lifted to me in what I again took to be support.

'We take 'em at Sarratt,' Haydon retorted. 'Why shouldn't Moscow Centre?'

I could feel the sweat running down my back, and I knew my voice was slipping. But I floundered on. 'Has anyone else in this photograph been identified?'

'As a matter of fact, yes.'

'What as?'

'Never mind.'

'What languages did she learn?'

Haydon had had enough of me. He lifted his eyes to Heaven as if appealing for the gift of patience. 'Well, they *all* learn English, darling, if *that's* what you're asking,' he drawled and, putting his chin in his hand, gave Smiley a long look.

I am not clairvoyant and I had no way of knowing what was passing between the two men, or what had passed already. But even allowing for the advantages of hindsight, I am sure I had the sensation of being caught between hostile camps. Even somebody as remote from Head Office politics as I was could not help hearing the rumble of the battle that was raging: how the great X had walked clean past the great Y in the corridor without so much as a 'Good morning'; how A had refused to sit at the same table with B in the canteen. And how Haydon's London Station was becoming a service within a service, gobbling up the regional directorates, taking over the special sections, the watchers, the listeners, right the way down to such humble beings as our postmen, who sat in dripping sorting offices, loyally steaming open mail with gas kettles permanently on the boil. It was even hinted that the true clash of Titans was between Bill Haydon and the reigning Chief, the last to call himself Control, and that Smiley as Control's cupbearer was more on his master's side than Haydon's.

But then it was also hinted that Smiley himself was under sentence – or, put more tactfully – contemplating an academic appointment so that he could take more care of his marriage.

Haydon looked jauntily at Smiley, but the jaunty look became a chill stare as he waited for Smiley to return it. The rest of us waited too. The embarrassment was that Smiley didn't return it. He was like a man declining to acknowledge a salute. He sat on the chaise longue with his eyebrows lifted, and his long eyelids turned down, and his round head tilted, seeming to study the Persian prayer mat that was another eccentric feature of Bill's room. And he simply went on studying it as if he were unaware of Haydon's interest in him, though we all knew – even I knew – that he wasn't. Then he puffed out his cheeks and pulled a frown of disapproval. And finally he stood – not dramatically, for George never had that far to go – and gathered up his papers.

'Well, I think we've had the meat of this, don't you, Bill?' he said. 'Control will see indoctrinated officers in one hour, please, if that's convenient, and we'll try to take a view. Ned, you and I have a small piece of Zurich history to clear up. Perhaps you'd drop by when Bill has done with you.'

Twenty minutes later I was sitting in Smiley's office.

'Do you believe that photograph?' he asked, with no pretence of talking about Zurich.

'I suppose I have to.'

'Why do you suppose that? Photographs can be faked. There is such a thing as disinformation. Moscow Centre has been known to go in for it now and then. They've even stooped to discrediting innocent people, I'm told. They have an entire department, as a matter of fact, devoted to little else. It runs to about five hundred officers.'

'Then why frame Bella? Why not go for Brandt or one of the crew?'

'What's Bill told you to do?'

'Nothing. He says I'll get my orders in due course.'

'You never answered his question. Do you think we should abort the network?'

'It's hard for me to say. I'm just the local link. The network's run direct from London Station.'

'Nevertheless.'

'We can't exfiltrate thirty agents. We'd start a war. If the supply lines are blown and the escape routes are closed, I don't see there's anything we can do for them at all.'

'So they're dead anyway,' he suggested, more in confirmation than question. A phone was ringing on his desk but he didn't pick it up. He continued to look at me with a merciful concern. 'Well, if they *are* dead, will you please remember it's not your fault, Ned?' he added kindly. 'Nobody expects you to take on Moscow Centre single-handed. It may be the Fifth Floor's fault, it may be mine. It certainly isn't yours.'

He nodded me to the door. I closed it after me and heard his phone stop ringing.

I returned to Hamburg the same night. Bella sounded excited when I rang, and sad that I wasn't rushing round to her at once.

'Where's Brandt?' she asked. She had no notion of telephone security. I said Brandt was fine, just fine. I felt guilty talking to her when I knew so much and she so little. I was to be natural towards her, Haydon had said: 'Whatever you did before, keep doing it or do it better. I don't want her guessing anything.' I should tell her that Brandt loved her, which he was apparently insisting on. I guessed that in his travail he was asking to see me. I hoped so, because I trusted him and he was my responsibility.

I tried not to feel upset for myself when there were so many larger tragedies round me, but it was hard. Until a few days ago, Brandt and the crew had been mine to care for. I had been their spokesman and champion. Now one of them was dead or worse, and the rest had been taken out of my hands. The network, though it had worked to London, had been my proxy family. Now it was like the remnants of a ghostly army, out of touch, floating between life and death.

Worst of all was my sense of dislocation, of holding a dozen conflicting theories in my head at once, and favouring each in turn. One minute I was insisting to myself that Bella was innocent, just as I had maintained to Haydon. The next I was asking myself how she could have communicated with her masters. The answer was, only too easily. She shopped, she went to cinemas, she went to school. She could meet couriers, fill and empty dead-letter boxes to her heart's content.

But no sooner had I gone this far than I ran to her defence. Bella was not *bad*. The photograph was a plant and the story about her father amounted to nothing. Smiley had said as much. There were a hundred ways in which the mission could have been blown without Bella having the least thing to do with it. Our operational security was tight, but not as tight as I would have wished. My predecessor had turned out to be corrupt. Might he not, in addition to inventing agents, have sold a few as well? And even if he hadn't, was it really so unreasonable of Brandt to suggest that the leak could have come from our side of the fence, not his?

*

Now I would not have you think that, alone in his cot that night, the young Ned unravelled single-handed the skein of treachery that later took all George Smiley's powers to expose. A source can be a plant, a plant can be ignored, an experienced intelligence officer can take a wrong decision – all without the assistance of a traitor within the Fifth Floor's gates. I knew that. I was not a child, and not one of your grey-cheeked Circus conspiracy-theorists either.

Nevertheless I did ponder, as any of us might when he is stretched to the limits of his allegiance to his Service. I pieced together from my worm's-eye view all the rumours that had reached me on the Circus grapevine. Stories of unaccountable failure and repeated scandal, of the mounting anger of our American Cousins. Of meaningless reorganisations, wasteful rivalries between men who were today immortals and tomorrow had resigned. Horror stories of incompetence being taken as proof of grand betrayal – and unnerving evidence of betrayal dismissed as incompetence.

If there is such a thing as growing up, you may say that sometime that night I made one of those leaps into maturity. I realised that the Circus was much the same as any other British institution, except that it was more so, since it played its games in the safety of sealed rooms, with other people's lives for counters. Yet I was pleased to have made my recognition. It gave me back the responsibility for my actions, which hitherto I had been a little too willing to lay at other people's feet. If my career till now had been a constant battle between submission and identity, then you might say that submission had maintained the upper hand. But that night I crossed some sort of border. I decided that from then on, I would pay more heed to my own instincts and desires, and less to the harness that I seemed unable to dispense with.

We met at the safe flat. If there was neutral ground to be found anywhere, it was there. She still knew nothing of the catastrophe. I had told her only that Brandt had been summoned to England. We made love at once, blindly and hungrily; then I waited for the clarity of after-love to begin my interrogation.

I began playfully stroking her hair, smoothing it against her head. Then I swept it back with both my hands, and scooped it into a rough bun.

'This way you look *very* stern,' I said, and kissed her, still holding it in place. 'Have you ever worn it like this?' I kissed her again.

'When I was a girl.'

'When was that?' I said, between our joined lips. 'You mean before Tadeo? When?'

'Until I went to the forest. Then I cut it off. Another woman did it with a knife.'

'Have you got a photograph of yourself like this?'

'In the forest we did not take photographs.'

'I mean before. When you wore it like a stern lady.'

She sat up. 'Why?'

'Just tell me.'

She was watching me with her almost colourless eyes. 'At school, they took our photographs. Why?'

'In groups? In classes? What sort of photographs?'

'Why?'

'Just tell me, Bella. I need to know.'

'They took photographs of us in our class, and they took photographs for our documents.'

'What documents?'

'For identity. For our passports.'

She did not mean a passport as we understand it. She meant a passport for moving about inside the Soviet Union. No free citizen could cross the road without one.

'A full-face photograph? Not smiling?'

'Yes.'

'What did you do with your old passport, Bella?'

She didn't remember.

'What did you wear for it – for the photograph?' I kissed her breasts. 'Not these. What did you wear?'

'A blouse and tie. What nonsense are you talking?'

'Bella, listen to me. Is there anyone you can think of, back at home, a schoolfriend, an old boyfriend, a relation, who would have a photograph of you with your hair back? Someone you could write to, perhaps, who could be contacted?'

She considered for a moment, staring at me. 'My aunt,' she said grumpily.

'What's her name?'

She told me.

'Where does she live?'

In Riga, she said. With Uncle Janek. I seized an envelope, sat her still naked at a table and made her write out their full address. Then I put a piece of plain writing paper before her and dictated a letter which she translated as she wrote.

'Bella.' I lifted her to her feet and kissed her tenderly. 'Bella, tell me something else. Did you ever go to any school, of any kind, except the schools in your own town?'

She shook her head.

'No holiday schools? Special schools? Language schools?'

'No.'

'Did you learn English at school?'

'Of course not. Otherwise I would speak English. What's happening to you, Ned? Why are you asking me these stupid questions?'

'The *Daisy* sailed into trouble,' I said, still face to face with her. 'There was shooting. Brandt wasn't hurt but others were. That's all I'm allowed to tell you. We're to fly back to London tomorrow, you and I together. They need to ask us some questions and find out what went wrong.'

She closed her eyes and began shaking. She opened her mouth and made a silent scream.

'I believe in you,' I said. 'I want to help you. And Brandt. That's the truth.'

Gradually she came back to me and put her head on my chest while she wept. She was a child again. Perhaps she had always been one. Perhaps, by helping me to grow up, she had increased the distance between us. I had brought a British passport for her. She had no nationality of her own. I made her stay the night with me and she clutched me like a drowning girl. Neither of us slept.

On the plane she held my hand but we were already continents apart. Then she spoke in a voice that I had not heard from her before. A firm, adult voice of sadness and disillusionment that reminded me of Stefanie's when she had delivered her Sibyl's warning to me on the island.

'*Es ist ein reiner Unsinn,*' she said. It is a pure nonsense.

'What is?'

She had taken away her hand. Not in anger, but in a kind of worldly despair. 'You tell them to put their feet into the water and you wait to see what happens. If they are not shot, they are heroes. If they are shot, they are martyrs. You gain nothing that is worth having and you encourage my people to kill themselves. What do you want us to do? Rise up and kill the Russian oppressor? Will you come and help us if we try? I don't think so. I think you are doing something because you cannot do nothing. I think you are not useful to us at all.'

I could never forget what Bella said, for it was also a dismissal of my love. And today I think of her each morning as I listen to the news before walking my dog. I wonder what we thought we were promising to those brave Balts in those days, and whether it was the same promise which we are now so diligently breaking.

This time it was Peter Guillam who was waiting at the airport, which was a relief to me, because his good looks and breezy manners seemed to give her confidence. For a chaperone he had brought Nancy from the watchers, and Nancy had made herself motherly for the occasion. Between them they led Bella through immigration to a grey van which belonged to the Sarratt inquisitors. I wished that someone could have thought to send a less formidable vehicle, because when she saw the van she stopped and looked back to me in accusation before Nancy grabbed her by the arm and shoved her in.

In the turbulent life of a case officer, I was learning, there was not always such a thing as an elegant goodbye.

I can only tell you what I next did, and what I later heard. I made for Smiley's office, and spent most of my day trying to catch him between meetings. Circus protocol required me to go first to Haydon, but I had already exceeded Haydon's brief by the questions I had put to Bella, and I suspected Smiley would give me a more sympathetic hearing. He listened to me; he took charge of Bella's letter and examined it.

'If we have it posted in Moscow and give a Finnish safe address for them to write back to, it might just work,' I urged him.

But, as so often with Smiley, I had the impression that he was thinking beyond me into realms from which I was excluded. He dropped the letter in a drawer and closed it.

'I rather think it won't be necessary,' he said. 'Let us hope not anyway.'

I asked him what they would do with Bella.

'I suppose much the same as they have done with Brandt,' he replied, waking sufficiently from his absorption to give me a sad smile. 'Take her through every detail of her life. Try to trip her up. Wear her down. They won't hurt her. Not physically. They won't tell her what they have against her. They'll just hope to break her cover. It seems that most of the men who looked after her in the forest were rounded up recently. That won't speak well for her, naturally.'

'What will they do with her afterwards?'

'Well, I think we can still prevent the worst, even if we can't prevent much else these days,' he replied, returning to his papers. 'Time you went on to Bill, isn't it? He'll be wondering what you're up to.'

And I remember the expression on his face as he dismissed me: the pain and frustration in it, and the anger.

Did Smiley have the letter posted as I suggested? Did the letter produce a photograph and did the photograph turn out to be the very one that Moscow Centre's forgers had dropped into their group photograph? I wish it were so neat, but in reality it never is, though I like to believe that my efforts on Bella's behalf had some influence on her release and resettlement in Canada, which occurred a few months later in circumstances that are a puzzle to me.

For Brandt refused to take her back, let alone go with her. Had Bella told him of our affair? Had someone else? I hardly think it possible, unless Haydon himself did it out of mischief. Bill hated all women and most men too, and liked nothing better than to turn people's affections inside out.

Brandt too was given a clean ticket and, after some resistance from the Fifth Floor, a gratuity to start him in a respectable walk of life. That is to say, he was able to buy a boat and take himself to the West Indies, where he resumed his old trade of smuggling, except that this time he chose arms to Cuba.

And the betrayal? The Brandt network had simply been too efficient for Haydon's stomach, Smiley told me later, so Bill had betrayed it as he had betrayed its predecessor, and tried to fix the blame on Bella. He had arranged for Moscow Centre to fake the evidence against her, which he then presented as coming from his spurious source Merlin, the provider of the Witchcraft material. Hard on the mole's tracks by then, Smiley had voiced his suspicions in high places, only to be sent into exile for being right. It took another two years for him to be brought back to clean the stable.

And there the story stood until our own internal *perestroika* began in earnest – in the winter of '89 – when Toby Esterhase, the ubiquitous survivor, conducted a middle-ranking Circus delegation to Moscow Centre as a first step to what our blessed Foreign Office insisted on calling a 'normalisation of the relationship between the two services.'

Toby's team was welcomed at Dzerzhinsky Square and shown many of the appointments, though not, one gathers, the torture chambers of the old Lubyanka, or the roof on which certain careless prisoners had occasionally lost their footing. Toby and his men were wined and dined. They were shown, as the Americans say, a time. They bought fur hats and pinned facetious badges on them and had themselves photographed in Dzerzhinsky Square.

And on the last day, as a special gesture of goodwill, they were escorted to the gallery of Centre's huge communications hall, where reports from all sources are received and processed. And it was here, as they were leaving the gallery, says Toby, that he and Peter Guillam in the same moment spotted a tall, flaxen, thickset fellow in half silhouette at the further end of the corridor, emerging from what was apparently the men's lavatory, for there was only one other door in that part of the corridor, and it was marked for women.

He was a man of some age, yet he strode out of the doorway like a bull. He paused, and for a long beat stared straight at them, as if in two minds whether to come towards them and greet them or retreat. Then he lowered his head and, as it seemed to them, with a smile, swung away from them and disappeared into another corridor. But not before they had ample opportunity to remark his seamanly roll and wrestler's shoulders.

Nothing goes away in the secret world; nothing goes away in the real one. If Toby and Peter are right – and there are those who still maintain that Russian hospitality had got the better of them – then Haydon had an even stronger reason to point the finger of suspicion at Bella, and away from Sea Captain Brandt.

Was Brandt bad from the beginning? If so, I had unwittingly furthered his recruitment and our agents' deaths. It is a dreadful thought and sometimes in the cold grey hours as I lie at Mabel's side, it comes home to haunt me.

And Bella? I think of her as my last love, as the right turning I never took. If Stefanie had unlocked the door of doubt in me, Bella pointed me towards the open world while there was still time. When I think of my women since, they are aftercare. And when I think of Mabel, I can only explain her as the lure of domesticity to a man returned from the front line. But the memory of Bella remains as fresh for me as on our first night in the safe flat overlooking the cemetery – though in my dreams she is always walking away from me, and there is reproach even in her back.

5

'**A** re you saying we could be housing another Haydon *now*?' a student named Maggs called out amid the groans of his colleagues. 'What's his motivation, Mr. Smiley? Who's paying him? What's his bag?'

I had had my doubts about Maggs ever since he had joined. He was earmarked for a cover career in journalism, and already had the worst characteristics of his future trade. But Smiley was unruffled.

'Oh well, I'm sure that in retrospect we owe Bill a great debt of thanks,' he replied calmly. 'He administered the needle to a Service that had been far too long a-dying.' He made a fussy little frown of perplexity. 'As to *new* traitors, I'm sure our present leader will have sown her discontents, won't she? Perhaps I'm one. I do find I become a great deal more radical in my old age.'

But believe me, we didn't thank Bill at the time.

There was Before the Fall and there was After the Fall and the Fall was Haydon, and suddenly there was not a man or woman in the Circus who could not tell you where he was and what he was doing when he heard the dreadful news. Old hands tell each other to this day of the silence in the corridors, the numbed, averted faces in the canteen, the unanswered telephones.

The greatest casualty was trust. Only gradually, like dazed people after an air attack, did we step shyly, one by one, from our shattered houses, and set to work to reconstruct the citadel. A fundamental reform was deemed necessary, so the Circus abandoned its ancient nickname and the warren of Dickensian corridors and crooked staircases in Cambridge Circus that had housed its shame, and built itself instead a vile steel-and-glass affair not far from Victoria, where the windows still blow out in a gale and the corridors reek of stale cabbage from the canteen, and type-writer-cleaning fluid. Only the English punish themselves with quite such dreadful prisons. Overnight we became, in formal parlance, the Service, though the name 'Circus' still occasionally crosses our lips in the same way as we speak of pounds, shillings and pence long after decimalisation.

The trust was broken because Haydon had been part of it. Bill was no upstart with a chip on his shoulder and a pistol in his pocket. He was exactly who he had always sneeringly described himself to be: Church and Spy Establishment, with uncles who sat on Tory Party committees, and a rundown estate in Norfolk with tenant farmers who called him 'Mr. William.' He was a strand of the finely spun web of English influence of which we had perceived ourselves the centre. And he had caught us in it.

In my own case – I still claim a certain distinction for this – I actually succeeded in hearing the news of Bill's arrest twenty-four hours after it had reached the rest of the Circus, for I was incarcerated in a windowless mediaeval cell at the back of a run of grand apartments in the Vatican. I was commanding a team of Circus eavesdroppers under the guidance of a hollow-eyed friar supplied to us by the Vatican's own secret service, who would rather have gone to the Russians themselves than seek the assistance of their secular colleagues a mile up the road in Rome. And our mission was to winkle a probe microphone into the audience room of a corrupt Catholic bishop who had got himself involved in a drugs-for-arms deal with one of our disintegrating colonies – well, why be coy? It was Malta.

With Monty and his boys flown in for the occasion, we had tiptoed through vaulted dungeons, up underground staircases, until we had reached this vantage point, from which we proposed to drill a fine hole through a course of old cement that ran between the blocks of a three-foot party wall. The hole by agreement was to be no more than two centimetres in diameter, wide enough for us to insert the elongated plastic drinking straw that would conduct the sound from the target room to our microphone, small enough to spare the hallowed masonry of the Papal palace. Today we would use more sophisticated equipment, but the seventies were the last of the steam age and probes were still the fashion. Besides, with the best will in the world, you don't show off your prize gadgets to official Vatican liaison, let alone to a friar in a black habit who looks as though he has stepped straight out of the Inquisition.

We drilled, Monty drilled, the friar watched. We poured water onto red-hot drill-heads, and onto our sweating hands and faces. We muffled the drone of our drills with liquid foam, and every few minutes we took readings to make sure we hadn't drilled our way into the holy man's apartment by mistake. For the aim was to stop the drill-head a centimetre short of entry, and listen from inside the membrane of the wallpaper or surface plaster.

Suddenly we were through, but worse than through. We were in thin air. A hasty sampling by vacuum produced only exotic threads of silk. A bemused silence descended on us. Had we struck furniture? Drapes? A bed? Or the hem of some unsuspecting prelate's robe? Had the audience room been altered since we had taken the reconnaissance photographs?

At which low point the friar was inspired to remember, in an appalled whisper, that the good bishop was a collector of priceless needlework, and we realised that the shreds of cloth we were staring at were not pieces of sofa or curtain, or even some priest's finery, but fragments of Gobelin tapestry. Excusing himself, the friar fled.

Now the scene changes to the old Kentish town of Rye, where two sisters named the Misses Quayle ran a tapestry-restoration business, and by a mercy – or, you may say, by the ineluctable laws of English social connection – their brother Henry was a retired member of the Service. Henry was run to earth, the sisters were roused from their beds, an RAF jet plane wafted them to Rome's military airport, from where a car sped them to our side. Then Monty calmly returned to the front of the building and ignited a smoke bomb which cleared half the Vatican and gave our augmented team four desperate hours in the target room. By mid-afternoon of the same day, the Gobelin was passably patched and our probe microphone snugly in place.

The scene changes yet again to the grand dinner given by our Vatican hosts. Swiss Guards stand menacingly at the doors. Monty, a white napkin at his throat, is seated between the sedate Misses Quayle and wiping the last of his cannelloni from his plate with a piece of bread while he regales them with accounts of his daughter's latest accomplishments at her riding school.

'Now you won't know this, Rosie, and there's no reason why you should, but my Beckie has the best pair of hands for her age in the whole of South Croydon – '

Then Monty stops dead in his tracks. He is reading the note I have passed him, delivered to me by hand of a messenger from our Rome Station: *Bill Haydon, Director of Circus Clandestine Operations, has confessed to being a Moscow Centre spy.*

Sometimes I wonder whether that was the greatest of all Bill's crimes: to steal for good the lightness we had shared.

I returned to London to be told that when there was more to tell me I would be told. A few mornings later Personnel informed me that I had been classified 'Tailor Halftone,' which was Circus jargon for 'unpostable to all but friendly countries.' It was like being told I would spend the rest of my life in a wheelchair. I had done nothing wrong, I was in no disgrace, quite the contrary. But in the trade, cover is virtue, and mine was blown.

I packed up my desk and gave myself the rest of the day off. I drove into the country and I still don't remember the drive, but there is a walk I do on the Sussex Downs, over whaleback chalk hills with cliffs five hundred feet high.

It took another month before I heard my sentence: 'You'll be back with the émigrés, I'm afraid,' Personnel said, with his customary distaste. 'And it's Germany again. Still, the allowances are quite decent, and the skiing isn't bad either, if you go high enough.'

6

I t was approaching midnight but Smiley's good spirits had increased with every fresh heresy. He's like a jolly Father Christmas, I thought, who hands round seditious leaflets with his gifts.

'Sometimes I think the most *vulgar* thing about the Cold War was the way we learned to gobble up our own propaganda,' he said, with the most benign of smiles. 'I don't *mean* to sound didactic, and of course in a way we'd done it all through our history. But in the Cold War, when our enemies lied, they lied to conceal the wretchedness of their system. Whereas when *we* lied, we concealed our virtues. Even from ourselves. We concealed the very things that made us right. Our respect for the individual, our love of variety and argument, our belief that you can only govern fairly with the consent of the governed, our capacity to see the other fellows' view – most notably in the countries we exploited, almost to death, for our own ends. In our supposed ideological rectitude, we sacrificed our compassion to the great god of indifference. We protected the strong against the weak, and we perfected the art of the public lie. We made enemies of decent reformers and friends of the most disgusting potentates. And we scarcely paused to ask ourselves how much longer we could defend our society by these means and remain a society worth defending.' A glance to me again. 'So it wasn't much wonder, was it, Ned, if we opened our gates to every con-man and charlatan in the anti-Communist racket? We got the villains we deserved. Ned knows. Ask Ned.'

At which Smiley, to the general delight, burst out laughing – and I, after a moment's hesitation, joined in and assured my students that I would tell them about it some day.

Perhaps you caught the show, as they say in the States. Perhaps you were part of the appreciative audience at one of the many rousing performances they gave on their tireless trail through the American mid-West, as they pressed the flesh and worked the rubber-chicken luncheons of the lecture circuit, a hundred dollars a plate and every plate a sell-out. We called it the Teodor-Latzi show. Teodor was the Professor's first name.

Perhaps you joined in one of the numberless standing Ovations as our two heroes humbly took centre stage, the Professor tall and resplendent in one of several costly new suits purchased for his tour, and the diminutive Latzi his chubby mute, his shallow eyes brimming with ideals. There were ovations before they started speaking and ovations when they had finished. No applause was loud enough for 'two great American Hungarians who, single-handed, kicked themselves a hole in the Iron Curtain.' I am quoting the Tulsa *Herald*.

Perhaps your all-American daughter dressed herself in the becoming costume of a Hungarian peasant girl and put flowers in her hair for the occasion – such things happened too. Perhaps you sent a donation to the League for the Liberation, Post Box something or other, Wilmington. Or did you read about our heroes in the *Reader's Digest* in your dentist's waiting room?

Or perhaps, like Peter Guillam, who was based in Washington at the time, you were honoured to be present at their grand world *première*, jointly stage-managed by our American Cousins, the Washington city police and the FBI, at no less a shrine of right-thinking than the austere and panelled Hay-Adams Hotel, just across the square from the White House. If so, you must have been rated a serious influence-maker. You had to be a front-line journalist or lobbyist at least to be admitted to the hushed conference room where every understated word had the authority of an engraved tablet, and men in bulging blazers watched tautly over your comfort and convenience. For who knew when the Kremlin would strike back? It was still that kind of time.

Or maybe you read their book, slipped by the Cousins to an obedient publisher on Madison Avenue and launched to a fanfare of docile critical acclaim before occupying the lower end of the non-fiction bestseller list for a spectacular two weeks. I hope you did, for though it appeared over their joint names, the fact is I wrote a slice of it myself, even if the Cousins took exception to my original title. The title of record was *The Kremlin's Killer*. I'll tell you what mine was later.

As usual, Personnel had got it wrong. For anybody who has lived in Hamburg, Munich is not Germany at all. It is another country. I never felt the remotest connection between the two cities, but when it came to spying, Munich like Hamburg was one of the unsung capitals of Europe. Even Berlin ran a poor second when it came to the size and visibility of Munich's invisible community. The largest and nastiest of our organisations was a body known best by the place that housed it, Pullach, where much too soon after 1945 the Americans had installed an unlovely assembly of old Nazi officers under a former general of Hitler's military intelligence. Their brief was to pay court to other old Nazis in East Germany and, by bribery, blackmail or an appeal to comradely sentiment, procure them for the West. It never seemed to occur to the Americans that the East Germans might be doing the same thing in reverse, though they did more of it and better.

So the German Service sat in Pullach, and the Americans sat with them, egging them on, then getting cold feet and egging them off. And where the Americans sat, there sat everybody else. And now and then frightful scandals broke, usually when one or other of this company of clowns literally forgot which side he was working for, or made a tearful confession in his cups, or shot his mistress or his boyfriend or himself, or popped up drunk on the other side of the Curtain to declare his loyalty to whomever he had not been loyal to so far. I never in my life knew such an intelligence bordello.

After Pullach came the codebreakers and security artists, and after these came Radio Liberty, Radio Free Europe and Radio Free Everywhere Else, and inevitably, since they were largely the same people, the émigré conspirators, who by now were feeling a little down on their luck but dared not say it. And much time was spent among these exiled bodies arguing out niceties about who would be Master of the Royal Horse when the monarchy was restored; and who would be awarded the Order of Saint Peter and the Hedgehog; or succeed to the Grand Duke's summer palace once the Communist chickens had been removed from its drawing rooms; or who would recover the crock of gold that had been sunk to the bottom of the Whatnotsee, always forgetting that the said lake had been drained thirty years ago by the Bolshevik usurpers, who had built a six-acre hydro-electric plant on the site before running out of water.

As if this were not enough, Munich played host to the wildest sort of All German aspiration, whose adherents regarded even the 1939 borders as a mere prelude to Greater German needs. East Prussians, Saxons, Pomeranians, Silesians, Balts and Sudeten Germans all protested the terrible injustice done to them, and drew fat pay-packets from Bonn for their grief. There were nights, as I trudged home to Mabel through the beery streets, when I fancied I could hear them singing their anthems behind Hitler's marching ghost.

Are they still in business as I write? Oh, I fear they are, and looking a lot less mad than in the days when it was my job to move among them. Smiley once quoted Horace Walpole to me, not a name that would otherwise have sprung naturally to my mind: This world is a comedy to those that think, said Walpole, a tragedy to those that feel. Well, for comedy Munich has her Bavarians. And for tragedy, she has her past.

My memory is patchy nearly twenty years later regarding the Professor's political antecedents. At the time, I fancied I understood them – indeed, I must have done, for most of my evenings with him were spent listening to his recitations of Hungarian history between the wars. And I am sure we put them into the book too – a chapter's worth, at least, if I could only lay my hands on a copy.

The problem was, he was so much happier evoking Hungary's past than her present. Perhaps he had learned, in a life of continual adjustment, that it is wise to limit one's concerns to issues safely consigned to history. There were the Legitimists, I remember, and they supported King Charles, who made a sudden return to Hungary in 1921, much to the consternation of the Allies, who ordered him smartly from the stage. I don't think the Professor could have been a day above five years old when this moving event occurred, but he spoke of it with tears in his enlightened eyes, and there was much in his bearing to suggest the transitory touch of monarchy. And when he mentioned the Treaty of Trianon, the refined white hand that held his wine glass trembled in restrained outrage.

'It was a *Diktat*, Herr Ned,' he protested to me in courtly reproof. 'Imposed upon us by you victors. You robbed us of two-thirds of our land under the Crown! You gave it to Czechoslovakia, Romania, Yugoslavia. Such scum you gave it to, Herr Ned! And we Hungarians were cultivated people! Why did you do it to us? For what?'

I could only apologise for my country's bad behaviour, just as I could only apologise for the League of Nations, which destroyed the Hungarian economy in 1931. Quite how the League achieved this reckless act I never understood, but I remember it had something to do with the wheat market, and the League's rigid policy of orthodox deflation.

Yet when we approached more contemporary matters, the Professor became strangely reticent in his opinions.

'It is another catastrophe' was all he would say. 'It is all a consequence of Trianon and the Jews.'

Shafts of evening sunlight sloped through the garden window on to Teodor's superb white head. He was a lion of a fellow, believe me, wide-browed and Socratic, like a grand conductor close to genius all the time, with sculpted hands and flowing locks, and a stoop of intellectual profundity. Nobody who looked so venerable could be shallow – not even when the learned eyes appeared a mite too small for their sockets, or slipped furtively to one side in the manner of a diner in a restaurant who catches sight of a better meal passing by.

No, no, he was a great, good man, and fifteen years our joe. If a man is tall, then clearly he has authority. If he has a golden voice, then his words are also golden. If he looks like Schiller, he must feel like Schiller. If the smile is remote and spiritual, then so for sure is the man within. Thus the visual society.

Except that just occasionally, as I think now, God amuses Himself by dealing us an entirely different man inside the shell. Some founder and are rumbled. Others expand until they meet the challenge of their looks. And a few do neither, but wear their splendours like a favour granted from above, blandly accepting the homage that is not their due.

The Professor's operational history is quickly told. Too quickly, for it was a mite banal. He was born in Debrecen, close to the Romanian border, an only son of indulgent parents of the small nobility who trimmed their sails to every wind. Through them, he inherited money and connections, a thing that happened more often in the so-called Socialist countries, even in those days, than you would suppose. He was a man of letters, a writer of articles for learned journals, a bit of a poet and a lover several times married. He wore his jackets like capes, the sleeves loose. All these luxuries he could well afford, on account of his privileges and discreet wealth.

In Budapest, where he taught a languid version of philosophy, he had acquired a modest following among his students, who discerned more fire in Teodor's words than he intended, for he was never cut out to be an orator, rhetoric being something for the rabble. Nevertheless, he had risen a certain distance to their needs. He had observed their passion, and as a natural conciliator he had responded by giving it a voice – moderate enough in all conscience, but a voice for all that, and one they respected, along with his beautiful manners and air of representing an older, better order. He was of an age, by then, to be warmed by youthful adulation, and he was always vain. And through vanity he allowed himself to be carried on the counter-revolutionary tide. So that when the Soviet tanks turned back from the border and surrounded Budapest on the terrible night of November 3, 1956, he had no choice but to run for his life, which he did, into the arms of British Intelligence.

The Professor's first act on arriving in Vienna was to telephone a Hungarian friend at Oxford, pressing him in his peremptory way for money, introductions and letters testifying to his excellence. This friend happened also to be a friend of the Circus, and it was the high season for recruitment.

Within months, the Professor was on the payroll. There was little courtship, no arch approach, no customary fan dance. The offer was made, and accepted as a due. Within a year, with generous American assistance, Professor Teodor had been set up in Munich, in a comfortable house beside the river, with a car and his devoted if distraught wife Helena, who had escaped with him – one suspected, somewhat to his regret. Henceforth, and for an extraordinary length of time, Professor Teodor had been the unlikely spearhead of our Hungarian attack, and not even Haydon had unseated him.

His cover job was Radio Free Europe's patrician-at-large on the subject of Hungarian history and culture, and it fitted him like a glove. He had never been much else. In addition, he lectured a little and gave private tuition – mainly, I noticed, to girls. His clandestine job, for which, thanks to the Americans, he was remarkably well paid, was to foster his links with the friends and former students he had left behind, to be a focus for them and a rallying point and, under guidance, to shape them into an operational network, though none, to my knowledge, had ever quite emerged. It was a visionary operation, and better on the page perhaps than on the ground. Yet it ran and ran. It ran for five years, and then another five and by the time I took up the great man's file, it had completed an extraordinary fifteen years. Some operations are like that, and stagnation favours them. They are not expensive, they are not conclusive, they don't necessarily lead anywhere – but then neither does political stalemate – they are free of scandal. And each year when the annual audit is taken, they are waved through without a vote, until their longevity becomes their justification.

Now I won't say the Professor had achieved nothing for us in all that time. To say so would not only be unfair, it would be derogatory to Toby Esterhase, himself of Hungarian origin, who on his reinstatement After the Fall had become the desk officer handling the Professor's case. Toby had paid a heavy price for his blind support of Haydon, and when he was given the Hungary desk – never the most exalted of Iron Curtain slots – the Professor promptly became the most important player in Toby's personal rehabilitation programme.

'Teodor, I would say, Ned – Teodor is our absolutely total star,' he had assured me before I left London, over a lunch he nearly paid for. 'Old school, total discretion, lot of years in the saddle, loyal like a leech. Teodor is our ace, totally.'

And certainly one of the Professor's more striking accomplishments had been to escape the Haydon axe – either because he had been lucky or, less charitably, because the Professor had never produced enough intelligence to merit the interest of a busy traitor. For I could not help noticing as I prepared myself for the takeover – my predecessor having dropped dead of a stroke while on leave in Ibiza – that whereas Teodor's personal file ran to several volumes, his product file was unusually slender. Partly this could be explained by the fact that his main function had been to spot talent rather than exploit it, partly that the few sources he had guided into our net over the long period he had been working for us were still relatively unproductive.

'Hungary, Ned, that's actually a damned hard target, I would say,' Toby assured me when I delicately pointed this out to him. 'It's too open. An open target, you get a lot of crap you know already. If you don't get the Crown Jewels, you get the common knowledge – who needs it? What Teodor produces for the Americans, it's fantastic.'

This seemed to be the nub. 'So what *does* he produce for them actually?' I asked. 'Apart from hearts and minds on the radio, and articles no one reads?'

Toby's smile became unpleasantly superior. 'Sorry, Ned, old boy. "Need to know," I'm afraid. You're not on the list for this one.'

A few days later, as protocol required, I called on Russell Sheriton in Grosvenor Square to say my goodbyes. Sheriton was the Cousins' Head of Station in London, but he was also responsible for their Western European operations. I bided my time, then dropped the name of Teodor.

'Ah now, that's for Munich to say, Ned,' Sheriton said quickly. 'You know me. Never trespass on another man's preserves.'

'But is he doing you any good? That's all I want to know. I mean joes do burn out, don't they? Fifteen years.'

'Well now, we thought he was doing *you* some good, Ned. To hear Toby speak, you'd think Teodor was propping up the free world single-handed.'

No, I thought. To hear Toby speak, you'd think Teodor was propping up Toby single-handed. But I was not cynical. In spying, as in much of life, it is always easier to say no than yes. I arrived in Munich prepared to believe that Teodor was the star Toby had cracked him up to be. All I wanted was to be assured.

And I was. At first I was. He was magnificent. I thought my marriage to Mabel had ridded me of such swift enthusiasms, and in a way it had, until the evening when he opened the door to me and I decided I had walked in on one of those perfectly preserved relics of mid-European history, and that all I could decently do was sit at his feet like the rest of his disciples and drink in his wisdom. This is what the Service is for! I thought. Such a man is worth saving on his own account! The culture, I thought. The breadth. The years and years of service.

He received me warmly but with a certain distance, as became his age and distinction. He offered me a glass of fine Tokay and treated me to a discourse on its provenance. No, I confessed, I knew little about Hungarian wines, but I was keen to learn. He talked music, of which I am also sadly ignorant, and played a few bars for me on his treasured violin, the very one he had brought with him when he escaped from Hungary, he explained, and made not by Stradivarius but someone infinitely better, whose name has long escaped me. I thought it a wonderful privilege to be running an agent who had fled with his violin. He talked theatre. A Hungarian theatrical company was presently on tour in Munich with an extraordinary *Othello*, and though Mabel and I had yet to see the production, his opinion of it enchanted me. He was dressed in what Germans call a *Hausjacke*, black trousers and a pair of splendidly polished boots. We talked of God and the world, we ate the best *gulyás* of my life, served by the distraught Helena, who whispered her excuses and left us. She was a tall woman and must once have been beautiful, but she preferred to wear the signs of her neglect. We rounded off the meal with an apricot Palinka.

'Herr Ned, if I may call you so,' said the Professor, 'there is one matter which weighs heavily on my mind, and which you will permit me to raise with you at the outset of our professional relationship.'

'Please do,' I said generously.

'Unfortunately, your most recent predecessor – a good man, of course' – he broke off, evidently unable to speak ill of the recent dead – 'and, like yourself, a man of culture – '

'Please,' I repeated.

'It concerns my British passport.'

'I didn't know you had one!' I exclaimed in surprise.

'That is the point. I haven't. One understands there are problems. It is so with all bureaucracies. Bureaucracies are the most evil of man's institutions, Herr Ned. They enshrine the worst of us and bring low the best of us. An exiled Hungarian living in Munich in the employment of an American organisation is not naturally eligible for British citizenship. I understand that. Nevertheless, after my many years of collaboration with your department, I am owed this passport. A temporary travel document is not a dignified alternative.'

'But I understood the Americans were giving you a passport! Wasn't that the deal right from the beginning? The Americans to be responsible for your citizenship and resettlement? That includes a passport, surely. It must!'

I was upset that a man who had given us so much of his life should have been denied this simple dignity. But the Professor had learned a more philosophical attitude.

'The Americans, Herr Ned, are a young people and a mercenary people. Having used the best of me, they can scarcely regard me as a man of the future. For the Americans, I belong already to the garbage heap of obsolescence.'

'But didn't they promise – subject to satisfactory service? I'm sure they did!'

He made a gesture I shall never forget. He lifted his hands from the table as if he were raising a prodigiously heavy rock. He brought them almost to the level of his shoulders, before letting them crash at full force back onto the table, the imaginary rock between them. And I remember his eyes, indignant from the exertion, accusing me in the silence. So much for your promises, he was saying. Yours and the Americans, both.

'Just get me my passport, Herr Ned.'

As a loyal case officer, concerned to do the best for my joe, I threw myself upon the problem. Knowing Toby of old, I decided to take an official tone from the beginning: no half promises, no vaporous reassurances for me. I informed Toby of Teodor's request and asked for guidance. He was my desk officer after all, my London anchor. If it was true that the Americans were sliding out of their undertaking to give the Professor citizenship, the matter would have to be dealt with in London or Washington, I said, not Munich. And if, for reasons outside my knowledge, a British passport was to be granted after all, this too would require the energetic endorsement of the Fifth Floor. The days were gone for good when the Home Office handed out free British citizenship to every ex-Circus Tom, Dick and Teodor. The Fall had seen to that.

I did not signal my request, but sent it by bag, which in Circus lore gives greater formality. I wrote a fighting letter and a couple of weeks later followed it with a reminder. But when the Professor asked for a progress report, I was non-committal. It's in the pipeline, I assured him; London does not take kindly to being hustled. But I still wondered why Toby took so long to answer.

Meanwhile, at my meetings with Teodor, I strove to unravel what precisely he was doing for us that made him the star of Toby's underpopulated firmament. My investigations were not made easier by the Professor's prickliness, and at first I wondered whether he was withholding his cooperation until the question of his passport was settled. Gradually I realised that where our secret work was concerned, this was his normal demeanour.

One of his more humdrum jobs was maintaining a one-roomed student flat in the Schwabing district, which he used as a safe address for receiving mail from certain of his Hungarian contacts. I persuaded him to take me there. He unlocked the door and there must have been a dozen envelopes lying on the mat, all with Hungarian stamps.

'My goodness, when did you last come here, Professor?' I asked him as I watched him gather them laboriously together.

He shrugged, I thought gracelessly.

'How many letters do you normally reckon to receive in a week, Professor?'

I took the envelopes from him and went through the postmarks. The oldest had been posted three weeks ago, the most recent, one. We moved to the tiny desk, which was covered in dust. With a sigh he settled himself in the chair, opened a drawer and withdrew a couple of bottles of chemicals and a paintbrush from a concealed recess. Taking up the first envelope, he examined it gloomily, then slit it open with a pocket knife.

'Who's it from?' I asked, with more curiosity than he appeared to consider warranted.

'Pali,' he replied gloomily.

'Pali at the Agriculture Ministry?'

'Pali from Debrecen. He has been visiting Romania.'

'What for? Not the toxic-weapons conference? That could be a scoop!'

'We shall see. An academic conference of some kind. His field is cybernetics. He is undistinguished.'

I watched him dip the brush into the first bottle and paint the back of the handwritten letter with it. He rinsed the brush in water and applied the second chemical. And it seemed to me he was determined to demonstrate his disdain for such menial employment. He repeated the process for every letter, sometimes varying the routine by spreading open the envelope and treating the inside of it, or by painting between the lines of the visible handwriting. In the same slow motion, he sat himself at an upright Remington and wearily tapped out in translation the texts that had emerged: anticipated mineral and power deficiencies in the new industries . . . bauxite quotas for mines in the Bakony Mountains . . . low metal content of iron ore recently extracted in the region of Miskolc . . . projected yield of maize and sugar-beet harvests in the region of some-where else . . . rumours of five-year plan to revitalise State railway network . . . disruptive action against Party officials in Sopron . . . I could almost hear the yawns of the Third Floor analysts as they waded through such turgid stuff. I remembered Toby's boast that Teodor was only interested in the highest quality of intelligence. If this was the highest, what in heaven's name was the lowest? Patience, I told myself. Great agents have to be humoured.

The next day I received a reply to my letter about the passport. The problem, Toby explained, was that there had been a lot of changes among the Cousins' Hungarian Section in recent years. An effort was now being made, he said – making suspicious use of the passive voice – to establish the terms of any undertakings given by the Americans or ourselves. Mean-while I should avoid discussing the matter with Teodor, he added – as if it were I, not the Professor, who was making the running.

The matter was still in the air three weeks later when I lunched with Milton Wagner at the Cosmo. Wagner was an old hand and my American opposite number. Now he was winding up his career as the Cousins' Chief of Eastern Operations, Munich. The Cosmo was the kind of place Americans make anywhere, with crisp potato skins and garlic dip, and club sandwiches impaled on enormous plastic hairpins.

'How are you getting along with our distinguished academic friend?' he asked, in his southern drawl, after we had despatched our other business.

'Splendidly,' I replied.

'Couple of our people seem to think Teodor's been having himself a free ride these how many years,' said Wagner lazily.

This time I said nothing.

'The boys back home have been holding a retrospective of his work. Not good, Ned. Not good at all. Some of the "Hello, Hungary" stuff he's been pushing out on the radio. It's been said before. They've found one passage makes a perfect fit with an article published in *Der Monat* back in '48. The original writer recognised his own words soon as he heard them on the air and flipped.' He helped himself liberally to ketchup. 'Could be any day now we haul him in for a full and frank exchange.'

'Probably going through a bad patch,' I said.

'Fifteen years is a long bad patch, Ned.'

'Is he aware you're checking on him?'

'In Radio Free Europe, Ned? Among Hungarians? *Gossip?* You must be joking.'

I could no longer contain my anxiety. 'But why has nobody warned London? Why haven't *you?*'

'Understand we did, Ned. Understand the message fell on pretty deaf ears. Bad time for you boys. Don't we know it.'

By now the momentous force of his news had got through to me. If the Professor was cheating with his broadcasts, whom else might he not be cheating?

'Milt, can I ask you a silly question?'

'Be my guest, Ned.'

'Has Teodor *ever* done good work for you? In all his time? Secret work? Very secret work, even?'

Wagner pondered this, determined to give the Professor the benefit of the doubt. 'Can't say he has, Ned. We did consider using him as an intermediary for one of our big fish one time, but we kind of didn't like the old man's manners.'

'Can I believe that?'

'Would I ever lie to you, Ned?'

So much for the fantastic work he's doing for the Americans, I thought. So much for the years of loyal service nobody can quite recall.

I signalled Toby straight away. I wasted time drafting different texts because my anger kept getting in the way. I understood only too well now why the Americans were refusing to give the Professor his passport, and why he had turned to us for one instead. I understood his air of last things, his listlessness, his lack of urgency: he was waiting to be sacked. I repeated Wagner's information and asked whether it was known to Head Office. If not, the Cousins were in default of their sharing agreement with us. If, on the other hand, the Cousins *had* warned us, why hadn't I been warned too?

Next morning I had Toby's slippery reply. It took a regal tone. I suspected he had got somebody to write it for him, for it was accent-free. The Cousins had given London a 'non-specific warning' he explained, that the Professor might be facing 'disciplinary enquiries at some future date on the subject of his broadcasts.' Head Office – by which I suspected he meant himself – had 'adopted the view' that the Professor's relationship with his American employers was not of direct concern to the Circus. Head Office also 'took the point' – who but Toby could have made it? – that with so much operational work to occupy him, the Professor could be excused for any 'small defects' in his cover work. If another cover job had to be found for the Professor, Head Office would 'take steps at the appropriate time.' One solution would be to place him with one of the tame magazines to which he was already an occasional contributor. But that was for the future. The Professor had fallen foul of his employers before, Toby reminded me, and he had ridden out the storm. This was true. A woman secretary had complained of his advances, and elements of the Hungarian community had taken exception to his anti-Semitic views.

For the rest, Toby advised me to cool down, bide my time, and – always a maxim of Toby's – act as if nothing had happened. Which was how matters stood one week and twelve hours later when the Professor telephoned me at ten at night, using the emergency wordcode and asking me in a strangled but imperious voice to come round to his house immediately, entering by way of the garden door.

My first thought was that he had killed someone, possibly his wife. I could not have been more wrong.

The Professor opened the back door, and closed it swiftly after me. The lights inside the house were dimmed. Somewhere in the gloom, a Biedermeier grandfather clock ticked like a big old bomb. At the entrance to the living room stood Helena, her hands to her mouth, smothering a scream. Twenty minutes had passed since Teodor's call, but the scream still seemed to be on the point of coming out of her.

Two armchairs stood before a dying fire. One was empty. I took it to be the Professor's. In the other, somewhat obscured from my line of sight, sat a silky, rounded man of forty, with a cap of soft black hair, and twinkling round eyes that said we were all friends, weren't we? His winged chair was high-backed and he had fitted himself into the angle of it like an aircraft passenger prepared for landing. His rather circular shoes stopped short of the floor, and it occurred to me they were East European shoes: marbled, of an uncertain leather, with moulded, heavy-treaded soles. His hairy brown suit was like a remodelled military uniform. Before him stood a table with a pot of mauve hyacinths on it, and beside the hyacinths lay a display of objects which I recognised as the instruments of silent killing: two garottes made of wooden toggles and lengths of piano wire; a screwdriver so sharpened that it was a stiletto; a Charter Arms .38 Undercover revolver with a five-shot cylinder, together with two kinds of bullet, six soft-nosed, and six rifled, with congealed powder squashed into the grooves.

'It is cyanide,' the Professor explained, in answer to my silent perplexity. 'It is an invention of the Devil. The bullet has only to graze the victim to destroy him utterly.'

I found myself wondering how the poisonous powder was supposed to survive the intense heat of a gun barrel.

'This gentleman is named Ladislaus Kaldor,' the Professor continued. 'He was sent by the Hungarian secret police to kill us. He is a friend. Kindly sit down, Herr Ned.'

With ceremony, Ladislaus Kaldor rose from his chair and pumped my hand as if we had concluded a profitable deal.

'Sir!' he cried happily, in English. 'Latzi. I am sorry, sir. Don't worry anything. Everybody call me Latzi. Herr Doktor. My friend. Please sit down. Yes.'

I remember how the scent of the hyacinths seemed to go so nicely with his smile. It was only slowly I began to realise I had no sense of danger. Some people convey danger all the time; others put it on when they are angry or threatened. But Latzi, when I was able to consult my instincts, conveyed only an enormous will to please. Which perhaps is all you need if you're a professional killer.

I did not sit down. A chorus of conflicting feelings was yelling in my head, but fatigue was not among them. The empty coffee cups, I was thinking. The empty plates with cake crumbs. Who eats cake and drinks coffee when his life is being threatened? Latzi was sitting again, smiling like a conjuror. The Professor and his wife were studying my face, but from different places in the room. They've quarrelled, I thought; crisis has driven them to their separate corners. An American revolver, I thought. But not the spare cylinder that serious players customarily carried. East European shoes, and with soles that leave a perfect print on every carpet or polished floor. Cyanide bullets that would burn off their cyanide in the barrel.

'How long's he been here?' I asked the Professor.

He shrugged. I hated his shrugs. 'One hour. Less.'

'More than one hour,' Helena contradicted him. Her indignant gaze was fixed upon me. Until tonight she had made a point of ignoring me, slipping past me like a ghost, smiling or scowling at the ground to show her disapproval. Suddenly she needed my support. 'He rang the bell at eight-forty-five exactly. I was listening to the radio. The programme changed.'

I glanced at Latzi. 'You speak German?'

'*Jawohl*, Herr Doktor!'

Back to Helena. 'Which programme?'

'The BBC World Service,' she said.

I went to the radio and switched it on. A reedy Oxford academic of unknown gender was bleating about Keats. Thank you, BBC. I switched it off.

'He rang the bell – who answered it?' I said.

'I did,' said the Professor.

'He did,' said Helena.

'Please,' said Latzi.

'And then?'

'He was standing on the doorstep, wearing a coat,' said the Professor.

'A raincoat,' Helena corrected him.

'He asked if I was Professor Teodor, I said yes. He gave his name, he said "Forgive me, Professor, I have come to kill you with a garotte or cyanide bullet but I do not wish to, I am your disciple and admirer. I wish to surrender to you and remain in the West." '

'He spoke Hungarian?' I asked.

'Naturally.'

'So you invited him in?'

'Naturally.'

Helena did not agree. 'No! First Teodor asked for *me*,' she insisted. I had not heard her correct her husband before tonight. Now she had done so twice in as many minutes. 'He calls to me and says, "Helena, we have a guest." I say, "Good." Then he asks Latzi into the house. I take his raincoat, I hang it in the hall, I make coffee. That is how it happened exactly.'

'And cake,' I said. 'You made cake.'

'The cake was made already.'

'Were you afraid?' I asked – for fear, like danger, was something else that was missing.

'I was disgusted, I was shocked,' she replied. 'Now I am afraid – yes, I am very afraid. We are all afraid.'

'And you?' I said to the Professor.

He shrugged again, as if to say I was the last man on earth to whom he would confide his feelings.

'Why don't you take your wife to the study?' I said.

He was disposed to argue, then changed his mind. Strangers arm in arm, they marched from the room.

I was alone with Latzi. I stood, he sat. Munich can be a very silent city. Even in repose his face smiled at me ingratiatingly. His small eyes still twinkled, but there was nothing I could read in them. He gave me a nod of encouragement, his smile broadened. He said 'Please,' and eased himself more comfortably into his chair. I made the gesture every Middle European understands. I held out my hand, palm upward, and passed my thumb across the tip of my forefinger. Still smiling, he rummaged in his inside jacket pocket and handed me his papers. They were in the name of Egon Braubach of Passau, born 1933, occupation artist. I never saw anyone who looked less like a Bavarian artist. They comprised one West German passport, one driver's licence and one social security document. None of them, it seemed to me, carried the least conviction. Neither did his shoes.

'When did you enter Germany?'

'This afternoon, Herr Doktor, this afternoon at five. Please.'

'Where from?'

'Vienna, please. Vienna,' he repeated, in a breathless rush, as if making me a gift of the entire city, and gave another wriggling motion of his rump, apparently to achieve greater subservience. 'I caught the first train to Munich this morning, Herr Doktor.'

'At what time?'

'At eight o'clock, sir. The eight-o'clock train.'

'When did you enter Austria?'

'Yesterday, Herr Doktor. It was raining. Please.'

'Which papers did you present at the Austrian border?'

'My Hungarian passport, Your Excellency. In Vienna I was given German papers.'

Sweat was forming on his upper lip. His German was fluent but unmistakably Balkan. He had travelled by train, he said: Budapest, Györ,

Vienna, Herr Doktor. His masters had given him a cold chicken and a bottle of wine for the journey. With best pickles, Your Honour, and paprika. More smiles. Arriving in Vienna, he had checked in at the Altes Kaiserreich Hotel, near the railway station, where a room had been reserved for him. A humble room, a humble hotel, Your Excellency, but I am a humble man. It was at the hotel, late at night, that he was visited by a Hungarian gentleman whom he had not seen before – 'But I suspect he was a diplomat, Herr Doktor. He was distinguished like yourself!' This gentleman gave him his money and documents, he explained – and the arsenal that lay before us on the table.

'Where are you staying in Munich?'

'It is a modest guesthouse on the edge of town, Herr Doktor,' he replied, with an apologetic smile. 'More a brothel. Yes, a brothel. One sees many men there, coming and going all the time.' He told me its name, and I had half a notion he was going to recommend a girl as well.

'Did they tell you to stay there?'

'For the discretion, Herr Doktor. The anonymity. Please.'

'Do you have luggage there?'

He gave the poor man's shrug, quite unlike the Professor's. 'A toothbrush,' he said. 'Some clothes. A bag, sir. Modest materials.'

In Hungary he was by vocation an agricultural journalist, he said, but he had made himself a second living working for the secret police, first as an informer, and more recently, for the money, as assassin. He had performed certain duties inside Hungary but preferred – forgive him, Excellency – not to say what these were until he was assured he would not be prosecuted in the West. The Professor was his first 'foreign duty,' but the thought of killing him had offended his sense of decorum.

'The Professor is a man of format, Herr Doktor! Of reputation! He is not some Jew or priest! Why should I kill this man? I'm a respectable human being, good heavens! I have my honour! Please!'

'Tell me your orders.'

They were not complicated. He was to ring the Herr Professor's doorbell, they had said – so he had rung it. The Professor was sure to be at home, since on Wednesdays he gave private tuition until nine, they had said. – The Professor was indeed at home. – He should describe himself as a friend of Pali from Debrecen. – He had taken the liberty not to describe himself in these terms. – Once inside the house, he should kill the Herr Professor by whatever means seemed appropriate, but preferably the garotte, since it was sure and silent, though there was always a regrettable danger of decapitation. He should kill Helena also, they said – perhaps kill her first, depending on who opened the door to him, they were not particular. It was for this contingency that he had brought a second garotte. With a garotte, Herr Doktor, he explained helpfully, one could never be sure of being able to disentangle the instrument after use. He should then telephone a number in Bonn, ask for Peter, and report that

'Susi will be staying with friends tonight' – Susi being the Professor's codename for the operation, Excellency. This was the signal for success, though in the present circumstance, Herr Doktor, it must be admitted that he had not been successful. Giggle.

'Telephone from here?' I asked.

'From this house, exactly. To Peter. Please. They are violent men, Herr Doktor. They threaten my family. I have no choice, naturally. I have a daughter. They gave me strict instructions: "From the Professor's house you will telephone Peter." '

This also surprised me. Since the Professor was identified to the Hungarian secret police as a Western asset – and had been for fifteen years – one might suppose they would be suspicious of his telephone.

'What do you do if you've failed?' I asked.

'If the duty cannot be fulfilled – if the Herr Professor has guests, or is for some reason not available – I am to ring from a phone box and say that Susi is on her way home.'

'From any particular phone box?'

'All phone boxes are suitable, Herr Doktor, in the event of a non-completion. Peter may then give further instructions, he may not. If not, I return at once to Budapest. Alternatively, Peter may say, "Try again tomorrow," or he may say, "Try in two days." It is all in the hands of Peter in this case.'

'What is the Bonn telephone number?'

He recited it.

'Turn out your pockets.'

A khaki handkerchief, some badly printed family snaps, including some of a young girl, presumably his daughter, three East European condoms, an open packet of Russian cigarettes, a wobbly tin penknife of obvious Eastern manufacture, a stub of unpainted pencil, 960 West German marks, some small change. The return half of a second-class rail ticket, Vienna – Munich – Vienna. I never in my life saw such miserably assembled pockets. Did the Hungarian Service have no despatchers? Checkers? What the Devil were they thinking of?

'And your raincoat,' I said, and watched him fetch it from the hall. It was brand-new. The pockets were empty. It was of Austrian manufacture and good quality. It must have cost serious Western money.

'Did you buy this in Vienna?'

'*Jawohl*, Herr Doktor. It was raining cats and dogs and I had no protection.'

'When?'

'Please?'

'What with?'

'Please?'

I discovered he could anger me quite quickly. 'You caught the first train this morning, right? It left Vienna before the shops opened, right? You didn't get your money till late last night when the Hungarian diplomat visited you. So when did you buy the coat and what did you use for money? Or did you steal it? Is that the answer?'

First he frowned; then he laughed indulgently at my breach of good manners. It was clear that he forgave me. He opened his hands to me in generosity. 'But I bought it last night, Herr Doktor! When I arrived at the station! With my personal *Valuten* that I brought with me from Hungary for shopping, naturally! I am not a liar! Please!'

'Did you keep the receipt?'

He shook his head sagely, advice to a younger man. 'To keep receipts, Herr Doktor? I give you this advice. To keep receipts is to invite questions about where you get your money. A receipt – it's like a spy in the pocket. Please.'

Too many excuses, I thought, releasing myself from the brilliance of his smile. Too many answers in one paragraph. All my instincts told me to trust nobody and nothing about the story that was being told me. It was not so much the sloppiness of the assassination plan that strained my credulity – the implausible documents, the contents of the pockets, the shoes – not even the basic improbability of the mission. I had seen enough of low-level Soviet satellite operations to regard such amateurishness as the norm. What disturbed me about these people was the unreality of their behaviour in my company, the feeling there was one story for me and one for them; that I had been brought here to perform a function, and the collective will required me to shut up and get on with it.

Yet at the same time I was trapped. I had no choice, and no time, but to take everything they had told me at face value. I was in the position of a doctor who, while suspecting a patient of malingering, has no option but to treat his symptoms. By the laws of the game, Latzi was a prize. It was not every day that a Hungarian assassin offered to defect to the West, no matter how incompetent he was. By the same token, the man was in considerable danger, since it was unthinkable that an assassination operation of this consequence could be launched without separate surveillance.

When in doubt, says the handbook, take the operational line. Were they watching the house? It was necessary to assume so, though it was not an easy house to watch, which was what had commended it to Teodor's handlers fifteen years ago. It stood at the end of a leafy cul-de-sac and backed on to the river. The way into the garden led along a deserted towpath. But the front porch was visible to anybody passing by, and Latzi could have already been observed entering it.

I went upstairs and from the landing window surveyed the road. The neighbouring houses were in darkness. I saw no sign of stray cars or people. My own car was parked in the next sidestreet, close to the river. I returned to the drawing room. The telephone was on the bookcase. I handed Latzi the receiver and watched him dial the number in Bonn. His hands were girlish and moist. Obligingly, he tilted the earpiece in my direction, and himself with it. He smelt of old blanket and Russian tobacco. The phone rang out, I heard a man's voice, very grumpy, speaking German. For somebody awaiting news of a killing, I thought, you're doing a good job of pretending you aren't.

A thick accent, presumably Hungarian: 'Hullo? Yes? Who is it?'

I nodded to Latzi to go ahead.

'Good evening, sir. I wish, please to speak to Mr. Peter.'

'What about?'

'Is this Mr. Peter, please? It is a private matter.'

'What do you want?'

'Is this Peter?'

'My name is Peter!'

'It is regarding Susi, Mr. Peter,' Latzi explained, with a sideways wink at me. 'Susi will not be coming home tonight, Mr. Peter. She will be staying with friends, I am afraid. Good friends. She will be looked after. Good night, Mr. Peter.'

He was about to replace the receiver, but I stayed his hand long enough to hear a growl of contempt or incomprehension the other end before he rang off.

Latzi smiled at me, very pleased with himself. 'He plays it well, Herr Doktor. A true professional, I would say. A fine actor, you agree?'

'Did you recognise the voice?'

'No, Herr Doktor. Alas, the voice is not familiar to me.'

I shoved open the study door. The Professor sat at his desk, his fists in front of him. Helena sat on the tutorial sofa. I felt a need to acquaint the Professor with my scepticism. I stepped into the room, closing the door behind me.

'The man Latzi, as you call him, is a criminal,' I said. 'Either he's some kind of confidence trickster, or he's a self-confessed murderer who came to Germany on false papers in order to kill you and your wife. Either way, you're within your rights to turn him over to the West German police and be done with him. Do you want to do that? Or do you want to leave the decisions to us? Which?'

To my surprise, he appeared for the first time that evening genuinely alarmed. Perhaps he had not expected to be challenged. Perhaps the proximity of his own death had dawned on him. Either way, I had the impression he was attaching more importance to my question than I understood. Helena had turned her eyes away from me and was watching him also. Critically. A woman waiting to be paid.

'Do whatever you must do,' he muttered.

'Then you must do as I ask. Both of you.'

'We are cooperative. We shall be – yes, cooperative. We have been – cooperative – for many years. Too many.'

I glanced at Helena.

'It will be my husband's responsibility,' she said.

I had no time to ponder the mysteries of this ominous statement. 'Then please put together some night things and be ready at the garden door in five minutes,' I said, and returned to the drawing room and Latzi.

I think he had been standing at the door, for he stepped quickly back as I entered, then clasped his hands to his chin and beamed at me, asking what was *gefällig* – what was my pleasure?

'Have you ever seen the Professor before tonight?'

'No, sir. Only photographs. One would admire him anywhere. A true aristocrat.'

'And his wife?'

'She is known to me, sir. Naturally.'

'How?'

'She was once an actress, Herr Doktor, one of the best in Budapest.'

'And you saw her on the stage?'

Another pause. 'No, sir.'

'Then where did you see her?'

He was trying to read me. I had the impression he was wondering whether she might have told me something, and he was trimming his answers accordingly.

'Theatre bills, Your Excellency. When she was young, her famous face was on every street corner. All young men loved her – I was no exception.'

'Where else?'

He saw that I had nothing. And I saw that he saw. 'So sad about a woman's looks, Herr Doktor. A man, he can remain impressive until he is eighty. A woman – ' he sighed.

I let him pack together his weapons, then took possession of them. I loaded the soft-nosed bullets into the revolver. As I did so, a thought occurred to me.

'When I walked in here, the cylinder was empty and the bullets were spread on the table.'

'Correct, Excellency.'

'When did you take the bullets out of the cylinder?' I asked.

'Before entering the house. So that I could demonstrate my peaceful intentions. Naturally.'

'Naturally.'

As we moved to the hall, I shoved the revolver into my waistband.

'If you take it into your head to run away, I shall shoot you in the back,' I explained to him, and had the satisfaction of seeing his little eyes swivel in alarm. Professional assassins, it seemed, did not take kindly to their own medicine.

I tossed him his raincoat and glanced round the room for other traces of him. There were none. I ordered silence and led the three of them into the garden and along the tow-path to my car. A famous actress, I thought, and not a word about it on the file. I put the Professor and Helena in the back, and Latzi in the front beside me. Then we sat still for five minutes while I waited for the slightest sign that we were being watched. Nothing. I drove as far as the main road and stopped again. Nothing. It was by now midnight and a new moon had risen among the stars. I circled the town, keeping a watch on my mirror, then took the autobahn south-west to the Starnbergersee, where we kept a safe house for briefing and debriefing joes in passage. It lay close to the lake's edge and was manned by two murderous long-haired wonders left over from London Station's Lamplighters Section. They were called Jeffrey and Arnold. Arnold was hovering in the doorway by the time we reached it. One hand was in the pocket of his kaftan. The other hung threateningly to his side.

'It's me, you buffoon,' I said softly.

Jeffrey showed the Professor and his wife to their bedroom while Arnold sat with Latzi in the drawing room. I went down the garden to the boathouse, where I was at last able to talk to Toby Esterhase on the safe telephone. He was amazingly composed. It was as if he had been expecting my call.

Toby arrived in Munich on the first flight from London next morning, wearing a beaver-lamb coat and a leather Trilby hat, and looking more the impresario than the beleaguered spy.

'Nedike, my God!' he cried, embracing me like a prodigal father. 'Listen, you look fantastic, I would say. Congratulations, okay? Nothing like a little excitement to bring the blooms to your cheeks. How's Mabel, actually? A marriage, that's something you got to water, same as a flower.'

I drove slowly and spoke, as best I could, dispassionately, giving him the fruits of my researches throughout the long night. I wanted him to know everything I knew by the time we reached the lake house.

Neither the Americans nor the West Germans had any trace of Latzi, I said. Neither, I gathered from Toby, had London.

'Latzi, that's an unwritten page, Ned. Totally,' Toby agreed, surveying the passing landscape with every sign of approval.

There was also no trace of his Bavarian covername, or of any of the covernames that Latzi claimed to have used on his 'duties' inside Hungary, I said.

Toby lowered his window to enjoy the fragrance of the fields.

Latzi's West German passport was a fake, I continued with determination, one of a batch recently run up by a low-grade forger in Vienna and sold on the private market.

Toby was mildly indignant. 'I mean who buys that crap, for God's sake?' he protested, as we passed a pair of palomino horses grazing in a paddock. 'With passports, these days, you get what you pay for actually. What you get for crap like that, it's six months in a stinking gaol.' And he shook his head sadly like a man whose warnings go unheeded until it's too late.

I blundered on. The phone number in Bonn belonged to the Hungarian military attaché, I said, whose first name was indeed listed as Peter. He was an identified Hungarian Intelligence officer. I allowed myself a restrained irony:

'That's a new one for us, isn't it, Tobe? A spy using his own name as a covername? I mean why bother any more? You're Toby, so we'll keep it a secret and call you Toby instead. Great.'

But Toby was too set on enjoying his day in Bavaria to be disturbed by the implications of my words. 'Nedike, believe me, those army guys, they're total idiots. Hungarian military intelligence, that's the same as Hungarian military music, know what I mean? They blow it out their arses actually.'

I continued my recitation. West German Security had a permanent tap running on the Hungarian attaché's telephone, I said. A cassette of Latzi's conversation with Peter was on its way to my office. From what I understood, it offered no surprises except to underline that Peter appeared genuinely unprepared for the call. Peter had neither made nor received further calls last night, I said, nor had there been any burst of diplomatic signals traffic from the roof of the Hungarian Embassy in Bonn. Peter had, however, complained to the Protocol Department of the West German Foreign Office about telephone harassment on his home line. This was not, I suggested, the act of a conspirator. Toby was less sure.

'Could be one thing, Ned, could be the other,' he said, leaning back in his seat and languidly tilting the flat of his hand both ways. 'A man thinks he's been compromised? So maybe it's not so stupid he makes a formal complaint once, brushes over his traces – why not?'

I gave him the rest. I was determined to. Latzi's description of the putative diplomat in Vienna tallied with that of one Leo Bakocs, Commercial Secretary and, like Peter, an identified Hungarian Intelligence officer, I said. Cousin Wagner was getting hold of a photograph for us to show to Latzi later in the day.

The name Bakocs brought a fond smile to Toby's lips. 'They drag *Leo* in on this? Listen, Leo's so vain he spies only on duchesses.' He laughed in jolly disbelief. 'Leo in some lousy hotel, handing over garottes to a smelly assassin? Tell me another, Ned. I mean.'

'It isn't me who's telling you,' I said. 'It's Latzi.'

Lastly, I said, I had despatched Jeffrey to the Munich whorehouse to pay Latzi's bill and collect his overnight bag. The only article of interest in his luggage was a set of pornographic photographs.

'It's the tension, Ned,' Toby explained magnanimously. 'In a foreign country, killing somebody you don't know, you need a little private company – know what I mean?'

In return, Toby had brought me nothing whatever, private or otherwise. I had imagined him on the phone all night, and perhaps he had been. But not in support of my enquiries.

'Maybe we have a party tonight,' he proposed. 'Harry Palfrey of Legal Department is coming over with a couple of guys from the Foreign Office. That's a nice fellow, Harry. Very English.'

I was bewildered. 'What branch of the Foreign Office?' I said. 'Who? Why Palfrey?'

But as Toby would say, questions are never dangerous until you answer them. We arrived at the lake house to find Arnold cooking eggs and bacon. The Professor and Latzi sat at one end of the table. Helena, a vegetarian, sat at the other, eating a nut bar from her handbag.

Arnold was blond and lank. His hair was done in a knot at the back. 'They had a bit of a dingdong, Ned,' he confided to me disapprovingly while Toby fell about the Professor's neck. 'The Professor and his missus, a real dogfight. I don't know who started it or what it was about, I wouldn't ask.'

'Did Latzi join in?'

'He was going to, Ned, but I told him to keep quiet. I don't like a man who comes between husband and wife, I never did.'

In retrospect, our discussions that day resemble an intricate minuet, beginning in our humble kitchen and ending in the courts of the Almighty Himself – more precisely in the beflagged conference room of the American Consulate General, where the inspiring features of President Nixon and Vice President Agnew smiled favourably on our endeavours.

For Toby, as I soon realised, far from doing nothing, had laid on an entire programme for himself, which he advanced from stage to stage with the dexterity of a ringmaster: In the kitchen, he listened to the whole story over again from Latzi and the Professor, while Helena chewed her nut bar. I had never seen Toby in full Hungarian flight before and found time to marvel at the transformation. With one sentence he had flung aside the unnatural corset of his Anglo-Saxon restraint and was back among his people. His eyes caught fire. He preened, and his back arched as if he were sitting on a parade horse.

'Ned, they say you have been quite fantastic actually,' he called to me down the table in the midst of all this. 'A tower of strength, they are saying, completely. I think maybe they will recommend you a Nobel prize!'

'Tell them to make it an Oscar, I'll accept,' I said sourly, and took myself for a walk down to the lakeside to recover my temper.

I returned to the house to find Toby and the Professor closeted in the drawing room, talking volubly. Toby's high respect for the Professor seemed, if anything, to have increased. Latzi was helping Arnold with the washing-up and they were both sniggering. Latzi had evidently been telling a dirty joke. Helena was nowhere to be seen. Next, it was Latzi's turn to sit alone with Toby, while the Professor and his wife walked uneasily at the lakeside, pausing every few steps to remonstrate with each other, until the Professor turned on his heel and strode back to the house.

Seizing the moment, I slipped out and joined Helena. Her lips were pursed and her face was sickly-white – whether from fear, anger or fatigue, I couldn't tell. When she spoke, she had to stop and begin again before the words would come.

'He is a *liar*,' she said. 'It is all lies! Lie, lie! He is a liar!'

'Who *is?*'

'They are *both* liars. From the day of birth, they *lie*. On their deathbeds, they *lie*.'

'So what's the truth?' I said.

'*Wait* is the truth!'

'Wait for what?'

'I have warned him. "If you do this, I shall tell the English." So we wait. If he does it, I shall tell you. If he repents, I shall spare him. I am his wife.'

She walked to the house, a stately woman. As she entered it, a black limousine pulled up in the drive and Harry Palfrey, the Circus legal adviser, emerged, accompanied by two other members of the English governing classes. I recognised the taller of them as Alan Barnaby, luminary of the Foreign Office's misnomered Information and Research Department, which traded in Communist counter propaganda at its sleaziest. Toby was shaking him warmly by the hand while with his other he beckoned me to join them. We went indoors and sat down.

At first I smouldered in silence. The players had been sent upstairs. Toby was doing the talking, the others listened to him with the special reverence their kind reserves for paupers or black men. I even found myself feeling a little protective of him – of Toby Esterhase, God help me, who protected no one but himself!

'What we are dealing with here, Alan, without talking out of turn actually, is a completely top source who is now expended,' Toby explained. 'A great joe, but his day is over.'

'You mean the Prof,' Barnaby said helpfully.

'They are on to him. They know his value too well. From certain clues I have obtained from Latzi, it's clear the Hungarians have a fat dossier on the Professor's operations. After all, I mean, why would they try to kill a fellow who is no use to us? A Hungarian assassination attempt – that's a *Good Housekeeping* certificate for the target, I would say.'

'We can't be responsible for the Professor's safety indefinitely,' Palfrey cautioned us with his loser's smile. 'We can give him protection for a bit, naturally. But we can't accept a life interest in him. He has to know that. We may have to get him to sign something just to make the point.'

The second Foreign Office man was round and shiny with a chain across his waistcoat. I had a childish urge to pull it and see if he squealed.

'Well, *I* think we may all be talking too much,' he said silkily. 'If the

Americans agree to take the pair of 'em off our hands, the Prof and his missus, we shan't have to worry, shall we? Best keep our heads down and our powder dry, what?'

Palfrey demurred. 'He should still sign a release for us, Norman. He has rather been playing us off against the Cousins in the last few years.'

Ever the protector of his own, Toby gave a knowing smile. 'All the best joes do this, I would say, Harry. One hand washes the other, even at Teodor's level. The question is, now that he is no longer usable, what have we got to lose except trouble actually? I mean, I am not the expert here,' he added, with an ingratiating smile at Barnaby.

'What about the assassin fellow?' said the man called Norman. 'Will he play ball as well? Bloody dangerous, isn't it, sitting up there like a duck in a tree?'

'Latzi is flexible,' said Toby. 'He is scared, he is also a complete patriot.' I would not have backed him on either of these points, but I was too sickened to interrupt. 'These *apparatchiks* when they step out of the system, they are in shock. Latzi is coping with it. He agonises over his family, but he is reconciled. If Teodor accepts, Latzi will accept also. With guarantees, naturally.'

'What sort of guarantees?' said the shiny Foreign Office man, so quickly that not even Harry Palfrey got in ahead of him.

Toby did not falter. 'Well, naturally the usual. Latzi and Teodor don't want to be thrown on to the rubbish heap when this one's over, I would say. Nor does Helena. American passports, a good bit of money at the end of the road, assistance and protection – I mean, that's basic so to speak.'

'The whole thing's a con,' I blurted. I had had enough.

Everybody was smiling at me. They would have smiled whatever I had said. They were that sort of crowd. If I had said I was a Hungarian double agent, they would have smiled. If I had said I was Adolf Hitler's reincarnated younger brother, they would have smiled. All but Toby, that is, whose face had acquired the lifelessness of someone who knows that all he can safely be at this moment is nobody at all.

'Now why on earth do you say that, Ned?' Barnaby was asking, awfully interested.

'Latzi's not a trained killer,' I said. 'I don't know what he is, but he isn't a killer. He was carrying an unloaded gun. No professional in his right mind does that. He's posing as a Bavarian artist, but he's wearing Hungarian clothes and half the junk in his pockets is Hungarian. I was standing over him when he made his phone call to Bonn. Fine, the attaché's first name is Peter. It's in the diplomatic list as Peter. Peter wasn't expecting that call in a month of Sundays. Latzi laid it on him. Listen to the German tape of their conversation.'

'Then what about the chap in Vienna, Ned?' said Barnaby, still determined to patronise me. 'The chap who gave him his money and his hardware? Eh? Eh?'

'They never met. We showed Latzi the photograph and he was delighted. 'That's the man,' he said. Oh sure: he'd seen a photograph somewhere else. Ask Helena, she knows. She's not telling at the moment, but if we put pressure on her, I'm sure she will.'

Toby came briefly alive. 'Pressure, Ned? Helena? Pressure, that's something you use when you know you can squeeze harder than the other fellow. That woman is crazy about her husband. She defends him to the grave actually.'

'The Professor's fallen foul of the Americans,' I said. 'They're rolling up his red carpet. He's desperate. If he didn't set up the assassination himself, Latzi did. The whole ploy is a device for him to cut his losses and make a new life.'

They waited for me to continue, all of them. It was as if they were waiting for the punchline. Finally Toby spoke. He had rediscovered his form.

'Nedike, how long since you slept actually?' he asked with an indulgent smile. 'Tell us, please.'

'What's that got to do with it?'

Toby was ostentatiously studying his watch. 'I think you have been now thirty hours without sleep, Ned. You took some pretty damn big decisions in that time – all good ones, I would say. I don't think we can blame you for having a bit of a reaction.'

It was as if I had never spoken. All heads had turned back to Toby.

'Well, *I* think it's rather important we take a peek at the cast,' Barnaby was saying as I headed for the door. 'Can we whistle them down, Toby? Question of how they'll shape up under the spotlights.'

'I think there's news value in doing this thing straight away, Barnaby,' Palfrey was saying, as I headed for the garden and sanity. 'Strike while the iron is hot. With me?'

'With you all the way, Harry. Hundred percent.'

I refused to be present for the first audition. I sulked in the kitchen and let Arnold minister to me while I pretended to listen to some story about his mother walking out on the fellow she'd been with for twenty years and shacking up with her childhood sweetheart. I watched Toby skip upstairs to fetch his champions, and scowled when the three men descended some minutes later, Latzi with his black hair slicked into a parting, the Professor with his jacket outside his shoulders, his seer's head struck forward in contemplation and his white mane flowing becomingly.

Then Helena came into the kitchen with tears streaming down her cheeks, so Arnold gave her a hug and fetched a blanket for her, because the spring morning was crisp and she was shivering. Then Arnold made her a camomile tea, and sat with his arm round her till Toby bustled in to say we were all expected at the American Consulate in two hours.

'Russell Sheriton is flying in from London, Pete de May from Bonn. They are mustard for it, Ned. Totally mustard. Washington throws its cap in the air, completely.' I do not recall whether Pete de May was grander than Sheriton or less grand. But grand enough. 'Ned, that Teodor's fantastic,' Toby assured me privately.

'Really? In what way?'

'You know what they told him? "What you are doing is damn risky, Professor. Do you think you can handle it?" You know what he replied? "Mr. Ambassador, risks are what we all take to protect civilised society." He's quiet, he's dignified. Latzi too. Ned, after this you get some sleep, okay? I phone Mabel.'

We rode in two cars, Toby with the Hungarians, myself with Palfrey and the Foreign Office. Opening the car door for me, Palfrey touched my arm and offered me some steel-edged advice. 'I think from now on, it's all hands pulling together, Ned. Tired is one thing. Talk about con-tricks is something else. Yes? Agreed?'

We must have numbered twenty head. The Consul General presided. He was a pallid mid-Westerner, an ex-lawyer like Palfrey, and kept talking anxiously about 'reprocussions.' Milton Wagner was seated between Sheriton and de May. It was clear to me that, whatever their private thoughts, Sheriton and Wagner had orders to keep their scepticism to themselves. Perhaps they too had recognised that there were worse ways of getting rid of useless agents than off-loading them onto the U.S. Information Services, who were represented by a quartet of troubled believers whose names I never learned.

Pullach was spoken for, naturally. Though not involved, they had sent their own observer, so we could be confident that our determinations would be the gossip of Potsdam by afternoon. They also insisted on making a voluble complaint about Vienna. It seemed that Pullach had a running battle with the Austrian police about forged passports, and suspected them of selling them to the Hungarians. Quite a lot of the meeting was taken up by an Oberst von-und-zu somewhere or other moaning about Austrian duplicity.

The three champions did not, of course, attend our deliberations, but sat in the waiting room. When sandwiches were passed round, a generous plate was sent out to them. And when they were finally called in, several of the lay members of the meeting broke into applause, which must have been the first of many times from then on when they heard the roar of the greasepaint.

But it was Helena's tears that stole the show. The Professor said his few words, and his halting dignity worked its predictable magic. Latzi followed him, and a cold chill fell over the room as he explained why he had carried the two garottes, which were then passed gingerly round the table with the rest of the exhibits. But when Helena stepped forward on the Professor's arm, I felt a lump rise to my throat, and knew that everyone in the room was feeling the same.

'I support my husband,' was all the great actress could declaim.

But it was enough to bring the room to its feet.

It was late evening before I managed to speak to her alone. We were washed out by then; even the irrepressible Latzi was exhausted. The captains and the kings had departed, Toby had departed. I was sitting with Arnold in the drawing room of the lake house. An American van, with blackened windows and two plainclothes marines aboard, was waiting in the drive, but our stars were learning to keep their public waiting. The day had been spent preparing afternoon press announcements and signing Palfrey's releases, which he turned out to have brought with him in his briefcase.

She entered hesitantly, as if she expected me to strike her, but the anger had been drained out of me.

'We shall get our passports,' she said, sitting down. 'It is the new world.'

Arnold slipped tactfully from the room, closing the door behind him.

'Who's Latzi?' I said.

'He is a friend of Teodor.'

'What else is he?'

'He is an actor. A bad, oh a *bad* actor from Debrecen.'

'Did he ever work for the secret police?'

She made a gesture of deprecation. 'He had connections. When Teodor needed to arrange himself with the authorities, Latzi was the go-between.'

'You mean, when Teodor needed to inform on his students?'

'Yes.'

'Did Latzi supply Teodor with his information while you were in Munich?'

'At first only a little. But when none came from other sources, more. Then much more. Latzi prepared the material for Teodor. Teodor sold it to the British and Americans. Otherwise we would have had no money.'

'Was Latzi getting help from the secret police to do this?'

'It was private. Things are changing in Hungary. It is no longer prudent to be involved with the authorities.'

I unlocked the door and watched her make her exit, head erect.

A few weeks later, back in London, I faced Toby with her story. He was neither surprised nor contrite.

'Women, Ned, that's a criminal class actually. Better we eat the soup, not stir it.'

A few weeks more and the Teodor-Latzi show was riding high. So was Toby. How much was he a part of it? How much did he know when? The whole of it? Did he dream up the entire piece of theatre in order to make the best of his imperilled agent and get him off his hands? I have often secretly suspected that the play was a three-hander, at the least, with Helena as the reluctant audience.

'Know what, Nedike?' Toby declared, throwing an affectionate arm around my shoulder. 'If you can't ride two horses at once, you better stay out of the Circus.'

You remember the pseudonymous Colonel Weatherby in the book? The master of disguises, at ease in seven European languages? Pimpernel leader of the East European resistance fighters? The man who 'flitted back and forth across the Iron Curtain as if it were of frailest gossamer'? That was me. Ned. I didn't write that part, thank God. It was the work of some venal sports journalist from Baltimore recruited by the Cousins. Mine was the introductory pen portrait of the great man, printed under the caption 'The Real Professor Teodor as I Knew Him,' and gouged out of me by Toby and the Fifth Floor. My working title for the book was *Tricks of the Trade*, but the Fifth Floor said that might be misunderstood. They promoted me instead.

But not before I had taken my indignation to George Smiley, who had just given up his job as acting chief and was on the point of removing himself for the nearly last time to the shadows of academia. I was back in London on a mid-tour break. It was a Friday evening and I ran him to earth in Bywater Street, packing for the weekend. He heard me out, he gave a small chuckle, then a larger chuckle. He muttered, '*Oh Toby*,' affectionately under his breath.

'But then they *do* assassinate, don't they, Ned,' he objected as he laboriously folded a tweed suit. 'The Hungarians, I mean. Even by East European standards, they're one of the foulest mobs there are, surely?'

Yes, I conceded, the Hungarians killed and tortured pretty much at will. But that didn't alter the fact that Latzi was a fake and Teodor was Latzi's accomplice, and as to Toby –

Smiley cut me short. 'Now, Ned, I think you're being a little bit prissy. Every church needs its saints. The anti-Communist church is no exception. And saints as a bunch are a pretty bogus lot, when you come down to it. But no one would pretend they don't have their uses, once they get the job. Do you think this shirt will do, or must I give it another iron?'

We sat in his drawing room sipping our Scotches and listening to the clamour of party-goers in Bywater Street.

'And did the ghost of Stefanie stalk the Munich pavements for you, Ned?' Smiley enquired tenderly, just when I was beginning to wonder whether he had dozed off.

I had long ceased to marvel at his capacity to put himself in my shoes.

'Now and then,' I replied.

'But not in the flesh? How sad.'

'I once rang one of her aunts,' I said. 'I'd had some silly row with Mabel and gone to a hotel. It was late. I expect I was a bit drunk.' I found myself wondering whether Smiley already knew, and decided I was being fanciful. 'Or I *think* it was an aunt. It could have been a servant. No, it was an aunt.'

'What did she say?'

' "Fräulein Stefanie is not at home." '

A long silence, but this time I did not make the mistake of thinking he had gone to sleep.

'Young voice?' he enquired thoughtfully.

'Quite.'

'Then perhaps it was Stefanie who answered.'

'Perhaps it was.'

We listened again to the raised voices in the street. A girl was laughing. A man was cross. Somebody hooted a horn and drove away. The sounds died. Stefanie's my Ann, I thought, as I walked back across the river to Battersea, where I had kept my little flat: the difference is, I never had the courage to let her disappoint me.

7

S miley had interrupted himself – some tale of a Central American diplomat with a passion for British model railways of a certain generation, and how the Circus had bought the man's lifelong allegiance with a Hornby Double-O shunting engine stolen from a London toy museum by Monty Arbuck's team. Everyone was laughing until this sudden reflective silence, while Smiley's troubled gaze fixed itself upon some point outside the room.

'And just occasionally we meet the reality we've been playing with,' he said quietly. 'Until it happens, we're spectators. The joes live out our dreams for us, and we case officers sit safe and snug behind our one-way mirrors, telling ourselves that seeing is feeling. But when the moment of truth strikes – if it ever does for you – well, from then on we become a little more humble about what we ask people to do for us.'

He never once glanced at me as he said this. He gave no hint of who was in his mind. But I knew, and he knew. And each knew the other knew that it was Colonel Jerzy.

*

I saw him and I said nothing to Mabel. Perhaps I was too surprised. Or
perhaps the old habits of dissembling die so hard that even today my first
response at any unexpected event is to suppress the spontaneous reaction.
We were watching the nine-o'clock news on television, which for Mabel
and myself has become a kind of Evensong these days, don't ask me why.
And suddenly I saw him. Colonel Jerzy. And instead of leaping from my
chair and shouting, 'My God! Mabel! Look, that fellow in the back there!
That's Jerzy!' – which would have been the healthy reaction of any
ordinary man – I went on watching the screen and sipping my whisky and
soda. Then, as soon as I was alone, I slipped a fresh tape into the video
machine so that I could be sure of catching the repeat when it came round
on 'Newsnight.' Since when – the incident is now six weeks old – I must
have watched it a dozen more times, for there is always some extra nuance
to be relished.

But I shall leave that part of the story to the end where it belongs. Better
to give you the events in the order they occurred, for there was more to
Munich than Professor Teodor, and there was more to spying in the wake
of Bill Haydon's exposure than waiting for the wounds to heal.

Colonel Jerzy was a Pole and I have never understood why so many Poles
have a soft spot for us. Our repeated betrayals of their country have
always seemed to me so disgraceful that if I were Polish, I would spit on
every passing British shadow, whether I had suffered under the Nazis or
the Russians – the British in their time having abandoned the poor Poles
to both. And I would certainly be tempted to plant a bomb under the so-
called 'competent department' of the British Foreign Office. Dear heaven,
what a phrase! As I write, the Poles are once more squeezed between the
unpredictable Russian Bear and the rather more predictable German Ox.
But you may be quite sure that if they should ever need a good friend to
help them out, the same 'competent department' of the British Foreign
Office will send its treacly regrets and plead a more enticing function up
the road.

Nevertheless, the record of my Service boasts a disproportionate rate of
success in Poland, and an almost embarrassing number of Polish men and
women who, with reckless Polish courage, have risked their necks
and those of their families in order to spy for 'England.'

No wonder then if, in the aftermath of Haydon, the casualty rate among
our Polish networks was correspondingly high. Thanks to Haydon, the
British had added yet another betrayal to their long list. As each new loss
followed the previous one with sickening inevitability, the air of mourning
in our Munich Station became almost palpable, and our sense of shame
was compounded by our helplessness. None of us had any doubt of what
had happened. Until the Fall, Polish Security – ably led by their Chief of
Operations, Colonel Jerzy – had held Haydon's treachery close to their
chests, contenting themselves with penetrating our existing networks and

using them as channels of disinformation – or, where they succeeded in turning them, playing them back at us with skill.

But After the Fall, the Colonel felt no further need of delicacy, and in the course of a few days savagely silenced those of our loyal agents whom till then he had allowed to remain in place. 'Jerzy's hitlist,' we called it as the tally rose almost daily, and in our frustration we developed a personal hatred of the man who had murdered our beloved joes, sometimes not bothering with the formalities of a trial, but letting his interrogators have their fun until the end.

It may seem odd to think of Munich as a springboard to Poland. Yet for decades Munich had been the command centre for a range of Polish operations. From the roof of our Consular annexe in a leafy suburb, our antennae had listened night and day for our Polish agents' signals – often no more than a blip compressed between words spoken on the open radio. And in return, on pre-determined schedules, we had transmitted comfort and fresh orders to them. From Munich we had despatched our Polish letters, impregnated with secret writing. And if our sources managed to travel outside Poland, it was from Munich again that we flew off to debrief and feast them and listen to their worries.

It was from Munich also, when the need was great enough, that our Station officers would cross into Poland, always singly and usually in the guise of a visiting businessman bound for a trade fair or exhibition. And in some roadside picnic spot or backstreet café, our emissaries would come briefly face to face with our precious joes, transact their business and depart, knowing they had refilled the lamp. For nobody who has not led a joe's life can imagine what loneliness of faith it brings. A well-timed cup of bad coffee shared with a good case officer can raise a joe's morale for months.

Which is how it happened that, one winter's day soon after the beginning of the second half of my tour in Munich (and the welcome departure of Professor Teodor and his appendages to America), I found myself flying into Gdansk on a LOT Polish Airlines flight from Warsaw, with a Dutch passport in my pocket describing me as Franz Joost of Nijmegen, born forty years before. According to my businessman's visa application, my mission was to inspect prefabricated agricultural buildings on behalf of a West German farming consortium. For I have some basic grounding as an engineer, and certainly enough to exchange visiting cards with officials from their Ministry of Agriculture.

My other mission was more complicated. I was looking for a joe named Oskar, who had returned to life six months after being given up for dead. Out of the blue, Oskar had sent us a letter to an old cover address, using his secret writing equipment and describing everything he had done and not done from the day he had first heard of the arrests till now. He had kept his nerve. He had remained at his job. He had anonymously denounced some blameless *apparatchik* in his Archives

Section in order to divert suspicion. He had waited, and after a few weeks the *apparatchik* disappeared. Encouraged, he waited again. Rumour reached him that the *apparatchik* had confessed. Given Colonel Jerzy's tender ministrations, this was not surprising. As the weeks went by, he began to feel safe again. Now he was ready to resume work if someone would tell him what to do. In earnest of this, he had stuck microdots to the third, fifth and seventh full stops of the letter, which were the pre-arranged positions. Blown up, they amounted to sixteen pages of top secret orders from the Polish Defence Ministry to Colonel Jerzy's department. The Circus analysts declared them 'likely and presumed reliable,' which, coming from them, was an ecstatic declaration of faith.

You must imagine now the excitement that Oskar's letter kindled in the Station, and even in myself, though I had never met him. Oskar! the believers cried. The old devil! Alive and kicking under the rubble! Trust Oskar to beat the rap! Oskar, our hardened Polish Admiralty clerk, based at Gdansk's coastal defence headquarters, one of the best the Station ever had!

Only the hardest-nosed, or those nearest to retirement, dismissed the letter as a lure. Saying 'no' in such cases is easy. Saying 'yes' takes nerve. Nevertheless, the nay-sayers are always heard the clearest, particularly after Haydon, and for a while there was a stalemate when no one had the nerve to jump either way. Buying time, we wrote to Oskar asking for more collateral. He wrote back angrily demanding to know whether he was trusted, and this time he insisted on a meeting. 'A meeting or nothing,' he said. And in Poland. Soon or never.

While Head Office continued to vacillate, I begged to be allowed to go to him. The unbelievers in my Station told me I was mad, the believers said it was the only decent thing to do. I was convinced by neither side, but I wanted clarity. Perhaps I also wanted it for myself, for Mabel had recently shown signs of withdrawing herself from our relationship and I was not disposed to rate myself too highly. Head Office sided with the noes. I reminded them of my naval background. Head Office dithered and said 'no, but maybe.' I reminded them of my bilinguality and the tested strength of my Netherlands identity, which our Dutch liaison condoned in exchange for favours in another field. Head Office measured the risks and the alternatives, and finally said, 'Yes, but only for two days.' Perhaps they had concluded that, after Haydon, I hadn't that many secrets to give away anyway. Hastily I put together my cover and set off before they could change their minds again. It was six below as my plane touched down at Gdansk airport; thick snow was lying in the streets, more was falling and the quiet gave me a greater sense of safety than was prudent. But I was taking no risks, believe me. I might be looking for clarity, but I was nobody's innocent any more.

Gdansk hotels are of a uniform frightfulness and mine was no exception. The lobby stank like a disinfected urinal; checking-in was as complicated as adopting a baby and took longer. My room turned out to be someone else's and she spoke no known language. By the time I had found another room, and a maid to remove the grosser traces of its previous inhabitant, it was dusk and time for me to make my arrival known to Oskar.

Every joe has his handwriting. In summer, said the file, Oskar liked to fish, and my predecessor had held successful conversations with him along the river bank. They had even caught a couple of fish together, though the pollution had made them inedible. But this was deep-frozen winter, when only children and masochists fished. In winter Oskar's habits changed and he liked to play billiards at a club for small officials near the docks. And this club had a telephone. To initiate a meeting, my predecessor, who spoke Polish, had only to call him there and conduct a cheery conversation built round the fiction that he was an old naval friend named Lech. Then Oskar would say, 'All right, I'll meet you tomorrow at my sister's for a drink,' which meant 'Pick me up in your car on the corner of so-and-so street in one hour's time.'

But I spoke no Polish. And besides, the rules of post-Haydon tradecraft dictated that no agent should be reactivated by means of past procedures.

In his letter, Oskar had provided the telephone numbers of three cafés, and the times at which he would try to be available in each of them – three because there was always the likelihood that one of the phones would be out of order or occupied. If none of the phone calls worked, then we would resort to a car pick-up, and Oskar had told me which tram stop I should stand at, and at what time. He had provided the registration number of his new blue Trabant.

And if all of this seems to place me in a passive role, that is because the iron rule for such meetings is that the agent in the field is king, and it's the agent who decides what is the safest course for him, and the most natural to his lifestyle. What Oskar was suggesting was not what I would have suggested, nor did I understand why we had to speak on the telephone before we met. But perhaps Oskar understood. Perhaps he was afraid of a trap. Perhaps he wanted to sample the reassurance of my voice before he took the plunge.

Or perhaps there was some sidelight I had yet to learn of: he was bringing a friend with him; he wished to be evacuated at once; he had changed his mind. For there is a second rule of tradecraft as rigid as the first, which says that the outrageous is to be regarded at all times as the norm. The good case officer *expects* the entire Gdansk telephone system to fail the moment he begins his call. He *expects* the tram stop to be at the centre of a road works, or that Oskar will that morning have driven his car into a lamp-post or developed a temperature of a hundred and four, or that his wife will have persuaded him to demand a million dollars in gold before resuming contact with us, or that her baby will have decided to be premature. The whole art – as I told my students till they hated me for it – is to rely on Sod's Law and otherwise nothing.

It was with this maxim in mind that, having spent a fruitless hour telephoning the three cafés, I placed myself at the agreed tram stop at ten past nine that night, and waited for Oskar's Trabant to grope its way towards me down the street. For though the snow had by now ceased to fall, the street was still no more than a pair of black tracks at one side of the tramlines, and the few cars that passed had the wariness of survivors returning from the front.

There is old Danzig the stately Hanseatic port, and there is Gdansk the Polish industrial slum. The tram stop was in Gdansk. To left and right of me as I waited, dour, low-lit concrete apartment houses hunched under the smouldering orange sky. Looking up and down the street, I saw not the smallest sign of human love or pleasure. Not a café, not a cinema, not a pretty light. Even the pair of drunks slumped in a doorway across the street seemed afraid to speak. One peal of laughter, one shout of goodfellowship or pleasure would have been a crime against the drabness of this outdoor prison. A car slipped by but it was not blue and it was not a Trabant. Its side windows were caked with snow, and even after it had passed I could not have told you how many people were inside. It stopped. Not at the side of the street, not on the pavement or in a turning or a layby, for mounds of snow blocked them all. It simply stopped in the twin black tracks of the road, and cut its engine, then its lights.

Lovers, I thought. If so, they were lovers blind to danger, for the road was two-way. A second car appeared, travelling in the same direction as the first. It too pulled up, but short of my tram stop. More lovers? Or merely a sensible driver allowing plenty of skidding distance between himself and the stationary car ahead of him? The effect was the same; there was one car to either side of me, and as I stood waiting, I saw that the two silent drunks were standing clear of their doorway and looking very sober. Then I heard the single footstep behind me, soft as a bedroom slipper in the snow, but close. And I knew that I must not make any sudden movement, certainly not a clever one. There was no springing free, there was no preemptive blow that would save me, because what I was beginning to fear in my imagination was either nothing or it was everything. And if it was everything, there was nothing I could do.

A man was standing to my left, close enough to touch me. He wore a fur coat and a leather hat and carried a collapsed umbrella that could have been a lead pipe shoved into a nylon sheath. Very well, like myself he was waiting for the tram. A second man was standing to my right. He smelt of horse. And very well, like his companion and myself, he too was waiting for the tram, even if he had ridden here on horseback. Then a man's voice spoke to me in mournful Polish English, and it came neither from my left nor my right, but from directly behind me, where I had heard the slippered footstep.

'Oskar will not be coming tonight, I am afraid, sir. He has been dead for six months.'

But by then he had given me time to think. A whole age, in fact. I knew of no Oskar. Oskar who? Coming where? I was a Dutchman who spoke only a limited amount of English, with a thick Dutch accent like my uncles and aunts in Nijmegen. I paused while I let his words have their effect on me; then I turned – but slowly and incuriously.

'You are confusing me, sir, I think,' I protested, in the slow singsong voice I had learned at my mother's knee. 'My name is Franz Joost, from Holland, and I do not think that I am waiting for anyone except the tram.'

And that was when the men on either side of me grabbed hold of me like good professionals, pinning my arms and knocking me off balance at the same moment, then dragging and toppling me all the way to the second car. But not before I had time to recognise the squat man who had addressed me, his damp grey jowls and sodden night-clerk's eyes. It was our very own Colonel Jerzy, the much publicised hero of the Protection of the Polish People's Republic, whose expressionless photograph had graced the front pages of several illustrious Polish newspapers around the time that he was gallantly arresting and torturing our agents.

There are deaths we unconsciously prepare for, depending on our choice of trades. An undertaker contemplates his funeral, the rich-man his destitution, the gaoler his imprisonment, the debauchee his impotence. An actor's greatest terror, I am told, is to watch the theatre empty itself while he wrestles in a void for his lines, and what else is that but a premature vision of his dying? For the civil servant, it is the moment when his protective walls of privilege collapse around him and he finds himself no safer than the next man, exposed to the gaze of the overt world, answering like a lying husband for his laxities and evasions. And most of my intelligence colleagues, if I am honest, came into this category: their greatest fear was to wake up one morning to read their real names *en clair* in the newspapers; to hear themselves spoken of on the radio and television, joked and laughed about and, worse yet, questioned by the public they believed they served. They would have regarded such public scrutiny as a greater disaster than being outwitted by the opposition, or blown to every kindred service round the globe. It would have been their death.

And for myself, the worst death, and therefore the greatest test, the one for which I had prepared myself ever since I passed through the secret door, was the one that was upon me now: to have my uncertain courage tested on the rack; to be reduced mentally and physically to my last component of endurance, knowing I had within me the power to stop the dying with a word – that what was going on inside me was mortal combat between my spirit and my body, and that those who were applying the pain were merely the hired mercenaries in this secret war within myself.

So that from the first blinding explosion of pain, my response was recognition: Hullo, I thought, you've come at last – my name is Joost, what's yours?

There was no ceremony, you see. He didn't sit me at a desk in the tried tradition of the screen and say, 'Either talk to me or you'll be beaten. Here is your confession. Sign it.' He didn't have them lock me in a cell and leave me to cook for a few days while I decided that confession was the better part of courage. They simply dragged me out of the car and through the gateway of what could have been a private house, then into a courtyard where the only footprints were our own, so that they had to topple me through the thick snow, slewing me on my heels, all three of them, punching me from one to the other, now in the face, now in the groin and stomach, now back to the face again, this time with an elbow or a knee. Then, while I was still double, kicking me like a half-stunned pig across the slithery cobble as if they couldn't wait to get indoors before they had me.

Then, once indoors, they became more systematic, as if the elegance of the old bare room had instilled in them a sense of order. They took me in turns, like civilised men, two of them holding me and one hitting me, a proper democratic rota, except that when it was Colonel Jerzy's fifth or fiftieth turn, he hit me so regretfully and so hard that I actually did die for a while, and when I came round I was alone with him. He was seated at a folding desk with his elbows on it, holding his unhappy head between his grazed hands as if he had a hangover, and reviewing with disappointment the answers I had given to the questions he had put to me between onslaughts, first lifting his head in order to study with disapproval my altered appearance, then shaking it painfully and sighing as if to say life really wasn't fair to him, he didn't know what more he could do to me to help me see the light. It dawned on me that more time had passed than I realised, perhaps several hours.

This was also the moment when the scene began to take on a resemblance to the one I had always imagined, with my tormentor sitting comfortably at a desk, brooding over me with a professional's concern, and myself spread-eagled against a scalding waterpipe, my arms hand-cuffed either side of a black concertina-style radiator, with corners that bit into the base of my spine like red-hot teeth. I had been bleeding from the mouth and nose and, I thought, from one ear as well, and my shirt front looked like a slaughterer's apron. But the blood had dried and I wasn't bleeding any more, which was another way of calculating the passage of time. How long does blood take to congeal in a big empty house in Gdansk when you are chained to a furnace and looking into the puppyish face of Colonel Jerzy?

It was terribly hard to hate him, and with the burning in my back it was becoming harder by the moment. He was my only saviour. His face stayed on me all the time now. Even when he turned his head downward to the table in private prayer, or got up and lit himself a filthy Polish cigarette and took a stretch around the room, his lugubrious gaze seemed to stay on me without reference to where the rest of him had gone. He turned his squat back to me. He gave me a view of his thick bald head and the pitted nape of his neck. Yet his eyes – treating with me, reasoning with me and sometimes, as it seemed, imploring me to ease his anguish – never left me for a second. And there was a part of me that really wanted to help him and it was becoming more and more strident with the burning. Because the burning was not a burning any more, it was pure pain, a pain indivisible and absolute, mounting like a scale that had no upper limit. So that I would have given almost anything to make him feel better – except myself. Except the part of me that made me separate from him, and was therefore my survival.

'What's your name?' he asked me, still in his Polish English.

'Joost.' He had to bend over me to hear me. 'Franz Joost.'

'From Munich,' he suggested, using my shoulder as a prop while he put his ear closer to my mouth.

'Born Nijmegen. Working for farmers in the Taunus, by Frankfurt.'

'You've forgotten your Dutch accent.' He shook me a little to wake me.

'You just don't hear it. You're a Pole. I want to see the Dutch Consul.'

'You mean British Consul.'

'Dutch.' And then I think I repeated the same word 'Dutch' several times, and went on repeating it till he threw cold water over me, then poured a little of it into my mouth to let me rinse and spit. I realised I was missing a tooth. Lower jaw, front left. Two teeth perhaps. It was hard to tell.

'Do you believe in God?' he asked me.

When he stared down at me like this, his cheeks fell forward like a baby's and his lips formed themselves in a kiss, so that he looked like a puzzled cherub.

'Not at the moment,' I said.

'Why not?'

'Get me the Dutch Consul. You've got the wrong man.'

I saw that he didn't like being told this. He wasn't used to being given orders or contradicted. He passed the back of his right hand across his lips, a thing he sometimes did before he hit me, and I waited for the blow. He began patting his pockets, I assumed for some instrument.

'No,' he remarked, with a sigh. 'You are mistaken. I have got the right man.'

He knelt to me and I thought he was preparing to kill me, because I had noticed that he was at his most murderous when he appeared most unhappy. But he was unlocking my handcuffs. When he had done so, he shoved his clenched fists under my armpits and hauled me – I almost thought helped me – to a spacious bathroom with an old, freestanding bath filled with warm water.

'Strip,' he said, and watched me dejectedly while I dragged off what remained of my clothes, too exhausted to care about what he would do to me once I was in the water: drown me, or cook me or freeze me, or drop in an electric wire.

He had my suitcase from the hotel. While I lay in the bath, he picked out clean clothes and tossed them on to a chair.

'You leave on tomorrow's plane for Frankfurt via Warsaw. There has been a mistake,' he said. 'We apologise. We shall cancel your business appointments and say you were the victim of a hit-and-run car.'

'I'll need more than an apology,' I said.

The bath was doing me no good. I was afraid that if I lay flat any longer, I would die again. I hauled myself into a crouch. Jerzy held out his forearm. I clutched it and stood upright, swaying dangerously. Jerzy helped me out of the bath, then handed me a towel and watched me gloomily while I dried myself and pulled on the clean clothes he had laid out for me.

He led me from the house and across the courtyard, carrying my case in one hand and bearing my weight with the other, because the bath had weakened me as well as easing the pain. I peered round for the henchmen but saw none.

'The cold air will be good for you,' he said, with the confidence of an expert.

He led me to a parked car, and it did not resemble either of the cars that had taken part in my arrest. A toy steering wheel lay on the back seat. We drove down empty streets. Sometimes I dozed. We reached a pair of white iron gates guarded by militia.

'Don't look at them,' he ordered me, and showed them his papers while I dozed again.

We got out of the car and stood on a grass clifftop. An inshore wind froze our faces. Mine felt big as two footballs. My mouth had moved into my left cheek. One eye had closed. There was no moon and the sea was a growl behind the salt mist. The only light came from the city behind us. Occasionally Phosphorous sparks slipped past us, or puffs of white spume spun away into the blackness. This is where I'm supposed to die, I thought as I stood beside him; first he beats me, then he gives me a warm bath, now he shoots me and shoves me over the cliff. But his hands were hanging glumly at his sides and there was no gun in them, and his eyes – what I could make out of them – were fixed on the starless darkness, not on me; so perhaps someone else was going to shoot me, someone already waiting in the dark. If I had had the energy, I could have killed Jerzy first. But I hadn't, and I didn't feel the need. I thought of Mabel, but without any sense of loss or gain. I wondered how she'd manage living on a pension, whom she'd find. *Fräulein Stefanie is not at home*, I remembered. . . . *Then perhaps it was Stefanie who answered*, Smiley was saying. . . . So many unanswered prayers, I was thinking. But so many never offered, either. I was feeling very drowsy.

At last Jerzy spoke, his voice no less despondent than before. 'I have brought you here because there isn't a microphone on earth can hear us. I wish to spy for your country. I need a good professional to act as intermediary. I have decided to choose you.'

Once more I lost my sense of time and place. But perhaps he had lost his too, for he had turned his back on the sea and, with his hand clutched to his leather hat to hold it against the wind, he had undertaken a mournful study of the inland lights, scowling at things that needed no scowling at, sometimes punching the wind-tears from his cheeks with his big fists.

'Why should anyone spy for Holland?' I asked him.

'Very well, I propose to spy for Holland,' he replied wearily, indulging a pedant. 'Therefore I need a good professional *Dutchman* who can keep his mouth shut. Knowing what fools you *Dutchmen* have employed against us in the past, I am understandably selective. However, you have passed the test. Congratulations. I select you.'

I thought it best to say nothing. Probably I didn't believe him.

'In the false compartment of your suitcase you will find a wad of Polish secret documents,' he continued, in a tone of dejection. 'At Gdansk airport you will have no Customs problems, naturally. I have given orders for them not to examine your luggage. For all they know, you are by now my agent. In Frankfurt, you are on home ground. I shall work to you and nobody else. Our next meeting will be in Berlin on May 5th. I shall be attending the May Day celebrations to mark the glorious victory of the proletariat.'

He was trying to light a fresh cigarette, but the wind kept putting out his matches. So he took his hat off and lit the cigarette inside the crown, lowering his fat face to it as if he were drinking water from a stream.

'Your people will wish to know my motive,' he continued when he had taken a deep draught of cigarette smoke. 'Tell them – ' Suddenly at a loss, he sank his head into his shoulders and peered round at me as if pleading for advice on how to deal with idiots. 'Tell them I'm bored. Tell them I'm sick of the work. Tell them the Party's a bunch of crooks. They know that anyway, but tell them. I'm a Catholic. I'm a Jew. I'm a Tartar. Tell them whatever the hell they want to hear.'

'They may want to know why you have chosen to come to the *Dutch*,' I said. 'Rather than to the Americans, or the French or whoever.'

He thought about that too, puffing at his cigarette in the darkness. 'You Dutch had some good joes,' he said ruminatively. 'I got to know some of them pretty well. They did a good job till that bastard Haydon came

along.' An idea occurred to him. 'Tell them my father was a Battle of
Britain pilot,' he suggested. 'Got himself shot down over Kent. That
should please them. You know Kent?'

'Why should a Dutchman know Kent?' I şaid.

If I had weakened, I could have told him that, before our so-called
'friendly' separation, Mabel and I had bought a house in Tunbridge Wells.
But I didn't, which was as well, because when Head Office came to check
the story out, there was no record of Jerzy's father having flown anything
larger than a paper kite. And when I put this to Jerzy several years later –
long after his loyalty to the perfidious British had been demonstrated
beyond all doubt – he just laughed, and said his father was an old fool
who cared for nothing but vodka and potatoes.

So why?

For five years Jerzy was my secret university of espionage, but his
contempt for motive – his own particularly – never relaxed. First we idiots
do what we want to do, he said; then we look round for justifications for
having done it. All men were idiots to him, he told me, and we spies were
the biggest idiots of all.

At first I suspected that he was spying for vengeance, and drew him out
on the people above him in the hierarchy who might have slighted him.
He hated them all, himself the most.

Then I decided he was spying for ideological reasons, and that his
cynicism was a disguise for the finer yearnings he had discovered in
his middle age. But when I attempted to use my wiles to break his cynicism
down – 'Your family, Jerzy, your mother, Jerzy. Admit you're proud to
have become a grandfather' – I found only more cynicism beneath. He felt
nothing for any of them, he retorted, but so icily that I concluded that he
did indeed, as he maintained, hate the entire human race, and that his
savagery, and perhaps his betrayal too, were the simple expression of this
hatred.

As to the West, it was run by the same idiots who ran everything in the
world, so what's the difference? And when I told him this simply was not
so, he became as defensive of his nihilist creed as any other zealot, and I
had to rein myself in for fear of angering him seriously.

So why? Why risk his neck, his life, his livelihood and the family he
hated, to do something for a world he despised?

The Church? I asked him that too, and significantly, as I think now, he
bridled. Christ was a manic depressive, he retorted. Christ needed to
commit suicide in public, so he provoked the authorities until they did
him the favour. 'Those God-thumper guys are all the same,' he said with
contempt. 'I've tortured them. I know.'

Like most cynics, he was a Puritan, and this paradox repeated itself in
him in several ways. When we offered to drop money for him, open a
Swiss bank account, the usual, he flew into a rage and declared he was not

some 'cheap informant.' When I picked a moment – on the instruction of Head Office – to assure him that if ever things went wrong, we would spare no effort to get him out and provide him with a new identity in the West, his contempt was absolute: 'I'm a Polish creep, but I would rather face a firing squad of my fellow creeps than die a traitor in some capitalist pigsty.'

As to life's other comforts, we could offer him nothing he had not got. His wife was a scold, he said, and going home after a heavy day at the office bored him. His mistress was a young fool, and after an hour with her he preferred a game of billiards to her conversation.

Then why? I kept asking myself when I had exhausted my checklist of the Service's standard-issue motives.

Meanwhile, Jerzy continued to fill our coffers. He was turning his Service inside out as neatly as Haydon had ever done with ours. When Moscow Centre gave him orders, we knew of them before he passed them to his underlings. He photographed everything that came within his reach; he took risks I begged him not to take. He was so heedless that sometimes he left me wondering whether, like the Christ he was so determined to deny, he was looking for a public death. It was only the unflagging efficiency of what we were pleased to call his cover work that protected him from suspicion. For that was the dark side of his balancing act: God help the Western agent, real or imagined, who was invited to make his voluntary confession at Jerzy's hands.

Only once in the five years that I ran him did he seem to let slip the clue I was searching for. He was tired to death. He had been attending a conference of Warsaw Pact Intelligence chiefs in Bucharest, in the midst of fighting off charges of brutality and corruption against his Service at home. We met in West Berlin, in a *pension* on the Kurfürstendamm which catered to the better type of representative. He was a really tired torturer. He sat on my bed, smoking and answering my follow-up questions about his last batch of material. He was red-eyed. When we had finished, he asked for a whisky, then another.

'No danger is no life,' he said, tossing three more rolls of film on the counterpane. 'No danger is dead.' He took out a grimy brown handkerchief and carefully wiped his heavy face with it. 'No danger, you do better stay home, look after the baby.'

I preferred not to believe it was danger he was talking about. What he was talking about, I decided, was feeling, and his terror that by ceasing to feel he was ceasing to exist – which perhaps was why he was so devoted to instilling feeling in others. For that moment, I thought I caught a glimpse of why he was sitting with me in the room breaking every rule in his book. He was keeping his spirit alive at a time of his life when it was beginning to look like dying.

The same night I dined with Stefanie at an Armenian restaurant ten minutes' walk from the *pension* where Jerzy and I had met. I had wangled her telephone number from a sister in Munich. She was as tall and beautiful as I remembered her, and determined to convince me she was happy. Oh, life was *perfect*, Ned, she declared. She was living with this *terribly* distinguished academic, not in his first youth any more – but look here, nor are we – and completely adorable and wise. She told me his name. It meant nothing to me. She said she was pregnant by him. It didn't show.

'And *you*, Ned, how did it go for *you*?' she asked, as if we were two generals reporting to each other from successful, but separate, campaigns.

I gave her my most confident smile, the one that had earned me the trust of my joes and colleagues in the years since I had seen her.

'Oh, I think it worked out pretty well actually, thanks, yes,' I said, with seeming British understatement. 'After all, you can't expect one person to be everything you need, can you? It's a pretty good partnership, I'd say. Good parallel living.'

'And you still do that work?' she said. 'Ben's work?'

'Yes.'

It was the first time either of us had mentioned him. He was living in Ireland, she said. A cousin of his had bought a tumbledown estate in County Cork. Ben sort of caretook for him while he wasn't there, stocking the river and looking after the farm and so on.

I asked whether she ever saw him.

'No,' she said. 'He won't.'

I would have driven her home, but she preferred a cab. We waited in the street till it came, and it seemed to take a terribly long time. As I closed the door on her, her head tipped forward as if she had dropped something on the floor. I waved her out of sight but she didn't wave back.

The nine-o'clock news was showing us an outdoor meeting of Solidarity in Gdansk, where a Polish Cardinal was exhorting an enormous crowd to moderation. Losing interest, Mabel settled the *Daily Telegraph* on her lap and resumed her crossword. At first the crowd heard the Cardinal noisily. Then, with the devotion Poles are famous for, they fell silent. After his address, the Cardinal moved among his flock, bestowing blessings and accepting homage. And as one dignitary after another was brought to him, I picked out Jerzy hovering in the background, like the ugly boy excluded from the feast. He had lost a lot of weight since he had retired, and I guessed that the social changes had not been kind to him. His jacket hung on him like someone else's; his once-formidable fists were hardly visible inside the sleeves.

Suddenly the Cardinal has spotted him, just as I had.

The Cardinal freezes as if in doubt of his own feelings, and for a moment makes himself neater somehow, almost in obedience, pressing in his elbows and drawing back his shoulders to attention. Then slowly his arms lift again and he gives an order to one of his attendants, a young priest who seems reluctant to obey it. The Cardinal repeats the order, the priest clears a path to Jerzy; the two men face each other, the secret policeman and the Cardinal. Jerzy winces, as if he has digestion pains. The Cardinal leans forward and speaks in Jerzy's ear. Awkwardly, Jerzy kneels to receive the Cardinal's blessing.

And each time I replay this moment I see Jerzy's eyes close apparently in pain. But what is he repenting? His brutality? His loyalty to a vanished cause? Or his betrayal of it? Or is squeezing the eyes shut merely the instinctive response of a torturer receiving the forgiveness of a victim?

I fish. I drop into my little reveries. My love of English landscape has, if possible, increased. I think of Stefanie and Bella, and my other half-had women. I lobby our Member of Parliament about the filthy river. He's a Conservative, but what on earth does he imagine he's conserving? I've joined one of the sounder environmentalist groups; I collect signatures on petitions. The petitions are ignored. I won't play golf, I never would. But I'll walk round with Mabel on a Wednesday afternoon, provided she's playing alone. I encourage her. The dog enjoys himself. Retirement is no time to be wandering lost, or puzzling how to reinvent mankind.

8

My students had decided to give Smiley a rough ride, just as they'd done to me from time to time. We'd be running along perfectly smoothly – a double session on natural cover, say, in the late afternoon – when one of them would start hectoring me, usually by adopting an anarchic stance which nobody in his right mind could sustain. Then a second would chime in, then all of them, so that if I didn't have my sense of humour shining-ready – and I'm only human – they'd be trampling me till the bell rang for close of play. And next day all would be forgotten: they'd have fed whatever little demon had got hold of them, and now they'd like to go back to learning, please, so where were we? At first I used to brood over these occasions, suspect conspiracy, hunt for ringleaders.

Then cautiously I came to recognise them as spontaneous expressions of resistance to the unnatural harness that these children had chosen to put on.

But when they started in on Smiley, their guest of honour and mine, even questioning the entire purpose of his life's work, my tolerance ended with a snap. And this time the offender was not Maggs, either, but the demure Clare, his girlfriend, who had sat so adoringly opposite Smiley throughout dinner.

'No, no, Ned,' Smiley protested, as I leapt angrily to my feet. 'Clare has a valid point. Nine times out of ten a good journalist *can* tell us quite as much about a situation as the spies can. Very often they're sharing the same sources anyway. So why not scrap the spies and subsidise the newspapers? It's a point that should be answered in these changeable times. Why not?'

Reluctantly I resumed my seat, while Clare, snuggling close against Maggs, continued to gaze angelically at her victim, while her colleagues smothered their grins.

But where I would have taken refuge in humour, Smiley elected to treat her sally seriously:

'It is perfectly true,' he agreed, 'that most of our work is either useless, or duplicated by overt sources. The trouble is, the spies aren't there to enlighten the public, but governments.'

And slowly I felt his spell re-unite them. They had moved their chairs to him in a disordered half-circle. Some of the girls were sprawled becomingly on the floor.

'And governments, like anyone else, trust what they pay for, and are suspicious of what they don't,' he said. Thus delicately passing beyond Clare's provocative question, he addressed a larger one: 'Spying is eternal,' he announced simply. 'If governments *could* do without it, they never would. They adore it. If the day ever comes when there are no enemies left in the world, governments will invent them for us, so don't worry. Besides – who says we only spy on enemies? All history teaches us that today's allies are tomorrow's rivals. Fashion may dictate priorities, but foresight doesn't. For as long as rogues become leaders, we shall spy. For as long as there are bullies and liars and madmen in the world, we shall spy. For as long as nations compete, and politicians deceive, and tyrants launch conquests, and consumers need resources, and the homeless look for land, and the hungry for food, and the rich for excess, your chosen profession is perfectly secure, I can assure you.'

And with the topic thus neatly turned back to their own future, he once more warned them of its perils:

'There's no career on earth more cockeyed than the one you've picked,' he assured them, with every sign of satisfaction. 'You'll be at your most postable while you're least experienced, and by the time you've learned the ropes, no one will be able to send you anywhere without a trade description round your necks. Old athletes know they've played their best games when they were in their prime. But spies in their prime are on the shelf, which is why they take so ungraciously to middle age, and start counting the cost of living how they've lived.'

Though his hooded gaze to all appearance remained fixed upon his brandy, I saw him cast a sideways glance at me. 'And then, at a certain age, you want the answer,' he continued. 'You want the rolled-up parchment in the inmost room that tells you who runs your lives and why. The trouble is, that by then you're the very people who know best that the inmost room is bare. Ned, you're not drinking. You're a brandy traitor. Fill him up, someone.'

It is an uncomfortable truth of the period of my life that follows that I recall it as a single search the object of which was unclear to me. And that the object, when I found him, turned out to be the lapsed spy Hansen.

And that, although in reality I was pursuing quite other goals and people along my eastward journey, all of them in retrospect seem to have been stages on my journey to him. I can put it no other way. Hansen in his Cambodian jungle was my Kurtz at the heart of darkness. And everything that happened to me on the way was a preparation for our meeting. Hansen's was the voice I was waiting to hear. Hansen held the answer to the questions I did not know I was asking. Outwardly, I was my stolid, moderate, pipe-smoking, decent self, a shoulder for weaker souls to rest their heads on. Inside, I felt a rampant incomprehension of my uselessness; a sense that, for all my striving, I had failed to come to grips with life; that in struggling to give freedom to others, I had found none for myself. At my lowest ebb, I saw myself as ridiculous, a hero in the style not of Buchan but of Quixote.

I took to writing down sardonic versions of my life, so that when, for instance, I reviewed the episodes I have described to you this far, I gave them picaresque titles that emphasised their futility: the Panda – I safeguard our Middle Eastern interests! Ben – I run to earth a British defector! Bella – I make the ultimate sacrifice! Teodor – I take part in a grand deception! Jerzy – I play the game to the end! Though with Jerzy, I had to admit, a positive purpose had been served, even if it was as short-lived as most intelligence, and as irrelevant to the human forces that have now engulfed his nation.

Like Quixote, I had set out in life vowing to check the flow of evil. Yet in my lowest moments I was beginning to wonder whether I had become a contributor to it. But I still looked to the world to provide me with the chance to make my contribution – and I blamed it for not knowing how to use me.

To understand this, you should know what had happened to me after Munich. Jerzy, whatever else he did to me, brought me a sort of prestige, and the Fifth Floor decided to invent a job for me as roving operational fixer, sent out on short assignments 'to appraise, and where possible

exploit opportunities outside the remit of the local Station' – thus my
brief, signed and returned to maker.

Looking back, I realise that the constant travel this entailed – Central
America one week, Northern Ireland the next, Africa, the Middle East,
Africa again – soothed the restlessness that was stalking me, and that
Personnel in all likelihood knew this, for I had recently embarked on a
senseless love affair with a girl called Monica, who worked in the Service's
Industrial Liaison Section. I had decided I needed an affair; I saw her in
the canteen and cast her in the part. It was as banal as that. One night it
was raining, and as I started to drive home, I saw her standing at a number
23 bus stop. Banality made flesh. I took her to her flat, I took her to her
bed, I took her to dinner and we tried to work out what we had done, and
came up with the convenient solution that we had fallen in love. It served
us well for several months, until tragedy abruptly called me to my senses.
By a mercy, I was back in London briefing myself for my next mission
when word came that my mother was failing. By an act of divine ill taste,
I was in bed with Monica when I took the call. But at least I was able to be
present for the event, which was lengthy, but unexpectedly serene.

Nevertheless, I found myself entirely unprepared for it. Somehow I had
taken for granted that, in the same way that I had managed to negotiate
myself round awkward hurdles in the past, I would do the same in the case
of my mother's death. I could not have been more mistaken. Very few
conspiracies, Smiley once remarked, survive contact with reality. And so
it was with the conspiracy that I had made with myself to let my mother's
death slip past me as a timely and necessary release from pain. I had not
taken into my calculations that the pain could be my own.

I was orphaned and elated both at once. I can describe it no other way.
My father had long been dead. Without my realising it, my mother had
done duty for both parents. In her death I saw the loss, not only of
my childhood, but of most of my adulthood as well. At last I stood
unencumbered before life's challenges, yet many of them were already
behind me – fudged, missed or botched. I was free to love at last, but
whom? Not, I am afraid, Monica, however much I might protest the
contrary and expect the reality to follow. Neither Monica nor my marriage
offered me the magic it was henceforth my duty as a survivor to pursue.
And when I looked at myself in the mirror of the undertaker's rose-tinted
lavatory after my night's vigil, I was horrified by what I saw. It was the
face of a spy branded by his own deception.

Have you seen it too, around you? On you? That face? In my case it was
so much my everyday companion that I had ceased to notice it until the
shock of death brought it home to me. We smile, but our withholding
makes our smile false. When we are exhilarated, or drunk – or, even as I
am told, make love – the reserve does not dissolve, the gyroscope stays
vertical, the monitory voice reminds us of our calling. Until gradually our
very withholding becomes so strident it is almost a security risk by itself.

So that today – if I go to a reunion, say, or we have a Sarratt old-boys' night – I can actually look round the room and see how the secret stain has come out in every one of us. I see the overbright face or the underlit one, but inside each I see the remnants of a life withheld. I hear the hoot of supposedly abandoned laughter and I don't have to mark down the source of it to know that nothing has been abandoned – not its owner, not its interior restrictions, nothing. In my younger days, I used to think it was just the inhibited British ruling classes who became that person. 'They were born into captivity and had no option from then on,' I would tell myself as I listened to their unconvincing courtesies, and returned their good-chap smiles. But, as only half a Briton, I had exempted myself from their misfortune – until that day in the undertaker's pink-tiled lavatory when I saw that the same shadow that falls across us all had fallen across me.

From that day on, I now believe, I saw only the horizon. I am starting so late! I thought. And from so far back! Life was to be a search, or nothing! But it was the fear that it was nothing that drove me forward. That's how I see it now. And so, please, must you see it, in the fragmented recollections that belong to this surreal passage of my life. In the eyes of the man I had become, every encounter was an encounter with myself. Every stranger's confession was my own, and Hansen's the most accusing – and therefore, ultimately, the most consoling. I buried my mother, I said goodbye to Monica and Mabel. The next day I departed for Beirut. Yet even that simple departure was attended by a disconcerting episode.

To brief myself for my mission, I had been sharing a room with a rather clever man called Giles Latimer, who had made a corner for himself in what was known as 'the Mad Mullah department,' studying the intricate and seemingly indecypherable web of Muslim fundamentalist groups operating out of Lebanon. The notion so beloved of the amateur terror industry that these bodies are all part of a superplot is nonsense. If only it were so – for then there might be some way to get at them! As it is, they slip about, grouping and regrouping like drops of water on a wet wall, and they are about as easy to pin down.

But Giles, who was an Arabist and a distinguished bridge player, had come as near to achieving the impossible as anyone was likely to, and my job was to sit at his feet in order to prepare myself for my mission. He was tall, angular and woolly. He was of my intake. His boyish manner was given extra youthfulness by the redness of his cheeks, though this was actually the consequence of clusters of tiny broken blood vessels. He was indefatigably, painfully gentlemanly, forever opening doors and leaping to his feet for women. In the spring weather I twice saw him get drenched to the skin on account of his habit of lending his umbrella to whoever was proposing to venture out of doors without one. He was rich but frugal, and a thoroughly good man, with a thoroughly good wife, who organised Service bridge drives and remembered the names of the junior staff and their families. Which made it all the more bizarre when his files started disappearing.

It was I, inadvertently, who first noticed the phenomenon. I was tracking a German girl called Britta on her odyssey through the terrorist training camps in the Shuf Mountains, and I requested a contingent file which contained sensitive intercept material about her. The material was American and limited by a subscription list, but when I had gone through the rigmarole of signing myself in, nobody could find it. Nominally it was marked to Giles, but so was almost everything, because Giles was Giles and his name was on every list around.

But Giles knew nothing of it. He remembered reading it, he could quote from it; he thought he had passed it on to me. It must have gone to the Fifth Floor, he said, or back to Registry. Or somewhere.

So the file was posted missing and the Registry bloodhounds were informed, and everything ran along normally for a couple of days until the same thing happened again, though this time it was Giles's own secretary who started the hunt when Registry called in all three volumes on a misty group called the Brothers of the Prophet, supposedly based in Damour.

Once again, Giles knew nothing: he had neither seen nor touched them. The Registry bloodhounds showed him his signature on the receipt. He flatly disowned it. And when Giles denied something, you didn't feel like challenging him. As I say, he was a man of transparent rectitude.

By now, the hunt was up in earnest and inventories were being taken left and right. Registry was in its last days before computerisation, and could still find what it was looking for, or know for sure that it was lost. Today somebody would shake his head and phone for an engineer.

What Registry discovered was that thirty-two files marked out to Giles were missing. Twenty-one of them were standard top secret, five had higher gradings, and six were of a category called RETAIN, which meant, I am afraid, that nobody of strong pro-Jewish sentiments should be admitted as a signatory. Parse that how you will. It was a squalid limitation and there were few of us who were not embarrassed by it. But this was the Middle East.

My first intimation of the scale of the crisis came from Personnel. It was a Friday morning. Personnel always liked the shelter of the weekend when he was about to wield his axe.

'Has Giles been *well* lately, Ned?' he asked me, with old-boy intimacy.

'Perfectly,' I said.

'He's a Christian, isn't he? Christian sort of chap. Pious.'

'I believe so.'

'Well, I mean we all are in a way, but is he a *heavy* sort of Christian, would you say, Ned? What's your opinion?'

'We've never discussed it.'

'Are you?'

'No.'

'Would you say, for example, he could be sympathetic to something like – say – the British-Israelite sect, or one of those sort of things, at all? Nothing against them, mind. Every man to his convictions, me.'

'Giles is very orthodox, very down the middle, I am sure. He's some sort of lay dignitary at his parish church. I believe he gives the odd Lenten Address, and that's about it.'

'That's what I've got down here,' Personnel complained, tapping his knuckles on a closed file. 'That's the picture I've got of him exactly, Ned. So what's up? Not always easy, my job, you know. Not always pleasant at all.'

'Why don't you ask him yourself?'

'Oh I know, I know, I must. Unless you would, of course. You could take him out to lunch – my expense, obviously. Feel his bones. Tell me what you think.'

'No,' I said.

His old-boy manner gave way to something a lot harder. 'I thought you'd say that. I worry about you sometimes, Ned. You're putting yourself about with the women and you're a touch stubborn for your health. It's the Dutch blood in you. Well, keep your mouth shut. That's an order.'

In the end it was Giles who took me out to lunch. Probably Personnel had played the game both ways, pitching some tale to Giles in reverse. Whether he had or not, at twelve-thirty Giles sprang suddenly to his feet and said, 'To hell with it, Ned. It's Friday. Come on, I'll give you lunch. Haven't had a pissy lunch for years.'

So we went to the Travellers', and sat at a table by the window and we drank a bottle of Sancerre very fast. And suddenly Giles began talking about a liaison trip he'd made recently to the FBI in New York. He kicked off quite normally; then his voice seemed to get stuck on one note, and his eyes got fixed on something only he could see. I put it down to the wine at first. Giles didn't look like a drinker and didn't drink like one. Yet there was great conviction in the way he spoke and – as he continued – a visionary intensity.

'Peculiar chaps actually, the Americans, Ned, you want to watch out for them. One doesn't think they're after one at first. One's hotel, for instance. You can always read the clues in a hotel. Too much smiling when you sign in. Too much interest in your luggage. They're watching you. Damned great high-rise greenhouse. Swimming pool on the top floor. You can look down on the helicopters going up the river. "Welcome, Mr. Lambert, and have a nice day, sir." I was using Lambert. I always do for America. The fourteenth floor they'd put me on. I'm a methodical chap. Always have been. Shoe-trees and that kind of thing. Can't help it. My father was the same. Shoes here, shirts there. Socks there. Suits in a certain order. We never have lightweight suits, do we, the English? You think they're lightweight. You choose lightweight. Your tailor tells you they're light-weight. "Lightest we've got, sir. We don't go any lighter." You'd think they'd have learned by now, the amount of American business they do. But they haven't. Cheers.'

He drank and I drank with him. I poured him some mineral water. He was sweating.

'Next day I come back to the hotel. Meetings all day long. Lot of trying to like each other. And I do, I mean they're nice chaps. Just – well, different. Different attitudes. Carry guns. Want results. There can't be any, though, can there? We all know that. The more fanatics you kill, the more there are of them. I know that, they don't. My father was an Arabist too, you know.'

I said I didn't. I said, 'Tell me about him.' I wanted to deflect him. I felt I would feel much better if he talked about his father instead of the hotel.

'So I walk in and they hand me my key. "Hey, hang on," I say. "This isn't floor fourteen. This is floor twenty-one. Mistake." I smile, naturally. Anyone can make a mistake. It's a woman this time. Very strong-looking woman. "It is not a mistake, Mr. Lambert. You're on the twenty-first floor. Your room is 2109." "No, no," I say. "It's 1409. Look here." I had this identity card they give you somewhere and I looked for it. Turned out my pockets while she watched, but couldn't find it. "Look," I said. "Believe me. I have that kind of memory. My room is 1409." She gets out the guest list, shows it to me. Lambert, 2109. I go up in the lift, unlock the room, it's all there. Shoes here. Shirts there. Socks there. Suits in the same order. Everything where I'd put it in the other room, down on the fourteenth floor. Know what they'd done?'

Again I said I didn't.

'Photographed it. Polaroid.'

'Why would they do that?'

'They wanted to mike me – 2109 was miked, 1409 was clean. No good to them, so they moved me up. They thought I was an Arab spy.'

'Why would they think that?'

'Because of my father. He was a Lawrence man. They knew that. They'd decided. That's what they do. Photograph your room.'

I scarcely remember the rest of lunch. I don't remember what we ate or what else we drank or anything at all. I have a recollection of Giles extolling Mabel at great length as the perfect Service wife, but perhaps that was my conscience. All I really remember is the two of us side by side in Giles's room back at Head Office, and Personnel standing in front of Giles's steel cupboard with the door removed, and the thirty-two missing files crammed higgledy-piggledy into the shelves – all the files Giles hadn't been able to cope with while he was having what Smiley called his 'Force Twelve nervous breakdown' in place.

And the reason for it, as I learned later? Giles too had found his Monica. What had unhinged him, ostensibly, was his passion for a twenty-year-old

girl in his village. His love for her, his guilt and despair had dictated that
he could no longer function. He had continued going through the day's
motions – naturally, he was a soldier – but his mind wouldn't play any
more. It had acquired its own preoccupations, even if he wouldn't own to
them.

What else had unhinged him, I leave that to you, and to our in-house
shrinks who seem to be daily gaining ground. Something to do, perhaps,
with the gap between our dreams and our realities. Something to do with
the gap between what Giles longed for when he was young, and what he'd
got now that he was nearly old. And the hard truth was, Giles had
frightened me. I felt he had gone ahead of me down the road I myself was
treading. I felt it as I drove to the airport; I felt it on the plane while I
thought about my mother. And downed several in-flight whiskies in order
not to feel it more.

I was still feeling it as I set out my own meagre wardrobe in Room 607
at the Commodore Hotel, Beirut, and the telephone began ringing a few
inches from my head. As I picked up the receiver, I had a wayward fancy I
was going to hear Ahmed at the front desk telling me I had been allocated
a new room on floor twenty-one. I was wrong. Surreal episode number
two had just announced itself.

Shooting had started, semi-automatic on the move. Most likely a bunch
of kids in a Japanese pickup hosing down the neighbourhood with AK
47s. It was one of those seasons in Beirut when you could set your watch
by the first excitements of the evening. But I had never minded too much
about the shooting. Shooting has a logic, if a haphazard one. It's directed
at you, or away from you. My personal phobia was car bombs – never
knowing, as you hurried along a pavement or dawdled in the sweating,
crawling traffic, whether a parked car was going to take out the entire
block with one huge heave, and leave you in such tiny shreds that there
was nothing worth a body bag, let alone a burial. The thing you noticed
about car bombs – I mean afterwards – was shoes. People blown clean out
of them, but the shoes intact. So that even after the bits of body had been
picked out and taken away, there was still the odd pair or two of wearable
shoes among the broken glass and smashed false teeth and shreds of
someone's suit. A little machine-gun fire, like now, or the odd hand-held
rocket, didn't trouble me as much as it did some people.

I lifted the receiver and when I heard a woman's voice I quickened, not
only because of my domestic ambiguities but because my errand was to
trace a German woman – the same Britta who had been taking lessons in
terror in the Shuf Mountains.

But it was not Britta. It was not Monica and not Mabel. The voice was
middle-American and scared. And I was Peter, remember – Peter Carter,
from a great British newspaper, even if its local correspondent had never
heard of me. I was reminding myself of this as I listened to her.

'Peter, for Christ's sake, I need to be with you,' she said in a single rush of breath. 'Peter, where the fuck have you been?'

A rattle of heavy machine-gun fire broke out, to be promptly silenced by the smack of a rocket-propelled grenade. The voice on the phone resumed in greater agitation.

'Jesus, Peter, why don't you call me? Okay, I said some shitty things. I spoiled your copy. I'm sorry. I mean, Jesus, what are we? Children? You know how I hate this stuff.'

A frenzy of rifle fire. Sometimes the kids just shot into the sky for effect.

Her voice rose steeply. 'Talk to me, Peter! Tell me something funny, will you, please? Something funny must be happening *somewhere* in the world! Peter, will you please answer me? You're not dead are you? You're not lying on the floor with your head blown off? Just nod for no. I don't want to die alone, Peter. I'm sociable. I love sociably, I die sociably. Peter, answer me. Please.'

'What room are you calling?' I said.

Dead silence. The really dead silence that gathers between bursts of gunfire.

'Who is this?' she demanded.

'This is Peter, but I don't think I'm your Peter. What room are you calling?'

'This room.'

'What number?'

'Room 607.'

'I'm afraid he must have checked out. I arrived in Beirut this afternoon. This is the room they gave me.'

A grenade exploded, answered by another. Out in the street, perhaps three blocks away, somebody screamed seriously. The scream ended.

'Is he dead?' she whispered.

I didn't answer.

'Could have been a woman,' she said.

'Could have been,' I agreed.

'Who are you? You British?'

'Yes.' Peter is too, I thought, without knowing why.

'What do you do?'

'For a living?'

'Just talk to me. Keep talking.'

'I'm a journalist,' I said.

'Like Peter?'

'I don't know what kind of journalist he is.'

'He's tough. The danger school. Are you tough?'

'Some things scare me, some don't.'

'Mice?'

'Mice scare me stiff.'

'Are you good?'

'As good as the news, I suppose. I don't write much any more. I'm editorial these days.'

'Married?'

'Are you?'

'Yes.'

'To Peter?'

'No, not Peter.'

'How long have you known him?'

'My husband?'

'No. Peter,' I said. I did not ask myself why I was more interested in her adultery than her marriage.

'You don't time things like that out here,' she said. 'A year, a couple of years – you don't talk that way. Not in Beirut. You're married too, aren't you? You didn't want to tell me till I told you first.'

'Yes, I am.'

'So tell me about her.'

'My wife?'

'Sure. Do you love her? Is she tall? Great Skin? Very British, stiff upper lip?'

I told her some harmless things about Mabel and invented some others, hating myself.

'I mean, who on earth can believe in sex after fifteen years of the same person?' she said.

I laughed but didn't answer.

'Are you faithful to her, Peter?'

'Infallibly,' I said, after a delay.

'Okay, let's do work. Go back to work. What are you doing out here? Something special? Tell me what you're doing.'

The spy in me dodged the question: 'I think it's time you told me what *you* do,' I said. 'Are you a journalist too?'

A stream of tracer tore into the sky. The firing followed.

Her voice turned weary, as if the fear had worn her out. 'I file copy, sure.'

'Who for?'

'A lousy wire service, what else? Fifty cents a line, till some big prick steals it and makes two grand in an afternoon. What's new?'

'What's your name?' I asked.

'I don't know. Maybe Annie. Call me Annie. Listen, you're real nice, know that? What do you do if a Doberman humps your leg?'

'Bark?'

'Fake an orgasm. I'm scared, Peter. Maybe I didn't make that clear. I need a drink.'

'Where are you?'

'Right here.'

'Where's here?'

'In the hotel, for Christ's sake. The Commodore. Standing in the lobby, smelling Ahmed's garlic and getting eyeballed by the Greek.'

'Who's the Greek?'

'Stavros. He pushes hard drugs and swears up and down they're soft. He's serious sleaze.'

I listened, and for the first time made out the babble of voices in the background. The shooting was over.

'Peter?'

'Yes.'

'Peter, put that light out.'

She must have known there was only one light working in the room, a rickety bedside light with a tilted parchment shade. It lay on a locker between the two divans. I turned it off. There were stars again.

'Unlock your door and leave it ajar. One inch. Got booze?'

'A bottle of Scotch,' I said.

'Vodka?'

'No.'

'Ice?'

'No.'

'I'll bring some. Peter?'

'Yes?'

'You're a good man. Anybody ever told you that?'

'Not for a long time.'

'Watch this space,' she said, and rang off.

She never came to me.

You may imagine it any way you like, as I did, all ways, while I sat on the divan, watching the door in the darkness and watching my life go by while I waited to hear her tread in the corridor.

After an hour I went downstairs. I sat in the bar and listened to every female American voice I could find. None fitted. I looked for someone who might call herself Annie and proposition a man she had only talked to on the telephone. I bribed Ahmed to tell me who had used the house phone from the lobby at nine o'clock that night, but his memory, for whatever reason, did not stretch to an emotional American woman.

I went so far as to try to establish the identity of the previous occupant of my room, and whether his first name was Peter, but Ahmed became mysteriously vague and said he had been in Tripoli visiting his old mother, and the hotel kept no lists.

Did the real Peter return in the nick of time and sweep her off? Did Stavros the Greek? Was she a whore? Was I? Was Ahmed pimping her? Was the phone call some kind of elaborate trick she played on newcomers to the hotel, to hook them on their first nervous night alone?

Or was she, as I prefer to think, simply a frightened woman missing her boyfriend and craving a body to hold on to when the nightly thunder of the city started driving her mad?

Whatever mystery she presented, I had learned something about myself even if it disconcerted me. I had learned how perilous was my solitude, how available I was, how much I needed to give love and receive it; and how fickle in me was that virtue which the Service called 'personal security,' compared with my growing hunger for connection. I thought of Monica and my hollow protestations of love which so failed to move the gods they were addressed to. I thought of Giles Latimer and his hopeless passion. And somehow the woman who called herself Annie seemed to belong to the same line of anguished messengers, all speaking from inside myself.

After the faceless girl came the faceless boy. That happened the next evening.

Exhausted, I had settled myself in the hotel lobby and I was drinking my Scotch alone. I had been visiting the camps round Sidon and my hand was still shaking from just another day in southern Lebanon. Now it was the magic hour of dusk, when Beirut's human animal kingdom agreed to put aside its feuds and assemble at the common watering hole. I have seen the same thing happen in the jungle. Perhaps you have too. At a single command, elephants, wart-hogs, gazelles, lions and giraffes tiptoe from the protective darkness of the trees and, mostly in silence, arrange themselves on the muddy flats. You could observe the Commodore lobby at the same hour, when the journalists came back from their day's excursions. As the electric glass doors, always a little too slow on their feet, sighed and grunted from their exertions, so the dark of the early Beirut night disgorged its motley: a Swedish television unit, fronted by a grey-faced blonde in designer denims; a photographer and correspondent from an American weekly; the wire men always in pairs; an elderly and utterly mysterious East German with his Japanese mistress. All had the same self-consciously undramatic way of entering, and pausing, and setting down the day's burden.

Not that their day was over. For the real journalists, there were films to be despatched, stories to be written and telexed and telephoned. Someone was missing and must be accounted for. So-and-so had taken a bad bullet, did his wife know? Nevertheless, with the closing of the glass doors behind them, their day was won back from the enemy. The hackpack was battening down the hatches for the night.

And as I watched, I waited – to meet a man who knew a man who knew another man who just might know the woman I had been sent to find. My day till then had yielded nothing, except another tour of the wretched of the earth.

Elsewhere in the lobby, other species were gathering, less glamorous but frequently more interesting to the observer: carpetbaggers and arms dealers and drug dealers and dark-suited minor diplomats, the pedlars in influence and information, switching at their worry-beads as their restless eyes darted from face to face about the room. And the spies – everyone's spies – trading openly, because in Beirut their trade was everyone's. There was not a man or woman in the place who had not got his source of inside information, if it was only Ahmed behind the counter, who for a few dollars and a smile would tell you the secrets of the uni-verse.

But the figure who had caught my eye was exotic even by the standards of the Commodore's menagerie. I did not see him enter. He must have come in behind a group. I saw him inside the lobby, framed against the darkness of the glass doors, dressed in a striped football shirt and a clean white nurse's scarf tied lightly round his head. If he had not been slender and flat-chested, I would not have been certain, at first sight, whether he was a woman pretending to be a man, or a man pretending to be a woman.

The security man had noticed him too. So had Ahmed the concierge behind his formidable counter. His two Kalashnikovs were propped against the wall behind him, just below the pigeon-holes where the room keys hung, and I saw Ahmed ease a half-step backward so that he had one within reach. A small hand-grenade in that lobby at that hour could have wiped out half the better rackets in the city.

But the apparition kept moving forward, either unaware or unheeding of the curiosity he was arousing. He was tall and young and agile, but rigid. He was like a person without will, summoned forward by his controller's voice. I saw him better now. He had dark glasses, black stubble and moustache. That was why his face had seemed so black. And the white nurse's scarf over his head. But it was the automaton's stiffness of his walk that set my skin tingling and made me wonder what kind of believer we might have on our hands.

He had reached the centre of the lobby. A few people made way for him. Some looked at him and looked away, others turned their backs in abstention, as if they knew and did not like him. Suddenly, under the brightness of the centre light, he seemed to be ascending. With his shrou-ded head forward and his arms barely moving, he was mounting his own scaffold on orders from above. I saw now that he was American. I saw it in the dipping knees and hanging wrists and slightly girlish hips. An all-American boy. His dark glasses were not dark enough, apparently, for a cloth eye-shade dangled from one long hand. It was of the kind that gamblers are supposed to wear, and night editors in forties films. He was six feet tall, at least. He wore sneakers, vestal white like his headscarf, and soundless.

An Arab freak? I wondered.

A crazed Zionist? There had been a few of those.

Stoned?

A high-school war tourist on the hippy trail, searching for kicks in the city of the damned?

Changing direction, he had begun talking to the receptionist, but at an angle facing into the lobby, already searching for the person he was enquiring for. Which was when I saw the red spots scattered over his cheeks and forehead, like hives or chicken pox, but more vivid. The bedbugs had eaten him in some stinking hostel, I decided. He had stuck his head through the windscreen of a clapped-out car. He started walking towards me. Stiffly again, without expression. Purposefully, a man used to being looked at. Angrily, the eyeshade dangling from his hand. Glowering at me blindly through his black glasses as I sat drinking. A woman had taken his arm. She wore a skirt and could have been the nurse who had given him his headscarf. They stood before me. Me and no one else.

'Sir? This is Sol, sir,' she said – or Mort, or Syd, or whatever. 'He's asking whether you're the journalist, sir.'

I said I was a journalist.

'From London, sir, visiting? Are you the editor, sir? Are you influential, sir?'

Influential I doubted, I said with a deprecating smile. I was on the managerial side, here on a brief swing.

'And going back to London, sir? Soon?'

In Beirut you learn not to talk in advance about your movements. 'Pretty soon,' I conceded, though the truth was I was planning to return south again next day.

'Can Sol speak with you a moment, sir, just speak? Sol needs very much to speak with a person who has influence with the major Western newspapers. The journalists here, he feels they've seen it all, they're jaded. Sol needs a voice from outside.'

I made space and she sat beside me while Sol very slowly lowered himself into a chair – this covered, silent, very clean man in his long football sleeves and headscarf. Seated finally, he laid his wrists over his knees, holding the eyeshade in both hands. Then he gave a long sigh and began to murmur to me.

'There's this thing I've written, sir. I'd like, please, to have it printed in your newspaper.'

His voice, though soft, was educated and polite. But it was lifeless and, like his movements, economical, as if each word hurt him to produce. Inside the lenses of his very dark glasses, I saw that his left eye was smaller than his right. Narrower. Not swollen, not closed by a punch, just altogether smaller than its partner, taken from a different face. And the spots were not bites, not hives, not cuts. They were craters, like the pockmarks of small-arms fire on a Beirut wall, stamped with heat and speed. Like craters also, the skin around them had risen but not closed.

His story followed without my asking for it. He was a relief volunteer,

sir, a third-year medical student from Omaha. He believed in peace, sir.
And he had been in this bombing, sir, down by the Corniche, in this
restaurant that had been one of the worst-hit places, just wiped out, you
should go down there and take a look, a place called Akhbar's, sir, where
a lot of Americans went, there was this car bomb and car bombs are the
worst. You can't get worse than car bombs for surprise.

I said I knew that.

Almost everyone in the restaurant had died except himself, sir, the
people nearest the wall just blew apart, he continued, unaware that he had
painted my own worst nightmare for me. And now he had this thing he
had written, he felt he had to say it, sir, a sort of mild statement about
peace, which he needed to print in my newspaper, maybe it would do some
good, he was thinking of like this weekend or maybe Monday. He'd like
to donate the fee to charity. He guessed it could be like a couple of hundred
dollars, maybe more. In the Beirut hospitals, that still bought people a
piece of hope.

'We need a pause, sir,' he explained, in his dead voice as the woman
fished a wad of typescript from his pocket for him. 'A pause for moderation. Just a break between wars to find the middle way.'

Only in the Commodore in Beirut could it have seemed natural that a
bomb-shocked peace-seeker should be pleading a hopeless cause to
a journalist who wasn't one. Nevertheless I promised to do what I could.
When I had done my business with the man I was waiting for – who knew
nothing, of course, had heard nothing, but perhaps, sir, if I spoke to
Colonel Asme in Tyre? – I settled in my room and with a glass at my elbow
began to read his offering, determined that, if it had any reasonable chance
of publication, I would twist the arm of one of our numberless Fleet Street
friendlies when I returned to London, and see it done.

It was a tragic piece, and quickly it became unreadable: a rambling,
emotional appeal to Jews, Christians and Muslims alike to remember their
own mothers and children, and live together in love. It urged the middle
ground of compromise and gave inaccurate examples from history. It
proposed a new religion 'like Joan of Arc would have given us only the
English wouldn't let her, so they burned her alive, disregarding her screams
and the will of the ordinary people.' This great new movement, he said,
would 'bind the Semitic races in a spiritual brotherhood of love and
tolerance.' Then it lost its way completely, and resorted to capital letters,
underlining, and rows of exclamation marks. So that by the time I reached
the end, it had ceased to be what it set out to be at all, and was talking
about 'this whole family, kids and grandparents, that was sitting up beside
the wall nearest to the epicentre.' And how they had all been blown to
pieces, not once, but over and over again, each time Sol allowed himself
to look into his anguished memory.

Suddenly I was writing the piece for him. To her. To Annie. First in my mind, then in the margin of his pages, then on a fresh sheet of A4 paper from my briefcase, which was quickly covered so I took another. I was sweating, the sweat was pouring off me like rain; it was that kind of Beirut night, quiet till now but with a damp, itchy heat rolling off the mountains and an evil grey smog like gunsmoke draping itself across the sea. I was writing, and wondering if she would ring again. I was writing as the bombed boy, to a girl I didn't know. I was writing – as I saw to my dismay when I awoke next morning – pretentious junk. I was proclaiming maverick affections, mouthing great sentiments, pontificating about the unbreakable cycle of human evil, about man's endless search for reasons to do the wrong thing.

A pause, the boy had said. A pause for moderation, a break between wars. I put him right on that. I put Annie right on it too. I told them that the only pauses in the history of human conflict had been pauses not for moderation but excess, pauses for the world to redivide itself, for the thugs and the victims to find each other, for greed and deprival to regroup. I wrote like an adolescent bleeding heart, and when the morning came and I saw the pages of my handwriting strewn over the floor around the empty whisky bottle, I could not believe this was the work of anyone I knew.

So I did the only thing I could think of. I put them in the handbasin and cremated them, then broke up the ash and scattered it in the lavatory and flushed it into the body-blocked sewers of Beirut. And when I had done that, I took myself for a punishing pelt along the waterfront, running as hard as I could go from whatever was coming after me.

I was running towards Hansen, away from myself, but I had one more stop to make along the way.

My German girl, Britta, turned out to be in Israel, in the middle of the Negev Desert, in a compound of stark grey huts near a village called Revivim. The huts had a ploughed strip round them, and a double peri-meter of barbed-wire fencing with a manned watchtower at each corner. If there were other European prisoners in the compound apart from her, I was not introduced to them. Her only companions that I saw were young Arab girls, mainly from poor villages in the West Bank or the Gaza, who had been talked or bullied by their Palestinian comrades into committing acts of savagery against the hated Zionist Occupiers, most often planting bombs in marketplaces or tossing them into civilian buses.

I arrived there by jeep from Beersheeba, driven by a hardy young Colonel of Intelligence whose father, while still a boy, had been trained as a Night Raider by the eccentric General Wingate during the British Man-date. The Colonel's father remembered Wingate squatting naked in his tent by candlelight, drawing out the battle plan in the sand. Every Israeli soldier seems to talk about his father and a good few talk about the British. After the Mandate, they think they know us for what we probably still

are: anti-Semitic, ignorant and imperialist, with just enough exceptions to
redeem us. Dimona, where the Israelis store their nuclear arsenal, was up
the road.

My sense of unreality had not left me. To the contrary, it had intensified.
It was as if I had lost the distance from the human condition that is
essential to our trade. My feelings and the feelings of others seemed to
count more with me than my observations. It is quite easy in the Lebanon,
if you drop your guard, to develop an unreasoning hatred of Israel. But I
had succumbed to a serious dose of the disease. Trudging through the mud
and stench of the shattered camps, crouching in the sandbagged hovels, I
convinced myself that the Israeli thirst for vengeance would not be stilled
until the accusing eyes of the last Palestinian child had been closed for
good.

Perhaps my young Colonel got a hint of this, for though I had flown in
from Cyprus it was still only a few hours since I had left Beirut, and
something of what I felt may still have been legible in my face.

'You get to see Arafat?' he asked, with a moody smile as we drove along
the straight road.

'No, I didn't.'

'Why not? He's a nice guy.'

I let that go.

'Why do you want to see Britta?'

I told him. There was no point in not doing so. It had taken all London's
powers of persuasion to get me the interview with her at all, and my hosts
were certainly not going to let me speak to her alone.

'We think she may be willing to talk to us about an old boyfriend,' I
said.

'Why would she do that?'

'He jilted her. She was angry with him.'

'Who's the boyfriend?' – as if he didn't know.

'He's Irish. He has the rank of adjutant in the IRA. He briefs bombers,
reconnoitres targets, supplies the equipment. She lived underground with
him in Amsterdam and Paris.'

'Like George Orwell, huh? *Down and Out?*'

'Like George Orwell.'

'How long ago he jilted her?'

'Six months.'

'Maybe she's not angry any more. Maybe she'll tell you go suck. For a
girl like Britta, six months is a hell of a long time.'

I asked whether she had talked much in her captivity. It was a delicate
question, since the Israelis were still not saying how long they had been
holding her, or how they had obtained her in the first place. The Colonel
was broad-faced and brown-skinned. His family came originally from
Russia. He wore parachute wings on his short-sleeved khaki shirt. He was
twenty-eight, a Sabra, born in Tel Aviv, engaged to a Sephardi from

Morocco. His father, the Night Raider, was now a dentist. All this he had told me in the first few minutes of our acquaintance, in a guttural English he had captured single-handed.

'Talked?' he repeated with a grim smile, in answer to my question. 'Britta? That lady didn't stop talking since she became a resident.'

Knowing a little of Israeli methods, I was not surprised, and I shuddered inwardly at the prospect of questioning a woman who had been subjected to them. It had happened to me in Ireland: a man buttoned to the neck who had stared at me like a dead man and confessed to everything.

'Do you interrogate her yourself?' I asked, noticing afresh his thick brown forearms and the uncompromising set of his jaw. And thinking, perhaps, of Colonel Jerzy.

He shook his head. 'Impossible.'

'Why?'

He seemed about to tell me something, then changed his mind. 'We got experts,' he said. 'Shin Bet guys, smart like Britta. Take their time with her. Family.'

I had heard about this loving family too, though I didn't say so. The Zionists had lured her into a trap, a bloodshot-eyed informant had whispered to me in Tyre. She had left the camps and gone to Athens with her new boyfriend, Said, and three of Said's friends, he said. Good boys. All able. The plan had been to shoot down an El Al plane as it made its approach to Athens airport. The boys had got themselves a hand-held rocket launcher and a rented house on the flightpath. Britta's job, as an unsuspicious-looking European, was to stand in a phone box at the airport with a thirty-dollar shortwave receiver and relay the control tower's instructions to the boys on the roof as the plane came in. Everything had been set fair, said my bone-weary informant. The rehearsals had gone like a dream. But on the day, the operation had fouled up.

Listening to him, I had filled in the rest of the story for myself, imagining how the Service would have done the job if we'd had the foreknowledge: two teams to assault the roof and the phone box simultaneously; the target plane, forewarned and empty, landing safely at Athens airport; the plane's homeward journey to Tel Aviv with the terrorists chained in their seats. I wondered what they would do with her. Whether they would put her on trial or trade her for favours in return.

'What happened to the boys she was with in Athens?' I asked the Colonel, ignoring London's injunction to show no curiosity in such matters.

'Boys? She knows nothing from boys. Athens? Where's Athens already? She's an innocent German tourist on vacation in Eilat. We kidnapped her, we drugged her, we imprisoned her, now we're framing her for propaganda. She invites us to prove the contrary because she knows we can't. You want any more information? Ask Britta, be our guest.'

His mood mystified me, the more so when, as we got out of the jeep, he laid a hand on my shoulder and wished me a sort of luck. 'She's all yours,' he said. '*Mazel tov.*'

I was beginning to dread what I might find.

A dumpy little woman in army uniform received us in her clean office. Prison staff never go short of cleaners, I thought. She was Captain Levi and she was Britta's unlikely gaoler. She spoke English the way a small-town American schoolmistress might speak it, but more slowly, with greater care. She had twinkly eyes and short grey hair and a look of kindly resignation. She had the dusty complexion of prison life, but when she put her hands together you felt she ought to be knitting for her grand-children.

'Britta is very intelligent,' she said apologetically. 'For an intelligent man to question an intelligent woman, that's sometimes difficult. Do you have a daughter, sir?'

I was not about to fill in my character profile for her so I said no, which happened also to be the truth.

'A pity. Never mind. Maybe you still get one. A man like you, you have time. You speak German?'

'Yes.'

'Then you are lucky. You can communicate with her in her language. That way you get to know her better. Britta and I, we can speak only English together. I speak it like my late husband, who was American. Britta speaks it like her late lover, who was Irish. Tel Aviv says we are to allow you two hours. Will you be happy with two hours? If you need more, we shall ask them – maybe they say yes. Maybe two hours will be too much. We shall see.'

'You are very kind,' I said.

'Kind, I don't know. Maybe we should be less kind. Maybe we are making kind too much. You will see.'

And with this, she sent for coffee and for Britta, while the Colonel and myself took up our places along one side of the plain wood table.

But Captain Levi did not sit at the table, I supposed because she was not part of the interview. She sat beside the door on a straight kitchen chair, her eyes lowered as if in preparation for a concert. Even when Britta walked in between two young wardresses, she only lifted her eyes as far as was necessary to watch the three women's feet pass her to the centre of the room and halt. One wardress pulled back a chair for Britta, the second unlocked her handcuffs. The wardresses left, and we settled to the table.

And I would like to paint for you the scene exactly as I saw it from where I sat: with the Colonel to my right, and Britta opposite us across the table, and the bowed grey head of Captain Levi almost directly behind her, but slightly to the left, wearing a reminiscent expression that was half a smile. Throughout our discussion she stayed like that, still as a waxwork. Her part-smile of familiarity never altered and never went away. There was concentration in her pose, and something of effort, so that I wondered whether she was straining to pick out phrases and words she could identify, perhaps from a combined knowledge of Yiddish and English, for Britta, being a Bremen girl, spoke a clear and authoritarian German, which makes comprehension easier.

And Britta, without a doubt, was a fine sample of her breed. She was 'blond as a bread roll,' as they say up there, tall and deep-shouldered and well-grown, with wide rather insolent blue eyes and a strong, attractive jaw. She had Monica's youth and Monica's height as well; and, as I could not avoid speculating, Monica's sensuality. My suspicion that they had been maltreating her vanished as soon as she walked in. She held herself like a ballerina, but with more intelligence and more of life's reality than is to be found in most dancers. She would have looked well in tennis gear or in a *dirndl* dress, and I suspected that in her time she had worn both. Even her prison tunic did not diminish her, for she had made herself a cloth belt out of something, and tied it at the waist, and she had brushed her fair hair over her shoulders in a cape. Her first gesture when her hands were freed was to offer me one, at the same time dropping a schoolgirl bob, whether out of irony or respect it was too soon to tell. Her grasp was like a boy's, but lingering. She wore no make-up but needed none.

'*Und mit wem hab' ich die Ehre?*' she enquired, either courteously or impishly. And whom do I have the honour to address?

'I'm a British official,' I said.

'Your name, please?'

'It's unimportant.'

'But you are very important!'

Prisoners when they are brought up from their cells often say silly things in their first flush, so I answered her with consideration.

'I'm working with the Israelis on aspects of your case. That's all you need to know.'

'Case? I am a case? How amusing. I thought I was a human being. Please sit down, Mr. Nobody,' she said, doing so herself.

So we sit as I have described, with Captain Levi's face behind her, a little out of focus like its expression. The Colonel had not stood up to greet Britta, and he barely bothered to look at her now she was sitting before him. He seemed suddenly to be without expectation. He glanced at his watch. It was of dull steel and like a weapon on his brown wrist. Britta's wrists were white and smooth like Monica's, but chafed with red rings from the handcuffs.

Suddenly she was lecturing me.

She began at once, as if she were resuming a tutorial, and in a sense she was, for I soon realised she lectured everyone this way, or everyone whom she had dismissed as bourgeois. She said she had a statement to make which she would like me to relay to my 'colleagues,' as she called them, since she felt that her position was not being sufficiently appreciated by the authorities. She was a prisoner of war, just as any Israeli soldier in

Palestinian hands was a prisoner of war, and entitled to the treatment and
privileges set out in the Geneva Convention. She was a tourist here, she
had committed no crime against Israel; she had been arrested solely on the
strength of her trumped-up record in other countries, as a deliberate act
of provocation against the world proletariat.

I gave a quick laugh, and she faltered. She was not expecting laughter.

'But look here,' I objected. 'Either you're a prisoner of war or you're an
innocent tourist. You can't be both.'

'The struggle is between the innocent and the guilty,' she retorted
without hesitation, and resumed her lecture. Her enemies were not limited
to Zionism, she said, but what she called the dynamic of bourgeois
domination, the repression of natural instincts, and the maintenance of
despotic authority disguised as 'democracy.'

Again I tried to interrupt her, but this time she talked straight through
me. She quoted Marcuse at me and Freud. She referred to the rebellion of
sons in puberty against their fathers, and the disavowal of this rebellion in
later years as the sons themselves became the fathers.

I glanced at the Colonel, but he seemed to be dozing.

The purpose of her 'actions' she said, and those of her comrades, was to
arrest this instinctual cycle of repression in all its forms – in the enslave-
ment of labour to materialism, in the repressive principle of 'progress'
itself – and to allow the real forces of society to surge, like erotic energy,
into new, unfettered forms of cultural creation.

'None of this is faintly interesting to me,' I protested. 'Just stop, please,
and listen to my questions.'

Acts of so-called 'terrorism' had therefore two clear purposes, she
continued, as if I had never spoken, of which the first was to disconcert
the armies of the bourgeois-materialist conspiracy, and the second to
instruct, by example, the pit-ponies of the earth, who had lost all knowledge of the light. In other words, to introduce ferment and awaken
consciousness at the most repressed human levels.

She wished to add that though she was not an adherent of Communism,
she preferred its teachings to those of capitalism, since Communism
provided a powerful negation of the ego-ideal which used property to
construct the human prison.

She favoured free sexual expression and – for those who needed them –
the use of drugs as a means of discovering the free self as contrasted
with the unfree self that is castrated by aggressive tolerance.

I turned to the Colonel. There is an etiquette of interrogation as there is
about everything else. 'Do we have to go on listening to this nonsense?
The lady is your prisoner, not mine,' I said. For I could hardly lay the law
down to her across his table.

The Colonel lifted his head high enough to glance at her with indifference. 'You want to go back down, Britta?' he asked her. 'You want bread

and water for a couple of weeks?' His German was as bizarre as his English. He seemed suddenly a lot older than his age, and wiser.

'I have more to say, thank you.'

'If you're going to stay up here, you answer his questions and you shut up,' said the Colonel. 'It's your choice. You want to leave now, it's fine by us.' He added something in Hebrew to Captain Levi, who nodded distantly. An Arab prisoner entered with a tray of coffee – four cups and a plate of sugar biscuits – and handed them round meekly, a coffee cup for each of us and one for Captain Levi, the biscuits at the centre of the table. An air of lassitude had settled over us. Britta stretched out her long arm for a biscuit, lazily, as if she were in her own home. The Colonel's hand crashed on the table just ahead of her as he removed the plate from her reach.

'So what do you wish to ask me, please?' Britta enquired of me, as if nothing at all had happened. 'Do you wish me to deliver the Irish to you? What other aspects of my case could interest the English, Mr. Nobody?'

'If you deliver us one particular Irishman, that will be fine,' I said. 'You lived with a man named Seamus for a year.'

She was amused. I had provided her with an opening. She studied me, and seemed to see something in my face she recognised. '*Lived* with him? That is an exaggeration. I slept with him. Seamus was only for sex,' she explained, with a mischievous smile. 'He was a convenience, an instrument. A *good* instrument, I would say. I was the same for him. You like sex? Sometimes another boy would join us, maybe sometimes a girl. We made combinations. It was irrelevant but we had fun.'

'Irrelevant to what?' I asked.

'To our work.'

'What work?'

'I have already described our work to you, Mr. Nobody. I have told you of its aims, and of our motivations. Humanitarianism is not to be equated with non-violence. We must fight to be free. Sometimes even the highest causes can only be served by violent methods. Do you not know that? Sex also can be violent.'

'What kind of violent methods was Seamus involved in?' I asked.

'We are speaking not of wanton acts but of the people's right of resistance against acts committed by the forces of repression. Are you a member of those forces or are you in favour of spontaneity, Mr. Nobody? Perhaps you should free yourself and join us.'

'He's a bomber,' I said. 'He blows up innocent people. His most recent target was a public house in southern England. He killed one elderly couple, the barman and the pianist, and I give you my word he didn't liberate a single deluded worker.'

'Is that a question or a statement, Mr. Nobody?'

'It's an invitation to you to tell me about his activities.'

'The public house was close to a British military camp,' she replied. 'It was providing infrastructure and comfort to Fascistic forces of oppression.'

Again her cool eyes held me in their playful gaze. Did I say she was attractive? What is attraction in such circumstances? She was wearing a calico tunic. She was an enforced penitent of crimes that she did not repent. She was alert in every part of herself, I could feel it, and she knew I felt it, and the divide between us enticed her.

'My department is considering offering you a sum of money on your release, payable, if you prefer, to somebody you nominate in the meantime,' I said. 'They want information that would lead to the arrest and conviction of your friend Seamus. They are interested in his past crimes, others he has yet to commit, safe addresses, contacts, habits and weaknesses.' She waited for me to go on, so, perhaps unwisely, I did. 'Seamus is not a hero. He's a pig. Not what you call a pig. A real pig. Nobody did bad things to him when he was young; his parents are decent people who run a tobacco shop in County Down. His grandfather was a policeman, a good one. Seamus is blowing people up for kicks because he's inadequate. That's why he treated you badly. He only exists when he's inflicting pain. The rest of the time he's a spoilt little boy.'

I had not scratched the surface of her steady stare.

'Are you inadequate, Mr. Nobody? I think perhaps you are. In your occupation, that is normal. You should join us, Mr. Nobody. You should take lessons with us, and we shall convert you to our cause. Then you will be adequate.'

You must understand that she did not raise her voice while she said this, or indulge in dramatics of any kind. She remained condescending and composed, even hospitable. The mischief in her lay deep and well-disguised. She had a healthy natural smile and it stayed with her all the time she spoke, while Captain Levi behind her continued to gaze into her own memories, perhaps because she did not understand what was being said.

The Colonel glanced at me in question. Not trusting myself to speak, I lifted my hands from the table, asking what's the point? The Colonel said something to Captain Levi, who in the disappointed manner of someone who has prepared a meal only to see it taken away uneaten, pressed a bell for the escort. Britta rose to her feet, smoothed her prison tunic over her breasts and hips and held out her hands for the handcuffs.

'How much money were they thinking of offering me, Mr. Nobody?' she enquired.

'None,' I said.

She dropped me another bob and walked between her guards towards the door, her hips flowing inside her calico tunic, reminding me of Monica's inside her dressing-gown. I was afraid she would speak again but she didn't. Perhaps she knew she had won the day, and anything more would spoil the effect. The Colonel followed her out and I was alone with Captain Levi. The half smile had not left her face.

'There,' she said. 'Now you know a little what it feels like to hear Britta's music.'

'I suppose I do.'

'Sometimes we communicate too much. Perhaps you should have spoken English to her. So long as she speaks English, I can care for her. She is a human being, she is a woman, she is in prison. And you may be sure she is in agony. She is courageous, and so long as she speaks English to me I can do my duty for her.'

'And when she speaks German to you?'

'What would be the point, since she knows I cannot understand her?'

'But if she did – and if you could understand her? What then?'

Her smile twisted and became slightly shameful. 'Then I think I would be frightened,' she replied in her slow American. 'I think if she ordered something of me, I would be tempted to obey her. But I do not let her order me. Why should I? I do not give her the power over me. I speak English and I stay the boss. I was for two years in concentration camp in Buchenwald, you see.' Still smiling at me, she delivered the rest in German, in the clenched, hushed whisper of the campnik: '*Man hört so scheussliche Echos in ihrer Stimme, wissen Sie.*' One hears such dreadful echoes in her voice, you see.

The Colonel was standing in the doorway waiting for me. As we walked downstairs, he put his hand once more on my shoulder. This time I knew why.

'Is she like that with all the boys?' I asked him.

'Captain Levi?'

'Britta.'

'Sure. With you a bit more, that's all. Maybe that's because you're English.'

Maybe it is, I thought, and maybe it's because she saw more in me than just my Englishness. Maybe she read my unconscious signals of availability. But whatever she saw in me, or didn't, Britta had provided the summation of my confusion until now. She had articulated my sense of trying to hold on to a world that was slipping away from me, my susceptibility to every stray argument and desire.

The summons to find Hansen arrived the same night, in the middle of a jolly diplomatic party given by my British Embassy host in Herzliyya.

9

E arnest Perigrew was quizzing Smiley about colonialism. Sooner or later, Perigrew quizzed everyone who came to Sarratt about colonialism, and his questions always hovered at the edge of outrage. He was a troubled boy, the son of British missionaries to West Africa, and one of those people the Service is almost bound to employ, on account of their rare knowledge and linguistic qualifications. He was sitting as usual alone, amid the shadows at the back of the library, his gaunt face thrust forward and one long hand held up as if to fend off ridicule. The question had started reasonably, then degenerated into a tirade against Britain's indifference towards her former enslaved subjects.

'Yes, well I think I rather agree with you,' said Smiley courteously, to the general surprise, when he had heard Perigrew to the end. 'The sad answer is, I'm afraid, that the Cold War produced in us a kind of *vicarious* colonialism. On the one hand we abandoned practically every article of our national identity to American foreign policy. On the other we bought ourselves a stay of execution for our vision of our colonial selves. Worse still, we encouraged the Americans to behave in the same way. Not that they needed our encouragement, but they were pleased to have it, naturally.'

Hansen had said much the same. And in much the same language. But where Smiley had lost little of his urbanity, Hansen had glared into my face with eyes lit by the red hells from which he had returned.

I flew from Israel to Bangkok because Smiley said Hansen had gone mad and knew too many secrets: a decypher yourself signal, care of the Head of Station, Tel Aviv. Smiley had charge of Service security at the time, with the courtesy rank of deputy chief. Whenever I heard of him, he seemed to be scuttling round plugging another leak or another scandal. I spent the weekend in a heatwave sweating my way through the stack of hand-delivered files and an hour on the telephone placating Mabel, who had fallen at the last fence of her annual race to become ladies' captain of our local golf club and was scenting intrigue.

I don't know why they're so hard on Mabel. Perhaps it's her way of plain talking that puts them off. I did what I could. I told her that nothing I had come upon in the Service could compare with the skulduggery of those Kent wives. I promised her a splendid holiday when I returned. I forget where the holiday was going to be because we never took it.

Hansen's file gave me a portrait of a type I had grown familiar with because we used a good few of them. I was one myself and Ben was another: the crossbred Englishman who adopts the Service as his country and endows it with a bunch of qualities it hasn't really got.

Like myself, Hansen was half a Dutchman. Perhaps that was why Smiley had chosen me. He was born in the long night of the German Occupation of Holland and raised in the shadow of Delft Cathedral. His mother, a counter clerk at Thomas Cook's, was of English parents who urged her to go back to London with them when the war broke out. She refused, choosing instead to marry a Delft curate, who a year afterwards got himself shot by a German firing squad, leaving his pregnant wife to fend for herself. Undaunted, she joined a British escape line and, by the time the war ended, had charge of a fully fledged network, with its own communications, informants, safe houses and the usual appointments. My mother's work with the Service had not been so different.

By what route the infant Hansen found his way to the Jesuits, the file did not relate. Perhaps the mother converted. Those were dark years still, and if expediency required it, she may have swallowed her Protestant convictions to buy the boy a decent education. Give the Jesuits his soul, she may have reasoned, and they will give him a brain. Or perhaps she sensed in her son from early on the mercurial nature that later ruled his life, and she determined to subordinate him to a stronger religious discipline than was offered by the easy-going Protestants. If so, she was wise. Hansen embraced the faith as he embraced everything else, with passion. The nuns had him, the brothers had him, the priests had him, the scholars had him. Till at twenty-one, schooled and devout but still a novice, he was packed off to a seminary in Indonesia to learn the ways of the heathen: Sumatra, Molucca, Java.

The Orient seems to have been an instinctive love of Hansen's as it is for many Dutchmen. The good Dutch, like Heine's proverbial pine tree, can stand on the shores of their flat little country and sniff the Asian scents of lemon grass and cooking pots on the chill sea air. Hansen arrived, he saw, he was conquered. Buddhism, Islam, the rites and superstitions of the remotest savages – he flung himself on all of them with a fervour that only intensified the deeper he penetrated into the jungle.

Languages also came naturally to him. To his native Dutch and English he had effortlessly added French and German. Now he acquired Tamil, Khmer, Thai, Sanskrit and more than a smattering of Cantonese, often hiking hundreds of miles of hill country in his quest for a missing dialect or ritualistic link. He wrote papers on philology, marriage rites, illumination and monkeys. He discovered lost temples in the depths of the jungle, and won prizes the Society forbade him to accept. After six years of fearless exploring and enquiring, he was not only the kind of academic showpiece Jesuits are famous for; he was also a full priest.

But few secrets can survive six years. Gradually the stories about him began to acquire a seamy edge. Hansen the skin artist. Hansen's appetites. Don't look now but here comes one of Hansen's girls.

It was the scale as well as the duration that did for him: the fact that once they started probing, they found no corner to his life that was immune, no journey that did not have its detour. A woman here or there – a boy or two – well, from what I have seen of priesthood round the globe, such peccadilloes are to be found more in the observance than the breach.

But this wholesale indulgence, in every kampong, in every tawdry sidestreet, this indefatigable debauchery, flaunted, as they now discovered, beneath their noses for more than a decade, with girls who by Western standards were barely eligible for their First Communion, let alone the marriage bed – and many of them under the Church's own protection – made Hansen suddenly and dramatically untenable. Faced with the evidence of such prolonged and dedicated sinning, his Superior responded more in grief than indignation. He ordered Hansen to return to Rome, and sent a letter ahead of him to the General of the Society. From Rome, he told Hansen sadly, he would most likely go to Loyola in Spain, where qualified Jesuit psychotherapists would help him come to terms with his regrettable weakness. After Loyola – well, a new beginning, perhaps a different hemisphere, a different decade.

But Hansen, like his mother before him, stubbornly declined to leave the place of his adoption.

At a loss, the Father Guardian packed him off to a distant mission in the hills run by a traditionalist of the sterner school. There Hansen suffered the barbarities of house arrest. He was watched over like a madman. He was forbidden to pass beyond the precincts of the house, denied books, paper, company, laughter. Men take to confinement in different ways, as they take differently to heights or cold or dying. Hansen took to it terribly, and after three months could bear no more. As his brother guardians escorted him to Mass, he hurled one of them down a staircase while the other fled. Then he headed back to Djakarta and, with neither money nor passport, went to ground in the brothels he knew well. The girls took him into their care, and in return he worked as pimp and bouncer. He gave out beer, washed glasses, ejected the unruly, heard confessions, gave succour, played with the children in the back room. I see him, as I know him now, doing all those things without fuss or complication. He was barely thirty and his desires burned bright as ever. Until one day, yielding as so often to an impulse, Hansen shaved, put on a clean shirt, and presented himself to the British Consul to claim his British soul.

And the Consul, being neither deaf nor blind, but a longstanding member of the Service, listened to Hansen's story, asked a humdrum question or two and, from behind a mask of apathy, sprang to action. For years he had been looking for a man of Hansen's gifts. Hansen's waywardness did not deter the Consul in the least. He liked it. He signalled London for background; he lent Hansen cautious sums of cash against receipts in triplicate, for he did not wish to show undue enthusiasm. When London came back with a white trace on Hansen's mother, indicating she was a former agent of the Service, the Consul's cup brimmed over.

Another month and Hansen was semi-conscious, which means he knew, but only half knew, but then again might not know, that he just could be half in touch with what one might loosely refer to as British Intelligence. Another two months and, restless as ever, he was taking a swing through southern Java ostensibly in search of ancient scrolls, in reality to report back to the Consul the strength of Communist subversion, which was his newly adopted anti-Christ. By the end of the year he was headed for London with the brand-new British passport he had wanted in his pocket, though not in his own name.

I turned to his potted training record, all six months of it. Clive Bellamy, a gangly, mischievous Etonian, was in charge of Sarratt. 'Excellent at all things practical,' he wrote in Hansen's end-of-course report. 'Has a first-rate memory, fast reactions, is self-sufficient. Needs to be ridden hard. If there's ever a mutiny on my ship, Hansen will be the first man I'll flog. Needs a big canvas and a first-rate controller.'

I turned to the operational record. No madness there either. Since Hansen was still Dutch, Head Office decided to keep him that way and play down his Englishness. Hansen bridled but they overruled him. At a time when the British abroad were being seen by everyone except themselves as Americans without the clout, Head Office would kill for a Swede and steal for a West German. Even Canadians, though more easily manufactured, were smiled on. Back in Holland, Hansen formalised his severance from the Jesuits and set about looking for new employment back East. A score of Oriental academic bodies were spread around the capitals of Western Europe in those days. Hansen did his rounds of them, gaining a promise here and a commitment there. A French Oriental news agency took him on as a stringer. A London weekly, nudged by Head Office, made a berth for him on condition they got him free. Till bit by bit his cover was complete – wide enough for him to have a reason to go anywhere and ask what questions he wanted, varied enough to be financially inscrutable, since no one would ever be able to tell which of his several employers were paying him how much for what. He was ready to be launched. British interests in South East Asia might have dwindled with her Empire, but the Americans were in there knee-deep with an official war running in Vietnam, an unofficial one in Cambodia and a secret one in Laos. In our unlovely rôle as camp follower, we were delighted to offer them Hansen's precious talents.

Espionage technology can do a lot. It can photograph crops and trenches, tanks and rocket sites and tyre-marks and the migration of the reindeer. It can flinch at the sound of a Russian fighter pilot breaking wind at forty thousand feet or a Chinese general belching in his sleep. But it can't replace human understanding. It can't tell you what's in the heart of a Cambodian farmer whose hill crops have been blown to smithereens by Dr. Kissinger's unmarked bombers, whose daughters have been sold into prostitution in the city, and whose sons have been lured into leaving the fields and fighting for an American puppet army, or urged, by way of family insurance, into the ranks of the Khmer Rouge. It can't read the lips of jungle fighters in black pyjamas whose most powerful weapon is the perverted Marxism of a blood-hungry Sorbonne-educated Cambodian psychopath. It can't sniff the exhaust fumes of an army that is unmechanised. Or break the codes of an army without radio. Or calculate the supplies of men who can nourish themselves on ground beetles and wood bark; or the morale of those who, having lost all they possess, have only the future to win.

But Hansen could. Hansen, the adopted Asian, could trek without food for a week, squat in the kampongs and listen to the murmur of the villagers, and Hansen could read the rising wind of their resistance long before it stirred the Stars and Stripes on the Embassy roofs of Phnom Penh and Saigon. And he could tell the bombers – and, to his later remorse, he did – he could tell the American bombers which villages were playing host to the Vietcong. He was a fisher of men, too. He could recruit helpers from every walk of life and instruct them how to see and hear and remember and report. He knew how little to tell them and how much, how to reward them and when not to.

For months, then years, Hansen functioned that way in the so-called 'liberated areas' of northern Cambodia where the Khmer Rouge nominally held sway, until the day he vanished from the village he had made his home. Vanished soundlessly, taking the inhabitants with him. Soon to be given up for dead, another jungle disappearance.

And remained dead until a short time ago, when he had come alive in a brothel in Bangkok.

'Take your time, Ned,' Smiley had urged me on the telephone to Tel Aviv. 'If you want to add a couple of days for jet-lag, it's quite all right by me.'

Which was Smiley-speak for 'Get to him as fast as you can and tell me I haven't got another king-sized scandal on my hands.'

Our Station Head in Bangkok was a bald, rude, moustachioed little tyrant called Rumbelow, whom I had never warmed to. The Service offers precious few prospects for men of fifty. Most are blown; many are too tired and disenchanted to care whether they are or not. Others head for private banking or big business, but the marriage seldom lasts. Something has happened to their way of thinking that unsuits them to the overt life. But a very few, of whom Toby Esterhase was one and Rumbelow another, pull off the trick of holding the Service hostage to their supposed assets.

Exactly what Rumbelow's were I never knew. Seedy, I am sure, for if he specialised in anything, it was human baseness. One rumour said he owned a couple of corrupt Thai generals who would work to him and to no one else. Another that he had managed to perform a grimy favour for a member of the royal household that was not transferable. Whatever his hold on them, the barons of the Fifth Floor would hear no ill of him. 'And for God's sake, don't rub up Rumbelow the wrong way, Ned,' Smiley had begged me. 'I'm sure he's a pain in the neck, but we do need him.'

I met him in my hotel room. To the overt world I was Mark Seymour, occupation accountant, and had no wish to parade myself at the Embassy or his house. I had been flying twenty hours. It was early evening. Rumbelow spoke like an Etonian bookmaker. Come to think of it, he looked like one as well.

'It was *sheerest* bloody coincidence we bumped into the bastard at all,' he told me huffily. 'One puts out one's feelers, naturally. One keeps one's ear to the proverbial ground. One knows the score. One's heard of other cases. One isn't insensitive. One doesn't like to think of one's joe trussed to a stick, being carted through the jungle for weeks on end, while the Khmer Rouge torture the hell out of him, naturally. Not an ostrich. Know the score. Your brown man doesn't obey the Queensberry Rules, you know,' he assured me, as if I had implied the opposite. And, plucking a handkerchief from the sleeve of his sweat-patched suit, he pummelled his stupid moustache with it. 'Your *average* joe would be yelling for a quick bullet after one night of it.'

'Are you sure that's what happened to him?'

'Not sure of anything, thank you, old boy. Rumour, that's all. How *can* I be sure, if the bastard won't even talk to us? Threatens violence if we try! For all *I* know, the KR never had sight nor sound of him. Never did trust a Dutchman, not out here – they think they own the bloody place. Hansen wouldn't be the first joe to lie doggo when things got too hot for him, then come bouncing back when it's all over, asking for his gong and his pension, not by any means. Still in possession of all his fingers and thumbs, by all accounts. Not missing any other part of his anatomy either, to judge by where he's holed out. Duffy Marchbanks spotted him. Remember Duffy? Good chap.'

With a sinking heart, yes, I remembered Duffy. I had remembered him when I saw his name in the file. He was a flamboyant crook based in Hong Kong, with a taste for fast deals in anything from opium to shellcases. For a few misguided years we had financed his office.

'Purest chance, it was, on Duffy's part. He'd popped up here on a flying visit. One day, that's all. One day, one night, then back to the missus and a book. Offshore leisure consortium wanted him to buy a hundred acres of prime coastland for them. Did his business, then off they all go to this girlie restaurant, Duffy and a bunch of his traders – Duffy's not averse to a bit of the other, never has been. Place called The Sea of Happiness, slap in the middle of the red-light quarter. Upmarket sort of establishment, as they go, I'm told. Private rooms, decent food if you like Hunanese, a straight deal and the girls leave you alone unless you tell 'em not to.'

At girlie restaurants, he explained, somehow contriving to suggest he had never personally been to one, young hostesses, dressed or undressed, sat between the guests and fed them food and drink while the men talked high matters of business. In addition, The Sea of Happiness offered a massage parlour, a discothèque and a live theatre on the ground floor.

'Duffy clinches the deal with the consortium, a cheque is passed, he's feeling his oats. So he decides to do himself a favour with one of the girls. Terms agreed, off they go to a cubicle. Girl says she's thirsty, how about a bottle of champagne to get her going? She's on commission, naturally – they all are. Never mind. Duffy's feeling expansive, so he says why not? Girl presses a bell, squawks into the intercom, next thing Duffy knows, in marches this bloody great European chap with an ice bucket and a tray. Sets it down, Duffy gives him twenty baht for himself, fellow says "Thank you" in English, polite enough but no smiles, clears out. It's Hansen. Jungle Hansen. Not a portrait . . . himself!'

'How does Duffy know that?'

'Seen his photograph, hasn't he?'

'Why?'

'Because we showed Duffy the bloody photograph, for heaven's sake, when Hansen went missing! We showed it to everyone we knew, all over the bloody hemisphere! We didn't say why – we just said if you spot this man, holler. Head Office's orders, thank you, not *my* idea. *I* thought it was bloody insecure.'

To calm himself, Rumbelow poured us both another whisky. 'Duffy roars back to his hotel, phones me at home straight away. Three in the morning. "It's your fellow," he tells me. "What fellow?" I say. "Fellow you sent me that pretty picture of, back in Hongkers a year ago or more. He's potboy at a whorehouse called The Sea of Happiness." You know how old Duffy talks. Loose. I sent Henry round next day. Bloody fool made a hash of it. You heard about that, I hope? Typical.'

'Did Duffy speak to Hansen? Ask him who he was? Anything?'

'Not a dickie bird. Looked clean through him. Duffy's a trouper. Salt of the earth. Always was.'

'Where's Henry?'

'Sitting downstairs in the lobby.'

'Call him up.'

Henry was Chinese, the son of a Kuomintang warlord in the Shan States and our resident chief agent, though I suspect he had long ago taken out reinsurance with the Thai police and was earning a quiet living playing both ends against the middle.

He was a podgy, over-eager, shiny fellow and he smiled too much. He wore a gold chain round his neck and carried a smart leather notebook with a gold pen in it. His cover work was translator. No translator I had ever met sported a Gucci notebook, but Henry was different.

'Tell Mark how you made a bloody fool of yourself at The Sea of

Happiness last Thursday evening,' Rumbelow ordered menacingly.

'Sure, Mike.'

'Mark,' I said.

'Sure, Mark.'

'His orders were to take a look. That's *all* he was to do,' Rumbelow barged in before Henry could tell anything at all. 'Take a look, sniff, get out, call me. Right, Henry? He was to spin the tale, sniff, *see* if he could spot Hansen anywhere, *not* approach him, report back to me. A discreet, no-contact reconnaissance. Sniff and tell. Now tell Mark what you did.'

First Henry had had a drink at the bar, he said; then he had watched the show. Then he had sent for the Mama San, who hurried over assuming he had a special wish. The Mama San was a Chinese lady from the same province as Henry's father, so they had an immediate bond.

He had shown the Mama San his translator's card and said he was writing an article about her establishment – the superb food, the romantic girls, the high standards of sensitivity and hygiene, particularly the hygiene. He said he had a commission from a German travel magazine that recommended only the best places.

The Mama San took the bait and offered him the run of the house. She showed him the private dining rooms, the kitchens, cubicles, toilets. She introduced him to the girls – and offered him one on the house, which he declined – to the head chef, the doorman and the bouncers, but not, as it happened, to the enormous round-eye whom Henry had by then spotted three times, once as he carried a tray of glasses from the private dining rooms to the kitchens, once crossing a corridor pushing a trolley of bottles and once emerging from an open steel doorway which apparently led to the drinks store.

'But who is your *farang* who carries the bottles for you?' Henry had cried out with amusement to the Mama San. 'Must he stay behind and work because he cannot pay his bill?'

The Mama San laughed also. Against *farangs*, or Westerners, all Asians feel naturally united. 'The *farang* lives with one of our Cambodian girls,' she replied with contempt, for Cambodians are rated even lower than *farangs* and Vietnamese in the Thai zoology. 'He met her here and fell in love with her, so he tried to buy her and make a lady out of her. But she refused to leave us. So he brings her to work every day, and stays until she is free to go home again.'

'What kind of *farang* is he? German? English? Dutch?'

The Mama San shrugged. What was the difference? Henry pressed her. But a *farang* who brings his woman to the brothel and pushes drinks about while she goes with other men, he insisted, and then takes her home again to his bed? This must be quite some girl!

'She is number nineteen,' said the Mama San, with a shrug. 'Her house name is Amanda. Would you like her?'

But Henry was too excited by his journalistic *coup* to be sidetracked.

'But the *farang*, what is his name? What is his history?' he cried in great amusement.

'He is called Ham Sin. He speaks Thai with us and Khmer with the girl but you must not put him in your magazine, because he is illegal.'

'I can disguise him. I can make it all disguised. Does the girl love him in return?'

'She prefers to be here at The Sea of Happiness with her friends,' the Mama San said primly.

Henry could not resist taking a look. The girls who were not with clients lounged on plush benches behind a glass wall, wearing numbers round their necks and nothing else, while they chatted to each other or tended their fingernails or stared vacuously at an ill-tuned television set. As Henry watched, number 19 stood up in response to a summons, picked up her little handbag and a wrap and walked from the room. She was very young. Many girls lied about their age in order to defeat the regulations – penniless Cambodians particularly. But this girl, said Henry, had looked no more than fifteen.

It was here that Henry's excess of zeal began to lead him astray. He said his goodbyes to the Mama San and drove his car into an alley opposite the rear entrance, where he settled down to wait. Soon after one o'clock the staff began leaving, among them Hansen, twice the height of anyone else, leading number 19 on his arm. In the square, Hansen and the girl looked round for a cab and Henry had the temerity to pull up his car beside them. Pimps and illegal cab drivers thrive at that hour of night, and Henry in his time had been both, so perhaps the move came naturally to him.

'Where you want to go, sir?' he called to Hansen in English. 'You want me to drive you?'

Hansen gave an address in a poor suburb five miles north. A price was agreed, Hansen and his girl got into the back of the car; they set off.

Now Henry began to lose his head in earnest. Flushed by his success, he decided for no reason he could afterwards explain that his best course of action would be to deliver his quarry and the girl to Rumbelow's house, which lay not north but west. He had not of course prepared Rumbelow for this bold manoeuvre; he had hardly prepared himself for it. He had no assurance that Rumbelow was at home, or in any condition, at one-thirty in the morning, to conduct a conversation with a former spy who had disappeared off the map for eighteen months. But reason, at that moment, did not predominate in Henry's mind. He was a joe, and there is not a joe in the world who does not, at one time or another in his life, do something totally daft.

'You like Bangkok?' Henry asked Hansen gaily, hoping to distract his passengers from the route he was taking.

No answer.

'You been here long?'

No answer.

'That's a nice girl. Very young. Very pretty. She your regular girl?'

The girl had her head on Hansen's shoulder. From what Henry could see in the mirror, she was already asleep. For some reason, this knowledge excited Henry further.

'You want a tailor, sir? All-night tailor, very good? I take you there. Good tailor.'

And he drove wildly into a sidestreet, pretending to look for his wretched tailor while he hurried towards Rumbelow's house.

'Why are you going west?' said Hansen, speaking for the first time. 'I don't want to go this way. I don't want a tailor. Get back on the main road.'

The last of Henry's commonsense deserted him. He was suddenly terrified by Hansen's size and Hansen's tactical advantage in sitting behind him. What if Hansen was armed? Henry jammed on the brakes and stopped the car.

'Mr. Hansen, sir, I am your friend!' he cried in Thai, much as he might plead for mercy. 'Mr. Rumbelow is your friend too. He's proud of you! He wants to give you a lot of money. You come with me, please. No problem. Mr. Rumbelow will be very happy to see you!'

That was the last speech Henry made that night, for the next thing he knew, Hansen had pushed the back of Henry's driving seat so hard that Henry's head nearly went through the windscreen. Hansen got out of the car and hauled Henry into the street. After that, Hansen lifted Henry to his feet and flung him across the road, to the dismay of a group of sleeping beggars, who began whimpering and clamouring while Hansen strode to where Henry lay and glared down at him.

'You tell Rumbelow, if he comes for me, I'll kill him,' he said in Thai.

Then he led the girl up the road in search of a better cab, one arm round her waist while she dozed.

By the time I had heard the two men's story to the end, I was suddenly dreadfully tired.

I sent them away, telling Rumbelow to call me next morning. I said that before I did anything else I was going to sleep off my jet-lag. I lay down and was at once wide awake. An hour later, I was presenting myself at The Sea of Happiness and buying a ticket for fifty dollars. I removed my shoes, as custom required, and moments later I was standing in a neon-lit cubicle in my stockinged feet, staring into the passive, much painted features of girl number 19.

She wore a cheap silk wrap with tigers on it, but it was open from the neck down. Underneath it she was naked. A heavy Japanese-style make-up covered her complexion. She smiled at me and thrust her hand swiftly towards my groin, but I replaced it at her side. She was so slight it seemed a mystery that she was equal to the work. She was longer-legged than most

Asian girls and her skin was unusually pale. She threw off her wrap and, before I could stop her, sprang on to the frayed chaise longue, where she arranged herself in what she imagined to be an erotic pose, caressing herself and uttering sighs of desire. She rolled on to her side with her rump thrust out, draping her black hair across her shoulder so that her tiny breasts poked through it. When I did not advance on her, she lay on her back and opened her thighs to me and bucked her pelvis, calling me 'darling' and saying 'please.' She flung herself away from me so that I could admire her back view, keeping her legs apart in invitation.

'Sit up,' I said, so she sat up and again waited for me to come to her.

'Put on your wrap,' I said.

When she appeared not to understand, I helped her into it. Henry had written the message for me in Khmer. 'I want to speak to Hansen,' it read. 'I am in a position to obtain Thai papers for yourself and your family.' I handed it to her and watched her study it. Could she read? I had no way of telling. I held out a plain white envelope addressed to Hansen. She took it and opened it. The letter was typed and its tone was not gentle. It contained two thousand baht.

'As an old friend of Father Vernon,' I had written, using the wordcode familiar to him, 'I must advise you that you are in breach of your contract with our company. You have assaulted a Thai citizen and your girlfriend is an illegal Cambodian immigrant. We may have no alternative but to pass this information to the authorities. My car is parked across the street. Give the enclosed money to the Mama San as payment to release you for the night, and join me in ten minutes.'

She left the cubicle, taking the letter with her. I had not realised till then how much noise there was in the corridor: the jangling music, the tinny laughter, the grumbles of desire, the swish of water down the ramshackle pipes.

I had left the car unlocked and he was sitting in the back, the girl beside him. Somehow I had not doubted he would bring the girl. He was big and powerful, which I knew already, and haggard. In the half darkness, with his black beard and hollowed eyes and his flattened hands curled tensely over the back of the passenger seat, he resembled one of the saints he had once worshipped, rather than the photographs on his file. The girl sat slumped and close to him, sheltering against his body. We had not gone a hundred metres before a rainburst crashed on us like a waterfall. I pulled in to the kerb while each of us stared through the drenched windscreen, watching the torrents of water swarm over the gutters and potholes.

'How did you get to Thailand?' I yelled in Dutch. The rain was thundering on the roof.

'I walked,' Hansen replied in English.

'Where did you come over?' I yelled, in English also.

He mentioned a town. It sounded like 'Orania Prathet.' The downpour

ended and I drove for three hours while the girl dozed and Hansen sat
guard over her, alert as a cat, and as silent. I had selected a beach hotel
advertised in the Bangkok *Nation*. I wanted to get him out of his own
setting, into one that I controlled. I drew the key and paid a night's lodging
in advance. Hansen and the girl followed me down a concrete path to the
beach. The bungalows stood in a half ring facing the sea. Mine was at one
end. I unlocked the door and went ahead of them. Hansen followed, after
him the girl. I switched on the light and the air-conditioning. The girl
hovered near the door, but Hansen kicked off his shoes and placed himself
at the centre of the room, casting round him with his hollowed eyes.

'Sit down,' I said. I pulled open the refrigerator door. 'Does she want a
drink?' I asked.

'Give her a Coca-Cola,' said Hansen. 'Ice. Got any limes in there?'

'No.'

He watched me on my knees in front of the refrigerator.

'How about you?' I asked.

'Water.'

I searched again: glasses, mineral water, ice. As I did so, I heard Hansen
say something tender to the girl in Khmer. She protested and he overrode
her. I heard him go into the bedroom and come out again. Climbing to my
feet, I saw the girl curled on the daybed that ran along one wall of the
room, and Hansen bending over her with a blanket, tucking her up. When
he had finished, he switched out the lamp above her and touched her cheek
with his fingertips before striding to the French window to stare at the sea.
A full red moon hung above the horizon. The rainclouds made black
mountains across the sky.

'What's your name?' he asked me.

'Mark,' I said.

'Is that your real name? Mark?'

The surest knowledge we have of one another comes from instinct. As I
watched Hansen's figure framed in the window and gazing out to sea, and
the moonlight picking out the lines and hollows of his ravaged face, I
knew that the lapsed priest had appointed me his confessor.

'Call me whatever you like,' I said.

You must think of a strong but uneasy English voice, the tone rich, the
manner shocked, as if its owner never expected it to say the things he is
hearing. The slight accent is East Indian Dutch. The bungalow is unlit,
designed for fornication, and gives on to a tiny illuminated swimming
pool and concrete rockery. Beyond this nonsense lies a superb and placid
Asian sea, with a wide moon-path, and stars sparkling in the water like
sunspots. A couple of fishermen stand upright in their sampans, tossing
their round nets into the water and drawing them slowly out again.

In the foreground you must set the jagged, towering figure of Hansen as
he prowls the room in his bare feet, now pausing at the French window,

now perching himself on the arm of a chair before slipping soundlessly away to another corner. And always the voice, now fierce, now ruminative, now shaken, and now, like his body, resting itself for minutes on end while it gathers strength for the next ordeal.

Stretched on her daybed, the Cambodian girl lies wrapped in a blanket, her forearm crooked Asian style beneath her head. Was she awake? Did she understand what he was saying? Did she care? Hansen cared. He could not pass her without stopping to gaze down at her, or fiddle with the blanket at her neck. Once, dropping to the floor beside her, he stared ardently into her closed eyes while he laid his palm on her brow as if to test her temperature.

'She needs limes,' he murmured. 'Coca-Cola is nothing for her. Limes.'

I had sent out for them already. They arrived, by hand of a boy from the front desk. There was business while Hansen squeezed them for her, then held her upright while she drank.

His first questions were a vague catechism about my standing in the Service. He wished to know with what authority I had been sent, with what instructions.

'I want no thanks for what I have done,' he warned me. 'There are no thanks for bombing villages.'

'But you may need help,' I said.

His response was to tell me formally that he would never again, in any circumstance, work for the Service. I could have told him that too, but I refrained. He had thought he was working for the British, he said, but he had been working for murderers. He had been another man when he did the things he did. He hoped the American pilots had been other men as well.

He asked after his sub-agent – the farmer so-and-so, the rice trader so-and-so. He asked about the stay behind network he had painstakingly built up against the certain day when the Khmer Rouge would break out of the jungle and help themselves to the cities, a thing that neither we nor the Americans, despite all the warnings, had ever quite believed would happen. But Hansen had believed it. Hansen was one of the warners. Hansen had told us time and again that Kissinger's bombs were dragon's teeth, even though Hansen had helped direct them to their targets.

'May I believe you?' he asked me when I assured him there had been no pattern of arrests among his sources.

'It's the truth,' I said, responding to the supplication in his voice.

'Then I didn't betray them,' he muttered in marvel. For a moment he sat and cupped his head in his hands, as if holding it together.

'If you were captured by the Khmer Rouge, nobody could expect you to stay silent, anyway,' I said.

'Silent! My God.' He almost laughed. 'Silent!' And, standing sharply, he swung away to the window again.

By the moonlight I saw tears of sweat clinging to his great bearded face.

I started to say something about the Service wishing to acquit itself honourably by him, but halfway through my speech he flung out his arms to their fullest extent, as if testing the limits of his confinement. Finding nothing to obstruct them, they fell back to his sides.

'The Service to hell,' he said softly. 'The West to bloody, bloody hell. We have no business making our wars here, peddling our religious recipes. We have sinned against Asia: the French, the British, the Dutch, now the Americans. We have sinned against the children of Eden. God forgive us.'

My tape recorder lay on the table.

We are in Asia. Hansen's Asia. The Asia sinned against. Listen to the frenetic chatter of the insects. Thais and Cambodians alike have been known to bet large sums on the number of times a bullfrog will burp. The room is twilit, the hour forgotten, the room forgotten also; the moon has risen out of sight. The Vietnam War is back with us, and we are in the Cambodian jungle with Hansen, and modern comforts are few, unless we include the American bombers that circle miles above us, like patient hawks, waiting for the computers to tell them what to destroy next: for instance, a team of oxen whose urine has been misread by secret sensors as the exhaust fumes of a military convoy; for instance, children whose chatter has been mistaken for military commands. The sensors have been hidden by American commandos along the supply routes Hansen has indicated to them – but unfortunately the sensors are not as well informed as Hansen is.

We are in what the American pilots call badland, though in the jungle definitions of good and bad are fluid. We are in a Khmer Rouge 'liberated area' that provides sanctuary for Vietcong troops who wish to attack the Americans in the flank rather than head-on from the north. Yet despite these appearances of war, we are among people with no collective perception of their enemies, in a region unmapped except by fighters. To hear Hansen speak, the region is as close to paradise as makes no difference, whether he speaks as priest, sinner, scholar or spy.

A few miles up the trail by jeep is an ancient Buddhist temple which, with the help of villagers, Hansen has excavated from the depths of vegetation, and which is the apparent reason for his being there, and for the notes he takes, and for the wireless messages he sends, and for the trickle of visitors who arrive usually just before nightfall, and depart at first light. The kampong where he lives is built on stilts in a clearing at the edge of a good river, in a plain of fertile fields that climb in steps to a rain forest. A blue mist is frequent. Hansen's house is set high up the slope in order to improve his radio reception and give a view of whatever enters and leaves the valley. In the wet season, it is his habit to leave the jeep in the village and trudge up to his house on foot. In the dry season, he drives into his compound, most often taking half the village children with him. As many as a dozen of them will be waiting to clamber over the tailboard for the five-minute ride from the village to his compound.

'Sometimes my daughter was among them,' Hansen said.

Neither Rumbelow nor the file had mentioned that Hansen had a daughter. If he had hidden her from us, he was gravely in breach of Service rules – though heaven knows, Service rules were about the last thing that mattered to either of us by then. Nevertheless he stopped speaking and glared at me in the darkness as if waiting for my reproof. But I preserved my silence, wishing to be the ear he had been waiting for, perhaps for years.

'While I was still a priest, I visited the temples of Cambodia,' he said. 'While I was there, I fell in love with a village woman and made her pregnant. In Cambodia it was the best time still. Sihanouk ruled. I remained with her until the child was born. A girl. I christened her Marie. I gave the mother money and returned to Djakarta, but I missed my child terribly. I sent more money. I sent money to the headman to look after them. I sent letters. I prayed for the child and her mother, and swore that one day I would care for them properly. As soon as I returned to Cambodia, I put the mother in my house, even though in the intervening years she had lost her beauty. My daughter had a Khmer name, but from the day she came to me I called her Marie. She liked that. She was proud to have me as her father.'

He seemed concerned to make clear to me that Marie was at ease with her European name. It was not an American name, he said. It was European.

'I had other women in my household, but Marie was my only child and I loved her. She was more beautiful than I had imagined her. But if she had been ugly and ungracious I would have loved her no less.' His voice acquired sudden strength and, as I heard it, warning. 'No woman, no man, no child, ever claimed my love in such a way. You may say that Marie is the only woman I have loved purely except for my mother.' He was staring at me in the darkness, challenging me to doubt his passion. But under Hansen's spell, I doubted nothing and had forgotten everything about myself, even my own mother's death. He was assuming me, occupying me.

'Once you have embarked upon the impossible concept of God, you will know that real love permits no rejection. Perhaps that is something only a sinner can properly understand. Only a sinner knows the scale of God's forgiveness.'

I think I nodded wisely. I thought of Colonel Jerzy. I was wondering why Hansen needed to explain that he could not reject his daughter. Or why his sinfulness was a concern to him when he spoke of her.

'That evening when I drove home from the temple, there were no children waiting for me in the kampong, though it was the dry season. I was disappointed because we had made a good find that day and I wanted to tell Marie about it. They must be having a school festival, I thought, but I could not think which one. I drove up the hill to the compound and called her name. The compound was empty. The gatehouse empty. The women's cookpots empty under the stilts. I called Marie again, then my wife. Then anybody. No one came. I drove back to the village. I went into the house of one of Marie's friends, then another and another, calling Marie. Even the pigs and chickens had disappeared. I looked for blood, for traces of fighting. There were none. But I found footprints leading into the jungle. I drove back to the compound. I took a spade and cached my radio in the forest, halfway between two tall trees that made a line due west, close to an old ant-hill shaped like a man. I hated all my work for you, all my lies, for you and for the Americans. I still do. I walked back to the house, uncached my codepads and equipment and destroyed them. I was glad to. I hated them also. I put on boots and filled a rucksack with food for a week. With my revolver I sent three bullets through the jeep's engine to immobilise it; then I followed the footprints into the jungle. The jeep was an insult to me, because you had bought it.'

Alone, Hansen had set off in pursuit of the Khmer Rouge. Other men – even men who were not Western spies – might have thought twice and a third time, even with their wife and daughter taken hostage. Not Hansen. Hansen had one thought and, absolutist that he was, he acted on it.

'I could not allow myself to be separated from God's grace,' he said. He was telling me, in case I did not know, that beyond the girl's survival lay the survival of his immortal soul.

I asked him how long he had marched for. He didn't know. To begin with he had marched only at night and lain up by day. But the daylight gnawed at him and gradually, against all jungle sense, it drew him forward. As he marched, he recalled every event of Marie's life from the night when he had lifted her from her mother's womb and, with a ritual bamboo stave, cut the cord and ordered the women in attendance to give him water so that he could wash her; and with the water, by his authority as priest and father, had christened her Marie after his own mother and the mother of Christ.

He remembered the nights when she had lain sleeping in his arms or in the rush crib at his feet. He saw her at her mother's breast in the firelight. He flailed himself for the dreadful years of separation in Djakarta and on his training course in England. He flailed himself for all the falsity of his work for the Service, and for his weakness, as he described it, his treachery against Asia. He was referring to his work of directing the American bombers.

He relived the hours he had spent telling her stories and singing her to sleep with English and Dutch songs. He cared only for his love for her, and his need of her, and for her need of him.

He was following the tracks because he had nothing else to follow. He knew now what had happened. It had happened to other kampongs, though none in Hansen's region. The fighters had surrounded the kampong at night and waited till dawn, when the able-bodied left for the fields. They had taken the able-bodied, then crept into the village and taken the elderly and the children, afterwards the livestock. They were provisioning themselves but they were also adding to their ranks. They were in a hurry or they would have ransacked the houses, but they wanted to return to the jungle before they were discovered. Soon, by the light of a full moon, Hansen came upon the first grisly proofs of his theory: the naked bodies of an old storekeeper and his wife, their hands bound behind their backs. Had they been unable to keep up? Were they too ugly? Had they argued?

Hansen marched faster. He was thanking God that Marie looked like a full Asian. In most children of mixed blood, the European strain would have been there for every Asian to see, but Hansen, though a giant, was dark-skinned and slim-bodied, and somehow with his Asian soul he had succeeded in engendering an Asian girl.

Next night another corpse lay beside the trail and Hansen approached it fearfully. It was Ong Sai, the argumentative schoolmistress. Her mouth was wide open. Shot while protesting, Hansen diagnosed, and pressed anxiously forward. In search of Marie, his pure love, the earth mother who was his daughter, the only keeper of his grace.

He wondered which sort of unit he was following. The shy boys who banged on your door at night to ask a little rice for the fighters? The grim-jawed cadres who regarded the Asian smile as an emblem of Western decadence? And there were the zombies, he remembered: freebooting packs of homeless who had clubbed together from necessity, more outlaws than guerrillas. But already in the group ahead of him he had an intimation of discipline. A less organised gang would have stayed to loot the village. They would have made camp to eat a meal and congratulate themselves. On the morning after he found Ong Sai, Hansen took special care to conceal himself while he slept.

'I had a premonition,' he said.

In the jungle you ignored premonition at your peril. He buried himself deep in the undergrowth and smeared himself with mud. He slept with his revolver in his hand. He woke at evening to the smell of woodsmoke and the shrill sound of shouting, and when he opened his eyes he found himself looking straight into the barrels of several automatic rifles.

He was talking about the chains. Jungle fighters, trained to travel light, humping a dozen sets of manacles for hundreds of kilometres – how had it happened? He was still mystified. Yet somebody had carried them, somebody had made a clearing and driven a stake into the centre of the clearing, and dropped the iron rings round the stake, and attached the twelve sets of chains to the twelve iron rings in order to tether twelve special prisoners to the rain and heat and cold and dark. Hansen described the pattern of the chains. To do so, he broke into French. I assumed he needed the protection of a different language. ' . . . *une tringle collective sur laquelle étaient enfilés des étriers . . . nous étions fixés par un pied . . . j'avais été mis au bout de la chaîne parce que ma cheville trop grosse ne passait pas . . . '*

I glanced at the girl. She lay, if it were possible, more inert than before. She could have been dead or in a trance. I realised Hansen was sparing her something he did not want her to hear.

By day, he said, still in French, our ankles were released, enabling us to kneel and even crawl, though never far, because we were tethered to the stake and had each other's bodies to contend with. Only by night, when our foot irons were fixed to heavy poles that made up the circumference of the enclosure, were we able to stretch full length. The availability of chains determined the number of special prisoners, who were drawn exclusively from the village bourgeoisie, he said. He recognised two village elders, and a stringy forty-year-old widow called Ra who had a reputation for prophecy. And the three rice-dealing brothers Liu, who were famous misers, one of whom looked already dead, for he lay curled round his chains like a hairless hedgehog. Only the sound of his sobbing proved he was alive.

And Hansen, with his horror of captivity? How had he responded to his chains?

'*Je les ai portées pour Marie,*' he answered in the swift, warning French I was learning to respect.

The prisoners who were not special were confined to a stockade at the clearing's edge, from which at intervals one of them was led or dragged to headquarters, a place out of sight behind a hillock. Questioning was brief. After a few hours' screaming, a single pistol shot would ring out and the uneasy quiet of the jungle would return. Nobody came back from questioning. The children, including Marie, were allowed to roam provided they did not approach the prisoners or venture up the hillock which hid the headquarters. The boldest of them had already struck up an acquaintance with the young fighters during the march, and were scurrying around them trying to perform errands or touch their guns.

But Marie had stayed apart from everyone. She sat in the dust of the clearing on the other side of the poles, watching over her father from dawn till night. Even when they hauled her mother from the stockade and her screams for Hansen rang out from behind the hillock, changing to screams for mercy and ending with the usual pistol shot, Marie's eyes never flinched from Hansen's face.

'Did she know?' I asked in French.

'The whole camp knew,' he replied.

'Had she been fond of her mother?'

Was it my imagination or had Hansen closed his eyes in the darkness?

'I was the father of Marie,' he replied. 'I was not the father of their relationship.'

How had I known that the mother and daughter had hated each other? Was it because I sensed that Hansen's love for Marie had been a jealous and demanding one – absolute, like all his loves, excluding rivals?

'I was not allowed to speak to her, nor she to me,' he was saying. 'Prisoners spoke to nobody on pain of death.'

Even a groan was enough, as one of the luckless Liu brothers learned when the guards reduced him to permanent silence with their rifle butts, and replaced him next morning with a cringing leftover from the stockade. But between Marie and her father no words were necessary. The stoicism Hansen saw in his daughter's face was the impassioned determination of his own heart as he lay bound and helpless in his chains. With Marie to support him, he could bear anything. Each would be the salvation of the other. Her love for him was as fierce and single-minded as his for her. He did not doubt it. For all his loathing of captivity, he thanked God he had followed her.

A day passed and another, but Hansen remained chained to the stake, burning in the sun, shaking in the evening cold, stinking in his own filth, his gaze and spirit fixed always upon Marie.

In his head, meanwhile, he was wrestling with the tactics of his situation.

From the start it had been clear to him that he was a celebrity. If they had been planning to capture a European, they would have made their attack before Hansen left his house, and searched the house afterwards. He was unexpected treasure, and they were waiting to hear what should be done with him. Others on the stake were fetched and disappeared, all but the one surviving Liu brother and the woman fortune teller, who after days of noisy questioning reappeared as camp trusties, abusing their former companions and trying by every means to ingratiate themselves with the soldiers.

An indoctrination class was formed, and each evening the children and selected survivors sat in a circle in the shade to be harangued by a young commissar with a red headband. While Hansen burned and froze, he could hear the commissar's shrill squawk, hour by hour, as he ranted against the hated imperialists. At first he resented these classes because they took Marie away from him. But when he made the effort, he could still lift his head high enough to see her straight body seated strictly at the far side of the circle, staring at him across the clearing. I will be your mother and your father and your friend, he told her. I will be your life, if I have to give up my own.

At other times he reproached himself with her spectacular beauty, regarding it as a punishment for his random lusts. Marie at twelve was without doubt the most beautiful in the camp, and though sex was forbidden to the cadres on the grounds that it was a bourgeois threat to their revolutionary will, Hansen could not help observe the effect that her thinly clothed figure had on the young fighters as they watched her pass; how their dulled eyes drank in her sprouting breasts and swinging haunches beneath the torn cotton frock, and their scowls darkened when they yelled at her. Worse still, he knew she was aware of their desire, and that her emerging womanhood responded to it.

Then a morning came when the routine of Hansen's captivity unaccountably improved, and his apprehensions deepened, for his benefactor was the young commissar in the red headband. Escorted by two soldiers, the commissar ordered Hansen to stand. When he was unable, the soldiers lifted him to his feet and, taking an arm each, let him stagger to a point along the river bank where an inlet made a natural pool.

'Wash,' the young commissar ordered.

For days – ever since they had bound him – Hansen had been vainly demanding the right to clean himself. On his first evening he had roared at them, 'Take me to the river!' They had beaten him. The next morning he had flung himself about on his chains, risking more beatings, yelling for a responsible comrade, all to assert his right to remain a person whom his captors could respect and consequently preserve.

Under the gaze of the soldiers, Hansen sufficiently rallied his racked limbs to bathe and – though it was a crucifixion – rub himself with the fine river mud before being led back to the stake. On each journey, he passed within a few feet of his beloved Marie in her habitual place beyond the ring of poles. Though his heart leapt at her nearness and the courage in her eyes, he could not suppress the suspicion that it was his own child who had purchased the rare comfort he was now enjoying. And when the commissar grunted a greeting to her, and Marie lifted her head and gave half a smile in return, the anguish of jealousy added itself to Hansen's pains.

After his bathe, they brought him rice – more than they had given him in all the time he had been their prisoner. And instead of making him eat it from the bowl like a dog, they untied his hands and let him use his fingers, so that he was able to secrete a small amount in his palm, and drop it down the front of his tunic before they chained him again.

All day long he thought of nothing but the pellet of rice inside his shirt, making sure no movement of his body crushed it. I will win her back, he thought. I will supplant the commissar in her admiration. When evening came and they again led him to the river, he achieved the miracle he had been planning. Staggering more dramatically than was necessary, he succeeded in dropping a pellet of rice at Marie's feet, unnoticed by his guards. As he passed by her again on his way back, he saw to his secret ecstasy that it had vanished.

Yet her face told him nothing. Only her eyes, straight and sometimes lifeless in their devotion, told him she returned his absolute love. I was deluding myself, he decided as they refastened his chains. She is learning the prisoner's tricks. She is chaste and will survive. That evening he listened with a new tolerance to the commissar's indoctrination class. Lead him on, he urged her in the telepathic dialogue he conducted with her constantly; lull him, bewitch him, gain his trust but give him nothing. And Marie must have heard him, because as the class broke up he saw the commissar beckon her over to him and rebuke her while she remained cowed and silent. He saw her head fall forward. He saw her walk away from him, her head still lowered.

Next day and for a week, Hansen repeated his trick, convinced he was unobserved except by Marie. The pellet of rice, rolling lightly over his stomach each time he shifted his body, became a source of vital comfort to him. I am nourishing her from my own breast. I am her guardian, the protector of her chastity. I am her priest, giving her Christ's Sacrament.

The rice was all that mattered to him. His concern was to contrive new ways to smuggle it to her, waiting till he was past her and flicking the pellet backward, letting it fall down the inside of his tattered trouser leg.

'I was inordinate,' he said softly, in the tone of a penitent.

And because he had been inordinate, God took Marie from him. Suddenly one morning when they unchained him and led him to the pool, there was no Marie waiting to receive her Sacrament. At the evening indoctrination class, he saw that she had been elevated to the commissar's side, and he thought he heard her voice above the rest, intoning the liturgical responses with a new self-confidence. When night fell, he picked out her silhouette among the soldiers' fires – an accepted member of their company, sharing their rice like a comrade. Next day he did not see her at all, nor the day after.

'I wished to die,' he said.

But in the evening as he waited in despair, prone and motionless, for the guards to chain his feet, it was the young commissar who marched towards him, and Marie, dressed in a black tunic, who trotted at his side.

'Is this man your father?' the commissar asked as they reached Hansen.

Marie's stare did not falter, but she seemed to be searching her memory for her reply. 'Angka is my father,' she said finally. 'Angka is the father of all oppressed.'

'Angka was the Party,' Hansen explained for me, without my asking. 'Angka was the Organisation that the Khmer Rouge prayed to. In the Khmer Rouge's ladder of beings, Angka was God.'

'So who is your mother?' the commissar asked Marie.

'My mother is Angka. I have no mother but Angka.'

'Who is this man?'

'He is an American agent,' Marie replied. 'He drops bombs on our villages. He kills our workers.'

'Why does he pretend he is your father?'

'He wishes to trick us by claiming to be our comrade.'

'Test the spy's chains. See that they are tight enough,' the commissar commanded.

Marie knelt to Hansen's feet, exactly as he had taught her to kneel in prayer. For a moment, like the healing touch of Christ, her hand closed over his festering ankles.

'Can you insert your fingers between the chain and ankle?' the commissar asked.

In his panic, Hansen behaved as he always did when his feet were being chained. He flexed his ankle muscles, hoping to give himself more freedom when he relaxed. He felt her finger probe the chain.

'I can insert my little finger,' she replied, holding it up while she kept her body in the line of sight between the commissar and Hansen's feet.

'Can you insert it with difficulty or easily?'

'I can insert my finger only with difficulty,' she lied.

Watching them march away, Hansen noticed something that alarmed him. With her black tunic, Marie had put on the stealthy waddle of the jungle fighter. All the same, for the first time since his capture, Hansen slept soundly in his chains. She is joining them in order to deceive them, he assured himself. God is protecting us. Soon we shall escape.

The official interrogator arrived by boat, a smooth-cheeked student with an earnest, frowning manner. In Hansen's mind, that was how he named him: the student. A reception committee led by the commissar met him at the river bank and escorted him over the hillock to headquarters. Hansen knew he was the interrogator because he was the only one who did not turn his head to look at the last remaining prisoner rotting in the heat. But he looked at Marie. He stopped in front of her, obliging everybody to stop with him. He stood before her; he held his studious face close to her while he asked her questions Hansen could not hear. He kept it there while he listened to her parrot answers. My daughter is the camp whore, thought Hansen in despair. But was she? Nothing he had ever heard about the Khmer Rouge suggested they appointed or even tolerated prostitutes in their midst. Everything suggested the contrary. 'Angka haït le sexuel,' a French anthropologist had said to him once.

Then they are ravishing her with their puritanism, he decided. They have locked her to them in a passion that is worse than a debauching. He lay with his face in the earth, praying to be allowed to take her sins of innocence upon himself.

I have no coherent picture of Hansen's interrogation for the reason he had little himself. I remembered my own treatment at the hands of Colonel Jerzy, and it was child's play by comparison. But Hansen's recollections had the same imprecision. That they tortured him goes without saying. They had built a wooden grid for the purpose. Yet they were also concerned to keep him alive, because between sessions they gave him food and even, if he remembered rightly, allowed him visits to the river bank, though it may have been a single visit broken by spells of unconsciousness.

There were also the sessions of writing, for in the literal mind of the student, no confession was real until it was written down. And the writing grew harder and harder and became a punishment in itself, even though they unstrapped him from the grid to make him do it.

As an interrogator, the student seems to have proceeded simultaneously on two intellectual fronts. When he was checked on the one, he shifted to the other.

You are an American spy, he said, and an agent of the counter-revolutionary puppet Lon Nol, also an enemy of the revolution. Hansen disagreed.

But you're also a Roman Catholic masquerading as a Buddhist, a poisoner of minds, a promoter of anti-Party superstitions, and a saboteur of the popular enlightenment, the student screamed at him.

In general, the student seems to have preferred making statements to asking questions: 'You will now please give all dates and places of your conspiratorial meetings with the counter-revolutionary puppet and American spy Lon Nol, naming all Americans present.'

Hansen insisted that no such meetings had occurred. But this gave the student no satisfaction. As the agony increased, Hansen recalled the names from an English folksong that his mother had used to sing him: Tom Pearse . . . Bill Brewer . . . Jan Stewer . . . Peter Gurney . . . Peter Davey . . . Dan'l Whiddon . . . Harry Hawk . . .

'You will now please write down the ringleader of this rabble,' the student said, turning a page of his notebook. The student's eyes, said Hansen, were often nearly closed. I remembered that about Jerzy too.

'Cobbleigh,' Hansen whispered, lifting his head from the desk where they had sat him. *Thomas Cobbleigh*, he wrote. *Tom for short. Covername Uncle.*

The dates were important because Hansen was concerned he would forget them once he had invented them, and be accused of inconsistency. He chose Marie's birthday and his mother's birthday and the date of his father's execution. He altered the year to suit Lon Nol's accession to power. For a conspiratorial place, he selected the walled gardens of Lon Nol's palace in Phnom Penh, which he had often admired on his way to a favourite *fumerie*.

His fear while he was confessing to this rubbish was that he would reveal true information by mistake, for it was by now clear to him that the student knew nothing about his real intelligence-gathering activities, and that the charges against him were based on the fact that he was a Westerner.

'You will please write down the name of each spy paid by you in the last five years, also each act of sabotage committed by you against the people.'

Not in all the days and nights that Hansen had passed anticipating his ordeal had he imagined he might fail on the score of creativity. He recited the names of martyrs whose agonies he had contemplated in order to prepare himself; of Oriental scholars safely dead; of authors of learned works on philology and linguistics. Spies, he said. All spies. And wrote them down, his hand jerking on the paper to the convulsions of the pain that continued to rack him long after they switched off the machine.

Writing desperately, he made a list of T. E. Lawrence's officers in the desert, which he remembered from his many readings of *The Seven Pillars of Wisdom*. He described how on Lon Nol's personal orders he had organised the poisoning of crops and cattle by Buddhist priests. The student put him back on the grid and increased the pain.

He described the clandestine classes he had held in imperialism, and how he had encouraged the spread of bourgeois sentiment and family virtues. The student opened his eyes, offered his commiserations and again increased the pain.

He gave them nearly everything. He described how he had lit beacons to guide American bombers, and distributed rumours that the bombers were Chinese. He was on the brink of telling them who had helped him to lead American commandos to the supply trails, when mercifully he fainted.

But throughout his ordeal it was still Marie with whom he lived in his heart, to whom he cried out in his pain, whose hands drew him back to life when his body was begging to relinquish it, whose eyes watched over him in love and pity. It was Marie to whom he sacrificed his suffering and for whom he swore to survive. As he lay between life and death, he had an hallucination in which he saw himself stretched out in the well of the student's boat and Marie in her black tunic seated over him, paddling them upriver to Heaven. But he still was not dead. They have not killed me. I have confessed to everything and they have not killed me.

But he had not confessed to everything. He had remained true to his helpers and he had not told them about his radio. And when they dragged him back next day and strapped him once more to the grid, he saw Marie sitting at the student's side, a copy of his confession lying before her on the table. Her hair was cropped, her expression closed.

'Are you familiar with the statements of this spy?' the student asked her.

'I am familiar with his statements,' she replied.

'Do the spy's statements accurately depict his lifestyle as you were able to observe it in his company?'

'No.'

'Why not?' the student asked, opening his notebook.

'They are not complete.'

'Explain why the spy Hansen's statements are not complete.'

'The spy Hansen kept a radio in his house which he used for signalling to the imperialist bombers. Also the names he has mentioned in his confession are fictitious. They are taken from a bourgeois English song which he sang to me when he was pretending to be my father. Also he received imperialist soldiers at our house at night and led them into the jungle. Also he has failed to mention that he has an English mother.'

The student appeared disappointed. 'What else has he failed to mention?' he asked, flattening a fresh page with the edge of his small hand.

'During his confinement, he has been guilty of many breaches of regulation. He has hoarded food and attempted to buy the collaboration of comrades in his plans to escape.'

The student sighed and made more notes. 'What else has he failed to mention?' he asked patiently.

'He has been wearing his foot chains improperly. When the chains were being fastened, he braced his feet illegally, leaving the chains loose for his escape.'

Until that moment Hansen had managed to persuade himself that Marie was playing a cunning game. No longer. The game was the reality.

'He is a whoremonger!' she screamed through her tears. 'He debauches our women by bringing them to his house and drugging them! He pretends to make a bourgeois marriage, then forces his wife to tolerate his decadent practices! He sleeps with girls of my own age! He pretends he is the father of our children and that our blood is not Khmer! He reads us bourgeois literature in Western languages in order to deprave us! He seduces us by taking us for rides in his jeep and singing imperialist songs to us!'

He had never heard her scream before. Nor evidently had the student, who appeared embarrassed. But she would not be checked. She persisted in denying him. She told them how he had forbidden her mother to love her. She was expressing a hatred for him that he knew was unfeigned, as absolute and inordinate as his love for her. Her body shook with the pent-up hatred of a misused woman, her features were crumpled with hatred and guilt. Her arm struck out and she pointed at him in the classic posture of accusation. Her voice belonged to someone he had never known.

'Kill him!' she screamed. 'Kill the despoiler of our people! Kill the corrupter of our Khmer blood! Kill the Western liar who tells us we are different from one another! Avenge the people!'

The student made a last note and ordered Marie to be led away. 'I prayed for her forgiveness,' Hansen said.

In the bungalow, I realised, it was dawn. Hansen was standing at the window, his eyes fixed on the misty plateau of the sea. The girl lay on the daybed where she had lain all night, her eyes closed, the empty Coca-Cola can beside her, her head still supported by her arm. Her hand, hanging down, looked worn and elderly. A terseness had entered Hansen's voice, and for a moment I feared that with morning he had decided to resent me. Then I realised it was not me he was at odds with but himself.

He was remembering his anger as they carried him, bound but not chained, to the stockade to sleep – if sleep is what you do when your body is dying of pain, and the blood is filling your ears and nose. Anger against himself, that he had implanted in his child so much loathing.

'I was her father still,' he said in French. 'I blamed Marie for nothing, myself for everything. If only I had made my escape earlier, instead of counting on her to help me. If only I had fought my way out when I was strong, instead of placing my reliance in a child. I should never have worked for you. My secret work had endangered her. I cursed you all. I still do.'

Did I speak? My concern was to say nothing that would obstruct his flow.

'She was drawn to them,' he said, making her excuses for her. 'They were her own people, jungle fighters with a faith to die for. Why should she reject them?

'I was the last obstacle to her acceptance by her people,' he said, explaining her. 'I was an intruder, a corrupter. Why should she believe I was her father when they were telling her I was not?'

Still lying in the stockade, he remembered her on the day the young commissar dressed her in her bridal black. He remembered her expression of distaste as she stared down at him, fouled and beaten, a beggar at her feet, a cringing Western spy. And beside her, the handsome commissar with his red headband. 'I am wedded to the Angka,' she was saying to him. 'The Angka answers all my questions.'

'I was alone,' he said.

Darkness fell in the stockade, and he supposed that if they were going to shoot him they would wait for daylight. But the notion that Marie would go through life knowing she had ordered her father's death appalled him. He imagined her in middle age. Who would help her? Who would confess her? Who would give her release and absolution? The idea of his death became increasingly alarming to him. It will be her death too.

At some point he must have dozed, he said, for when dawn came he found a bowl of rice on the floor of the stockade and he knew it had not been there the night before; even in his agony he would have smelt it. Not rolled into pellets, the rice, not hoarded against the naked skin, but a white mound of it, enough for five days. At first he was too tired to be surprised. Lying on his stomach to eat, he noticed the quiet. By this hour the clearing should have been alive with the sounds of soldiers waking for the day: Singsong voices and washing noises from the river bank, the clatter of pans and rifles, the chant of slogans led by the commissar. Yet when he paused to listen, even the birds and monkeys seemed to have stopped their shrieking and he heard no human sounds at all.

'They had gone,' he said, from somewhere behind me. 'They had decamped in the night, taking Marie with them.'

He ate more rice and dozed again. Why have they not killed me? Marie has talked them out of it. Marie has bought me my life. Hansen set to work chafing his bonds against the wall of the stockade. By nightfall, covered in sores and flies, he was lying on the river bank, washing his wounds. He crawled back to the stockade to sleep, and next morning, with the remainder of his rice, he set off. This time, having no prisoners or livestock, they had left no tracks.

All the same, he went in search of her.

For months, Hansen thinks five or six, he remained in the jungle, moving from village to village, never settling, trusting no one – I suspect a little crazed. Wherever he could, he enquired after Marie's unit, but there was too little to describe it by and his quest became indiscriminate. He heard of units that had fighting girls. He heard of units that consisted of girls only. He heard of girls being sent into the towns as whores to gather information. He imagined Marie in all these situations. One night he crept back to his old house hoping she had taken refuge there. The village had been burned.

I asked him whether his cached wireless had been disturbed.

'I didn't look,' he replied. 'I didn't care. I hated you all.'

Another night he called on Marie's aunt, who lived in a remote village, but she hurled pans at him and he had to flee. Yet his determination to rescue his daughter was stronger than ever, for he knew now that he must rescue her from herself. She is cursed with my absolutism, he thought. She is violent and headstrong; it is I who am to blame. I have locked her in the prison of my own impulses. Only a father's love could ever have blinded him to this knowledge. Now his eyes were open. He saw her drawn to cruelty and inhumanity as a means of proving her devotion. He saw her reliving his own erratic quest, yet deprived of his intellectual and religious disciplines – vaguely believing, like himself, that her assumption into a great vision would bring her self-fulfilment.

Of his walk to the Thai border he said little. He headed southwest towards Pailin. He had heard there was a camp there for Khmer refugees. He crossed mountains and malarial marshes. Once arrived, he besieged the tracing centres and pinned her description on camp noticeboards. How he achieved this without papers, money or connections, yet kept his presence in Thailand secret, is a mystery to me still. But Hansen was a trained and hardened agent, even if he denied us. He was not disposed to let much stop him. I asked why he did not turn to Rumbelow for help, but he shook off the idea contemptuously.

'I was not an imperialist agent any more. I believed in nothing but my daughter.'

One day in the office of a relief organisation, he met an American woman who thought she remembered Marie.

'She left,' she said cautiously.

Hansen pressed her. Marie was one of a group of half a dozen girls, said the woman. They were whores but they had the assurance of fighters. When they were not entertaining men, they kept themselves apart from everyone and were tough to handle. One day they broke bounds. She had heard they were picked up by the Thai police. She never saw them again.

The woman who said this appeared unsure whether to say what else was on her mind, but Hansen gave her no choice.

'We were afraid for her,' she said. 'She gave different names for herself. She gave conflicting accounts of how she came to us. The doctors argued over whether she was mad. Somewhere along her journey, she had lost track of who she was.'

Hansen presented himself to the Thai police and, by threats or animal persuasion, traced Marie to a police hostel run for the enjoyment of the officers. They never asked him who he was, it seems, or what he had for papers. He was a round-eye, a *farang*, who spoke Khmer and Thai. Marie had stayed three months, then vanished, they said. She was strange, said a kindly sergeant.

'What is strange?' Hansen asked.

'She would speak only English,' the sergeant replied.

There was another girl, a friend of Marie's, who had stayed longer and married one of the corporals. Hansen obtained her name.

He had ceased speaking.

'And did you find her?' I asked after a long silence.

I knew the answer already, as I had known it from halfway through his story, without knowing that I knew. He was sitting at the girl's head, which he was gently stroking. Slowly she sat upright and with her little, old hands rubbed her eyes, pretending she had been asleep. I think she had listened to us all night.

'It was all she understood any more,' Hansen explained in English, while he continued to stroke her head. He was speaking of the brothel where he had found her. 'She wanted no big choices, did you, Marie? No big words, no promises.' He pressed her to him. 'She wishes only to be admired. By her own people. By us. All of us must love Marie. That is what comforts her.'

I think he mistook my reticence for reproach, for his voice rose. 'She wishes to be harmless. Is that so bad? She wishes to be left alone, as all of them wish. It would be a good thing if more of us wished the same. Your bombers and your spies and your big talk are not for her. She is not the child of Dr. Kissinger. She asks only for a small existence where she can give pleasure and hurt no one. Which is worse? Your brothel or hers? Get out of Asia. You should never have come, any of you. I am ashamed I ever helped you. Leave us alone.'

'I shall tell Rumbelow very little of this,' I said as I rose to leave.

'Tell him what you like.'

From the doorway, I took a last look at them. The girl was staring at me as I believe she had stared at Hansen from outside the circle of chains, her eyes unflinching, deep and still. I thought I knew what was in her mind. I had paid for her and not had her. She was wondering whether I wanted my money's worth.

Rumbelow drove me to the airport. Like Hansen, I would have preferred to do without him, but we had matters to discuss.

'You promised him *how* much?' he cried in horror.

'I told him he was entitled to a resettlement grant and all the protection we can give him. I told him you would be sending him a cashier's cheque for fifty thousand dollars.'

Rumbelow was furious. '*Me* give *him* fifty thousand dollars? My dear man, he'll be drunk for six months and spill his life story all over Bangkok. What about that Cambodian whore of his? She's in the know, I'll bet.'

'Don't worry,' I said. 'He turned me down.'

This news astonished Rumbelow so profoundly that he ran out of indignation altogether, preserving instead a wounded silence that lasted us the rest of the journey.

On the plane I drank too much and slept too little. Once, waking from a bad dream, I was guilty of a seditious thought about Rumbelow and the Fifth Floor. I wished I could pack off the whole tribe of them on Hansen's march into the jungle, Smiley included. I wished I could make them throw everything over for a flawed and impossible passion, only to see the object of it turn against them, proving there is no reward for love except the experience of loving, and nothing to be learned by it except humility.

Yet I was content, as I am content to this day whenever I think of Hansen. I had found what I was looking for – a man like myself, but one who in his search for meaning had discovered a worthwhile object for his life; who had paid every price and not counted it a sacrifice; who was paying it still and would pay it till he died; who cared nothing for compromise, nothing for his pride, nothing for ourselves or the opinion of others; who had reduced his life to the one thing that mattered to him, and was free. The slumbering subversive in me had met his champion. The would-be lover in me had found a scale by which to measure his own trivial preoccupations.

So that when a few years later I was appointed Head of the Russia House, only to watch my most valuable agent betray his country for his love, I could never quite muster the outrage required of me by my masters. Personnel was not all stupid when he packed me off to the Interrogators' Pool.

10

Maggs, my unpleasing crypto journalist, was trying to draw Smiley on the amoral nature of our work. He was wanting Smiley to admit that anything went, as long as you got away with it. I suspect he was actually wanting to hear this maxim applied to the whole of life, for he was ruthless as well as mannerless, and wished to see in our work some kind of licence to throw aside his few remaining scruples.

But Smiley would not give him this satisfaction. At first he appeared ready to be angry, which I hoped he would be. If so, he checked himself. He started to speak, but stopped again, and faltered, leaving me wondering whether it was time to call a halt to the proceedings. Until, to my relief, he rallied, and I knew he had merely been distracted by some private memory among the thousands that made up his secret self.

'You see,' he explained – replying, as so often, to the spirit rather than the letter of the question – 'it really is essential in a free society that the people who do our work should remain unreconciled. It's true that we are obliged to sup with the Devil, and not always with a very long spoon. And as everyone knows – ' a sly glance at Maggs produced a gust of grateful laughter – 'the Devil is often far better company than the Godly, isn't he? All the same, our obsession with virtue won't go away. Self-interest is so *limiting*. So is expediency.' He paused again, still deep inside his own thoughts. 'All I'm really saying, I suppose, is that if the temptation to humanity does assail you now and then, I hope you won't take it as a weakness in yourselves, but give it a fair hearing.'

The cufflinks, I thought, in a flash of inspiration. George is remembering the old man.

For a long time I could not fathom why the story had continued to haunt me for so long. Then I realised I had happened upon it at a period when my relationship with my son Adrian had hit a low point. He was talking of not bothering with university, and getting himself a well-paid job instead. I mistook his restlessness for materialism and his dreams of independence for laziness, and one night I lost my temper and insulted him, and was duly ashamed of myself for weeks thereafter. It was during one of those weeks that I unearthed the story.

Then I remembered also that Smiley had had no children, and that perhaps his ambiguous part in the affair was to some extent explained by this. I was slightly chilled by the thought that he might have been filling an emptiness in himself by redressing a relationship he had never had.

Finally I remembered that just a few days after coming upon the papers, I had received the letter that anonymously denounced poor Frewin as a

Russian spy. And that there were certain mystical affinities between Frewin and the old man, to do with dogged loyalty and lost worlds. All this for context, you understand, for I never knew a case yet that was not made up of a hundred others.

Finally there was the fact that, as so often in my life, Smiley turned out once again to have been my precursor, for I had no sooner settled myself at my unfamiliar desk in the Interrogators' Pool than I found his traces everywhere: in our dusty archives, in back numbers of our duty officer's log and in the reminiscent smiles of our senior secretaries, who spoke of him with the old vestal's treacly awe, part as God, part as teddy bear and part – though they were always quick to gloss over this aspect of his nature – as killer shark. They would even show you the bone-china cup and saucer by Thomas Goode of South Audley Street – where else? – a present to George from Ann, they explained dotingly, which George had bequeathed to the Pool after his reprieve and rehabilitation to Head Office – and, of course, like the Grail itself, the Smiley cup could never possibly be *drunk* from by a mere mortal.

The Pool, if you have not already gathered as much, is by way of being the Service's Siberia, and Smiley, I was comforted to discover, had served out not one exile there but two: the first, for his gall in suggesting to the Fifth Floor that it might be nursing a Moscow Centre mole to its bosom; and the second, a few years later, for being right. And the Pool has not only the monotony of Siberia but its remoteness also, being situated not in the main building but in a run of cavernous offices on the ground floor of a gabled pile in Northumberland Avenue at the northern end of Whitehall.

And, like so much of the architecture around it, the Pool has seen great days. It was set up in the Second World War to receive the offerings of strangers, to listen to their suspicions and calm their fears or – if they had indeed stumbled on a larger truth – misguide or scare them into silence.

If you thought you had glimpsed your neighbour late at night, for instance, crouched over a radio transmitter; if you had seen strange lights winking from a window and were too shy or untrusting to inform your local police station; if the mysterious foreigner on the bus who questioned you about your work had reappeared at your elbow in your local pub; if your secret lover confessed to you – out of loneliness or bravado or a desperate need to make himself more interesting in your eyes – that he was working for the German Secret Service – why then, after a correspondence with some spurious assistant to some unheard-of Whitehall Under-Secretary, you would quite likely, of an early evening, be summoned to brave the blitz, and find yourself being guided heart-in-mouth down the flaking, sandbagged corridor, on your way to Room 909, where a Major Somebody or a Captain Somebody Else, both bogus as three-dollar bills, would courteously invite you to state your matter frankly without fear of repercussion.

And occasionally, as the covert history of the Pool records, great things were born, and are still occasionally born today, of these inauspicious beginnings, though business is not a patch on what it used to be, and much of the Pool's work is now given over to such chores as unsolicited offers of service, anonymous denunciations like the one levelled at poor Frewin and even – in support of the despised security services – positive vetting enquiries, which are the worst Siberias of all, and about as far as you can get from the high-wire operations of the Russia House without quitting the Service altogether.

All the same, there is more than mere humility to be learned from these chastisements. An intelligence officer is nothing if he has lost the will to listen, and George Smiley, plump, troubled, cuckolded, unassuming, indefatigable George, forever polishing his spectacles on the lining of his tie, puffing to himself and sighing in his perennial distraction, was the best listener of us all.

Smiley could listen with his hooded, sleepy eyes; he could listen by the very inclination of his tubby body, by his stillness and his understanding smile. He could listen because with one exception, which was Ann, his wife, he expected nothing of his fellow souls, criticised nothing, condoned the worst of you long before you had revealed it. He could listen better than a microphone because his mind lit at once upon essentials; he seemed able to spot them before he knew where they were leading.

And that was how George had come to be listening to Mr. Arthur Wilfred Hawthorne of 12, The Dene, Ruislip, half a lifetime before me, in the very same Room 909 where I now sat, curiously turning the yellowed pages of a file marked 'Destruction Pending' which I had unearthed from the shelves of the Pool's strongroom.

I had begun my quest idly – you may even say frivolously – much as one might pick up an old copy of the *Tatler* in one's club. And suddenly I realised I had stumbled on page after page of Smiley's familiar, guarded handwriting, with its sharp little German t's and twisted Greek e's, and signed with his legendary symbol. Where he was forced to appear in the drama in person – and you could feel him seeking any means to escape this vulgar ordeal – he referred to himself merely as 'D.O.,' short for Duty Officer. And since he was notorious for his hatred of initials, you are made once more aware of his reclusive, if not downright fugitive nature. If I had discovered a missing Shakespeare folio, I could not have been more excited. Everything was there: Hawthorne's original letter, transcripts of the microphoned interviews, initialled by Smiley himself, even Hawthorne's signed receipts for his travel money and out-of-pocket expenses.

My dull care was gone. My relegation no longer oppressed me, neither did the silence of the great empty house to which I was condemned. I was sharing them with George, waiting for the clip of Arthur Hawthorne's loyal boots as he was marched down the corridor and into Smiley's presence.

'Dear Sir,' he had written to 'The Officer in Charge of Intelligence, Ministry of Defence.' And already, because we are British, his class is branded on the page – if only by the strangely imperious use of capitals so dear to uneducated people. I imagined much effort in the penning, and perhaps a dictionary at the elbow. 'I wish, Sir, to Request an Interview with your Staff regarding a Person who has done Special Work for British Intelligence at the highest Level, and whose Name is as Important to my Wife and myself as it may be to your good Selves, and which I am accordingly forbidden to Mention in this Letter.'

That was all. Signed 'Hawthorne, A. W., Warrant Officer Class II, retired.' Arthur Wilfred Hawthorne, in other words, as Smiley's researches revealed when he consulted the voters' list, and followed up his findings with an examination of the War Office files. Born 1915, Smiley painstakingly recorded on Hawthorne's personal particulars sheet. Enlisted 1939, served with the Eighth Army from Cairo to El Alamein. Ex-Sergeant Major Arthur Wilfred Hawthorne, twice wounded in battle, three commendations and one gallantry medal for his trouble, demobilised without a stain on his character, 'the best example of the best fighting man in the world,' wrote his commandant, in a glowing if hyperbolic commendation.

And I knew that Smiley, as a good professional, would have taken up his post well ahead of his client's arrival, just as I myself had done these last months: at the same scuffed yellow desk of wartime pine, singed brown along the leading edge – legend has it by the Hun; with the same mossy telephone, letters as well as numbers on the dial; the same hand-tinted photograph of the Queen, sitting on a horse when she was twenty. I see George frowning studiously at his watch, then pulling a sour face as he peered round him at the usual mess, for there had been a running battle for as long as anyone could remember about who was supposed to clean the place, the Ministry or ourselves. I see him tug a handkerchief from his sleeve – laboriously again, for no gesture ever came to George without a struggle – and wipe the grime off the seat of his wooden chair, then do the same in advance for Hawthorne on the other side of the desk. Then, as I had done myself a few times, perform a similar service for the Queen, setting her frame straight and bringing back the sparkle to her young, idealistic eyes.

For I imagined George already studying the feelings of his subject, as any good intelligence officer must. An ex-sergeant major would expect a certain order about him, after all. Then I see Hawthorne himself, punctual to the minute, as the janitor showed him in, his best suit buttoned like a battledress, the polished toecaps of his boots glistening like conkers in the gloom. Smiley's description of him on the encounter sheet was sparse but trenchant: height five seven, grey hair close cut, clean-shaven, groomed appearance, military bearing. Other characteristics: suppressed limp of the left leg, army boots.

'Hawthorne, sir,' he snapped, and held himself to attention till Smiley with difficulty persuaded him to sit.

Smiley was Major Nottingham that day and had an impressive card with his photograph to prove it. In my pocket as I read his account of the case lay a similar card in the name of Colonel Ned Ascot. Don't ask me why Ascot except to note that, in choosing a place-name for my alias, I was yet again unconsciously copying one of Smiley's little habits.

'What regiment are you from, sir, if you don't mind my asking?' Hawthorne enquired of Smiley as he sat.

'The General List, I'm afraid,' said Smiley, which is the only way we are allowed to answer.

But I am sure it came hard to Smiley, as it would to me, to have to describe himself as some kind of non-combatant.

As evidence of his loyalty, Hawthorne had brought his medals wrapped in a piece of gun cloth. Smiley obligingly went through them for him.

'It's about our son, sir,' the old man said. 'I've got to ask you. The wife – well, she won't hear of it any more, she says it's a load of his nonsense. But I told her I've got to ask you. Even if you refuse to answer, I told her, I won't have done my duty by my son if I didn't ask on his account.'

Smiley said nothing but I am sure his silence was sympathetic.

'Ken was our only boy, you see, Major, so it's natural,' said Hawthorne apologetically.

And still Smiley let him take his time. Did I not say he was a listener? Smiley could draw answers from you to questions he had never put, just by the sincerity of his listening.

'We're not asking for secrets, Major. We're not asking to know what can't be known. But Mrs. Hawthorne is failing, sir, and she needs to know whether it's true before she goes.' He had prepared the question exactly. Now he put it. 'Was our boy, or was he not – was Ken – in the course of what appeared to be a criminal career, operating behind enemy lines in Russia?'

And here you might say that for once I was ahead of Smiley, if only because after five years in the Russia House I had a pretty good idea of the operations we had conducted in the past. I felt a smile come to my face, and my interest in the story, if it was possible, increased.

But to Smiley's face, I am sure, came nothing at all. I imagine his features settling into a Mandarin immobility. Perhaps he fiddled with his spectacles, which always gave the impression of belonging to a larger man. Finally he asked Hawthorne – but earnestly, never a hint of scepticism – why he supposed this might be the case.

'Ken told me he was, sir, that's why.' And still nothing on Smiley's side, except an ever-open door. 'Mrs. Hawthorne wouldn't visit Ken in prison, you see. I would. Every month. He was doing five years for grievous bodily harm, plus three more for being habitual. We had PD in those days, preventive detention. We're in the prison canteen there, me and Ken, sitting together at a table. And suddenly Ken puts his head close to mine, and he says to me in this low voice he's got, "Don't come here again, Dad. It's difficult for me. I'm not really locked up, you see. I'm in Russia. They had to bring me back special, just to show me to you. I'm working behind the lines, but don't tell Mum. Write to me – that's not a problem, they'll send it on. And I'll write back same as if I was a prisoner here, which is what I pretend to be, because you can't get better cover than a prison. But the truth is, Dad, I'm serving the old country just like you did when you was with the Desert Rats, which is why the best of us are put on earth." I didn't ask to see Ken after that. I felt I had to obey orders. I wrote to him, of course. In the prison. Hawthorne and then his number. And three months later he'd write back on prison paper like it was a different boy writing to me every time. Sometimes the big heavy writing, like he was angry, sometimes small and quick, like he hadn't had the time. Once or twice there was even the foreign words in there that I didn't understand, crossed out mainly, like he was having difficulty with his own language. Sometimes he'd drop me a clue. "I'm cold but safe," he'd say. "Last week I had a bit more exercise than I needed," he'd say. I didn't tell the wife because he said I wasn't to. Besides, she wouldn't have believed him. When I offered her his letters, she pushed them away – they hurt too much. But when Ken died we went and saw his body all cut to pieces in the prison morgue. Twenty stab wounds and nobody to blame. She didn't weep, she doesn't, but they might as well have stabbed her. And on the way home on the bus I couldn't help it. "Ken's a hero," I said to her. I was trying to wake her up because she'd gone all wooden. I got hold of her by the sleeve and gave her a bit of a shake to make her listen. "He's not a dirty convict," I said. "Not our Ken. He never was. And it wasn't convicts who done him in, either. It was the Red Russians." I told her about the cufflinks too. "Ken's romancing," she said. "Same as he always did. He doesn't know the difference, he never did, which has been his trouble all along." '

Interrogators, like priests and doctors, have a particular advantage when it comes to concealing their feelings. They can ask another question, which is what I would have done myself.

'What cufflinks, Sergeant Major?' Smiley said, and I see him lowering his long eyelids and sinking his head into his neck as he once more prepared himself to listen to the old man's tale.

' "There's no medals, Dad," Ken says to me. "Medals wouldn't be secure. You have to be gazetted to get a medal, there'd be too many in the know. Otherwise I'd have a medal same as you. Maybe an even better one, if I'm honest, like the Victoria Cross, because they stretch us as far as we can go and sometimes further. But if you do right in the job, you earn your cufflinks and they keep them for you in a special safe. Then once a year there's this big dinner at a certain place I'm not allowed to mention, with the champagne and butlers you wouldn't believe, and all us Russia boys go to it. And we put on our tuxedos and we wear the cufflinks, same as a uniform but secret. And we have this party, with the speeches and the handshakes, like a special investiture, same as you had for your medals, I expect, in this place I'm not allowed to mention. And when the party's over, we hand the cufflinks back. We have to, for the security. So if ever I go missing, or if something happens to me, just you write to them at the Secret Service and ask them for the Russia cufflinks for your Ken. Maybe they'll say they never heard of me, maybe they'll say, 'What cufflinks?' But maybe they'll make you a compassionate exception and let you have them, because they sometimes do. And if they do – you'll know that everything I ever did wrong was more right than you can imagine. Because I'm my dad's boy, right down the line, and the cufflinks will prove it to you. That's all I'm saying, and it's more than I'm allowed." '

Smiley asked first for the boy's full name. Then for the boy's date of birth. Then he asked about his schooling and qualifications, which were predictably dismal, both. I see him acting quiet and businesslike as he takes down the details: Kenneth Branham Hawthorne, the old soldier told him – Branham, that was his mother's maiden name, sir; he sometimes used it for what they called his crimes – born Folkestone, July 14, 1946, sir, twelve months after I came back from the war. I wouldn't have a child earlier, although the wife wanted it, sir, I didn't think it right. I wanted our boy brought up in peace, sir, with both his living parents to look after him, Major, which is the right of any child, I say, even if it's not as usual as it ought to be.

Smiley's next task was not half as easy as it might seem, whatever the improbabilities of Kenneth Hawthorne's story. Smiley was never one to deny a good man, or even a bad one, the benefit of the doubt. The Circus of those days possessed no such thing as a reliable central index of its resources, and what passed for one was shamefully and often deliberately incomplete, for rival outfits guarded their sources jealously and poached from their neighbours when they saw the chance.

True, the old man's story bristled with unlikelihoods. In purist terms it was grotesque, for example, to imagine a group of secret agents meeting once a year to dine, thus breaking the most elementary rule of 'need to know.' But worse things could happen in the lawless world of the irregulars, as Smiley was aware. And it took all his powers of ingenuity and persuasion to satisfy himself that Hawthorne was nowhere on their books: not as a runner, not as a lamplighter or a scalphunter, not as a signalman and not as any other of the beloved tradenames with which these seedy operators glamourised their ranks.

And when he had exhausted the irregulars he turned to the armed services, the security services and the Royal Ulster Constabulary, any one of which might conceivably have employed – if on some much more modest basis than the boy described – a violent criminal of Ken Hawthorne's character.

For one thing at least seemed certain: the boy's criminal record was a nightmare. It would have been hard to imagine a grimmer record of persistent and often bestial behaviour. As Smiley crossed and recrossed the boy's history, through childhood to adolescence, reform school to prison, there seemed to be no transgression, from pilfering to sadistic assault, that Kenneth Branham Hawthorne, born Folkestone 1946, had not stooped to.

Till at the end of a full week, Smiley appears reluctantly to have admitted to himself what in another part of his head he must have known all along. Kenneth Hawthorne, for whatever sad reasons, had been an unredeemable and habitual monster. The death he had suffered at the hands of his fellow prisoners was no more than he deserved. His past was written and complete, and his tales of heroism on behalf of some mythical British intelligence service were merely the last chapter in his lifelong effort to steal his father's glory.

It was mid-winter. It was a foul grey, sleet-driven evening on which to drag an old soldier back across London to a barren interviewing room in Whitehall. And Whitehall in the meagre lighting of those days was a citadel still at war, even if its guns were somewhere else. It was a place of military austerity, heartless and imperial; of lowered voices and blacked windows, of rare and hurried footsteps and averted eyes. Smiley was in the War too, remember, even if he was sitting behind German lines. I can hear the puttering of the paraffin Aladdin stove which the Circus had grudgingly approved to supplement the faulty ministerial radiators. It has the sound of a wireless transmitter operated by a freezing hand.

Hawthorne had not come alone to hear Major Nottingham's reply. The old soldier had brought his wife, and I can even tell you how she looked, for Smiley had written of her in his log and my imagination has long painted in the rest.

She had a buckled sick body wrapped in Sunday best. She wore a brooch in the design of her husband's regimental badge. Smiley invited her to sit, but she preferred her husband's arm. Smiley stood across the desk from them, the same burned, yellowed desk where I had sat in exile these last months. I see him standing almost to attention, with his rounded shoulders uncharacteristically straightened, his stubby fingers curled at the seams of his trousers in traditional army manner.

Ignoring Mrs. Hawthorne, he addressed the old soldier, man to man. 'You understand I have absolutely nothing to say to you at all, Sergeant Major?'

'I do, sir.'

'I never heard of your son, you understand? Kenneth Hawthorne is not a name to me, nor to any of my colleagues.'

'Yes, sir.' The old man's gaze was fixed parade-ground style above Smiley's head. But his wife had her eyes fiercely turned on Smiley's all the time, even if she found it hard to fix on them through the thick lenses of his spectacles.

'He has never in his life worked for any British department of government, whether secret or otherwise. He was a common criminal all his life. Nothing more. Nothing at all.'

'Yes, sir.'

'I deny absolutely that he was ever a secret agent in the service of the Crown.'

'Yes, sir.'

'You understand also that I can answer no questions, give you no explanations, and that you will never see me again or be received at this building?'

'Yes, sir.'

'You understand finally that you may never speak of this moment to a living soul? However proud you may be of your son? That there are others still alive who must be protected?'

'Yes, sir. I understand, sir.'

Opening the drawer of our desk, Smiley took out a small red Cartier box, which he handed to the old man. 'I happened to find this in my safe,' he said.

The old man passed the box to his wife without looking at it. With firm fingers, she forced it open. Inside lay a pair of superb gold cufflinks with a tiny English rose set discreetly in a corner, hand-engraved, a marvel of fine work. Her husband still did not look. Perhaps he didn't have to; perhaps he didn't trust himself. Closing the box, she parted the clasp of her scuffed purse and popped it inside. Then snapped the purse shut again, so loudly you would think she was slamming down the lid on her son's tomb. I have listened to the tape; it too is waiting to be destroyed.

The old man still said nothing. They were too proud to bother with Smiley as they left.

And the cufflinks? you ask – where did Smiley get the cufflinks from? I had my answer not from the yellowing records of Room 909 but from Ann Smiley herself, quite by chance one evening in a splendid Cornish castle near Saltash where we both happened to be guests. Ann was on her own, and chastened. Mabel had a golf tournament. It was long after the Bill Haydon business, but Smiley still could not bear to have her near him. When dinner was over, the guests dispersed themselves in groups, but Ann stayed close to me, I supposed as a substitute for being close to George. And I asked her, half intuitively, whether she had ever given George a pair of cufflinks. Ann was always at her most beautiful when she was alone.

'Oh those,' she said, as if she scarcely remembered. 'You mean the ones he gave to the old man.'

Ann had given them to George on their first anniversary, she said. After her fling with Bill, he had decided they should be put to better use.

*

But *why*, exactly, did George decide that? I wondered.

At first it seemed perfectly clear to me. This was Smiley's soft centre. The old cold warrior was revealing his bleeding heart.

Like most things with George – maybe.

Or an act of vengeance against Ann perhaps? Or against his other faithless love, the Circus, at a time when the Fifth Floor was locking him out of the house?

Gradually I arrived at a slightly different theory, which I may as well pass on to you, since one thing is certain, and that is that George himself will not enlighten us.

Listening to the old soldier, Smiley recognised one of those rare moments when the Service could be of real value to real people. For once, the mythology of espionage would be used not to disguise yet another tale of incompetence or betrayal, but to leave an old couple with their dreams. For once, Smiley could look at an intelligence operation and say with absolute confidence that it had worked.

11

'A nd some interrogations,' said Smiley, gazing into the dancing flames of the log fire, 'are not interrogations at all, but communions between damaged souls.'

He had been talking about his debriefing of the Moscow Centre spymaster, codename Karla, whose defection he had secured. But for me, he was talking only of poor Frewin, of whom, so far as I know, he had never heard.

The letter denouncing Frewin as a Soviet spy arrived on my desk on a Monday evening, posted first class in the S.W.1 area of London on the Friday, opened by Head Office Registry on the Monday morning and marked by the Assistant Registrar on duty 'HIP to see,' HIP being the unlikely acronym of the Head of the Interrogators' Pool; in other words, myself, and in the opinion of some the 'H' ought to be an 'R' – you Rest in Peace at the Interrogators' Pool. It was five o'clock by the time the Head Office green van unloaded its humble package at Northumberland Avenue, and in the Pool such late intrusions were customarily ignored until next morning. But I was trying to change all that and, having anyway nothing else to do, I opened the envelope at once.

Two pink trace slips were pinned to the letter, each bearing a pencilled note. Head Office's notes to the Pool always had the ring of instructions addressed to an idiot. The first read, 'FREWIN C presumed identical with FREWIN Cyril Arthur, Foreign Office cypher clerk,' followed by Frewin's positive vetting reference and white file number, which was a cumbersome way of telling me there was nothing recorded against him. The second said, 'MODRIAN S presumed identical with MODRIAN Sergei,' followed by a further string of references, but I didn't bother with them. After my five years in the Russia House, Sergei Modrian was plain Sergei to me, as he had been to the rest of us: old Sergei, the crafty Armenian, head boy of Moscow Centre's generously over-staffed residence at the Soviet Embassy in London.

If I had had any lingering wish to postpone my reading of the letter till tomorrow, Sergei's name dispelled it. The letter might be bunkum, but I was playing on home ground.

To the Director,
The Security Department,
The Foreign Office,
Downing Street, SW.

Dear Sir,

This is to inform you, that C. Frewin, a Foreign Office cypher clerk with constant and regular access to *Top Secret and Above*, has been keeping surreptitious company with S. Modrian, First Secretary at the Soviet Embassy in London, for the last four years, and has not revealed same in his annual vetting returns. Secret materials have been passed. Mr. Modrian's whereabouts are no longer known, in view of the fact that he has recently been recalled to the Soviet Union. The said Frewin still resides at the Chestnuts, Beavor Drive, Sutton, and Modrian has been present there at least on one occasion. C. Frewin is now living a *highly solitary life*.

Yours sincerely,
A. Patriot.

Electronically typed. Plain white A4 paper, no watermark. Dated, over-punctuated, accurately spelt and crisply folded. And no address of sender. There never is.

Having nothing much else to do that evening, I had a couple of Scotches at The Sherlock Holmes, then wandered round to Head Office, where I checked myself into the Registry reading room and drew the files. Next morning at the surgery hour of ten I took my place in Burr's waiting room, having first spelt my name to his glossy personal assistant, who seemed never to have heard of me. Brock, from Moscow Station, was ahead of me in the queue. We talked intently about cricket till his name was called, and managed not to refer to the fact that he had worked for me in the Russia House, most recently on the Blair case. A couple of minutes later, Peter Guillam drifted in clutching a bunch of files and looking hung-over. He had recently become Head of Secretariat for Burr.

'Don't mind if I squeeze ahead of you, do you, old boy? I've been sent for urgently. Bloody man seems to expect me to work in my sleep. What's your problem?'

'Leprosy,' I said.

There is nowhere quite like the Service – except possibly Moscow – for becoming an unperson overnight. In the upheavals that had followed Barley Blair's defection, not even Burr's predecessor, the nimble Clive, had kept his foothold on the slippery Fifth Floor deck. When last heard of, he was on his way to take up the salubrious post of Head of Station, Guyana. Only our craven legal adviser, Harry Palfrey, seemed as usual to have weathered the changes, and as I entered Burr's shiny executive suite, Palfrey was slipping stealthily out of the other door – but not quite quickly enough, so he treated me to a rhapsodic smile instead. He had recently grown himself a moustache for greater integrity.

'Ned! Marvellous! We must do that lunch,' he breathed in an excited whisper, and disappeared below the waterline.

Like his office, Burr was all modern man. Where he came from was a mystery to me, but then I was no longer in the swim. Someone had told me advertising, someone else the City, someone else the Inns of Court. One wit in the Pool mailroom said he came from nowhere at all: that he had been born as found, smelling of aftershave and power, in his two-piece executive blue suit and his patent black shoes with side buckles. He was big and floating and absurdly young. Grasping his soft hand, you at once relaxed your grip for fear of denting it. He had Frewin's file in front of him on his executive desk, with my loose minute – written late last night – pinned to the cover.

'Where does the letter come from?' he demanded in his dry North Country cadence, before I had sat down.

'I don't know. It's well informed. Whoever wrote it did his homework.'

'Probably Frewin's best friend,' said Burr, as if that was what best friends were known for.

'He's got Modrian's dates right, he's got Frewin's access right,' I said. 'He knows the positive vetting routine.'

'Not a work of art, though, is it? Not if you're an insider? Most likely a colleague. Or his girl. What do you want to ask me?'

I had not expected this quick fire interrogation. After six months in the Pool, I wasn't used to being hurried.

'I suppose I need to know whether you want me to pursue the case,' I said.

'Why shouldn't I?'

'It's outside the Pool's normal league. Frewin's access is formidable. His section handles some of the most delicate signals traffic in Whitehall. I assumed you'd prefer to pass it to the Security Service.'

'Why?'

'It's their bailiwick. If it's anything at all, it's a straight security enquiry.'

'It's our information, our shout, our letter,' Burr retorted, with a bluntness that secretly warmed my heart. 'To hell with them. When we know what we've got, we'll decide where we go with it. All that those churchy buggers across the Park can think of is a judgeproof prosecution and a bunch of medals to hand around. I collect intelligence for the marketplace. If Frewin's bad, maybe we can keep him going and turn him round. He might even get us alongside Brother Modrian back in Moscow. Who knows? The security artists don't, that's for sure.'

'Then presumably you'd prefer to hand the case to the Russia House,' I said doggedly.

'Why should I do that?'

I had assumed I would make an unappetising figure to him, for he was still of an age to find failure immoral. Yet he seemed to be asking me to tell him why he shouldn't count on me.

'The Pool has no charter to function operationally,' I explained. 'We run a front office and listen to the lonely hearts. We've no charter to conduct clandestine investigations or run agents, and no mandate to pursue suspects with Frewin's sort of access.'

'You can run a phone tap, can't you?'

'If you get me a warrant I can.'

'You can brief watchers, can't you? You've done that a few times, they say.'

'Not unless you authorise it personally.'

'Suppose I do? The Pool's also empowered to make vetting enquiries. You can play Mr. Plod. You're good at it, by all accounts. This is a vetting matter, right? And Frewin's due for a vetting top-up, right? So vet him.'

'In positive vetting cases, the Pool is obliged to clear all enquiries with the Security Service in advance.'

'Assume it's done.'

'I can't do that unless I have it in writing.'

'Oh yes you can. You're not a Service hack. You're the great Ned. You've broken as many rules as you've stuck to, you have, I've read you up. You know Modrian, too.'

'Not well.'

'How well?'

'I had dinner with him once and played squash with him once. That's hardly knowing him.'

'Squash where?'

'At the Lansdowne.'

'How did that come about?'

'Modrian was formally declared to us as the Embassy's Moscow Centre link. I was trying to put together a deal with him on Barley Blair. A swap.'

'Why didn't you succeed?'

'Barley wouldn't go along with us. He'd done his own deal already. He wanted his girl, not us.'

'What's his game like?'

'Tricky.'

'Did you beat him?'

'Yes.'

He interrupted his own flow while he looked me over. It was like being studied by a baby. 'And you can handle it, can you? You're not under too much stress? You've done some good things in your time. You've a heart too, which is more than I can say for some of the capons in this outfit.'

'Why should I be under stress?'

No answer. Or not yet. He seemed to be chewing at something just behind his thick lips.

'Who believes in marriage these days, for Christ's sake?' he demanded. His regional drawl had thickened. It was as if he had abandoned restraint. 'If you want to live with your girl, live with her is my advice. We've cleared her, she's nobody's worry, she's not a bomb thrower or a secret sympathiser or a druggie, what's your bother? She's a nice girl in a nice way of life, and you're a lucky fellow. Do you want the case, or do you not?'

For a moment I was robbed of an answer. There was nothing surprising in Burr knowing of my affair with Sally. In our world you put those things on record before the record puts them on you, and I had already endured my obligatory confessional with Personnel. No, it was Burr's capacity for intimacy that had silenced me, the speed with which he had got under my skin.

'If you'll cover me and give me the resources, of course I'll take it,' I said.

'So get on with it, then. Keep me informed but not too much – don't bullshit me, always give me bad news straight. He's a man without qualities, our Cyril is. You've read Robert Musil, I dare say, haven't you?'

'I'm afraid I haven't.'

He was pulling open Frewin's file. I say 'pulling' because his doughy hands gave no impression of having done anything before: now we are going to see how this file opens; now we are going to address ourselves to this strange object called a pencil.

'He's got no hobbies, no stated interests beyond music, no wife, no girl, no parents, no money worries, not even any bizarre sexual appetites, poor devil,' Burr complained, flipping to a different part of the file. When on earth had he found time to read it? I asked myself. I presumed the early hours. 'And how the hell a man of your experience, whose job is dealing with modern civilisation and its discontentments, can manage without the wisdom of Robert Musil is a question which at a calmer moment I shall require you to answer.' He licked his thumb and turned another page. 'He's one of five,' he said.

'I thought he was an only child.'

'Not his brothers and sisters, you mug, his work. There's five clerks in his dreary cyphers office and he's one of them. They all handle the same stuff; they're all the same rank, work the same hours, think the same dirty thoughts.' He looked straight at me, a thing he had not done before. 'If he did it, what's his motive? The writer doesn't say. Funny, that. They usually do. Boredom – how about that? Boredom and greed, they're the only motives left these days. Plus getting even, which is eternal.' He went back to the file. 'Cyril's the only one not married, notice that? He's a poofter. So am I. I'm a poofter, you're a poofter. We're all poofters. It's just a question which bit of yourself ends on top. He's no hair, see that?' I caught a flash of Frewin's photograph as he waved it past me and talked on. He had a daunting energy. 'Still that's no crime, I dare say, baldness, any more than marriage is. I should know, I've had three and I'm still not done. That's no normal denunciation, is it? That's why you're here. That letter knows what it's talking about. You don't think Modrian wrote it, do you?'

'Why should he have done?'

'I'm asking, Ned, don't fox with me. Wicked thoughts are what keep me going. Perhaps Modrian thought he'd leave a little confusion in his wake when he went back to Moscow. He's a scheming little monkey, Modrian, when he puts his mind to it. I've been reading him too.'

When? I thought again. When on earth did you find the time?

For another twenty minutes he zigzagged back and forth, tossing possibilities at me, seeing how they came back. And when I finally stepped exhausted into the anteroom, I walked straight into Peter Guillam again.

'Who the hell is Leonard Burr?' I asked him, still dazed.

Peter was astonished that I didn't know. 'Burr? My dear chap. Leonard was Smiley's Crown Prince for years. George rescued him from a fate worse than death at All Souls.'

Of Sally, my reigning extramarital girlfriend, what should I tell you? She was free, and spoke to the captive in me. Monica had been within my walls. Monica was a woman of the Service, bound and not bound to me by the same set of rules. But to Sally I was just a middle-aged civil servant who had forgotten to have any fun. She was a designer and sometime dancer whose passion was theatre, and she thought the rest of life unreal. She was tall and she was fair and rather wise, and sometimes I think she must have reminded me of Stefanie.

'Meet you, skipper?' Gorst cried over the telephone. 'Top up our Cyril? It'll be my pleasure, sir!'

We met the next day in a Foreign Office interviewing room. I was Captain York, another dreary vetting officer doing his rounds. Gorst

was head of Frewin's Cypher Section, which was better known as the
Tank: a lecher in a beadle's suit, a waddling, smirking man with prising
elbows and a tiny mouth that wriggled like a worm. When he sat, he
scooped up the skirts of his jacket as if he were exposing himself from
behind. Then he kicked out a plump leg like a chorus girl, before laying it
suggestively over the thigh of the other.

'Saint Cyril, that's what we call Mr. Frewin,' he announced blithely.
'Doesn't drink, doesn't smoke, doesn't swear, certified virgin. End of
vetting interview.' Extracting a cigarette from a packet of ten, he tapped
the tip of it on his thumbnail, then moistened it with his busy tongue.
'Music's his only weakness. Loves the *operah*. Goes to the *operah* regular
as clockwork. Never cared for it myself. Can't make out whether it's actors
singing or singers acting.' He lit his cigarette. I could smell the lunchtime
beer on his breath. 'I'm not too fond of fat women, either, to be frank.
Specially when they scream at me.' He tipped his head back and blew out
smoke rings, savouring them as if they were emblems of his authority.

'May I ask how Frewin gets on with the rest of the staff these days?' I
said, playing the honest journeyman as I turned a page of my notebook.

'Swimmingly, your grace. Par-fectly.'

'The archivists, registrars, secretaries – no trouble on that front?'

'Not a finger. Not a mini-digit.'

'You all sit together?'

'In a big room and I'm the titular head of it. Very *tit*-ular indeed.'

'And I've had it said to me he's something of a misogynist,' I said,
fishing.

Gorst gave a shrill laugh. 'Cyril? A *misogynist?* Bollocks. He just hates
the girls. Won't speak to them, not apart from good morning. Won't come
to the pre-Christmas party if he can help it, in case he has to kiss them
under the mistletoe.' He recrossed his legs, indicating that he had decided
to make a statement. 'Cyril Arthur Frewin – Saint Cyril – is a highly
reliable, eminently conscientious, totally bald, incredibly boring clerk of
the old school. Saint Cyril, though punctilious to a fault, has in my view
reached his natural promotion ceiling in his line of country or profession.
Saint Cyril is set in his ways. Saint Cyril does what he does, one hundred
percent. Amen.'

'Politics?'

'Not in my house, thank you.'

'And he's not workshy?'

'Did I say he was, squire?'

'No, to the contrary, I was quoting from the file. If there's extra work to
be done, Cyril will always roll his sleeves up, stay on in the lunch hour, the
evenings and so forth. That's still the case, is it? No slackening off of his
enthusiasm?'

'Our Cyril is ready to oblige at all hours, to the pleasure of those who
have families, wives or a nice piece of Significant Other to return to. He'll

do the early mornings, he'll do lunch hours, he'll do evening watch, except for *operah* nights, of course. Cyril never counts the cost. Latterly, I will admit, he has been slightly less inclined to martyr himself, but that is no doubt a purely temporary suspension of service. Our Cyril does have his little moods. Who does not, your eminence?'

'So recently a slackening off, you would say?'

'Not of his work, never. Cyril is your total workslave, always has been. Merely of his willingness to be put upon by his more human colleagues. Come five-thirty these days, Saint Cyril packs up his desk and goes home with the rest of us. He does not, for instance, offer to replace the late shift and remain solo incommunicado till nine o'clock and lock up, which was what he used to do.'

'You can't put a date to that change of habit, can you?' I enquired as boringly as I could manage, turning dutifully to a fresh page of my notebook.

Curiously enough, Gorst could. He pursed his lips. He frowned. He raised his girlish eyebrows and pressed his chins into his grimy shirt collar. He made a vast show of ruminating. And he finally remembered. 'The last time Cyril Frewin did young Burton's evening watch was Midsummer's Day. I keep a log, you see. Security. I also have quite an impressive memory, which I don't always care to reveal.'

I was secretly impressed, but not by Gorst. Three days after Modrian left London for Moscow, Cyril Frewin had ceased to work late, I was thinking. I had other questions that were clamouring to be asked. Did the Tank boast electronic typewriters? Did the cypher clerks have access to them? Did Gorst? But I was afraid of arousing his suspicions.

'You mentioned his love of opera,' I said. 'Could you tell me a little more about that?'

'No I could not, since we do not get blow-by-blow accounts, and we do not ask for them. However, he does come in wearing a pressed dark suit on his *operah* days, if he doesn't bring his dinner jacket in a suitcase, and he does impart what I would refer to as a state of high if controlled excitement somewhat similar to other forms of anticipation, which I will not mention.'

'But he has a regular seat, for instance? A subscription seat? It's only for the record. As you say, he's a bit short of relaxing pastimes otherwise.'

'As I think I told you, squire, alas, me and *operah* were not made for each other. Put down "opera buff" on his form and you're covered for your relaxing pastime is my advice.'

'Thank you. I will.' I turned another page. 'And really no enemies that you can think of?' I said, my pencil hovering over my notebook.

Gorst became serious. The beer was wearing off. 'Cyril is laughed at, Captain, I'll admit. But he takes it in good part. Cyril is not disliked.'

'No one who would speak ill of him, for instance?'

'I can think of no single reason whatever why anyone should speak ill of Cyril Arthur Frewin. The British civil servant, he may be sullen but he's not malicious. Cyril does his duty, as we all do. We're a happy ship. I wouldn't mind if you put that down, too.'

'I gather he went to Salzburg for Christmas this year. And previous years too, is that right?'

'That is correct. Cyril always takes his leave at Christmas. He goes to Salzburg, he hears the music. It's the one point on which he will make no concession to the rest of the Tank. There's some of the young ones try to complain about it, but I won't let them. "Cyril makes it up to you in other ways," I tell them. "Cyril's got his seniority, he loves his trip to Salzburg for the music, he has his little ways, and that's how it's going to stay." '

'Does he leave a holiday address behind when he goes?'

Gorst didn't know, but at my request he telephoned his personnel department and obtained it. The same hotel, the last four years running. He's been keeping company with Modrian for four years too, I thought, remembering the letter. Four years of Salzburg, four years of Modrian, ending in a *highly solitary life*.

'Does he take a friend, would you know?'

'Cyril never had a friend in his life, skipper.' Gorst yawned. 'Not one he'd take on holiday, that's for sure. Shall we do a lunch next time? They tell me you boys have very nifty expense accounts when you care to give them a tickle.'

'Does he talk about his Salzburg trips at all when he comes back? The fun he's had – the music he's heard – anything like that?' Thanks to Sally, I suppose, I had learned that people were expected to have fun.

Having made a brief show of thinking, Gorst shook his head. 'If Cyril has fun, squire, it's very, very private,' he said, with a last smirk.

That wasn't Sally's idea of fun at all.

From my office at the Pool I booked a secure line to Vienna and spoke to Toby Esterhase, who with his infinite talent for survival had recently been made Head of Station.

'I want you to shake out the Weisse Rose in Salzburg for me, Toby. Cyril Frewin, British subject. Stayed there every Christmas for the last four years. I want to know when he arrived, how long he stayed, whether he's stayed there before, who with, how much the bills come to and what he gets up to. Concert tickets, excursions, meals, women, boys, celebrations – anything you can get. But don't raise local eyebrows, whatever you do. Be a divorce agent or something.'

Toby was predictably appalled. 'Ned, listen to me. Ned, this is actually completely impossible. I'm in Vienna, okay? Salzburg, that's like the other side of the globe. This city is buzzing like a beehouse. I need more staff, Ned. You got to tell Burr. He doesn't understand the pressures here. Get me two more guys, we do anything you want, no problem. Sorry.'

He asked for a week. I said three days. He said he'd try his best and I believed him. He said he had heard a rumour that Mabel and I had broken up. I denied it.

Ever since I can remember, watchers have been most at home in condemned houses handy for bus routes and the airport. Monty's choice for his own headquarters was an unlikely Edwardian palazzo in Baron's Court. From the tiled hall, a stone staircase curled grandly through five pokey floors to a stained-glass skylight. As I climbed, doors flew open and shut like a French farce as his strange crew, in varying stages of undress, scurried between changing room, cafeteria and briefing room, their eyes averted from the stranger. I arrived in a garret once a painter's studio. Somewhere a women's foursome was playing noisy ping-pong. Closer at hand, two male voices were singing Blake's 'Jerusalem' under the shower.

I had not set eyes on Monty for a long time, but neither the years between nor his promotion to Head Watcher had aged him. A few grey hairs, a sharper edge to his hollow cheeks. He was not a natural conversationalist, and for a while we just sat and sipped our tea.

'Frewin, then,' he said finally.

'Frewin,' I said.

Like a marksman, Monty had a way of making his own particular area of quiet. 'Frewin's a funny one, Ned. He's not being normal. Now of course we don't know what normal is, do we, not really, not for Cyril, not apart from what you pick up from hearsay and that. Postman, milkman, neighbours, the usual. Everyone talks to a window cleaner, you'd be amazed. Or a Telecom engineer who's lost his way with a junction box. We've only been on him two days, all the same.'

With Monty, when he talked like this, you just pinned your ears back and bided your time.

'And nights, of course,' he added. 'If you count nights. Cyril's not sleeping, that's for sure. More prowling, judging by his windows and his teacups in the morning. And his music. One of his neighbours is thinking of complaining to him. She never has before, but she might this time. "Whatever's come over him?" she says. "Handel for breakfast is one thing, but Handel at three in the morning's a bit of another." She thinks he's having his change. She says men get like that at his age, same as women. We wouldn't know about that, would we?'

I grinned. And again bided my time. '*She* does, though,' Monty said reflectively. 'Her old man's gone off with a supply teacher from the comprehensive. She's not at all sure she'll have him back. Nearly raped our pretty boy who'd come to read the meter. Here – how's Mabel?' he demanded.

I wondered whether he too had heard the rumour; but I decided that if he had, he would not have asked me.

'Fine,' I said.

'Cyril used to take a newspaper on the train. The *Telegraph*, need you ask. Cyril doesn't hold with Labour – he says they're common. But he doesn't buy a paper any more. He sits. Sits and stares. That's all he does. Our bloke had to give him a nudge yesterday when they pulled up at Victoria. He'd gone off in a daydream. Going home last night, he tapped out the whole score of an opera on his briefcase. Nancy says it was Vivaldi. I suppose she knows. Remember Pauli Skordeno?'

I said I did. Diversions were part of Monty's way. Like, 'How's Mabel?' for instance.

'Pauli's doing seven years in Barbados for bothering a bank. What gets into them, Ned? He never put a foot wrong while he was watching. Never late, never naughty with his expenses, lovely memory, lovely eye, good nose. Burglaries galore we did. London, the Home Counties, the Midlands, the civil-rights boys, the disarmers, the Party, the naughty diplomats – we did the lot. Did Pauli ever get rumbled? Not once. The moment he goes private, he's all fingers and thumbs and boasting to the bloke next door to him in the bar. I think they *want* to be caught, that's my opinion. I think it's wanting recognition after all the years of being nobody.'

He sipped his tea. 'Cyril's other kick, apart from music, is his radio. He loves his radio. Only receiving, mind, as far as anybody knows. But he's got one of those fancy German sets with the fine tuning and big speakers for his concerts, and he didn't buy it locally because when it went on the blink the local shop had to send it off to Wiesbaden. Three months it took, and cost a fortune. He doesn't run a car, he doesn't hold with them. He shops by bus Saturday mornings, he's a stay-at-home except for his Christmases in Austria. No pets, he doesn't mix. Entertaining, forget it. No house-guests, lodgers, receives no mail except the bills, pays everything regular, doesn't vote, doesn't go to church, doesn't have a television. His cleaning lady says he reads a lot, mainly big books. She only comes once a week, usually when he's not there, and we didn't dare get close to her. A big book for her is anything bigger than a Bible-study pamphlet. His phone bills are modest, he's got six thousand in a building society, owns his house and maintains a well-managed bank account fluctuating between six and fourteen hundred, except Christmas times when it drops to around two hundred because of his holiday.'

Monty's sense of the proprieties again required us to make a detour, this time to discuss our children. My son Adrian had just won a modern languages scholarship to Cambridge, I said. Monty was hugely impressed. Monty's only son had just passed his law exam with flying colours. We agreed that kids were what made life worth living.

'Modrian,' I said when the formalities were once more over. 'Sergei.'

'I remember the gentleman well, Ned. We all do. We used to follow him round the clock some days. Except at Christmas, of course, when he took his home leave. . . . Hullo! Are you thinking what I'm thinking? We all take leave at Christmas?'

'It had crossed my mind,' I said.

'We didn't even bother to pretend with Modrian, not after a while, you couldn't. *Oh*, he was a slippery eel, though. I could have walloped him sometimes, I really could. Pauli Skordeno got so angry with him once he let his tyres down outside the Victoria and Albert while he was inside sussing out a dead-letter box. I never reported it, I didn't have the heart.'

'Am I not right in thinking Modrian was also an opera buff, Monty?'

Monty's eyes became quite round, and I had the rare pleasure of seeing him surprised.

'Oh my Lord, Ned,' he exclaimed. 'Oh dear, oh dear. You're right. Sergei was a Covent Garden subscriber – of course he was, same as Cyril. We must have taken him there and fetched him – oh, a dozen times. He could have used a cab if he'd had any mercy, but he never did. He liked wearing us out in the traffic.'

'If we could know the performances he went to, and where he sat – if you could get them – we could try and match them up with Frewin's.'

Monty had fallen into a theatrical silence. He frowned, then scratched his head. 'You don't think this is all a touch too *easy* for us, do you, Ned?' he asked. 'I get suspicious when everything fits in a pretty pattern, don't you?'

'I won't be part of your pattern,' Sally had said to me the night before. 'Patterns are for breaking.'

'He *sings* Ned,' Mary Lasselles murmured while she arranged my white tulips in a pickle jar. 'He sings *all* the time. Night and day, it doesn't matter. I think he missed his vocation.'

Mary was as pale as a nightnurse and as dedicated. A luminous virtue lit her unpowdered face and shone from her clear eyes. A shock of white, like the mark of early widowhood, capped her bobbed hair.

Of the many callings that comprise the over-world of intelligence, none requires as much devotion as that of the sisterhood of listeners. Men are no good at it. Only women are capable of such passionate espousal of the destiny of others. Condemned to windowless cellars, engulfed by tracks of grey-clad cable and banks of Russian-style tape recorders, they occupy a nether region populated by absent lives which they know more intimately than those of their closest friends or relations. They never see their quarries, never meet them, never touch them or sleep with them. Yet the whole force of their personalities is beamed upon these secret loves. On microphones and telephones they hear them blandish, weep, smoke, eat, argue and couple. They hear them cook, belch, snore and worry. They endure their children, in-laws and babysitters without complaint, as well as their tastes in television. These days, they even ride with them in cars, take them shopping, sit with them in cafés and bingo halls. They are the secret sharers of the trade.

Passing me a pair of earphones, Mary put on her own and, folding her hands beneath her chin, closed her eyes for better listening. So I heard

Cyril Frewin's voice for the first time, singing himself a passage from *Turandot* while Mary Lasselles with her eyes shut smiled in her enchantment. His voice was mellow and, to my untutored ear, as pleasing as it clearly was to Mary.

I sat up straight. The singing had stopped. I heard a woman's voice in the background, then a man's, and they were speaking Russian.

'Mary, who the hell's that?'

'His teachers, darling. Radio Moscow's Olga and Boris, five days a week, 6 a.m. sharp. This is yesterday morning.'

'You mean he's teaching himself *Russian*?'

'Well, he listens to it, darling. How much of it is going into his little head is anybody's guess. Every morning, sharp at six, Cyril does his Olga and Boris. They're visiting the Kremlin today. Yesterday they were shopping at Gum.'

I heard Frewin mutter unintelligibly in the bath, I heard him call out 'Mother' in the night, while he tossed restlessly in bed. FREWIN Ella, I remembered, deceased, mother to FREWIN Cyril Arthur, q.v. I have never understood why Registry insists on opening personal files for the dead relatives of suspected spies.

I listened to him arguing with the British Telecom engineers' department after he had waited the statutory twenty minutes to be connected with them. His voice was edgy, full of unexpected emphases.

'Well, *next* time you elect to identify a *fault* on my line, I would be *highly* grateful if you would kindly inform *me* as the subscriber *prior* to barging into my house when my *cleaning* woman happens to be in, and leaving particles of *wire* on the carpet and bootmarks on the kitchen *floor* . . .'

I listened to him phone the Covent Garden opera house to say he would not be taking up his subscription ticket this Friday. This time his tone was self-pitying. He explained that he was ill. The kind lady the other end said there was a lot of it about.

I listened to him talking to the butcher in anticipation of my visit, which Foreign Office Personnel had set for tomorrow morning at his house.

'Mr. Steele, this is Mr. Cyril Frewin. Good morning. I shall *not* be able to come *in* to you on Saturday, owing to the fact that I have a conference at my *house*. I would therefore be *grateful* if you would kindly deliver four *good* lamb chops for me on the Friday evening as you pass by on your way home. Will that be convenient, Mr. Steele? Also a jar of your pre-mixed mint *sauce*. No, I have red currant jelly already, thank you. Will you attach your *bill*, please?'

To my over-acute ear, he sounded like a man preparing to abandon ship.

'I'll take the engineers again, please, Mary,' I said. Having twice more listened to Frewin's dogmatic tones of complaint to British Telecom, I gave her a distracted kiss and stepped into the evening air. Sally had said, 'Come round,' but I was in no mood to spend an evening professing love to her and listening to music I secretly detested.

I returned to the Pool. The Service laboratories had completed their examination of the anonymous letter. A Markus electronic, model number so-and-so, probably Belgian manufacture, new or little used, was the best they could suggest. They believed they would be able to identify another document issuing from the same machine. Could I get one? End of report. The laboratories were still wrestling with the characteristics of the new generation of machines.

I rang Monty at his lair in Baron's Court. Frewin's complaint to the engineers was still ringing in my memory: his pauses, like unnatural commas, his use of the word *highly*, his habit of punching the unlikely word to achieve vindictive emphasis.

'Did your fellows notice a typewriter in Cyril's house, Monty, by any chance, while they were kindly mending his telephone?' I asked.

'No, Ned. There was no typewriter, Ned – not one they saw, put it that way.'

'Could they have missed it?'

'Easily, Ned. It was soft-pedalling only. No opening desks or cupboards, no photographing, not too much familiarity with his cleaning lady either, or she'll worry afterwards. It was "See what you can, get out fast, and be sure you leave a mess or he'll smell a rat." '

I thought of phoning Burr, but I didn't. My case officer's possessiveness was taking over, and I was damned if I was going to share Frewin with anyone, not even the man who had entrusted him to me. A hundred twisted threads were running through my head, from Modrian to Gorst to Boris and Olga to Christmas to Salzburg to Sally. In the end, I wrote Burr a minute setting out most of what I had discovered and confirming that I would 'make a first reconnaissance' of Frewin tomorrow morning when I interviewed him for his routine vetting clearance.

To go home? To go to Sally? Home was a hateful little service flat in St. James's, where I was supposed to be sorting myself out – though that's the last thing any man does when he sits alone with a bottle of Scotch and a reproduction painting of 'The Laughing Cavalier,' dithering between his dreams of freedom and his addiction to what holds him prisoner. Sally was my Alternative Life, but I knew already I was too set to jump the wall and reach it.

Preferring to remain at my desk, therefore, I fetched myself a whisky from the safe and browsed through Modrian's file. It told me nothing I didn't already know, but I wanted him at the front of my head. Sergei Modrian, tried and tested Moscow Centre professional. A charmer, a bit of a dancer, a befriender, a smiling Armenian with a mercury tongue. I had liked him. He had liked me. In our profession, since we may like no one beyond a point, we can forgive a lot for charm.

My direct line was ringing. I thought for a moment it would be Sally, for contrary to regulations I had given her the number. It was Toby and he sounded pleased with himself. He usually did. He didn't mention Frewin by name. He didn't mention Salzburg. I guessed he was ringing from his flat, and I'd a shrewd notion he was in bed and not alone.

'Ned? Your man's a joke. Books himself a single room for two weeks, checks in, pays his two weeks in advance, gives the staff their Christmas box, pats the kids, makes nice to everybody. Next morning he disappears, does it every year. Ned, can you hear me? Listen, the guy's crazy. No phone calls out, one meal, two *Apfelsaft*, no explanations, taxi to the station. Keep my room, don't let it, maybe I'll be back tomorrow, maybe in a few days, I don't know. After twelve days, back he comes, no explanations, tips the staff some more, everybody happy like a heathen. They call him "the ghost." Ned, you got to talk nice to Burr for me. You owe me now. Toby works his fingers to the bone, tell him. Old star like you, a young fellow like Burr, he'll listen to you, costs you nothing. I need another man out here, maybe two. Tell him, Ned, hear me? Cheers.'

I stared at the wall, the one I couldn't scale; I stared at Modrian's file, I remembered Monty's dictum about too easy. I suddenly wanted Sally terribly, and had some cloudy notion that by solving the mystery of Frewin I would convert my recurring spurts for freedom into one bold leap. But as I reached for the phone to talk to her, it started to ring again.

'They fit,' said Monty in a flat voice. He had managed to check Frewin's opera attendance. 'It's Sergei and Cyril every time. When *he* goes, so does *he*. When *he* doesn't, neither does *he*. Maybe that's why he doesn't go any more. Got it?'

'And the seats?' I asked.

'Side by side, darling. What do you expect? Front to back?'

'Thanks, Monty,' I said.

Do I have to tell you how I spent that interminable night? Have you never telephoned your own son, listened to his unhappy jibes and had to remind yourself that he is yours? Talked frankly to an understanding wife about your inadequacies, not knowing what on earth they were? Have you never reached out for your mistress, cried 'I love you' and remained a mystified spectator to her untroubled fulfilment, before leaving her once more, to walk the London streets as if they were a foreign city? Have you never, from all the other sounds of dawn, picked out the wet chuckle of a magpie and fixed on it for your whole life long while you lie wide-eyed on your beastly single bed?

I arrived at Frewin's house at half past nine, having dressed myself as boringly as I could contrive, and that must have been boringly indeed, for I am not a natty dresser at the best of times, though Sally has appalling ideas about how she might improve my style. Frewin and I had agreed on ten but I told myself I wanted the element of surprise. Perhaps the truth was, I needed his company. A postman's van was parked up the street. A builder's truck with an aerial stood beyond it, telling me Monty's men were at their posts.

I forget what month it was but I know it was autumn, both in my private life and in the prim cul-de-sac of steep brick houses. For I see a disc of white sun hanging behind the pollarded chestnut trees that had given the place its name, and I smell to this day the scent of bonfires and autumn air in my nostrils urging me to leave London, leave the Service, take to Sally and the world's real countryside. And I remember the whirr of small birds as they lifted from Frewin's telephone line on their way to somewhere better. And a cat in the next-door garden rising on its rear paws to box a drowsy butterfly.

I dropped the latch to the garden gate and crunched up the prim gravel path to the Seven Dwarfs semi-detached, with its bottle-glass windows and thatched porch. I reached out my hand for the bell, but the front door flew away from me. It was ribbed, and studded with fake coach bolts, and it shot back as if it had been blasted by a street bomb, almost sucking me after it into the dark tiled hall. Then the door stood still, and Frewin stood beside it, a bald centurion to his own endangered house.

He was taller than I had realised by a wrestler's head. His thick shoulders were braced to receive my attack, his eyes were fixed on me in scared hostility. Yet even at this first moment of encounter I sensed no contest in him, only a sort of heroic vulnerability made tragic by his bulk. I entered his house, and knew I was entering a madness. I had known it all night long. In desperation we find a natural kinship with the mad. I had known that for much longer.

'Captain York? Yes, well, welcome, sir. Welcome indeed. Personnel of their goodness *did* advise me you were coming. They don't always. But this time they did. Come in, please. You have your *duty* to do, Captain, as I have mine.' His vast, soggy hands were lifted for my coat but seemed unable to grapple with it. So they hovered above my neck as if to strangle or embrace me while he went on talking. 'We're all on the same side and no hard feelings, I say. I liken your job to airport security, personally, it's the same parameters. If they don't search *me*, they won't search the villains either, will they? It's the logical approach to the matter, in my view.'

Heaven knows what lost original he thought he was copying as he delivered these over-prepared words, but at least they freed him from his frozen state. His hands descended to my coat and helped me out of it, and I can feel now the reverence with which they did so, as if unveiling something exciting to us both.

'You fly a lot then, do you, Mr. Frewin?' I asked.

He hung my coat on a hanger, and the hanger on a vile reproduction coat-tree. I waited for an answer but none came. I was thinking of his air travel to Salzburg, and I wondered whether he was too, and whether his conscience was speaking out of him in the tension of my arrival. He marched ahead of me to the drawing room, where by the light of the leaded bay window I was able to examine him at my ease, for he was already busy with the next article of his urgent hospitality: this time, an electric coffee percolator filled but not switched on – did I want the milk, or the sugar or the both, Captain? And the milk, Captain, was it hot or cold? And how about a home-made biscuit for you, Captain?

'You really made them yourself?' I asked as I fished one from the jar.

'Any fool who can read can cook,' said Frewin, with a chaotic grin of superiority, and I could see at once why Gorst would loathe him.

'Well, I can read, but I certainly can't cook,' I replied, with a rueful shake of my head.

'What's your first name, Captain?'

'Ned,' I replied.

'Well, that's because you're married, Ned, I expect. Your wife has robbed you of your self-sufficiency. I've seen it too often in my life. In comes the wife, out goes the independence. I'm Cyril.'

And you're ducking my question about your air travel, I thought, refusing to allow him this attempted incursion into my private territory.

'If *I* ran this country,' Frewin announced over his shoulder to me while he poured, 'which I am *pleased* to say I shall never have the opportunity to *do*' – his voice was acquiring the didactic drumbeat of his conversation with the engineers – 'I would make an *absolute* law that *everyone*, regardless of colour, sex or creed, would take *cooking* as an obligatory subject *while* at school.'

'Good idea,' I said, accepting a mug of coffee, 'very sound,' and helped myself to sugar from the yellow beehive pot, which nestled like a missile in his damp paw. He had turned to me all at once, shoulders, waist and head together. His bare eyes, unfringed and unprotected, gazed down on me with a radiant and doting innocence.

'Play any games at all, Ned?' he enquired softly, tipping his head to one side for added confidentiality.

'A spot of golf, Cyril,' I lied. 'How about you?'

'Hobbies at all, Ned?'

'Well, I do like to do the odd watercolour when I'm on holiday,' I said, borrowing again from Mabel.

'Drive a car, do you, Ned? I expect you boys have to have all the skills at your fingertips, don't you?'

'Just an old Rover.'

'What year is it, then? What vintage, Ned? There's many a good tune played on an old fiddle, they say.'

His energy was not just in his person, I realised as I gave him the first date that occurred to me; it spilled into every object that came within his sphere. Into the reproduction horse-brasses that glistened like military cap-badges from his vigorous polishing. Into the polished fire grate and wood floor and the resplendent surface of his dining table. Into the very chair where I now sat and meekly sipped my coffee, for its arms were concealed in linen covers so pressed and spotless that I was reluctant to put hands on them. And I knew without his telling me that, cleaning woman or none, he tended all these things himself, that he was their servant and dictator, in the kingdom of his boundless wasted energy.

'Where do you live then, Ned?'

'Me? Oh well, London, really.'

'What part then, Ned? What district? Somewhere nice, or do you have to be slightly anonymous for your work?'

'Well, we're not really allowed to say, I'm afraid.'

'London born, are you? Hastings, me.'

'Sort of suburbs. You know. Pinner, say.'

'You must retain your discretion, Ned. Always. Your discretion is your dignity. Let nobody take it from you. It's your professional integrity, discretion is. Remember that. It could come in handy.'

'Thanks,' I said, affecting a sheepish laugh. 'I will.'

He was feeding on me with his eyes. He reminded me of my dog Lizzie when she watches me for a signal – unblinking, body ready to go. 'Shall we start, then?' he said. 'Want to sound the "off"? As soon as it's official, tell me. "Cyril. The red light's on." That's all you have to say.'

I laughed, shaking my head again, as if to say he was a card.

'It's only routine, Cyril,' I said. 'My goodness, you must know the questions by heart after all these years. Mind if I smoke?' I laboriously lit my pipe and dropped the match into the ashtray he was pressing on me. Then I resumed my study of his room. Along the walls, do-it-yourself shelves filled with do-it-yourself books, every one of them of global resonance: *The World's One Hundred Greatest Men; Gems of All the World's Literature; Music of the Great Ages in Three Volumes*. Next to them, his gramophone records in cases, all classical. And in the corner, the gramophone itself, a splendid teak affair with more control buttons than a simpleton like myself could master.

'Well now, if you like painting watercolours, Ned, why don't you try the music too?' he suggested, following my eye. 'It's the finest consolation in the world, good music is, properly played, if you choose right. I could put you on the right lines if you wanted.'

I puffed for a while. A pipe is a great weapon for playing slow against someone else's haste. 'I rather think I'm tone deaf, actually, Cyril. I have made the occasional effort, but I don't know, I sort of lose heart really . . . '

My heresy – drawn, I am afraid, from inconclusive debates I had had with Sally – was already too much for him. He had sprung to his feet, his face a mask of horror and concern as he seized the biscuit jar and thrust it at me as if only food would save me.

'Now, Ned, that is not *right*, if I may say so! There is no such *thing* as a tone-deaf *person!* Take two, go on, there's plenty more in the kitchen.'

'I'll stick to my pipe if you don't mind.'

'Tone deafness, Ned, is merely a *term*, an expression, I will go so far as to say an *excuse*, designed to cover up, to disguise, a purely *temporary*, self-imposed *psychological* resistance to a certain world which your conscious mind is refusing you permission to enter! It is *merely* a fear of the unknown which is holding you *back*. Let me give you the example of certain acquaintances of mine . . . '

He ran on and I let him, while he dabbed at me with his forefinger, and with the other hand clutched the biscuit jar against his heart. I listened to him, I watched him, I expressed my admiration at the appropriate moments. I fished for my black notebook and removed the garter of black elastic from it as a signal to him that I was ready to begin, but he ignored me and ranted on. I imagined Mary Lasselles in her lair, smiling dreamily while her loved one lectured me. And Monty's boys and girls in their surveillance vans outside, cursing him and yawning while they waited to change shifts. And for all I knew, Burr too – all of them hostages to Frewin's endless anecdote about a married couple he had had for neighbours when he lived in Surbiton, whom he had taught to share his musical appreciation.

'Anyway, I can tell my masters at PVHQ that music is still your great love,' I suggested with a smile when he had finished.

'PV' for Positive Vetting, you understand, and 'HQ' for Headquarters. My part as the downtrodden security workhorse required a higher authority than my own. Then, opening the notebook on my knee, I spread the pages, and with my unpainted government-issue pencil wrote the name FREWIN at the top of the left-hand page.

'Ah well, if you're talking about *love*, Ned – you *could* say music was my great love, yes. And music, to quote the bard, is the food of love. However, I'd *prefer* to say, it depends how you *define* love. What *is* love? That's your real question, Ned. *Define love.*'

God's coincidences are sometimes too vulgar to be borne. 'Well, I suppose *I* define it rather broadly,' I said doubtfully, my pencil poised. 'How do *you* define it?'

He shook his head and began energetically stirring his coffee, all his thick fingers gathered round the neck of one tiny Apostle spoon.

'Is this on the record?' he asked.

'It could be. Please yourself.'

'Commitment is how *I* define love. A great *number* of people speak of love as if it were some kind of *nirvana*. It isn't. I happen to know that. Love is not *separate* from life. It's not *beyond* it or *superior* to it. Love is *within* life. Love is totally *integral* to life, and what you get *out* of it depends on the ways and means whereby you invest your *efforts* and your loyalty. Our Lord taught us that *perfectly* clearly, not that I'm a God-man personally, I'm a rationalist. Love is *sacrifice* and love is hard work. Love is *also* sweat and tears, exactly as your great music has to be in order to qualify. By that token, yes, I'll grant you, Ned, *music* is my first love, if you follow me.'

I was following him only too well. I had made similar half-hearted representations to Sally, only to have them swept aside. I knew also that in his beleaguered state of mind there was no such thing to him as a casual question, let alone a casual answer – anymore than there was to me, even if my systems of concealment were more sophisticated than his.

'I don't think I'll write that down,' I said. 'I think I'll regard it as what we call deep background.' In earnest of which, I pencilled a couple of words in the notebook, as a memo to myself and a sign to him that we were going on the record. 'All right, let's do the meat-and-potatoes work first,' I suggested, 'or PVHQ will say I'm dragging my feet as usual. Have you joined the Communist Party since you were last spoken to by one of our representatives, Cyril, or have you managed to restrain yourself?'

'I have not,' he said, with a smirk.

'Haven't joined or haven't restrained yourself?'

A broader smirk. 'The first. I like you, Ned. I cherish wit when I find it, I always have done. Not that we're overburdened with it at my place of work. Where wit's concerned, I'd be inclined to refer to the Tank as a total desert.'

'No friendship or peace groups?' I continued, affecting disappointment. 'Fellow-travelling organisations? Taken out membership to any homosexual or otherwise deviant-oriented clubs, formed a secret passion for any under-age choirboys lately?'

'No to the lot, thank you,' said Frewin, now smiling broadly.

'Run up vast debts, causing you to live beyond your means? Set up some tasteful redhead in the style to which she is not accustomed? Acquired a Ferrari motorcar on the hire purchase?'

'My needs remain as modest as they have always been, thank you. I am not of a materialist or self-indulgent nature, as you may have gathered. I rather abhor materialism, frankly. There's too much of it these days. Far.'

'And no to the rest?'

'All no.'

I was jotting all the time, making annotations against an imaginary checklist.

'So you wouldn't be flogging secrets for money then,' I commented, turning a page and adding a couple of ticks. 'And you have not launched yourself upon a course of foreign language instruction without first obtaining the consent of your employing department in writing, I take it?' My pencil was poised once more. 'Sanskrit? Hebrew? Urdu? Serbo-Croat?' I suggested. 'Russian?'

He was standing very still and staring at me, but I pretended to be unaware of this.

'Hottentot?' I continued facetiously. 'Estonian?'

'Since when's *that* been on the list?' Frewin demanded aggressively.

'Hottentot?'

I waited.

'Languages. A language isn't a defect. It's an attribute. An accomplishment! You don't have to list all your accomplishments, just to get cleared!'

I tilted back my head in reminiscence. 'Addendum to the Positive Vetting procedure, November 5, 1967,' I recited. 'I always remember that one. Fireworks Day. Special circular to all employing departments, yours included, requiring advance notice in writing of all intended language instruction courses. Recommended by Judicial Steering Committee, approved by Cabinet.'

He had turned his back to me. 'I regard this as a totally out-of-court question and I refuse to answer it in any shape or form. Write that down.'

I puffed through my pipe smoke.

'I said write it down!'

'I wouldn't say that, Cyril, if I were you. They'll be cross with you.'

'Let them be.'

I drew on my pipe again. 'I'll put it to you the way HQ put it to me, shall I? "What's all this nonsense Cyril's been getting up to with his chums Boris and Olga?" they said. "Ask him that one – then see what he comes up with." '

Still turned away from me, he was scowling indignantly from place to place around the room, appealing to his polished world to witness my profanity. I waited for the explosion I was sure would come. But instead he peered at me in hurt reproach. *Us*, he was saying, *friends – and you do this to me*. And in the way that the brain in stress can handle a multitude of images at once, I saw before me, not Frewin, but a typist I had once interrogated in our Embassy in Ankara: how she had rolled back the sleeve of her cardigan and thrust out her arm at me and showed me the festering cigarette burns she had inflicted on herself the night before our interview. 'Don't you think you have made me suffer enough?' she asked. Yet it was not I who had made her suffer; it was the twenty-five-year-old Polish diplomat for whom she had sacrificed every secret she possessed.

I took my pipe from my mouth and gave him a reassuring laugh. 'Come on, Cyril. Aren't Boris and Olga two of the characters on this Russian course you're doing on the sly? Papering their house together? Going off to stay at Auntie Tanya's dacha, all that? You're doing the standard Radio Moscow language course, five days a week, 6 a.m. sharp, that's what they told me. "Ask him about Boris and Olga," they say. "Ask him why he's learning Russian on the q.t." So I'm asking you. That's all.'

'They'd no business knowing I was doing that course,' he muttered, still grappling with the implications of my question. 'Bloody sniffer dogs. It was private. Privately selected, privately pursued. They can get lost. So can you.'

I laughed. But I was also put out. 'Now don't be like that, Cyril. You know the rules as well as I do. It's not your style to ignore a regulation. It's not mine either. Russian is Russian, and reporting is reporting. It's only a matter of getting it down in writing. I didn't make up the regulations. I get a brief, the same as anyone else.' I was talking to his back again. He had taken refuge at the bay window, and was gazing out at the rectangle that was his garden.

'What's their names?' he demanded.

'Olga and Boris,' I repeated patiently.

This enraged him. 'The people who brief you, idiot! I'm going to enter a complaint about them! Snooping, that's what it is. It's bloody brutal in this day and age. I'm holding you to blame too, frankly. What's their names?'

I still didn't answer him. I preferred to let the fury bank up in him.

'Number one,' he announced in a louder voice, still staring at his mud patch. 'Are you writing this down? Number one, I am not taking a language course within the meaning of the Act. A language course is going to a school or class, it is sitting on a bench with a bunch of snivelling typists with bad breath, it is submitting to the sneers of an uncouth instructor. Number two. I *do*, however, listen to *radio*, it being one of my *continuing* pleasures to scan the wavebands for examples of the quaint or esoteric. Write that down and I'll sign it. Finish, okay? Then take yourself off. I'm done with you, thank you, up to here. Nothing personal. It's them.'

'Which was how you stumbled on Boris and Olga,' I suggested helpfully, writing again. 'Got it. You scanned the wavebands and there they were. Boris and Olga. Nothing wrong in that, Cyril. Stick with it and you might even land yourself a language allowance, if you pass the test. It's only a few bob, I suppose, but it's better in your pocket than theirs, I always say.' I continued writing, but slowly, letting him hear the maddening scratch of my government-issue pencil. 'It's always the *not* reporting that bothers them most,' I confided, apologising for the foibles of my masters. ' "If he hasn't told us about Olga and Boris, what else hasn't he told us?" You can't blame them, I suppose. Their jobs are on the line, same as ours.'

Turn another page. Lick tip of pencil. Make another annotation. I was beginning to feel the excitement of the chase. Love as commitment, he had said, love as part of life, love as effort, love as sacrifice. But love for whom? I drew a heavy pencil line and turned a page:

'Can we pass on to your Iron Curtains, please, Cyril?' I asked in my weariest voice. 'HQ are devils for Iron Curtains. I wondered whether you'd any fresh names to add to the list of those you've already given us these past years. The last one' – I flipped to the back of the notebook – 'my goodness, that was aeons ago. A gentleman from East Germany, a member of a local choral society you joined. Is there no one you can think of since at all? They're a bit after you now, Cyril, I'll admit, now that they've caught you not reporting the language course.'

His disillusionment in me was again sliding into anger. Once again he began punching the unlikely words. But this time it was as if he were punching me.

'You will find *all* my Iron Curtain contacts, past and present, *such* as they are, *duly* listed *and* submitted to my superiors, according to regulations. *If* you had troubled yourself to *obtain* this data from Foreign Office Personnel Department *prior* to this interview – and I mean why they send me a hack like you – '

I decided to cut him short. I did not think it useful that he should be allowed to reduce me to nothing. To insignificance, yes. But not to nothing, for I was the servant of a higher authority. I pulled a sheet of paper from the back of my notebook. 'Look, now, here you are, I've got them. All your Iron Curtains on one page. There's only been five ever, in your whole twenty years. HQ cleared, I see, the lot. Well, so they would be, as long as you report them.' I put the sheet back in my notebook. 'Anyone to add, then? Who's to add? Think now, Cyril. Don't be hasty. They know an awful lot, my people. They shock me sometimes. Take your time.'

He took his time. And more time. And more. Finally he took the line of self-pity.

'I'm not a *diplomat*, Ned,' he complained in a small voice. 'I'm not out doing the gay hurrah every night, Belgravia, Kensington, St. John's Wood, medals and white tie, rubbing shoulders with the great, am I? I'm a clerk. I'm not that man at all.'

'What man's that, Cyril?'

'I like a treat, that's different. I like a friend best.'

'I know you do, Cyril. HQ knows too.'

A fresh resort to anger to mask his rising panic. Deafening body language as he clenches his great fists and lifts his elbows. 'There is not a single *name* on that list that has *crossed* my path since I reported the *persons* concerned. The names in that list related *entirely* to the most *completely* casual encounters, which had no follow-up *whatsoever.*'

'But what about new people since?' I pleaded patiently. 'You'll not get past them, Cyril. I don't, so why should you?'

'If there was anyone to add, any contact at all, even a Christmas card from someone, you may rest assured I would have been the first to add him. Finish. Done. Over. Next question, thank you.'

Diplomat, I noted. *Him*, I noted. *Christmas*. Salzburg. I became if anything more laborious.

'That's not quite the answer they want, Cyril,' I said as I wrote in my notebook. 'That sounds a bit too much like flannel, frankly. They want a "yes" or a "no," or an "if yes, who?" They want a straight answer and they're not settling for flannel. "He didn't own up to his language, so why should we think he's owning up to his Iron Curtains?" That's what they're thinking, Cyril. That's what they're going to say to me too. It'll all come back on me in the end,' I warned him, still writing.

Once again I could feel that my ponderousness was a torture to him. He was pacing, snapping his fingers at his sides. He was muttering, working his jaw menacingly, growling again about getting names. But I was far too busy writing in my notebook to notice any of this. I was old Ned, Burr's Mr. Plod, doing his duty by HQ.

'How's about this then, Cyril?' I said at last. And, holding up my notebook, I read aloud to him what I had written: " 'I, Cyril Frewin, solemnly declare that I have not made the acquaintance, however briefly, of any Soviet or Eastern Bloc citizen, other than those already listed by me, in the last twelve months. Dated and signed Cyril." '

I relit my pipe and studied the bowl in order to make quite sure it was drawing. I put the burned-out match in the matchbox, and the matchbox in my pocket. My voice, already slowed to a walking pace, now became a crawl.

'Alternatively, Cyril, and I say this advisedly, if there *is* anyone like that in your life, now's your chance to tell me. And them. I'll treat everything you say in confidence; so will they, depending what I tell them of it, which isn't always everything, not by any means. Nobody's a saint, after all. And HQ probably wouldn't clear them if they were.'

Intentionally or otherwise, I had touched the fuse in him. He had been waiting for an excuse and now I had delivered it.

'Saint? Who's talking *saint*? Don't *you* call me bloody saint, I won't have it! Saint Cyril, they call me, did you know that? Of course you did, you're taunting me!'

Taut-faced and rude. Battering me with words. Frewin against the ropes, slugging anything that came at him. 'If there *were* such a person – which there is not – I would *not* have told *you* or your snooping PV lot – I would have reported the matter *in writing*, according to regulations, to personnel department *at* the – '

For the second time, I allowed myself to cut him short. I didn't like him conducting the rhythm of our exchanges. 'But there really isn't anyone, is that right?' I said, as pressingly as my passive rôle allowed. 'There's no one? You haven't been to any functions – parties, get-togethers, meetings – official, unofficial – in London, outside London, abroad even – at which a citizen of an Iron Curtain country was remotely present?'

'Do I have to continue saying no?'

'Not if the answer's yes,' I replied, with a smile he didn't like.

'The answer is no. No, no, no. Repeat no. Got it?'

'Thank you. So I can put *none*, can I? That means no one, not even a Russian. And you can sign it. Yes?'

'Yes.'

'Meaning no?' I suggested, making another weak joke. 'I'm sorry, Cyril, but we do have to be crystal clear, otherwise HQ will fall on us from a great height. Look, I've written it down for you. Sign it.'

I handed him my pencil and he signed. I wanted to instil the habit in him. He handed back my notebook, smiling tragically at me. He had lied to me and he needed my comfort in his wretchedness. So I granted it to him – if only, I am afraid, because I wanted to take it away again very soon. I stowed the notebook in my inside pocket, stood up, and gave a big stretch as if announcing a break in our discussions, seeing that a tricky point was behind us. I rubbed my back a bit, an old man's ache.

'What's all that digging you've been doing out there, Cyril?' I said. 'Building your own deep shelter, are you? Hardly necessary these days, I'd have thought.'

Looking past him, my eye had fallen on a pile of new bricks stacked in a corner of the mud patch, with a tarpaulin tied over the top of them. An unfinished trench, about two feet deep, cut across the lawn towards them.

'I am *building* a *pond*,' Frewin retorted, seizing gratefully on my facetious diversion. '*I happen* to be very fond of *water*.'

'A goldfish pond, Cyril?'

'An *ornamental* pond.' His good humour came sailing back. He relaxed, he smiled, and his smile was so warm and unaffected that I found myself smiling in return. 'What I intend to do, Ned,' he explained, drawing near to me in friendship, 'is construct three separate levels of water, beginning four feet above the existing ground, descending over eighteen-inch intervals to that trench. I shall then illuminate each pool from beneath with the aid of a concealed lamp. I shall then pump the water with an electric pump. And at night, instead of drawing the curtains, I shall be able to look out on to my own private display of illuminated pools and waterfalls!'

'And play your music!' I cried, responding in full measure to his enthusiasm. 'I think that's splendid, Cyril. Genius. I'm most impressed, I really am. I'd like my wife to see that. How was Salzburg, by the way?'

He actually reels, I thought, watching his head swing away from me. I hit him and he reels, and I wait till he recovers consciousness before I hit him again.

'You go to Salzburg for the music, they tell me. Quite a Mecca for you musicians, they tell me, Salzburg. Do they do opera at Christmas, or is it all carols and anthems you go for?'

They must have closed off the street, I thought, listening to the enormous silence. I wondered whether Frewin was thinking the same as he went on staring into the garden.

'Why should you care?' he answered. 'You're a musical ignoramus. You said so. As well as being a very considerable snooper.'

'Verdi? I've heard of Verdi. Mozart? He was Austrian, wasn't he? I saw the film. I'll bet they do you Mozart for Christmas. They'd have to. Which ones do they do?'

Silence again. I sat down and once again prepared myself to write to his dictation.

'Do you go alone?' I asked.

'Of course I do.'

'Do you always?'

'Of course I do.'

'Last time too?'

'Yes!'

'Do you stay alone?' I asked.

He laughed loudly. 'Me? Not for one minute. Not me. There's dancing girls waiting for me in my room when I arrive. They're changed every day.'

'But music night after night after night, the way you like it?'

'Who says what I like?'

'Fourteen nights of it. Twelve, I suppose, if you count the travel.'

'Could be twelve. Could be fourteen. Could be thirteen. What does it matter?' He was still concussed. He was talking from a long way off.

'Which is what you go for. To Salzburg. And what you pay for. Yes? Yes, Cyril? Give me a signal, please, Cyril. I keep thinking I'm losing you. And it was what you went for this Christmas too?'

He nodded.

'Concerts, night after night? Opera? Carols?'

'Yes.'

'Only the trouble is, you see, HQ says you only stayed the one night. You arrived on the first day as booked, they say,.and you were off again next morning. You paid the full whack for your room, all two weeks, but the hotel never saw hide nor hair of you from your second day till you came back at the end of your holiday. So quite reasonably, really, HQ are asking where the bloody hell you went.' I took my boldest leap so far. 'And who with. They're asking whether you've got someone on the side. Like Boris and Olga, but real.'

I turned a couple more pages of my notebook, and in the deep silence the rustle was like falling bricks. His terror was infecting me. It was like a shared evil. The truth lay a membrane from us, yet the dread of it seemed to be as terrible to the man who was trying to keep it outside the door as to myself, who was trying to let it in.

'All we need to do is get it down on paper, Cyril,' I said. 'Then we can forget it. Nothing like writing something down for getting it out of the way, I say. It's no crime to have a friend. Even a foreign one isn't a crime, as long as he's written down. He *is* foreign, I take it? Only, I notice a certain hesitation in you here. He must be quite some friend, I will say, if you gave up all that music for him.'

'He's nowhere. He doesn't exist. He's gone. I was in his way.'

'Well, he hadn't gone at Christmas time, had he? Not if you were together with him. Was he Austrian, Cyril?'

Frewin was lifeless. He was dead with his eyes open. I had hit him once too often.

'All right, then, he's French,' I suggested more loudly, trying to jerk him from his introspection. 'Was he a Frenchie, Cyril, your chum? . . . They wouldn't mind about a Frenchie, even if they don't like them. Come on, Cyril, how about a Yank then? They can't object to a Yank!' No answer. 'Not Irish, was he? I hope not, for your sake!'

I did the laughing for him, but nothing stirred him from his melancholy. Still at the window, he had crooked his thumb and was boring the knuckle joint into his forehead, as if trying to make a bullet hole. Had he whispered something?

'I didn't catch you, Cyril!'

'He's above all that.'

'Above nationality?'

'He's above it.'

'You mean he's a diplomat?'

'He didn't *come* to Salzburg, can't you bloody listen?' He swung round at me and began screaming. 'You're bloody spastic, you know that? Never mind the answers, you can't even *ask* right! No wonder the country's in a mess! Where's your savvy gone? Where's your human understanding, for a change?'

I stood up again. Slowly. Keep him watching me. Give my back another rub. I wandered down the room. I shook my head as if to say this simply would not do.

'I'm trying to help you, Cyril. If you went to Salzburg and stayed there, that's one scenario. If you went on somewhere else – well, that's quite another. If your chum is Italian, say. And if you pretended to go to Salzburg but went – oh, I don't know – to Rome, say, or Milan, even Venice – well, that's another. I can't do it all for you. It's not fair and they wouldn't thank me if I did.'

He was wide-eyed. He was transferring his madness to me, appointing himself the sane one. I refilled my pipe, giving it my entire attention while I went on talking.

'You're a hard man to please, Cyril' – tamping the tobacco with my forefinger – 'you're a tease, if you want to know. "Don't touch me here, take your hand away from there, you can do this but only once." I mean, what *am* I allowed to talk about?'

I struck a match and held it to the bowl, and as I did so I saw that he had transferred his knuckles to his eyes in order not to be in the room. But I pretended not to notice. 'All right, we'll forget Salzburg. If Salzburg is hurtful, put Salzburg aside and let's go back to your Iron Curtains. Yes? Agreed?'

His hands slipped slowly from his face. No answer, but no outright rejection either. I went on talking. He wanted me to. I could sense his reliance on my words as a bridge between the real world and the inner hell where he was living. He wanted me to do the talking for both of us. I felt I had to make his confession for him, which was why I decided to play my most perilous card.

'So suppose, for argument's sake, Cyril, we were to add the name of Sergei Modrian to this list and call it a day,' I suggested carelessly, almost covering over my words in my efforts to sound unthreatening. 'Just to be on the safe side,' I added cheerfully. 'What do you say?' His head was still hanging downward, his face cut off from me. Chatting cheerfully, I expanded on my latest helpful proposal for HQ. ' "All right," we say to them, "so take your wretched Mr. Modrian. Don't play around with us any more, we'll come clean. Have him and go home. Ned and Cyril have got work to do." '

He was dangling, smiling like a hanged man. In the profound silence that had settled over the neighbourhood, I had the sensation of hearing my words resounding from the rooftops. But Frewin seemed barely to have heard them.

'Modrian's the one they want you to own up to, Cyril,' I continued reasonably. 'They told me. If you say *yes* to Modrian – and if I write him down, which I'm doing, and you allow me to, and I notice you're not stopping me, are you? – nobody can accuse either one of us of being less than frank with them. "Yes, I am a chum of Sergei Modrian and screw the lot of you" – how's that? "*And* I went with him to wherever we went, *and* we did this, we did that, we agreed to do certain other things, and we had a lovely time, or we didn't. And anyway, what's all the *glasnost* for, if I'm still being forbidden to associate with an extremely civilised Russian?" . . . How's that? Never mind the gaps for the moment, we can fill all those in later. Then, the way I see it, they can pack up the file for another year and we can all get on with our weekend.'

'Why?'

I affected not to understand.

'Why can they pack up the file then?' he demanded, as suspicions crowded in on him. 'When they've been who they are? They're not going to turn round and say "What's the point?" Nobody does. Not when they've been one thing. They stay who they are. They don't become other people. They can't.'

'Come off it, Cyril!' He had sunk into his own thoughts and was becoming hard to reach. '*Cyril!*'

'What then? What's up? Don't shout.'

'So what's wrong with being Russian these days? HQ would be *far* more worried if Sergei was a Frenchie! I only suggested Frenchie as a trap. I regret that now, I apologise. But a Russian these days – for heaven's sake, we're not just talking friendly nations, we're talking partners! *You* know

HQ. They're always behind the times. So's Gorst. Our job's to set the trend. Are you hearing me, Cyril?'

And that was where, for a moment, I thought I had lost the whole game – lost his complicity, lost his dependence, lost the willing suspension of his disbelief. He wandered past me like a sleepwalker. He stood himself at his bay window again, where he remained contemplating his half-dug pool and all the other half-built dreams of his life, which he must have known by now would never be completed.

Then, to my relief, he started talking. Not about what he had done. Not about who he had done it with. But why.

'You don't know what it means, do you, to be locked up all day with a bunch of morons?'

I thought at first he was complaining of his future, till I realised he was talking about the Tank.

'Listening to their filthy jokes all day, choking on their fags and their B.O.? Not *you*, you're privileged, however humble you make yourself out. Day after day of it, sniggers about tits and knickers and periods and little bits on the side? "Come on, Saint, tell us a naughty joke for a change! You're a deep one, I'll bet, Saint! What are you into – gym slips? Bit of the rough? What's the Saint's little fancy of a Saturday night?" ' His energy had returned to him in full force, and with it, to my astonishment, an unexpected gift for mimicry. He was mincing at me, playing the music-hall queen, a ghastly soft grin twisting his hairless face. ' "Heard the one about the Boy Scouts and the Girl Guides, Saint? The excitement was in tents. Get *you!*" You wouldn't know about that, would you? "Do you pull it now and then, Saint? Give it a little jerk occasionally, just to make sure it's there? You'll go blind, you know. It'll drop off. I'll bet you've got a big one, haven't you? A real donkey knock, all the way down your leg and tucked into your garter." . . . You've never had that, have you, all day long, in the office, in the canteen? You're a gentleman. Know what they gave me April Fool's Day? A top secret incoming from Paris, Frewin's eyes only, decypher yourself, manual, ha ha. *Flash priority*, get the joke? I didn't. So I go into the cubicle and get out the books, don't I? And I decypher it, don't I? Manual. Everyone's got his head down. Nobody laughing or spoiling it. I do the first six groups and it's filth, some filthy joke all about a French letter. Gorst had done it. He'd had the boys at the Paris Embassy send it specially as a joke. "Steady on, Saint, keep your hair on, give us a smile. It was only a joke, Saint, can't you take a joke?" That's what Personnel said too, when I complained. Horseplay, they said. Pranks are good for morale. Think of it as a compliment, they said, show a little sporting instinct. If I hadn't had my music, I'd have killed myself long ago. I considered it, I don't mind telling you. Trouble was, I wouldn't see their faces when they found out what they'd done.'

A traitor needs two things, Smiley had once remarked bitterly to me at the time of Haydon's betrayal of the Circus: somebody to hate, and somebody to love. Frewin had told me whom he hated. Now he began to talk about whom he loved.

'I'd been all over the world that night – Puerto Rico, Cape Verde, Jo'burg – and there wasn't anything that took my fancy. I like the amateurs best, as a rule, the hacks. They've got more wit, which is what I like, I told you. I didn't even know it was morning. I've got these thick curtains up there, three hundred quids' worth, interlined. It's meat and drink to me after the Tank, the quiet is.'

A different smile had come up on him, a small boy's smile on his birthday.

' "Good morning to you, Boris, my friend," says Olga. "How are you feeling this morning?' Then she says it in Russian and Boris replies that he's feeling a bit low. He's often low, Boris is. He's prone to Slav depressions. Olga takes care of him, mind. She'll have a joke, but it's never cruelly meant. They have a fight now and then too – well, it's only natural, seeing they do everything together. But they always make it up in the same programme. They don't bear a grudge from day to day. Olga couldn't do that, to be frank. It's out with it and that's it, with Olga. Then they'll have a laugh together. That's how they are. Constructive. Friendly. Clean spoken. Musical too, naturally – well, they would be, being Russian. I wasn't that keen on Tchaikovsky till I heard them discussing him. But afterwards I came round to him straight away. Boris has got quite advanced tastes in music actually. Olga – well, she's a bit easy to please. Still, they're only actors, I suppose, reading their lines. But you forget that when you're listening to them, trying to learn the language. You believe in them.'

And you send your written work in, he was saying.

For free correction and advice, he was saying.

You don't even have to write to Moscow after the first time. They've got this box number in Luxembourg.

He had fallen quiet but not dangerously so. Nevertheless I was becoming scared that his trance might end too soon. I took myself out of his line of sight, and stood in a corner of the room behind him.

'What address did you give them, Cyril?'

'This one, of course. What else have I got to give them, then? A country house in Shropshire? A villa in Capri?'

'Did you give them your own name too?'

'Of course I didn't. Well, Cyril, yes. I mean anyone can be Cyril.'

'Good man,' I said approvingly. 'Cyril who?'

'Nemo,' he announced proudly. 'Mr. C. Nemo. "Nemo" is Latin for "nobody," in case you didn't know.'

Mr. C. Nemo. Like Mr. A. Patriot, perhaps.

'Did you put your occupation?'

'Not my real one. You're being stupid again.'

'So what did you put?'

'Musician.'

'Did they ask for your age?'

'Of course they did. They had to. They had to know you were eligible, in case you won the prize. They can't give prizes to minors, can they? No one can.'

'And status – married or single – you told them that too?'

'I *had* to put my status, didn't I, with the prize being available to *couples!* They can't give a *prize* to *one* person and leave his wife out, it wouldn't be gracious.'

'What work did you send in – the first time round, for instance – do you remember?'

He decided to take further exception to my stupidity.

'Thickhead. What do you think I sent them? Bloody logarithms? You write in you get the forms, you enrol, you get the Luxembourg box number, you get the book, you're one of them. After that you do what Boris and Olga tell you to do in the programme, don't you? "Complete the exercise on page 9. Answer the questions on page 12." Haven't you been to school then?'

'And you were good. HQ says you've got a mind like an encyclopaedia when you use it. They told me.' I was beginning to learn how much he relished flattery.

'I was *more* than good, as a matter of fact, thank you, HQ. If you *wish* to know, I was in the nature of being their *top pupil*. Certain *notes* were sent to me by certain *tutors* and some of them had a highly congratulatory *tone*,' he added, with the wild grin that came over him when he was praised. 'It gave me quite a filip, if you wish to know, walking into the Tank of a Monday morning with one of their little *notes* in my pocket and not saying anything. I thought, I could tell some of *you* a tale if I wanted. I didn't, though. I preferred my privacy. I preferred my friendships. I wasn't going to have those animals making filthy comments about Olga and Boris, thank you.'

'And you wrote back to these tutors?'

'Only as Nemo.'

'But you didn't fool with them otherwise?' I asked, trying to fathom what restraints, if any, were in his mind as he embarked on this first illicit love affair. 'I mean, if they asked you a plain question, you'd give them a plain answer. You weren't coy.'

'I was *not* coy! I had no *cause* to be! I took great care to be courteous, the same as my tutors were. They were high professors, some of them, academicians. I was *grateful* and I was *diligent*. That was the least they deserved, considering there was no fee and it was voluntary and in the interests of human understanding.'

The hunter in me again. I was calculating the moves they would have made as they played him along. I was working out how I would have played him myself, if the Circus had dreamed up anything so perfect.

'And I suppose, as you improved, they passed you on from plain printed exercises to the more ambitious stuff – composition, essays?'

'When it was deemed by the Board of Tutors in Moscow that I was ripe for it, yes, they moved me up to freestyle.'

'Do you remember the subjects they set you?'

He laughed his superior laugh. 'You think I'd forget them? Five nights at each one of them with the dictionary? Two hours' sleep if I'm lucky? Wake up, will you, Ned!'

I gave a rueful little laugh as I wrote to his dictation.

' "My Life" was the first one. I told them about the Tank, not mentioning names, of course, or the nature of our work, naturally. Nevertheless, a certain element of social comment was present, I won't deny it. I thought the Board had a right to know, specially with the *glasnost* in the pipeline and everything easing up for the benefit of all mankind.'

'What was the next one?'

' "My Home." I told them about my plans for the pond. They liked that. And my cooking. One of them was quite a major cook. After that they gave me "My Favourite Pastime," which could have been redundant but wasn't.'

'You described your love of music, I suppose?'

'Wrong.'

The rest of his answer rings in my ears today: as an accusation, as a cry of sympathy from a fellow sufferer; as a blind prayer flung into the ether by a man who, like myself, was desperate for love before it was too late.

'I elected "Good Company" as my favourite pastime, if you really wish to know,' he said as the wild smile came racing back to his cheeks. 'The fact that I had not *had* much good company in my life hitherto did not *deter* me from relishing the few occasions when it *had* come my way.' He seemed to forget that he had spoken, for he began again, in words I might have used of Sally: 'I had a feeling I had *renounced* something in my life which I *now* wished to reclaim,' he said.

'And did they admire your advanced work too? Were they impressed by it?' I asked as I diligently wrote this down.

He was smirking again. 'Moderately, I assume. Marginally. Here and there. With reservations, naturally.'

'Why do you assume that?'

'Because, unlike some, they had the grace and generosity to show their appreciation. That's why.'

And they showed it, said Frewin – I scarcely needed to press him further – they showed it in the person of one Sergei Modrian, First Secretary Cultural, of the Soviet Embassy in London, in his capacity as Radio

Moscow's devoted local emissary despatched to answer Frewin's prayer.

Like all good angels, Modrian arrived without warning, on Frewin's doorstep one dank November Saturday, bearing with him the gifts of his high office: one bottle of Moskovskaya vodka, one tin of Sevruga caviar, and one foully printed artbook about the Bolshoi Ballet. And one grandly typed letter appointing Mr. C. Nemo to be an Honorary Student of Moscow State University, in recognition of his unique progress in the Russian language.

But the greatest gift of all was Modrian's own magical person, custom-trained to provide the good company Frewin had so loudly craved in his prize-winning essay for the Board.

We had arrived at our destination. Frewin was calm, Frewin was in triumph; Frewin, for however long, was fulfilled. His voice had broken free of its confinements; his plain face was lit with the smile of a man who had known true love and was longing to impart his luck. If there had been anyone in the world for whom I could ever have smiled in the same way, I would have been a different man.

'*Modrian*, Ned? Sergei Modrian? Oh, Ned, I mean we're talking the total top league here. One look at him, I knew. None of your half measures here, I thought. This one's the whole hog. We had the same sense of humour, of course, straight off. Acid. No wool across the eyes. The same interests too, right down to composers.' He attempted a more detached tone, but in vain. 'It is very *rare* in life, in my experience, for two human beings to be naturally compatible in each and every respect – bar women, where I have to admit that Sergei's experience far outran my own. Sergei's attitude to women' – he was trying hard to be disapproving – 'I'll put it this way: if it had been anyone else behaving in that manner, I would have been hard put to it to approve.'

'Did he introduce you to women, Cyril?'

His expression switched to one of adamant rejection. 'He assuredly did not, thank you. Nor would I have permitted him to. Nor would he have regarded such introductions as coming within the ambit of our relationship.'

'Not even on your trips to Russia together?' I ventured, taking another leap for him.

'Nowhere, thank you. It would have ruined them, as a matter of fact. Killed them stone dead.'

'So it's all hearsay, what they say about his women?'

'No, it's not. It's what Sergei told me himself. Sergei Modrian had a totally ruthless attitude to women. His colleagues confirmed this to me privately. Ruthless.'

I found time to marvel at Modrian's psychological dexterity – or was it the dexterity of his masters? Between Modrian the ruthless pursuer of women, and Frewin the ruthless rejecter of them, there was indeed a natural bond.

'So you met his colleagues too,' I said. 'In Moscow, presumably. At Christmas.'

'Only the ones he trusted. Their respect for him was incredible. Or Leningrad. I wasn't fussy, I'd no right to be. I was an honoured guest. I went along with whatever they'd arranged for me.'

I kept my eyes on my notebook. God knows what I was writing by then. Gobbledygook. Afterwards, there were whole tracts I couldn't read a word of. I selected my absolutely dullest tone.

'And was all this in honour of your remarkable linguistic abilities, Cyril? Or were you already providing informal services for Modrian by then? Like giving him information or whatever. Translating and so on. A lot do it, I'm told. They're not supposed to, of course. But you can't blame people – can you? – wanting to help the *glasnost* along, now it's come. We've waited long enough. Only, I've got to put the proper history to this, Cyril. They'll skin me otherwise.'

I did not dare look up. I simply kept writing. I turned a page and wrote: *keep talking, keep talking, keep talking*. And still I did not look up.

I heard him whisper something I couldn't understand. I heard him mutter, 'It's *not*. I didn't. I never bloody did.' I heard him complain more loudly: 'Don't *say* that, do you mind? Don't you ever say that again, you and your HQ. "Giving him information" – what's all that about? They're wrong words. *I'm talking to you, Ned!*'

I looked up, sucking on my pipe and smiling. 'Are you, Cyril? Of course you are. I'm sorry. You're my sixth in a week, to be honest. They're all doing the *glasnost* these days. It's the fashion. I'm beginning to feel my age.'

He decided to comfort me. He sat down. Not in the chair, but on its arm. He put on an avuncular, friend-to-friend manner that reminded me of my preparatory-school headmaster.

'You're by way of being a liberal yourself, aren't you, Ned? You've got the face for it anyway, even if you are a bit of a toady for HQ.'

'I suppose I'm a sort of free thinker in my way, yes,' I conceded. 'Though I do have my pension to consider, naturally.'

'Of course you are! You favour a mixed economy, don't you? You don't like public poverty and private wealth any more than I do. Humanity above ideology, you believe in that? Stop the derailed train of capitalism destroying all before it in its path? Of course you do! You've got a sensible concern for the environment, I dare say. Badgers, whales, fur coats, power stations. Even a vision of sharing, where it doesn't impinge. Brothers and sisters marching together towards common goals, culture and music for all! Freedom of movement and choice of allegiance! Peace! Well, then.'

'Makes good enough sense to me,' I said.

'You're not old enough to have done the thirties; neither am I. I wouldn't have held with them if I had been. We're *good men*, that's all we are. *Reasonable men*. That's what Sergei was too. You and Sergei – I can see it in your face, Ned, it's no good your trying to hide it, you're birds of a feather. So don't go painting me black and you white, because we're like minds, same as me and Sergei were. On the same side against the wickedness, the lack of culture, the filth. We're "the unrecognised aristoc-racy" – that's what Sergei called us. He was right. You're one too, that's all I'm saying. I mean, who else is there? Who's the alternative to what we see around us every day, the degradation, the waste, the disrespect? Who are we going to listen to, up there in the attic at night, twiddling the dials? Not the yuppies, that's for sure. Not the pigs-in-clover lot – what have they got to say? Not the make-more spend-more be-more school, they're no help. Not the knickers-and-tits brigade, either. And we're not going to convert to Islam in a hurry, are we, not while they go round pinching countries off each other and doing the poison gas. So I mean what's the alternative for a feeling man, a man of conscience, now the Russians are abandoning their responsibilities right and left and putting on the hair shirt? Who's out there for us? Where's the vision any more? Where's the relief? The friendship? Someone's got to fill the gap. I can't be left in the air. I can't be without. Not after Sergei, Ned – I'd die. Sergei was the most important man on earth to me. Drink, meat and laughter, Sergei was. He was my total meaning. What's going to happen? That's what I want to know. There's some heads could roll, in my view. Sergei had the ideology. I don't see it in you – I don't think I do anyway. I get a glimpse of it, a longing here and there, then I'm not at all sure. I don't know you've got the quality.'

'Try me,' I said.

'I don't know you've got the wit. The dance. I thought that as you came in. I compared you with Sergei in my mind, and I'm afraid I found you seriously wanting. Sergei didn't shuffle in like a deadbeat; he took me by storm. Rings the bell, marches in as if he's bought the place, sits down where you're sitting, but more awake – not that he ever sat anywhere long, Sergei didn't, he was a shocking fidget, even at the opera. Then he grins like an elf and lifts up a glass of his own vodka. "Congratulations, Mr. Nemo," he says. "Or may I call you C? You've won the competition and I'm the first prize." '

He passed the back of his hand across his mouth, and I realised that he was wiping away a grin. 'He was a real flyer, Sergei was.'

He was laughing, so I laughed with him. Modrian was his false freedom, I was thinking. As Sally is mine.

'He hadn't even taken his coat off,' he continued. 'He went straight into his pitch. "Now the first thing we've got to talk about is the ceremony," he says. "Nothing flashy, Mr. Nemo, just a couple of friends of mine, who happen to be Boris and Olga, plus one or two high dignitaries from the

Board, and a small reception for a few of your many admirers in Moscow."

'At your Embassy?' I said. 'I'm not coming there. My office would kill me – you don't know Gorst.'

' "No, no, Mr. Nemo," he says. "No, no, Mr. C. *I'm* not talking about the Embassy – who cares about the Embassy? *I'm* talking about Moscow State University foreign language school and the official inauguration of your honorary studentship with full civilian honours."

'I thought I was dead at first. My heart had stopped beating. I could feel it. I'd never been beyond Dover in my life, let alone Russia, although I was Foreign Office. "Come to Moscow?" I said. "You're off your head," I said. "I'm a cypher clerk, not a trade union leader with an ulcer. I can't come to Moscow at the drop of a hat," I said. "Even if there is a prize at the end of it, and Olga and Boris waiting to shake my hand, and studentships and I don't know what. You don't seem to understand the position at all. I'm in highly sensitive work," I said. "The people aren't that sensitive, but the work is. I've got constant and regular access to top secret and above. I'm not just anybody off the street, into your plane to Moscow and nobody's the wiser. I thought I put that in my essays, some of them." '

' "Then come to Salzburg," he says. "Who's counting? Take a plane to Salzburg, say you're doing the music there, slip up to Vienna, I'll have the air tickets ready – all right, it's Aeroflot but it's only two hours – no nonsense with the passports when we arrive, we'll keep the ceremony family, who's the wiser?" Then he hands me this document like a scroll, all with the burned edges and that, the full formal invitation, signed by the whole Board, English one side, Russian the other. I read the English, I don't mind telling you. I wasn't going to sit in front of him with a dictionary for an hour, was I? I'd have looked a total idiot, me a top language student.' He paused – a little shamefully, I thought. 'Then I told him my name,' he said. 'I shouldn't have done, really, but I'd had enough of being Nemo. I wanted to be me.'

Now you must lose me for a minute, as I lost Cyril. Until now, I had managed to stay abreast of his references. Where I had dared, I had even led them. Now suddenly he was running free and I was struggling to keep up with him. He was in Russia, but I wasn't. He'd given me no warning that we'd gone there. He was talking about Boris and Olga, not how they sounded any more, but how they looked; and how Boris had flung his arms round him, and how Olga had given him a demure but heartfelt Russian kiss – he didn't hold with kissing as a rule, Ned, but with the Russians it wasn't Gorst's kind of kissing at all, so you didn't mind. You even got to expect it, Ned, it being all part of what Russians regard as comradely. Frewin was looking twenty years younger and talking about being made a fuss of, all the birthdays that he'd never had. Olga and Boris in the flesh, Ned, no side to them, just natural, same as they were in their lessons.

' "Congratulations, Cyril," she says to me, "on your completely phenomenal progress in the Russian language." Well, through interpreters, naturally, I wasn't *that* far on, as I told her. Then Boris puts his arm round me. "We're proud to be of assistance, Cyril," he says. "There's a lot of our students fall by the wayside, to be truthful, but those as don't make up for all the rest." '

And by then at last I had pieced together the scene that he was painting for me in such broad, unpredicated strokes: his first Christmas in Russia, and for Frewin, I had no doubt, his first good Christmas anywhere, and Sergei Modrian playing ringmaster at his side. They are in a great room somewhere in Moscow, with chandeliers and speeches and a presentation, and fifty handpicked extras from Moscow Central Casting, and Frewin in paradise, which is exactly where Modrian wishes him to be.

Then, as abruptly as Frewin had treated me to this memory, he abandoned it. The light went out of his eyes, his head tipped to one side, and he beetled his eyebrows as if in judgment at his own behaviour.

Prudently, I returned him to time present. 'So where is it?' I said. 'The scroll he gave you. Here? The scroll, Cyril. Appointing you. Where?'

He stared at me, slowly waking. 'I had to give it back to Sergei. "When we're in Moscow, Cyril," he said, "you shall have it hanging on your wall and framed in gold. Not here. I wouldn't put you in the danger." He'd thought of everything, Sergei had, and he was quite right, what with you and your HQ snooping on me night and day.'

I allowed no pause, no alteration in my voice, not even in the direction of casualness. I lowered my eyes again and dug once more in my inside pocket. I was his candidate as Sergei's replacement, and he was courting me. He was showing me his tricks and asking me to take him on. Instinct told me to make him work harder for me. I addressed myself to the notebook again, and I spoke exactly as if I were asking him the name of his maternal grandfather.

'So when did you start giving Sergei all these great British secrets?' I said. 'Well, what we *call* secrets, anyway. Obviously what was secret a few years ago is not going to be the same as what's secret today, is it? We didn't win the Cold War by secrecy, did we? We won it with the openness. The *glasnost*.'

It was the second time I had mentioned passing over secrets, but on this occasion, when I crossed the Rubicon for him, he came with me. Yet he seemed not even to notice he was on the other side.

'Correct. That's how we won it. And Sergei didn't even want the secrets at first, either. "Secrets, Cyril, they're unimportant to me," he said. "Secrets, Cyril, in the changing world in which we live, I'm pleased to say, they're a drug on the market," he said. "I'd rather keep our friendship on a non-official basis. However, if I *do* require something in that line, you may count on me to let you know." In the meantime, he said, it would be quite sufficient if I wrote him a few unofficial reports on the quality of Radio Moscow's programmes just to keep his bosses happy. Whether the reception was good enough, for example. You'd think they'd know that, really, but they don't. You never know with Russians where you're going to strike the ignorance in them, to be frank. That's not a criticism, it's a fact. He'd like my opinion of the course as well, he said, the standard of instruction generally, any suggestions I might have for Boris and Olga in the future, me being somewhat of an unusual pupil in my own right.'

'So what changed it?'

'Changed what? Be lucid, please, Ned. I'm not nobody, you know. I'm not Mr. Nemo. I'm Cyril.'

'What changed Sergei's reluctance to take secrets from you?' I said.

'His Embassy did. The diehards. The barbarians. They always do. They prevailed on him. They declined to recognise the course of history; they preferred to remain total troglodytes in their caves and continue with their ridiculous Cold War.'

I said I did not understand him. I said he was a bit above my head.

'Yes, well I'm not surprised. I'll put it this way. There was a lot of them in that Embassy didn't like the time given over to cultural friendship, for a start. There was this internal rivalry going on between the camps. I was an impotent spectator. The *doves*, they were in favour of the culture, naturally, and above all they were in favour of the *glasnost*. They saw culture filling the vacuum left behind by the withdrawal of hostilities. Sergei explained that to me. But the hawks – *including* the Ambassador, I regret to say – wanted Sergei concentrating more on the continuation of old attitudes, what's left of them, gathering intelligence and generally acting in an aggressive and conspiratorial manner regardless of the changes in the world climate. The Embassy diehards didn't care about Sergei being an idealist, not at all. Well, they wouldn't, would they, any more than what Gorst does. Sergei had to tread a highly precarious path, frankly, a bit for one side, then a bit for the other. So did I, it was duty. We'd do our culture together, a bit of language, a bit of art or music; then we'd do some secrets to satisfy the hawks. We had to justify ourselves to all parties, same as you with your HQ and me with the Tank.'

He was fading, I was losing him. I had to use the whip. 'So *when?*' I asked impatiently.

'When what?'

'Don't be clever with me, Cyril, do you mind? I've got to get this down. Look at the time. *When* did you start giving Sergei Modrian information, *what* did you give him, what for, how *much* for, when did it stop, and why, when it could perfectly well have continued? I'd like a weekend, Cyril, if you don't mind. So would my wife. I'd like to put my feet up in front of the telly. I'm not paid overtime, you know. It's strictly piecework, what they offer. One candidate's the same as another, when it comes to payday.

We're living in a time of cost effectiveness, in case you haven't noticed.
They tell me we could be privatised if we're not careful.'

He didn't hear me. He didn't want to. He was wandering, in his body
and in his mind, looking for distraction, for somewhere to hide. My anger
was not all simulated. I was beginning to hate Modrian. I was angry about
how much we depended on the credulity of the innocent in order to
survive. It was sickening me that a trickster like Modrian had contrived
to turn Frewin's loneliness to treachery. I felt threatened by the notion of
love as the antithesis of duty.

I stood up smartly, anger still my ally. Frewin was perched listlessly on
the edge of a carved Arthurian stool with the Royal Navy's ensign stitched
into the seat.

'Show me your toys,' I ordered him.

'What toys? I'm a man, if you don't mind, not an infant. It's my house.
Don't tell me what to do.'

I was remembering Modrian's tradecraft, the stuff he used, the way he
equipped his agents. I was remembering my own tradecraft, from the days
when I had run Frewin's counterparts against the Soviet target, even if
they were not quite as mad as Frewin. I was imagining how I would have
handled a high-access walk-in like Frewin, living on borrowed sanity.

'I want to see your camera, don't I?' I said petulantly. 'Your high-speed
transmitter, right, Cyril? Your signals plan. Your one-time codepads. Your
crystals. Your white carbons for your secret writing. Your concealment
devices. I want to see them, Cyril, I want to put them in my briefcase for
Monday; then I want to go home and watch Arsenal against United. That
may not be your taste, but it happens to be mine. So can we move this
along a bit and cut out the bullshit, *please?*'

The madness was running out, I could feel it. He was drained and so
was I. He sat head down and knees spread, staring dully at his hands. I
could sense the end beginning in him – the moment when the penitent
grows tired of his confession and of the emotions that compelled it.

'Cyril, I'm getting a bit edgy,' I said.

And when he still didn't respond, I strode to his telephone, the same one
that Monty's fake engineer had made permanently live. I dialled Burr's
direct line and heard his fancy secretary the other end, the same one who
hadn't known my name.

'Darling?' I said. 'I'm going to be about another hour, if I'm lucky. I've
got a slow one. Yes, all right, I know, I'm sorry. Well, I said I'm sorry. Yes,
of course.'

I rang off and stared at him accusingly. He climbed slowly to his feet
and led me upstairs. His attic was a spare bedroom, roof high. His radio
receiver stood on a table in the corner – German, just as Monty had said.
I switched it on while he watched me, and we heard an accented female
Russian voice talking indignantly about Moscow's criminal mafia.

'Why do they *do* that?' Frewin burst out at me, as if I were responsible.

'The Russians. Why do they run down their own country all the time? They never used to. They were proud. I was proud too. All the cornfields, the classlessness, the chess, the cosmonauts, the ballet, the athletes. It was paradise till they started running it down. They've forgotten the good in themselves. It's bloody disgraceful. That's what I told Sergei.'

'Then why do you still listen to them?' I said.

He was almost weeping, but I pretended not to notice.

'For the message, don't I?'

'Make it snappy, will you, Cyril!'

'Telling me I'm reactivated. That I'm wanted again. "Come back, Cyril. All is forgiven, love, Sergei." That's all I need to hear.'

'How would they say that?'

'White paint.'

'Go on.'

' "There's white paint on the dog, Olga." . . . "We need a spot of white paint on the bookshelf, Boris." . . . "Oh dear, oh dear, Olga, look at the cat, someone has dipped her tail in white paint. I hate cruelty," says Boris. Why don't they say it when I'm listening?'

'Let's just stick to the method, can we? All right, you hear the message. On the radio. Olga or Boris says "white paint." Or they both do. *Then* what do you do?'

'Look in my signals plan.'

I held out my hand, commanding him with my snapping fingers. 'Hurry!' I said.

He hurried. He found a wooden hairbrush. Pulling the bristles from the casing, he shoved his big fingers into the gap and hauled out a piece of soft, flammable paper with times of the day and wavebands printed in parallel. He offered it to me, hoping it would satisfy. I took it from him without pleasure and snapped it into my notebook, glancing at my watch at the same moment.

'Thanks,' I said curtly. 'More, please, Cyril. I need a codebook and a transmitter. Don't tell me you haven't got them, I'm not in the mood.'

He was grappling with a tin of talcum powder, tugging at the base, trying desperately to please me. He talked nervously while he shook the powder into the handbasin.

'I was respected, you see, Ned, you don't get that a lot. There's three of these. Olga and Boris tell me which to use, like with the white paint except it was the composers. Tchaikovsky was number three, Beethoven was number two, Bach was one. They did them alphabetical to help me remember. You get the glimpses but you don't get the friends, not normally, do you? Not unless you meet Sergei or one of his lot.'

The powder was all poured away. Three radio crystals lay in his palm, together with a tiny codepad and an eye-glass to enlarge it.

'He had all I'd got, Sergei did. I gave it to him. He'd tell me a thing, I'd add it to my life. I'd have a mood, he'd get me straight again. He

understood. He could see right into me. It gave me a feeling of being
known, which I liked. It's gone now. It's been posted back to Moscow.'

His rambling was scaring me. So was his feverish desire to pacify me. If
I had been his hangman, he would have been gratefully loosening his tie.

'Your transmitter,' I snapped. 'What the hell's the good of a crystal and
a codepad if you can't send!'

At the same terrible pace, he bent his swelled body to the floor and
rolled back a corner of the tufted Wilton carpet.

'I haven't got a knife actually, Ned,' he confessed.

Neither had I, but I dared not leave him, I dared not break my command
over him. I crouched beside him. He was peering vaguely at a loose
floorboard, trying to raise it with his thick fingertips. Clenching my fist, I
punched one end of the board, and had the satisfaction of seeing the other
end lift.

'Help yourself,' I said.

It was old stuff, I could have guessed, nothing they cared about any
more – a rig of grey boxes, a squash transmitter, a lash-up to be fitted to
his receiver. Yet he handed it to me proudly, in its tangled mess.

A terrible anxiety had entered his eyes. 'All I am now, you see, Ned, I'm
a hole,' he explained. 'I don't mean to be morbid, do I, but I don't exist.
This house isn't anything either. I used to love it. It looked after me, same
as I looked after it. We'd have been nothing without each other, this house
and me. It's hard for you to understand that, I dare say, if you have a wife,
what a house is. She'd come between you. You and the house, I mean.
Your wife. You and him. Modrian. I loved him, Ned. I was infatuated.
"You're too much, Cyril," he used to say. "Cool down. Relax. Take a
holiday. You're hallucinating." I couldn't. Sergei was my holiday.'

'Camera,' I ordered.

He didn't read me at once. He was obsessed with Modrian. He looked
at me, but it was Modrian he saw.

'Don't be like that,' he said, not understanding.

'Camera!' I yelled. 'For Christ's sake, Cyril, don't you *ever* have a
weekend?'

He stood at his wardrobe. Camelot sword blades carved on oak doors.

'Camera!' I shouted louder as he still hesitated. 'How can you slip film
to a good friend at the opera if you haven't photographed your files in the
first place?'

'Take it easy, Ned. Cool down, will you? Please.' Grinning in a superior
way, he reached a hand into the wardrobe. But his eyes were ogling me,
Saying 'Now watch this.' He groped in the wardrobe, smiling at
me mysteriously. He pulled out a pair of opera glasses and trained them
on me, first the right way, then back to front. Then he handed them to me
so that I could do the same to him. I took them in my hands and felt their
unnatural weight at once. I turned the central dial until it clicked. He was
nodding at me, encouraging me, saying 'Yes, Ned, that's the way.' He

grabbed a book from the bookshelf and opened it at the centre, *All the World's Dancers* illustrated. A young girl was doing a *pas de chat*. Sally too had been at ballet school. He unbuckled the neck strap and I saw that the short end did duty as a measuring chain. He took the binoculars from me and trained them on the book, measured the distance and turned the dial till it clicked.

'See?' he said proudly. '*Comprenez*, do you? They made it specially. For me. For opera nights. Sergei designed it personally. There's a lot of idleness in Russia, but Sergei had to have the best. I'd stay in late at the Tank. I'd photograph the whole weekly float for him if I felt like it, then give him the film while we were sitting in the stalls. I'd give it to him in one of the arias, usually – it was a sort of joke between us.' He handed the binoculars back to me and drifted down the room, scrabbling his fingertips on his bare scalp as if he had a full head of hair. Then he held out his hands like someone testing the atmosphere for rain.

'Sergei had the best of me, Ned, and he's gone. *C'est la vie*, I say. Now it's up to you. Have you got the courage? Have you got the wit? That's why I wrote to you. I had to. I was empty. I didn't know you, but I needed you. I wanted a good man who understood me. A man I could trust again. It's up to you, Ned. Now's your chance. Jump out of yourself and live, I say, while there is yet time. That wife of yours is a bit of a bully, by the sound of her. You'd be well advised to tell her to live her own life instead of yours. I should have advertised, shouldn't I?' A terrible smile, which he turned full upon me. 'Single man, non-smoker, fond of music and wit. I peruse those columns sometimes – who doesn't? I contemplate replying sometimes, except I'd never know how to break it off if I wasn't suited. So I wrote you a letter, didn't I? It was like writing to God in a way, till you came along in your shabby coat and asked a lot of spotty questions, no doubt drafted by HQ. It's time you stood on your own feet, Ned, same as me. You're cowed, that's your trouble. Your wife is partly to blame, in my opinion. I listened to your voice while you were apologising and I was not impressed. You won't reach out to take. Still, I reckon I could make something of you, and you could make something of me, too. You could help me dig my pool. I could show you music. That's evens, right? Nobody's impervious to music. I only did it because of Gorst.' His voice leapt in horror. '*Ned!* Leave that alone, do you mind! Take your thieving hands off my property, Ned. *Now!*'

I was fingering his Markus typewriter. It was in the wardrobe where he kept his opera glasses, stowed under a few shirts. Signed A. Patriot, I thought. '*A*' standing for *Anyone's* I thought. Anyone who loved him. I'd guessed already and he'd told me already, but the sight of it had excited both of us with a sense of ending.

'So why did you break it off with Sergei?' I asked him, still fingering the keys.

But this time he didn't rise to my flattery. '*I* didn't break it off. *He* did. I haven't ended it now, not if you're stepping into his shoes. Put that away. Cover it over the way you found it, thank you.'

I did as he asked. I hid the evidence of the typewriter.

'What did he say?' I asked carelessly. 'How.did he break it to you? Or did he write and run?' I was thinking of Sally again.

'Not a lot. You don't need a lot of words when someone's stuck in London and you're in Moscow. The silence speaks for itself.'

He wandered over to his radio and sat before it. I followed close on his heels, ready to restrain him.

'Let's plug her in, shall we, have a nice listen. I could still get a "Come back, Cyril," you never know.'

I watched him set up his transmitter, then fling open the leaded window and toss out the hairline-aerial, which was like a fishing line with a lead sinker but no hook. I watched him peer at his signals plan and type out SOS and his callsign on his squash recorder. Then he linked the recorder to the transmitter and, with a *whizz*, sent it into the ether. He did this several times before he switched over to receive, but nothing came and he didn't expect it to; he was showing me that it never would again.

'He did *tell* me it was over,' he said, staring at the dials. 'I'm not accusing him. He did *say*.'

'*What* was over? Spying?'

'Oh no, not spying, that'll go on for ever, won't it? Communism, really. He said Communism was just another minority religion these days, but we hadn't woken up to the fact. "Time to hang up your boots, Cyril. Better not come to Russia if you're rumbled, Cyril. You'd be a bit of an embarrassment to the new climate. We might have to give you back as a gesture. We're out of date, you see, you and me. Moscow Centre's decided. It's hard currency that talks to Moscow these days. They need all the pounds and dollars they can get. So I'm afraid we're on the shelf, you and me, we're *de trop* and slightly *déjà vu*, not to say a rather large embarrassment to all concerned. Moscow can't afford to be seen running Foreign Office cypher clerks with access to top secret and above, and they rather regard you and me as more of a liability than an asset, which is the reason why they're calling me home. My advice to you, Cyril, therefore, is to take a nice long holiday, see a doctor and get some sun and rest, because between you and me you're showing signs of being slightly barking. We'd like to do right by you but we're a bit strapped for hard currency, to be frank. If you'd like a modest couple of thousand, I'm sure we can do you a small something in a Swiss bank, but the larger sums are unavailable till further notice." He was like a different person talking to me, to be honest, Ned,' he continued, in a tone of valiant incomprehension. 'We'd been these great friends and he didn't want me any more. "Don't take life so hard, Cyril," he says. He keeps telling me I'm under strain, too many people inside my head. He's right really, I suppose. I lived the wrong life, that's all. You don't know till it's too late, though, do you, sometimes?

You think you're one person, you turn out to be another, same as opera. Still, not to worry, I say. Fight another day. Say not the struggle naught availeth. All grist to the mill. Yes.'

He had pulled back his soft shoulders and inflated himself somehow, seeing himself as a person superior to events. 'Right, then,' he said, and we returned spryly to the drawing room.

We had finished. All that remained was to mop up the missing answers and obtain an inventory of what he had betrayed.

We had finished, but it was I, not Frewin, who was resisting the final step. Sitting on the arm of the sofa, he turned his head away from me, smiling over-brightly and offering me his long neck for the knife. But he was waiting for a strike that I was refusing to deliver. His round bald head was craned tensely upward while he leaned away from me as if saying, 'Do it now, hit me here.' But I couldn't do it. I made no move towards him. I had the notebook in my hand, and enough written down for him to sign and destroy himself. But I didn't move. I was on his stupid side, not theirs. Yet what side was that? Was love an ideology? Was loyalty a political party? Or had we, in our rush to divide the world, divided it the wrong way, failing to notice that the real battle lay between those who were still searching, and those who, in order to prevail, had reduced their vulnerability to the lowest common factor of indifference? I was on the brink of destroying a man for love. I had led him to the steps of his own scaffold, pretending we were taking a Sunday stroll together.

'Cyril?'

I had to repeat his name.

'What is it?'

'I'm supposed to take a signed statement from you.'

'You can tell HQ that I was furthering understanding between great nations,' he said helpfully. I had the feeling that if he had been able, he would have told them for me. 'Tell them I was putting an end to the mindless and incredible hostility I had observed for many years in the Tank. That should keep them quiet.'

'Well, they did guess it would be something like that,' I said. 'It's just that there's a bit more to it than you understand.'

'Also, put in that I wish for a posting. I should like to leave the Tank forthwith and earn out my retirement in a non-classified appointment. I'll accept demotion, I've decided. I'm not short of a bob or two. I'm not proud. A change of work is better than a holiday, I say. Where are you going, Ned? The facilities are the other way.'

I was heading for the door. I was heading for sanity and escape. It was as if my world had reduced itself to this dreadful room. 'Just back to the office, Cyril. For an hour or so. I can't produce your statement out of a hat for you, you know. It's got to be properly drawn up on the right forms and so forth. Never mind about the weekend. I never like weekends anyway, to be truthful. Holes in the universe, if you want my secret opinion, weekends are.' Why was I speaking with his cadences? 'Not to worry, Cyril. I'll see myself out. You get some rest.'

I wanted to escape before they came. Looking past Frewin's head to the window, I could see Monty and two of his boys climbing out of their van, and a black police car pulling up outside the house – for the Service, thank God, has no powers of arrest.

But Frewin was talking again, the way the dying go on talking after you think they're dead.

'I can't be left alone, Ned, you see. Not any more. I can't explain it to a stranger, Ned, what I've done, not all over again, no one can.'

I heard a footfall on the gravel, then the ring of the doorbell. Frewin's head came up and his eyes found mine and I watched the knowledge dawn in them, and fade in disbelief, and dawn again. I kept my gaze on him while I opened the front door. Palfrey was standing at Monty's shoulder. Behind them stood two uniformed police officers and a man called Redman, better known as Bedlam, from the Service's team of shrinks.

'Marvellous, Ned,' Palfrey murmured, in a hasty aside to me as the others brushed past us into the drawing room. 'An absolute *coup*. You'll get a medal, I'll see to it.'

They had put handcuffs on him. It had not occurred to me that they would do that. They had handcuffed his hands behind his back, which made him lift his chin. I walked with him to the van and helped him into it, but by then he had found some kind of dignity of his own, and was no longer bothering whose hand was on his elbow.

'It's not everyone can crack a Modrian-trained spook between breakfast and lunchtime,' said Burr with dour satisfaction. We were eating a muted dinner at Cecconi's, where he had insisted on taking me the same evening. 'Our dear brethren across the Park are beside themselves with rage, anger, indignation and envy, which is never bad either.' But he was speaking to me from a world I had temporarily taken leave of.

'He cracked himself,' I said.

Burr looked sharply at me. 'I won't have that, Ned. I've not seen a hand played better. You were a whore. You had to be. We're all whores. Whores who pay. I've had enough of your melancholy, come to think of it – sitting over there in Northumberland Avenue, sulking like a stormcloud, caught between your women. If you can't take a decision, that's a decision. Leave your little love and go back to Mabel, if you want my advice, which you don't. I went back to mine last week and it's bloody murder.'

Despite myself I discovered I was laughing.

'So what I've decided is this,' Burr continued when he had generously consented to another enormous plate of pasta. 'You're to abandon sulking as a way of life, and you're to abandon the Interrogators' Pool, in which, in my humble opinion, you have been studying your own narcissistic reflection for somewhat too long. And you're to unroll your mat on the

Fifth Floor and replace Peter Guillam as my Head of Secretariat, which will suit your Calvinist disposition and rid me of a thoroughly idle officer.'

I did what he suggested – all of it. Not because he had suggested it, but because he had spoken into my mind. I told Sally of my decision the next night and, if nothing else, the wretchedness of the occasion served to ease my memories of Frewin. For a few months, at her request, I continued writing to her from Tunbridge Wells, but it became as difficult as writing home from school. Sally was the last of what Burr had called my little loves. Perhaps I had had a notion that, added together, they would make up one big one.

12

'S o it's over,' said Smiley. The glow of the dying fire lit the panelled library, gilding its gappy shelves of dusty books on travel and adventure, and the old, cracked leather of its armchairs, and the foxed photographs of its vanished battalions of uniformed officers with walking sticks; and finally our own assorted faces, turned to Smiley on his throne of honour. Four generations of the Service lounged about the room, but Smiley's quiet voice and the haze of cigar smoke seemed to bind us in a single family.

I did not remember ever quite inviting Toby to join us, but certainly the staff had been expecting him and the mess waiters had scurried out to greet him as he arrived. In his wide, watered-silk lapels and waistcoat with its Balkan frogging, he looked every inch the *Rittmeister*.

Burr had hastened directly from Heathrow, changing into his dinner jacket in the back of his chauffeur-driven Rover in deference to George. He had entered almost unremarked, with that soundless dancer's walk of his that big men seem to manage naturally. Then Monty Arbuck spotted him and at once gave up his seat. Burr had recently become the first man to make Coordinator before the age of thirty-five.

And at Smiley's feet lounged my last intake of students, the girls like cut flowers in their evening dresses, the boys keen and fresh-faced after their end-of-course exertions in Argyll.

'It's over,' Smiley repeated.

Was it his sudden stillness that alerted us? His altered voice? Or some almost priestly gesture that he made, a stiffening of his tubby body in piety or resolution? I couldn't have told you then, I can't tell you now. But I know I caught no one's eye, yet with his words I felt at once a kind of tensing among us, as if Smiley were calling us to arms – yet what he was talking about had as much to do with laying them down as taking them up.

'It's over, and so am I. Absolutely over. Time you rang down the curtain on yesterday's cold warrior. And please don't ask me back, ever again. The new time needs new people. The worst thing you can do is imitate us.'

I think he had intended to end there, but with George you do better not to guess. For all I know, he had committed his entire closing speech to memory before he came, worked on it, rehearsed it word for word. In either case our silence now commanded him, as did our need of ceremony. Indeed, so thorough was our dependence on him at that moment that if he had turned and walked from the room without offering us another word, our disappointment would have turned our love to gall.

'I only ever cared about the *man*,' Smiley announced. And it was typical of his artfulness that he should have opened with a riddle, then waited a moment before setting out to explain it. 'I never gave a fig for the ideologies, unless they were mad or evil, I never saw institutions as being worthy of their parts, or policies as much other than excuses for not feeling. *Man*, not the mass, is what our calling is about. It was *man* who ended the Cold War in case you didn't notice. It wasn't weaponry, or technology, or armies or campaigns. It was just *man*. Not even Western man either, as it happened, but our sworn enemy in the East, who went into the streets, faced the bullets and the batons and said: we've had enough. It was *their* emperor, not ours, who had the nerve to mount the rostrum and declare he had no clothes. And the ideologies trailed after these impossible events like condemned prisoners, as ideologies do when they've had their day. Because they have no heart of their own. They're the whores and angels of our striving selves. One day, history may tell us who really won. If a democratic Russia emerges – why then, Russia will have been the winner. And if the West chokes on its own materialism, then the West may still turn out to have been the loser. History keeps her secrets longer than most of us. But she has one secret that I will reveal to you tonight in the greatest confidence. Sometimes there are no winners at all. And sometimes nobody needs to lose. You asked me how we should think of Russia today.'

Was that really what we had asked him? What else explained his change of direction? We had talked loosely of the crumbling Soviet Empire, it was true; we had pondered the rise and rise of Japan and the historical shifts of economic power. And in the to-and-fro after dinner, yes, there had been a few passing references to my time in the Russia House, and a few questions touching on the Middle East and Smiley's work with the Fishing Rights Committee, which, thanks to Toby, had become common knowledge. But I don't think that was the question George was choosing to answer now.

'You ask,' he went on, 'can we ever trust the Bear? You seem to be amused, yet a bit unseated, by the notion that we can talk to the Russians like human beings and find common cause with them in many fields. I will give you several answers at once.

'The first is no, we can never trust the Bear. For one reason, the Bear doesn't trust himself. The Bear is threatened and the Bear is frightened and the Bear is falling apart. The Bear is disgusted with his past, sick of his present and scared stiff of his future. He often was. The Bear is broke, lazy, volatile, incompetent, slippery, dangerously proud, dangerously armed, sometimes brilliant, often ignorant. Without his claws, he'd be just another chaotic member of the Third World. But he isn't without his claws, not by any means. And he can't pull his soldiers back from foreign parts overnight, for the good reason that he can't house them or feed them or employ them, and he doesn't trust them either. And since this Service is the hired keeper of our national mistrust, we'd be neglecting our duty if we relaxed for one second our watch on the Bear, or on any of his unruly cubs. That's the first answer.

'The second answer is yes, we can trust the Bear completely. The Bear has never been so trustworthy. The Bear is begging to be part of us, to submerge his problems in us, to have his own bank account with us, to shop in our High Street and be accepted as a dignified member of our forest as well as his – all the more so because his society and economy are in tatters, his natural resources are pillaged and his managers incompetent beyond belief. The Bear needs us so desperately that we may safely trust him to need us. The Bear longs to wind back his dreadful history and emerge from the dark of the last seventy or seven hundred years. We are his daylight.

'The problem is, we Westerners do not find it in us naturally to trust the Bear, whether he's a White Bear or a Red Bear, or both kinds of bear at once, which is what he is at the moment. The Bear may be in perdition without us, but there are lots of us who believe that's exactly where he belongs. Just as there were people in 1945 who argued that a defeated Germany should remain a rubble desert for the rest of human history.'

Smiley paused and seemed to wonder whether he had said enough. He glanced towards me but I refused to catch his eye. The waiting silence must have convinced him to go on.

'The Bear of the future will be whatever we make of him, and the reasons for making something of him are several. The first is common decency. When you've helped a man to escape from wrongful imprisonment, the least you can do is provide him with a bowl of soup and the means to take his place in a free world. The second is so obvious it makes me a little intemperate to have to mention it at all. Russia – even Russia alone, shorn of all her conquests and possessions – is a vast country with a vast population in a crucial part of the globe. Do we leave the Bear to rot? – encourage him to become resentful, backward, an over-armed nation outside our camp? Or make a partner of him in a world that's changing its shape every day?'

He picked up his balloon glass and peered thoughtfully into it while he swirled the last of his brandy. And I sensed that he was finding it harder to take his leave than he had expected.

'Yes. Well,' he muttered, as if somehow defending himself against his own assertions. 'It's not only our minds we're going to have to reconstruct, either. It's the over-mighty modern State we've built for ourselves as a bastion against something that isn't there any more. We've given up far too many freedoms in order to be free. Now we've got to take them back.'

He gave a shy grin, and I knew that he was trying to break his own spell upon us.

'So while you're out there striving loyally for the State, perhaps you'll do me a small favour and lean on its pillars from time to time. It's got a lot too big for its boots of late. It would be nice if you would cut it down to size. Ned, I'm a bore. Time you sent me home.'

He stood up abruptly, as if shaking himself free of something that threatened to hold him too tight. Then, very deliberately, he treated himself to a last slow look round the room – not at the students any more, but at the old photographs and trophies of his time, apparently committing them to memory. He was taking leave of his house after he had bequeathed it to his heirs. Then, with a great flurry, he launched a search for his spectacles, before he discovered he was wearing them. Then he drew back his shoulders and marched purposefully to the door as two students hastened to open it for him.

'Yes. Well. Goodnight. And thanks. Oh, and tell them to spy on the ozone layer, will you, Ned? It's dreadfully hot in St. Agnes for the time of year.'

He left without looking back.

13

The rituals of retirement from the Service are probably no more harrowing than any other professional leavetaking, but they have their own poignancy. There are the ceremonies of remembering – lunches with old contacts, office parties, brave handshakes with tearful senior secretaries, courtesy visits to friendly services. And there are the ceremonies of forgetting, where snip by snip you sever yourself from the special knowledge not given to other mortals. For someone who has spent a lifetime in the Service, including three years in Burr's inmost Secretariat, these can be lengthy and repetitive affairs, even if the secrets themselves have retired long before you. Closeted in Palfrey's musty lawyer's office, mercifully quite often in the glow of a good lunch, I signed away one piece after another of my past, obediently mumbling after him the same shy little English oath, and listening each time to his insincere warnings of retribution should I be tempted by vanity or money to transgress.

And I would be deceiving us both if I pretended that the cumulative burden of these ceremonies did not slowly weigh me down, and make me wish that my day of execution could be brought forward – or, better still, regarded as accomplished. For day by day I began to feel like the man who is reconciled to death but has to spend the last of his energies consoling those who will survive him.

It was a considerable relief to me, therefore, when seated once more in Palfrey's wretched lair with three days still to go before my final freedom or imprisonment, I received a peremptory summons to Burr's presence.

'I've got a job for you. You'll hate it,' he assured me, and slammed down the phone.

He was still fuming when I reached his gaudy modern office. 'You're to read his file, then drive into the country and reason with him. You're not to offend him, but if you should happen to break his neck by accident you'll not find me over-critical.'

'Who is he?'

'Some leftover relic of Percy Alleline's. One of those beer-bellied tycoons from the City that Percy liked to play his golf with.'

I glanced at the cover of the top volume. 'BRADSHAW,' I read, 'Sir Anthony Joyston.' And in small letters underneath: 'asset index,' meaning that the fileholder was perceived as an ally of the Service.

'You're to crawl to him, that's an order. Appeal to his better nature,' said Burr in the same acid tone. 'Strike the elder statesman's note. Bring him back into the fold.'

'Who says I am?'

'The sainted Foreign Office. Who do you think?'

'Why don't they do their own crawling?' I said, peering curiously at the career synopsis on page 1. 'I thought that was what they were paid for.'

'They tried. They sent a Junior Minister, cap in hand. Sir Anthony is crawlproof. He also knows too much. He can name names and point fingers. Sir Anthony Bradshaw' – Burr announced, raising his voice in a North Country salvo of indignation – 'Sir Anthony *Joyston* Bradshaw,' he corrected himself, 'is one of England's natural shits, who in the course of affecting to be of service to his country has picked up more knowledge of the disreputable activities of Her Majesty's Government than HMG ever picked up from Sir Anthony in regard to her adversaries. He accordingly has HMG by the balls. Your brief is to invite him, very courteously, to relax his grip. Your weapons for this task are your grey locks and your palpable good nature, which I have observed that you are not above putting to perfidious use. He's expecting you at five this evening and he likes punctuality. Kitty's cleared a desk for you in the anteroom.'

It was not long before Burr's outrage was explained to me. There are few things more riling in our trade than having to cope with the unappetising leftovers of one's predecessors, and Sir Anthony Joyston Bradshaw, self-styled merchant venturer and City magnate, was a gruesome example of the type. Alleline had befriended him – at his club, where else? Alleline had recruited him. Alleline had sponsored him through a string of shady transactions of dubious value to anybody but Sir Anthony, and there were uncomfortable suggestions that Alleline might have taken a cut. Where scandal had threatened, Alleline had sheltered Sir Anthony under the Circus's compendious umbrella. Worse still, many of the doors that Alleline had opened for Bradshaw appeared to have stayed open, for the reason that nobody had thought to close them. And it was through one of these that Bradshaw had now walked, to the shrill outrage of the Foreign Office and half of Whitehall.

I drew an Ordnance Survey map from Library and a Ford Granada from the car pool. At half past two, with the file pretty much in my head, I set off. Sometimes you forget how beautiful England is. I passed through Newbury and climbed a winding hill lined with beech trees whose long shadows were cut like trenches into the golden stubble. A smell of cricket fields filled the car. I mounted a crest, castles of white cloud waited to receive me. I must have been thinking of my childhood, I suppose, for I had a sudden urge to drive straight into them, a thing I had often dreamed of as a boy. The car dipped again and fell free, and suddenly a whole valley opened below me, strewn with hamlets, churches, folding fields and forests.

I passed a pub, and soon a great pair of closed and gilded gates appeared between stone gateposts capped by carved lions. Beside them stood a neat white gatehouse newly thatched. A fit young man lowered his face to my open window and studied me with sniper's eyes.

'To see Sir Anthony,' I said.

'Name, sir?'

'Carlisle,' I replied, using an alias for the last time.

The boy disappeared into the lodge; the gates opened, then closed as soon as I was through them. The park was bordered by a high brick wall – there must have been a couple of miles of it. Fallow deer lay in the shade of chestnut trees. The drive lifted and the house appeared before me. It was golden and immaculate and very large. The centre section was William and Mary. The wings looked later, but not much. A lake lay before it, vegetable gardens and greenhouses behind. The old stables had been converted to offices, with clever outside staircases and glazed external corridors. A gardener was watering the orangerie.

The drive skirted the lake and brought me to the front sweep. Two Arab mares and a llama eyed me over the fence of a lunging ring. A young butler came down the steps, dressed in black trousers and a linen jacket.

'Shall I park your car round the back, Mr. Carlisle, once you've been introduced?' he asked. 'Sir Anthony does like a clear facade, when he can get one, sir.'

I gave him the keys and followed him up the wide steps. There were nine, though I can't imagine why I counted, except that it was something we had taught on the Sarratt awareness course, and in recent weeks my life seemed to have become less a continuation than a mosaic of past ages and experiences. If Ben had come striding up to me and grasped my hand, I don't think I would have been particularly surprised. If Monica or Sally had appeared to accuse me, I would have had my answers ready.

I entered a huge hall. A splendid double staircase rose to an open landing. Portraits of noble ancestors, all men, stared down at me, but somehow I didn't believe they were of one family, or could have lived here long without their women. I passed through a billiards room and noticed that the table and cues were new. I suppose I saw everything so clearly because I was treating each experience as my last. I followed the butler through a stately drawing room and traversed a second room that was got up as a hall of mirrors, and a third that was supposed to be informal, with a television set the size of one of those old ice-cream tricycles that used to call at my preparatory school on sunny evenings just like this. I arrived at a pair of majestic doors and waited while the butler knocked. Then waited again for a response. If Bradshaw were an Arab, he would keep me standing here for hours, I thought, remembering Beirut.

Finally I heard a male voice drawl 'Come,' and the butler took a pace into the room and announced, 'A Mr. Carlisle, Sir Anthony, from London.'

I had not told him I had come from London.

The butler stepped aside and gave me a first view of my host, though it took a little longer before my host had his first view of Mr. Carlisle.

He was sitting at a twelve-foot desk with brass inlay and cabriole legs. Modern oil paintings of spoilt children hung behind him. His correspondence was stacked in trays of thick stitched hide. He was a big, well-nourished man, and clearly a big worker also, for he had stripped to his shirt, which was blue with a midwife's white collar, and he was working in his braces, which were red. Also he was too busy to acknowledge me. First he read, using a gold pen to guide his eye. Then he signed, using the gold pen to write. Then he meditated, still in a downward direction, using the tip of the gold pen as a focus for his great thoughts. His gold cufflinks were as big as old pennies. Then at last he laid the pen down and, with a wounded – even accusatory – air, he raised his head, first to discover me, then to measure me by standards I had yet to ascertain.

At the same moment, by a happy chance of nature, a shaft of low sunlight from the French windows landed on his face, and I was able to measure him in return: the self-sadness of his pouchy eyes, as if he should be pitied for his wealth, the straight small mouth set tense and crooked in the puckered chins, the air of resolution formed of weakness, of boyhood suspicions in a grown-up world. At forty-five, this fattened child was unappeased, blaming some absent parent for his comforts.

Suddenly, Bradshaw was walking towards me. Stalking? Wading? There is an English walk these days peculiar to men of power, and it is a confection of several things at once. Self-confidence is one, lazy sportiveness another. But there is also menace in it, and impatience, and a leisured arrogance, which comes with the crablike splaying of elbows that give way to nobody, and the boxer's slouch of the shoulders, and the playful springiness in the knees. You knew long before you shook his hand that he had no truck with a whole category of life that ranged from art to public transport. You were silently forewarned to keep your distance if you were that kind of fool.

'You're one of Percy's boys,' he told me, in case I didn't know, while he sampled my hand, and was duly disappointed. 'Well, well. Long time no see. Must be ten years. More. Have a drink. Have champagne. Have what you like.' An order: 'Summers. Get us a bottle of shampoo, bucket of ice, two glasses, then bugger off. And nuts!' he shouted after him. 'Cashews. Brazils. Masses of fucking nuts – like nuts?' he enquired of me, with a sudden and disarming intimacy.

I said I did.

'Good. Me too. Love 'em. You've come to read me the riot act. Right? Go on. Not made of glass.'

He was flinging open the French windows so that I could have a better view of what he owned. He had chosen a different walk for this manoeuvre, more march, more swinging of the arms to the rhythm of unheard martial music. When he had opened the doors, he gave me his back to look at, and kept his arms up, palms propped against the door posts, like a martyr waiting for the arrow. And the City haircut, I thought: thick at the collar and little horns above the ears. In golds and browns and greens, the valley faded softly into eternity. A nanny and a small child were walking among the deer. She wore a brown hat with the brim up all the way round and a brown uniform like a Girl Guide's. The lawn was set for croquet.

'We're just appealing to you, that's all, Sir Anthony,' I said. 'Asking you another favour, like the ones you did for Percy. After all, it was Percy who got you your knighthood, wasn't it?'

'Fuck Percy. Dead, isn't he? Nobody gives me anything, thank you. Help myself to it. What do you want? Spit it out, will you? I've had one sermon already. Portly Savoury from the Foreign Office. Used to flog him when he was my fag at school. Wimp then, wimp now.'

The arms stayed up there, the back was braced and aggressive. I might have spoken, but I felt strangely off key. Three days before my retirement, I was beginning to feel I hardly knew the real world at all. Summers brought champagne, uncorked it and filled two glasses, which he handed to us on a silver tray. Bradshaw snatched one and strode into the garden. I trailed after him to the centre of a grass alley. Azaleas and rhododendrons grew high to either side of us. At the farther end, a fountain played in a stone pond.

'Did you get a lordship of the manor when you bought this house?' I asked, thinking a little small talk might give me time to collect myself.

'Suppose I did?' Bradshaw retorted, and I realised he did not wish to be reminded that he had bought his house rather than inherited it.

'Sir Anthony,' I said.

'Well?'

'It's concerning your relationship with a Belgian company called Astrasteel.'

'Never heard of 'em.'

'But you are associated with them, aren't you?' I said, with a smile.

'Aren't now, never was. Told Savoury the same.'

'But you have holdings in Astrasteel, Sir Anthony,' I protested patiently.

'Zilch. Absolutely buggerall. Different bloke, wrong address. Told him.'

'But you do have a one hundred percent holding in a company called Allmetal of Birmingham Limited, Sir Anthony. And Allmetal of Birmingham does own a company called Eurotech Funding & Imports Limited of Bermuda, doesn't it? And Eurotech of Bermuda does own Astrasteel of Belgium, Sir Anthony. So we may take it that a certain loose association might be said to exist between yourself on the one hand, and the company that is owned by the company you own on the other.' I was still smiling, still reasoning with him, joking him along.

'No holdings, no dividends, no influence over Astrasteel's affairs. Arm's length, whole thing. Told Savoury, tell the same to you.'

'Nevertheless, when you were invited by Alleline – back in the old days, I know, but not so long ago, was it? – to make deliveries of certain commodities to certain countries not strictly on the official shopping list for those commodities, Astrasteel *was* the company you used. And

Astrasteel did what you told them to do. Because if they hadn't done, Percy would not have come to you – would he? You'd have been no use to him.' My smile felt stiff on my face. 'We're not *policemen*, Sir Anthony, we're not the *taxman*. I'm merely indicating to you certain relationships that stand – as you insist – beyond the law's reach, and were indeed designed – with Percy's active help – to do just that.'

My speech sounded so ill composed to me, so unpointed, that I assumed at first that Bradshaw did not propose to bother with it at all.

And in a way I was right, for he merely shrugged and said, 'Fuck's that got to do with anything?'

'Well quite a lot actually.' I could feel my blood beginning to rise, and there was nothing I could do to check it. 'We're asking you to lay off. Stop. You've got your knighthood, you're worth a fortune, you have a duty to your country today just as you had twelve years ago. So get out of the Balkans and stop stirring it with the Serbs and stop stirring it in Central Africa, stop offering them guns galore on tick, and stop trying to cash in on wars that may never happen if you and other like-minded spirits keep your fingers out of them. You're British. You've more money in your pocket than most of us will touch in a lifetime. Stop. Just stop. That's all we're asking. Times have changed. We're not playing those games any more.'

For a moment I fancied I had impressed him, for he turned his unlit gaze on me, and looked me over as if I were someone who might after all be worth buying. Then his interest flickered out again and he relapsed into despondency.

'It's your country talking to you, Bradshaw,' I said, now with real anger. 'For Christ's sake, man, what more do you *need*? Haven't you got even the vestige of a conscience?'

I will give you Bradshaw's reply as I transcribed it, for at Burr's request I had slipped a recorder into my jacket pocket, and Bradshaw's sawing nasal tones ensured a perfect reproduction. I will give you his voice too, as nearly as I can write it down. He spoke English as if it were his second language, but it was the only one he had. He spoke in what my son Adrian tells me is called 'slur,' which is a slack-mouthed Belgravia cockney that contrives to make *mice* out of *mouse* and dispenses almost entirely with the formality of pronouns. It has a vocabulary, naturally: nothing rises but it *escalates*, no opportunity is without a *window*, no minor event occurs that is not *sensational*. It also has a pedantic inaccuracy which is supposed to distinguish it from the unwashed, and explains gems like 'as for you and I.' But even without my tape recorder, I like to think I would have remembered every word, for his speech was like an evening war-cry from a world I was leaving to itself.

'I'm sorry,' he began, which was a lie to start with. 'Did I understand you were appealing to my *conscience*? Good. Right. Make a statement for the record. Mind? Statement begins here. Point One. There *is* only one point actually. *I don't give a fart.* The difference between me and other charlies is, *I* admit it. If a horde of niggers – yes, I said *niggers*, I meant *niggers* – if these *niggers* shot each other dead with my toys tomorrow and I made a bob out of it, great news by me. Because if *I* don't sell 'em the goods, some *other* charlie will. Government used to understand that. If they've gone soft, tough titty on 'em. Point Two. Question: heard what the tobacco boys are up to these days? Flogging off high-toxic tobacco to the fuzzy-wuzzies and telling 'em it makes 'em horny and cures the common cold. Tobacco boys give a fart? Sit at home having nervous breakdowns about spreading lung cancer among the natives? The fuck they do. Doing a little creative selling, period. Take drugs. Don't use 'em personally. Don't need 'em. Never mind. If willing seller is doing business with willing buyer, my advice is step aside, let them slug it out, and bloody good luck to 'em. If drugs don't kill 'em, the atmosphere will or they'll get barbecued by the global warming. British, you said. Matter of fact, rather proud of it. Also rather proud of one's *school*. Empire man. Happens to be the tradition one's inherited. When people get in one's way, I break 'em. Or they break me. Discipline is rather up one's street too, actually. *Order.* Accepting responsibilities of one's class and education, and beating the foreigner at his own game. Thought you people were rather committed to that one, too. Error, apparently. Failure of communication. What one cares about is quality of life. This life. *Standards* actually. Old word. Don't care. *These* standards. Pompous, you're thinking. All right, I'm pompous. Fuck you. I'm Pharaoh, right? If a few thousand slaves have to die so that I can build this pyramid, nature. And if they can make *me* die for *their* fucking pyramid, bloody good on 'em. Know what I've got in my cellar? Iron rings. Rusty iron rings, built into the walls when this house was built. Know what they were for? Slaves. *That's* nature too. Original owner of this house – man who *built* this house – man who *paid* for it, man who sent his architect to Italy, learn his trade – that man owned slaves, and had his slave quarters in the cellar of this house. Think there aren't slaves today? Think capital doesn't *depend* on slaves? Jesus Christ, what kind of shop do you run? One doesn't normally talk philosophy, but I'm afraid one doesn't like being preached to either. Won't have it, you see. Not in my house, thank you. Annoys me. Don't bug easily, rather famous for one's cool. But one does have a certain view of nature; one gives work to people and one takes one's share.'

I said nothing, and that is on the tape too.

In the face of an absolute, what can you say? All my life I had battled against an institutionalised evil. It had had a name, and most often a country as well. It had had a corporate purpose, and had met a corporate end. But the evil that stood before me now was a wrecking infant in our own midst, and I became an infant in return, disarmed, speechless and betrayed. For a moment, it was as if my whole life had been fought against the wrong enemy. Then it was as if Bradshaw had personally stolen the fruits of my victory. I remembered Smiley's aphorism about the right people losing the Cold War, and the wrong people winning it, and I thought of repeating it to him as some sort of insult, but I would have been beating the air. I thought of telling him that now we had defeated Communism, we were going to have to set about defeating capitalism, but that wasn't really my point: the evil was not in the system, but in the man. And besides, by then he was asking me whether I wanted to stay to dinner, at which I politely declined, and left.

In the event, it was Burr who gave me dinner, and I am pleased to say I don't remember much about it. Two days later, I turned in my Head Office pass.

You see your face. It's no one you remember. You wonder where you put your love, what you found, what you were after. You want to say: 'I slew the dragon, I left the world a safer place.' You can't really, not these days. Perhaps you never could.

We have a good life, Mabel and I. We don't talk about things we can't change. We don't cross each other. We're civilised. We've bought a cottage on the coast. There's a long garden there I'd like to get my hands on, plant a few trees, make a vista to the sea. There's a sailing club for poor kids I'm involved in; we bring them down from Hackney, they enjoy it. There's a move to draft me for the local council. Mabel does the church. I go back to Holland now and then. I still have a few relations there.

Burr drops in from time to time. I like that in him. He gets on well with Mabel, as you'd expect. He doesn't try to be wise. He chats to her about her watercolours. He's not judgmental. We open a good bottle, cook a chicken. He brings me up to date, drives back to London. Of Smiley, nothing, but that's the way he wanted it. He hates nostalgia, even if he's part of other people's.

There's no such thing as retirement, really. Sometimes there's knowing too much, and not being able to do much about it, but that's just age, I'm sure. I think a lot. I'm stepping out with my reading. I talk to people, ride on buses. I'm a newcomer to the overt world but I'm learning.

A Murder of Quality

There are probably a dozen great schools of whom it will be confidently asserted that Carne is their deliberate image. But he who looks among their common rooms for the D'Arcys, Fieldings, and Hects will search in vain.

JOHN LE CARRÉ

1. Black Candles

T he greatness of Carne School has been ascribed by common consent to Edward VI, whose educational zeal is ascribed by history to the Duke of Somerset. But Carne prefers the respectability of the monarch to the questionable politics of his adviser, drawing strength from the conviction that Great Schools, like Tudor Kings, were ordained in Heaven.

And indeed its greatness is little short of miraculous. Founded by obscure monks, endowed by a sickly boy king, and dragged from oblivion by a Victorian bully, Carne had straightened its collar, scrubbed its rustic hands and face and presented itself shining to the courts of the twentieth century. And in the twinkling of an eye, the Dorset bumpkin was London's darling: Dick Whittington had arrived. Carne had parchments in Latin, seals in wax, and Lammas Land behind the Abbey. Carne had property, cloisters and woodworm, a whipping block and a line in the Doomsday Book – then what more did it need to instruct the sons of the rich?

And they came; each Half they came (for terms are not elegant things), so that throughout a whole afternoon the trains would unload sad groups of black-coated boys on to the station platform. They came in great cars that shone with mournful purity. They came to bury poor King Edward, trundling handcarts over the cobbled streets or carrying tuck boxes like little coffins. Some wore gowns, and when they walked they looked like crows, or black angels come for the burying. Some followed singly like undertakers' mutes, and you could hear the clip of their boots as they went. They were always in mourning at Carne; the small boys because they must stay and the big boys because they must leave, the masters because respectability was underpaid; and now, as the Lent Half (as the Easter term was called) drew to its end, the cloud of gloom was as firmly settled as ever over the grey towers of Carne.

Gloom and the cold. The cold was crisp and sharp as flint. It cut the faces of the boys as they moved slowly from the deserted playing fields after the school match. It pierced their black topcoats and turned their stiff, pointed collars into icy rings round their necks. Frozen, they plodded from the field to the long walled road which led to the main tuck shop and the town, the line gradually dwindling into groups, and the groups into pairs. Two boys who looked even colder than the rest crossed the road and made their way along a narrow path which led towards a distant but less populated tuck shop.

'I think I shall die if ever I have to watch one of those beastly rugger games again. The noise is fantastic,' said one. He was tall with fair hair, and his name was Caley.

'People only shout because the dons are watching from the pavilion,' the other rejoined; 'that's why each house has to stand together. So that the house dons can swank about how loud their houses shout.'

'What about Rode?' asked Caley. 'Why does he stand with us and make us shout, then? He's not a house don, just a bloody usher.'

'He's sucking up to house dons all the time. You can see him in the quad between lessons buzzing round the big men. All the junior masters do.' Caley's companion was a cynical red-haired boy called Perkins, Captain of Fielding's house.

'I've been to tea with Rode,' said Caley.

'Rode's hell. He wears brown boots. What was tea like?'

'Bleak. Funny how tea gives them away. Mrs Rode's quite decent, though – homely in a plebby sort of way: doyleys and china birds. Food's good: Women's Institute, but good.'

'Rode's doing Corps next Half. That'll put the lid on it. He's so *keen*, bouncing about all the time. You can tell he's not a gentleman. You know where he went to school?'

'No.'

'Branxome Grammar. Fielding told my Mama, when she came over from Singapore last Half.'

'God. Where's Branxome?'

'On the coast. Near Bournemouth. I haven't been to tea with anyone except Fielding.' Perkins added after a slight pause, 'You get roast chestnuts and crumpets. You're never allowed to thank him, you know. He says emotionalism is only for the lower classes. That's typical of Fielding. He's not like a don at all. I think boys bore him. The whole house goes to tea with him once a Half, he has us in turn, four at a time, and that's about the only time he talks to most men.'

They walked on in silence for a while until Perkins said:

'Fielding's giving another dinner party tonight.'

'He's pushing the boat out these days,' Caley replied, with disapproval. 'Suppose the food in your house is worse than ever?'

'It's his last Half before he retires. He's entertaining every don and all the wives separately by the end of the Half. Black candles every evening. For mourning. Hells extravagant.'

'Yes. I suppose it's a sort of gesture.'

'My Pater says he's a queer.'

They crossed the road and disappeared into the tuck shop, where they continued to discuss the weighty affairs of Mr Terence Fielding, until

Perkins drew their meeting reluctantly to a close. Being a poor hand at science, he was unfortunately obliged to take extra tuition in the subject.

The dinner party to which Perkins had alluded that afternoon was now drawing to a close. Mr Terence Fielding, senior housemaster of Carne, gave himself some more port and pushed the decanter wearily to has left. It was his port, the best he had. There was enough of the best to last the Half – and after that, be damned. He felt a little tired after watching the match, and a little drunk, and a little bored with Shane Hecht and her husband. Shane was so hideous. Massive and enveloping, like a faded Valkyrie. All that black hair. He should have asked someone else. The Snows for instance, but he was too clever. Or Felix D'Arcy, but D'Arcy interrupted. Ah well, a little later he would annoy Charles Hecht, and Hecht would get in a pet and leave early.

Hecht was fidgeting, wanting to light his pipe, but Fielding damn well wouldn't have it. Hecht could have a cigar if he wanted to smoke. But his pipe could stay in his dinner-jacket pocket, where it belonged, or didn't belong, and his athletic profile could remain unadorned.

'Cigar, Hecht?'

'No thanks, Fielding. I say, do you mind if I . . . '

'I can recommend the cigars. Young Havelake sent them from Havana. His father's ambassador there, you know.'

'Yes, dear,' said Shane tolerantly; 'Vivian Havelake was in Charles's troop when Charles was commandant of the Cadets.'

'Good boy, Havelake,' Hecht observed, and pressed his lips together to show he was a strict judge.

'It's amusing how things have changed.' Shane Hecht said this rapidly with a rather wooden smile, as if it weren't really amusing. 'Such a grey world we live in, now.'

'I remember before the war when Charles inspected the Corps on a white horse. We don't do that kind of thing now, do we? I've got nothing against Mr Iredale as commandant, nothing at all. What *was* his regiment, Terence, do you know? I'm sure he does it very nicely, whatever they do now in the Corps – he gets on so well with the boys, doesn't he? His wife's such a nice person . . . I wonder why they can never keep their servants. I hear Mr Rode will be helping out with the Corps next Half.'

'Poor little Rode,' said Fielding slowly; 'running about like a puppy, trying to earn his biscuits. He tries so hard; have you seen him cheering at school matches? He'd never seen a game of rugger before he came here, you know. They don't play rugger at grammar schools – it's all soccer. Do you remember when he first came, Charles? It was fascinating. He lay very low at first, drinking us in: the games, the vocabulary, the manners. Then, one day it was as if he had been given the power of speech, and he spoke in our language. It was amazing, like plastic surgery. It was Felix D'Arcy's work of course – I've never seen anything quite like it before.'

'Dear Mrs Rode,' said Shane Hecht in that voice of abstract vagueness which she reserved for her most venomous pronouncements: 'So sweet . . . and such simple taste, don't you think? I mean, whoever would have dreamed of putting those china ducks on the .wall? Big ones at the front and little ones at the back. Charming, don't you think? Like one of those teashops. I wonder where she bought them. I must ask her. I'm told her father lives near Bournemouth. It must be so lonely for him, don't you think? Such a vulgar place; no one to talk to.'

Fielding sat back and surveyed his own table. The silver was good. The best in Carne, he had heard it said, and he was inclined to agree. This Half he had nothing but black candles. It was the sort of thing people remembered when you'd gone: 'Dear old Terence – marvellous host. He dined every member of the staff during his last Half you know, wives too. Black candles, rather touching. It broke his heart giving up his house.' But he must annoy Charles Hecht. Shane would like that. Shane would egg him on because she hated Charles, because within her great ugly body she was as cunning as a snake.

Fielding looked at Hecht and then at Hecht's wife, and she smiled back at him, the slow rotten smile of a whore. For a moment Fielding thought of Hecht pasturing in that thick body: it was a scene redolent of Lautrec . . . yes, that was it! Charles pompous and top-hatted, seated stiffly upon the plush coverlet; she massive, pendulous and bored. The image pleased him: so perverse to consign that fool Hecht from the Spartan cleanliness of Carne to the brothels of nineteenth-century Paris . . .

Fielding began talking, pontificating rather, with an air of friendly objectivity which he knew Hecht would resent.

'When I look back on my thirty years at Carne, I realise I have achieved rather less than a road sweeper.' They were watching him now – 'I used to regard a road sweeper as a person inferior to myself. Now, I rather doubt it. Something is dirty, he makes it clean, and the state of the world is advanced. But I – what have I done? Entrenched a ruling class which is distinguished by neither talent, culture, nor wit; kept alive for one more generation the distinctions of a dead age.'

Charles Hecht, who had never perfected the art of not listening to Fielding, grew red and fussed at the other end of the table.

'Don't we teach them, Fielding? What about our successes, our scholarships?'

'I have never taught a boy in my life, Charles. Usually the boy wasn't clever enough; occasionally, I wasn't. In most boys, you see, perception dies with puberty. In a few it persists, though where we find it we take good care at Carne to kill it. If it survives our efforts the boy wins a scholarship . . . Bear with me, Shane; it's my last Half.'

'Last Half or not, you're talking through your hat, Fielding,' said Hecht, angrily.

'That is traditional at Carne. These successes, as you call them, are the

failures, the rare boys who have not learned the lessons of Carne. They
have ignored the cult of mediocrity. We can do nothing for them. But for
the rest, for the puzzled little clerics and the blind little soldiers, for them
the truth of Carne is written on the wall, and they hate us.'

Hecht laughed rather heavily.

'Why do so many come back, then, if they hate us so much? Why do
they remember us and come and see us?'

'Because we, dear Charles, are the writing on the wall! The one lesson
of Carne they never forget. They come back to read *us*, don't you see? It
was from us they learnt the secret of life: that we grow old without
growing wise. They realised that nothing happened when we grew up: no
blinding light on the road to Damascus, no sudden feeling of maturity.'
Fielding put his head back and gazed at the clumsy Victorian moulding on
the ceiling, and the halo of dirt round the light rose.

'We just got a little older. We made the same jokes, thought the same
thoughts, wanted the same things. Year in, year out, Hecht, we were the
same people, not wiser, not better; we haven't had an original thought
between us for the last fifty years of our lives. They saw what a trick it all
was, Carne and us: our academic dress, our schoolroom jokes, our wise
little offerings of guidance. And that's why they come back year after year
of their puzzled, barren lives to gaze fascinated at you and me, Hecht, like
children at a grave, searching for the secret of life and death. Oh, yes, they
have learned *that* from us.'

Hecht looked at Fielding in silence for a moment.

'Decanter, Hecht?' said Fielding, in a slightly conciliatory way, but
Hecht's eyes were still upon him.

'If that's a joke . . . ' he began, and his wife observed with satisfaction
that he was very angry indeed.

'I wish I knew, Charles,' Fielding replied with apparent earnestness. 'I
really wish I knew. I used to think it was clever to confuse comedy with
tragedy. Now I wish I could distinguish them.' He rather liked that.

They had coffee in the drawing-room, where Fielding resorted to gossip,
but Hecht was not to be drawn. Fielding rather wished he had let him light
his pipe. Then he recalled his vision of the Hechts in Paris, and it restored
him. He had been rather good this evening. There were moments when he
convinced himself.

While Shane fetched her coat, the two men stood together in the hall,
but neither spoke. Shane returned, an ermine stole, yellow with age,
draped over her great white shoulders. She inclined her head to the right,
smiled and held out her hand to Fielding, the fingers down.

'Terence, darling,' she said, as Fielding kissed her fat knuckles; 'so kind.
And in your last Half. You must dine with us before you go. So sad. So
few of us left.' She smiled again, half closing her eyes to indicate emotional
disturbance, then followed her husband into the street. It was still bitterly
cold and snow was in the air.

Fielding closed and carefully bolted the door behind them – perhaps a fraction earlier than courtesy required – and returned to the dining-room. Hecht's port glass was still about half full. Fielding picked it up and carefully poured the contents back into the decanter. He hoped Hecht wasn't too upset; he hated people to dislike him. He snuffed the black candles and damped their wicks between his forefinger and thumb. Switching on the light, he took from the sideboard a sixpenny notebook, and opened it. It contained his list of dining guests for the remainder of the Half. With his fountain pen he placed a neat tick against the name Hecht. They were done. On Wednesday he would have the Rodes. The husband was quite good value, but she, of course, was hell . . . It was not always the way with married couples. The wives as a rule were so much more sympathetic.

He opened the sideboard and took from it a bottle of brandy and a tumbler. Holding them both in the same hand, he shuffled wearily back to the drawing-room, resting his other hand on the wall as he went. God! He felt old, suddenly; that thin line of pain across the chest, that heaviness in the legs and feet. Such an effort being with people – on stage all the time. He hated to be alone, but people bored him. Being alone was like being tired, but unable to sleep. Some German poet had said that; he'd quoted it once, 'You may sleep but I must dance.' Something like that.

'That's how I am,' thought Fielding. 'That's how Carne is, too; an old satyr dancing to the music.' The music grew faster and their bodies older, but they must dance on – there were young men waiting in the wings. It had been funny once dancing the old dances in a new world. He poured himself some more brandy. He'd be pleased to leave in a way, even though he'd have to go on teaching somewhere else.

But it had its beauty, Carne . . . The Abbey Close in spring . . . the flamingo figures of boys waiting for the ritual of worship . . . the ebb and flow of children, like the seasons of the year, and the old men dying among them. He wished he could paint; he would paint the pageant of Carne in the fallow browns of autumn . . . What a shame, thought Fielding, that a mind so perceptive of beauty had no talent for creation.

He looked at his watch. Quarter to twelve. Nearly time to go out . . . to dance, and not to sleep.

2. *The Thursday Feeling*

It was Thursday evening and the *Christian Voice* had just I been put to bed. This was scarcely a historic event in Fleet Street. The pimply boy from Dispatch who took away the ragged pile of page-proofs showed no more ceremony than was strictly demanded by the eventual prospect of his Christmas bonus. And even in this respect he had learned that the secular journals of Unipress were more provident of material charity than the *Christian Voice*; charity being in strict relationship to circulation.

Miss Brimley, the journal's editor, adjusted the air cushion beneath her and lit a cigarette. Her secretary and sub-editor – the appointment carried both responsibilities – yawned, dropped the aspirin bottle into her hand-bag, combed out her ginger hair and bade Miss Brimley good night, leaving behind her as usual the smell of strongly scented powder and an empty paper-tissue box. Miss Brimley listened contentedly to the clipping echo of her footsteps as it faded down the corridor. It pleased her to be alone at last, tasting the anticlimax. She never failed to wonder at herself, how every Thursday morning brought the same slight uneasiness as she entered the vast Unipress building and stood a little absurdly on one escalator after the other, like a drab parcel on a luxury liner. Heaven knows, she had run the *Voice* for fourteen years, and there were those who said its layout was the best thing Unipress did. Yet the Thursday feeling never left her, the wakeful anxiety that one day, perhaps today, they wouldn't be ready when the dispatch boy came. She often wondered what would happen then. She had heard of failures elsewhere in that vast combine, of features disapproved and staff rebuked. It was a mystery to her why they kept the *Voice* at all, with its expensive room on the seventh floor and a circulation which, if Miss Brimley knew anything, hardly paid for the paperclips.

The *Voice* had been founded at the turn of the century by old Lord Landsbury, together with a Nonconformist daily newspaper and the *Temperance Gazette*. But the *Gazette* and the daily were long since dead, and Landsbury's son had woken one morning not long ago to find his whole business and every man and woman of it, every stick of furniture, ink, paper-clips, and galley-pins, bought by the hidden gold of Unipress.

That was three years ago and every day she had waited for her dismissal. But it never came; no directive, no question, no word. And so, being a sensible woman, she continued exactly as before and ceased to wonder.

And she was glad. It was easy to sneer at the *Voice*. Every week it offered humbly and without fanfares evidence of the Lord's intervention in the world's affairs, retold in simple and somewhat unscientific terms the early history of the Jews, and provided over a fictitious signature motherly advice to whomever should write and ask for it. The *Voice* scarcely concerned itself with the fifty-odd millions of the population who had never heard of it. It was a family affair, and rather than abuse those who were not members, it did its best for those who were. For them it was kind, optimistic, and informative. If a million children were dying of the plague in India, you may be sure that the weekly editorial described the miraculous escape from fire of a Methodist family in Kent. The *Voice* did not advise you how to disguise the encroaching wrinkles round your eyes, or control your spreading figure; did not dismay you, if you were old, by its own eternal youth. It was itself middle-aged and middle class, counselled caution to girls and charity to all. Nonconformity is the most conservative of habits and families which took the *Voice* in 1903 continued to take it in 1960.

Miss Brimley was not quite the image of her journal. The fortunes of war and the caprice of Intelligence work had thrown her into partnership with the younger Lord Landsbury, and for the six years of war they had worked together efficiently and inconspicuously in an unnamed building in Knightsbridge. The fortunes of peace rendered both unemployed, but Landsbury had the good sense, as well as the generosity, to offer Miss Brimley a job. The *Voice* had ceased publication during the war, and no one seemed anxious to renew it. At first Miss Brimley had felt a little ashamed at reviving and editing a journal which in no way expressed her own vague deism, but quite soon, as the touching letters came in and the circulation recovered, she developed an affection for her job – and for her readers – which outweighed her earlier misgivings. The *Voice* was her life and its readers her preoccupation. She struggled to answer their odd, troubled questions, sought advice of others where she could not provide it herself, and, in time, under a handful of pseudonyms, became, if not their philosopher, their guide, friend, and universal aunt.

Miss Brimley put out her cigarette, absently tidied the pins, paperclips, scissors, and paste into the top right-hand drawer of her desk, and gathered together the afternoon mail from her in-tray which, because it was Thursday, she had left untouched. There were several letters addressed to Barbara Fellowship, under which name the *Voice* had, since its foundation, answered both privately and through its published columns the many problems of its correspondents. They could wait until tomorrow. She rather enjoyed the 'problem post', but Friday morning was when she read it. She opened the little filing cabinet at her elbow and dropped the letters into a box file at the front of the compartment. As she did so, one of them fell on its back and she noticed with surprise that the sealed flap was embossed with an elegant blue dolphin. She picked the envelope out of the cabinet and looked at it curiously, turning it over several times. It was of pale grey paper, very faintly lined. Expensive – perhaps hand-made. Beneath the dolphin was a tiny scroll on which she could just discern the legend, *Regem defendere diem videre*. The postmark was Carne, Dorset.

That must be the school crest. But why was Carne familiar to her? Miss Brimley was proud of her memory, which was excellent, and she was vexed when it failed her. As a last resort she opened the envelope with her faded ivory paper knife and read the letter.

Dear Miss Fellowship,

I don't know if you are a real person but it doesn't matter, because you always give such good, kind answers. It was me who wrote last June about the pastry mix. I am not mad and I know my husband is trying to kill me. Could I please come and see you as soon as it's convenient? I'm sure you'll believe me, and understand that I am normal. Could it be *as soon as possible* please, I am so afraid of the long nights. I don't know who else to turn to. I could try Mr Cardew at the Tabernacle but he wouldn't believe me and Dad's too sensible. I might as well be dead. There's something not quite right about him. At night sometimes when he thinks I'm asleep he just lies watching the darkness. I know it's wrong to think such wicked things and have fear in our hearts, but I can't help it.

I hope you don't get many letters like this.

Yours faithfully,

Stella Rode (Mrs)

née Glaston

She sat quite still at her desk for a moment, looking at the address in handsome blue engraving at the top of the page: 'North Fields, Carne School, Dorset.' In that moment of shock and astonishment one phrase forced itself upon her mind. 'The value of intelligence depends on its breeding.' That was John Landsbury's favourite dictum. Until you know the pedigree of the information you cannot evaluate a report. Yes, that was what he used to say: 'We are not democratic. We close the door on intelligence without parentage.' And she used to reply: 'Yes, John, but even the best families had to begin somewhere.'

But Stella Rode *had* parentage. It all came back to her now. She was the Glaston girl. The girl whose marriage was reported in the editorial, the girl who won the summer competition; Samuel Glaston's daughter from Branxome. She had a card in Miss Brimley's index.

Abruptly she stood up, the letter still in her hand, and walked to the uncurtained window. Just in front of her was a contemporary window-box of woven white metal. It was odd, she reflected, how she could never get anything to grow in that window-box. She looked down into the street, a slight, sensible figure leaning forward a little and framed by the incandescent fog outside; fog made yellow from the stolen light of London's streets. She could just distinguish the street lamps far below, pale and sullen. She suddenly felt the need for fresh air, and on an impulse quite alien to her usual calm, she opened the window wide. The quick cold and the angry surge of noise burst in on her, and the insidious fog followed.

The sound of traffic was constant, so that for a moment she thought it was the turning of some great machine. Then above its steady growl she heard the newsboys. Their cries were like the cries of gulls against a gathering storm. She could see them now, sentinels among the hastening shadows.

It might be true. That had always been the difficulty. Right through the war it was the same restless search. It might be true. It was no use relating reports to probability when there was no quantum of knowledge from which to start. She remembered the first intelligence from France on flying bombs, wild talk of concrete runways in the depths of a forest. You had to resist the dramatic, you had to hold out against it. Yet it might be true. Tomorrow, the day after, those newsboys down there might be shouting it, and Stella Rode *née* Glaston might be dead. And if that was so, if there was the remotest chance that this man was plotting to kill this woman, then she, Ailsa Brimley, must do what she could to prevent it. Besides, Stella Glaston had a claim on her assistance if anyone did: both her father and her grandfather had taken the *Voice*, and when Stella married five years ago Miss Brimley had put a couple of lines about it in the editorial. The Glastons sent her a Christmas card every year. They were one of the original families to subscribe . . .

It was cold at the window, but she remained there, still fascinated by the half hidden shadows joining and parting beneath her, and the useless street lights burning painfully among them. She began to imagine him as one of those shadows, pressing and jostling, his murderer's eyes turned to sockets of dark. And suddenly she was frightened and needed help.

But not the police, not yet. If Stella Rode had wanted that she would have gone herself. Why hadn't she? For love? For fear of looking a fool? Because instinct was not evidence? They wanted fact. But the fact of murder was death. Must they wait for that?

Who would help? She thought at once of Landsbury, but he was farming in Rhodesia. Who else had been with them in the war? Fielding and Jebedee were dead, Steed-Asprey vanished. Smiley – where was he? George Smiley, the cleverest and perhaps the oddest of them all. Of course, Miss Brimley remembered now. He made that improbable marriage and went back to research at Oxford. But he hadn't stayed there . . . The marriage had broken up . . . What *had* he done after that?

She returned to her desk and picked up the S–Z directory. Ten minutes later she was sitting in a taxi, heading for Sloane Square. In her neatly gloved hand she held a cardboard folder containing Stella Rode's card from the index and the correspondence which had passed between them at the time of the summer competition. She was nearly at Piccadilly when she remembered she'd left the office window open. It didn't seem to matter much.

'With other people it's Persian cats or golf. With me it's the *Voice* and my readers. I'm a ridiculous spinster, I know, but there it is. I won't go to the police until I've tried *something*, George.'

'And you thought you'd try me?'

'Yes.'

She was sitting in the study of George Smiley's house in Bywater Street; the only light came from the complicated lamp on his desk, a black spider of a thing shining brightly on to the manuscript notes which covered the desk.

'So you've left the Service?' she said.

'Yes, yes, I have.' He nodded his round head vigorously, as if reassuring himself that a distasteful experience was really over, and mixed Miss Brimley a whisky and soda. 'I had another spell there after . . . Oxford. It's all very different in peacetime, you know,' he continued.

Miss Brimley nodded.

'I can imagine it. More time to be bitchy.' Smiley said nothing, just lit a cigarette and sat down opposite her.

'And the people have changed. Fielding, Steed, Jebedee. All gone.' She said this in a matter-of-fact way as she took from her large sensible handbag Stella Rode's letter. 'This is the letter, George.'

When he had read it, he held it briefly towards the lamp, his round face caught by the light in a moment of almost comic earnestness. Watching him, Miss Brimley wondered what impression he made on those who did not know him well. She used to think of him as the most forgettable man she had ever met; short and plump, with heavy spectacles and thinning hair, he was at first sight the very prototype of an unsuccessful middle-aged bachelor in a sedentary occupation. His natural diffidence in most practical matters was reflected in his clothes, which were costly and unsuitable, for he was clay in the hands of his tailor, who robbed him.

He had put down the letter on the small marquetry table beside him, and was looking at her owlishly.

'This other letter she sent you, Brim. Where is it?'

She handed him the folder. He opened it and after a moment read aloud Stella Rode's other letter:

Dear Miss Fellowship,

I would like to submit the following suggestion for your 'Kitchen Hints' competition.

Make your basic batch of cake mixture once a month. Cream equal quantities of fat and sugar and add one egg for every six ounces of the mixture. For puddings and cakes, add flour to the required quantity of basic mixture.

This will keep well for a month.

I enclose stamped addressed envelope.

Yours sincerely,

Stella Rode (*née* Glaston)

PS – Incidentally, you can prevent wire wool from rusting by keeping it in a jar of soapy water. Are we allowed two suggestions? If so, please can this be my second?

'She won the competition,' Miss Brimley observed, 'but that's not the point. This is what I want to tell you, George. She's a Glaston, and the Glastons have been reading the *Voice* since it started. Stella's grandfather was old Rufus Glaston, a Lancashire pottery king; he and John Landsbury's father built chapels and tabernacles in practically every village in the Midlands. When Rufus died the *Voice* put out a memorial edition and old Landsbury himself wrote the obituary. Samuel Glaston took on his father's business, but had to move south because of his health. He ended up near Bournemouth, a widower with one daughter, Stella. She's the last of all that family. The whole lot are as down to earth as you could wish, Stella included, I should think. I don't think any of them is likely to be suffering from delusions of persecution.'

Smiley was looking at her in astonishment.

'My dear Brim, I can't possibly take that in. How on earth do you know all this?'

Miss Brimley smiled apologetically.

'The Glastons are easy – they're almost part of the magazine. They send us Christmas cards, and boxes of chocolates on the anniversary of our foundation. We've got about five hundred families who form what I call our Establishment. They were in on the *Voice* from the start and they've kept up ever since. They write to us, George; if they're worried they write and say so; if they're getting married, moving house, retiring from work, if they're ill, depressed, or angry, they write. Not often, Heaven knows; but enough.'

'How do you remember it all?'

'I don't. I keep a card index. I always write back you see . . . only . . . '

'Yes?'

Miss Brimley looked at him earnestly.

'This is the first time anyone has written because she's frightened.'

'What do you want me to do?'

'I've only had one bright idea so far. I seem to remember Adrian Fielding had a brother who taught at Carne . . . '

'He's a housemaster there, if he hasn't retired.'

'No, he retires this Half – it was in *The Times* some weeks ago, in that little bit on the Court page where Carne always announces itself. It said: "Carne School reassembles today for the Lent Half. Mr T. R. Fielding will retire at the end of the Half, having completed his statutory fifteen years as a housemaster." '

Smiley laughed.

'Really, Brim, your memory is absurd!'

'It was the mention of Fielding . . . Anyway, I thought you could ring him up. You must know him.'

'Yes, yes. I know him. At least, I met him once at Magdalen High Table. But – ' Smiley coloured a little.

'But what, George?'

'Well, he's not quite the man his brother was, you know.'

'How could he be?' Miss Brimley rejoined a little sharply. 'But he can tell you something about Stella Rode. And her husband.'

'I don't think I could do that on the telephone. I think I'd rather go and see him. But what's to stop you ringing up Stella Rode?'

'Well, I can't tonight, can I? Her husband will be in. I thought I'd put a letter in the post to her tonight telling her she can come to see me any time. But,' she continued, making a slight, impatient movement with her foot, 'I want to do something *now*, George.'

Smiley nodded and went to the telephone. He rang directory inquiries and asked for Terence Fielding's number. After a long delay he was told to ring Carne School central exchange, who would connect him with whomever he required. Miss Brimley, watching him, wished she knew a little more about George Smiley, how much of that diffidence was assumed, how vulnerable he was.

'The best,' Adrian had said. 'The strongest and the best.'

But so many men learnt strength during the war, learnt terrible things, and put aside their knowledge with a shudder when it ended.

The number was ringing now. She heard the dialling tone and for a moment was filled with apprehension. For the first time she was afraid of making a fool of herself, afraid of becoming involved in unlikely explanations with angular, suspicious people.

'Mr Terence Fielding, please . . . ' A pause.

'Fielding, good evening. My name is George Smiley; I knew your brother well in the war. We have in fact met . . . Yes, yes, quite right – Magdalen, was it not, the summer before last? Look, I wonder if I might come and see you on a personal matter . . . it's a little difficult to discuss on the telephone. A friend of mine has received a rather disturbing letter from the wife of a Carne master . . . Well, I – Rode, Stella Rode; her husband . . . '

He suddenly stiffened, and Miss Brimley, her eyes fixed upon him, saw with alarm how his chubby face broke into an expression of pain and disgust. She no longer heard what he was saying. She could only watch the dreadful transformation of his face, the whitening knuckles of his hand clutching the receiver. He was looking at her now, saying something . . . it was too late. Stella Rode was dead. She had been murdered late on Wednesday night. They'd actually been dining with Fielding the night it happened.

3. The Night of the Murder

T he seven-five from Waterloo to Yeovil is not a popular train, though it provides an excellent breakfast. Smiley had no difficulty in finding a first-class compartment to himself. It was a bitterly cold day, dark and the sky heavy with snow. He sat huddled in a voluminous travelling coat of Continental origin, holding in his gloved hands a bundle of the day's papers. Because he was a precise man and did not care to be hurried, he had arrived thirty minutes before the train was due to depart. Still tired after the stresses of the previous night, when he had sat up talking with Ailsa Brimley until Heaven knew what hour, he was disinclined to read. Looking out of the window on to an almost empty station, he caught sight, to his great surprise, of Miss Brimley making her way along the platform, peering in at the windows, a carrier bag in her hand. He lowered the window and called to her.

'My dear Brim, what are you doing here at this dreadful hour? You should be in bed.'

She sat down opposite him and began unpacking her bag and handing him its contents: thermos, sandwiches, and chocolate.

'I didn't know whether there was a breakfast car,' she explained; 'and besides, I wanted to come and see you off. You're such a dear, George, and I wish I could come with you, but Unipress would go mad if I did. The only time they notice you is when you're not there.'

'Haven't you seen the papers?' he asked.

'Just briefly, on the way here. They seem to think it wasn't him, but some madman . . .'

'I know, Brim. That's what Fielding said, wasn't it?' There was a moment's awkward silence.

'George, am I being an awful ass, letting you go off like this? I was sure last night, but now I wonder . . .'

'After you left I rang Ben Sparrow of Special Branch. You remember him, don't you? He was with us in the war. I told him the whole story.'

'George! At three in the morning?'

'Yes. He's ringing the Divisional Superintendent at Carne. He'll tell him about the letter, and that I'm coming down. Ben had an idea that a man named Rigby would be handling the case. Rigby and Ben were at police college together.' He looked at her kindly for a moment. 'Besides, I'm a man of leisure, Brim. I shall enjoy the change.'

'Bless you, George,' said Miss Brimley, woman enough to believe him. She got up to go, and Smiley said to her:

'Brim, if you should need any more help or anything, and can't get hold of me, there's a man called Mendel who lives in Mitcham, a retired police inspector. He's in the book. If you get hold of him and mention me, he'll do what he can for you. I've booked a room at the Sawley Arms.'

Alone again, Smiley surveyed uneasily the assortment of food and drink which Miss Brimley had provided. He had promised himself the luxury of breakfast in the restaurant car. He would keep the sandwiches and coffee for later, that would be the best thing; for lunch, perhaps. And he would breakfast properly.

In the restaurant car Smiley read first the less sensational reports on the death of Stella Rode. It appeared that on Wednesday evening Mr and Mrs Rode had been guests at dinner of Mr Terence Fielding, the senior housemaster at Carne and brother of the late Adrian Fielding, the celebrated French scholar who had vanished during the war while specially employed by the War Office. They had left Mr Fielding's house together at about ten to eleven and walked the half mile from the centre of Carne to their house, which stood alone at the edge of the famous Carne playing fields. As they reached their house Mr Rode remembered that he had left at Mr Fielding's house some examination papers which urgently required correction that night. (At this point Smiley remembered that he had failed to pack his dinner-jacket, and that Fielding would almost certainly ask him to dine.) Rode determined to walk back to Fielding's house and collect the papers, therefore, starting back at about five past eleven. It appears that Mrs Rode made herself a cup of tea and sat down in the drawing-room to await his return.

Adjoining the back of the house is a conservatory, the inner door of which leads to the drawing-room. It was there that Rode eventually found his wife when he returned. There were signs of a struggle, and certain inexpensive articles of jewellery were missing from the body. The confusion in the conservatory was terrible. Fortunately there had been a fresh fall of snow on Wednesday afternoon, and detectives from Dorchester were examining the footprints and other traces early on Thursday morning. Mr Rode had been treated for shock at Dorchester Central Hospital. The police wished to interview a woman from the adjacent village of Pylle who was locally known as 'Mad Janie' on account of her eccentric and solitary habits. Mrs Rode, who was well known in Carne for her energetic work on behalf of the International Refugee Year, had apparently shown a charitable interest in her welfare, and she had vanished without trace since the night of the murder. The police were currently of the opinion that the murderer had caught sight of Mrs Rode through the drawing-room window (she had not drawn the curtains) and that Mrs Rode had admitted the murderer at the front door in the belief that it was her husband returning from Mr Fielding's house. The Home Office pathologist had been asked to conduct a post-mortem examination.

The other reports were not so restrained: 'Murder most foul has desecrated the hallowed playing fields of Carne' one article began, and another, 'Science teacher discovers murdered wife in blood-spattered conservatory'. A third screamed, 'Mad woman sought in Carne murder'. With an expression of distaste, Smiley screwed up all the newspapers except the *Guardian* and *The Times* and tossed them on to the luggage rack.

He changed at Yeovil for a local line to Sturminster, Okeford and Carne. It was something after eleven o'clock when he finally arrived at Carne station.

He telephoned the hotel from the station and sent his luggage ahead by taxi. The Sawley Arms was only full at Commemoration and on St Andrew's Day. Most of the year it was empty; sitting like a prim Victorian lady, its slate roof in the mauve of half-mourning, on ill-tended lawns midway between the station and Carne Abbey.

Snow still lay on the ground, but the day was fine and dry, and Smiley decided to walk into the town and arrange to meet the police officer conducting the investigation of the murder. He left the station, with its foretaste of Victorian austerity, and walked along the avenue of bare trees which led towards the great Abbey tower, flat and black against the colourless winter sky. He crossed the Abbey Close, a serene and beautiful square of medieval houses, the roofs snow-covered, the white lawns shaded with pin strokes of grass. As he passed the west door of the Abbey, the soft snow creaking where he trod, the clock high above him struck the half-hour, and two knights on horseback rode out from their little castle over the door, and slowly raised their lances to each other in salute. Then, as if it were all part of the same clockwork mechanism, other doors all round the Close opened too, releasing swarms of black-coated boys who stampeded across the snow towards the Abbey. One boy passed so close that his gown brushed against Smiley's sleeve. Smiley called to him as he ran past:

'What's going on?'

'Sext,' shouted the boy in reply, and was gone.

He passed the main entrance to the school and came at once upon the municipal part of the town, a lugubrious nineteenth-century fairyland in local stone, stitched together by a complexity of Gothic chimneys and crenel windows. Here was the town hall, and beside it, with the flag of St George floating at its masthead, the Carne Constabulary Headquarters, built ninety years ago to withstand the onslaughts of archery and battering rams.

He gave his name to the Duty Sergeant, and asked to see the officer investigating the death of Mrs Rode. The Sergeant, an elderly, inscrutable man, addressed himself to the telephone with a certain formality, as if he were about to perform a difficult conjuring trick. To Smiley's surprise, he was told that Inspector Rigby would be pleased to see him at once, and a police cadet was summoned to show him the way. He was led at a spanking pace up the wide staircase in the centre of the hall, and in a matter of moments found himself before the Inspector.

He was a very short man, and very broad. He could have been a Celt from the tin-mines of Cornwall or the collieries of Wales. His dark grey hair was cut very close; it came to a point in the centre of his brow like a devil's cap. His hands were large and powerful, he had the trunk and stance of a wrestler, but he spoke slowly, with a Dorset burr to his soft voice. Smiley quickly noticed that he had one quality rare among small men: the quality of openness. Though his eyes were dark and bright and the movements of his body swift, he imparted a feeling of honesty and straight dealing.

'Ben Sparrow rang me this morning, sir. I'm very pleased you've come. I believe you've got a letter for me.'

Rigby looked at Smiley thoughtfully over his desk, and decided that he liked what he saw. He had got around in the war and had heard a little, just a very little, of the work of George Smiley's Service. If Ben said Smiley was all right, that was good enough for him – or almost. But Ben had said more than that.

'Looks like a frog, dresses like a bookie, and has a brain I'd give my eyes for. Had a very nasty war. Very nasty indeed.'

Well, he looked like a frog, right enough. Short and stubby, round spectacles with thick lenses that made his eyes big. And his clothes *were* odd. Expensive, mind, you could see that. But his jacket seemed to drape where there wasn't any room for drape. What did surprise Rigby was his shyness. Rigby had expected someone a little brash, a little too smooth for Carne, whereas Smiley had an earnest formality of manner which appealed to Rigby's conservative taste.

Smiley took the letter from his wallet and put it on the desk, while Rigby extracted an old pair of gold-rimmed spectacles from a battered metal case and adjusted the ends carefully over his ears.

'I don't know if Ben explained,' said Smiley, 'but this letter was sent to the correspondence section of a small Nonconformist journal to which Mrs Rode subscribed.'

'And Miss Fellowship is the lady who brought you the letter?'

'No; her name is Brimley. She is the editor of the magazine. Fellowship is just a pen-name for the correspondence column.'

The brown eyes rested on him for a moment.

'When did she receive this letter?'

'Yesterday, the seventeenth. Thursday's the day they go to press, their busy day. The afternoon mail doesn't get opened till the evening, usually. This was opened about six o'clock, I suppose.'

'And she brought it straight to you?'

'Yes.'

'Why?'

'She worked for me during the war, in my department. She was reluctant to go straight to the police – I was the only person she could think of who wasn't a policeman,' he added stupidly. 'Who could help, I mean.'

'May I ask what you yourself, sir, do for a living?'

'Nothing much. A little private research on seventeenth-century Germany.' It seemed a very silly answer.

Rigby didn't seem bothered.

'What's this earlier letter she talks about?'

Smiley offered him the second envelope, and again the big, square hand received it.

'It appears she won this competition,' Smiley explained. 'That was her winning entry. I gather she comes from a family which has subscribed to the magazine since its foundation. That's why Miss Brimley was less inclined to regard the letter as nonsense. Not that it follows.'

'Not that what follows?'

'I meant that the fact that her family had subscribed to a journal for fifty years does not logically affect the possibility that she was unbalanced.'

Rigby nodded, as if he saw the point, but Smiley had an uncomfortable feeling that he did not.

'Ah,' said Rigby, with a slow smile. 'Women, eh?'

Smiley, completely bewildered, gave a little laugh. Rigby was looking at him thoughtfully.

'Know any of the staff do you, sir?'

'Only Mr Terence Fielding. We met at an Oxford dinner some time ago. I thought I'd call round and see him. I knew his brother pretty well.'

Rigby appeared to stiffen slightly at the mention of Fielding, but he said nothing, and Smiley went on:

'It was Fielding I rang when Miss Brimley brought me the letter. He told me the news. That was last night.'

'I see.'

They looked at one another again in silence. Smiley discomfited and slightly comic, Rigby appraising him, wondering how much to say.

'How long are you staying?' he said at last.

'I don't know,' Smiley replied. 'Miss Brimley wanted to come herself, but she has her paper to run. She attached great importance, you see, to doing all she could for Mrs Rode, even though she was dead. Because she was a subscriber, I mean. I promised to see that the letter arrived quickly in the right hands. I don't imagine there's much else I can do. I shall probably stay on for a day or two just to have a word with Fielding . . . go to the funeral, I suppose. I've booked in at the Sawley Arms.'

'Fine hotel, that.'

Rigby put his spectacles carefully back into their case and dropped the case into a drawer.

'Funny place, Carne. There's a big gap between the Town and Gown, as we say; neither side knows nor likes the other. It's fear that does it, fear and ignorance. It makes it hard in a case like this. Oh, I can call on Mr Fielding and Mr D'Arcy and they say, "Good day, Sergeant," and give me a cup of tea in the kitchen, but I can't get among them. They've got their own community, see, and no one outside it can get in. No gossip in the pubs, no contacts, nothing . . . just cups of tea and bits of seed cake, and being called Sergeant.' Rigby laughed suddenly, and Smiley laughed with him in relief. 'There's a lot I'd like to ask them, a lot of things; who liked the Rodes and who didn't, whether Mr Rode's a good teacher and whether his wife fitted in with the others. I've got all the facts I want, but I've got no clothes to hang on them.' He looked at Smiley expectantly. There was a very long silence.

'If you want me to help, I'd be delighted,' said Smiley at last. 'But give me the facts first.'

'Stella Rode was murdered between about ten past eleven and quarter to twelve on the night of Wednesday the sixteenth. She must have been struck fifteen to twenty times with a cosh or bit of piping or something. It was a terrible murder . . . terrible. There are marks all over her body. At a guess I would say she came from the drawing-room to the front door to answer the bell or something, when she opened the door she was struck down and dragged to the conservatory. The conservatory door was unlocked, see?'

'I see . . . It's odd that he should have known that, isn't it?'

'The murderer may have been hiding there already: we can't tell from the prints just there. He was wearing boots – Wellington boots, size $10\frac{1}{2}$. We would guess from the spacing of the footprints in the garden that he was about six foot tall. When he had got her to the conservatory he must have hit her again and again – mainly on the head. There's a lot of what we call travelled blood in the conservatory, that's to say, blood spurted from an open artery. There's no sign of that anywhere else.'

'And no sign of it on her husband?'

'I'll come to that later, but the short answer is, no.' He paused a moment and continued:

'Now, I said there were footprints, and so there were. The murderer came through the back garden. Where he came from and went to, Heaven alone knows. You see, there are no tracks leading away – not Wellingtons. None at all. Of course, it's possible the outgoing tracks followed the path to the front gate and got lost in all the to-ing and fro-ing later that night. But I don't think we'd have lost them even then.' He glanced at Smiley, then went on:

'He left one thing behind him in the conservatory – an old cloth belt, navy blue, from a cheap overcoat by the look of it. We're working on that now.'

'Was she . . . robbed or anything?'

'No sign of interference. She was wearing a string of green beads round her neck, and they've gone, and it looks as though he tried to get the rings off her finger, but they were too tight.' He paused.

'I need hardly tell you that we've had reports from every corner of the country about tall men in blue overcoats and gumboots. But none of them had wings as far as I know. Or seven-league boots for jumping from the conservatory to the road.'

They paused, while a police cadet brought in tea on a tray. He put it on the desk, looked at Smiley out of the corner of his eye and decided to let the Inspector pour out. He guided the teapot round so that the handle was towards Rigby and withdrew. Smiley was amused by the immaculate condition of the tray cloth, by the matching china and tea-strainer, laid before them by the enormous hands of the cadet. Rigby poured out the tea and they drank for a moment in silence. There was, Smiley reflected, something devastatingly competent about Rigby. The very ordinariness of the man and his room identified him with the society he protected. The nondescript furniture, the wooden filing cupboards, the bare walls, the archaic telephone with its separate earpiece, the brown frieze round the wall and the brown paint on the door, the glistening linoleum and the faint smell of carbolic, the burbling gas-fire, and the calendar from the Prudential – these were the evidence of rectitude and moderation; their austerity gave comfort and reassurance. Rigby continued:

'Rode went back to Fielding's house for the examination papers. Fielding confirms that, of course. He arrived at Fielding's house at about 11.35, near as Fielding can say. He hardly spent any time there at all – just collected his papers at the door – they were in a small writing-case he uses for carrying exercise books. He doesn't remember whether he saw anyone on the road. He thinks a bicycle overtook him, but he can't be sure. If we take Rode's word for it, he walked straight home. When he got there he rang the bell. He was wearing a dinner-jacket and so he hadn't got his key with him. His wife was expecting him to ring the bell, you see. That's the devil of it. It was a moonlit night, mind, and snow on the ground, so you could see a mighty long way. He called her, but she didn't answer. Then he saw footprints going round to the side of the house. Not just footprints, but blood marks and the snow all churned up where the body had been dragged to the conservatory. But he didn't know it was blood in the moonlight, it just showed up dark, and Rode said afterwards he thought it was the dirty water from the gutters running over on to the path.

'He followed the prints round until he came to the conservatory. It was darker in there and he fumbled for the light switch, but it didn't work.'

'Did he light a match?'

'No, he didn't have any. He's a non-smoker. His wife didn't approve of smoking. He moved forward from the door. The conservatory walls are mainly glass except for the bottom three feet, but the roof is tiled. The moon was high that night, and not much light got in at all, except through the partition window between the drawing-room and the conservatory – but she'd only had the little table light on in the drawing-room. So he groped his way forward, talking all the time, calling Stella, his wife. As he went, he tripped over something and nearly fell. He knelt down and felt with his hands, up and down her body. He realised that his hands were covered in blood. He doesn't remember much after that, but there's a senior master living a hundred yards up the road – Mr D'Arcy his name is, lives with his sister, and he heard him screaming on the road. D'Arcy went out to him. Rode had blood all over his hands and face and seemed to be out of his mind. D'Arcy rang the police and I got there at about one o'clock that morning. I've seen some nasty things in my time, but this is the worst. Blood everywhere. Whoever killed her must have been covered in it. There's an outside tap against the conservatory wall. The tap had been turned on, probably by the murderer to rinse his hands. The boffins have found traces of blood in the snow underneath it. The tap was lagged recently by Rode I gather . . . '

'And fingerprints?' Smiley asked. 'What about them?'

'Mr Rode's were everywhere. On the floor, the walls and windows, on the body itself. But there were other prints; smudges of blood, little more, made with a gloved hand probably.'

'And they were the murderer's?'

'They had been made *before* Rode made his. In some cases Rode's prints were partly superimposed on the glove prints.'

Smiley was silent for a moment.

'These examination papers he went back for. Were they as important as all that?'

'Yes. I gather they were. Up to a point anyway. The marks had to be handed in to Mr D'Arcy by midday on Friday.'

'But why did he take them to Fielding's in the first place?'

'He didn't. He'd been invigilating exams all afternoon and the papers were handed in to him at six o'clock. He put them in his little case and had them taken to Fielding's by a boy – head boy in Mr Fielding's house, name of Perkins. Rode was on Chapel duty last week, so he didn't have time to return home before dinner.'

'Where did he change then?'

'In the Tutors' Robing Room, next to the Common Room. There are facilities there, mainly for games tutors who live some distance from Carne.'

'The boy who brought this case to Fielding's house – who was he?'

'I can't tell you much more than I've said. His name is Perkins; he's head of Mr Fielding's house. Fielding has spoken to him and confirmed Rode's statement . . . House tutors are very possessive about their boys, you know . . . don't like them to be spoken to by rough policemen.' Rigby seemed to be slightly upset.

'I see,' Smiley said at last, helplessly, and then: 'But how do you explain the letter?'

'It isn't only the letter we've got to explain.'

Smiley looked at him sharply.

'What do you mean?'

'I mean,' said Rigby slowly, 'that Mrs Rode did several pretty queer things in the last few weeks.'

4. *Town and Gown*

'**M**rs Rode was Chapel, of course,' Rigby continued, 'and we've quite a community in Carne. Truth to tell,' he added with a slow smile, 'my wife belongs to it.'

'A couple of weeks ago our Minister called round to see me. It was in the evening, about half past six, I suppose. I was just thinking of going home, see. He walked in here and sat himself down where you're sitting now. He's a big fellow, the Minister, a fine man; comes from up North, where Mrs Rode came from. Cardew, his name is.'

'The Mr Cardew in the letter?'

'That's him. He knew all about Mrs Rode's family before the Rodes ever came here. Glaston's quite a name up North, and Mr Cardew was very pleased when he heard that Stella Rode was Mr Glaston's daughter; very pleased indeed. Mrs Rode came to the Tabernacle regular as clock-work, you can imagine, and they like to see that round here. My wife was pleased as Punch, I can tell you. It was the first time, I suppose, that anyone from the School had done that. Most of the Chapel people here are tradespeople – what we call the locals.' Rigby smiled again. 'It isn't often that Town and Gown come together, so to speak. Not here.'

'How about her husband? Was he Chapel too?'

'Well, he had been, so she told Mr Cardew. Mr Rode was born and bred in Branxome, and all his family were Chapel people. That's how Mr and Mrs Rode first met, I gather – at Branxome Tabernacle. Ever been there, have you? A fine church, Branxome, right up on the hill there, overlooking the sea.'

Smiley shook his head and Rigby's wide brown eyes rested on him thoughtfully for a moment.

'You should,' he said, 'you should go and see that. It seems,' he continued, 'that Mr Rode turned Church of England when he came to Carne. Even tried to persuade his wife to do the same. They're very strong at the

School. I heard that from my wife, as a matter of fact. I never let her gossip as a rule, being a policeman's wife and that, but Mr Cardew told her that himself.'

'I see,' said Smiley.

'Well now, Cardew came and saw me. He was all worried and bothered with himself. He didn't know what he should make of it, but he wanted to talk to me as a friend and not as a policeman.' Rigby looked sour, 'When people say that to me, I always know that they want to talk to me as a policeman. Then he told me his story. Mrs Rode had called to see him that afternoon. He'd been out visiting a farmer's wife over in Okeford and didn't come home until half past five or thereabouts, so Mrs Cardew had had to talk to her and hold the fort until the Minister came home. Mrs Rode was white as a sheet, sitting very still by the fire. As soon as the Minister arrived, Mrs Cardew left them alone and Stella Rode started talking about her husband.'

He paused. 'She said Mr Rode was going to kill her. In the long nights. She seemed to have a kind of fixation about being murdered in the long nights. Cardew didn't take it too seriously at first, but thinking about it afterwards, he decided to let me know.'

Smiley looked at him sharply.

'He couldn't make out what she meant. He thought she was out of her mind. He's a down-to-earth man, see, although he's a Minister. I think he was probably a bit too firm with her. He asked her what put this dreadful thought into her head, and she began to weep. Not hysterical, apparently, but just crying quietly to herself. He tried to calm her down, promised to help her any way he could, and asked her again what had given her this idea. She just shook her head, then got up, walked over to the door, still shaking her head in despair. She turned to him, and he thought she was going to say something, but she didn't. She just left.'

'How very curious,' said Smiley, 'that she lied about that in her letter. She went out of her way to say she *hadn't* told Cardew.'

Rigby shrugged his great shoulders.

'If you'll pardon me,' he said, 'I'm in a darned awkward position. The Chief Constable would sooner cut his throat than call in Scotland Yard. He wants an arrest and he wants one quick. We've got enough clues to cover a Christmas tree; footprints, time of the murder, indication of murderer's clothing, and even the weapon itself.'

Smiley looked at him in surprise.

'You've *found* the weapon, then?'

Rigby hesitated. 'Yes, we've found it. There's hardly a soul knows this, sir, and I'll trouble you to remember that. We found it the morning after the murder, four miles north of Carne on the Okeford road, tossed into a ditch. Eighteen inches of what they call coaxial cable. Know what that is, do you? It comes in all sizes, but this piece is about two inches in diameter. It has a copper rod running down the middle and plastic insulation between the rod and the outer cover. There was blood on it: Stella Rode's blood group, and hairs from her head, stuck to the blood. We're keeping that very dark indeed. By the Grace of God, it was found by one of our own men. It pinpoints the line of the murderer's departure.'

'There's no doubt, I suppose, that it *is* the weapon?' Smiley asked lamely.

'We found particles of copper in the wounds on the body.'

'It's odd, isn't it,' Smiley suggested reflectively, 'that the murderer should have carried the weapon so far before getting rid of it? Specially if he was walking. You'd think he'd want to get rid of it as soon as he could.'

'It is odd. Very odd. The Okeford road runs beside the canal for half of those four miles; he could have pitched the cable into the canal anywhere along there. We'd never have been the wiser.'

'Was the cable old?'

'Not particularly. Just standard type. It could have come from almost anywhere.' Rigby hesitated a minute, then burst out:

'Look, sir, this is what I am trying to say. The circumstances of this case demand a certain type of investigation: wide-scale search, detailed laboratory work, mass inquiry. That's what the Chief wants, and he's right. We've no case against the husband at all, and to be frank he's precious little use to us. He seems a bit lost, a bit vague, contradicting himself on little things that don't matter, like the date of his marriage or the name of his doctor. It's shock, of course, I've seen it before. I know all about your letter, sir, and it's damned odd, but if you can tell me how he could have produced Wellington boots out of a hat and got rid of them afterwards, battered his wife to death without leaving more than a few smudges of blood on himself, and got the weapon four miles from the scene of the crime, all within ten minutes of being at Fielding's house, I'll be grateful to you. We're looking for a stranger, six foot tall, wearing newish Dunlop Wellington boots size $10\frac{1}{2}$, leather gloves and an old blue overcoat stained with blood. A man who travels on foot, who was in the area of North Fields between 11.10 and 11.45 on the night of the murder, who left in the direction of Okeford, taking with him one and a half feet of coaxial cable, a string of green beads and an imitation diamond clip, valued at twenty-three and six. We're looking for a maniac, a man who kills for pleasure or the price of a meal.' Rigby paused, smiled wistfully and added, 'Who can fly fifty feet through the air? But with information like this how else should we spend our time? What else can we look for? I can't put men on to chasing shadows when there's work like that to be done.'

'I understand that.'

'But I'm an old policeman, Mr Smiley, and I like to know what I'm about. I don't like looking for people I can't believe in, and I don't like being cut off from witnesses. I like to meet people and talk to them, nose about here and there, get to know the country. But I can't do that, not at the school. Do you follow me? So we've got to rely on laboratories, tracker dogs, and nation-wide searches, but somehow in my bones I don't think it's altogether one of those cases.'

'I read in the paper about a woman, a Mad Janie . . . '

'I'm coming to that. Mrs Rode was a kindly woman, easy to talk to. I always found her so, anyway. Some of the women at Chapel took against her, but you know what women are. It seems she got friendly with this Janie creature. Janie came begging, selling herbs and charms at the back door; you know the kind of thing. She's queer, talks to birds and all that. She lives in a disused Norman chapel over Pylle. Stella Rode used to give her food and clothes – the poor soul was often as not half-starved. Now Janie's disappeared. She was seen early Wednesday night on the lane towards North Fields and hasn't been seen since. That don't mean a thing. These people come and go in their own way. They'll be all over the neighbourhood for years, then one day they're gone like snow in the fire. They've died in a ditch, maybe, or they've took ill and crept away like a cat. Janie's not the only queer one round here. There's a lot of excitement because we found a spare set of footprints running along the fringe of trees at the far end of the garden. They were a woman's prints by the look of them, and at one point they come quite close to the conservatory. Could be a gypsy or a beggar woman. Could be anything, but I expect it's Janie right enough. I hope to Heaven it was, sir; we could do with an eyewitness, even a mad one.'

Smiley stood up. As they shook hands, Rigby said, 'Goodbye, sir. Ring me any time, any time at all.' He scribbled a telephone number on the pad in front of him, tore off the sheet and gave it to Smiley. 'That's my home number.' He showed Smiley to the door, seemed to hesitate, then he said, 'You're not a Carnian yourself by any chance, are you, sir?'

'Good heavens, no.'

Again Rigby hesitated. 'Our Chief's a Carnian. Ex-Indian Army. Brigadier Havelock. This is his last year. He's very interested in this case. Doesn't like me messing around the school. Won't have it.'

'I see.'

'He wants an arrest quickly.'

'And outside Carne, I suppose?'

'Good-bye, Mr Smiley. Don't forget to ring me. Oh, another thing I should have mentioned. That bit of cable . . . '

'Yes?'

'Mr Rode used a length of the same stuff in a demonstration lecture on elementary electronics. Mislaid it about three weeks ago.'

Smiley walked slowly back to his hotel.

My dear Brim,

As soon as I arrived I handed your letter over to the CID man in charge of the case – it was Rigby, as Ben had supposed: he looks like a mixture of Humpty-Dumpty and a Cornish elf – very short and broad – and I don't think he's anyone's fool.

To begin at the middle – our letter didn't have quite the effect we expected; Stella Rode evidently told Cardew, the local Baptist Minister, two weeks ago, that her husband was trying to kill her in the long nights, whatever they are. As for the circumstances of the murder – the account in the *Guardian* is substantially correct.

In fact, the more Rigby told me, the less likely it became that she was killed by her husband. Almost everything pointed away from him. Quite apart from motive, there is the location of the weapon, the footprints in the snow (which indicate a tall man in Wellingtons), the presence of unidentified glove-prints in the conservatory. Add to that the strongest argument of all: whoever killed her must have been covered in blood – the conservatory was a dreadful sight, Rigby tells me. Of course, there *was* blood on Rode when he was picked up by his colleague in the lane, but only smears which could have resulted from stumbling over the body in the dark. Incidentally, the footprints only go into the garden and not out.

As things stand at the moment, there is, as Rigby points out, only one interpretation – the murderer was a stranger, a tramp, a madman perhaps, who killed her for pleasure or for her jewellery (which was worthless) and made off along the Okeford road, throwing the weapon into a ditch. (But why carry it four miles – and why not throw it into the canal the other side of the ditch? The Okeford road crosses Okemoor, which is all cross-dyked to prevent flooding.) If this interpretation is correct, then I suppose we attribute Stella's letter and her interview with Cardew to a persecuted mind, or the premonition of death, depending on whether we're superstitious. If that is so, it is the most monstrous coincidence I have ever heard of. Which brings me to my final point.

I rather gathered from what Rigby *didn't* say that his Chief Constable was treading on his tail, urging him to scour the country for tramps in bloodstained blue overcoats (you remember the belt). Rigby, of course, has no alternative but to follow the signs and do as his Chief expects – but he is clearly uneasy about something – either something he hasn't told me, or something he just feels in his bones. I think he was sincere when he asked me to tell him anything I found out about the *School* end – the Rodes themselves, the way they fitted in, and so on. Carne's monastery walls are still pretty high, he feels . . .

So I'll just sniff around a bit, I think, and see what goes on. I rang Fielding when I got back from the police station and he's asked me to supper tonight. I'll write again as soon as I have anything to tell you.

George.

Having carefully sealed the envelope, pressing down the corners with his thumbs, Smiley locked his door and made his way down the wide marble staircase, treading carefully on the meagre coconut matting that ran down the centre. There was a red wooden letter box in the hall for the use of residents, but Smiley, being a cautious man, avoided it. He walked to the pillar box at the corner of the road, posted his letter and wondered what to do about lunch. There were, of course, the sandwiches and coffee provided by Miss Brimley. Reluctantly he returned to the hotel. It was full of journalists, and Smiley hated journalists. It was also cold, and he hated the cold. And there was something very familiar about sandwiches in a hotel bedroom.

5. Cat and Dog

It was just after seven o'clock that evening when George Smiley climbed the steps which led up to the front door of Mr Terence Fielding's house. He rang, and was admitted to the hall by a little plump woman in her middle fifties. To his right a log fire burned warmly on a pile of wood ash and above him he was vaguely aware of a minstrel gallery and a mahogany staircase, which rose in a spiral to the top of the house. Most of the light seemed to come from the fire, and Smiley could see that the walls around him were hung with a great number of paintings of various styles and periods, and the chimneypiece was laden with all manner of *objets d'art*. With an involuntary shudder, he noticed that neither the fire nor the pictures quite succeeded in banishing the faint smell of school – of polish bought wholesale, of cocoa and community cooking. Corridors led from the hall, and Smiley observed that the lower part of each wall was painted a dark brown or green according to the inflexible rule of school decorators. From one of these corridors the enormous figure of Mr Terence Fielding emerged.

He advanced on Smiley, massive and genial, with his splendid mane of grey hair falling anyhow across his forehead, and his gown billowing behind him.

'Smiley? Ah! You've met True, have you – Miss Truebody, my house-keeper? Marvellous this snow, isn't it? Pure Bruegel! Seen the boys skating by the Eyot? Marvellous sight! Black suits, coloured scarves, pale sun; all there, isn't it, all there! Bruegel to the life. Marvellous!' He took Smiley's coat and flung it on to a decrepit deal chair with a rush seat which stood in the corner of the hall.

'You like that chair – you recognise it?'

'I don't think I do,' Smiley replied in some confusion.

'Ah, you should, you know, you should! Had it made in Provence before the war. Little carpenter I knew. Place it now? Facsimile of Van Gogh's yellow chair; some people recognise it.' He led the way down a corridor and into a large comfortable study adorned with Dutch tiles, small pieces of Renaissance sculpture, mysterious bronzes, china dogs and unglazed vases; and Fielding himself towering magnificent among them.

As senior housemaster of Carne, Fielding wore, in place of the customary academic dress, a wonderful confection of heavy black skirts and legal bib, like a monk in evening dress. All this imparted a suggestion of clerical austerity in noted contrast to the studied flamboyance of his personality. Evidently conscious of this, he sought to punctuate the solemnity of his uniform and give to it a little of his own temperament, by adorning it with flowers carefully chosen from his garden. He had scandalised the tailors of Carne, whose frosted windows carried the insignia of royal households, by having buttonholes let into his gown. These he would fill according to his mood with anything from hibernia to bluebells. This evening he wore a rose, and from its freshness Smiley deduced that he had this minute put it into place, having ordered it specially.

'Sherry wine or Madeira?'

'Thank you; a glass of sherry.'

'Tart's drink, Madeira,' Fielding called, as he poured from a decanter, 'but boys like it. Perhaps that's why. They're frightful flirts.' He handed Smiley a glass and added, with a dramatic modification of his voice:

'We're all rather subdued at the moment by this dreadful business. We've never had anything quite like it, you know. Have you seen the evening papers?'

'No, I'm afraid I haven't. But the Sawley Arms is packed with journalists of course.'

'They've really gone to town. They've got the Army out in Hampshire, playing about with mine-detectors. God knows what they expect to find.'

'How have the boys taken it?'

'They adore it! My own house has been particularly fortunate, of course, because the Rodes were dining here that night. Some oaf from the police even wanted to question one of my boys.'

'Indeed,' said Smiley innocently. 'What on earth about?'

'Oh, God knows,' Fielding replied abruptly, and then, changing the subject, he asked, 'You knew my brother well, didn't you? He talked about you, you know.'

'Yes, I knew Adrian very well. We were close friends.'

'In the war, too?'

'Yes.'

'Were you in his crowd, then?'

'What crowd?'

'Steed-Asprey, Jebedee. All those people.'

'Yes.'

'I never really heard how he died. Did you?'

'No.'

'We didn't see much of one another in later years, Adrian and I. Being a fraud, I can't afford to be seen beside the genuine article,' Fielding declared, with something of his earlier panache. Smiley was spared the embarrassment of a reply by a quiet knock at the door, and a tall red-haired boy came timidly into the room.

'I've called the Adsum, sir, if you're ready, sir.'

'Damn,' said Fielding, emptying his glass. 'Prayers.' He turned to Smiley. 'Meet Perkins, my head prefect. Musical genius, but a problem in the schoolroom. That right, Tim? Stay here or come as you like. It only lasts ten minutes.'

'Rather less tonight, sir,' said Perkins. 'It's the Nunc Dimittis.'

'Thank God for small mercies,' Fielding declared, tugging briefly at his bib, as he led Smiley at a spanking pace out into the corridor and across the hall, with Perkins stalking along behind them. Fielding was speaking all the time without bothering to turn his head:

'I'm glad you've chosen this evening to come. I never entertain on Fridays as a rule because everyone else does, though none of us quite knows what to do about entertaining at the moment. Felix D'Arcy will be coming tonight, but that's hardly entertaining. D'Arcy's a professional. Incidentally, we normally dress in the evening, but it doesn't matter.'

Smiley's heart sank. They turned a corner and entered another corridor.

'We have prayers at all hours here. The Master's revived the seven Day Hours for the Offices: Prime, Terce, Sext and so on. A surfeit during the Half, abstinence during the holidays, that's the system, like games. Useful in the house for roll-calls, too.' He led the way down yet another corridor, flung open a double door at the end of it and marched straight into the dining-room, his gown filling gracefully behind him. The boys were waiting for him.

'More sherry? What did you think of prayers? They sing quite nicely, don't they? One or two good tenors. We tried some plainsong last Half; quite good, really quite good. D'Arcy will be here soon. He's a frightful toad. Looks like a Sickert model fifty years after – all trousers and collar. However, you're lucky his sister isn't accompanying him. She's worse!'

'What's his subject?' They were back in Fielding's study.

'Subject! I'm afraid we don't have subjects here. None of us has read a word on any subject since we left University.' He lowered his voice and added darkly, 'That's if we *went* to University. D'Arcy teaches French. D'Arcy is Senior Tutor by election, bachelor by profession, sublimated pansy by inclination . . . ' he was standing quite still now, his head thrown back and his right hand stretched out towards Smiley, '. . . and his subject is other people's shortcomings. He is principally, however, self-appointed majordomo of Carne protocol. If you wear a gown on a bicycle, reply incorrectly to an invitation, make a fault in the *placement* of your dinner guests or speak of a colleague as 'Mister', D'Arcy will find you out and admonish you.'

'What are the duties of Senior Tutor, then?' Smiley asked, just for something to say.

'He's the referee between the classics and the scientists; arranges the timetable and vets the exam. results. But principally, poor man, he must reconcile the Arts with the Sciences.' He shook his head sagely. 'And it takes a better man than D'Arcy to do that. Not, mind you,' he added wearily, 'that it makes the least difference who wins the extra hour on Friday evenings. Who cares? Not the boys, poor dears, that's certain.'

Fielding talked on, at random and always in superlatives, sometimes groping in the air with his hand as if to catch the more elusive metaphors; now of his colleagues with caustic derision, now of boys with compassion if not with understanding; now of the Arts with fervour – and the studied bewilderment of a lonely disciple.

'Carne isn't a school. It's a sanatorium for intellectual lepers. The symptoms began when we came down from University; a gradual putre-faction of our intellectual extremities. From day to day our minds die, our spirits atrophy and rot. We watch the process in one another, hoping to forget it in ourselves.' He paused, and looked reflectively at his hands.

'In me the process is complete. You see before you a dead soul, and Carne is the body I live in.' Much pleased by this confession, Fielding held out his great arms so that the sleeves of his gown resembled the wings of a giant bat; 'the Vampire of Carne', he declared, bowing deeply. '*Alcoholique et poète!*' A bellow of laughter followed this display.

Smiley was fascinated by Fielding, by his size, his voice, the wanton inconstancy of his temperament, by his whole big-screen style; he found himself attracted and repelled by this succession of contradictory poses; he wondered whether he was supposed to take part in the performance, but Fielding seemed so dazzled by the footlights that he was indifferent to the audience behind them. The more Smiley watched, the more elusive seemed the character he was trying to comprehend: changeful but sterile, daring but fugitive; colourful, unbounded, ingenuous, yet deceitful and perverse. Smiley began to wish he could acquire the material facts of Fielding – his means, his ambitions and disappointments.

His reverie was interrupted by Miss Truebody. Felix D'Arcy had arrived.

No candles, and a cold supper admirably done by Miss Truebody. Not claret, but hock, passed round like port. And at last, at long last, Fielding mentioned Stella Rode.

They had been talking rather dutifully of the Arts and the Sciences. This would have been dull (for it was uninformed) had not D'Arcy constantly been goaded by Fielding, who seemed anxious to exhibit D'Arcy in his worst light. D'Arcy's judgements of people and problems were largely coloured by what he considered 'seemly' (a favourite word) and by an effeminate malice towards his colleagues. After a while Fielding asked who was replacing Rode during his absence, to which D'Arcy said, 'No one,' and added unctuously:

'It was a terrible shock to the community, this affair.'

'Nonsense,' Fielding retorted. 'Boys love disaster. The further we are from death the more attractive it seems. They find the whole affair most exhilarating.'

'The publicity has been most unseemly,' said D'Arcy, 'most. I think that has been prominent in the minds of many of us in the Common Room.' He turned to Smiley:

'The press, you know, is a constant worry here. In the past it could never have happened. Formerly our great families and institutions were not subjected to this intrusion. No, indeed not. But today all that is changed. Many of us are compelled to subscribe to the cheaper newspapers for this very reason. One Sunday newspaper mentioned no fewer than four of Hecht's old boys in one edition. All of them in an unseemly context, I may say. And of course such papers never fail to mention that the boy is a Carnian. You know, I suppose, that we have the young Prince here. (I myself have the honour to supervise his French studies.) The young Sawley is also at Carne. The activity of the press during his parents' divorce suit was deplorable. Quite deplorable. The Master wrote to the Press Council, you know. I drafted the letter myself. But on this tragic occasion they have excelled themselves. We even had the press at Compline last night, you know, waiting for the Special Prayer. They occupied the whole of the two rear pews on the west side. Hecht was doing Chapel Duty and tried to have them removed.' He paused, raised his eyebrows in gentle reproach and smiled. 'He had no business to, of course, but that never stopped the good Hecht.' He turned to Smiley, 'One of our *athletic* brethren,' he explained.

'Stella was too common for you, Felix, wasn't she?'

'Not at all,' said D'Arcy quickly. 'I would not have you say that of me, Terence. I am by no means discriminatory in the matter of class; merely of manners. I grant you, in that particular field, I found her wanting.'

'In many ways she was just what we needed,' Fielding continued, addressing Smiley and ignoring D'Arcy. 'She was everything we're forced to ignore – she was red-brick, council estates, new towns, the very anti-thesis of Carne!' He turned suddenly to D'Arcy and said, 'But to you, Felix, she was just bad form.'

'Not at all; merely unsuitable.'

Fielding turned to Smiley in despair.

'Look,' he said. 'We talk academic here, you know, wear academic dress and hold high table dinners in the Common Room; we have long graces in

Latin that none of us can translate. We go to the Abbey and the wives sit in the hencoop in their awful hats. But it's a charade. It means nothing.'

D'Arcy smiled wanly.

'I cannot believe, my dear Terence, that anyone who keeps such an excellent table as yourself can have so low an opinion of the refinements of social conduct.' He looked to Smiley for support and Smiley dutifully echoed the compliment. 'Besides, we know Terence of old at Carne. I am afraid we are accustomed to his roar.'

'I know why you disliked that woman, Felix. She was honest, and Carne has no defence against that kind of honesty.'

D'Arcy suddenly became very angry indeed.

'Terence, I will not have you say this. I simply will not have it. I feel I have a certain duty at Carne, as indeed we all have, to restore and maintain those standards of behaviour which suffered so sadly in the war. I am sensible that this determination has made me on more than one occasion unpopular. But such comment or advice as I offer is never – I beg you to notice this – is *never* directed against personalities, only against behaviour, against unseemly lapses in conduct. I will acknowledge that more than once I was compelled to address Rode on the subject of his wife's conduct. That is a matter quite divorced from personalities, Terence. I will not have it said that I disliked Mrs Rode. Such a suggestion would be disagreeable at all times, but under the present tragic circumstances it is deplorable. Mrs Rode's own . . . background and education did not naturally prepare her for our ways; that is quite a different matter. It does, however, illustrate the point that I wish to emphasise, Terence: it was a question of enlightenment, not of criticism. Do I make myself clear?'

'Abundantly,' Fielding answered dryly.

'Did the other wives like her?' Smiley ventured.

'Not entirely,' D'Arcy replied crisply.

'The wives! My God!' Fielding groaned, putting his hand to his brow. There was a pause.

'Her clothes, I believe, were a source of distress to some of them. She also frequented the public laundry. This, too, would not make a favourable impression. I should add that she did not attend our church . . . '

'Did she have any close friends among the wives?' Smiley persisted.

'I believe young Mrs Snow took to her.'

'And you say she was dining here the night she was murdered?'

'Yes,' said Fielding quietly, 'Wednesday. And it was Felix and his sister who took in poor Rode afterwards . . . ' He glanced at D'Arcy.

'Yes, indeed,' said D'Arcy abruptly. His eyes were on Fielding, and it seemed to Smiley that something had passed between them. 'We shall never forget, never . . . Terence, if I may talk shop for just one moment, Perkins's construe is abysmal; I declare I have never seen work like it. Is he unwell? His mother is a most cultured woman, a cousin of the Samfords, I am told.'

Smiley looked at him and wondered. His dinner-jacket was faded, green with age. Smiley could almost hear him saying it had belonged to his grandfather. The skin of his face was so unlined that he somehow suggested fatness without being fat. His voice was pitched on one insinuating note, and he smiled all the time, whether he was speaking or not. The smile never left his smooth face, it was worked into the malleable fabric of his flesh, stretching his lips across his perfect teeth and opening the corners of his red mouth, so that it seemed to be held in place by the invisible fingers of his dentist. Yet D'Arcy's face was far from unexpressive; every mark showed. The smallest movement of his mouth or nose, the quickest glance or frown, were there to read and interpret. And he wanted to change the subject. Not away from Stella Rode (for he returned to discussing her himself a moment later), but away from the particular evening on which she died, away from the precise narration of events. And what was more, there was not a doubt in Smiley's mind that Fielding had seen it too, that in that look which passed between them was a pact of fear, a warning perhaps, so that from that moment Fielding's manner changed, he grew sullen and preoccupied, in a way that puzzled Smiley long afterwards.

D'Arcy turned to Smiley and addressed him with cloying intimacy.

'*Do* forgive my deplorable descent into Carne gossip. You find us a little cut off, here, do you not? We are often held to be cut off, I know. Carne is a "Snob School", that is the cry. You may read it every day in the gutter press. And yet, despite the claims of the *avant-garde*,' he said, glancing slyly at Fielding, 'I may say that *no one* could be less of a snob than Felix D'Arcy.' Smiley noticed his hair. It was very fine and ginger, growing from the top and leaving his pink neck bare.

'Take poor Rode, for instance. I certainly don't hold Rode's background against him in any way, poor fellow. The grammar schools do a splendid job, I am sure. Besides, he settled down here very well. I told the Master so. I said to him that Rode had settled down well; he does Chapel duty quite admirably – that was the very point I made. I hope I have played my part, what is more, in helping him to fit in. With careful instruction, such people can, as I said to the Master, learn our customs and even our manners; and the Master agreed.'

Smiley's glass was empty and D'Arcy, without consulting Fielding, filled it for him from the decanter. His hands were polished and hairless, like the hands of a girl.

'But,' he continued, 'I must be honest. Mrs Rode did not adapt herself so willingly to our ways.' Still smiling, he sipped delicately from his glass. He wants to put the record straight, thought Smiley.

'She would never really have fitted in at Carne; that is my opinion – though I am sure I never voiced it while she was alive. Her background was against her. The fault was not hers – it was her background which, as I say, was unfortunate. Indeed, if we may speak frankly and in confidence, I have reason to believe it was her past that brought about her death.'

'Why do you say that?' asked Smiley quickly, and D'Arcy replied with a glance at Fielding, 'It appears she was expecting to be attacked.'

'My sister is devoted to dogs,' D'Arcy continued. 'You may know that already perhaps. King Charles spaniels are her *forte*. She took a first at the North Dorset last year and was commended at Cruft's shortly afterwards for her "Queen of Carne". She sells to America, you know. I dare say there are few people in the country with Dorothy's knowledge of the breed. The Master's wife found occasion to say the very same thing a week ago. Well, the Rodes were our neighbours, as you know, and Dorothy is not a person to neglect her neighbourly duties. Where duty is concerned, you will not find her discriminatory, I assure you. The Rodes also had a dog, a large mongrel, quite an intelligent animal, which they brought with them. (I have little idea where they came from, but that is another matter.) They appeared quite devoted to the dog, and I have no doubt they were. Rode took it with him to watch the football until I had occasion to advise him against it. The practice was giving rise to unseemly humour among the boys. I have found the same thing myself when exercising Dorothy's spaniels.

'I shall come to the point presently. Dorothy uses a vet called Harriman, a superior type of person who lives over toward Sturminster. A fortnight ago she sent for him. "Queen of Carne" was coughing badly and Dorothy asked Harriman to come over. A bitch of her quality is not to be taken lightly, I assure you.'

Fielding groaned, and D'Arcy continued, oblivious:

'I happened to be at home, and Harriman stayed for a cup of coffee. He is, as I say, a superior type of person. Harriman made some reference to the Rodes' dog and then the truth came out; Mrs Rode had had the dog destroyed the previous day. She said it had bitten the postman. Some long and confused story; the Post Office would sue, the police had been round, and I don't know what else. And, anyway, she said, the dog couldn't really protect, it could only warn. She had said so to Harriman, "It wouldn't do any good." '

'Wasn't she upset about losing the dog?' asked Smiley.

'Oh, indeed, yes. Harriman said she was in tears when she arrived. Mrs Harriman had to give her a cup of tea. They suggested she should give the dog another chance, put it in kennels for a while, but she was adamant, quite adamant. Harriman was most perplexed. So was his wife. When they discussed it afterwards they agreed that Mrs Rode's behaviour had not been quite normal. Not normal at all, in fact. Another curious fact was the condition of the dog: it had been maltreated, seriously so. Its back was marked as if from beatings.'

'Did Harriman follow up this remark she made? About not doing any good? What did Harriman make of it?' Smiley was watching D'Arcy intently.

'She repeated it to Mrs Harriman, but she wouldn't explain it. However, I think the explanation is obvious enough.'

'Oh?' said Fielding.

D'Arcy put his head on one side and plucked coyly at the lobe of his ear. 'We all have a little of the detective in us,' he said. 'Dorothy and I talked it over after the – death. We decided that Stella Rode had formed some unsavoury association before coming to Carne, which had recently been revived . . . possibly against her will. Some violent ruffian – an old admirer – who would resent the improvement in her station.'

'How badly was the postman bitten by the dog?' Smiley asked.

D'Arcy turned to him again.

'That is the extraordinary thing. That is the very crux of the story, my dear fellow: the postman hadn't been bitten at all. Dorothy inquired. Her whole story was an absolute string of lies from beginning to end.'

They rose from the table and made their way to Fielding's study, where Miss Truebody had put the coffee. The conversation continued to wander back and forth over Wednesday's tragedy. D'Arcy was obsessed with the indelicacy of it all – the persistence of journalists, the insensitivity of the police, the uncertainty of Mrs Rode's origin, the misfortune of her husband. Fielding was still oddly silent, sunk in his own thoughts, from which he occasionally emerged to glance at D'Arcy with a look of hostility. At exactly a quarter to eleven D'Arcy pronounced himself tired, and the three of them went into the great hall, where Miss Truebody produced a coat for Smiley and a coat and muffler and cap for D'Arcy. Fielding accepted D'Arcy's thanks with a sullen nod. He turned to Smiley:

'That business you rang me about. What was it exactly?'

'Oh – a letter from Mrs Rode just before she was murdered,' said Smiley vaguely, 'the police are handling it now, but they do not regard it as . . . significant. Not significant at all. She seems to have had a sort of' – he gave an embarrassed grin 'persecution complex. Is that the expression? However, we might discuss it some time. You must dine with me at the Sawley before I go back. Do you come to London at all? We might meet in London perhaps, at the end of the Half.'

D'Arcy was standing in the doorway, looking at the new fall of snow which lay white and perfect on the pavement before him.

'Ah,' he said, with a little knowing laugh, 'the long nights, eh, Terence, the long nights.'

6. *Holly for the Devil*

'What are the long nights?' Smiley asked, as he and D'Arcy walked briskly away from Fielding's house through the new snow towards the Abbey Close.

'We have a proverb that it always snows at Carne in the long nights. That is the traditional term here for the nights of Lent,' D'Arcy replied. 'Before the Reformation the monks of the Abbey kept a vigil during Lent between the Offices of Compline and Lauds. You may know that already perhaps. As there is no longer a religious order attached to the Abbey, the custom has fallen into disuse. We continue to observe it, however, by the saying of Compline during Lent. Compline was the last of the Canonical Day Hours and was said before retiring for the night. The Master, who has a great respect for traditions of this kind, has reintroduced the old words for our devotions. Prime was the dawn Office, as you are no doubt aware. Terce was at the third hour of daylight – that is to say at 9.0 a.m. Thus we no longer refer to Morning Prayer, but to Terce. I find it delightful. Similarly, during Advent and Lent we say Sext at midday in the Abbey.'

'Are all these services compulsory?'

'Of course. Otherwise it would be necessary to make arrangements for those boys who did not attend. That is not desirable. Besides, you forget that Carne is a religious foundation.'

It was a beautiful night. As they crossed the Close, Smiley looked up at the tower. It seemed smaller and more peaceful in the moonlight. The whiteness of the new snow lit the very sky itself; the whole Abbey was so sharply visible against it that even the mutilated images of saints were clear in every sad detail of their defacement, wretched figures, their purpose lost, with no eyes to see the changing world.

They reached the cross-roads to the south of the Abbey.

'The parting of the ways, I fear,' said D'Arcy, extending his hand.

'It's a beautiful night,' Smiley replied quickly, 'let me come with you as far as your house.'

'Gladly,' said D'Arcy dryly.

They turned down North Fields Lane. A high stone wall ran along one side; and on the other the great expanse of playing fields, twenty or more rugby pitches, bordered the road for over half a mile. They walked this distance in silence, until D'Arcy stopped and pointed with his stick past Smiley towards a small house on the edge of the playing fields.

'That's North Fields, the Rodes' house. It used to belong to the head groundsman, but the school added a wing a few years ago, and now it's a staff house. My own house is rather larger, and lies farther up the road. Happily, I am fond of walking.'

'Was it along here that you found Stanley Rode that night?'

There was a pause, then D'Arcy said: 'It was nearer to my house, about a quarter of a mile farther on. He was in a terrible condition, poor fellow, terrible. I am myself unable to bear the sight of blood. If I had known how he would look when I brought him into the house, I do not think I could have done it. Mercifully, my sister Dorothy is a most competent woman.'

They walked on in silence, until Smiley said: 'From what you were saying at dinner, the Rodes were a very ill-assorted couple.'

'Precisely. If her death had happened any other way, I would describe it as providential: a blessed release for Rode. She was a thoroughly mischievous woman, Smiley, who made it her business to hold her husband up to ridicule. I believe it was intentional. Others do not. I do, and I have my reasons. She took pleasure in deriding her husband.'

'And Carne too, no doubt.'

'Just so. This is a critical moment in Carne's development. Many public schools have conceded to the vulgar clamour for change – change at any price. Carne, I am pleased to say, has not joined these Gadarene swine. That makes it more important than ever that we protect ourselves from within as well as from without.' He spoke with surprising vehemence.

'But was she really such a problem? Surely her husband could have spoken to her?'

'I never encouraged him to do so, I assure you. It is not my practice to interfere between man and wife.'

They reached D'Arcy's house. A high laurel hedge entirely concealed the house from the road, except for two multiple chimney-stacks which were visible over the top of it, confirming Smiley's impression that the house was large and Victorian.

'I am not ashamed of the Victorian taste,' said D'Arcy as he slowly opened the gate; 'but then, I am afraid we are not close to the modern idiom at Carne. This house used to be the rectory for North Fields Church, but the church is now served by a priest-in-charge from the Abbey. The vicarage is still within the school's gift, and I was fortunate enough to receive it. Good night. You must come for sherry before you go. Do you stay long?'

'I doubt it,' Smiley replied, 'but I am sure you have enough worries at the moment.'

'What do you mean?' D'Arcy said sharply.

'The press, the police and all the attendant fuss.'

'Ah yes, just so. Quite so. Nevertheless, our community life must continue. We always have a small party in the middle of the Half, and I feel it is particularly important that we should do so on this occasion. I will send a note to the Sawley tomorrow. My sister would be charmed. Good night.' He clanged the gate to, and the sound was greeted by the frantic barking of dogs from somewhere behind the house. A window opened and a harsh female voice called:

'Is that you, Felix?'

'Yes, Dorothy.'

'Why do you have to make such a bloody noise? You've woken those dogs again.' The window closed with a significant thud, and D'Arcy, without so much as a glance in Smiley's direction, disappeared quickly into the shadow of the house.

Smiley set off along the road again, back towards the town. After walking for about ten minutes he stopped and looked again towards the Rodes' house a hundred yards across the playing fields. It lay in the shadow of a small coppice of fir trees, dark and secret against the white fields. A narrow lane led towards the house; there was a brick pillar-box on one corner and a small oak sign-post, quite new, pointed along the lane, which must, he decided, lead to the village of Pylle. The legend upon the sign was obscured by a film of snow, and Smiley brushed it away with his hand, so that he could read the words 'North Fields', done in a contrived suburban Gothic script which must have caused D'Arcy considerable discomfort. The snow in the lane was untrodden; obviously more had fallen recently. There could not be much traffic between Pylle and Carne. Glancing quickly up and down the main road he began making his way along the lane. The hedge rose high on either side, and soon Smiley could see nothing but the pale sky above him, and the straggling willow wands reaching towards it. Once he thought he heard the sound of a footstep, close behind him, but when he stopped he heard nothing but the furtive rustle of the laden hedges. He grew more conscious of the cold: it seemed to hang in the still damp of the sunken road, to clutch and hold him like the chill air of an empty house. Soon the hedge on his left gave way to a sparse line of trees, which Smiley judged to belong to the coppice he had seen from the road. The snow beneath the trees was patchy, and the bare ground looked suddenly ugly and torn. The lane took him in a gradual curve to the left and, quite suddenly the house stood before him, gaunt and craggy in the moonlight. The walls were brick and flint, half obscured by the mass of ivy which grew in profusion across them, tumbling over the porch in a tangled mane.

He glanced towards the garden. The coppice which bordered the lane encroached almost as far as the corner of the house, and extended to the far end of the lawn, screening the house from the playing fields. The murderer had reached the house by a path which led across the lawn and through the trees to the lane at the farthest end of the garden. Looking carefully at the snow on the lawn, he was able to discern the course of the path. The white glazed door to the left of the house must lead to the conservatory . . . And suddenly he knew he was afraid – afraid of the house, afraid of the sprawling dark garden. The knowledge came to him like an awareness of pain. The ivy walls seemed to reach forward and hold him, like an old woman cosseting an unwilling child. The house was large, yet dingy, holding to itself unearthly shapes, black and oily in the sudden contrasts of moonlight. Fascinated despite his fear, he moved towards it. The shadows broke and reformed, darting swiftly and becoming still, hiding in the abundant ivy, or merging with the black windows.

He observed in alarm the first involuntary movement of panic. He was afraid, then suddenly the senses joined in one concerted cry of terror, where sight and sound and touch could no longer be distinguished in the frenzy of his brain. He turned round and ran back to the gate. As he did so, he looked over his shoulder towards the house.

A woman was standing in the path, looking at him, and behind her the conservatory door swung slowly on its hinges.

For a second she stood quite still, then turned and ran back towards the conservatory. Forgetting his fear, Smiley followed. As he reached the corner of the house he saw to his astonishment that she was standing at the door, rocking it gently back and forth in a thoughtful, leisurely way, like a child. She had her back to Smiley, until suddenly she turned to him and spoke, with a soft Dorset drawl, and the childish lilt of a simpleton:

'I thought you was the Devil, Mister, but you'm got no wings.'

Smiley hesitated. If he moved forward, she might take fright again and run. He looked at her across the snow, trying to make her out. She seemed to be wearing a bonnet or shawl over her head, and a dark cape over her shoulders. In her hand she held a sprig of leaves, and these she gently waved back and forth as she spoke to him.

'But you'm carn't do nothin', Mister, 'cos I got the holly fer to hold yer. So you do bide there, Mister, for little Jane can hold yer.' She shook the leaves vehemently towards him and began laughing softly. She still had one hand upon the door, and as she spoke her head lolled to one side.

'You bide away from little Jane, Mister, however pretty she'm do be.'

'Yes, Jane,' said Smiley softly, 'you're a very pretty girl, I can see that; and that's a pretty cape you're wearing, Jane.'

Evidently pleased with this, she clutched the lapels of her cape and turned slowly round, in a child's parody of a fine lady.

As she turned, Smiley saw the two empty sleeves of an overcoat swinging at her sides.

'There's some do laugh at Janie,' she said, a note of petulance in her voice, 'but there's not many seen the Devil fly, Mister. But Janie seed 'im, Janie seed 'im. Silver wings like fishes 'e done 'ad, Janie saw.'

'Where did you find that coat, Janie?'

She put her hands together and shook her head slowly from side to side.

'He'm a bad one. Ooh, he'm a bad one, Mister,' and she laughed softly. 'I seed 'im flying, riding on the wind,' she laughed again, 'and the moon be'ind 'im, lightin' up the way! They'm close as sisters, moon and Devil.'

On an impulse Smiley seized a handful of ivy from the side of the house and held it out to her, moving slowly forward as he did so.

'Do you like flowers, Janie? Here are flowers for Janie; pretty flowers for pretty Janie.' He had nearly reached her when with remarkable speed she ran across the lawn, disappeared into the trees and ran off down the lane. Smiley let her go. He was drenched in sweat.

As soon as he reached the hotel he telephoned Detective Inspector Rigby.

7. *King Arthur's Church*

T he coffee lounge of the Sawley Arms resembles nothing so much as the Tropical Plants Pavilion at Kew Gardens. Built in an age when cactus was the most fashionable of plants and bamboo its indispensable companion, the lounge was conceived as the architectural image of a jungle clearing. Steel pillars, fashioned in segments like the trunk of a palm tree, supported a high glass roof whose regal dome replaced the African sky. Enormous urns of bronze or green-glazed earthenware contained all that was elegant and prolific in the cactus world, and between them very old residents could relax on sofas of spindly bamboo, sipping warm coffee and re-living the discomforts of safari.

Smiley's efforts to obtain a bottle of whisky and a syphon of soda at half past eleven at night were not immediately rewarded. It seemed that, like carrion from the carcass, the journalists had gone. The only sign of life in the hotel was the night porter, who treated his request with remote disapproval and advised him to go to bed. Smiley, by no means naturally persistent, discovered a half-crown in his overcoat pocket and thrust it a little irritably into the old man's hand. The result, though not magical, was effective, and by the time Rigby had made his way to the hotel, Smiley was seated in front of a bright gas fire in the coffee lounge with glasses and a whisky bottle before him.

Smiley retold his experiences of the evening with careful accuracy.

'It was the coat that caught my eye. It was a heavy overcoat like a man's,' he concluded. 'I remembered the blue belt and . . . ' He left the sentence unfinished. Rigby nodded, got up and walked briskly across the lounge and through the swing doors to the porter's desk. Ten minutes later, he returned.

'I think we'd better go and pull her in,' he said simply. 'I've sent for a car.'

'We?' asked Smiley.

'Yes, if you wouldn't mind. What's the matter? Are you frightened?'

'Yes,' he replied. 'Yes, I am.'

The village of Pylle lies to the south of North Fields, upon a high spur which rises steeply from the flat, damp pastures of the Carne valley. It consists of a handful of stone cottages and a small inn where you may drink beer in the landlord's parlour. Seen from Carne playing fields, the village could easily be mistaken for an outcrop of rock upon a tor, for the hill on which it stands appears conical from the northern side. Local historians claim that Pylle is the oldest settlement in Dorset, that its name is Anglo-Saxon for harbour, and that it served the Romans as a port when all the lowlands around were covered by the sea. They will tell you, too, that King Arthur rested there after seven months at sea, and paid homage to Saint Andrew, the patron saint of sailors, on the site of pylle Church, where he burned a candle for each month he had spent afloat; and that in the church, built to commemorate his visit and standing to this day lonely and untended on the hillside, there is a bronze coin as witness to his visit – the very one King Arthur gave to the verger before he set sail again for the Isle of Avalon.

Inspector William Rigby, himself a keen local historian, gave Smiley a somewhat terse précis of Pylle's legendary past as he drove cautiously along the snow-covered lanes.

'These small, out-of-the-way villages are pretty strange places,' he concluded. 'Often only three or four families, all so inbred you can no more sort them out than a barnful of cats. That's where your village idiots come from. They call it the Devil's Mark; I call it incest. They hate to have them in the village, you know – they'll drive them away at any price, like trying to wash away their shame, if you follow me.'

'I follow you.'

'This Jane's the religious sort. There's one or two of them turn that way. The villagers at Pylle are all Chapel now, see, so there's been no use for King Arthur's Church since Wesley. It's empty, falling to bits. There's a few from the valley go up to see it, for its history, like, but no one cares for it, or didn't, not till Janie moved in.'

'Moved in?'

'Yes. She's taken to cleaning the church out night and day, bringing in wild flowers and such. That's why they say she's a witch.'

They passed Rode's house in silence and after turning a sharp bend began climbing the long steep hill that led to Pylle village. The snow in the lane was untouched and apart from occasional skidding they progressed without difficulty. The lower slopes of the hill were wooded, and the lane dark, until suddenly they emerged to find themselves on a smooth plateau, where a savage wind blew the fine snow like smoke across the fields, whipping it against the car. The snow had risen in drifts to one side of the lane, and the going became increasingly difficult.

Finally Rigby stopped the car and said:

'We'll walk from here, sir, if you don't mind.'

'How far is it?'

'Short and sour, I'd say. That's the village straight ahead.'

Through the windscreen, Smiley could discern behind the drifting veils of blown snow two low buildings about a quarter of a mile away. As he looked, a tall, muffled figure advanced towards them along the lane.

'That's Ted Mundy,' said Rigby with satisfaction, 'I told him to be here. He's the sergeant from Okeford.' He leaned out of the car window and called merrily:

'Hullo, Ted there, you old buzzard, how be?' Rigby opened the back door of the car and the sergeant climbed in. Smiley and Mundy were briefly introduced.

'There's a light in the church,' said Mundy, 'but I don't know whether Janie's there. I can't ask no one in the village, see, or I'd have the whole lot round me. They thought she'd gone for good.'

'Does she sleep there then, Ted? She got a bed there or something?' Rigby asked, and Smiley noticed with pleasure that his Dorset accent was more pronounced when he spoke to Mundy.

'So they say, Bill. I couldn't find no bed when I looked in there Saturday. But I tell you an odd thing, Bill. It seems Mrs Rode used to come up here sometimes, to the chapel, to see Janie.'

'I heard about that,' said Rigby shortly. 'Now which way's the church, Ted?'

'Over the hill,' said Mundy. 'Outside the village, in a paddock.' He turned to Smiley. 'That's quite common round here, sir, as I expect you know.' Mundy spoke very slowly, choosing his words. 'You see, when they had the plague they left their dead in the villages and moved away; not far though, on account of their land and the church. Terrible it was, terrible.' Somehow Mundy managed to imply that the Black Death was a fairly recent disaster in those parts, if not actually within living memory.

They got out of the car, forcing the doors against the strong wind, and made their way towards the village, Mundy leading and Smiley in third place. The driven snow, fine and hard, stung their faces. It was an unearthly walk, high on that white hill on such a night. The curve of the bleak hill's crest and the moaning of the wind, the snow cloud which sped across the moon, the dismal, unlit cottages so cautiously passed, belonged to another corner of the world.

Mundy led them sharply to the left, and Smiley guessed that by avoiding the centre of the village he hoped to escape the notice of its inhabitants. After about twenty minutes' walking, often through deep snow, they found themselves following a low hedge between two fields. In the furthest corner of the right-hand field they saw a pale light glimmering across the snow, so pale that at first Smiley had to look away from it, then run his eyes back along the line of that distant hedge to make sure he was not deceived. Rigby stopped, beckoning to the others.

'I'll take over now,' he said. He turned to Smiley. 'I'd be obliged, sir, if you'd stand off a little. If there's any trouble we don't want you mixed up in it, do we?'

'Of course.'

'Ted Mundy, you come up by me.'

They followed the hedge until they came to a stile. Through the gap in the hedge they saw the church clearly now, a low building more like a tithe barn than a church. At one end a pale glow, like the uncertain light of a candle, shone dimly through the leaded windows.

'She's there,' said Mundy, under his breath, as he and Rigby moved forward, Smiley following some distance behind.

They were crossing the field now, Rigby leading, and the church drawing ever closer. New sounds disturbed the moaning of the storm: the parched creak of a door, the mutter of a crumbling roof, the incessant sigh of wind upon a dying house. The two men in front of Smiley had stopped, almost in the shadow of the church wall, and were whispering together. Then Mundy walked quietly away, disappearing round the corner of the church. Rigby waited a moment, then approached the narrow entrance in the rear wall, and pushed the door.

It opened slowly, creaking painfully on its hinges. Then he disappeared into the church. Smiley was waiting outside when suddenly above all the sounds of night he heard a scream, so taut and shrill and clear that it seemed to have no source, but to ride everywhere upon the wind, to mount the ravaged sky on wings; and Smiley had a vision of Mad Janie as he had seen her earlier that night, and he heard again in her demented cry the dreadful note of madness. For a moment he waited. The echo died. Then slowly, terrified, he walked through the snow to the open doorway.

Two candles and an oil lamp on the bare altar shed a dim light over the tiny chapel. In front of the altar, on the sanctuary step, sat Jane, looking vaguely towards them. Her vacuous face was daubed with stains of green and blue, her filthy clothes were threaded with sprigs of evergreen and all about her on the floor were the bodies of small animals and birds.

The pews were similarly decorated with dead creatures of all kinds; and on the altar, broken twigs and little heaps of holly leaves. Between the candles stood a crudely-fashioned cross. Stepping forward past Rigby, Smiley walked quickly down the aisle, past the lolling figure of Jane, until he stood before the altar. For a moment he hesitated, then turned and called softly to Rigby.

On the cross, draped over its three ends like a crude diadem, was a string of green beads.

8. Flowers for Stella

H e woke with the echo of her scream in his ears. He had meant to sleep late, but his watch said half past seven. He put on his bedside lamp, for it was still half-dark, and peered owlishly round the room. There were his trousers, flung over the chair, the legs still sodden from the snow. There were his shoes; he'd have to buy another pair. And there beside him were the notes he had made early that morning before going to sleep, transcriptions from memory of some of Mad Jane's monologue on the journey back to Carne, a journey he would never forget. Mundy had sat with her in the back. She spoke to herself as a child does, asking questions and then in the patient tones of an adult for whom the reply is self-evident, providing the answer.

One obsession seemed to fill her mind: she had seen the devil. She had seen him flying on the wind, his silver wings stretched out behind him. Sometimes the recollection amused her, sometimes inflated her with a sense of her own importance or beauty, and sometimes it terrified her, so that she moaned and wept and begged him to go away. Then Mundy would speak kindly to her, and try to calm her. Smiley wondered whether policemen grew accustomed to the squalor of such things, to clothes that were no more than stinking rags wound round wretched limbs, to puling imbeciles who clutched and screamed and wept. She must have been living on the run for nights on end, finding her food in the fields and dustbins since the night of the murder . . . What had she done that night? What had she seen? Had she killed Stella Rode? Had she seen the murderer, and fancied *him* to be the devil flying on the wind? Why should she think that? If Janie did not kill Stella Rode, what had she seen that so frightened her that for three long winter nights she prowled in terror like an animal in the forest? Had the devil within taken hold of Janie and given power to her arm as she struck down Stella? Was that the devil who rode upon the wind?

But the beads and the coat and the footprints which were not hers – what of them? He lay there thinking, and achieving nothing. At last it was time to get up: it was the morning of the funeral.

As he was getting out of bed the telephone rang. It was Rigby. His voice sounded strained and urgent. 'I want to see you,' he said. 'Can you call round?'

'Before or after the funeral?'

'Before, if possible. What about now?'

'I'll be there in ten minutes.'

Rigby looked, for the first time since Smiley had met him, tired and worried. 'It's Mad Janie,' he said. 'The Chief thinks we should charge her.'

'What for?'

'Murder,' Rigby replied crisply, pushing a thin file across the table. 'The old fool's made a statement . . . a sort of confession.'

They sat in silence while Smiley read the extraordinary statement. It was signed with Mad Janie's mark – J. L. – drawn in a childish hand in letters an inch high. The constable who had taken it down had begun by trying to condense and simplify her account, but by the end of the first page he had obviously despaired. At last Smiley came to the description of the murder:

'So I tells my darling, I tells her: "You are a naughty creature to go with the devil," but her did not hearken, see, and I took angry with her, but she paid no call. I can't abide them as go with devils in the night, and I told her. She ought to have had holly, mister, there's the truth. I told her, mister, but she never would hearken, and that's all Janie's saying, but she drove the devil off, Janie did, and there's one will thank me, that's my darling and I took her jewels for the saints I did, to pretty out the church, and a coat for to keep me warm.'

Rigby watched him as he slowly replaced the statement on the desk.

'Well, what do you think of it?'

Smiley hesitated. 'It's pretty good nonsense as it stands,' he replied at last.

'Of course it is,' said Rigby, with something like contempt. 'She saw something, Lord knows what, when she was out on the prowl; stealing, I shouldn't wonder. She may have robbed the body, or else she picked up the beads where the murderer dropped them. We've traced the coat. Belonged to a Mr Jardine, a baker in Carne East. Mrs Jardine gave it to Stella Rode last Wednesday morning for the refugees. Janie must have pinched it from the conservatory. That's what she meant by "a coat for to keep me warm". But she no more killed Stella Rode than you or I did. What about the footprints, the glove-marks in the conservatory? Besides, she's not strong enough, Janie isn't, to heave that poor woman forty feet through the snow. This is a man's work, as anyone can see.'

'Then what exactly . . . ?'

'We've called off the search, and I'm to prepare a case against one Jane Lyn of the village of Pylle for the wilful murder of Stella Rode. I wanted to tell you myself before you read it all over the papers. So that you'd know how it was.'

'Thanks.'

'In the meantime, if there's any help I can give you, we're still willing.' He hesitated, seemed about to say something, then to change his mind.

As he made his way down the wide staircase Smiley felt useless and very angry, which was scarcely the right frame of mind in which to attend a funeral.

*

It was an admirably conducted affair. Neither the flowers nor the congregation exceeded what was fitting to the occasion. She was not buried at the Abbey, out of deference perhaps to her simplicity of taste, but in the parish churchyard not far from North Fields. The Master was detained that day, as he was on most days, and had sent instead his wife, a small, very vague woman who had spent a long time in India. D'Arcy was much in evidence, fluttering here and there before the ceremony like an anxious beadle; and Mr Cardew had come to guide poor Stella through the unfamiliarities of High Anglican procedure. The Hechts were there, Charles all in black, scrubbed and shining, and Shane in dramatic weeds, and a hat with a very broad brim.

Smiley, who, like the others, had arrived early in anticipation of the unwholesome public interest which the ceremony might arouse, found himself a seat near the entrance of the church. He watched each new arrival with interest, waiting for his first sight of Stanley Rode.

Several tradesmen arrived, pressed into bulging serge and black ties, and formed a small group south of the aisle, away from the staff and their wives. Soon they were joined by other members of the town community, women who had known Mrs Rode at the Tabernacle; and then by Rigby, who looked straight at Smiley and gave no sign. Then on the stroke of three a tall old man walked slowly through the doorway, looking straight before him, neither knowing nor seeing anyone. Beside him was Stanley Rode.

It was a face which at first sight meant nothing to Smiley, seeming to have neither the imprint of temperament nor the components of character; it was a shallow, ordinary face, inclining to plumpness, and lacking quality. It matched his short, ordinary body and his black, ordinary hair; it was suitably compressed into an expression of sorrow. As Smiley watched him turn into the centre aisle and take his place among the principal mourners, it occurred to him that Rode's very walk and bearing successfully conveyed something entirely alien to Carne. If it is vulgar to wear a pen in the breast pocket of your jacket, to favour Fair Isle pullovers and brown ties, to bob a little and turn your feet out as you walk, then Rode beyond a shadow of doubt was vulgar, for though he did not now commit these sins, his manner implied them all.

They followed the coffin into the churchyard and gathered round the open grave. D'Arcy and Fielding were standing together, seemingly intent upon the service. The tall, elderly figure who had entered the churchyard with Rode was now visibly moved, and Smiley guessed that he was Stella's father, Samuel Glaston. As the service ended, the old man walked quickly away from the crowd, nodding briefly to Rode, and disappeared into the church. He seemed to struggle as he went, like a man walking against a strong wind.

The little group moved slowly away from the graveside, until only Rode remained, an oddly stiff figure, taut and constrained, his eyes wide but somehow sightless, his mouth set in a strict, pedagogic line. Then, as Smiley watched, Rode seemed to wake from a dream; his body suddenly relaxed and he too walked slowly but quite confidently away from the grave towards the small group which by now had reassembled at the churchyard gate. As he did so, Fielding, at the edge of the group, caught sight of him approaching and, to Smiley's astonishment, walked deliberately and quite quickly away with an expression of strong distaste. It was not the calculated act of a man wishing to insult another, for it attracted the notice neither of Rode nor of anyone else standing by. Terence Fielding, for once, appeared to be in the grip of a genuine emotion, and indifferent to the impression he created.

Reluctantly Smiley approached the group. Rode was rather to one side, the D'Arcys were there, and three or four members of the staff. No one was talking much.

'Mr Rode?' he inquired.

'That's right, yes.' He spoke slowly, a trace of an accent carefully avoided.

'I'm representing Miss Brimley of the *Christian Voice*.'

'Oh, yes.'

'She was most anxious that the journal should be represented. I thought you would like to know that.'

'I saw your wreath; very kind, I am sure.'

'Your wife was one of our most loyal supporters,' Smiley continued. 'We regarded her almost as one of the family.'

'Yes, she was very keen on the *Voice*.' Smiley wondered whether Rode was always as impassive as this, or whether bereavement had made him listless.

'When did you come?' Rode asked suddenly.

'Yesterday.'

'Making a week-end of it, eh?'

Smiley was so astonished that for a moment he could think of nothing to say. Rode was still looking at him, waiting for an answer.

'I have one or two friends here . . . Mr Fielding . . . '

'Oh, Terence.' Smiley was convinced that Rode was not on Christian-name terms with Fielding.

'I would like, if I may,' Smiley ventured, 'to write a small obituary for Miss Brimley. Would you have any objection?'

'Stella would have liked that.'

'If you are not too upset, perhaps I could call round tomorrow for one or two details?'

'Certainly.'

'Eleven o'clock?'

'It will be a pleasure,' Rode replied, almost pertly, and they walked together to the churchyard gate.

9. *The Mourners*

It was a cheap trick to play on a man who had suddenly lost his wife. Smiley knew that. As he gently unlatched the gate and entered the drive, where two nights ago he had conducted his strange conversation with Jane Lyn, he acknowledged that in calling on Rode under any pretext at such a time he was committing a thoroughly unprincipled act. It was a peculiarity of Smiley's character that throughout the whole of his clandestine work he had never managed to reconcile the means to the end. A stringent critic of his own motives, he had discovered after long observation that he tended to be less a creature of intellect than his tastes and habits might suggest; once in the war he had been described by his superiors as possessing the cunning of Satan and the conscience of a virgin, which seemed to him not wholly unjust.

He pressed the bell and waited.

Stanley Rode opened the door. He was very neatly dressed, very scrubbed.

'Oh hullo,' he said, as if they were old friends. 'I say, you haven't got a car, have you?'

'I'm afraid I left it in London.'

'Never mind.' Rode sounded disappointed. 'Thought we might have gone out for a drive, had a chat as we went. I get a bit fed-up, kicking around here on my own. Miss D'Arcy asked me to stay over at their place. Very good people they are, very good indeed; but somehow I didn't wish it, not yet.'

'I understand.'

'Do you?' They were in the hall now, Smiley was getting out of his overcoat, Rode waiting to receive it. 'I don't think many do – the loneliness I mean. Do you know what they've done, the Master and Mr D'Arcy? They meant it well, I know. They've farmed out all my correcting – my exam. correcting, you understand. What am I supposed to do here, all on my own? I've no teaching, nothing; they've all taken a hand. You'd think they wanted to get rid of me.'

Smiley nodded vaguely. They moved towards the drawing-room, Rode leading the way.

'I know they did it for the best, as I said. But after all, I've got to spend the time somehow. Simon Snow got some of my division to correct. Have you met him by any chance? Sixty-one per cent he gave one boy – sixty-one. The boy's an absolute fool; I told Fielding at the beginning of the Half that he wouldn't possibly get his remove. Perkins his name is, a nice enough boy; head of Fielding's house. He'd have been lucky to get thirty per cent ... sixty-one, Snow gave him. I haven't seen the papers yet, of course, but it's impossible, quite impossible.'

They sat down.

'Not that I don't want the boy to get on. He's a nice enough boy, nothing special, but well-mannered. Mrs Rode and I meant to have him here to tea this Half. We would have done, in fact, if it hadn't been for ... ' There was a moment's silence. Smiley was going to speak when Rode stood up and said:

'I've a kettle on the stove, Mr ... '

'Smiley.'

'I've a kettle on the stove, Mr Smiley. May I make you a cup of coffee?' That little stiff voice with the corners carefully defined, like a hired morning suit, thought Smiley.

Rode returned a few minutes later with a tray and measured their coffee in precise quantities, according to their taste.

Smiley found himself continually irritated by Rode's social assumptions, and his constant struggle to conceal his origin. You could tell at the time, from every word and gesture, what he was; from the angle of his elbow as he drank his coffee, from the swift, expert pluck at the knee of his trouser leg as he sat down.

'I wonder,' Smiley began, 'whether perhaps I might now ... '

'Go ahead, Mr Smiley.'

'We are, of course, largely interested in Mrs Rode's association with ... our Church.'

'Quite.'

'You were married at Branxome, I believe.'

'Branxome Hill Tabernacle; fine church.' D'Arcy wouldn't have liked the way he said that; cocksure lad on a motor-bike. Pencils in the outside pocket.

'When was that?'

'September, fifty-one.'

'Did Mrs Rode engage in charitable work in Branxome? I know she was very active here.'

'No, not at Branxome, but a lot here. She had to look after her father at Branxome, you see. It was refugee relief she was keen on here. That didn't get going much until late 1956 – the Hungarians began it, and then this last year ... '

Smiley peered thoughtfully at Rode from behind his spectacles, forgot himself, blinked, and looked away.

'Did she take a large part in the social activities of Carne? Does the staff have its own Women's Institute and so on?' he asked innocently.

'She did a bit, yes. But, being Chapel, she kept mainly with the Chapel people from the town ... you should ask Mr Cardew about that; he's the Minister.'

'But may I say, Mr Rode, that she took an active part in school affairs
as well?'

Rode hesitated.

'Yes, of course,' he said.

'Thank you.'

There was a moment's silence, then Smiley continued: 'Our readers
will, of course, remember Mrs Rode as the winner of our Kitchen Hints
competition. Was she a good cook, Mr Rode?'

'Very good, for plain things, not fancy.'

'Is there any little fact that you would specially like us to include,
anything she herself would like to be remembered by?'

Rode looked at him with expressionless eyes. Then he shrugged.

'No, not really. I can't think of anything. Oh, you could say her father
was a magistrate up North. She was proud of that.'

Smiley finished his coffee and stood up.

'You've been very patient with me, Mr Rode. We're most grateful, I
assure you. I'll take care to send you an advance copy of our notice.'

'Thanks. I did it for her, you see. She liked the *Voice*; always did. Grew
up with it.'

They shook hands.

'By the way, do you know where I can find old Mr Glaston? Is he staying
in Carne or has he returned to Branxome?'

'He was up here yesterday. He's going back to Branxome this afternoon.
The police wanted to see him before he left.'

'I see.'

'He's staying at the Sawley.'

'Thank you. I might try and see him before I go.'

'When do you leave, then?'

'Quite soon, I expect. Good-bye, then, Mr Rode. Incidentally – ' Smiley
began.

'Yes?'

'If ever you're in London and at a loose end, if ever you want a chat . . .
and a cup of tea, we're always pleased to see you at the *Voice*, you know.
Always.'

'Thanks. Thanks very much, Mr – '

'Smiley.'

'Thanks, that's very decent. No one's said that to me for a long time. I'll
take you up on that one day. Very good of you.'

'Good-bye.' Again they shook hands; Rode's was dry and cool. Smooth.

He returned to the Sawley Arms, sat himself at a desk in the empty
residents' lounge and wrote a note to Mr Glaston:

Dear Mr Glaston,
    I am here on behalf of Miss Brimley of the *Christian Voice*. I have

some letters from Stella which I think you would like to see. Forgive me for bothering you at this sad moment: I understand you are leaving Carne this afternoon and wondered if I might see you before you left.

He carefully sealed the envelope and took it to the reception desk. There was no one there, so he rang the bell and waited. At last a porter came, an old turnkey with a grey, bristly face, and after examining the envelope critically for a long time, he agreed, against an excessive fee, to convey it to Mr Glaston's room. Smiley stayed at the desk, waiting for his answer.

Smiley himself was one of those solitaries who seem to have come into the world fully educated at the age of eighteen. Obscurity was his nature, as well as his profession. The byways of espionage are not populated by the brash and colourful adventurers of fiction. A man who, like Smiley, has lived and worked for years among his country's enemies learns only one prayer: that he may never, never be noticed. Assimilation is his highest aim, he learns to love the crowds who pass him in the street without a glance; he clings to them for his anonymity and his safety. His fear makes him servile – he could embrace the shoppers who jostle him in their impatience, and force him from the pavement. He could adore the officials, the police, the bus conductors, for the terse indifference of their attitudes.

But this fear, this servility, this dependence, had developed in Smiley a perception for the colour of human beings: a swift, feminine sensitivity to their characters and motives. He knew mankind as a huntsman knows his cover, as a fox the wood. For a spy must hunt while he is hunted, and the crowd is his estate. He could collect their gestures and their words, record the interplay of glance and movement, as a huntsman can record the twisted bracken and the broken twig, or as a fox detects the signs of danger.

Thus, while he waited patiently for Glaston's reply and recalled the crowded events of the last forty-eight hours, he was able to order and assess them with detachment. What was the cause of D'Arcy's attitude to Fielding, as if they were unwilling partners to a shabby secret? Staring across the neglected hotel gardens towards Carne Abbey, he was able to glimpse behind the lead roof of the Abbey the familiar battlements of the school: keeping the new world out and the old world secure. In his mind's eye he saw the Great Court now, as the boys came out of Chapel: the black-coated groups in the leisured attitudes of eighteenth-century England. And he remembered the other school beside the police station: Carne High School; a little tawdry place like a porter's lodge in an empty graveyard, as detached from the tones of Carne as its brick and flint from the saffron battlements of School Hall.

Yes, he reflected, Stanley Rode had made a long, long journey from the Grammar School at Branxome. And if he killed his wife, then the motive, Smiley was sure, and even the means, were to be found in that hard road to Carne.

*

'It was kind of you to come,' said Glaston; 'kind of Miss Brimley to send you. They're good people at the *Voice*; always were.' He said this as if 'good' were an absolute quality with which he was familiar.

'You'd better read the letters, Mr Glaston. The second one will shock you, I'm afraid, but I'm sure you'll agree that it would be wrong of me not to show it to you.' They were sitting in the lounge, the mammoth plants like sentinels beside them.

He handed Glaston the two letters, and the old man took them firmly and read them. He held them a good way from him to read, thrusting his strong head back, his eyes half closed, the crisp line of his mouth turned down at the corners. At last he said:

'You were with Miss Brimley in the war, were you?'

'I worked with John Landsbury, yes.'

'I see. That's why she came to you?'

'Yes.'

'Are you Chapel?'

'No.'

He was silent for a while, his hands folded on his lap, the letters before him on the table.

'Stanley was Chapel when they married. Then he went over. Did you know that?'

'Yes.'

'Where I come from in the North, we don't do that. Chapel was something we'd stood up for and won. Almost like the Vote.'

'I know.'

His back was as straight as a soldier's. He looked stern rather than sad. Quite suddenly, his eyes turned towards Smiley, and he looked at him long and carefully.

'Are you a schoolmaster?' he asked, and it occurred to Smiley that in his day Samuel Glaston had been a very shrewd man of business.

'No . . . I'm more or less retired.'

'Married?'

'I was.'

Again the old man fell silent, and Smiley wished he had left him alone.

'She was a great one for chatter,' he said at last.

Smiley said nothing.

'Have you told the police?'

'Yes, but they knew already. That is, they knew that Stella thought her husband was going to murder her. She'd tried to tell Mr Cardew . . . '

'The Minister?'

'Yes. He thought she was overwrought and . . . deluded.'

'Do you think she wasn't?'

'I don't know. I just don't know. But from what I have heard of your daughter I don't believe she was unbalanced. *Something* roused her suspicions, something frightened her very much. I don't believe we can just disregard that. I don't believe it was a coincidence that she was frightened before she died. And therefore I don't believe that the beggar-woman murdered her.'

Samuel Glaston nodded slowly. It seemed to Smiley that the old man was trying to show interest, partly to be polite, and partly because if he did not it would be a confession that he had lost interest in life itself.

Then, after a long silence, he carefully folded up the letters and gave them back. Smiley waited for him to speak, but he said nothing.

After a few moments Smiley got up and walked quietly from the room.

10. *Little Women*

S hane Hecht smiled, and drank some more sherry. 'You must be dreadfully important,' she said to Smiley, 'for D'Arcy to serve decent sherry. What are you, *Almanach de Gotha?*'

'I'm afraid not. D'Arcy and I were both dining at Terence Fielding's on Friday night and D'Arcy asked me for sherry.'

'Terence is *wicked*, isn't he? Charles loathes him. I'm afraid they see Sparta in *quite* different ways ... Poor Terence. It's his last Half, you know.'

'I know.'

'So sweet of you to come to the funeral yesterday. I hate funerals, don't you? Black is so insanitary. I always remember King George V's funeral. Lord Sawley was at Court in those days, and gave Charles two tickets. So kind. I always think it's *spoilt* us for ordinary funerals in a way. Although I'm never quite *sure* about funerals, are you? I have a suspicion that they are largely a lower-class recreation; cherry brandy and seed cake in the parlour. I think the tendency of people like ourselves is for a *quiet* funeral these days; no flowers, just a short obituary and a memorial service later.' Her small eyes were bright with pleasure. She finished her sherry and held out her empty glass to Smiley.

'Would you mind, dear? I hate sherry, but Felix is so mean.'

Smiley filled her glass from the decanter on the table.

'Dreadful about the murder, wasn't it? That beggar-woman must be mad. Stella Rode was such a nice person, I always thought ... and so *unusual*. She did such clever things with the same dress . . . But she had such curious friends. All for Hans the woodcutter and Pedro the fisherman, if you know what I mean.'

'Was she popular at Carne?'

Shane Hecht laughed gently: 'No one is popular at Carne . . . but she wasn't easy to like . . . She would wear black crêpe on Sundays . . . Forgive me, but do the lower classes always do that? The townspeople liked her, I believe. They adore anyone who betrays Carne. But then she was a Christian Scientist or something.'

'Baptist, I understand,' said Smiley unthinkingly.

She looked at him for a moment with unfeigned curiosity. 'How sweet,' she murmured. 'Tell me, what *are* you?'

Smiley made some facetious reply about being unemployed, and realised that it was only by a hair's-breadth that he had avoided explaining himself to Shane Hecht like a small boy. Her very ugliness, her size and voice, coupled with the sophisticated malice of her conversation, gave her the dangerous quality of command. Smiley was tempted to compare her with Fielding, but for Fielding other people scarcely existed. For Shane Hecht they did exist: they were there to be found wanting in the minute tests of social behaviour, to be ridiculed, cut off and destroyed.

'I read in the paper that her father was quite well off. From the North. Second generation. Remarkable really how *unspoilt* she was . . . so natural . . . You wouldn't think she *needed* to go to the launderette or to make friends with beggars . . . Though, of course, the Midlands are different, aren't they? Only about three good families between Ipswich and Newcastle. Where did you say you came from, dear?'

'London.'

'How nice. I went to tea with Stella once. Milk in first and Indian. So different,' and she looked at Smiley suddenly and said, 'I'll tell you something. She almost aroused an admiration in me, I found her so insufferable. She was one of those tiresome little snobs who think that only the humble are virtuous.' Then she smiled and added, 'I even agreed with Charles about Stella Rode, and that's saying something. If you're a student of mankind, do go and have a look at him, the contrast is riveting.' But at that moment they were joined by D'Arcy's sister, a bony, virile woman with untidy grey hair and an arrogant, hunting mouth.

'Dorothy darling,' Shane murmured; 'such a lovely party. So *kind*. And so *exciting* to meet somebody from London, don't you think? We were talking about poor Mrs Rode's funeral.'

'Stella Rode may have been damn' bad form, Shane, but she did a lot for my refugees.'

'Refugees?' asked Smiley innocently.

'Hungarians. Collecting for them. Clothes, furniture, money. One of the few wives who *did* anything.' She looked sharply at Shane Hecht, who was smiling benignly past her towards her husband: 'Busy little creature, she was; didn't mind rolling her sleeves up, going from door to door. Got her little women on to it too at the Baptist chapel and brought in a mass of stuff. You've got to hand it to them, you know. They've got *spirit*. Felix, more sherry!'

There were about twenty in the two rooms, but Smiley, who had arrived a little late, found himself attached to a group of about eight who stood nearest the door: D'Arcy and his sister; Charles and Shane Hecht; a young mathematician called Snow and his wife; a curate from the Abbey and Smiley himself, bewildered and mole-like behind his spectacles. Smiley looked quickly round the room, but could see no sign of Fielding.

' . . . Yes,' Dorothy D'Arcy continued, 'she was a good little worker, very . . . right to the end. I went over there on Friday with that parson man from the tin tabernacle – Cardew – to see if there was any refugee stuff to tidy up. There wasn't a thing out of place – every bit of clothing she had was all packed up and addressed; we just had to send it off. She was a damn' good little worker, I will say. Did a splendid job at the bazaar, you know.'

'Yes, darling,' said Shane Hecht sweetly. 'I remember it well. It was the day I presented her to Lady Sawley. She wore such a *nice* little hat – the one she wore on Sundays, you know. And *so* respectful. She called her "my lady".' She turned to Smiley and breathed: 'Rather feudal, don't you think, dear? I always like that: so few of us left.'

The mathematician and his wife were talking to Charles Hecht in a corner and a few minutes later Smiley managed to extricate himself from the group and join them.

Ann Snow was a pretty girl with a rather square face and a turned-up nose. Her husband was tall and thin, with an agreeable stoop. He held his sherry glass between straight, slender fingers as if it were a chemical retort and when he spoke he seemed to address the sherry rather than his listener; Smiley remembered them from the funeral. Hecht was looking pink and rather cross, sucking at his pipe. They talked in a desultory way, their conversation dwarfed by the exchanges of the adjoining group. Hecht eventually drifted away from them, still frowning and withdrawn, and stood ostentatiously alone near the door.

'Poor Stella,' said Ann Snow after a moment's silence. 'Sorry,' she added. 'I can't get her out of my mind yet. It seems mad, just mad. I mean why should she *do* it, that Janie woman?'

'Did you like Stella?' Smiley asked.

'Of course we did. She was sweet. We've been here four Halves now, but she was the only person here who's ever been *kind* to us.' Her husband said nothing, just nodded at his sherry. 'Simon wasn't a boy at Carne, you see – most of the staff were – so we didn't know anyone and no one was really interested. They all pretended to be terribly pleased with us, of course, but it was Stella who really . . . '

Dorothy D'Arcy was descending on them. 'Mrs Snow,' she said crisply,

'I've been meaning to talk to you. I want you to take over Stella Rode's job on the refugees.' She cast an appraising look in Simon's direction: 'The Master's very keen on refugees.'

'Oh, my goodness!' Ann Snow replied, aghast. 'I couldn't possibly, Miss D'Arcy, I . . . '

'Couldn't? Why couldn't you? You helped Mrs Rode with her stall at the bazaar, didn't you?'

'So that's where she got her clothes from,' breathed Shane Hecht behind them. Ann was fumbling on:

'But . . . well I haven't quite got Stella's nerve, if you understand what I mean; and besides, she was a Baptist: all the locals helped her and gave her things, and they all liked her. With me it would be different.'

'Lot of damn' nonsense,' declared Miss D'Arcy, who spoke to all her juniors as if they were grooms or erring children; and Shane Hecht beside her said: 'Baptists are the people who don't like private pews, aren't they? I do so agree – one feels that if one's paid one simply has to go.'

The curate, who had been talking cricket in a corner, was startled into mild protest: 'Oh, come, Mrs Hecht, the private pew had many advantages . . . ' and embarked on a diffuse apologia for ancient custom, to which Shane listened with every sign of the most assiduous interest. When at last he finished she said: 'Thank you, William dear, so sweet,' turned her back on him and added to Smiley in a stage whisper: 'William Trumper – one of Charles's old pupils – such a triumph when he passed his Certificate.'

Smiley, anxious to dissociate himself from Shane Hecht's vengeance on the curate, turned to Ann Snow, but she was still at the mercy of Miss D'Arcy's charitable intentions, and Shane was still talking to him:

'The only Smiley I ever heard of married Lady Ann Sercombe at the end of the war. She left him soon afterwards, of course. A very curious match. I understand he was quite unsuitable. She was Lord Sawley's cousin, you know. The Sawleys have been connected with Carne for four hundred years. The present heir is a pupil of Charles; we often dine at the Castle. I never did hear what became of Ann Sercombe . . . she went to Africa, you know . . . or was it India? No, it was America. So tragic. One doesn't talk about it at the Castle.' For a moment the noise in the room stopped. For a moment, no more, he could discern nothing but the steady gaze of Shane Hecht upon him, and knew she was waiting for an answer. And then she released him as if to say: 'I could crush you, you see. But I won't, I'll let you live,' and she turned and walked away.

He contrived to take his leave at the same time as Ann and Simon Snow. They had an old car and insisted on running Smiley back to his hotel. On the way there, he said:

'If you have nothing better to do, I would be happy to give you both dinner at my hotel. I imagine the food is dreadful.'

The Snows protested and accepted, and a quarter of an hour later they were all three seated in a corner of the enormous dining-room of the Sawley Arms, to the great despondency of three waiters and a dozen generations of Lord Sawley's forebears, puffy men in crumbling pigment.

'We really got to know her our second Half,' Ann Snow ran on. 'Stella didn't do much mixing with the other wives – she'd learnt her lesson by then. She didn't go to coffee parties and things, so it was really luck that we did meet. When we first came there wasn't a staff house available for us: we had to spend the first Half in a hotel. We moved in to a little house in Bread Street at the end of our second Half. Moving was chaos – Simon was examining for the scholarships and we were terribly broke, so we had to do everything we possibly could for ourselves. It was a wet Thursday morning when we moved. The rain was simply teeming down; but none of our good pieces would get in through the front door, and in the end Mulligan's just dumped me on the doorstep and let me sort it out.' She laughed, and Smiley thought what an agreeable child she was. 'They were absolutely foul. They would have just driven off, I think, but they wanted a cheque as soon as they'd done the delivery, and the bill was pounds more than the estimate. I hadn't got the cheque-book, of course. Simon had gone off with it. Mulligan's even threatened to take all the stuff away again. It was monstrous. I think I was nearly in tears.' She nearly is now, thought Smiley. 'Then out of the blue Stella turned up. I can't think how she even knew we were moving – I'm sure no one else did. She'd brought an overall and an old pair of shoes and she'd come to help. When she saw what was going on she didn't bother with the men at all, just went to a phone and rang Mr Mulligan himself. I don't know what she said to him, but she made the foreman talk to him afterwards and there was no more trouble after that. She was terribly happy – happy to *help*. She was that sort of person. They took the door right out and managed to get everything in. She was marvellous at helping without managing. The rest of the wives,' she added bitterly, 'are awfully good at managing, but don't help at all.'

Smiley nodded, and discreetly filled their glasses.

'Simon's leaving,' Ann said, suddenly confidential. 'He's got a grant and we're going back to Oxford. He's going to do a DPhil and get a University job.'

They drank to his success, and the conversation turned to other things until Smiley asked: 'What's Rode himself like to work with?'

'He's a good schoolmaster,' said Simon, slowly, 'but tiring as a colleague.'

'Oh, he was *quite* different from Stella,' said Ann; 'terribly Carne-minded. D'Arcy adopted him and he got the bug. Simon says all the grammar school people go that way – it's the fury of the convert. It's sickening. He even changed his religion when he got to Carne. Stella didn't, though; she wouldn't dream of it.'

'The Established Church has much to offer Carne,' Simon observed, and Smiley enjoyed the dry precision of his delivery.

'Stella can't exactly have hit it off with Shane Hecht,' Smiley probed gently.

'Of *course* she didn't!' Ann declared angrily. 'Shane was horrid to her, always sneering at her because she was honest and simple about the things she liked. Shane hated Stella – I think it was because Stella didn't *want* to be a lady of quality. She was quite happy to be herself. That's what really worried Shane. Shane likes people to compete so that she can make fools of them.'

'So does Carne,' said Simon, quietly.

'She was awfully good at helping out with the refugees. That was how she got into real trouble.' Ann Snow's slim hands gently rocked her brandy glass.

'Trouble?'

'Just before she died. Hasn't anyone told you? About her frightful row with D'Arcy's sister?'

'No.'

'Of course, they wouldn't have done. Stella never gossiped.'

'Let me tell you,' said Simon. 'It's a good story. When the Refugee Year business started, Dorothy D'Arcy was fired with charitable enthusiasm. So was the Master. Dorothy's enthusiasms always seem to correspond with his. She started collecting clothes and money and packing them off to London. All very laudable, but there was a perfectly good town appeal going, launched by the Mayor. That wasn't good enough for Dorothy, though: the school must have its own appeal; you can't mix your charity. I think Felix was largely behind it. Anyway, after the thing had been going for a few months the refugee centre in London apparently wrote to Dorothy and asked whether anyone would be prepared to accommodate a refugee couple. Instead of publicising the letter, Dorothy wrote straight back and said she would put them up herself. So far so good. The couple turned up, Dorothy and Felix pointed a proud finger at them and the local press wrote it all up as an example of British humanity.

'About six weeks later, one afternoon, these two turned up on Stella's doorstep. The Rodes and the D'Arcys are neighbours, you see, and anyway Stella had tried to take an interest in Dorothy's refugees. The woman was in floods of tears and the husband was shouting blue murder, but that didn't worry Stella. She had them straight into the drawing-room and gave them a cup of tea. Finally, they managed to explain in basic English that they had run away from the D'Arcys because of the treatment they received. The girl was expected to work from morning till night in the kitchen, and the husband was acting as unpaid kennel-boy for those beastly spaniels that Dorothy breeds. The ones without noses.'

'King Charles,' Ann prompted.

'It was about as awful as it could be. The girl was pregnant and he was a fully qualified engineer, so neither of them were exactly suited to domestic service. They told Stella that Dorothy was away till the evening – she'd gone to a dog show. Stella advised them to stay with her for the time being, and that evening she went round and told Dorothy what had happened. She had quite a nerve, you see. Although it wasn't nerve really. She just did the simple thing. Dorothy was furious, and demanded that Stella should return "her refugees" immediately. Stella replied that she was sure that they wouldn't come, and went home. When Stella got home she rang up the refugee people in London and asked their advice. They sent a woman down to see Dorothy and the couple, and the result was that they returned to London the following day . . . You can imagine what Shane Hecht would have made of that story.'

'Didn't she ever find out?'

'Stella never told anyone except us, and we didn't pass it on. Dorothy just let it be known that the refugees had gone to some job in London, and that was that.'

'How long ago did this happen?'

'They left exactly three weeks ago,' said Ann to her husband. 'Stella told me about it when she came to supper the night you were in Oxford for your interview. That was three weeks ago tonight.' She turned to Smiley:

'Poor Simon's been having an awful time. Felix D'Arcy unloaded all Rode's exam. correcting on to him. It's bad enough doing one person's correction – two is frantic.'

'Yes,' replied Simon reflectively. 'It's been a bad week. And rather humiliating in a way. Several of the boys who were up to me for science last Half are now in Rode's forms. I'd regarded one or two of them as practically unteachable, but Rode seems to have brought them on marvellously. I corrected one boy's paper – Perkins – sixty-one per cent for elementary science. Last Half he got fifteen per cent in a much easier paper. He only got his remove because Fielding raised hell. He was in Fielding's house.'

'Oh I know – a red-haired boy, a prefect.'

'Good Lord,' cried Simon. 'Don't say you know him?'

'Oh, Fielding introduced us,' said Smiley vaguely. 'Incidentally – no one else ever mentioned that incident to you about Miss D'Arcy's refugees, did they? Confirmed it, as it were?'

Ann Snow looked at him oddly. 'No. Stella told us about it, but of course Dorothy D'Arcy never referred to it at all. She must have *hated* Stella, though.'

He saw them to their car, and waited despite their protests while Simon cranked it. At last they drove off, the car bellowing down the silent street. Smiley stood for a moment on the pavement, an odd, lonely figure peering down the empty road.

11. A Coat to Keep Her Warm

A dog that had not bitten the postman; a devil that rode upon the wind; a woman who knew that she would die; a little, worried man in an overcoat standing in the snow outside his hotel, and the laborious chime of the Abbey clock telling him to go to bed.

Smiley hesitated, then with a shrug crossed the road to the hotel entrance, mounted the step and entered the cheap, yellow light of the residents' hall. He walked slowly up the stairs.

He detested the Sawley Arms. That muted light in the hall was typical: inefficient, antiquated and smug. Like the waiters in the dining-room and the lowered voices in the residents' lounge, like his own hateful bedroom with its blue and gilt urns, and the framed tapestry of a Buckinghamshire garden.

His room was bitterly cold; the maid must have opened the window. He put a shilling in the meter and lit the gas. The fire bubbled grumpily and went out. Muttering, Smiley looked around for some paper to write on, and discovered some, much to his surprise, in the drawer of the writing desk. He changed into his pyjamas and dressing-gown and crawled miserably into bed. After sitting there uncomfortably for some minutes he got up, fetched his overcoat and spread it over the eiderdown. A coat for to keep her warm . . .

How did her statement read? 'There's one will thank me, that's my darling and I took her jewels for the saints I did, and a coat for to keep me warm . . . ' The coat had been given to Stella last Wednesday for the refugees. It seemed reasonable to assume from the way the statement read that Janie had taken the coat from the outhouse at the same time as she took the beads from Stella's body. But Dorothy D'Arcy had been round there on Friday morning – of course she had, with Mr Cardew – she was talking about it at her party that very evening: 'There wasn't a thing out of place – every bit of clothing she had was all packed up and addressed – a damn' good little worker, I will say . . . ' Then why hadn't Stella packed the overcoat? If she packed everything else, why not the overcoat too?

Or had Janie stolen the coat earlier in the day, before Stella made her parcel? If that was so, it went some way to weakening the case against her. But it was not so. It was not so because it was utterly improbable that Janie should steal a coat in the afternoon and return to the house the same evening.

'Start at the beginning,' Smiley muttered, a little sententiously, to the crested paper on his lap. 'Janie stole the coat at the same time as she stole the beads – that is, after Stella was dead. Therefore either the coat was not packed with the other clothes, or . . . '

Or what? *Or somebody else somebody who was not Stella Rode, packed up the clothes after Stella had died and before Dorothy D'Arcy and Mr Cardew went round to North Fields on Friday morning. And why the devil, thought Smiley, should anyone do that?*

It had been one of Smiley's cardinal principles in research, whether among the incunabula of an obscure poet or the laboriously gathered fragments of intelligence, not to proceed beyond the evidence. A fact, once logically arrived at, should not be extended beyond its natural significance. Accordingly he did not speculate with the remarkable discovery he had made, but turned his mind to the most obscure problem of all: motive for murder.

He began writing:

'Dorothy D'Arcy – resentment after refugee fiasco. As a motive for murder – definitely thin.' Yet why did she seem to go out of her way to sing Stella's praises?

'Felix D'Arcy – resented Stella Rode for not observing Carne's standards. As a motive for murder – ludicrous.

'Shane Hecht – hatred.

'Terence Fielding – in a sane world, no conceivable motive.'

Yet was it a sane world? Year in year out they must share the same life, say the same things to the same people, sing the same hymns. They had no money, no hope. The world changed, fashion changed; the women saw it second-hand in the glossy papers, took in their dresses and pinned up their hair, and hated their husbands a little more. Shane Hecht – did she kill Stella Rode? Did she conceal in the sterile omniscience of her huge body not only hatred and jealousy, but the courage to kill? Was she frightened for her stupid husband, frightened of Rode's promotion, of his cleverness? Was she really so angry when Stella refused to take part in the rat race of gentility?

Rigby was right – it was impossible to know. You had to be ill, you had to be sick to understand, you had to be there in the sanatorium, not for weeks, but for years, had to be one in the line of white beds, to know the smell of their food and the greed in their eyes. You had to hear it and see it, to be part of it, to know their rules and recognise their transgressions. This world was compressed into a mould of anomalous conventions: blind, pharisaical but real.

Yet some things were written plain enough: the curious bond which tied Felix D'Arcy and Terence Fielding despite their mutual dislike; D'Arcy's reluctance to discuss the night of the murder; Fielding's evident preference for Stella Rode rather than her husband; Shane Hecht's contempt for everyone.

He could not get Shane out of his mind. If Carne were a rational place, and somebody had to die, then Shane Hecht should clearly be the one. She was a depository of other people's secrets, she had an infallible sense of weakness. Had she not found even Smiley out? She had taunted him with his wretched marriage, she had played with him for her own pleasure. Yes, she was an admirable candidate for murder.

But why on earth should Stella die? Why and how? Who tied up the parcel after her death? And why?

He tried to sleep, but could not. Finally, as the Abbey clock chimed three, he put the light on again and sat up. The room was much warmer and at first Smiley wondered if someone had switched on the central heating in the middle of the night, after it had been off all day. Then he became aware of the sound of rain outside; he went to the window and parted the curtains. A steady rain was falling; by tomorrow the snow would be washed away. Two policemen walked slowly down the road; he could hear the squelch of their boots as they trod in the melting snow. Their wet capes glistened in the arc of the street lamp.

And suddenly he seemed to hear Rigby's voice: 'Blood everywhere. Whoever killed her must have been covered in it.' And then Mad Janie calling to him across the moonlit snow: 'Janie seed 'im . . . silver wings like fishes . . . flying on the wind . . . there's not many seen the devil fly . . .' Of course: the parcel! He remained a long time at the window, watching the rain. Finally, content at last, he climbed back into bed and fell asleep.

He tried to telephone Miss Brimley throughout the morning. Each time she was out and he left no message. Eventually, at about midday, he spoke to her:

'George, I'm terribly sorry – some missionary is in London – I had to go for an interview and I've got a Baptist Conference this afternoon. They've both got to be in this week. Will first thing tomorrow do?'

'Yes,' said Smiley. 'I'm sure it will.' There was no particular hurry. There were one or two ends he wanted to tie up that afternoon, anyway.

12. *Uncomfortable Words*

H e enjoyed the bus. The conductor was a very surly man with a great deal to say about the bus company, and why it lost money. Gently encouraged by Smiley, he expanded wonderfully so that by the time they arrived at Sturminster he had transformed the Directors of the Dorset and General Traction Company into a herd of Gadarene swine charging into the abyss of voluntary bankruptcy. The conductor directed Smiley to the Sturminster kennels, and when he alighted in the tiny village, he set out confidently towards a group of cottages which stood about a quarter of a mile beyond the church, on the Okeford road.

He had a nasty feeling he wasn't going to like Mr Harriman. The very fact that D'Arcy had described him as a superior type of person inclined Smiley against him. Smiley was not opposed to social distinctions but he liked to make his own.

A notice stood at the gate: '*Sturminster Kennels, proprietor C. J. Reid-Harriman, Veterinary Surgeon. Breeder of Alsatian and Labrador Dogs. Boarding.*'

A narrow path led to what seemed to be a backyard. There was washing everywhere, shirts, underclothes, and sheets, most of it khaki. There was a rich smell of dog. There was a rusted hand-pump with a dozen or so dog leads draped over it, and there was a small girl. She watched him sadly as he picked his way through the thick mud towards the door. He pulled on the bell-rope and waited. He tried again, and the child said:

'It doesn't work. It's bust. It's been bust for years.'

'Is anyone at home?' Smiley asked.

'I'll see,' she replied coolly, and after another long look at him she walked round the side of the house and disappeared from view. Then Smiley heard from inside the house the sound of someone approaching, and a moment later the door opened.

'Good day to you.' He had sandy hair and a moustache. He wore a khaki shirt and a khaki tie of a lighter shade; old Service dress trousers and a tweed jacket with leather buttons.

'Mr Harriman?'

'Major,' he replied lightly. 'Not that it matters, old boy. What can we do for you?'

'I'm thinking of buying an Alsatian,' Smiley replied, 'as a guard dog.'

'Surely. Come in, won't you. Lady wife's out. Ignore the child: she's from next door. Just hangs around; likes the dogs.' He followed Harriman into the living-room and they sat down. There was no fire.

'Where are you from?' Harriman asked.

'I'm staying at Carne at the moment; my father lives over at Dorchester. He's getting on and he's nervous, and he wants me to find him a good dog. There's a gardener to look after it in the daytime, feed it and exercise it and so on. The gardener doesn't live in at night, of course, and it's at night that the old man gets so worried. I've been meaning to get him a dog for some time – this recent business at Carne rather brought it home to me.' Harriman ignored the hint.

'Gardener good chap?'

'Yes, very.'

'You don't want anything brilliant,' said Harriman. 'You want a good, steady type. I'd take a bitch if I were you.' His hands were dark brown, his wrists too. His handkerchief was tucked into his cuff. Smiley noticed that his wrist-watch faced inwards, conforming with the obscure rites of the military *demi-monde* from which he seemed to come.

'What will it do, a dog like that? Will it attack, or what?'

'Depends how she's trained, old boy; depends how she's trained. She'll warn, though; that's the main thing. Frighten the fellers away. Shove a notice up, "Fierce Dog", let her sniff at the tradesmen a bit and the word will get around. You won't get a burglar within a mile of the place.'

They walked out into the garden again, and Harriman led the way to an enclosure with half a dozen Alsatian puppies yapping furiously at them through the wire.

'They're good little beasts, all of them,' he shouted. 'Game as hell.' He unlocked the door and finally emerged with a plump bitch puppy chewing fiercely at his jacket.

'This little lady might do you,' he said. 'We can't show her – she's too dark.'

Smiley pretended to hesitate, allowed Harriman to persuade him and finally agreed. They went back into the house.

'I'd like to pay a deposit,' said Smiley, 'and collect her in about ten days. Would that be all right?' He gave Harriman a cheque for five pounds and again they sat down, Harriman foraging in his desk for inoculation certificates and pedigrees. Then Smiley said:

'It's a pity Mrs Rode didn't have a dog, isn't it? I mean, it might have saved her life.'

'Oh, she *had* a dog, but she had it put down just before she was killed,' said Harriman. 'Damned odd story between ourselves. She was devoted to the beast. Odd little mongrel, bit of everything, but she loved it. Brought it here one day with some tale about it biting the postman, got me to put it down – said it was dangerous. It wasn't anything of the sort. Some friends of mine in Carne made inquiries. No complaints anywhere. Postman liked the brute. Damned silly sort of lie to tell in a small community. Bound to be found out.'

'Why on earth did she tell it then?'

Harriman made a gesture which particularly irritated Smiley. He ran his forefinger down the length of his nose, then flicked either side of his absurd moustache very quickly. There was something shamefaced about the whole movement, as if he were assuming the ways of senior officers, and fearful of rebuke.

'She was trouble,' he said crisply. 'I can spot 'em. I've had a few in the regiment, wives who are trouble. Little simpering types. Butter-wouldn't-melt, holier-than-thou. Arrange the flowers in the church and all that – pious as you please. I'd say she was the hysterical kind, self-dramatising, weeping all over the house for days on end. Anything for a bit of drama.'

'Was she popular?' Smiley offered him a cigarette.

'Shouldn't think so. Thanks. She wore black on Sundays, I gather. Typical. We used to call them "crows" out East, the ones who wore black – Sunday virgins. They were OD mostly – other denominations. Not C of E – some were Romans, mind . . . I hope I'm not . . . '

'Not at all.'

'You never know, do you? Can't stand 'em myself; no prejudice, but I don't like Romans – that's what my old father used to say.'

'Did you know her husband?'

'Not so well, poor devil, not so well.'

Harriman, Smiley reflected, seemed to have a great deal more sympathy for the living than the dead. Perhaps soldiers were like that. He wouldn't know.

'He's terribly cut up, I hear. Dreadful shock – fortunes of war, eh?' he added and Smiley nodded. 'He's the other type. Humble origin, good officer qualities, credit to the mess. Those are the ones that cut up most, the ones women get at.'

They walked along the path to the gate. Smiley said goodbye, and promised to return in a week or so to collect the puppy. As he walked away Harriman called to him:

'Oh – incidentally . . . '

Smiley stopped and turned round.

'I'll pay that cheque in, shall I, and credit you with the amount?'

'Of course,' said Smiley. 'That will do very well,' and he made his way to the bus stop pondering on the strange byways of the military mind.

The same bus took him back to Carne, the same conductor railed against his employers, the same driver drove the entire distance in second gear. He got out at the station and made his way to the red-brick Tabernacle. Gently opening the Gothic door, made of thickly-varnished ochre pine, he stepped inside. An elderly woman in an apron was polishing the heavy brass chandelier which hung over the centre aisle. He waited a moment, then tiptoed up to her and asked for the Minister. She pointed towards the vestry door. Obeying her mimed directions, he crossed to it, knocked and waited. A tall man in a clerical collar opened the door.

'I'm from the *Christian Voice*,' said Smiley quietly. 'Can I have a word with you?'

Mr Cardew led him through the side entrance and into a small vegetable garden, carefully tilled, with bright yellow paths running between the empty beds. The sun shone through the crisp air. It was a cold, beautiful day. They crossed the garden and entered a paddock. The ground was hard despite last night's rain, and the grass short. They strolled side by side, talking as they went.

'This is Lammas Land, belonging to the School. We hold our fêtes here in the summer. It's very practical.'

Cardew seemed a little out of character. Smiley, who had a rather childish distrust of clergymen, had expected a Wesleyan hammer, a wordy, forbidding man with a taste for imagery.

'Miss Brimley, our editor, sent me,' Smiley began. 'Mrs Rode subscribed to our journal; her family has taken it since it began. She was almost a part of the family. We wanted to write an obituary about her work for the Church.'

'I see.'

'I managed to have a word with her husband; we wanted to be sure to strike the right note.'

'What did he say?'

'He said I should speak to you about her work – her refugee work particularly.'

They walked on in silence for a while, then Cardew said, 'She came from up North, near Derby. Her father used to be a man of substance in the North – though money never altered him.'

'I know.'

'I've known the family for years, off and on. I saw her old father before the funeral.'

'What may I say about her work for the Church, her influence on the Chapel community here? May I say she was universally loved?'

'I'm afraid,' said Cardew, after a slight pause, 'that I don't hold much with that kind of writing, Mr Smiley. People are never universally loved, even when they're dead.' His North Country accent was strong.

'Then what may I say?' Smiley persisted.

'I don't know,' Cardew replied evenly. 'And when I don't know, I usually keep quiet. But since you're good enough to ask me, I've never met an angel, and Stella Rode was no exception.'

'But was she not a leading figure in refugee work?'

'Yes. Yes, she was.'

'And did she not encourage others to make similar efforts?'

'Of course. She was a good worker.'

They walked on together in silence. The path across the field led downwards, then turned and followed a stream which was almost hidden by the tangled gorse and hawthorn on either side. Beyond the stream was a row of stark elm trees, and behind them the familiar outline of Carne.

'Is that all you wanted to ask me?' said Cardew suddenly.

'No,' replied Smiley. 'Our editor was very worried by a letter she received from Mrs Rode just before her death. It was a kind of . . . accusation. We put the matter before the police. Miss Brimley reproaches herself in some way for not having been able to help her. It's illogical, perhaps, but there it is. I would like to be able to assure her that there was no connexion between Stella Rode's death and this letter. That is another reason for my visit . . .'

'Whom did the letter accuse?'

'Her husband.'

'I should tell your Miss Brimley,' said Cardew slowly, and with some emphasis, 'that she has nothing whatever for which to reproach herself.'

13. The Journey Home

I t was Monday evening. At about the time that Smiley returned to his hotel after his interview with Mr Cardew, Tim Perkins, the Head of Fielding's house, was taking his leave of Mrs Harlowe, who taught him the 'cello. She was a kindly woman, if neurotic, and it distressed her to see him so worried. He was quite the best pupil that Carne had sent her, and she liked him.

'You played foully today, Tim,' she said as she wished him good-bye at the door, 'quite foully. You needn't tell me – you've only got one more Half and you still haven't got three passes in A Level and you've got to get your remove, and you're in a tizz. We won't practise next Monday if you don't want – just come and have buns and we'll play some records.'

'Yes, Mrs Harlowe.' He strapped his music-case on to the carrier of his bicycle.

'Lights working, Tim?'

'Yes, Mrs Harlowe.'

'Well, don't try and beat the record tonight, Tim. You've plenty of time till Boys' Tea. Remember the lane's still quite slippery from the snow.'

Perkins said nothing. He pushed the bicycle on to the gravel path and started towards the gate.

'Haven't you forgotten something, Tim?'

'Sorry, Mrs Harlowe.'

He turned back and shook hands with her in the doorway. She always insisted on that.

'Look, Tim, what *is* the matter? Have you done something silly? You can tell me, can't you? I'm not Staff, you know.'

Perkins hesitated, then said:

'It's just exams, Mrs Harlowe.'

'Are your parents all right? No trouble at home?'

'No, Mrs Harlowe; they're fine.' Again he hesitated, then: 'Good night, Mrs Harlowe.'

'Good night.'

She watched him close the gate behind him and cycle off down the narrow lane. He would be in Carne in a quarter of an hour; it was downhill practically all the way.

Usually he loved the ride home. It was the best moment of the week. But tonight he hardly noticed it. He rode fast, as he always did; the hedge raced against the dark sky and the rabbits scuttled from the beam of his lamp, but tonight he hardly noticed them.

He would have to tell somebody. He should have told Mrs Harlowe; he wished he had. She'd know what to do. Mr Snow would have been all right, but he wasn't up to him for science any longer, he was up to Rode. That was half the trouble. That and Fielding.

He could tell True – yes, that's who he'd tell, he'd tell True. He'd go to Miss Truebody tonight after evening surgery and he'd tell her the truth. His father would never get over it, of course, because it meant failure and perhaps disgrace. It meant not getting to Sandhurst at the end of next Half, it meant more money they couldn't afford . . .

He was coming to the steepest part of the hill. The hedge stopped on one side and instead there was a marvellous view of Sawley Castle against the night sky, like a backcloth for *Macbeth*. He loved acting – he wished the Master let them act at Carne.

He leant forward over the handlebars and allowed himself to gather speed to go through the shallow ford at the bottom of the hill. The cold air bit into his face, and for a moment he almost forgot . . . Suddenly he braked; felt the bike skid wildly beneath him.

Something was wrong; there was a light ahead, a flashing light, and a familiar voice calling to him urgently across the darkness.

14. *The Quality of Mercy*

T he Public Schools Committee for Refugee Relief (Patroness: Sarah, Countess of Sawley) has an office in Belgrave Square. It is not at all clear whether this luxurious situation is designed to entice the wealthy or encourage the dispossessed – or, as some irreverent voices in Society whispered, to provide the Countess of Sawley with an inexpensive *pied-à-terre* in the West End of London. The business of assisting refugees has been suitably relegated to the south of the river, to one of those untended squares in Kennington which are part of London's architectural schizophrenia. York Gardens, as the square is called, will one day be discovered by the world, and its charm lost, but go there now, and you may see real children playing hopscotch in the road, and their mothers, shod in bedroom slippers, abusing them from doorways.

Miss Brimley, dispatched on her way by Smiley's telephone call the previous morning, had the rare gift of speaking to children as if they were human beings, and thus discovered without difficulty the dilapidated, unnamed house which served the Committee as a collecting centre. With the assistance of seven small boys, she pulled on the bell and waited patiently. At last she heard the clatter of feet descending an uncarpeted staircase, and the door was opened by a very beautiful girl. They looked at one another with approval for a moment.

'I'm sorry to be a nuisance,' Miss Brimley began, 'but a friend of mine in the country has asked me to make some inquiries about a parcel of clothes that was sent up a day or two ago. She's made rather a stupid mistake.'

'Oh, goodness, how awful,' said the girl pleasantly. 'Would you like to come in? Everything's frightfully chaotic, I'm afraid, and there's nothing to sit on, but we can give you powdered coffee in a mug.'

Miss Brimley followed her in, closing the door firmly on the seven children, who were edging gently forward in her wake. She was in the hall, and everywhere she looked there were parcels of every kind, some wrapped in jute with smart labels, some in brown paper, torn and clumsy, some in crates and laundry baskets, old suitcases and even an antiquated cabin trunk with a faded yellow label on it which read: 'Not wanted on voyage.'

The girl led the way upstairs to what was evidently the office, a large room containing a deal table littered with correspondence, and a kitchen chair. An oil stove sputtered in one corner, and an electric kettle was steaming in a melancholy way beside it. 'I'm sorry,' said the girl as they entered the room, 'but there just isn't anywhere to talk downstairs. I mean, one can't talk on one leg like the Incas. Or isn't it Incas? Perhaps it's Afghans. However did you find us?'

'I went to your West End office first,' Miss Brimley replied, 'and they told me I should come and see you. I think they were rather cross. After that I relied on children. They always know the way. You are Miss Dawney, aren't you?'

'Lord, no. I'm the sort of daily help. Jill Dawney's gone to see the Customs people at Rotherhithe – she'll be back at tea time if you want to see her.'

'Gracious, my dear, I'm sure I shan't keep you two minutes. A friend of mine who lives in Carne – ('Goodness! How grand,' said the girl) she's a sort of cousin really, but it's simpler to call her a friend, isn't it? – gave an

old grey dress to the refugee people last Thursday and now she's convinced
she left her brooch pinned to the bodice. I'm sure she hasn't done anything
of the sort, mind you – she's a scatter-brain creature – but she rang me
yesterday morning in a dreadful state and made me promise to come
round at once and ask. I couldn't come yesterday, unfortunately – tied to
my little paper from dawn till dusk. But I gather you're a bit behind, so it
won't be too late?'

'Gosh, no! We're miles behind. That's all the stuff downstairs, waiting
to be unpacked and sorted. It comes from the voluntary reps. at each
school – sometimes boys and sometimes Staff – and they put all the clothes
together and send them up in big parcels, either by train or ordinary mail,
usually by train. We sort them here before sending abroad.'

'That's what I gathered from Jane. As soon as she realised she'd made
this mistake she got hold of the woman doing the collecting and sending,
but of course it was too late. The parcel had gone.'

'How frantic . . . Do you know when the parcel was sent off?'

'Yes. On Friday morning.'

'From Carne? Train or post?'

Miss Brimley had been dreading this question, but she made a guess:
'Post, I believe.'

Darting past Miss Brimley, the girl foraged among the pile of papers on
her desk and finally produced a stiff-backed exercise book with a label
on it marked 'Ledger'. Opening it at random, she whisked quickly back
and forth through the pages, licking the tip of one finger now and then in
a harassed sort of way.

'Wouldn't have arrived till yesterday at the earliest,' she said. 'We
certainly won't have opened it yet. Honestly, I don't know how we shall
ever cope, and with Easter coming up we shall just get worse and worse.
On top of that, half our stuff is rotting in the Customs sheds – hullo, here
we are!' She pushed the ledger over to Miss Brimley, her slim finger
pointing to a pencilled entry in the central column: 'Carne, parcel post, 27
lb.'

'I wonder,' said Miss Brimley, 'whether you would mind awfully if we
had a quick look inside?'

They went downstairs to the hall.

'It's not quite as hideous as it looks,' the girl called over her shoulder.
'All the Monday lot will be nearest the door.'

'How do you know where they come from if you can't read the postmark?' asked Miss Brimley as the girl began to forage among the parcels.

'We issue volunteer reps. with our printed labels. The labels have an
originator's number on. In other cases we just ask them to write the name
of the school in capitals on the outside. You see, we simply can't allow
covering letters; it would be *too* desperate. When we get a parcel all we
have to do is send off a printed card acknowledging with thanks receipt of
a parcel of such and such a date weighing so and so much. People who

aren't reps. won't send parcels to this address, you see – they'll send to the advertised address in Belgrave Square.'

'Does the system work?'

'No,' replied the girl, 'it doesn't. The reps. either forget to use our labels or they run out and can't be bothered to tell us. Ten days later they ring up in a rage because they haven't had an acknowledgement. Reps. change, too, without letting us know, and the packing and labelling instructions don't get passed on. Sometimes the boys will suddenly decide to do it themselves, and no one tells them the way to go about it. Lady Sarah gets as mad as a snake if parcels turn up at Head Office – they all have to be carted over here for repacking and inventories.'

'I see.' Miss Brimley watched anxiously as the girl foraged among the parcels, still talking.

'Did you say your friend actually *taught* at Carne? She must be terribly grand. I wonder what the Prince is like: he looks rather soft in his photographs. My cousin went to Carne – he's an utter wet. Do you know what he told me? During Ascot week they all . . . Hello! Here we are!' The girl stood up, a large square parcel in her arms, and carried it to a table which stood in the shadow of the staircase. Miss Brimley, standing beside her as she began carefully to untie the stout twine, looked curiously at the printed label. In its top left-hand corner was stamped the symbol which the Committee had evidently allocated to Carne: C4. After the four the letter B had been written in with ballpoint pen.

'What does the B mean?' asked Miss Brimley.

'Oh, that's a local arrangement at Carne. Miss D'Arcy's the rep. there, but they've done so well recently that she coopted a friend to help with dispatch. When we acknowledge we always mention whether it was A or B. B must be terribly keen, whoever she is.'

Miss Brimley forbore from inquiring what proportion of the parcels from Carne had originated from Miss D'Arcy, and what proportion from her anonymous assistant.

The girl removed the string and turned the parcel upside down in order to liberate the overlap of wrapping paper. As she did so Miss Brimley caught sight of a faint brown smudge, no more, about the size of a shilling, near the join. It was consistent with her essential rationalism that she should search for any explanation other than that which so loudly presented itself. The girl continued the work of unwrapping, saying suddenly: 'I say, Carne was where they had that dreadful murder, wasn't it – that master's wife who got killed by the gipsy? It really *is* awful, isn't it, how much of that kind of thing goes on? Hm! Thought as much,' she remarked, suddenly interrupting herself. She had removed the outer paper, and was about to unwrap the bundle inside when her attention was evidently arrested by the appearance of the inner parcel.

'What?' Miss Brimley said quickly.

The girl laughed. 'Oh, only the packing,' she said. 'The C4Bs are usually so neat – quite the best we get. This is quite different. Not the same person at all. Must be a stand-in. I thought so from the outside.'

'How can you be so sure?'

'Oh, it's like handwriting. We can tell.' She laughed again, and without more ado removed the last wrapping. 'Grey dress, you said, didn't you? Let's see.' With both hands she began picking clothes from the top of the pile and laying them to either side. She was nearly half-way through when she exclaimed, 'Well, *honestly!* They must be having a brain-storm,' and drew from the bundle of part-worn clothes a transparent plastic mackintosh, a very old pair of leather gloves, and a pair of rubber overshoes.

Miss Brimley was holding the edge of the table very tightly. The palms of her hands were throbbing.

'Here's a cape. Damp, too,' the girl added in disgust, and tossed the offending articles on to the floor beside the table. Miss Brimley could only think of Smiley's letter: 'Whoever killed her must have been covered in blood.' Yes, and whoever killed her wore a plastic cape and a hood, rubber overshoes and those old leather gloves with the terra-cotta stains. Whoever killed Stella Rode had not chanced upon her in the night, but had plotted long ahead, had waited. 'Yes,' thought Miss Brimley, 'had waited for the long nights.'

The girl was talking to her again: 'I'm afraid it really isn't here.'

'No, my dear,' Miss Brimley replied, 'I see that. Thank you. You've been very sweet.' Her voice faltered for a moment, then she managed to say: 'I think, my dear, you should leave the parcel exactly as it is now, the wrapping and everything in it. Something very dreadful has happened, and the police will want to . . . know about it and see the parcel . . . You must trust me, my dear – things aren't quite what they seem . . . ' And somehow she escaped to the comforting freedom of York Gardens and the large-eyed wonder of its waiting children.

She went to a telephone box. She got through to the Sawley Arms and asked a very bored receptionist for Mr Smiley. Total silence descended on the line until the Trunks operator asked her to put in another three and sixpence. Miss Brimley replied sharply that all she had so far had for her money was a three-minute vacuum; this was followed by the unmistakable sound of the operator sucking her teeth, and then, quite suddenly, by George Smiley's voice:

'George, it's Brim. A plastic mackintosh, a cape, rubber overshoes, and some leather gloves that look as though they're stained with blood. Smudges on some of the wrapping paper too by the look of it.'

A pause.

'Handwriting on the outside of the parcel?'

'None. The Charity organisers issue printed labels.'

'Where is the stuff now? Have you got it?'

'No. I've told the girl to leave everything exactly as it is. It'll be all right for an hour or two . . . George, are you there?'

'Yes.'

'Who did it? Was it the husband?'

'I don't know. I just don't know.'

'Do you want me to do anything – about the clothes, I mean? Phone Sparrow or anything?'

'No. I'll see Rigby at once. Good-bye, Brim. Thanks for ringing.'

She put back the receiver. He sounded strange, she thought. He seemed to lose touch sometimes. As if he'd switched off.

She walked north-west towards the Embankment. It was long after ten o'clock – the first time she'd been late for Heaven knows how long. She had better take a taxi. Being a frugal woman, however, she took a bus.

Ailsa Brimley did not believe in emergencies, for she enjoyed a discipline of mind uncommon in men and even rarer in women. The greater the emergency, the greater her calm. John Landsbury had remarked upon it: 'You have sales resistance to the dramatic, Brim; the rare gift of contempt for what is urgent. I know of a dozen people who would pay you five thousand a year for telling them every day that what is important is seldom urgent. Urgent equals ephemeral, and ephemeral equals unimportant.'

She got out of the bus, carefully putting the ticket in the rubbish compartment. As she stood in the warm sunlight of the street she caught sight of the hoardings advertising the first edition of the evening papers. If it hadn't been for the sun, she might never have looked; but the sun dazzled her and made her glance downwards. And so she did see; she read it in the plump black of the wet newsprint, in the prepacked hysteria of Fleet Street: 'All-night search for missing Carne boy.'

15. *The Road to Fielding*

S| miley put down the receiver and walked quickly past the reception desk towards the front door. He must see Rigby at once. Just as he was leaving the hotel he heard his name called. Turning, he saw his old enemy, the night porter, braving the light of day, beckoning to him like Charon with his grey hand.

'They've been on to you from the police station,' he observed with undisguised pleasure. 'Mr Rigby wants you, the Inspector. You're to go there at once. At once, see?'

'I'm on my way there now,' Smiley replied irritably, and as he pushed his way through the swing doors he heard the old man repeat; 'At once, mind; they're waiting for you.'

Making his way through the Carne streets, he reflected for the hundredth time on the obscurity of motive in human action: there is no true thing on earth. There is no constant, no dependable point, not even in the purest logic or the most obscure mysticism; least of all in the motives of men when they are moved to act violently.

Had the murderer, now so near discovery, found contentment in the meticulous administration of his plans? For now it was clear beyond a doubt; this was a murder devised to the last detail, even to the weapon inexplicably far from the place of its use; a murder with clues cast to mislead, a murder planned to look unplanned, a murder for a string of beads. Now the mystery of the footprints was solved: having put the overshoes into the parcel, the murderer had walked down the path to the gate, and his own prints had been obscured by the subsequent traffic of feet.

Rigby looked tired.

'You've heard the news, sir, I suppose?'

'What news?'

'About the boy, the boy in Fielding's house, missing all night?'

'No.' Smiley felt suddenly sick. 'No, I've heard nothing.'

'Good Lord, I thought you knew! Half past eight last night Fielding rang us here. Perkins, his head boy, hadn't come back from a music lesson with Mrs Harlowe, who lives over to Longemede. We put out an alert and started looking for him. They sent a patrol car along the road he should have come back on – he was cycling, you see. The first time they didn't see anything, but on the way back the driver stopped the car at the bottom of Longemede Hill, just where the water-splash is. It occurred to him the lad might have taken a long run at the water-splash from the top of the hill, and come to grief in the dip. They found him half in the ditch, his bike beside him. Dead.'

'Oh, my dear God.'

'We didn't let on to the press at first. The boy's parents are in Singapore. The father's an Army officer. Fielding sent them a telegram. We've got on to the War Office, too.'

They were silent for a moment, then Smiley asked, 'How did it happen?'

'We've closed the road and we've been trying to reconstruct the accident. I've got a detective over there now, just having a look. Trouble is, we couldn't do much till the morning. Besides, the men trampled everywhere; you can't blame them. It looks as though he must have fallen near the bottom of the hill and hit his head on a stone: his right temple.'

'How did Fielding take it?'

'He was very shaken. Very shaken indeed. I wouldn't have believed it, to be quite honest. He just seemed to ... give up. There was a lot that had to be done – telegraph the parents, get in touch with the boy's uncle at Windsor, and so on. But he just left all that to Miss Truebody, his house-keeper. If it hadn't been for her, I don't know how he'd have managed. I was with him for about half an hour, then he just broke down, completely, and asked to be left alone.'

'How do you mean, broke down?' Smiley asked quickly.

'He cried. Wept like a child,' said Rigby evenly. 'I'd never have thought it.'

Smiley offered Rigby a cigarette and took one himself.

'I suppose,' he ventured, 'it was an accident?'

'I suppose so,' Rigby replied woodenly.

'Perhaps,' said Smiley, 'before we go any farther, I'd better give you my news. I was on my way to see you when you rang. I've just heard from Miss Brimley.' And in his precise, rather formal way he related all that Ailsa Brimley had told him, and how he had become curious about the contents of the parcel.

Smiley waited while Rigby telephoned to London. Almost mechanically, Rigby described what he wanted done: the parcel and its contents were to be collected and arrangements made to subject them immediately to forensic examination; the surfaces should be tested for finger-prints. He would be coming up to London himself with some samples of a boy's handwriting and an examination paper; he would want the opinion of a handwriting expert. No, he would be coming by train on the 4.25 from Carne, arriving at Waterloo at 8.05. Could a car be sent to the station to collect him? There was silence, then Rigby said testily, 'All right, I'll take a ruddy taxi,' and rang off rather abruptly. He looked at Smiley angrily for a moment, then grinned, plucked at his ear and said:

'Sorry, sir; getting a bit edgy.' He indicated the far wall with his head and added, 'Fighting on too many fronts, I suppose. I shall have to tell the Chief about that parcel, but he's out shooting at the moment – only pigeon, with a couple of friends, he won't be long – but I haven't mentioned your presence here in Carne, as a matter of fact, and if you don't mind I'll ... '

'Of course,' Smiley cut in quickly. 'It's much simpler if you keep me out of it.'

'I shall tell him it was just a routine inquiry. We shall have to mention Miss Brimley later ... but there's no point in making things worse, is there?'

'No.'

'I shall have to let Janie go, I suppose . . . She was right, wasn't she? Silver wings in the moonlight.'

'I wouldn't – no, I wouldn't let her go, Rigby,' said Smiley with unaccustomed vehemence. 'Keep her with you as long as you can possibly manage. No more accidents, for heaven's sake. We've had enough.'

'Then you don't believe Perkins's death was an accident?'

'Good Lord, no,' cried Smiley suddenly, 'and nor do you, do you?'

'I've put a detective on to it,' Rigby replied coolly. 'I can't take the case myself. I shall be needed on the Rode murder. The Chief will have to call the Yard in now; there'll be hell to pay, I can tell you. He thought it was all over bar the shouting.'

'And in the meantime?'

'In the meantime, sir, I'm going to do my damnedest to find out who killed Stella Rode.'

'If,' said Smiley slowly, 'if you find fingerprints on that mackintosh, which I doubt, will you have anything . . . local . . . to compare them with?'

'We've got Rode's, of course, and Janie 's.'

'But not Fielding's?'

Rigby hesitated.

'As a matter of fact, we have,' he said at last. 'From long ago. But nothing to do with this kind of thing.'

'It was during the war,' said Smiley. 'His brother told me. Up in the North. It was hushed up, wasn't it?'

Rigby nodded. 'So far as I heard, only the D'Arcys knew; and the Master, of course. It happened in the holidays – some Air Force boy. The Chief was very helpful . . . '

Smiley shook hands with Rigby and made his way down the familiar pine staircase. He noticed again the vaguely institutional smell of floor polish and carbolic soap, like the smell at Fielding's house.

He walked slowly back towards the Sawley Arms. At the point where he should have turned left to his hotel, however, he hesitated, then seemed to change his mind. Slowly, almost reluctantly, he crossed the road to the Abbey Close, and walked along the southern edge towards Fielding's house. He looked worried, almost frightened.

16. A Taste for Music

Miss Truebody opened the door. The rims of her eyes were pink, as though she had been weeping.

'I wonder if I might see Mr Fielding? To say good-bye.'

She hesitated: 'Mr Fielding's very upset. I doubt whether he'll want to see anyone.' He followed her into the hall and watched her go to the study door. She knocked, inclined her head, then gently turned the handle and let herself in. It was a long time before she returned. 'He'll be out shortly,' she said, without looking at him. 'Will you take off your coat?' She waited while he struggled out of his overcoat, then took it from him and hung it beside the Van Gogh chair. They stood together in silence, both looking towards the study door.

Then, quite suddenly, Fielding was standing in the half open doorway, unshaven and in his shirt-sleeves. 'For Christ's sake,' he said thickly. 'What do you want?'

'I just wanted to say good-bye, Fielding, and to offer you my condolences.'

Fielding looked at him hard for a moment; he was leaning heavily against the doorway. 'Well, good-bye. Thank you for calling.' He waved one hand vaguely in the air. 'You needn't have bothered really, need you?' he added rudely. 'You could have sent me a card, couldn't you?'

'I could have done, yes; it just seemed so very tragic, when he was so near success.'

'What do you mean? What the devil do you mean?'

'I mean in his work . . . the improvement. Simon Snow was telling me all about it. Amazing really, the way Rode brought him on.'

A long silence, then Fielding spoke: 'Good-bye, Smiley. Thanks for coming.' He was turning back into the study as Smiley called:

'Not at all . . . not at all. I suppose poor Rode must have been bucked with those exam. results, too. I mean it was more or less a matter of life and death for Perkins, passing that exam, wasn't it? He wouldn't have got his remove next Half if he'd failed in science. They might have superannuated him, I suppose, even though he was head of the house; then he couldn't have sat for the Army. Poor Perkins, he had a lot to thank Rode for, didn't he? And you, too, Fielding, I'm sure. You must have helped him wonderfully . . . both of you did, you and Rode; Rode and Fielding. His parents ought to know that. They're rather hard up, I gather; the father's in the Army, isn't he, in Singapore? It must have been a great effort keeping the boy at Carne. It will comfort them to know how much was done for him, won't it, Fielding?'

Smiley was very pale. 'You've heard the latest, I suppose,' he continued.

'About that wretched gipsy woman who killed Stella Rode? They've decided she's fit to plead. I suppose they'll hang her. That'll be the third death, won't it? You know, I'll tell you an odd thing – just between ourselves, Fielding. I don't believe she did it. Do you? I don't believe she did it at all.'

He was not looking at Fielding. He had clasped his little hands tightly behind his back, and he stood with his shoulders bowed and his head inclined to one side, as though listening for an answer.

Fielding seemed to feel Smiley's words like a physical pain. Slowly he shook his head:

'No he said; 'no. Carne killed them; it was Carne. It could only happen here. It's the game we play: the exclusion game. Divide and rule!' He looked Smiley full in the face, and shouted: 'Now for God's sake go! You've got what you want, haven't you? You can pin me on your little board, can't you?' And then, to Smiley's distress, he began sobbing in great uncontrollable gulps, holding his hand across his brow. He appeared suddenly grotesque, stemming the childish tears with his chalky hand, his cumbersome feet turned inwards. Gently, Smiley coaxed him back into the study, gently sat him before the dead fire. Then he began talking to him softly and with compassion.

'If what I think is true, there isn't much time,' he began. 'I want you to tell me about Tim Perkins – about the exam.'

Fielding, his face buried in his hands, nodded.

'He would have failed, wouldn't he? He would have failed and not got his remove; he'd have had to leave.' Fielding was silent. 'After the exam. that day, Rode gave him the writing-case to bring here, the case that contained the papers; Rode was doing chapel duty that week and wouldn't be going home before dinner, but he wanted to correct the papers that night, after his dinner with you.'

Fielding took his hands from his face and leant back in his chair, his great head tilted back, his eyes closed. Smiley continued:

'Perkins came home, and that evening he brought the case to you, as Rode told him to, for safe keeping. Perkins, after all, was head of your house, a responsible boy . . . He gave you the case and you asked him how he'd done in the exam.'

'He wept,' said Fielding suddenly. 'He wept as only a child can.'

'And after breaking down he told you he had cheated? That he had looked up the answers and copied them on to his paper. Is that right? And after the murder of Stella Rode he remembered what else he had seen in the suitcase?'

Fielding was standing up. 'No! Don't you see? Tim wouldn't have cheated to save his life! That's the whole point, the whole bloody irony of it,' he shouted. 'He never cheated at all. I cheated for him.'

'But you couldn't! You couldn't copy his handwriting!'

'He wrote with a ball-pen. It was only formulae and diagrams. When he'd gone, and left me alone with the case, I looked at his paper. It was hopeless – he'd only done two out of seven questions. So I cheated for him. I just cribbed them from the science book, and wrote them with blue ballpoint, the kind we all use. Abbots' sell them. I copied his hand as best I could. It only needed about three lines of figures. The rest was diagrams.'

'Then it was you who opened the case? You who saw . . . '

'Yes. It was me, I tell you, not Tim! He couldn't cheat to save his life! But Tim paid for it, don't you see? When the marks were published. Tim must have known something was wrong with them. After all, he'd only attempted two questions out of seven and yet he'd got sixty-one per cent. But he knew *nothing* else, *nothing!*'

For a long time neither spoke. Fielding was standing over Smiley, exultant with the relief of sharing his secret, and Smiley was looking vaguely past him, his face drawn in deep concentration.

'And of course,' he said finally, 'when Stella was murdered, you knew who had done it.'

'Yes,' replied Fielding. 'I knew that Rode had killed her.'

Fielding poured himself a brandy and gave one to Smiley. He seemed to have recovered his self-control. He sat down and looked at Smiley thoughtfully for a time.

'I've got no money,' he said at last. 'None. Nobody knows that except the Master. Oh, they know I'm more or less broke, but they don't know *how* broke. Long ago I made an ass of myself. I got into trouble. It was in the war, when staff was impossible. I had a boys' house and was practically running the school – D'Arcy and I. We were running it together, and the Master running us. Then I made an ass of myself. It was during the holidays. I was up North at the time, giving a course of talks at an RAF educational place. And I stepped out of line. Badly. They pulled me in. And along came D'Arcy wearing his country overcoat and bringing the Master's terms: Come back to Carne, my dear fellow, and we'll say no more about it; go on running your house, my dear fellow, and giving of your wisdom. There's been no publicity. We know it will never happen again, my dear fellow, and we're dreadfully hard up for staff. Come back as a temporary. So I did, and I've been one ever since, going cap in hand to darling D'Arcy every December asking for my contract to be renewed. And, of course – no pension. I shall have to teach at a crammer's. There's a place in Somerset where they'll take me. I'm seeing their Headmaster in London on Thursday. It's a sort of breaker's yard for old dons. The Master had to know, because he gave me a reference.'

'That was why you couldn't tell anyone? Because of Perkins?'

'In a way, yes. I mean they'd want to know all sorts of things. I did it for Tim, you see. The Governors wouldn't have liked that much . . . inordinate affection . . . It looks bad, doesn't it? But it wasn't that kind of affection,

Smiley, not any more. You never heard him play the 'cello. He wasn't marvellous, but just sometimes he would play so beautifully, with a kind of studious simplicity, that was indescribably good. He was an awkward boy, and when he played well it was such a surprise. You should have heard him play.'

'You didn't want to drag him into it. If you told the police what you had seen it would ruin Tim too?'

Fielding nodded. 'In the whole of Carne, he was the one thing I loved.'

'Loved?' asked Smiley.

'For God's sake,' said Fielding in an exhausted voice, 'why not?'

'His parents wanted him to go to Sandhurst; I didn't, I'm afraid. I thought that if I could keep him here another Half or two I might be able to get him a music scholarship. That's why I made him Head of House: I wanted his parents to keep him on because he was doing so well.' Fielding paused. 'He was a rotten Head of House,' he added.

'And what exactly was in the writing-case,' Smiley asked, 'when you opened it that evening to look at Tim's exam. paper?'

'A sheet of transparent plastic . . . it may have been one of those pack-away cape things – an old pair of gloves, and a pair of home-made galoshes.'

'Home-made?'

'Yes. Hacked from a pair of Wellington boots, I should think.'

'That's all?'

'No. There was a length of heavy cable, I presumed for demonstrating something in his science lessons. It seemed natural enough in winter to carry waterproofs about. Then, after the murder, I realised how he had done it.'

'Did you know,' Smiley asked him, '*why* he had done it?'

Fielding seemed to hesitate: 'Rode's a guinea-pig,' he began, 'the first man we've had from a grammar school. Most of us are old Carnians ourselves, in fact. Focused when we start. Rode wasn't, and Carne thrilled him. The very name Carne means quality, and Rode loved quality. His wife wasn't like that. She had her standards and they were different, but just as good. I used to watch Rode in the Abbey sometimes on Sunday mornings. Tutors sit at the end of pews, right by the aisle, you know. I used to watch his face as the choir processed past him in white and scarlet, and the Master in his doctor's robes and the Governors and Guardians behind him. Rode was drunk – drunk with the pride of Carne. We're heady wine for the grammar school men, you know. It must have hurt him terribly that Stella wouldn't share any of that. You could see it did. The night they came to dinner with me, the night she died, they argued. I never told anyone, but they did. The Master had preached a sermon at Compline that evening: "Hold fast to that which is good." Rode talked about it at dinner; he couldn't take much drink, you know, he wasn't used to it. He was full of this sermon and of the eloquence of the Master. She never came to the Abbey – she went to that drab tabernacle by the station. He went on and on about the beauty of the Abbey service, the dignity, the reverence. She kept quiet till he'd finished, then laughed, and said: "Poor old Stan. You'll always be Stan to me." I've never seen anyone so angry as he was then. He went quite pale.'

Fielding swept his white hair from his eyes and went on, with something like the old panache: 'I've watched her, too, at meals. Not just here, but at dinner parties elsewhere, when we've both been invited. I've watched her do the simplest things – like eating an apple. She'd peel it in one piece, round and round till the whole peel fell off. Then she'd cut the apple and dice the quarters, getting it all ready before she ate it. She might have been a miner's wife preparing it for her husband. She must have *seen* how people do things here, but it never occurred to her that she ought to copy them. I admire that. So do you, I expect. But Carne doesn't – and Rode didn't; above all, Rode didn't. He'd watch her, and I think he grew to hate her for not conforming. He came to see her as the bar to his success, the one factor which would deprive him of a great career. Once he'd reached that conclusion, what could he do? He couldn't divorce her – that would do him more harm than remaining married to her. Rode knew what Carne would think of divorce; we're a Church foundation, remember. So he killed her. He plotted a squalid murder, and with his little scientist's mind he gave them all the clues they wanted. Fabricated clues. Clues that would point to a murderer who didn't exist. But something went wrong; Tim Perkins got sixty-one per cent. He'd got an impossible mark – he must have cheated. He'd had the opportunity – he'd had the papers in the case. Rode put his little mind to it and decided what had happened: Tim had opened the case and he'd seen the cape and the boots and the gloves. And the cable. So Rode killed him too.'

With surprising energy, Fielding got up and gave himself more brandy. His face was flushed, almost exultant.

Smiley stood up. 'When did you say you'll be coming to London? Thursday, wasn't it?'

'Yes. I had arranged to lunch with my crammer man at one of those dreadful clubs in Pall Mall. I always go into the wrong one, don't you? But I'm afraid there's not much point in my seeing him now, is there, if all this is going to come out? Not even a crammer's will take me then.'

Smiley hesitated.

'Come and dine with me that evening. Spend the night if you want. I'll ask one or two other people. We'll have a party. You'll feel better by then. We can talk a bit. I might be able to help you . . . for Adrian's sake.'

'Thank you. I should like to. Interview apart, I've got some odds and ends to clear up in London, anyway.'

'Good. Quarter to eight. Bywater Street, Chelsea, number 9A.' Fielding wrote it down in his diary. His hand was quite steady.

'Black tie?' asked Fielding, his pen poised, and some imp made Smiley reply:

'I usually do, but it doesn't matter.' There was a moment's silence.

'I suppose,' Fielding began tentatively, 'that all this *will* come out in the trial, about Tim and me? I'll be ruined if it does, you know, ruined.'

'I don't see how they can prevent it.'

'I feel much better now, anyway,' said Fielding; 'much.'

With a cursory good-bye, Smiley left him alone. He walked quickly back to the police station, reasonably confident that Terence Fielding was the most accomplished liar he had met for a long time.

17. *Rabbit Run*

H e knocked on Rigby's door and walked straight in.
'I'm awfully afraid you'll have to arrest Stanley Rode,' he began, and recounted his interview with Fielding.

'I shall have to tell the Chief,' said Rigby doubtfully. 'Would you like to repeat all that in front of him? If we're going to pull in a Carne master, I think the Chief had better know first. He's just come back. Hang on a minute.' He picked up the telephone on his desk and asked for the Chief Constable. A few minutes later they were walking in silence down a carpeted corridor. On either wall hung photographs of rugby and cricket teams, some yellow and faded from the Indian sun, others done in a sepia tint much favoured by Carne photographers in the early part of the century. At intervals along the corridor stood empty buckets of brilliant red, with FIRE printed carefully in white on the outside. At the far end of the corridor was a dark oak door. Rigby knocked and waited. There was silence. He knocked again and was answered with a cry of 'Come!'

Two very large spaniels watched them come in. Behind the spaniels, at an enormous desk, Brigadier Havelock, O.B.E., Chief Constable of Carne, sat like a water rat on a raft.

The few strands of white hair which ran laterally across his otherwise bald head were painstakingly adjusted to cover the maximum area. This gave him an oddly wet look, as if he had just emerged from the river. His moustache, which lavishly compensated for the scarcity of other hair, was yellow and appeared quite solid. He was a very small man, and he wore a brown suit and a stiff white collar with rounded corners.

'Sir,' Rigby began, 'may I introduce Mr Smiley from London?'

He came out from behind his desk as if he were giving himself up, unconvinced but resigned. Then he pushed out a little, knobbly hand and said, 'From London, eh? How d'you do, sir,' all at once, as if he'd learnt it by heart.

'Mr Smiley's here on a private visit, sir,' Rigby continued. 'He is an acquaintance of Mr Fielding.'

'Quite a card, Fielding, quite a card,' the Chief Constable snapped.

'Yes, indeed, sir,' said Rigby, and went on:

'Mr Smiley called on Mr Fielding just now, sir, to take his leave before returning to London.' Havelock shot a beady glance at Smiley, as if wondering whether he were fit to make the journey.

'Mr Fielding made a kind of statement, which he substantiated with new evidence of his own. About the murder, sir.'

'Well, Rigby?' he said challengingly. Smiley intervened:

'He said that the husband had done it; Stanley Rode. Fielding said that when his head boy brought him Rode's writing-case containing the examination papers . . . '

'What examination papers?'

'Rode was invigilating that afternoon, you remember. He was also doing chapel duty before going on to dinner at Fielding's house. As an expediency, he gave the papers to Perkins to take . . . '

'The boy who had the accident?' Havelock asked.

'Yes.'

'You know a lot about it,' said Havelock darkly.

'Fielding said that when Perkins brought him the case, Fielding opened it. He wanted to see how Perkins had done in the science paper. It was vital to the boy's future that he should get his remove,' Smiley went on.

'Oh, work's the only thing now,' said Havelock bitterly. 'Wasn't the way when I was a boy here, I assure you.'

'When Fielding opened the case, the papers were inside. So was a plastic cape, an old pair of leather gloves, and a pair of rubber overshoes, cut from Wellingtons.'

A pause.

'Good God! Good God! Hear that, Rigby? That's what they found in the parcel in London. Good God!'

'Finally, there was a length of cable, heavy cable, in the case as well. It was this writing-case that Rode went back for, you remember, on the night of the murder,' Smiley concluded. It was like feeding a child – you couldn't overload the spoon.

There was a very long silence indeed. Then Rigby, who seemed to know his man, said:

'Motive was self-advancement in the profession, sir. Mrs Rode showed no desire to improve her station, dressed in a slovenly manner and took no part in the religious life of the school.'

'Just a minute,' said Havelock. 'Rode planned the murder from the start, correct?'

'Yes, sir.'

'He wanted to make it look like robbery with violence.'

'Yes, sir.'

'Having collected the writing-case, he walked back to North Fields. Then what does he do?'

'He puts on the plastic cape and hood, overshoes and gloves. He arms himself with the weapon, sir. He lets himself in by the garden gate, crosses the back garden, goes to the front door and rings the bell, sir. His wife comes to the door. He knocks her down, drags her to the conservatory and murders her. He rinses the clothes under the tap and puts them in the parcel. Having sealed the parcel, he walks down the drive this time to the front gate, following the path, sir, knowing that his own footprints will soon be obscured by other people's. Having got to the road, where the snow was hard and showed no prints, he turned round and re-entered the house, playing the part of the distressed husband, taking care, when he discovers the body, sir, to put his own finger-prints over the glove-marks. There was one article that was too dangerous to send, sir. The weapon.'

'All right, Rigby. Pull him in. Mr Borrow will give you a warrant if you want one; otherwise I'll ring Lord Sawley.'

'Yes, sir. And I'll send Sergeant Low to take a full statement from Mr Fielding, sir?'

'Why the devil didn't he speak up earlier, Rigby?'

'Have to ask him that, sir,' said Rigby woodenly, and left the room.

'You a Carnian?' Havelock asked, pushing a silver cigarette-box across the desk.

'No. No, I'm afraid not,' Smiley replied.

'How d'you know Fielding?'

'We met at Oxford after the war.'

'Queer card, Fielding, very queer. Say your name was Smiley?'

'Yes.'

'There was a fellow called Smiley married Ann Sercombe, Lord Sawley's cousin. Damned pretty girl, Ann was, and went and married this fellow. Some funny little beggar in the Civil Service with an OBE and a gold watch. Sawley was damned annoyed.' Smiley said nothing. 'Sawley's got a son at Carne. Know that?'

'I read it in the press, I think.'

'Tell me – this fellow Rode. He's a grammar school chap, isn't he?'

'I believe so, yes.'

'Damned odd business. Experiments never pay, do they? You can't experiment with tradition.'

'No. No, indeed.'

'That's the trouble today. Like Africa. Nobody seems to understand you can't build society overnight. It takes centuries to make a gentleman.' Havelock frowned to himself and fiddled with the paper-knife on his desk.

'Wonder how he got his cable into that ditch, the thing he killed her with. He wasn't out of our sight for forty-eight hours after the murder.'

'That,' said Smiley, 'is what puzzles me. So does Jane Lyn.'

'What d'you mean?'

'I don't believe Rode would have had the nerve to walk back to the house after killing his wife knowing that Jane Lyn had seen him do it. Assuming, of course, that he *did* know, which seems likely. It's too cool . . . too cool altogether.'

'Odd, damned odd,' muttered Havelock. He looked at his watch, pushing his left elbow outwards to do so, in a swift equestrian movement which Smiley found comic, and a little sad. The minutes ticked by. Smiley wondered if he should leave, but he had a vague feeling that Havelock wanted his company.

'There'll be a hell of a fuss,' said Havelock. 'It isn't every day you arrest a Carne tutor for murder.' He put down the paper-knife sharply on the desk.

'These bloody journalists ought to be horsewhipped!' he declared. 'Look at the stuff they print about the Royal Family. Wicked, wicked!' He got up, crossed the room and sat himself in a leather armchair by the fire. One of the spaniels went and sat at his feet.

'What made him do it, I wonder. What the devil made him do it? His own wife, I mean; a fellow like that.' Havelock said this simply, appealing for enlightenment.

'I don't believe,' said Smiley slowly, 'that we can ever entirely know what makes anyone do anything.'

'My God, you're dead right . . . What do you do for a living, Smiley?'

'After the war I was at Oxford for a bit. Teaching and research. I'm in London now.'

'One of those clever coves, eh?'

Smiley wondered when Rigby would return.

'Know anything about this fellow's family? Has he got people, or anything?'

'I think they're both dead,' Smiley answered, and the telephone on Havelock's desk rang sharply. It was Rigby. Stanley Rode had disappeared.

18. After the Ball

He caught the 1.30 train to London. He just made it after an argument at his hotel about the bill. He left a note for Rigby giving his address and telephone number in London and asking him to telephone that night when the laboratory tests were completed. There was nothing else for him to do in Carne.

As the train pulled slowly out of Carne and one by one the familiar landmarks disappeared into the cold February mist, George Smiley was filled with a feeling of relief. He hadn't wanted to come, he knew that. He'd been afraid of the place where his wife had spent her childhood, afraid to see the fields where she had lived. But he had found nothing, not the faintest memory, neither in the lifeless outlines of Sawley Castle, nor in the surrounding countryside, to remind him of her. Only the gossip remained, as it would while the Hechts and the Havelocks survived to parade their acquaintance with the first family in Carne.

He took a taxi to Chelsea, carried his suitcase upstairs and unpacked with the care of a man accustomed to living alone. He thought of having a bath, but decided to ring Ailsa Brimley first. The telephone was by his bed. He sat on the edge of the bed and dialled the number. A tinny model-voice sang: 'Unipress, good afternoon,' and he asked for Miss Brimley. There was a long silence, then, 'Ah'm afraid Miss Brimley is in conference. Can someone else answer your query?'

Query, thought Smiley. Good God! Why on earth query – why not question or inquiry?

'No,' he replied. 'Just tell her Mr Smiley rang.' He put back the receiver and went into the bathroom and turned on the hot tap. He was fiddling with his cuff-links when the telephone rang. It was Ailsa Brimley:

'George? I think you'd better come round at once. We've got a visitor. Mr Rode from Carne. He wants to talk to us.' Pulling on his jacket, he ran out into the street and hailed a taxi.

19. Disposal of a Legend

he descending escalator was packed with the staff of Unipress, homebound and heavy-eyed. To them, the sight of a fat, middle-aged gentleman bounding up the adjoining staircase provided unexpected entertainment, so that Smiley was hastened on his way by the jeers of office-boys and the laughter of typists. On the first floor he paused to study an enormous board carrying the titles of a quarter of the national dailies. Finally, under the heading of 'Technical and Miscellaneous', he spotted the *Christian Voice*, Room 619. The lift seemed to go up very slowly. Formless music issued from behind its plush, while a boy in a monkey jacket flicked his hips on the heavier beats. The golden doors parted with a sigh, the boy said 'Six', and Smiley stepped quickly into the corridor. A moment or two later he was knocking on the door of Room 619. It was opened by Ailsa Brimley.

'George, how nice,' she said brightly. 'Mr Rode will be dreadfully pleased to see you.' And without any further introduction she led him into her office. In an armchair near the window sat Stanley Rode, tutor of Carne, in a neat black overcoat. As Smiley entered he stood up and held out his hand. 'Good of you to come, sir,' he said woodenly. 'Very.' The same flat manner, the same cautious voice.

'How can I help you?' asked Smiley.

They all sat down. Smiley offered Miss Brimley a cigarette and lit it for her.

'It's about this article you're writing about Stella,' he began. 'I feel awful about it really, because you've been so good to her, and her memory, if you see what I mean. I know you wish well, but I don't want you to write it.'

Smiley said nothing, and Ailsa was wise enough to keep quiet. From now on it was Smiley's interview. The silence didn't worry him, but it seemed to worry Rode.

'It wouldn't be right; it wouldn't do at all. Mr Glaston agreed; I spoke to him yesterday before he left and he agreed. I just couldn't let you write that stuff.'

'Why not?'

'Too many people know, you see. Poor Mr Cardew, I asked him. He knows a lot; and a lot about Stella, so I asked him. He understands why I gave up Chapel too; I couldn't bear to see her going there every Sunday and going down on her knees.' He shook his head. 'It was all wrong. It just made a fool of your faith.'

'What did Mr Cardew say?'

'He said we should not be the judges. We should let God judge. But I said to him it wouldn't be right, those people knowing her and knowing what she'd done, and then reading all that stuff in the *Voice*. They'd think it was crazy. He didn't seem to see that, he just said to leave it to God. But I can't, Mr Smiley.'

Again no one spoke for a time. Rode sat quite still, save for a very slight rocking movement of his head. Then he began to talk again:

'I didn't believe old Mr Glaston at first. He said she was bad, but I didn't believe it. They lived up on the hill then, Gorse Hill, only a step from the Tabernacle; Stella and her father. They never seemed to keep servants for long, so she did most of the work. I used to call in Sunday mornings sometimes after church. Stella looked after her father, cooked for him and everything, and I always wondered how I'd ever have the nerve to ask Mr Glaston for her. The Glastons were big people in Branxome. I was teaching at Grammar School in those days. They let me teach part-time while I read for my degree, and I made up my mind that if I passed the exam, I'd ask her to marry me.

'The Sunday after the results came out I went round to the house after morning service. Mr Glaston opened the door himself. He took me straight into the study. You could see half the potteries in Poole from the window, and the sea beyond. He sat me down and he said: "I know what you're here for, Stanley. You want to marry Stella. But you don't know her," he said, "you don't know her." "I've been visiting two years, Mr Glaston," I said, "and I think I know my mind." Then he started talking about her. I never thought to hear a human being talk like that of his own child. He said she was bad – bad in her heart. That she was full of malice. That was why no servants would stay at the Hill. He told me how she'd lead people on, all kind and warm, till they'd told her everything, then she'd hurt them, saying wicked, wicked things, half true, half lies. He told me a lot more besides, and I didn't believe it, not a word. I think I lost my head; I called him a jealous old man who didn't want to lose his housekeeper, a lying, jealous old man who wanted his child to wait on him till he died. I said it was him who was bad, not Stella, and I shouted at him liar, liar. He didn't seem to hear, just shook his head, and I ran out into the hall and called Stella. She'd been in the kitchen, I think, and she came to me and put her arms round me and kissed me.

'We were married a month later, and the old man gave her away. He shook my hand at the wedding and called me a fine man, and I thought what an old hypocrite he was. He gave us money – to me, not her – two thousand pounds. I thought perhaps he was trying to make up for the dreadful things he'd said, and later I wrote to him and said I forgave him. He never answered and I didn't see him often after that.

'For a year or more we were happy enough at Branxome. She was just what I thought she'd be, neat and simple. She liked to go for walks and kiss at the stiles; she liked to be a bit grand sometimes, going to the Dolphin for dinner all dressed up. It meant a lot to me then, I don't mind admitting, going to the right places with Mr Glaston's daughter. He was Rotary and on the Council and quite a figure in Branxome. She used to tease me about it – in front of other people too, which got me a bit. I remember one time we went to the Dolphin, one of the waiters there was a bloke called Johnnie Raglan. We'd been to school together. Johnnie was a bit of a tear-about and hadn't done anything much since he'd left school except run after girls and get into trouble. Stella knew him, I don't know how, and she waved to him as soon as we'd sat down. Johnnie came over and Stella made him bring another chair and sit with us. The Manager looked daggers, but he didn't dare to do anything because she was Samuel Glaston's daughter. Johnnie stayed there all the meal and Stella talked to him about school and what I was like. Johnnie was pleased as punch and got cheeky, saying I'd been a swat and a good boy and all the rest, and how Johnnie had knocked me about – lies most of it, and she egged him on. I went for her afterwards and said I didn't pay good money at the Dolphin to hear Johnnie Raglan tell a lot of tall stories, and she turned on me fast like a cat. It was her money, she said, and Johnnie was as good as me any day. Then she was sorry and kissed me and I pretended to forgive her.'

Sweat was forming on his face; he was talking fast, the words tripping over each other. It was like a man recalling a nightmare, as if the memory were still there, the fear only half gone. He paused and looked sharply at Smiley as if expecting him to speak, but Smiley seemed to be looking past him, his face impassive, its soft contours grown hard.

'Then we went to Carne. I'd just started reading *The Times* and I saw the advert. They wanted a science tutor and I applied. Mr D'Arcy interviewed me and I got the job. It wasn't till we got to Carne that I knew that what her father had said was true. She hadn't been very keen on Chapel before, but as soon as she got here she went in for it in a big way. She knew it would look wrong, that it would hurt me. Branxome's a fine big church, you see; there was nothing funny about going to Branxome Tabernacle. But at Carne it was different; Carne Tabernacle's a little out-of-the-way place with a tin roof. She wanted to be different, to spite the school and me, by playing the humble one. I wouldn't have minded if she'd been sincere, but she wasn't, Mr Cardew knew that. He got to know Stella, Mr Cardew did. I think her father told him; anyway, Mr Cardew was up North before, and he knew the family well. For all I know he wrote to Mr Glaston, or went and saw him or something.

'She began there well enough. The townspeople were all pleased enough to see her – a wife from the School coming to the Tabernacle, that had never happened before. Then she took to running the appeal for the refugees – to collecting clothes and all that. Miss D'Arcy was running it for the school, Mr D'Arcy's sister, and Stella wanted to beat her at her own game – to get more from the Chapel people than Miss D'Arcy got from the School. But I knew what she was doing, and so did Mr Cardew, and so did the townspeople in the end. She listened. Every drop of gossip and dirt, she hoarded it away. She'd come home of an evening sometimes – Wednesdays and Fridays she did her Chapel work – and she'd throw off her coat and laugh till I thought she'd gone mad.

' "I've got them! I've got them all," she'd say, "I know all their little secrets and I've got them in the hollow of my hand, Stan." That's what she'd say. And those that realised grew to be frightened of her. They all gossiped, Heaven knows, but not to profit from it, not like Stella. Stella was cunning; anything decent, anything good, she'd drag it down and spoil it. There were a dozen she'd got the measure of. There was Mulligan the furniture man; he's got a daughter with a kid near Leamington. Somehow she found out the girl wasn't married – they'd sent her to an aunt to have her baby and begin again up there. She rang up Mulligan once, something to do with a bill for moving Simon Snow's furniture, and she said "Greetings from Leamington Spa, Mr Mulligan. We need a little cooperation." She told me that – she came home laughing her head off and told me. But they got her in the end, didn't they? They got their own back!'

Smiley nodded slowly, his eyes now turned fully upon Rode.

'Yes,' he said at last, 'they got their own back.'

'They thought Mad Janie did it, but I didn't. Janie'd as soon have killed her own sister as Stella. They were as close as moon and stars, that's what Stella said. They'd talk together for hours in the evenings when I was out late on Societies or Extra Tuition. Stella cooked food for her, gave her clothes and money. It gave her a feeling of power to help a creature like Janie, and have her fawning round. Not because she was kind, but because she was cruel.

'She'd brought a little dog with her from Branxome, a mongrel. One day a few months ago I came home and found it lying in the garage whimpering, terrified. It was limping and had blood on its back. She'd beaten it. She must have gone mad. I knew she'd beaten it before, but never like that; never. Then something happened – I shouted at her and she laughed and then I hit her. Not hard, but hard enough. In the face. I gave her twenty-four hours to have the dog destroyed or I'd tell the police. She screamed at me – it was her dog and she'd damn' well do what she liked with it – but next day she put on her little black hat and took the dog to the vet. I suppose she told him some tale. She could spin a good tale about anything, Stella could. She kind of stepped into a part and played it right through. Like the tale she told the Hungarians. Miss D'Arcy had some refugees to stay from London once and Stella told them such a tale they ran away and had to be taken back to London. Miss D'Arcy paid for their fares and everything, even had the welfare officer down to see them and try and put things right. I don't think Miss D'Arcy ever knew who'd got at them, but I did – Stella told me. She laughed, always that same laugh: "There's your fine lady, Stan. Look at her charity now."

'After the dog, she took to pretending I was violent, cringing away whenever I came near, holding her arm up as though I was going to hit her again. She even made out I was plotting to murder her: she went and told Mr Cardew I was. She didn't believe it herself, she'd laugh about it sometimes. She said to me: "It's no good killing me now, Stan; they'll all know who's done it." But other times she'd whine and stroke me, begging me not to kill her. "You'll kill me in the long nights!" She'd scream it out – it was the words that got her, the long nights, she liked the sound of them the way an actor does, and she'd build a whole story round them. "Oh, Stan," she'd say, "keep me safe in the long nights." You know how it is when you never meant to do anything anyway, and someone goes on begging you not to do it? You think you might do it after all, you begin to consider the possibility.'

Miss Brimley drew in her breath rather quickly. Smiley stood up and walked over to Rode.

'Why don't we go back to my house for some food?' he said. 'We can talk this over quietly. Among friends.'

They took a taxi to Bywater Street. Rode sat beside Ailsa Brimley, more relaxed now, and Smiley, opposite him on a drop-seat, watched him and wondered. And it occurred to him that the most important thing about Rode was that he had no friends. Smiley was reminded of Büchner's fairy tale of the child left alone in an empty world who, finding no one to talk to, went to the moon because it smiled at him, but the moon was made of rotten wood. And when the sun and moon and stars had all turned to nothing, he tried to go back to the earth, but it had gone.

Perhaps because Smiley was tired, or perhaps because he was getting a little old, he felt a movement of sudden compassion towards Rode, such as children feel for the poor and parents for their children. Rode had tried so hard – he had used Carne's language, bought the right clothes, and thought as best he could the right thoughts, yet remained hopelessly apart, hopelessly alone.

He lit the gas-fire in the drawing-room while Ailsa Brimley went to the delicatessen in the King's Road for soup and eggs. He poured out whisky and soda and gave one to Rode, who drank it in short sips, without speaking.

'I had to tell somebody,' he said at last. 'I thought you'd be a good person. I didn't want you to print that article, though. Too many knew, you see.'

'How many really knew?'

'Only those she'd gone for, I think. I suppose about a dozen towns-people. And Mr Cardew, of course. She was terribly cunning, you see. She didn't often pass on gossip. She knew to a hair how far she could go. Those who knew were the ones she'd got on the hook. Oh, and D'Arcy,

Felix D'Arcy, he knew. She had something special there, something she never told me about. There were nights when she'd put on her shawl and slip out, all excited as if she was going to a party. Quite late sometimes, eleven or twelve. I'd never ask her where she was going because it only bucked her, but sometimes she'd nod at me all cunning and say, "You don't know, Stan, but D'Arcy does. D'Arcy knows and he can't tell," and then she'd laugh again and try and look mysterious, and off she'd go.'

Smiley was silent for a long time, watching Rode and thinking. Then he asked suddenly: 'What was Stella's blood group, do you know?'

'Mine's B. I know that. I was a donor at Branxome. Hers was different.'

'How do you know that?'

'She had a test before we were married. She used to suffer from anaemia. I remember hers being different, that's all. Probably A. I can't remember for sure. Why?'

'Where were you registered as a donor?'

'North Poole Transfusion Centre.'

'Will they know you there still? Are you still recorded there?'

'I suppose so.'

The front door bell rang. It was Ailsa Brimley, back from her shopping.

Ailsa installed herself in the kitchen, while Rode and Smiley sat in the warm comfort of the drawing-room.

'Tell me something else,' said Smiley, 'about the night of the murder. Why did you leave the writing-case behind? Was it absent-mindedness?'

'No, not really. I was on Chapel duty that night, so Stella and I arrived separately at Fielding's house. She got there before I did and I think Fielding gave the case to her – right at the start of the evening so that it wouldn't get forgotten. He said something about it later that evening. She'd put the case beside her coat in the hall. It was only a little thing about eighteen inches by twelve. I could have sworn she was carrying it as we stood in the hall saying good-bye, but I must have been mistaken. It wasn't till we got to the house that she asked me what I'd done with it.'

'*She* asked *you* what you'd done with it?'

'Yes. Then she threw a temper and said I expected her to remember everything. I didn't particularly want to go back, I could have rung Fielding and arranged to collect it first thing next morning, but Stella wouldn't hear of it. She made me go. I didn't like to tell the police all this stuff about us quarrelling, it didn't seem right.'

Smiley nodded. 'When you got back to Fielding's you rang the bell?'

'Yes. There's the front door, then a glass door inside, a sort of french window to keep out draughts. The front door was still open, and the light was on in the hall. I rang the bell and collected the case from Fielding.'

They had finished supper when the telephone rang.

'Rigby here, Mr Smiley. I've got the laboratory results. They're rather puzzling.'

'The exam. paper first: it doesn't tally?'

'No, it doesn't. The boffins here say all the figures and writing were done with the same ballpoint pen. They can't be sure about the diagrams but they say the legend on all the diagrams corresponds to the rest of the script on the sheet.'

'All done by the boy after all in fact?'

'Yes. I brought up some other samples of his hand-writing for comparison. They match the exam. paper right the way through. Fielding couldn't have tinkered with it.'

'Good. And the clothing? Nothing there either?'

'Traces of blood, that's all. No prints on the plastic.'

'What was her blood group, by the way?'

'Group A.'

Smiley sat down on the edge of the bed. Pressing the receiver to his ear, he began talking quietly. Ten minutes later he was walking slowly downstairs. He had come to the end of the chase, and was already sickened by the kill.

It was nearly an hour before Rigby arrived.

20. *The Dross of the River*

Albert Bridge was as preposterous as ever; bony steel, rising to Wagnerian pinnacles, against the patient London sky; the Thames crawling beneath it with resignation, edging its filth into the wharves of Battersea, then sliding towards the mist down river.

The mist was thick. Smiley watched the driftwood, as it touched it, turning first to white dust, then seeming to lift, dissolve and vanish.

This was how it would end, on a foul morning like this when they dragged the murderer whimpering from his cell and put the hempen rope round his neck. Would Smiley have the courage to recall this two months from now, as the dawn broke outside his window and the clock rang out the time? When they broke a man's neck on the scaffold and put him away like the dross of the river?

He made his way along Beaumont Street towards the King's Road. The milkman chugged past him in his electric van. He would breakfast out this

morning, then take a cab to Curzon Street and order the wine for dinner.
He would choose something good. Fielding would like that.

Fielding closed his eyes and drank, his left hand held lightly across his
chest.

'Divine,' he said, 'divine!' And Ailsa Brimley, opposite him, smiled
gently.

'How are you going to spend your retirement, Mr Fielding?' she asked.
'Drinking Frankenwein?'

His glass still held before his lips, he looked into the candles. The silver
was good, better than his own. He wondered why they were only dining
three. 'In peace,' he replied at last. 'I have recently made a discovery.'

'What's that?'

'That I have been playing to an empty house. But now I'm comforted to
think that no one remembers how I forgot my words or missed an entry.
So many of us wait patiently for our audience to die. At Carne no one will
remember for more than a Half or two what a mess I've made of life. I was
too vain to realise that until recently.' He put the glass down in front of
him and smiled suddenly at Ailsa Brimley. 'That is the peace I mean. Not
to exist in anyone's mind, but my own; to be a secular monk, safe and
forgotten.'

Smiley gave him more wine: 'Miss Brimley knew your brother Adrian
well in the war. We were all in the same department,' he said. 'She was
Adrian's secretary for a while. Weren't you, Brim?'

'It's depressing how the bad live on,' Fielding declared. 'Rather embarrassing. For the bad, I mean.' He gave a little gastronomic sigh. 'The
moment of truth in a good meal! *Übergangsperiode* between *entremets*
and dessert,' and they all laughed, and then were silent. Smiley put down
his glass, and said:

'The story you told me on Thursday, when I came and saw you . . . '

'Well?' Fielding was irritated.

'About cheating for Tim Perkins . . . how you took the paper from the
case and altered it . . . '

'Yes?'

'It isn't true.' He might have been talking about the weather. 'They've
examined it and it isn't true. The writing was all one person's . . . the boy's.
If anyone cheated, it must have been the boy.'

There was a long silence. Fielding shrugged.

'My dear fellow, you can't expect me to believe that. These people are
practically moronic.'

'Of course, it doesn't necessarily signify anything. I mean you could be
protecting the boy, couldn't you? By lying for him, for his honour so to
speak. Is that the explanation?'

'I've told you the truth,' he replied shortly. 'Make what you want of it.'

'I mean, I can see a situation where there might have been collusion, where you were moved by the boy's distress when he brought you the papers; and on the spur of the moment you opened the case and took out his paper and told him what to write.'

'Look here,' said Fielding hotly, 'why don't you keep off this? What's it got to do with you?' And Smiley replied with sudden fervour:

'I'm trying to help, Fielding. I beg you to believe me, I'm trying to help. For Adrian's sake. I don't want there to be . . . more trouble than there need, more pain. I want to get it straight before Rigby comes. They've dropped the charge against Janie. You know that, don't you? They seem to think it's Rode, but they haven't pulled him in. They could have done, but they haven't. They just took more statements from him. So you see, it matters terribly about the writing-case. Everything hangs by whether you really saw inside it; and whether Perkins did. Don't you see that? If it was Perkins who cheated after all, if it was only the boy who opened the case and not you, then they'll want to know the answer to a very important question: *they'll want to know how you knew what was inside it.*'

'What are you trying to say?'

'They're not really moronic, you know. Let's start from the other end for a moment. Suppose it was you who killed Stella Rode, suppose you had a reason, a terribly good reason, and they knew what that reason might be; suppose you went ahead of Rode after giving him the case that night – by bicycle, for instance, like Janie said, riding on the wind. If that were really so, none of those things you saw would have been in the case at all. You could have made it up. And when later the exam. results came out and you realised that Perkins had cheated, then you guessed he had seen inside the case, had seen that it contained nothing, *nothing but exam. papers.* I mean that would explain why you had to kill the boy.' He stopped and glanced towards Fielding. 'And in a way,' he added almost reluctantly, 'it makes better sense, doesn't it?'

'And what, may I ask, was the reason you speak of?'

'Perhaps she blackmailed you. She certainly knew about your conviction in the war from when she was up North. Her father was a magistrate, wasn't he? I understand they've looked up the files. The police, I mean. It was her father who heard the case. She knew you're broke and need another job and she kept you on a hook. It seems D'Arcy knew too. She told him. She'd nothing to lose; he was in on the story from the start, he'd never allow the papers to get hold of it; she knew that, she knew her man. Did *you* tell D'Arcy as well, Fielding? I think you may have done. When she came to you and told you she knew, jeered and laughed at you, you went to D'Arcy and told him. You asked him what to do. And he said – what would he say? – perhaps he said find out what she wants. But she wanted nothing; not money at least, but something more pleasing, more gratifying to her twisted little mind: she wanted to command and own you. She loved to conspire, she summoned you to meetings at absurd times and places; in woods, in disused churches, and above all at night. And she wanted nothing from you but your will, she made you listen to her boasts and her mad intrigues, made you fawn and cringe, then let you run away till the next time.' He looked up again. 'They might think along those lines, you see. That's why we need to know who saw inside the case. And who cheated in the exam.' They were both looking at him, Ailsa in horror, Fielding motionless, impassive.

'If they think that,' asked Fielding at last, 'how do they suppose I knew Rode would come back for the case that night?'

'Oh, they knew she was expecting you to meet her that night, after the dinner at your house.' Smiley threw this off as if it were a tedious detail, 'It was part of the game she liked to play.'

'How do they know that?'

'From what Rode says,' Smiley continued, 'Stella was carrying the case in the hall, actually had it in her hand. When they arrived at North Fields she was without it; she flew into a rage and accused him of forgetting it. She made him go back for it. You see the inference?'

'Oh, clearly,' said Fielding, and Smiley heard Ailsa Brimley whisper his name in horror.

'In other words, when Stella devised this trick to gratify her twisted will, you saw it as an opportunity to kill her, putting the blame on a non-existent tramp, or, failing that, on Rode, as a second line of defence. Let us suppose you had been meaning to kill her. You had meant, I expect, to ride out there one night when Rode was teaching late. You had your boots and your cape, even the cable stolen from Rode's room, and you meant to lay a false trail. But what a golden opportunity when Perkins turned up with the hand-case! Stella wanted her meeting – the forgotten hand-case was agreed upon as the means of achieving it. That, I fear, is the way their minds may work. And you see, they *know* it wasn't Rode.'

'How do they know? How *can* they know? He's got no alibi.' Smiley didn't seem to hear. He was looking towards the window, and the heavy velvet curtains stirring uneasily.

'What's that? What are you looking at?' Fielding asked with sudden urgency, but Smiley did not answer.

'You know, Fielding,' he said at last, 'we just don't know what people are like, we can never tell; there isn't any truth about human beings, no formula that meets each one of us. And there are some of us – aren't there? – who are nothing, who are so labile that we astound ourselves; we're the chameleons. I read a story once about a poet who bathed himself in cold fountains so that he could recognise his own existence in the contrast. He had to reassure himself, you see, like a child being hateful to its parents. You might say he had to make the sun shine on him so that he could see his shadow and feel alive.'

Fielding made an impatient movement with his hand. 'How do you know it wasn't Rode?'

'The people who are like that – there really are some, Fielding – do you know their secret? They can't feel anything inside them, no pleasure or pain, no love or hate; they're ashamed and frightened that they can't feel. And their shame, this shame, Fielding, drives them to extravagance and colour; they must make themselves feel that cold water, and without that they're nothing. The world sees them as showmen, fantasists, liars, as sensualists perhaps, not for what they are: the living dead.'

'How do you know? How do you know it wasn't Rode?' Fielding cried with anger in his voice, and Smiley replied: 'I'll tell you.'

'If Rode murdered his wife, he had planned to do so long ago. The plastic cape, the boots, the weapon, the intricate timing, the use of Perkins to carry the case to your house – these are evidence of long premeditation. Of course one could ask: if that's so, why did he bother with Perkins at all – why didn't he keep the case with him all the time? But never mind. Let's see how he does it. He walks home with his wife after dinner, having deliberately forgotten the writing-case. Having left Stella at home, he returns to your house to collect it. It was a risky business, incidentally, leaving that case behind. Quite apart from the fact that one would expect him to have locked it, his wife might have noticed he hadn't got it as they left – or you might have noticed, or Miss Truebody – but luckily no one did. He collects the case, hurries back, kills her, fabricating the clues which mislead the police. He thrusts the cape, boots and gloves into the refugees' parcel, ties it up and prepares to make good his escape. He is alarmed by Mad Janie, perhaps, but reaches the lane and re-enters the house as Stanley Rode. Five minutes later he is with the D'Arcys. From then on for the next forty-eight hours he is under constant supervision. Perhaps you didn't know this, Fielding, but the police found the murder weapon four miles down the road in a ditch. They found it within ten hours of the murder being discovered, long before Rode had a chance to throw it there.

'This is the point, though, Fielding. This is what they can't get over. I suppose it would be possible to make a phoney murder weapon. Rode could have taken hairs from Stella's comb, stuck them with human blood to a length of coaxial cable and planted the thing in a ditch *before* he committed the murder. But the only blood he could use was his own – which belongs to a different blood group. The blood on the weapon they found belonged to Stella's blood group. He didn't do it. There's a rather more concrete piece of evidence, to do with the parcel. Rigby had a word with Miss Truebody yesterday. It seems she telephoned Stella Rode on the morning of the day she was murdered. Telephoned at your request, Fielding, to say a boy would be bringing some old clothes up to North Fields on Thursday morning – would she be sure to keep the parcel open till then? . . . What did Stella threaten to do, Fielding? Write an anonymous letter to your next school?'

Then Smiley put his hand on Fielding's arm and said: 'Go now, in God's name go now. There's very little time, for Adrian's sake go now,' and Ailsa Brimley whispered something he could not hear.

Fielding seemed not to hear. His great head was thrown back, his eyes half closed, his wine glass still held between his thick fingers.

And the front-door bell rang out, like the scream of a woman in an empty house.

Smiley never knew what made the noise, whether it was Fielding's hands on the table as he stood up, or his chair, falling backwards. Perhaps it was not a noise at all, but simply the shock of violent movement when it was least expected; the sight of Fielding, who a moment before had sat lethargic in his chair, springing forward across the room. Then Rigby was holding him, had taken Fielding's right arm and done something to it so that Fielding cried out in pain and fear, swinging round to face them under the compulsion of Rigby's grip. Then Rigby was saying the words, and Fielding's terrified gaze fell upon Smiley.

'Stop him, stop him, Smiley, for God's sake! They'll hang me.' And he shouted the last two words again and again: 'Hang me, hang me,' until the detectives came in from the street, and shoved him without ceremony into a waiting car.

Smiley watched the car go. It didn't hurry, just picked its way down the wet street and disappeared. He remained there long after it had gone, looking towards the end of the road, so that passers-by stared oddly at him, or tried to follow his gaze. But there was nothing to see. Only the half-lit street, and the shadows moving along it.